Great American Short Novels

Great American Short Novels

EDITED BY

WILLIAM PHILLIPS

A Permanent Library Book

1 9 5 0

DIAL PRESS : *NEW YORK*

PERMANENT LIBRARY BOOKS

The Permanent Library makes available to the general reader those works of the world's great writers which have long been out of print, or which are not readily obtainable. They give a better understanding of the wide range of the talents of these masters of literature. The volumes are carefully edited, durably bound and tastefully designed. The average length is in excess of 700 pages.

THE GREAT SHORT NOVELS OF HENRY JAMES
edited by PHILIP RAHV *$5.00*

THE SHORT NOVELS OF DOSTOEVSKY
with an introduction by THOMAS MANN *$5.00*

GREEK PLAYS IN MODERN TRANSLATION
edited by DUDLEY FITTS *$5.00*

GREAT AMERICAN SHORT NOVELS
edited by WILLIAM PHILLIPS *$4.00*

THE PERMANENT GOETHE
edited by THOMAS MANN *$5.00*

THE SHORT NOVELS OF BALZAC
with an introduction by JULES ROMAINS *$4.00*

THE SHORT NOVELS OF TOLSTOY
edited by PHILIP RAHV *$4.00*

THE SHORT STORIES OF DOSTOEVSKY
with an introduction by WILLIAM PHILLIPS *$4.00*

THE BOSTONIANS
by HENRY JAMES *$3.00*

In Preparation:

GREAT FRENCH SHORT NOVELS
GREAT ITALIAN SHORT NOVELS
THE PSYCHOANALYTIC READER

Copyright 1946 Dial Press

Fifth Printing

Printed in the United States of America
by The Haddon Craftsmen, Inc., Scranton, Pa.

Contents

Grateful acknowledgment is made to Random House, Inc. for permission to reprint *Melanctha* by Gertrude Stein; to Charles Scribner's Sons for permission to reprint *The Great Gatsby* by F. Scott Fitzgerald; to D. Appleton-Century Co., Inc. for permission to reprint *False Dawn* by Edith Wharton; to Harcourt, Brace & Co., Inc. to reprint *Pale Horse, Pale Rider* by Katherine Anne Porter from *Pale Horse, Pale Rider,* copyright, 1936, 1937 and 1939, by Katherine Anne Porter. By permission of Harcourt, Brace and Company, Inc. and to Harper & Brothers for permission to reprint *The Pilgrim Hawk* by Glenway Wescott.

Introduction

THE short novel—"the shapely *nouvelle*," as Henry James called it—cannot be said to have any claims on American nativity, either in origin or in accomplishment. It has had a long European history, and it has from time to time absorbed the talent of such masters of European fiction as Balzac, Goethe, Dostoevsky, Tolstoy, Mann.

Yet there is a sense in which the short novel seems peculiarly appropriate to our national experience and literary tradition. Not that it has ever threatened to displace the full-length, massive narrative; but it has served to capture moments of experience and impressions of the American mind that might have been lost had the writer felt the need to document fully his situations or press home their relation to the larger perspectives of American life. It has been noted again and again that the fast and episodic movements of American history as well as the lack of an old and *felt* tradition have forced each novelist to create anew a sense of the American scene. Hawthorne, Melville, James, Wharton, Dreiser, Hemingway—to mention only a few outstanding figures—each in his turn expressed a new version of American existence. But it has been in the short novel that some of these authors, and others who never gave themselves to the longer form, were able to express the essentials of their art and their primary response to the moods of the time, with a kind of creative spontaneity.

Henry James, who was certainly one of the most conscious of American writers, was one of the first to be drawn to the short novel, and some of his finest work was produced in that medium. His many references to it suggest a kind of fascination with the form, and in one of his prefaces, where he is ostensibly counterposing it to the "short" story, that packageable item that has become a fetish of the harassed editor, James noted the possibility of combining economy with variety in the *nouvelle*, making it so tempting and so rewarding a vehicle for fiction:

"Among forms, moreover, we had had, on the dimensional ground

—for length and breadth—our ideal, the beautiful and blest *nouvelle*; the generous and enlightened hour for which appeared thus at last to shine. It was under the star of the *nouvelle* that in other languages, a hundred interesting and charming results, such studies on the minor scale as the best of Turgenieff's, of Balzac's, of Maupassant's, had been all economically arrived at . . . . It had taken the blank misery of our Anglo-Saxon sense of such matters to organize, as might be said, the general indifference to this fine type of composition. In that dull view a 'short story' was a 'short story,' and that was the end of it. Shades and differences, varieties and styles, the value above all of the idea happily *developed*, languished to extinction, under the hard-and-fast rule of the 'from six to eight thousand words'—when, for one's benefit, the rigour was a little relaxed. For myself, I delighted in the shapely *nouvelle*—as, for that matter, I had from time to time and here and there been almost encouraged to show."

Since James wrote this aggrieved plea, at once personal and objective, for a form that has its own felicities, springing almost inevitably from at least one level of the literary mind, the short novel has become an accepted and important genre that has enlisted the gifts at one time or another of most of our leading writers of fiction. I would hesitate to say just how much of this is due to a kind of instinctive recognition of the fitness of the form to the spontaneities or the compulsions or the lack of cultural stamina, so characteristic of the native tradition. The fact is, however, that these traits of social as well as literary life in America have been realized in what might be called the *illuminations* of the *nouvelle*. So remarkable a novel, for example, as *The Great Gatsby* has the quality of an incomplete vision; and in his recently published letters, it is clear that F. Scott Fitzgerald himself was aware of the gaps in background and the ambiguities of conception to be found in the work. And yet these flaws—if one can call them such—can be ascribed to the unity and intensity of Fitzgerald's *idea* of life in the twenties.

This is the reason for this collection, which is an attempt to bring together for the first time some of the most distinguished American short novels in such a way as to demonstrate the continuity of the form in this country and to indicate that these works are at the peak of our native talent. I would not care to describe the contents of this volume as the "best" *nouvelles*, partly because any such characterization raises the spectre of so many questions of personal taste and criteria that are usually resolved only by the last word, or, eventually, by history. Besides, the entire notion of a collection of the "best," bequeathed to us by the cultural reformism of the nineteenth century, and advanced most conscientiously by Matthew Arnold, is a rather pale and neutral standard, more appropriate, it seems to me, to the vaults of a museum than to a literary selection. Principles of choice are necessarily complex, and the eight short novels in this anthology have been chosen, it is true, primarily for their literary merit, but such considerations as representativeness and historical importance have also been weighed.

Benito Cereno, for example, can be said to be the first really distinguished short novel produced by an American author, and it has even been regarded by some critics as the most perfect American story. Melville's biographer, John Freeman, described it as "a flaming instance of the author's pure genius." Perhaps this is an overestimation, but there is no doubt of its impeccable structure, its superbly controlled pace, and its quality of complete self-containment. Of Melville's shorter works only *Billy Budd* is comparable in stature; and while the latter is in some ways a more explicit and dramatic novelette, I find *Benito Cereno* unusually interesting for its fusion of Melville's basic themes into the pure structure of the story. (Melville's critics have tended to slur over this aspect of the work.)

Beneath the narrative calm of *Benito Cereno*, one can discern the symbolism of good and evil, of innocence, violence and loneliness, that runs through all of Melville's work. It should be noted, in this respect, that Melville used an old travel book, Delano's *Voyages and Travels* as a source for *Benito Cereno*, but he transformed the original captain of the slave ship, who was a dark and scheming character, into a pawn of innocence, a victim of the "destructive element" that pursues man and overwhelms him in the most unexpected and distant places. And this primary meaning of Cereno's life is maintained by the supreme artistry of keeping Delano's attitude toward him constant, for even while Delano is baffled by the perverse practices on board the helpless ship he is drawn to Cereno by a compassion for his undefinable weakness.

The genius of Henry James, and his delight with the form of the *nouvelle*, yielded so many little masterpieces that any selection of one of them must appear somewhat arbitrary. Still, it seems to me that *Washington Square* is one of his most characteristic short novels, and it does at least rank with the outstanding ones. It may lack the thematic preoccupations of some of his other works, such as that of the spell of Europe in *Daisy Miller*, for instance, or the fateful incapacity to complete oneself, as in *The Beast in The Jungle*; but, on the other hand, it does exhibit many of the typical Jamesian ironies and accents within the restrained charm of its social world. We recognize the conscientious adventurer, the heiress, this time on the innocent and solidly virtuous side, the conscious authority of the father, and, in Aunt Lavinia, the person who lives her life through the destiny of another. The failure of the three main characters, Dr. Sloper, Catherine, Townsend—Lavinia is successful in that she thrives on the failures of the situation—is a tragedy of status, of the inability to step outside their moral and social selves. All are, after all, right in their own way, yet their fulfillment is, at the same time, a failure of self-realization. And, it should be added, these Jamesian meanings are carried by an unexcelled sureness and grace of movement.

Stephen Crane is commonly taken to be the forerunner of realism in this country, and the publication of his short novel, *The Red Badge of Courage*, is supposed to have provided the shock for the change in literary attitude. The truth is, however, that this novel is realistic only in a thematic sense, for its style and sensibility have little in common with the method of additive detail associated with the modern realistic school. It is rather *Maggie*, a somewhat earlier novel that created less of a stir than the *Red Badge of Courage*, that foreshadowed the development of truly naturalistic writing not only of the serious but of the popular variety as well. And it seems to me an act of remarkable creative discipline on Crane's part to have maintained a genuine literary integrity and spareness in a story that contains all the sentimental ingredients of the five-and-dime novel. William Dean Howells, himself a crusader for the under side of life in literature, was one of the first enthusiasts of *Maggie*, of which he said: "I think what strikes me most in the story of *Maggie* is that quality of fatal necessity which dominates Greek tragedy. . . . Another effect is that of an ideal of artistic beauty which is present in the working out of this poor girl's squalid romance as in any classic fable. . . . " In this respect, one of the most impressive signs of Crane's artistry is in the irony of the theatre scene, where Maggie responds with her full romantic being to the sentimentalities on the stage that Crane takes off just enough to set them apart. We observe also in *Maggie*, all the pathos, sometimes shallow and only dimly conscious, of the underdog, that makes up the mood as well as the subject of what we now call "social realism."

Even more important, however, in terms of the medium, is the fact that *Maggie* is completely keyed to the shorter form: had Crane chosen to stretch it into the full-dress novel, it is hard to see how he could have avoided a thoroughly unctuous and dripping story. As Mencken put it: "His [Crane's] method . . . was grossly ill-adapted to the novel, properly so-called. He had, so to speak, no literary small talk; he could not manage what the musicians call passage work. His superlative skill lay in the handling of isolated situations; he knew exactly how to depict them with a dazzling brilliance, and he knew, too, how to analyze them with a penetrating insight. . . . "

After *Maggie*, the selections are all products of this century, and one would naturally expect them to be characteristically modern in their sensibility. But while Edith Wharton's *False Dawn* was published in the twenties, many years after *Melanctha*, by Gertrude Stein, whom we still think of as an *avant-guardist*, it has much in common with the feelings of the earlier period. In fact, Edith Wharton may be said to have linked, or at least to have spanned, the literary movements of the present and past century. And this transitional quality is better illustrated in *False Dawn*, among her novelettes, than, say, the more highly publicized *Ethan Frome*, which for all its effectiveness, has always seemed to me to be something of a set piece, a *tour-de-force* of a great talent projecting itself ahead in time. At any rate, *False Dawn* has the ease and casualness of an assimilated background, as it touches on the cultural changes of a newly-born and rapidly shifting social world.

The active Jamesian influence on Edith Wharton's writing has often been commented on; and it is especially evident in *False Dawn*, a novel of upper class motivations in a period setting. Aside from the obvious stylistic echoes, there are such apparent Jamesian themes as the lure of the old world and the conflicts within status, but, on the whole, as Edmund Wilson has pointed out, Edith Wharton is given to much more literal distinctions, while her emphasis is usually social—or sociological. Thus the tensions within the Raycie family point up the barriers of generation in a society that is constantly creating or importing its traditions, and the classic contradiction between the acquisition of wealth and its cultural disposal by its heirs. Edith Wharton's ironies, too, as in the eventual discovery of the true value of Lewis Raycie's pictures, or the snobbish references by the elder Raycie to Ruskin and Poe, are mostly on the side of progress—or backwardness. And in this explicitness of attitude, in the fact that the perceptiveness of *False Dawn* in no way depends on a feeling for social ambiguities, lies the modernity of the novel. Essentially, Lewis Raycie is an unsophisticated version of the pale-faced zealot of art in contemporary fiction, while his father is the prototype of the self-confident philistine who would like to round out his prejudices.

The four novelettes by Gertrude Stein, Fitzgerald, Katherine Anne Porter, Wescott, are all unmistakably modern products. All possess the concentrated perceptiveness, the anxieties of isolation, and the psychological half-tones of contemporary writing. Gertrude Stein has applied her experiments in primitive syntax to a kind of intensive résumé of the life of a young negress; Fitzgerald, in a more conventional form, has carried the symbolism of loneliness into a highly-charged and glamorous social world; Katherine Anne Porter's *Pale Horse, Pale Rider* is a fable of the futilities of life and death in a time of war, through the medium of an apparently simple love-story; *The Pilgrim Hawk* is a tale of broken contacts, of uncontrollable hungers that are neither understood nor satisfied. All of the central characters in these short novels—Melanctha, Gatsby, Daisy, Miranda, Mrs. Cullen—are thrown back on themselves by some fatality that cuts their human ties.

In the case of Melanctha, it is her restlessness and "disloyalty," concealing some generic anxiety—plus a faint suggestion of sexual perversity—that lead her not only to violate all her human relations, but, ultimately, to destroy herself. Incidentally, the character of Melanctha is a remarkable fusion of her personal and her social history, marking the first—perhaps the only—treatment of the Negro in American fiction without exaggerated pathos, or patronization, or justification. The humanity of all the people in this novel carries the accents of the Negro in the organic way that the fiction of any country can be said to have its national characteristics.

In *The Great Gatsby*, which has been described by T. S. Eliot as "the first step that American fiction has taken since Henry James," Fitzgerald has projected the harassed solitude of a man obsessed with the urge to incarnate in himself the great success drives of the twenties. Gatsby had, as Fitzgerald says, "something gorgeous about him, some heightened sensitivity to the promises of life." Hence even his ultimate failure takes on a façade of the mysterious, the heroic, the triumphant. Apparently, Fitzgerald could not disengage the myth from the reality, for in a sense they were one, especially since, as Fitzgerald tells us in his letters, he began to identify himself with Gatsby somewhere midway in the narrative. As a result, Gatsby declines to a feeble image of himself, while the "I" of the novel gradually increases in importance, until at the end, he virtually absorbs the meaning of the story while remaining apart from it. Commenting on the common frustration of all the characters, Nick Carraway picks up the thread of isolation and weaves it into another pattern, possibly that of his own life: "Tom and Gatsby, Daisy and Jordan and I," he says, "were all Westerners, and perhaps we possessed some deficiency in common which made us subtly unadaptable to Eastern life."

Pale Horse, Pale Rider, set in World War I, but apparently composed some years later, is to my knowledge, the most meaningful and superbly written story of either this or the last conflict. Katherine Anne Porter's gifts as a prose writer have been commonly recognized—gifts, incidentally, that have so far been employed only in the short novel and short story—but they seem to have distracted critics from the content of her work. Yet the effectiveness of *Pale Horse, Pale Rider* is largely due to the presence, in somewhat transposed form, of the basic human themes of the war. Thus Adam, the flawless male, carries the fatalism of death in a way that is partially dissociated from his civilian existence, and his actual dying has all the anonymity and lack of detail of a reported casualty. Miranda, on the other hand, becomes the visible sufferer, her illness being not only a symbol of the anxiety of one left behind, but also a reenactment of the ritual of life and death that Adam has gone through. Both face "oblivion," though it is only through the consciousness of Miranda that this "awful knowledge" unfolds. Before either of them is stricken, Miranda knew "that there was nothing ahead for Adam or for her," but the full weight of its meaning hits her as she comes out of her delirium, when, still ignorant of Adam's death, she cries out with a desperate intuition of what is in store for her, "Please open the window, please, I smell death in here."

The Pilgrim Hawk, published in 1942, brings us to the end of our collection, fittingly enough with a novelette that represents an important side of the modern sensibility. Wescott's earlier writing showed an unusual grasp of the idiom of sensitivity, applied to the typical young man of modern times, groping for his ego, and moved by the dual feeling of withdrawal and belonging to the world. In *The*

Pilgrim Hawk, however, this characteristic mood is projected into the symbolic situation of the man, wife and hawk, with Wescott, himself, making us aware of the yearnings and frustrations contained in the story, partly by assuming the role of the sensitive observer, partly through his identification with the thwarted Mrs. Cullen. And yet, we are still left at the end with the feeling that humanity is beyond our reach, either as something to be entered into or simply to be understood. Even the hawk is an ambiguous figure as he shifts in meaning, sometimes being an extension of Cullen's decrepit sensuality, at other times a projection of Mrs. Cullen's primal hungers. "It might have been," says Wescott, "a baby, and he a lover, or was it the other way around?" At the risk of inflating its meaning, one is tempted to say of the grim hawk that it might be taken as a symbol of the *unknown* that obsesses the modern sensibility and produces its feeling of mystery and irrationality.

All in all, these eight short novels, ranging from Melville's search for some moral equivalent of the human dilemma to Wescott's image of personal isolation, touch on the basic themes of American experience as they have found their way into American literature.

WILLIAM PHILLIPS

Benito Cereno

1855

HERMAN MELVILLE

Benito Cereno

I
N THE year 1799, Captain Amasa Delano, of Duxbury, in Massachusetts, commanding a large sealer and general trader, lay at anchor, with a valuable cargo, in the harbour of St. Maria—a small, desert, uninhabited island towards the southern extremity of the long coast of Chili. There he had touched for water.

On the second day, not long after dawn, while lying in his berth, his mate came below, informing him that a strange sail was coming into the bay. Ships were then not so plenty in those waters as now. He rose, dressed, and went on deck.

The morning was one peculiar to that coast. Everything was mute and calm; everything grey. The sea, though undulated into long roods of swells, seemed fixed, and was sleeked at the surface like waved lead that has cooled and set in the smelters' mould. The sky seemed a grey mantle. Flights of troubled grey fowl, kith and kin with flights of troubled grey vapours among which they were mixed, skimmed low and fitfully over the waters, as swallows over meadows before storms. Shadows present, foreshadowing deeper shadows to come.

To Captain Delano's surprise, the stranger, viewed through the glass, showed no colours; though to do so upon entering a haven, however uninhabited in its shores, where but a single other ship might be lying, was the custom among peaceful seamen of all nations. Considering the lawlessness and loneliness of the spot, and the sort of stories, at that day, associated with those seas, Captain Delano's surprise might have deepened into some uneasiness had he not been a person of a singularly undistrustful good nature, not liable, except on extraordinary and repeated excitement, and hardly then, to indulge in personal alarms, any way involving the imputation of malign evil in man. Whether, in view of what humanity is capable, such a trait implies, along with a benevolent heart, more than ordinary quickness and accuracy of intellectual perception, may be left to the wise to determine.

3

But whatever misgivings might have obtruded on first seeing the stranger, would almost, in any seaman's mind, have been dissipated by observing that, the ship, in navigating into the harbour, was drawing too near the land, for her own safety's sake, owing to a sunken reef making out off her bow. This seemed to prove her a stranger, indeed, not only to the sealer, but the island; consequently, she could be no wonted freebooter on that ocean. With no small interest, Captain Delano continued to watch her—a proceeding not much facilitated by the vapours partly mantling the hull, through which the far matin light from her cabin streamed equivocally enough; much like the sun—by this time crescented on the rim of the horizon, and apparently, in company with the strange ship, entering the harbour—which, wimpled by the same low, creeping clouds, showed not unlike a Lima intriguante's one sinister eye peering across the Plaza from the Indian loop-hole of her dusk *saya-y-manta*.

It might have been but a deception of the vapours, but, the longer the stranger was watched, the more singular appeared her manœuvres. Ere long it seemed hard to decide whether she meant to come in or no—what she wanted, or what she was about. The wind, which had breezed up a little during the night, was now extremely light and baffling, which the more increased the apparent uncertainty of her movements.

Surmising, at last, that it might be a ship in distress, Captain Delano ordered his whale-boat to be dropped, and, much to the wary opposition of his mate, prepared to board her, and, at the least, pilot her in. On the night previous, a fishing-party of the seamen had gone a long distance to some detached rocks out of sight from the sealer, and, an hour or two before day-break, had returned, having met with no small success. Presuming that the stranger might have been long off soundings, the good captain put several baskets of the fish, for presents, into his boat, and so pulled away. From her continuing too near the sunken reef, deeming her in danger, calling to his men, he made all haste to apprise those on board of their situation. But, some time ere the boat came up, the wind, light though it was, having shifted, had headed the vessel off, as well as partly broken the vapours from about her.

Upon gaining a less remote view, the ship, when made signally visible on the verge of the leaden-hued swells, with the shreds of fog here and there raggedly furring her, appeared like a whitewashed monastery after a thunder-storm, seen perched upon some dun cliff among the Pyrenees. But it was no purely fanciful resemblance which now, for a moment, almost led Captain Delano to think that nothing less than a ship-load of monks was before him. Peering over the bulwarks were what really seemed, in the hazy distance, throngs of dark cowls; while, fitfully revealed through the open port-holes, other dark moving figures were dimly descried, as of Black Friars pacing the cloisters.

Upon a still nigher approach, this appearance was modified, and the true character of the vessel was plain—a Spanish merchantman of the first class; carrying negro slaves, amongst other valuable freight, from one colonial port to another. A very large, and, in its time, a very fine vessel, such as in those days were at intervals encountered along that main; sometimes superseded Acapulco treasure-ships, or retired frigates of the Spanish king's navy, which, like superannuated Italian palaces, still, under a decline of masters, preserved signs of former state.

As the whale-boat drew more and more nigh, the cause of the peculiar pipe-clayed aspect of the stranger was seen in the slovenly neglect pervading her. The spars, ropes, and great part of the bulwarks, looked woolly, from long unacquaintance with the scraper, tar, and the brush. Her keel seemed laid, her ribs put together, and she launched, from Ezekiel's Valley of Dry Bones.

In the present business in which she was engaged, the ship's general model and rig appeared to have undergone no material change from their original warlike and Froissart pattern. However, no guns were seen.

The tops were large, and were railed about with what had once been octagonal net-work, all now in sad disrepair. These tops hung overhead like three ruinous aviaries, in one of which was seen perched, on a ratlin, a white noddy, a strange fowl, so called from its lethargic somnambulistic character, being frequently caught by hand at sea. Battered and mouldy, the castellated forecastle seemed some ancient turret, long ago taken by assault, and then left to decay. Towards the stern, two high-raised quarter galleries—the balustrades here and there covered with dry, tindery sea-moss—opening out from the unoccupied state-cabin, whose dead lights, for all the mild weather, were hermetically closed and caulked—these tenantless balconies hung over the sea as if it were the grand Venetian canal. But the principal relic of faded grandeur was the ample oval of the shield-like stern-piece, intricately carved with the arms of Castile and Leon, medallioned about by groups of mythological or symbolical devices; uppermost and central of which was a dark satyr in a mask, holding his foot on the prostrate neck of a writhing figure, likewise masked.

Whether the ship had a figure-head, or only a plain beak, was not quite certain, owing to canvas wrapped about that part, either to protect it while undergoing a refurbishing, or else decently to hide its decay. Rudely painted or chalked, as in a sailor freak, along the forward side of a sort of pedestal below the canvas, was the sentence, "*Seguid vuestro jefe,*" (follow your leader); while upon the tarnished head-boards, near by, appeared, in stately capitals, once gilt, the ship's name, "SAN DOMINICK," each letter streakingly corroded with tricklings of copper-spike rust; while, like mourning weeds, dark festoons of sea-grass slimily swept to and fro over the name, with every hearse-like roll of the hull.

As at last the boat was hooked from the bow along toward the gangway amidship, its keel, while yet some inches separated from the hull, harshly grated as on a sunken coral reef. It proved a huge bunch of conglobated barnacles adhering below the water to the side like a wen; a token of baffling airs and long calms passed somewhere in those seas.

Climbing the side, the visitor was at once surrounded by a clamorous throng of whites and blacks, but the latter outnumbering the former more than could have been expected, negro transportation-ship as the stranger in port was. But, in one language, and as with one voice, all poured out a common tale of suffering; in which the negresses, of whom there were not a few, exceeded the others in their dolorous vehemence. The scurvy, together with a fever, had swept off a great part of their number, more especially the Spaniards. Off Cape Horn, they had narrowly escaped shipwreck; then, for days together, they had lain tranced without wind; their provisions were low; their water next to none; their lips that moment were baked.

While Captain Delano was thus made the mark of all eager tongues, his one eager glance took in all the faces, with every other object about him.

Always upon first boarding a large and populous ship at sea, especially a foreign one, with a nondescript crew such as Lascars or Manilla men, the impression varies in a peculiar way from that produced by first entering a strange house with strange inmates in a strange land. Both house and ship, the one by its walls and blinds, the other by its high bulwarks like ramparts, hoard from view their interiors till the last moment; but in the case of the ship there is this addition: that the living spectacle it contains, upon its sudden and complete disclosure, has, in contrast with the blank ocean which zones it, something of the effect of enchantment. The ship seems unreal; these strange costumes, gestures, and faces, but a shadowy tableau just emerged from the deep, which directly must receive back what it gave.

Perhaps it was some such influence as above is attempted to be described which, in Captain Delano's mind, heightened whatever, upon a staid scrutiny, might have seemed unusual; especially the conspicuous figures of four elderly grizzled negroes, their heads like black, doddered willow tops, who, in venerable contrast to the tumult below them, were couched sphinx-like, one on the starboard cat-head, another on the larboard, and the remaining pair face to face on the opposite bulwarks above the main-chains. They each had bits of unstranded old junk in their hands, and, with a sort of stoical self-content, were picking the junk into oakum, a small heap of which lay by their sides. They accompanied the task with a continuous, low, monotonous chant; droning and drooling away like so many grey-headed bag-pipers playing a funeral march.

The quarter-deck rose into an ample elevated poop, upon the forward verge of which, lifted, like the oakum-pickers, some eight feet above the general throng, sat along in a row, separated by regular spaces, the cross-legged figures of six other blacks; each with a rusty hatchet in his hand, which, with a bit of brick and a rag, he was engaged like a scullion in scouring; while between each two was a small stack of hatchets, their rusted edges turned forward awaiting a like operation. Though occasionally the four oakum-pickers would briefly address some person or persons in the crowd below, yet the six hatchet-polishers neither spoke to others, nor breathed a whisper among themselves, but sat intent upon their task, except at intervals, when, with the peculiar love in negroes of uniting industry with pastime, two-and-two they sideways clashed their hatchets together, like cymbals, with a barbarous din. All six, unlike the generality, had the raw aspect of unsophisticated Africans.

But that first comprehensive glance which took in those ten figures, with scores less conspicuous, rested but an instant upon them, as, impatient of the hubbub of voices, the visitor turned in quest of whomsoever it might be that commanded the ship.

But as if not unwilling to let nature make known her own case among his suffering charge, or else in despair of restraining it for the time, the Spanish captain, a gentlemanly, reserved-looking, and rather young man to a stranger's eye, dressed with singular richness, but bearing plain traces of recent sleepless cares and disquietudes, stood passively by, leaning against the main-mast, at one moment casting a dreary, spiritless look upon his excited people, at the next an unhappy glance toward his visitor. By his side stood a black of small stature, in whose rude face, as occasionally, like a shepherd's dog, he mutely turned it up into the Spaniard's, sorrow and affection were equally blended.

Struggling through the throng, the American advanced to the Spaniard, assuring him of his sympathies, and offering to render whatever assistance might be in his power. To which the Spaniard returned, for the present, but grave and ceremonious acknowledgments, his national formality dusked by the saturnine mood of ill health.

But losing no time in mere compliments, Captain Delano returning to the gangway, had his baskets of fish brought up; and as the wind still continued light, so that some hours at least must elapse ere the ship could be brought to the anchorage, he bade his men return to the sealer, and fetch back as much water as the whaleboat could carry, with whatever soft bread the steward might have, all the remaining pumpkins on board, with a box of sugar, and a dozen of his private bottles of cider.

Not many minutes after the boat's pushing off, to the vexation of all, the wind entirely died away, and the tide turning, began drifting back the ship helplessly seaward. But trusting this would not long last, Captain Delano sought with good hopes to cheer up the strangers, feeling no small satisfaction that, with persons in their condition he could—thanks to his frequent voyages along the Spanish main—converse with some freedom in their native tongue.

While left alone with them, he was not long in observing some things tending to heighten his first impressions; but surprise was lost in pity, both for the Spaniards and blacks, alike evidently reduced from scarcity of water and provisions; while long-continued suffering seemed to have brought out the less good-natured qualities of the negroes, besides, at the same time, impairing the Spaniard's authority over them. But, under the circumstances, precisely this condition of things was to have been anticipated. In armies, navies, cities, or families—in nature herself—nothing more relaxes good order than misery. Still, Captain Delano was not without the idea, that had Benito Cereno been a man of greater energy, misrule would hardly have come to the present pass. But the debility, constitutional or induced by the hardships, bodily and mental, of the Spanish captain, was too obvious to be overlooked. A prey to settled dejection, as if long mocked with hope he would not now indulge it, even when it had ceased to be a mock, the prospect of that day or evening at furthest, lying at anchor, with plenty of water for his people, and a brother captain to counsel and befriend, seemed in no perceptible degree to encourage him. His mind appeared unstrung, if not still more seriously affected. Shut up in these oaken walls, chained to one dull round of command, whose unconditionality cloyed him, like some hypochondriac abbot he moved slowly about, at times suddenly pausing, starting, or staring, biting his lip, biting his finger-nails, flushing, paling, twitching his beard, with other symptoms of an absent or moody mind. This distempered spirit was lodged, as before hinted, in as distempered a frame. He was rather tall, but seemed never to have been robust, and now with nervous suffering was almost worn to a skeleton. A tendency to some pulmonary complaint appeared to have been lately confirmed. His voice was like that of one with lungs half gone, hoarsely suppressed, a husky whisper. No wonder that, as in this state he tottered about, his private servant apprehensively followed him. Sometimes the negro gave his master his arm, or took his handkerchief out of his pocket for him; performing these and similar offices with that affectionate zeal which transmutes into something filial or fraternal acts in themselves but menial; and which has gained for the negro the repute of making the most pleasing body servant in the world; one, too, whom a master need be on no stiffly superior terms with, but may treat with familiar trust; less a servant than a devoted companion.

Marking the noisy indocility of the blacks in general, as well as what seemed the sullen inefficiency of the whites, it was not without humane satisfaction that Captain Delano witnessed the steady good conduct of Babo.

But the good conduct of Babo, hardly more than the ill-behaviour of others, seemed to withdraw the half-lunatic Don Benito from his cloudy languor. Not that such precisely was the impression made by the Spaniard on the mind of his visitor. The Spaniard's individual unrest was, for the present, but noted as a conspicuous feature in the ship's general affliction. Still, Captain Delano was not a little concerned at what he could not help taking for the time to be Don Benito's unfriendly indifference toward himself. The Spaniard's manner, too, conveyed a sort of sour and gloomy disdain, which he seemed at no pains to disguise. But this the American in charity ascribed to the harassing effects of sickness, since, in former instances, he had noted that there are peculiar natures on whom prolonged physical suffering seems to cancel every social instinct of kindness; as if forced to black bread themselves, they deemed it but equity that each person coming nigh them should, indirectly, by some slight or affront, be made to partake of their fare.

But ere long Captain Delano bethought him that, indulgent as he was at the first, in judging the Spaniard, he might not, after all, have exercised charity enough. At bottom it was Don Benito's reserve which displeased him; but the same reserve was shown toward all but his personal attendant. Even the formal reports which, according to sea-usage, were at stated times made to him by some petty underling (either a white, mulatto or black), he hardly had patience enough to listen to, without betraying contemptuous aversion. His manner upon such occasions was, in its degree, not unlike that which might be supposed to have been his imperial countryman's, Charles V., just previous to the anchoritish retirement of that monarch from the throne.

This splenetic disrelish of his place was evinced in almost every function pertaining to it. Proud as he was moody, he condescended to no personal mandate. Whatever special orders were necessary, their delivery was delegated to his body-servant, who in turn transferred them to their ultimate destination, through runners, alert Spanish boys or slave boys, like pages or pilot-fish within easy call continually hovering round Don Benito. So that to have beheld this undemonstrative invalid gliding about, apathetic and mute, no landsman could have dreamed that in him was lodged a dictatorship beyond which, while at sea, there was no earthly appeal.

Thus, the Spaniard, regarded in his reserve, seemed as the involuntary victim of mental disorder. But, in fact, his reserve might, in some degree, have proceeded from design. If so, then in Don Benito was evinced the unhealthy climax of that icy though conscientious policy, more or less adopted by all commanders of large ships, which, except in signal emergencies, obliterates alike the manifestation of sway with every trace of sociality; transforming the man into a block, or rather into a loaded cannon, which, until there is call for thunder, has nothing to say.

Viewing him in this light, it seemed but a natural token of the perverse habit induced by a long course of such hard self-restraint, that, notwithstanding the present condition of his ship, the Spaniard should still persist in a demeanour, which, however harmless—or it may be, appropriate—in a well-appointed vessel, such as the *San Dominick* might have been at the outset of the voyage, was anything but judicious now. But the Spaniard perhaps thought that it was with captains as with gods: reserve, under all events, must still be their cue. But more probably this appearance of slumbering dominion might have been but an attempted disguise to conscious imbecility—not deep policy, but shallow device. But be all this as it might, whether Don Benito's manner was designed or not, the more Captain Delano noted its pervading reserve, the less he felt uneasiness at any particular manifestation of that reserve toward himself.

Neither were his thoughts taken up by the captain alone. Wonted to the quiet orderliness of the sealer's comfortable family of a crew, the noisy confusion of the *San Dominick's* suffering host repeatedly challenged his eye. Some prominent breaches not only of discipline but of decency were observed. These Captain Delano could not but ascribe, in the main, to the absence of those subordinate deck-officers to whom, along with higher duties, is entrusted what may be styled the police department of a populous ship. True, the old oakumpickers appeared at times to act the part of monitorial constables to their countrymen, the blacks; but though occasionally succeeding in allaying trifling outbreaks now and then between man and man, they could do little or nothing toward establishing general quiet. The *San Dominick* was in the condition of a transatlantic emigrant ship, among whose multitude of living freight are some individuals, doubtless, as little troublesome as crates and bales; but the friendly remonstrances of such with their ruder companions are of not so much avail as the unfriendly arm of the mate. What the *San Dominick* wanted was, what the emigrant ship has, stern superior officers. But on these decks not so much as a fourth mate was to be seen.

The visitor's curiosity was roused to learn the particulars of those mishaps which had brought about such absenteeism, with its consequences; because, though deriving some inkling of the voyage from the wails which at the first moment had greeted him, yet of the details no clear understanding had been had. The best account would, doubtless, be given by the captain. Yet at first the visitor was loth to ask it, unwilling to provoke some distant rebuff. But plucking up courage, he at last accosted Don Benito, renewing the expression of his benevolent interest, adding, that did he (Captain Delano) but know the particulars of the ship's misfortunes, he would, perhaps, be better able in the end to relieve them. Would Don Benito favour him with the whole story?

Don Benito faltered; then, like some somnambulist suddenly interfered with, vacantly stared at his visitor, and ended by looking down on the deck. He maintained this posture so long, that Captain Delano, almost equally disconcerted, and involuntarily almost as rude, turned suddenly from him, walking forward to accost one of the Spanish seamen for the desired information. But he had hardly gone five paces, when with a sort of eagerness Don Benito invited him back, regretting his momentary absence of mind, and professing readiness to gratify him.

While most part of the story was being given, the two captains stood on the after part of the main-deck, a privileged spot, no one being near but the servant.

"It is now a hundred and ninety days," began the Spaniard, in his husky whisper, "that this ship, well officered and well manned, with several cabin passengers—some fifty Spaniards in all—sailed from Buenos Ayres bound to Lima, with a general cargo, Paraguay tea and the like—and," pointing forward, "that parcel of negroes, now not more than a hundred and fifty, as you see, but then numbering over three hundred souls. Off Cape Horn we had heavy gales. In one moment, by night, three of my best officers, with fifteen sailors, were lost, with the main-yard; the spar snapping under them in the slings, as they sought, with heavers, to beat down the icy sail. To lighten the hull, the heavier sacks of mata were thrown into the sea, with most of the water-pipes lashed on deck at the time. And this last necessity it was, combined with the prolonged detentions afterwards experienced, which eventually brought about our chief causes of suffering. When—"

Here there was a sudden fainting attack of his cough, brought on, no doubt, by his mental distress. His servant sustained him, and drawing a cordial from his pocket placed it to his lips. He a little revived. But unwilling to leave him unsupported while yet imperfectly restored, the black with one arm still encircled his master, at the same time keeping his eye fixed on his face, as if to watch for the first sign of complete restoration, or relapse, as the event might prove.

The Spaniard proceeded, but brokenly and obscurely, as one in a dream.

—"Oh, my God! rather than pass through what I have, with joy I would have hailed the most terrible gales; but—"

His cough returned and with increased violence; this subsiding, with reddened lips and closed eyes he fell heavily against his supporter.

"His mind wanders. He was thinking of the plague that followed the gales," plaintively sighed the servant; "my poor, poor master!" wringing one hand, and with the other wiping the mouth. "But be patient, Señor," again turning to Captain Delano, "these fits do not last long; master will soon be himself."

Don Benito reviving, went on; but as this portion of the story was very brokenly delivered, the substance only will here be set down.

It appeared that after the ship had been many days tossed in storms off the Cape, the scurvy broke out, carrying off numbers of the whites and blacks. When at last they had worked round into the Pacific, their spars and sails were so damaged, and so inadequately handled by the surviving mariners, most of whom were become invalids, that, unable to lay her northerly course by the wind, which was powerful, the unmanageable ship for successive days and nights was blown northwestward, where the breeze suddenly deserted her, in unknown waters, to sultry calms. The absence of the water-pipes now proved as fatal to life as before their presence had menaced it. Induced, or at least aggravated, by the more than scanty allowance of water, a malignant fever followed the scurvy; with the excessive heat of the lengthened calm, making such short work of it as to sweep away, as by billows, whole families of the Africans, and a yet larger number, proportionably, of the Spaniards, including, by a luckless fatality, every officer on board. Consequently, in the smart west winds eventually following the calm, the already rent sails having to be simply dropped, not furled, at need, had been gradually reduced to the beggar's rags they were now. To procure substitutes for his lost sailors, as well as supplies of water and sails, the captain at the earliest opportunity had made for Baldivia, the southernmost civilized port of Chili and South America; but upon nearing the coast the thick weather had prevented him from so much as sighting that harbour. Since which period, almost without a crew, and almost without canvas and almost without water, and at intervals giving its added dead to the sea, the *San Dominick* had been battle-dored about by contrary winds, inveigled by currents, or grown weedy in calms. Like a man lost in woods, more than once she had doubled upon her own track.

"But throughout these calamities," huskily continued Don Benito, painfully turning in the half embrace of his servant, "I have to thank those negroes you see, who, though to your inexperienced eyes appearing unruly, have, indeed, conducted themselves with less of restlessness than even their owner could have thought possible under such circumstances."

Here he again fell faintly back. Again his mind wandered: but he rallied, and less obscurely proceeded.

"Yes, their owner was quite right in assuring me that no fetters would be needed with his blacks; so that while, as is wont in this transportation, those negroes have always remained upon deck— not thrust below, as in the Guineamen—they have, also from the beginning, been freely permitted to range within given bounds at their pleasure."

Once more the faintness returned—his mind roved—but, recovering, he resumed:

"But it is Babo here to whom, under God, I owe not only my own preservation, but likewise to him, chiefly, the merit is due, of pacifying his more ignorant brethren, when at intervals tempted to murmurings."

"Ah, master," sighed the black, bowing his face, "don't speak of me; Babo is nothing; what Babo has done was but duty."

"Faithful fellow!" cried Captain Delano. "Don Benito, I envy you such a friend; slave I cannot call him."

As master and man stood before him, the black upholding the white, Captain Delano could not but bethink him of the beauty of that relationship which could present such a spectacle of fidelity on the one hand and confidence on the other. The scene was heightened by the contrast in dress, denoting their relative positions. The Spaniard wore a loose Chili jacket of dark velvet; white small clothes and stockings, with silver buckles at the knee and instep; a high-crowned sombrero, of fine grass; a slender sword, silver mounted, hung from a knot in his sash; the last being an almost invariable adjunct, more for utility than ornament, of a South American gentleman's dress to this hour. Excepting when his occasional nervous contortions brought about disarray, there was a certain precision in his attire, curiously at variance with the unsightly disorder around; especially in the belittered Ghetto, forward of the main-mast, wholly occupied by the blacks.

The servant wore nothing but wide trousers, apparently, from their coarseness and patches, made out of some old topsail; they were clean, and confined at the waist by a bit of unstranded rope, which, with his composed, deprecatory air at times, made him look something like a begging friar of St. Francis.

However unsuitable for the time and place, at least in the blunt-thinking American's eyes, and however strangely surviving in the midst of all his afflictions, the toilette of Don Benito might not, in fashion at least, have gone beyond the style of the day among South Americans of his class. Though on the present voyage sailing from Buenos Ayres, he had avowed himself a native and resident of Chili, whose inhabitants had not so generally adopted the plain coat and once plebeian pantaloons; but, with a becoming modification, adhered to their provincial costume, picturesque as any in the world. Still, relatively to the pale history of the voyage, and his own pale face, there seemed something so incongruous in the Spaniard's apparel, as almost to suggest the image of an invalid courtier tottering about London streets in the time of the plague.

The portion of the narrative which, perhaps, most excited interest, as well as some surprise, considering the latitudes in question, was the long calms spoken of, and more particularly the ship's so long drifting about. Without communicating the opinion, of course, the American could not but impute at least part of the detentions both to clumsy seamanship and faulty navigation. Eyeing Don Benito's small, yellow hands, he easily inferred that the young captain had not got into command at the hawse-hole but the cabin-window, and if so, why wonder at incompetence, in youth, sickness, and aristocracy united? Such was his democratic conclusion.

But drowning criticism in compassion, after a fresh repetition of his sympathies, Captain Delano having heard out his story, not only engaged, as in the first place, to see Don Benito and his people supplied in their immediate bodily needs, but, also, now further promised to assist him in procuring a large permanent supply of water, as well as some sails and rigging; and, though it would involve no small embarrassment to himself, yet he would spare three of his best seamen for temporary deck officers; so that without delay the ship might proceed to Concepcion, there fully to refit for Lima, her destined port.

Such generosity was not without its effect, even upon the invalid. His face lighted up; eager and hectic, he met the honest glance of his visitor. With gratitude he seemed overcome.

"This excitement is bad for master," whispered the servant, taking his arm, and with soothing words gently drawing him aside.

When Don Benito returned, the American was pained to observe that his hopefulness, like the sudden kindling in his cheek, was but febrile and transient.

Ere long, with a joyless mien, looking up toward the poop, the host invited his guest to accompany him there, for the benefit of what little breath of wind might be stirring.

As during the telling of the story, Captain Delano had once or twice started at the occasional cymballing of the hatchet-polishers, wondering why such an interruption should be allowed, especially in that part of the ship, and in the ears of an invalid; and, moreover, as the hatchets had anything but an attractive look, and the handlers of them still less so, it was, therefore, to tell the truth, not without some lurking reluctance, or even shrinking, it may be, that Captain Delano, with apparent complaisance, acquiesced in his host's invitation. The more so, since with an untimely caprice of punctilio, rendered distressing by his cadaverous aspect, Don Benito, with Castilian bows, solemnly insisted upon his guest's preceding him up the ladder leading to the elevation; where, one on each side of the last step, sat four armorial supporters and sentries, two of the ominous file. Gingerly enough stepped good Captain Delano between them, and in the instant of leaving them behind, like one running the gantlet, he felt an apprehensive twitch in the calves of his legs.

But when, facing about, he saw the whole file, like so many organ-grinders, still stupidly intent on their work, unmindful of everything beside, he could not but smile at his late fidgeting panic.

Presently, while standing with Don Benito, looking forward upon the decks below, he was struck by one of those instances of insubordination previously alluded to. Three black boys, with two Spanish boys, were sitting together on the hatches, scraping a rude wooden platter, in which some scanty mess had recently been cooked. Suddenly, one of the black boys, enraged at a word dropped by one of his white companions, seized a knife, and though called to forbear by one of the oakum-pickers, struck the lad over the head, inflicting a gash from which blood flowed.

In amazement, Captain Delano inquired what this meant. To which the pale Benito dully muttered, that it was merely the sport of the lad.

"Pretty serious sport, truly," rejoined Captain Delano. "Had such a thing happened on board the *Bachelor's Delight,* instant punishment would have followed."

At these words the Spaniard turned upon the American one of his sudden, staring, half-lunatic looks; then, relapsing into his torpor, answered, "Doubtless, doubtless, Señor."

Is it, thought Captain Delano, that this helpless man is one of those paper captains I've known, who by policy wink at what by power they cannot put down? I know no sadder sight than a commander who has little of command but the name.

"I should think, Don Benito," he now said, glancing toward the oakum-picker who had sought to interfere with the boys, "that you would find it advantageous to keep all your blacks employed, especially the younger ones, no matter at what useless task, and no matter what happens to the ship. Why, even with my little band, I find such a course indispensable. I once kept a crew on my quarter-deck thrumming mats for my cabin, when, for three days, I had given up my ship—mats, men, and all—for a speedy loss, owing to the violence of a gale in which we could do nothing but helplessly drive before it."

"Doubtless, doubtless," muttered Don Benito.

"But," continued Captain Delano, again glancing upon the oakum-pickers and then at the hatchet-polishers, near by, "I see you keep some at least of your host employed."

"Yes," was again the vacant response.

"Those old men there, shaking their pows from their pulpits," continued Captain Delano, pointing to the oakum-pickers, "seem to act the part of old dominies to the rest, little heeded as their admonitions are at times. Is this voluntary on their part, Don Benito, or have you appointed them shepherds to your flock of black sheep?"

"What posts they fill, I appointed them," rejoined the Spaniard in an acrid tone, as if resenting some supposed satiric reflection.

"And these others, these Ashantee conjurors here," continued Captain Delano, rather uneasily eyeing the brandished steel of the hatchet-polishers, where in spots it had been brought to a shine, "this seems a curious business they are at, Don Benito?"

"In the gales we met," answered the Spaniard, "what of our general cargo was not thrown overboard was much damaged by the brine. Since coming into calm weather, I have had several cases of knives and hatchets daily brought up for overhauling and cleaning."

"A prudent idea, Don Benito. You are part owner of ship and cargo, I presume; but not of the slaves, perhaps?"

"I am owner of all you see," impatiently returned Don Benito, "except the main company of blacks, who belonged to my late friend, Alexandro Aranda."

As he mentioned this name, his air was heart-broken, his knees shook; his servant supported him.

Thinking he divined the cause of such unusual emotion, to confirm his surmise, Captain Delano, after a pause, said, "And may I ask, Don Benito, whether—since awhile ago you spoke of some cabin passengers—the friend, whose loss so afflicts you, at the outset of the voyage accompanied his blacks?"

"Yes."

"But died of the fever?"

"Died of the fever.—Oh, could I but—"

Again quivering, the Spaniard paused.

"Pardon me," said Captain Delano slowly, "but I think that, by a sympathetic experience, I conjecture, Don Benito, what it is that gives the keener edge to your grief. It was once my hard fortune to lose at sea a dear friend, my own brother, then supercargo. Assured of the welfare of his spirit, its departure I could have borne like a man; but that honest eye, that honest hand—both of which had so often met mine—and that warm heart; all, all—like scraps to the dogs—to throw all to the sharks! It was then I vowed never to have for fellow-voyager a man I loved, unless, unbeknown to him, I had provided every requisite, in case of a fatality, for embalming his mortal part for interment on shore. Were your friend's remains now on board this ship, Don Benito, not thus strangely would the mention of his name affect you."

"On board this ship?" echoed the Spaniard. Then, with horrified gestures, as directed against some spectre, he unconsciously fell into the ready arms of his attendant, who, with a silent appeal toward Captain Delano, seemed beseeching him not again to broach a theme so unspeakably distressing to his master.

This poor fellow now, thought the pained American, is the victim of that sad superstition which associates goblins with the deserted body of man, as ghosts with an abandoned house. How unlike are we made! What to me, in like case, would have been a solemn satisfaction, the bare suggestion, even, terrifies the Spaniard into this trance. Poor Alexandro Aranda! what would you say could you here see your friend—who, on former voyages, when you for months were left behind, has, I dare say, often longed, and longed, for one peep at you—now transported with terror at the least thought of having you anyway nigh him.

At this moment, with a dreary graveyard toll, betokening a flaw, the ship's forecastle bell, smote by one of the grizzled oakum-pickers, proclaimed ten o'clock through the leaden calm; when Captain Delano's attention was caught by the moving figure of a gigantic black, emerging from the general crowd below, and slowly advancing toward the elevated poop. An iron collar was about his neck, from which depended a chain, thrice wound round his body; the terminating links padlocked together at a broad band of iron, his girdle.

"How like a mute Atufal moves," murmured the servant.

The black mounted the steps of the poop, and, like a brave prisoner, brought up to receive sentence, stood in unquailing muteness before Don Benito, now recovered from his attack.

At the first glimpse of his approach, Don Benito had started, a resentful shadow swept over his face; and, as with the sudden memory of bootless rage, his white lips glued together.

This is some mulish mutineer, thought Captain Delano, surveying, not without a mixture of admiration, the colossal form of the negro.

"See, he waits your question, master," said the servant.

Thus reminded, Don Benito, nervously averting his glance, as if shunning, by anticipation, some rebellious response, in a disconcerted voice, thus spoke:

"Atufal, will you ask my pardon now?"

The black was silent.

"Again, master," murmured the servant, with bitter upbraiding eyeing his countryman; "Again, master; he will bend to master yet."

"Answer," said Don Benito, still averting his glance, "say but the one word pardon, and your chains shall be off."

Upon this, the black, slowly raising both arms, let them lifelessly fall, his links clanking, his head bowed; as much as to say, "No, I am content."

"Go," said Don Benito, with inkept and unknown emotion.

Deliberately as he had come, the black obeyed.

"Excuse me, Don Benito," said Captain Delano, "but this scene surprises me; what means it, pray?"

"It means that that negro alone, of all the band, has given me peculiar cause of offence. I have put him in chains; I—"

Here he paused; his hand to his head, as if there were a swimming there, or a sudden bewilderment of memory had come over him; but meeting his servant's kindly glance seemed reassured, and proceeded:

"I could not scourge such a form. But I told him he must ask my pardon. As yet he has not. At my command, every two hours he stands before me."

"And how long has this been?"

"Some sixty days."

"And obedient in all else? And respectful?"

"Yes."

"Upon my conscience, then," exclaimed Captain Delano, impulsively, "he has a royal spirit in him, this fellow."

"He may have some right to it," bitterly returned Don Benito; "he says he was king in his own land."

"Yes," said the servant, entering a word, "those slits in Atufal's ears once held wedges of gold; but poor Babo here, in his own land, was only a poor slave; a black man's slave was Babo, who now is the white's."

Somewhat annoyed by these conversational familiarities, Captain Delano turned curiously upon the attendant, then glanced inquiringly at his master; but, as if long wonted to these little informalities, neither master nor man seemed to understand him.

"What, pray, was Atufal's offence, Don Benito?" asked Captain Delano; "if it was not something very serious, take a fool's advice, and, in view of his general docility, as well as in some natural respect for his spirit, remit his penalty."

"No, no, master never will do that," here murmured the servant to himself, "proud Atufal must first ask master's pardon. The slave there carries the padlock, but master here carries the key."

His attention thus directed, Captain Delano now noticed for the first time that, suspended by a slender silken cord, from Don Benito's neck hung a key. At once, from the servant's muttered syllables divining the key's purpose, he smiled and said: "So, Don Benito—padlock and key—significant symbols, truly."

Biting his lip, Don Benito faltered.

Though the remark of Captain Delano, a man of such native simplicity as to be incapable of satire or irony, had been dropped in playful allusion to the Spaniard's singularly evidenced lordship over the black; yet the hypochondriac seemed in some way to have taken it as a malicious reflection upon his confessed inability thus far to break down, at least, on a verbal summons, the entrenched will of the slave. Deploring this supposed misconception, yet despair-ing of correcting it, Captain Delano shifted the subject; but finding his companion more than ever withdrawn, as if still slowly digesting the lees of the presumed affront above-mentioned, by-and-by Captain Delano likewise became less talkative, oppressed, against his own will, by what seemed the secret vindictiveness of the morbidly sensitive Spaniard. But the good sailor himself, of a quite contrary disposition, refrained, on his part, alike from the appearance as from the feeling of resentment, and if silent, was only so from contagion.

Presently the Spaniard, assisted by his servant, somewhat discourteously crossed over from Captain Delano; a procedure which, sensibly enough, might have been allowed to pass for idle caprice of ill-humour, had not master and man, lingering round the corner of the elevated skylight, begun whispering together in low voices. This was unpleasing. And more: the moody air of the Spaniard, which at times had not been without a sort of valetudinarian stateliness, now seemed anything but dignified; while the menial familiarity of the servant lost its original charm of simple-hearted attachment.

In his embarrassment, the visitor turned his face to the other side of the ship. By so doing, his glance accidentally fell on a young Spanish sailor, a coil of rope in his hand, just stepped from the deck to the first round of the mizzen-rigging. Perhaps the man would not have been particularly noticed, were it not that, during his ascent to one of the yards, he, with a sort of covert intentness, kept his eye fixed on Captain Delano, from whom, presently, it passed, as if by a natural sequence, to the two whisperers.

His own attention thus redirected to that quarter, Captain Delano gave a slight start. From something in Don Benito's manner just then, it seemed as if the visitor had, at least partly, been the subject of the withdrawn consultation going on—a conjecture as little agreeable to the guest as it was little flattering to the host.

The singular alternations of courtesy and ill-breeding in the

Spanish captain were unaccountable, except on one of two suppositions—innocent lunacy, or wicked imposture.

But the first idea, though it might naturally have occurred to an indifferent observer, and, in some respects, had not hitherto been wholly a stranger to Captain Delano's mind, yet, now that, in an incipient way, he began to regard the stranger's conduct something in the light of an intentional affront, of course the idea of lunacy was virtually vacated. But if not a lunatic, what then? Under the circumstances, would a gentleman, nay, any honest boor, act the part now acted by his host? The man was an impostor. Some low-born adventurer, masquerading as an oceanic grandee; yet so ignorant of the first requisites of mere gentlemanhood as to be betrayed into the present remarkable indecorum. That strange ceremoniousness, too, at other times evinced, seemed not uncharacteristic of one playing a part above his real level. Benito Cereno—Don Benito Cereno—a sounding name. One, too, at that period, not unknown, in the surname, to supercargoes and sea captains trading along the Spanish Main, as belonging to one of the most enterprising and extensive mercantile families in all those provinces; several members of it having titles; a sort of Castilian Rothschild, with a noble brother, or cousin, in every great trading town of South America. The alleged Don Benito was in early manhood, about twenty-nine or thirty. To assume a sort of roving cadetship in the maritime affairs of such a house, what more likely scheme for a young knave of talent and spirit? But the Spaniard was a pale invalid. Never mind. For even to the degree of simulating mortal disease, the craft of some tricksters had been known to attain. To think that, under the aspect of infantile weakness, the most savage energies might be couched—those velvets of the Spaniard but the velvet paw to his fangs.

From no train of thought did these fancies come; not from within, but from without; suddenly, too, and in one throng, like hoar frost; yet as soon to vanish as the mild sun of Captain Delano's good-nature regained its meridian.

Glancing over once again toward Don Benito—whose side-face, revealed above the skylight, was now turned toward him—Captain Delano was struck by the profile, whose clearness of cut was refined by the thinness incident to ill-health, as well as ennobled about the chin by the beard. Away with suspicion. He was a true off-shoot of a true hidalgo Cereno.

Relieved by these and other better thoughts, the visitor, lightly humming a tune, now began indifferently pacing the poop, so as not to betray to Don Benito that he had at all mistrusted incivility, much less duplicity; for such mistrust would yet be proved illusory, and by the event; though, for the present, the circumstance which had provoked that distrust remained unexplained. But when that little mystery should have been cleared up, Captain Delano thought he might extremely regret it, did he allow Don Benito to become aware that he had indulged in ungenerous surmises. In short, to the Spaniard's black-letter text, it was best, for a while, to leave open margin.

Presently, his pale face twitching and overcast, the Spaniard, still supported by his attendant, moved over toward his guest, when, with even more than his usual embarrassment, and a strange sort of intriguing intonation in his husky whisper, the following conversation began:

"Señor, may I ask how long you have lain at this isle?"

"Oh, but a day or two, Don Benito."

"And from what port are you last?"

"Canton."

"And there, Señor, you exchanged your seal-skins for teas and silks, I think you said?"

"Yes. Silks, mostly."

"And the balance you took in specie, perhaps?"

Captain Delano, fidgeting a little, answered—

"Yes; some silver; not a very great deal, though."

"Ah—well. May I ask how many men have you on board, Señor?"

Captain Delano slightly started, but answered:

"About five-and-twenty, all told."

"And at present, Señor, all on board, I suppose?"

"All on board, Don Benito," replied the captain now with satisfaction.

"And will be to-night, Señor?"

At this last question, following so many pertinacious ones, for the soul of him Captain Delano could not but look very earnestly at the questioner, who, instead of meeting the glance, with every token of craven discomposure dropped his eyes to the deck; presenting an unworthy contrast to his servant, who, just then, was kneeling at his feet adjusting a loose shoe-buckle; his disengaged face meantime, with humble curiosity, turned openly up into his master's downcast one.

The Spaniard, still with a guilty shuffle, repeated his question: "And—and will be to-night, Señor?"

"Yes, for aught I know," returned Captain Delano,—"but nay," rallying himself into fearless truth, "some of them talked of going off on another fishing party about midnight."

"Your ships generally go—go more or less armed, I believe, Señor?"

"Oh, a six-pounder or two, in case of emergency," was the intrepidly indifferent reply, "with a small stock of muskets, sealing-spears, and cutlasses, you know."

As he thus responded, Captain Delano again glanced at Don Benito, but the latter's eyes were averted; while abruptly and awkwardly shifting the subject, he made some peevish allusion to the calm, and then, without apology, once more, with his attendant, withdrew to the opposite bulwarks, where the whispering was resumed.

At this moment, and ere Captain Delano could cast a cool thought upon what had just passed, the young Spanish sailor before mentioned was seen descending from the rigging. In act of stooping over to spring inboard to the deck, his voluminous, unconfined frock, or shirt, of coarse woollen, much spotted with tar, opened out far down the chest, revealing a soiled under-garment of what seemed the finest linen, edged, about the neck, with a narrow blue ribbon, sadly faded and worn. At this moment the young sailor's eye was again fixed on the whisperers, and Captain Delano thought he observed a lurking significance in it, as if silent signs of some freemason sort had that instant been interchanged.

This once more impelled his own glance in the direction of Don Benito, and, as before, he could not but infer that himself formed the subject of the conference. He paused. The sound of the hatchet-polishing fell on his ears. He cast another swift side-look at the two. They had the air of conspirators. In connection with the late questionings, and the incident of the young sailor, these things now begat such return of involuntary suspicion, that the singular guilelessness of the American could not endure it. Plucking up a gay and humorous expression, he crossed over to the two rapidly, saying: "Ha, Don Benito, your black here seems high in your trust; a sort of privy-counsellor, in fact."

Upon this, the servant looked up with a good-natured grin, but the master started as from a venomous bite. It was a moment or two before the Spaniard sufficiently recovered himself to reply; which he did, at last, with cold constraint: "Yes, Señor, I have trust in Babo."

Here Babo, changing his previous grin of mere animal humour into an intelligent smile, not ungratefully eyed his master.

Finding that the Spaniard now stood silent and reserved, as if involuntarily, or purposely giving hint that his guest's proximity was inconvenient just then, Captain Delano, unwilling to appear uncivil even to incivility itself, made some trivial remark and moved off; again and again turning over in his mind the mysterious demeanour of Don Benito Cereno.

He had descended from the poop, and, wrapped in thought, was passing near a dark hatchway, leading down into the steerage, when, perceiving motion there, he looked to see what moved. The same instant there was a sparkle in the shadowy hatchway, and he saw one of the Spanish sailors, prowling there, hurriedly placing his hand in the bosom of his frock, as if hiding something. Before the man could have been certain who it was that was passing, he slunk below out of sight. But enough was seen of him to make it sure that he was the same young sailor before noticed in the rigging.

What was that which so sparkled? thought Captain Delano. It was no lamp—no match—no live coal. Could it have been a jewel? But how come sailors with jewels?—or with silk-trimmed under-shirts either? Has he been robbing the trunks of the dead cabin passengers? But if so, he would hardly wear one of the stolen articles on board ship here. Ah, ah—if now that was, indeed, a secret sign I saw passing between this suspicious fellow and his captain awhile since; if I could only be certain that in my uneasiness my senses did not deceive me, then—

Here, passing from one suspicious thing to another, his mind revolved the point of the strange questions put to him concerning his ship.

By a curious coincidence, as each point was recalled, the black wizards of Ashantee would strike up with their hatchets, as in ominous comment on the white stranger's thoughts. Pressed by such enigmas and portents, it would have been almost against nature, had not, even into the least distrustful heart, some ugly misgivings obtruded.

Observing the ship now helplessly fallen into a current, with enchanted sails, drifting with increased rapidity seaward; and noting that, from a lately intercepted projection of the land, the sealer was hidden, the stout mariner began to quake at thoughts which he barely durst confess to himself. Above all, he began to feel a ghostly dread of Don Benito. And yet when he roused himself, dilated his chest, felt himself strong on his legs, and coolly considered it—what did all these phantoms amount to?

Had the Spaniard any sinister scheme, it must have reference not so much to him (Captain Delano) as to his ship (the *Bachelor's Delight*). Hence the present drifting away of the one ship from the other, instead of favouring any such possible scheme, was, for the time at least, opposed to it. Clearly any suspicion, combining such contradictions, must need be delusive. Beside, was it not absurd to think of a vessel in distress—a vessel by sickness almost dismanned of her crew—a vessel whose inmates were parched for water—was it not a thousand times absurd that such a craft should, at present, be of a piratical character; or her commander, either for himself or those under him, cherish any desire but for speedy relief and refreshment? But then, might not general distress, and thirst in particular, be affected? And might not that same undiminished Spanish crew, alleged to have perished off to a remnant, be at that very moment lurking in the hold? On heart-broken pretence of entreating a cup of cold water, fiends in human form had got into lonely dwellings, nor retired until a dark deed had been done. And among the Malay pirates, it was no unusual thing to lure ships after them into their treacherous harbours, or entice boarders from a declared enemy at sea, by the spectacle of thinly manned or vacant decks, beneath which prowled a hundred spears with yellow arms ready to upthrust them through the mats. Not that Captain Delano had entirely credited such things. He had heard of them—and now, as stories, they recurred. The present destination of the ship was the anchorage. There she would be near his own vessel. Upon gaining that vicinity, might not the *San Dominick*, like a slumbering volcano, suddenly let loose energies now hid?

He recalled the Spaniard's manner while telling his story. There was a gloomy hesitancy and subterfuge about it. It was just the manner of one making up his tale for evil purposes, as he goes. But if that story was true, what was the truth? That the ship had unlawfully come into the Spaniard's possession? But in many of its details, especially in reference to the more calamitous parts, such as the fatalities among the seamen, the consequent prolonged beating about, the past sufferings from obstinate calms, and still continued suffering from thirst; in all these points, as well as others, Don Benito's story had corroborated not only the wailing ejaculations of the indiscriminate multitude, white and black, but likewise—what seemed impossible to be counterfeit—by the very expression and play of every human feature, which Captain Delano saw. If Don Benito's story was throughout an invention, then every soul on board, down to the youngest negress, was his carefully drilled recruit in the plot: an incredible inference. And yet, if there was ground for mistrusting the Spanish captain's veracity, that inference was a legitimate one.

In short, scarce an uneasiness entered the honest sailor's mind but, by a subsequent spontaneous act of good sense, it was ejected. At last he began to laugh at these forebodings; and laugh at the strange ship for, in its aspect someway siding with them, as it were; and laugh, too, at the odd-looking blacks, particularly those old scissors-grinders, the Ashantees; and those bed-ridden old knitting-women, the oakum-pickers; and in a human way, he almost began to laugh at the dark Spaniard himself, the central hobgoblin of all.

For the rest, whatever in a serious way seemed enigmatical, was now good-naturedly explained away by the thought that, for the most part, the poor invalid scarcely knew what he was about; either sulking in black vapours, or putting random questions without sense or object. Evidently, for the present, the man was not fit to be entrusted with the ship. On some benevolent plea withdrawing the command from him, Captain Delano would yet have to send her to Concepcion in charge of his second mate, a worthy person and good navigator—a plan which would prove no wiser for the *San Dominick* than for Don Benito; for—relieved from all anxiety, keeping wholly to his cabin—the sick man, under the good nursing of his servant, would probably, by the end of the passage, be in a measure restored to health and with that he should also be restored to authority.

Such were the American's thoughts. They were tranquillizing. There was a difference between the idea of Don Benito's darky preordaining Captain Delano's fate, and Captain Delano's lightly arranging Don Benito's. Nevertheless, it was not without something of relief that the good seaman presently perceived his whale-boat in the distance. Its absence had been prolonged by unexpected detention at the sealer's side, as well as its returning trip lengthened by the continual recession of the goal.

The advancing speck was observed by the blacks. Their shouts attracted the attention of Don Benito, who, with a return of courtesy, approaching Captain Delano, expressed satisfaction at the coming of some supplies, slight and temporary as they must necessarily prove.

Captain Delano responded; but while doing so, his attention was drawn to something passing on the deck below: among the crowd climbing the landward bulwarks, anxiously watching the coming boat, two blacks, to all appearances accidentally incommoded by one of the sailors, flew out against him with horrible curses, which the sailor someway resenting, the two blacks dashed him to the deck and jumped upon him, despite the earnest cries of the oakum-pickers.

"Don Benito," said Captain Delano quickly, "do you see what is going on there? Look!"

But, seized by his cough, the Spaniard staggered, with both hands to his face, on the point of falling. Captain Delano would have supported him, but the servant was more alert, who, with one hand sustaining his master, with the other applied the cordial. Don Benito, restored, the black withdrew his support, slipping aside a little, but dutifully remaining within call of a whisper. Such discretion was here evinced as quite wiped away, in the visitor's eyes, any blemish of impropriety which might have attached to the attendant, from the indecorous conferences before mentioned; showing, too, that if the servant were to blame, it might be more the master's fault than his own, since when left to himself he could conduct thus well.

His glance thus called away from the spectacle of disorder to the more pleasing one before him, Captain Delano could not avoid again congratulating Don Benito upon possessing such a servant, who, though perhaps a little too forward now and then, must upon the whole be invaluable to one in the invalid's situation.

"Tell me, Don Benito," he added, with a smile—"I should like to have your man here myself—what will you take for him? Would fifty doubloons be any object?"

"Master wouldn't part with Babo for a thousand doubloons," murmured the black, overhearing the offer, and taking it in earnest, and, with the strange vanity of a faithful slave appreciated by his master, scorning to hear so paltry a valuation put upon him by a stranger. But Don Benito, apparently hardly yet completely restored, and again interrupted by his cough, made but some broken reply.

Soon his physical distress became so great, affecting his mind, too, apparently, that, as if to screen the sad spectacle, the servant gently conducted his master below.

Left to himself, the American, to while away the time till his boat should arrive, would have pleasantly accosted some one of the few Spanish seamen he saw; but recalling something that Don Benito had said touching their ill conduct, he refrained, as a ship-master indisposed to countenance cowardice or unfaithfulness in seamen.

While, with these thoughts, standing with eye directed forward toward that handful of sailors—suddenly he thought that some of them returned the glance and with a sort of meaning. He rubbed his eyes, and looked again; but again seemed to see the same thing. Under a new form, but more obscure than any previous one, the old suspicions recurred, but, in the absence of Don Benito, with less of panic than before. Despite the bad account given of the sailors, Captain Delano resolved forthwith to accost one of them. Descending the poop, he made his way through the blacks, his movement drawing a queer cry from the oakum-pickers, prompted by whom the negroes, twitching each other aside, divided before him; but, as if curious to see what was the object of this deliberate visit to their Ghetto, closing in behind, in tolerable order, followed the white stranger up. His progress thus proclaimed as by mounted kings-at-arms, and escorted as by a Caffre guard of honour, Captain Delano, assuming a good-humoured, off-hand air, continued to advance; now and then saying a blithe word to the negroes, and his eye curiously surveying the white faces, here and there sparsely mixed in with the blacks, like stray white pawns venturously involved in the ranks of the chessmen opposed.

While thinking which of them to select for his purpose, he chanced to observe a sailor seated on the deck engaged in tarring the strap of a large block, with a circle of blacks squatted round him inquisitively eyeing the process.

The mean employment of the man was in contrast with something superior in his figure. His hand, black with continually thrusting it into the tar-pot held for him by a negro, seemed not naturally allied to his face, a face which would have been a very fine one but for its haggardness. Whether this haggardness had aught to do with criminality, could not be determined; since, as intense heat and cold, though unlike, produce like sensations, so innocence and guilt, when, through casual association with mental pain, stamping any visible impress, use one seal—a hacked one.

Not again that this reflection occurred to Captain Delano at the time, charitable man as he was. Rather another idea. Because observing so singular a haggardness to be combined with a dark eye, averted as in trouble and shame, and then, however illogically, uniting in his mind his own private suspicions of the crew with the confessed ill-opinion on the part of their captain, he was insensibly operated upon by certain general notions, which, while disconnecting pain and abashment from virtue, as invariably link them with vice.

If, indeed, there be any wickedness on board this ship, thought Captain Delano, be sure that man there has fouled his hand in it, even as now he fouls it in the pitch. I don't like to accost him. I will speak to this other, this old Jack here on the windlass.

He advanced to an old Barcelona tar, in ragged red breeches and dirty night-cap, cheeks trenched and bronzed, whiskers dense as thorn hedges. Seated between two sleepy-looking Africans, this mariner, like his younger shipmate, was employed upon some rigging—splicing a cable—the sleepy-looking blacks performing the inferior function of holding the outer parts of the ropes for him.

Upon Captain Delano's approach, the man at once hung his head below its previous level; the one necessary for business. It appeared as if he desired to be thought absorbed, with more than common fidelity, in his task. Being addressed, he glanced up,·but with what seemed a furtive, diffident air, which sat strangely enough on his weatherbeaten visage, much as if a grizzly bear, instead of growling and biting, should simper and cast sheep's eyes. He was asked several questions concerning the voyage—questions purposely referring to several particulars in Don Benito's narrative—not previously corroborated by those impulsive cries greeting the visitor on first coming on board. The questions were briefly answered, confirming all that remained to be confirmed of the story. The negroes about the windlass joined in with the old sailor, but, as they became talkative, he by degrees became mute, and at length quite glum, seemed morosely unwilling to answer more questions, and yet, all the while, this ursine air was somehow mixed with his sheepish one.

Despairing of getting into unembarrassed talk with such a centaur, Captain Delano, after glancing round for a more promising counte-

nance, but seeing none, spoke pleasantly to the blacks to make way
for him; and so, amid various grins and grimaces, returned to the
poop, feeling a little strange at first, he could hardly tell why, but
upon the whole with regained confidence in Benito Cereno.

How plainly, thought he, did that old whiskerando yonder betray
a consciousness of ill-desert. No doubt, when he saw me coming, he
dreaded lest I, apprised by his captain of the crew's general mis-
behaviour, came with sharp words for him, and so down with his
head. And yet—and yet, now that I think of it, that very old fellow,
if I err not, was one of those who seemed so earnestly eyeing me
here awhile since. Ah, these currents spin one's head round almost
as much as they do the ship. Ha, there now's a pleasant sort of
sunny sight; quite sociable, too.

His attention had been drawn to a slumbering negress, partly
disclosed through the lace-work of some rigging, lying, with youthful limbs carelessly disposed, under the lee of the bulwarks, like a
doe in the shade of a woodland rock. Sprawling at her lapped breasts
was her wide-awake fawn, stark naked, its black little body half
lifted from the deck, crosswise with its dam's; its hands, like two
paws, clambering upon her; its mouth and nose ineffectually rooting
to get at the mark; and meantime giving a vexatious half-grunt,
blending with the composed snore of the negress.

The uncommon vigour of the child at length roused the mother.
She started up, at distance facing Captain Delano. But, as if not at
all concerned at the attitude in which she had been caught, delightedly she caught the child up, with maternal transports, covering
it with kisses.

There's naked nature, now; pure tenderness and love, thought
Captain Delano, well pleased.

This incident prompted him to remark the other negresses more
particularly than before. He was gratified with their manners; like
most uncivilized women, they seemed at once tender of heart and
tough of constitution; equally ready to die for their infants or fight
for them. Unsophisticated as leopardesses; loving as doves. Ah!
thought Captain Delano, these perhaps are some of the very women
whom Mungo Park saw in Africa, and gave such a noble account of.

These natural sights somehow insensibly deepened his confidence
and ease. At last he looked to see how his boat was getting on; but
it was still pretty remote. He turned to see if Don Benito had returned; but he had not.

To change the scene, as well as to please himself with a leisurely observation of the coming boat, stepping over into the mizzen-chains he clambered his way into the starboard quarter-gallery; one of those abandoned Venetian-looking water-balconies previously mentioned; retreats cut off from the deck. As his foot pressed the half-damp, half-dry seamosses matting the place, and a chance phantom cats-paw—an islet of breeze, unheralded, unfollowed—at this ghostly cats-paw came fanning his cheek, as his glance fell upon the row of small, round dead-lights, all closed like coppered eyes of the coffined, and the state-cabin door, once connecting with the gallery, even as the dead-lights had once looked out upon it, but now caulked fast like a sarcophagus lid, to a purple-black, tarred-over panel, threshold, and post; and he bethought him of the time, when that state-cabin and this state-balcony had heard the voices of the Spanish king's officers, and the forms of the Lima viceroy's daughters had perhaps leaned where he stood—as these and other images flitted through his mind, as the cats-paw through the calm, gradually he felt rising a dreamy inquietude, like that of one who alone on the prairie feels unrest from the repose of the noon.

He leaned against the carved balustrade, again looking off toward his boat; but found his eye falling upon the ribboned grass, trailing along the ship's water-line, straight as a border of green box; and parterres of sea-weed, broad ovals and crescents, floating nigh and far, with what seemed long formal alleys between, crossing the terraces of swells, and sweeping round as if leading to the grottoes below. And overhanging all was the balustrade by his arm, which, partly stained with pitch and partly embossed with moss, seemed the charred ruin of some summer-house in a grand garden long running to waste.

Trying to break one charm, he was but becharmed anew. Though upon the wide sea, he seemed in some far inland country; prisoner in some deserted château, left to stare at empty grounds, and peer out at vague roads, where never wagon or wayfarer passed.

But these enchantments were a little disenchanted as his eye fell on the corroded main-chains. Of an ancient style, massy and rusty in link, shackle and bolt, they seemed even more fit for the ship's present business than the one for which probably she had been built.

Presently he thought something moved nigh the chains. He rubbed his eyes, and looked hard. Groves of rigging were about the chains; and there, peering from behind a great stay, like an Indian from behind a hemlock, a Spanish sailor, a marlingspike in his hand, was seen, who made what seemed an imperfect gesture toward the balcony—but immediately, as if alarmed by some advancing step along the deck within, vanished into the recesses of the hempen forest, like a poacher.

What meant this? Something the man had sought to communicate, unbeknown to any one, even to his captain. Did the secret involve aught unfavourable to his captain? Were those previous misgivings of Captain Delano's about to be verified? Or, in his haunted mood at the moment, had some random, unintentional motion of the man, while busy with the stay, as if repairing it, been mistaken for a significant beckoning?

Not unbewildered, again he gazed off for his boat. But it was temporarily hidden by a rocky spur of the isle. As with some eagerness he bent forward, watching for the first shooting view of its beak, the balustrade gave way before him like charcoal. Had he not clutched an outreaching rope he would have fallen into the sea. The crash, though feeble, and the fall, though hollow, of the rotten fragments, must have been overheard. He glanced up. With sober curiosity peering down upon him was one of the old oakum-pickers, slipped from his perch to an outside boom; while below the old negro —and, invisible to him, reconnoitring from a port-hole like a fox from the mouth of its den—crouched the Spanish sailor again. From something suddenly suggested by the man's air, the mad idea now darted into Captain Delano's mind; that Don Benito's plea of indisposition, in withdrawing below, was but a pretence: that he was engaged there maturing some plot, of which the sailor, by some means gaining an inkling, had a mind to warn the stranger against; incited, it may be, by gratitude for a kind word on first boarding the ship. Was it from foreseeing some possible interference like this, that Don Benito had, beforehand, given such a bad character of his sailors, while praising the negroes; though, indeed, the former seemed as docile as the latter the contrary? The whites, too, by nature, were the shrewder race. A man with some evil design, would not he be likely to speak well of that stupidity which was blind to his depravity, and malign that intelligence from which it might not be hidden? Not unlikely, perhaps. But if the whites had dark secrets concerning Don Benito, could then Don Benito be any way in complicity with the blacks? But they were too stupid. Besides, who ever heard of a white so far a renegade as to apostatize from his very species almost, by leaguing in against it with negroes? These difficulties recalled former ones. Lost in their mazes, Captain Delano, who had now regained the deck, was uneasily advancing along it, when he observed a new face: an aged sailor seated cross-legged near the main hatchway. His skin was shrunk up with wrinkles like a pelican's empty pouch; his hair frosted; his countenance grave and composed. His hands were full of ropes, which he was working into a large knot. Some blacks were about him obligingly dipping the strands for him, here and there, as the exigencies of the operation demanded.

Captain Delano crossed over to him, and stood in silence survey- ing the knot; his mind, by a not uncongenial transition, passing from its own entanglements to those of the hemp. For intricacy such a knot he had never seen in an American ship, or indeed any other. The old man looked like an Egyptian priest, making gordian knots for the temple of Ammon. The knot seemed a combination of double-bow-line-knot, treble-crown-knot, back-handed-well-knot, knot-in-and-out-knot, and jamming-knot.

At last, puzzled to comprehend the meaning of such a knot, Cap- tain Delano, addressed the knotter:—

"What are you knotting there, my man?"

"The knot," was the brief reply, without looking up.

"So it seems; but what is it for?"

"For some one else to undo," muttered back the old man, plying his fingers harder than ever, the knot being now nearly completed.

While Captain Delano stood watching him, suddenly the old man threw the knot toward him, and said in broken English,—the first heard in the ship,—something to this effect—"Undo it, cut it, quick." It was said lowly, but with such condensation of rapidity, that the long, slow words in Spanish, which had preceded and followed, almost operated as covers to the brief English between.

For a moment, knot in hand, and knot in head, Captain Delano stood mute; while, without further heeding him, the old man was now intent upon other ropes. Presently there was a slight stir behind Captain Delano. Turning, he saw the chained negro, Atufal, stand- ing quietly there. The next moment the old sailor rose, muttering, and, followed by his subordinate negroes, removed to the forward part of the ship, where in the crowd he disappeared.

An elderly negro, in a clout like an infant's, and with a pepper and salt head, and a kind of attorney air, now approached Captain De- lano. In tolerable Spanish, and with a good-natured, knowing wink,

he informed him that the old knotter was simple-witted, but harmless; often playing his old tricks. The negro concluded by begging
the knot, for of course the stranger would not care to be troubled
with it. Unconsciously, it was handed to him. With a sort of congé,
the negro received it, and turning his back ferreted into it like a detective Custom House officer after smuggled laces. Soon, with some
African word, equivalent to pshaw, he tossed the knot overboard.

All this is very queer now, thought Captain Delano, with a
qualmish sort of emotion; but as one feeling incipient seasickness,
he strove, by ignoring the symptoms, to get rid of the malady. Once
more he looked off for his boat. To his delight, it was now again in
view, leaving the rocky spur astern.

The sensation here experienced, after at first relieving his uneasiness, with unforeseen efficiency, soon began to remove it. The
less distant sight of that well-known boat—showing it, not as before,
half blended with the haze, but with outline defined, so that its in-
dividuality, like a man's, was manifest; that boat, *Rover* by name,
which, though now in strange seas, had often pressed the beach of
Captain Delano's home, and, brought to its threshold for repairs,
had familiarly lain there, as a Newfoundland dog; the sight of that
household boat evoked a thousand trustful associations, which, contrasted with previous suspicions, filled him not only with lightsome
confidence, but somehow with half humorous self-reproaches at his
former lack of it.

"What, I, Amasa Delano—Jack of the Beach, as they called me
when a lad—I, Amasa; the same that, duck-satchel in hand, used to
paddle along the waterside to the schoolhouse made from the old
hulk;—I, little Jack of the Beach, that used to go berrying with
cousin Nat and the rest; I to be murdered here at the ends of the
earth, on board a haunted pirate-ship by a horrible Spaniard?—Too
nonsensical to think of! Who would murder Amasa Delano? His
conscience is clean. There is some one above. Fie, fie, Jack of the
Beach! you are a child indeed; a child of the second childhood, old
boy; you are beginning to dote and drule, I'm afraid."

Light of heart and foot, he stepped aft, and there was met by
Don Benito's servant, who, with a pleasing expression, responsive
to his own present feelings, informed him that his master had recovered from the effects of his coughing fit, and had just ordered him
to go present his compliments to his good guest, Don Amasa, and

say that he (Don Benito) would soon have the happiness to rejoin him.

There now, do you mark that? again thought Captain Delano, walking the poop. What a donkey I was. This kind gentleman who here sends me his kind compliments, he, but ten minutes ago, dark-lantern in hand, was dodging round some old grind-stone in the hold, sharpening a hatchet for me, I thought. Well, well; these long calms have a morbid effect on the mind, I've often heard, though I never believed it before. Ha! glancing toward the boat; there's *Rover*; a good dog; a white bone in her mouth. A pretty big bone though, seems to me.—What? Yes, she has fallen afoul of the bubbling tide-rip there. It sets her the other way, too, for the time. Patience.

It was now about noon, though, from the greyness of everything, it seemed to be getting toward dusk.

The calm was confirmed. In the far distance, away from the influence of land, the leaden ocean seemed laid out and leaded up, its course finished, soul gone, defunct. But the current from landward, where the ship was, increased; silently sweeping her further and further toward the tranced waters beyond.

Still, from his knowledge of those latitudes, cherishing hopes of a breeze, and a fair and fresh one, at any moment, Captain Delano, despite present prospects, buoyantly counted upon bringing the *San Dominick* safely to anchor ere night. The distance swept over was nothing; since, with a good wind, ten minutes' sailing would retrace more than sixty minutes' drifting. Meantime, one moment turning to mark "Rover" fighting the tide-rip, and the next to see Don Benito approaching, he continued walking the poop.

Gradually he felt a vexation arising from the delay of his boat; this soon merged into uneasiness; and at last, his eye falling continually, as from a stage-box into the pit, upon the strange crowd before and below him, and by-and-by recognizing there the face— now composed to indifference—of the Spanish sailor who had seemed to beckon from the main chains, something of his old trepidations returned.

Ah, thought he—gravely enough—this is like the ague: because it went off, it follows not that it won't come back.

Though ashamed of the relapse, he could not altogether subdue it; and so, exerting his good nature to the utmost, insensibly he came to a compromise.

Yes, this is a strange craft; a strange history, too, and strange folks on board. But—nothing more.

By way of keeping his mind out of mischief till the boat should arrive, he tried to occupy it with turning over and over, in a purely speculative sort of way, some lesser peculiarities of the captain and crew. Among others, four curious points recurred.

First, the affair of the Spanish lad assailed with a knife by the slave boy; an act winked at by Don Benito. Second, the tyranny in Don Benito's treatment of Atufal, the black; as if a child should lead a bull of the Nile by the ring in his nose. Third, the trampling of the sailor by the two negroes; a piece of insolence passed over without so much as a reprimand. Fourth, the cringing submission to their master of all the ship's underlings, mostly blacks; as if by the least inadvertence they feared to draw down his despotic displeasure.

Coupling these points, they seemed somewhat contradictory. But what then, thought Captain Delano, glancing toward his now nearing boat,—what then? Why, this Don Benito is a very capricious commander. But he is not the first of the sort I have seen; though it's true he rather exceeds any other. But as a nation—continued he in his reveries—these Spaniards are all an odd set; the very word Spaniard has a curious, conspirator, Guy-Fawkish twang to it. And yet, I dare say, Spaniards in the main are as good folks as any in Duxbury, Massachusetts. Ah, good! At last "Rover" has come.

As, with its welcome freight, the boat touched the side, the oakum-pickers, with venerable gestures, sought to restrain the blacks, who, at the sight of three gurried water-casks in its bottom, and a pile of wilted pumpkins in its bow, hung over the bulwarks in disorderly raptures.

Don Benito with his servant now appeared; his coming, perhaps, hastened by hearing the noise. Of him Captain Delano sought permission to serve out the water, so that all might share alike, and none injure themselves by unfair excess. But sensible, and, on Don Benito's account, kind as this offer was, it was received with what seemed impatience; as if aware that he lacked energy as a commander, Don Benito, with the true jealousy of weakness, resented as an affront any interference. So, at least, Captain Delano inferred.

In another moment the casks were being hoisted in, when some of the eager negroes accidentally jostled Captain Delano, where he stood by the gangway; so that, unmindful of Don Benito, yielding to the impulse of the moment, with good-natured authority he bade the blacks stand back; to enforce his words making use of a half-mirthful, half-menacing gesture. Instantly the blacks paused, just where they were, each negro and negress suspended in his or her posture, exactly as the word had found them—for a few seconds continuing so—while, as between the responsive posts of a telegraph, an unknown syllable ran from man to man among the perched oakum-pickers. While Captain Delano's attention was fixed by this scene, suddenly the hatchet-polishers half rose, and a rapid cry came from Don Benito.

Thinking that at the signal of the Spaniard he was about to be massacred, Captain Delano would have sprung for his boat, but paused, as the oakum-pickers, dropping down into the crowd with earnest exclamations, forced every white and every negro back, at the same moment, with gestures friendly and familiar, almost jocose, bidding him, in substance, not be a fool. Simultaneously the hatchet-polishers resumed their seats, quietly as so many tailors, and at once, as if nothing had happened, the work of hoisting in the casks was resumed, whites and blacks singing at the tackle.

Captain Delano glanced toward Don Benito. As he saw his meagre form in the act of recovering itself from reclining in the servant's arms, into which the agitated invalid had fallen, he could not but marvel at the panic by which himself had been surprised on the darting supposition that such a commander, who upon a legitimate occasion, so trivial, too, as it now appeared, could lose all self-command, was, with energetic iniquity, going to bring about his murder.

The casks being on deck, Captain Delano was handed a number of jars and cups by one of the steward's aides, who, in the name of Don Benito, entreated him to do as he had proposed: dole out the water. He complied, with republican impartiality as to this republican element, which always seeks one level, serving the oldest white no better than the youngest black; excepting, indeed, poor Don Benito, whose condition, if not rank, demanded an extra allowance. To him, in the first place, Captain Delano presented a fair pitcher of the fluid; but, thirsting as he was for fresh water, Don Benito quaffed not a drop until after several grave bows and salutes: a reciprocation of courtesies which the sight-loving Africans hailed with clapping of hands.

Two of the less wilted pumpkins being reserved for the cabin table, the residue were minced up on the spot for the general regalement. But the soft bread, sugar, and bottled cider, Captain Delano would have given the Spaniards alone, and in chief Don Benito; but the latter objected; which disinterestedness, on his part, not a little pleased the American; and so mouthfuls all around were given alike to whites and blacks; excepting one bottle of cider, which Babo insisted upon setting aside for his master.

Here it may be observed that as, on the first visit of the boat, the American had not permitted his men to board the ship, neither did he now; being unwilling to add to the confusion of the decks.

Not uninfluenced by the peculiar good humour at present prevailing, and for the time oblivious of any but benevolent thoughts, Captain Delano, who from recent indications counted upon a breeze within an hour or two at furthest, despatched the boat back to the sealer with orders for all the hands that could be spared immediately to set about rafting casks to the watering-place and filling them. Likewise he bade word be carried to his chief officer, that if against present expectation the ship was not brought to anchor by sunset, he need be under no concern, for as there was to be a full moon that night, he (Captain Delano) would remain on board ready to play the pilot, should the wind come soon or late.

As the two captains stood together, observing the departing boat— the servant as it happened having just spied a spot on his master's velvet sleeve, and silently engaged rubbing it out—the American expressed his regrets that the *San Dominick* had no boats; none, at least, but the unseaworthy old hulk of the long-boat, which, warped as a camel's skeleton in the desert, and almost as bleached, lay potwise inverted amidships, one side a little tipped, furnishing a subterraneous sort of den for family groups of the blacks, mostly women and small children; who, squatting on old mats below, or perched above in the dark dome, on the elevated seats, were descried, some distance within, like a social circle of bats, sheltering in some friendly cave; at intervals, ebon flights of naked boys and girls, three or four years old, darting in and out of the den's mouth.

"Had you three or four boats now, Don Benito," said Captain Delano, "I think that, by tugging at the oars, your negroes here might help along matters some.—Did you sail from port without boats, Don Benito?"

"They were stove in the gales, Señor."

"That was bad. Many men, too, you lost then. Boats and men.— Those must have been hard gales, Don Benito."

"Past all speech," cringed the Spaniard.

"Tell me, Don Benito," continued his companion with increased interest, "tell me, were these gales immediately off the pitch of Cape Horn?"

"Cape Horn?—who spoke of Cape Horn?"

"Yourself did, when giving me an account of your voyage," answered Captain Delano with almost equal astonishment at this eating of his own words, even as he ever seemed eating his own heart, on the part of the Spaniard. "You yourself, Don Benito, spoke of Cape Horn," he emphatically repeated.

The Spaniard turned, in a sort of stooping posture, pausing an instant, as one about to make a plunging exchange of elements, as from air to water.

At this moment a messenger-boy, a white, hurried by, in the regular performance of his function carrying the last expired half-hour forward to the forecastle, from the cabin time-piece, to have it struck at the ship's large bell.

"Master," said the servant, discontinuing his work on the coat sleeve, and addressing the rapt Spaniard with a sort of timid apprehensiveness, as one charged with a duty, the discharge of which, it was foreseen, would prove irksome to the very person who had imposed it, and for whose benefit it was intended, "master told me never mind where he was, or how engaged, always to remind him, to a minute, when shaving-time comes. Miguel has gone to strike the half-hour afternoon. It is *now*, master. Will master go into the cuddy?"

"Ah—yes," answered the Spaniard, starting, somewhat as from dreams into realities; then turning upon Captain Delano, he said that ere long he would resume the conversation.

"Then if master means to talk more to Don Amasa," said the servant, "why not let Don Amasa sit by master in the cuddy, and master can talk, and Don Amasa can listen, while Babo here lathers and strops."

"Yes," said Captain Delano, not unpleased with this sociable plan, "yes, Don Benito, unless you had rather not, I will go with you."

"Be it so, Señor."

As the three passed aft, the American could not but think it another strange instance of his host's capriciousness, this being shaved with such uncommon punctuality in the middle of the day. But he deemed it more than likely that the servant's anxious fidelity had something to do with the matter; inasmuch as the timely interruption served to rally his master from the mood which had evidently been coming upon him.

The place called the cuddy was a light deck-cabin formed by the poop, a sort of attic to the large cabin below. Part of it had formerly been the quarters of the officers; but since their death all the partitionings had been thrown down, and the whole interior converted into one spacious and airy marine hall; for absence of fine furniture and picturesque disarray, of odd appurtenances, somewhat answering to the wide, cluttered hall of some eccentric bachelor-squire in the country, who hangs his shooting-jacket and tobacco-pouch on deer antlers, and keeps his fishing-rod, tongs, and walking-stick in the same corner.

The similitude was heightened, if not originally suggested, by glimpses of the surrounding sea; since, in one aspect, the country and the ocean seem cousins-german.

The floor of the cuddy was matted. Overhead, four or five old muskets were stuck into horizontal holes along the beams. On one side was a claw-footed old table lashed to the deck; a thumbed missal on it, and over it a small, meagre crucifix attached to the bulkhead. Under the table lay a dented cutlass or two, with a hacked harpoon, among some melancholy old rigging, like a heap of poor friar's girdles. There were also two long, sharp-ribbed settees of malacca cane, black with age, and uncomfortable to look at as inquisitors' racks, with a large, misshapen arm-chair, which, furnished with a rude barber's crutch at the back, working with a screw, seemed some grotesque Middle Age engine of torment. A flag locker was in one corner, exposing various coloured bunting, some rolled up, others half unrolled, still others tumbled. Opposite was a cumbrous washstand, of black mahogany, all of one block, with a pedestal, like a font, and over it a railed shelf, containing combs, brushes, and other implements of the toilet. A torn hammock of stained grass swung near; the sheets tossed, and the pillow wrinkled up like a brow, as if whoever slept here slept but illy, with alternate visitations of sad thoughts and bad dreams.

The further extremity of the cuddy, overhanging the ship's stern, was pierced with three openings, windows or port holes, according as men or cannon might peer, socially or unsocially, out of them. At present neither men nor cannon were seen, though huge ring-bolts and other rusty iron fixtures of the wood-work hinted of twenty-four-pounders.

Glancing toward the hammock as he entered, Captain Delano said, "You sleep here, Don Benito?"

"Yes, Señor, since we got into mild weather."

"This seems a sort of dormitory, sitting-room, sail-loft, chapel, armoury, and private closet together, Don Benito," added Captain Delano, looking round.

"Yes, Señor; events have not been favourable to much order in my arrangements."

Here the servant, napkin on arm, made a motion as if waiting his master's good pleasure. Don Benito signified his readiness, when, seating him in the malacca arm-chair, and for the guest's convenience drawing opposite it one of the settees, the servant commenced operations by throwing back his master's collar and loosening his cravat.

There is something in the negro which, in a peculiar way, fits him for avocations about one's person. Most negroes are natural valets and hair-dressers; taking to the comb and brush congenially as to the castanets, and flourishing them apparently with almost equal satisfaction. There is, too, a smooth tact about them in this employment, with a marvelous, noiseless, gliding briskness, not ungraceful in its way, singularly pleasing to behold, and still more so to be the manipulated subject of. And above all is the great gift of good humour. Not the mere grin or laugh is here meant. Those were unsuitable. But a certain easy cheerfulness, harmonious in every glance and gesture; as though God had set the whole negro to some pleasant tune.

When to all this is added the docility arising from the unaspiring contentment of a limited mind, and that susceptibility of blind attachment sometimes inhering in indisputable inferiors, one readily perceives why those hypochondriacs, Johnson and Byron—it may be something like the hypochondriac, Benito Cereno—took to their hearts, almost to the exclusion of the entire white race, their serving men, the negroes, Barber and Fletcher. But if there be that in the negro which exempts him from the inflicted sourness of the morbid or cynical mind, how, in his most prepossessing aspects, must he appear to a benevolent one? When at ease with respect to exterior things, Captain Delano's nature was not only benign, but familiarly and humourously so. At home, he had often taken rare satisfaction in sitting in his door, watching some free man of colour at his work or play. If on a voyage he chanced to have a black sailor, invariably he was on chatty, and half-gamesome terms with him. In fact, like most men of a good, blithe heart, Captain Delano took to negroes, not philanthropically, but genially, just as other men to Newfoundland dogs.

Hitherto the circumstances in which he found the *San Dominick* had repressed the tendency. But in the cuddy, relieved from his former uneasiness, and, for various reasons, more sociably inclined than at any previous period of the day, and seeing the coloured servant, napkin on arm, so debonair about his master, in a business so familiar as that of shaving, too, all his old weakness for negroes returned.

Among other things, he was amused with an odd instance of the African love of bright colours and fine shows, in the black's informally taking from the flag-locker a great piece of bunting of all hues, and lavishly tucking it under his master's chin for an apron.

The mode of shaving among the Spaniards is a little different from what it is with other nations. They have a basin, specially called a barber's basin, which on one side is scooped out, so as accurately to receive the chin, against which it is closely held in lathering; which is done, not with a brush, but with soap dipped in the water of the basin and rubbed on the face.

In the present instance salt-water was used for lack of better; and the parts lathered were only the upper lip, and low down under the throat, all the rest being cultivated beard.

These preliminaries being somewhat novel to Captain Delano he sat curiously eyeing them, so that no conversation took place, nor for the present did Don Benito appear disposed to renew any.

Setting down his basin, the negro searched among the razors, as for the sharpest, and having found it, gave it an additional edge by expertly stropping it on the firm, smooth, oily skin of his open palm; he then made a gesture as if to begin, but midway stood suspended for an instant, one hand elevating the razor, the other professionally dabbling among the bubbling suds on the Spaniard's lank neck. Not unaffected by the close sight of the gleaming steel, Don Benito nervously shuddered, his usual ghastliness was heightened by the lather, which lather, again, was intensified in its hue by the contrasting sootiness of the negro's body. Altogether the scene was somewhat peculiar, at least to Captain Delano, nor, as he saw the two thus postured, could he resist the vagary, that in the black he saw a headsman, and in the white, a man at the block. But this was one of those antic conceits, appearing and vanishing in a breath, from which, perhaps, the best regulated mind is not free.

Meantime the agitation of the Spaniard had a little loosened the bunting from around him, so that one broad fold swept curtain-like over the chair-arm to the floor, revealing, amid a profusion of armorial bars and ground-colours—black, blue and yellow—a closed castle in a blood-red field diagonal with a lion rampant in a white.

"The castle and the lion," exclaimed Captain Delano—"why, Don Benito, this is the flag of Spain you use here. It's well it's only I, and not the King, that sees this," he added with a smile, "but"—turning toward the black,—"it's all one, I suppose, so the colours be gay," which playful remark did not fail somewhat to tickle the negro.

"Now, master," he said, readjusting the flag, and pressing the head gently further back into the crotch of the chair; "now master," and the steel glanced nigh the throat.

Again Don Benito faintly shuddered.

"You must not shake so, master.—See, Don Amasa, master always shakes when I shave him. And yet master knows I never yet have drawn blood, though it's true, if master will shake so, I may some of these times. Now, master," he continued. "And now, Don Amasa, please go on with your talk about the gale, and all that, master can hear, and between times master can answer."

"Ah yes, these gales," said Captain Delano; "but the more I think of your voyage, Don Benito, the more I wonder, not at the gales, terrible as they must have been, but at the disastrous interval following them. For here, by your account, have you been these two months and more getting from Cape Horn to St. Maria, a distance which I myself, with a good wind, have sailed in a few days. True, you had calms, and long ones, but to be becalmed for two months, that is, at least, unusual. Why, Don Benito, had almost any other gentleman told me such a story, I should have been half disposed to a little incredulity."

Here an involuntary expression came over the Spaniard, similar to that just before on the deck, and whether it was the start he gave, or a sudden gawky roll of the hull in the calm, or a momentary unsteadiness of the servant's hand; however it was, just then the razor drew blood, spots of which stained the creamy lather under the throat; immediately the black barber drew back his steel, and remaining in his professional attitude, back to Captain Delano, and face to Don Benito, held up the trickling razor, saying, with a sort of half humorous sorrow, "See, master,—you shook so—here's Babo's first blood."

No sword drawn before James the First of England, no assassination in that timid King's presence, could have produced a more terrified aspect than was now presented by Don Benito.

Poor fellow, thought Captain Delano, so nervous he can't even bear the sight of barber's blood; and this unstrung, sick man, is it credible that I should have imagined he meant to spill all my blood, who can't endure the sight of one little drop of his own? Surely, Amasa Delano, you have been beside yourself this day. Tell it not when you get home, sappy Amasa. Well, well, he looks like a murderer, doesn't he? More like as if himself were to be done for. Well, well, this day's experience shall be a good lesson.

Meantime, while these things were running through the honest seaman's mind, the servant had taken the napkin from his arm, and to Don Benito had said: "But answer Don Amasa, please, master, while I wipe this ugly stuff off the razor, and strop it again."

As he said the words, his face was turned half round, so as to be alike visible to the Spaniard and the American, and seemed by its expression to hint, that he was desirous, by getting his master to go on with the conversation, considerately to withdraw his attention from the recent annoying accident. As if glad to snatch the offered relief, Don Benito resumed, rehearsing to Captain Delano, that not only were the calms of unusual duration, but the ship had fallen in with obstinate currents and other things he added, some of which were but repetitions of former statements, to explain how it came to pass that the passage from Cape Horn to St. Maria had been so exceedingly long, now and then mingling with his words, incidental praises, less qualified than before, to the blacks for their general good conduct.

These particulars were not given consecutively, the servant now and then using his razor, and so, between the intervals of shaving, the story and panegyric went on with more than usual huskiness.

To Captain Delano's imagination, now again not wholly at rest, there was something so hollow in the Spaniard's manner, with apparently some reciprocal hollowness in the servant's dusky comment of silence, that the idea flashed across him, that possibly master and man, for some unknown purpose, were acting out, both in word and deed, nay, to the very tremor of Don Benito's limbs, some juggling play before him. Neither did the suspicion of collusion lack apparent support, from the fact of those whispered conferences before mentioned. But then, what could be the object of enacting this play of the barber before him? At last, regarding the notion as a whimsy, insensibly suggested, perhaps, by the theatrical aspect of Don Benito in his harlequin ensign, Captain Delano speedily banished it.

The shaving over, the servant bestirred himself with a small bottle of scented waters, pouring a few drops on the head, and then diligently rubbing; the vehemence of the exercise causing the muscles of his face to twitch rather strangely.

His next operation was with comb, scissors and brush; going round and round, smoothing a curl here, clipping an unruly whisker-hair there, giving a graceful sweep to the temple-lock, with other impromptu touches evincing the hand of a master; while, like any resigned gentleman in barber's hands, Don Benito bore all, much less uneasily, at least, than he had done the razoring; indeed, he sat so pale and rigid now, that the negro seemed a Nubian sculptor finishing off a white statue-head.

All being over at last, the standard of Spain removed, tumbled up, and tossed back into the flag-locker, the negro's warm breath blowing away any stray hair which might have lodged down his master's neck; collar and cravat readjusted; a speck of lint whisked off the velvet lapel; all this being done; backing off a little space, and pausing with an expression of subdued self-complacency, the servant for a moment surveyed his master, as, in toilet at least, the creature of his own tasteful hands.

Captain Delano playfully complimented him upon his achievement; at the same time congratulating Don Benito.

But neither sweet waters, nor shampooing, nor fidelity, nor sociality, delighted the Spaniard. Seeing him relapsing into forbidding gloom, and still remaining seated, Captain Delano, thinking that his presence was undesired just then, withdrew, on pretence of seeing whether, as he had prophesied, any signs of a breeze were visible.

Walking forward to the mainmast, he stood awhile thinking over the scene, and not without some undefined misgivings, when he heard a noise near the cuddy, and turning, saw the negro, his hand to his cheek. Advancing, Captain Delano perceived that the cheek was bleeding. He was about to ask the cause, when the negro's wailing soliloquy enlightened him.

"Ah, when will master get better from his sickness; only the sour heart that sour sickness breeds made him serve Babo so; cutting Babo with the razor, because, only by accident, Babo had given master one little scratch; and for the first time in so many a day, too. Ah, ah, ah," holding his hand to his face.

Is it possible, thought Captain Delano; was it to wreak in private his Spanish spite against this poor friend of his, that Don Benito, by his sullen manner, impelled me to withdraw? Ah, this slavery breeds ugly passions in man! Poor fellow!

He was about to speak in sympathy to the negro, but with a timid reluctance he now re-entered the cuddy.

Presently master and man came forth; Don Benito leaning on his servant as if nothing had happened.

But a sort of love-quarrel, after all, thought Captain Delano.

He accosted Don Benito, and they slowly walked together. They had gone but a few paces, when the steward—a tall, rajah-looking mulatto, orientally set off with a pagoda turban formed by three or four Madras handkerchiefs wound about his head, tier on tier—approaching with a salaam, announced lunch in the cabin.

On their way thither, the two captains were preceded by the mulatto, who, turning round as he advanced, with continual smiles and bows, ushered them in, a display of elegance which quite completed the insignificance of the small bare-headed Babo, who, as if not unconscious of inferiority, eyed askance the graceful steward. But in part, Captain Delano imputed his jealous watchfulness to that peculiar feeling which the full-blooded African entertains for the adulterated one. As for the steward, his manner, if not bespeaking much dignity of self-respect, yet evidenced his extreme desire to please; which is doubly meritorious, as at once Christian and Chesterfieldian.

Captain Delano observed with interest that while the complexion of the mulatto was hybrid, his physiognomy was European; classically so.

"Don Benito," whispered he, "I am glad to see this usher-of-the-golden-rod of yours; the sight refutes an ugly remark once made to me by a Barbados planter that when a mulatto has a regular European face, look out for him; he is a devil. But see, your steward here has features more regular than King George's of England; and yet there he nods, and bows, and smiles; a king, indeed—the king of kind hearts and polite fellows. What a pleasant voice he has, too?"

"He has, Señor."

"But, tell me, has he not, so far as you have known him, always proved a good, worthy fellow?" said Captain Delano, pausing, while with a final genuflexion the steward disappeared into the cabin; "come, for the reason just mentioned, I am curious to know."

"Francesco is a good man," rather sluggishly responded Don Benito, like a phlegmatic appreciator, who would neither find fault nor flatter.

"Ah, I thought so. For it were strange indeed, and not very creditable to us white-skins, if a little of our blood mixed with the African's, should, far from improving the latter's quality, have the sad effect of pouring vitriolic acid into black broth; improving the hue, perhaps, but not the wholesomeness."

"Doubtless, doubtless, Señor, but"—glancing at Babo—"not to speak of negroes, your planter's remark I have heard applied to the Spanish and Indian intermixtures in our provinces. But I know nothing about the matter," he listlessly added.

And here they entered the cabin.

The lunch was a frugal one. Some of Captain Delano's fresh fish and pumpkins, biscuit and salt beef, the reserved bottle of cider, and the *San Dominick's* last bottle of Canary.

As they entered, Francesco, with two or three coloured aids, was hovering over the table giving the last adjustments. Upon perceiving their master they withdrew, Francesco making a smiling congé, and the Spaniard, without condescending to notice it, fastidiously remarking to his companion that he relished not superfluous attendance.

Without companions, host and guest sat down, like a childless married couple, at opposite ends of the table, Don Benito waving Captain Delano to his place, and, weak as he was, insisting upon that gentleman being seated before himself.

The negro placed a rug under Don Benito's feet, and a cushion behind his back, and then stood behind, not his master's chair, but Captain Delano's. At first, this a little surprised the latter. But it was soon evident that, in taking his position, the black was still true to his master; since by facing him he could the more readily anticipate his slightest want.

"This is an uncommonly intelligent fellow of yours, Don Benito," whispered Captain Delano across the table.

"You say true, Señor."

During the repast, the guest again reverted to parts of Don Benito's story, begging further particulars here and there. He inquired how it was that the scurvy and fever should have committed such wholesale havoc upon the whites, while destroying less than half of the blacks. As if this question reproduced the whole scene of plague before the Spaniard's eyes, miserably reminding him of his solitude in a cabin where before he had had so many friends and officers round him, his hand shook, his face became hueless, broken words escaped; but directly the sane memory of the past seemed replaced by insane terrors of the present. With starting eyes he stared before him at vacancy. For nothing was to be seen but the hand of his servant pushing the Canary over toward him. At length a few sips served partially to restore him. He made random reference to the different constitutions of races, enabling one to offer more resistance to certain maladies than another. The thought was new to his companion.

Presently Captain Delano, intending to say something to his host concerning the pecuniary part of the business he had undertaken for him, especially—since he was strictly accountable to his owners—with reference to the new suit of sails, and other things of that sort; and naturally preferring to conduct such affairs in private, was desirous that the servant should withdraw; imagining that Don Benito for a few minutes could dispense with his attendance. He, however, waited awhile; thinking that, as the conversation proceeded, Don Benito, without being prompted, would perceive the propriety of the step.

But it was otherwise. At last catching his host's eye, Captain Delano, with a slight backward gesture of his thumb, whispered, "Don Benito, pardon me, but there is an interference with the full expression of what I have to say to you."

Upon this the Spaniard changed countenance; which was imputed to his resenting the hint, as in some way a reflection upon his servant. After a moment's pause, he assured his guest that the black's remaining with him could be of no disservice; because since losing his officers he had made Babo (whose original office, it now appeared, had been captain of the slaves) not only his constant attendant and companion, but in all things his confidant.

After this, nothing more could be said; though, indeed, Captain Delano could hardly avoid some little tinge of irritation upon being left ungratified in so inconsiderable a wish, by one, too, for whom he intended such solid services. But it is only his querulousness, thought he; and so filling his glass he proceeded to business.

The price of the sails and other matters was fixed upon. But while this was being done, the American observed that, though his original offer of assistance had been hailed with hectic animation, yet now when it was reduced to a business transaction, indifference and apathy were betrayed. Don Benito, in fact, appeared to submit to hearing the details more out of regard to common propriety, than from any impression that weighty benefit to himself and his voyage was involved.

Soon, this manner became still more reserved. The effort was vain to seek to draw him into social talk. Gnawed by his splenetic mood, he sat twitching his beard, while to little purpose the hand of his servant, mute as that on the wall, slowly pushed over the Canary.

Lunch being over, they sat down on the cushioned transom; the servant placing a pillow behind his master. The long continuance of the calm had now affected the atmosphere. Don Benito sighed heavily, as if for breath.

"Why not adjourn to the cuddy," said Captain Delano; "there is more air there." But the host sat silent and motionless.

Meantime his servant knelt before him, with a large fan of feathers. And Francesco, coming in on tiptoes, handed the negro a little cup of aromatic waters, with which at intervals he chafed his master's brow, smoothing the hair along the temples as a nurse does a child's. He spoke no word. He only rested his eye on his master's, as if, amid all Don Benito's distress, a little to refresh his spirit by the silent sight of fidelity.

Presently the ship's bell sounded two o'clock; and through the cabin-windows a slight rippling of the sea was discerned; and from the desired direction.

"There," exclaimed Captain Delano, "I told you so, Don Benito, look!"

He had risen to his feet, speaking in a very animated tone, with a view the more to rouse his companion. But though the crimson curtain of the stern-window near him that moment fluttered against his pale cheek, Don Benito seemed to have even less welcome for the breeze than the calm.

Poor fellow, thought Captain Delano, bitter experience has taught him that one ripple does not make a wind, any more than one swallow a summer. But he is mistaken for once. I will get his ship in for him, and prove it.

Briefly alluding to his weak condition, he urged his host to remain quietly where he was, since he (Captain Delano) would with pleasure take upon himself the responsibility of making the best use of the wind.

Upon gaining the deck, Captain Delano started at the unexpected figure of Atufal, monumentally fixed at the threshold, like one of those sculptured porters of black marble guarding the porches of Egyptian tombs.

But this time the start was, perhaps, purely physical. Atufal's presence, singularly attesting docility even in sullenness, was contrasted with that of the hatchet-polishers, who in patience evinced their industry; while both spectacles showed, that lax as Don Benito's general authority might be, still, whenever he chose to exert it, no man so savage or colossal but must, more or less, bow.

Snatching a trumpet which hung from the bulwarks, with a free step Captain Delano advanced to the forward edge of the poop, issuing his orders in his best Spanish. The few sailors and many negroes, all equally pleased, obediently set about heading the ship toward the harbour.

While giving some directions about setting a lower stu'n'-sail, suddenly Captain Delano heard a voice faithfully repeating his orders. Turning, he saw Babo, now for the time acting, under the pilot, his original part of captain of the slaves. This assistance proved valuable. Tattered sails and warped yards were soon brought into some trim. And no brace or halyard was pulled but to the blithe songs of the inspirited negroes.

Good fellows, thought Captain Delano, a little training would make fine sailors of them. Why see, the very women pull and sing, too. These must be some of those Ashantee negresses that make such capital soldiers, I've heard. But who's at the helm? I must have a good hand there.

He went to see.

The *San Dominick* steered with a cumbrous tiller, with large horizontal pullies attached. At each pulley-end stood a subordinate black, and between them, at the tiller-head, the responsible post, a Spanish seaman, whose countenance evinced his due share in the general hopefulness and confidence at the coming of the breeze.

He proved the same man who had behaved with so shamefaced an air on the windlass.

"Ah,—it is you, my man," exclaimed Captain Delano—"well, no more sheep's-eyes now;—look straightforward and keep the ship so. Good hand, I trust? And want to get into the harbour, don't you?"

"Sí Señor," assented the man with an inward chuckle, grasping the tiller-head firmly. Upon this, unperceived by the American, the two blacks eyed the sailor askance.

Finding all right at the helm, the pilot went forward to the forecastle, to see how matters stood there.

The ship now had way enough to breast the current. With the approach of evening, the breeze would be sure to freshen.

Having done all that was needed for the present, Captain Delano, giving his last orders to the sailors, turned aft to report affairs to Don Benito in the cabin; perhaps additionally incited to rejoin him by the hope of snatching a moment's private chat while his servant was engaged upon deck.

From opposite sides, there were, beneath the poop, two approaches to the cabin; one further forward than the other, and consequently communicating with a longer passage. Marking the servant still above, Captain Delano, taking the nighest entrance—the one last named, and at whose porch Atufal still stood—hurried on his way, till, arrived at the cabin threshold, he paused an instant, a little to recover from his eagerness. Then, with the words of his intended business upon his lips, he entered. As he advanced toward the Spaniard, on the transom, he heard another footstep, keeping time with his. From the opposite door, a salver in hand, the servant was likewise advancing.

"Confound the faithful fellow," thought Captain Delano; "what a vexatious coincidence."

Possibly, the vexation might have been something different, were it not for the buoyant confidence inspired by the breeze. But even as it was, he felt a slight twinge, from a sudden involuntary association in his mind of Babo with Atufal.

"Don Benito," said he, "I give you joy; the breeze will hold, and will increase. By the way, your tall man and time-piece, Atufal, stands without. By your order, of course?"

Don Benito recoiled, as if at some bland satirical touch, delivered with such adroit garnish of apparent good-breeding as to present no handle for retort.

He is like one flayed alive, thought Captain Delano; where may one touch him without causing a shrink?

The servant moved before his master, adjusting a cushion; recalled to civility, the Spaniard stiffly replied: "You are right. The slave appears where you saw him, according to my command; which is, that if at the given hour I am below, he must take his stand and abide my coming."

"Ah now, pardon me, but that is treating the poor fellow like an ex-king denied. Ah, Don Benito," smiling, "for all the license you permit in some things, I fear lest, at bottom, you are a bitter hard master."

Again Don Benito shrank; and this time, as the good sailor thought, from a genuine twinge of his conscience.

Conversation now became constrained. In vain Captain Delano called attention to the now perceptible motion of the keel gently cleaving the sea; with lack-lustre eye, Don Benito returned words few and reserved.

By-and-by, the wind having steadily risen, and still blowing right into the harbour, bore the *San Dominick* swiftly on. Rounding a point of land, the sealer at distance came into open view.

Meantime Captain Delano had again repaired to the deck, remaining there some time. Having at last altered the ship's course, so as to give the reef a wide berth, he returned for a few moments below.

I will cheer up my poor friend, this time, thought he.

"Better and better, Don Benito," he cried as he blithely re-entered; "there will soon be an end to your cares, at least for awhile. For when, after a long, sad voyage, you know, the anchor drops into the haven, all its vast weight seems lifted from the captain's heart. We are getting on famously, Don Benito. My ship is in sight. Look through this sidelight here; there she is; all a-taunt-o! The *Bachelor's Delight*, my good friend. Ah, how this wind braces one up. Come, you must take a cup of coffee with me this evening. My old steward will give you as fine a cup as ever any sultan tasted. What say you, Don Benito, will you?"

At first, the Spaniard glanced feverishly up, casting a longing look toward the sealer, while with mute concern his servant gazed into his face. Suddenly the old ague of coldness returned, and dropping back to his cushions he was silent.

"You do not answer. Come, all day you have been my host; would you have hospitality all on one side?"

"I cannot go," was the response.

"What? it will not fatigue you. The ships will lie together as near as they can, without swinging foul. It will be little more than stepping from deck to deck; which is but as from room to room. Come, come, you must not refuse me."

"I cannot go," decisively and repulsively repeated Don Benito.

Renouncing all but the last appearance of courtesy, with a sort of cadaverous sullenness, and biting his thin nails to the quick, he glanced, almost glared, at his guest; as if impatient that a stranger's presence should interfere with the full indulgence of his morbid hour. Meantime the sound of the parted waters came more and more gurglingly and merrily in at the windows; as reproaching him for his dark spleen; as telling him that, sulk as he might, and go mad with it, nature cared not a jot; since, whose fault was it, pray?

But the foul mood was now at its depth, as the fair wind at its height.

There was something in the man so far beyond any mere unsociality or sourness previously evinced, that even the forbearing good-nature of his guest could no longer endure it. Wholly at a loss to account for such demeanour, and deeming sickness with eccentricity, however extreme, no adequate excuse, well satisfied, too, that nothing in his own conduct could justify it, Captain Delano's pride began to be roused. Himself became reserved. But all seemed one to the Spaniard. Quitting him, therefore, Captain Delano once more went to the deck.

The ship was now within less than two miles of the sealer. The whale-boat was seen darting over the interval.

To be brief, the two vessels, thanks to the pilot's skill, ere long in neighborly style lay anchored together.

Before returning to his own vessel, Captain Delano had intended communicating to Don Benito the practical details of the proposed services to be rendered. But, as it was, unwilling anew to subject himself to rebuffs, he resolved, now that he had seen the *San Dominick* safely moored, immediately to quit her, without further allusion to hospitality or business. Indefinitely postponing his ulterior plans, he would regulate his future actions according to future circumstances. His boat was ready to receive him; but his host still tarried below. Well, thought Captain Delano, if he has little breeding, the more need to show mine. He descended to the cabin to bid a ceremonious, and, it may be, tacitly rebukeful adieu. But to his great satisfaction, Don Benito, as if he began to feel the weight of that treatment with which his slighted guest had, not indecorously, retaliated upon him, now supported by his servant, rose to his feet, and grasping Captain Delano's hand, stood tremulous; too much agitated to speak. But the good augury hence drawn was suddenly dashed, by his resuming all his previous reserve, with augmented gloom, as, with half-averted eyes, he silently reseated himself on his cushions. With a corresponding return of his own chilled feelings, Captain Delano bowed and withdrew.

He was hardly midway in the narrow corridor, dim as a tunnel, leading from the cabin to the stairs, when a sound, as of the tolling for execution in some jail-yard, fell on his ears. It was the echo of the ship's flawed bell, striking the hour, drearily reverberated in this subterranean vault. Instantly, by a fatality not to be withstood, his mind, responsive to the portent, swarmed with superstitious suspicions. He paused. In images far swifter than these sentences, the minutest details of all his former distrusts swept through him.

Hitherto, credulous good-nature had been too ready to furnish excuses for reasonable fears. Why was the Spaniard, so superfluously punctilious at times, now heedless of common propriety in not accompanying to the side his departing guest? Did indisposition forbid? Indisposition had not forbidden more irksome exertion that day. His last equivocal demeanour recurred. He had risen to his feet, grasped his guest's hand, motioned toward his hat; then, in an instant, all was eclipsed in sinister muteness and gloom. Did this imply one brief, repentant relenting at the final moment, from some iniquitous plot, followed by remorseless return to it? His last glance seemed to express a calamitous, yet acquiescent farewell to Captain Delano for ever. Why decline the invitation to visit the sealer that evening? Or was the Spaniard less hardened than the Jew, who refrained not from supping at the board of him whom the same night he meant to betray? What imported all those day-long enigmas and contradictions, except they were intended to mystify, preliminary to some stealthy blow? Atufal, the pretended rebel, but punctual shadow, that moment lurked by the threshold without. He seemed a sentry, and more. Who, by his own confession, had stationed him there? Was the negro now lying in wait?

The Spaniard behind—his creature before: to rush from darkness to light was the involuntary choice.

The next moment, with clenched jaw and hand, he passed Atufal, and stood unarmed in the light. As he saw his trim ship lying peacefully at her anchor, and almost within ordinary call; as he saw his household boat, with familiar faces in it, patiently rising and falling on the short waves by the *San Dominick's* side; and then, glancing about the decks where he stood, saw the oakum-pickers still gravely plying their fingers; and heard the low, buzzing whistle and industrious hum of the hatchet-polishers, still bestirring themselves over their endless occupation; and more than all, as he saw the benign aspect of Nature, taking her innocent repose in the evening; the screened sun in the quiet camp of the west shining out like the mild light from Abraham's tent; as his charmed eye and ear took in all these, with the chained figure of the black, the clenched jaw and hand relaxed. Once again he smiled at the phantoms which had mocked him, and felt something like a tinge of remorse, that, by indulging them even for a moment, he should, by implication, have betrayed an almost atheist doubt of the everwatchful Providence above.

There was a few minutes' delay, while, in obedience to his orders, the boat was being hooked along to the gangway. During this interval, a sort of saddened satisfaction stole over Captain Delano, at thinking of the kindly offices he had that day discharged for a stranger. Ah, thought he, after good actions one's conscience is never ungrateful, however much so the benefited party may be.

Presently, his foot, in the first act of descent into the boat, pressed the first round of the side-ladder, his face presented inward upon the deck. In the same moment, he heard his name courteously sounded; and, to his pleased surprise, saw Don Benito advancing—an unwonted energy in his air, as if, at the last moment, intent upon making amends for his recent discourtesy. With instinctive good feeling, Captain Delano, revoking his foot, turned and reciprocally advanced. As he did so, the Spaniard's nervous eagerness increased, but his vital energy failed; so that, the better to support him, the servant, placing his master's hand on his naked shoulder, and gently holding it there, formed himself into a sort of crutch.

When the two captains met, the Spaniard again fervently took the hand of the American, at the same time casting an earnest glance into his eyes, but, as before, too much overcome to speak.

I have done him wrong, self-reproachfully thought Captain Delano; his apparent coldness has deceived me; in no instance has he meant to offend.

Meantime, as if fearful that the continuance of the scene might too much unstring his master, the servant seemed anxious to terminate it. And so, still presenting himself as a crutch, and walking between the two captains, he advanced with them toward the gangway; while still, as if full of kindly contrition, Don Benito would not let go the hand of Captain Delano, but retained it in his, across the black's body.

Soon they were standing by the side, looking over into the boat, whose crew turned up their curious eyes. Waiting a moment for the Spaniard to relinquish his hold, the now embarrassed Captain Delano lifted his foot, to overstep the threshold of the open gangway; but still Don Benito would not let go his hand. And yet, with an agitated tone, he said, "I can go no further; here I must bid you adieu. Adieu, my dear, dear Don Amasa. Go—go!" suddenly tearing his hand loose, "go, and God guard you better than me, my best friend."

Not unaffected, Captain Delano would now have lingered; but catching the meekly admonitory eye of the servant, with a hasty farewell he descended into his boat, followed by the continual adieus of Don Benito, standing rooted in the gangway.

Seating himself in the stern, Captain Delano, making a last salute, ordered the boat shoved off. The crew had their oars on end. The bowsman pushed the boat a sufficient distance for the oars to be lengthwise dropped. The instant that was done, Don Benito sprang over the bulwarks, falling at the feet of Captain Delano; at the same time, calling towards his ship, but in tones so frenzied, that none in the boat could understand him. But, as if not equally obtuse, three Spanish sailors, from three different and distant parts of the ship, splashed into the sea, swimming after their captain, as if intent upon his rescue.

The dismayed officer of the boat eagerly asked what this meant. To which, Captain Delano, turning a disdainful smile upon the unaccountable Benito Cereno, answered that, for his part, he neither knew nor cared; but it seemed as if the Spaniard had taken it into his head to produce the impression among his people that the boat wanted to kidnap him. "Or else—give way for your lives," he wildly added, starting at a clattering hubbub in the ship, above which rang the tocsin of the hatchet-polishers; and seizing Don Benito by the throat he added, "this plotting pirate means murder!" Here, in apparent verification of the words, the servant, a dagger in his hand, was seen on the rail overhead, poised, in the act of leaping, as if with desperate fidelity to befriend his master to the last; while, seemingly to aid the black, the three Spanish sailors were trying to clamber into the hampered bow. Meantime, the whole host of negroes, as if inflamed at the sight of their jeopardized captain, impended in one sooty avalanche over the bulwarks.

All this, with what preceded, and what followed, occurred with such involutions of rapidity, that past, present, and future seemed one.

Seeing the negro coming, Captain Delano had flung the Spaniard aside, almost in the very act of clutching him, and, by the unconscious recoil, shifting his place, with arms thrown up, so promptly grappled the servant in his descent, that with dagger presented at Captain Delano's heart, the black seemed of purpose to have leaped there as to his mark. But the weapon was wrenched away, and the assailant dashed down into the bottom of the boat, which now, with disentangled oars, began to speed through the sea.

At this juncture, the left hand of Captain Delano, on one side, again clutched the half-reclined Don Benito, heedless that he was in a speechless faint, while his right foot, on the other side, ground the prostrate negro; and his right arm pressed for added speed on the after oar, his eye bent forward, encouraging his men to their utmost.

But here, the officer of the boat, who had at last succeeded in beating off the towing Spanish sailors, and was now, with face turned aft, assisting the bowsman at his oar, suddenly called to Captain Delano, to see what the black was about; while a Portuguese oarsman shouted to him to give heed to what the Spaniard was saying.

Glancing down at his feet, Captain Delano saw the freed hand of the servant aiming with a second dagger—a small one, before concealed in his wool—with this he was snakishly writhing up from the boat's bottom, at the heart of his master, his countenance lividly vindictive, expressing the centred purpose of his soul; while the Spaniard, half-choked, was vainly shrinking away, with husky words, incoherent to all but the Portuguese.

That moment, across the long benighted mind of Captain Delano, a flash of revelation swept, illuminating in unanticipated clearness

Benito Cereno's whole mysterious demeanour, with every enigmatic event of the day, as well as the entire past voyage of the *San Dominick*. He smote Babo's hand down, but his own heart smote him harder. With infinite pity he withdrew his hold from Don Benito. Not Captain Delano, but Don Benito, the black, in leaping into the boat, had intended to stab.

Both the black's hands were held, as, glancing up toward the *San Dominick*, Captain Delano, now with the scales dropped from his eyes, saw the negroes, not in misrule, not in tumult, not as if frantically concerned for Don Benito, but with mask torn away, flourishing hatchets and knives, in ferocious piratical revolt. Like delirious black dervishes, the six Ashantees danced on the poop. Prevented by their foes from springing into the water, the Spanish boys were hurrying up to the topmost spars, while such of the few Spanish sailors, not already in the sea, less alert, were descried, helplessly mixed in, on deck, with the blacks.

Meantime Captain Delano hailed his own vessel, ordering the ports up, and the guns run out. But by this time the cable of the *San Dominick* had been cut; and the fag-end, in lashing out, whipped away the canvas shroud about the beak, suddenly revealing, as the bleached hull swung round toward the open ocean, death for the figurehead, in a human skeleton; chalky comment on the chalked words below, *"Follow your leader."*

At the sight, Don Benito, covering his face, wailed out: "'Tis he, Aranda! my murdered, unburied friend!"

Upon reaching the sealer, calling for ropes, Captain Delano bound the negro, who made no resistance, and had him hoisted to the deck. He would then have assisted the now almost helpless Don Benito up the side; but Don Benito, wan as he was, refused to move, or be moved, until the negro should have been first put below out of view. When, presently assured that it was done, he no more shrank from the ascent.

The boat was immediately despatched back to pick up the three swimming sailors. Meantime, the guns were in readiness, though, owing to the *San Dominick* having glided somewhat astern of the sealer, only the aftermost one could be brought to bear. With this, they fired six times; thinking to cripple the fugitive ship by bringing down her spars. But only a few inconsiderable ropes were shot away. Soon the ship was beyond the guns' range, steering broad out of the bay; the blacks thickly clustering round the bowsprit, one moment with taunting cries toward the whites, the next with upthrown gestures hailing the now dusky expanse of ocean—cawing crows escaped from the hand of the fowler.

The first impulse was to slip the cables and give chase. But, upon second thought, to pursue with whale-boat and yawl seemed more promising.

Upon inquiring of Don Benito what firearms they had on board the *San Dominick*, Captain Delano was answered that they had none that could be used; because, in the earlier stages of the mutiny, a cabin-passenger, since dead, had secretly put out of order the locks of what few muskets there were. But with all his remaining strength, Don Benito entreated the American not to give chase, either with ship or boat; for the negroes had already proved themselves such desperadoes, that, in case of a present assault, nothing but a total massacre of the whites could be looked for. But, regarding this warning as coming from one whose spirit had been crushed by misery, the American did not give up his design.

The boats were got ready and armed. Captain Delano ordered twenty-five men into them. He was going himself when Don Benito grasped his arm.

"What! have you saved my life, Señor, and are you now going to throw away your own?"

The officers also, for reasons connected with their interests and those of the voyage, and a duty owing to the owners, strongly objected against their commander's going. Weighing their remonstrances a moment, Captain Delano felt bound to remain; appointing his chief mate—an athletic and resolute man, who had been a privateer's man, and, as his enemies whispered, a pirate—to head the party. The more to encourage the sailors, they were told, that the Spanish captain considered his ship as good as lost; that she and her cargo, including some gold and silver, were worth upwards of ten thousand doubloons. Take her, and no small part should be theirs. The sailors replied with a shout.

The fugitives had now almost gained an offing. It was nearly night; But the moon was rising. After hard, prolonged pulling, the boats came up on the ship's quarters, at a suitable distance laying upon their oars to discharge their muskets. Having no bullets to return, the negroes sent their yells. But, upon the second volley, Indian-like, they hurtled their hatchets. One took off a sailor's fingers. Another struck the whale-boat's bow, cutting off the rope there, and remaining stuck in the gunwale, like a woodman's axe. Snatching it, quivering from its lodgment, the mate hurled it back. The returned gauntlet now stuck in the ship's broken quarter-gallery, and so remained.

The negroes giving too hot a reception, the whites kept a more respectful distance. Hovering now just out of reach of the hurtling hatchets, they, with a view to the close encounter which must soon come, sought to decoy the blacks into entirely disarming themselves of their most murderous weapons in a hand-to-hand fight, by foolishly flinging them, as missiles, short of the mark, into the sea. But ere long perceiving the stratagem, the negroes desisted, though not before many of them had to replace their lost hatchets with handspikes; an exchange which, as counted upon, proved in the end favourable to the assailants.

Meantime, with a strong wind, the ship still clove the water; the boats alternately falling behind, and pulling up, to discharge fresh volleys.

The fire was mostly directed toward the stern, since there, chiefly, the negroes, at present, were clustering. But to kill or maim the negroes was not the object. To take them, with the ship, was the object. To do it, the ship must be boarded; which could not be done by boats while she was sailing so fast.

A thought now struck the mate. Observing the Spanish boys still aloft, high as they could get, he called to them to descend to the yards, and cut adrift the sails. It was done. About this time, owing to causes hereafter to be shown, two Spaniards, in the dress of sailors and conspicuously showing themselves, were killed; not by volleys, but by deliberate marksman's shots; while, as it afterwards appeared, during one of the general discharges, Atufal, the black, and the Spaniard at the helm likewise were killed. What now, with the loss of the sails, and loss of leaders, the ship became unmanageable to the negroes.

With creaking masts she came heavily round to the wind; the prow slowly swinging into view of the boats, its skeleton gleaming in the horizontal moonlight, and casting a gigantic ribbed shadow upon the water. One extended arm of the ghost seemed beckoning the whites to avenge it.

"Follow your leader!" cried the mate; and, one on each bow, the boats boarded. Scaling-spears and cutlasses crossed hatchets and handspikes. Huddled upon the long-boat amidships, the negresses raised a wailing chant, whose chorus was the clash of the steel.

For a time, the attack wavered; the negroes wedging themselves to beat it back; the half-repelled sailors, as yet unable to gain a footing, fighting as troopers in the saddle, one leg sideways flung over the bulwarks, and one without, plying their cutlasses like carters' whips. But in vain. They were almost overborne, when, rallying themselves into a squad as one man, with a huzza, they sprang inboard; where, entangled, they involuntarily separated again. For a few breaths' space there was a vague, muffled, inner sound as of submerged sword-fish rushing hither and thither through shoals of black-fish. Soon, in a reunited band, and joined by the Spanish seamen, the whites came to the surface, irresistibly driving the negroes toward the stern. But a barricade of casks and sacks, from side to side, had been thrown up by the mainmast. Here the negroes faced about, and though scorning peace or truce, yet fain would have had a respite. But, without pause, overleaping the barrier, the unflagging sailors again closed. Exhausted, the blacks now fought in despair. Their red tongues lolled, wolf-like, from their black mouths. But the pale sailors' teeth were set; not a word was spoken; and, in five minutes more, the ship was won.

Nearly a score of the negroes were killed. Exclusive of those by the balls, many were mangled; their wounds—mostly inflicted by the long-edged scaling-spears—resembling those shaven ones of the English at Preston Pans, made by the poled scythes of the Highlanders. On the other side, none were killed, though several were wounded; some severely, including the mate. The surviving negroes were temporarily secured, and the ship, towed back into the harbour at midnight, once more lay anchored.

Omitting the incidents and arrangements ensuing, suffice it that, after two days spent in refitting, the two ships sailed in company for Concepcion in Chili, and thence for Lima in Peru; where, before the vice-regal courts, the whole affair, from the beginning, underwent investigation.

Though, midway on the passage, the ill-fated Spaniard, relaxed from constraint, showed some signs of regaining health with freewill; yet, agreeably to his own foreboding, shortly before arriving at Lima, he relapsed, finally becoming so reduced as to be carried ashore in arms. Hearing of his story and plight, one of the many religious institutions of the City of Kings opened an hospitable refuge to him, where both physician and priest were his nurses, and a member of the order volunteered to be his one special guardian and consoler, by night and by day.

The following extracts, translated from one of the official Spanish documents, will, it is hoped, shed light on the preceding narrative, as well as, in the first place, reveal the true port of departure and true history of the *San Dominick's* voyage, down to the time of her touching at the island of Santa Maria.

But, ere the extracts come, it may be well to preface them with a remark.

The document selected, from among many others, for partial translation, contains the deposition of Benito Cereno; the first taken in the case. Some disclosures therein were, at the time, held dubious for both learned and natural reasons. The tribunal inclined to the opinion that the deponent, not undisturbed in his mind by recent events, raved of some things which could never have happened. But subsequent depositions of the surviving sailors, bearing out the revelations of their captain in several of the strangest particulars, gave credence to the rest. So that the tribunal, in its final decision, rested its capital sentences upon statements which, had they lacked confirmation, it would have deemed it but duty to reject.

. . . .

I, Don José de Abos and Padilla, His Majesty's Notary for the Royal Revenue, and Register of this Province, and Notary Public of the Holy Crusade of this Bishopric, etc.

Do certify and declare, as much as is requisite in law, that, in the criminal cause commenced the twenty-fourth of the month of September, in the year seventeen hundred and ninety-nine, against the Senegal negroes of the ship *San Dominick*, the following declaration before me was made.

Declaration of the first witness, Don Benito Cereno.

The same day, and month, and year, His Honour Doctor Juan Martinez de Dozas, Councillor of the Royal Audience of this Kingdom, and learned in the law of this Intendancy, ordered the captain of the ship *San Dominick*, Don Benito Cereno, to appear; which he did in his litter, attended by the monk Infelez; of whom he received, before Don José de Abos and Padilla, Notary Public of the Holy Crusade, the oath, which he took by God, our Lord, and a sign of the Cross; under which he promised to tell the truth of whatever he should know and should be asked;—and being interrogated agreeably to the tenor of the act commencing the process, he said, that on the twentieth of May last, he set sail with his ship from the port of Valparaiso, bound to that of Callao; loaded with the produce of the country and one hundred and sixty blacks, of both sexes, mostly belonging to Don Alexandro Aranda, gentleman, of the city of Mendoza; that the crew of the ship consisted of thirty-six men, beside the persons who went as passengers; that the negroes were in part as follows:

[*Here, in the original, follows a list of some fifty names, descriptions, and ages, compiled from certain recovered documents of Aranda's, and also from recollections of the deponent, from which portions only are extracted.*]

—One, from about eighteen to nineteen years, named José, and this was the man that waited upon his master, Don Alexandro, and who speaks well the Spanish, having served him four or five years; . . . a mulatto, named Francesco, the cabin steward, of a good person and voice, having sung in the Valparaiso churches, native of the province of Buenos Ayres, aged about thirty-five years. . . . A smart negro, named Dago, who had been for many years a grave-digger among the Spaniards, aged forty-six years. . . . Four old negroes, born in Africa, from sixty to seventy, but sound, caulkers by trade, whose names are as follows:—the first was named Muri, and he was killed (as was also his son named Diamelo); the second, Nacta; the third, Yola, likewise killed; the fourth, Ghofan; and six full-grown negroes, aged from thirty to forty-five, all raw, and born among the Ashantees—Martiniqui, Yan, Lecbe, Hapenda, Yambaio, Akim; four of whom were killed; . . . a powerful negro named Atufal, who, being supposed to have been a chief in Africa, his owners set great store by him. . . . And a small negro of Senegal, but some years among the Spaniards, aged about thirty, which negro's name was Babo; . . . that he does not remember the names of the others, but that still expecting the residue of Don Alexandro's papers will be found, will then take due account of them all, and remit to the court; . . . and thirty-nine women and children of all ages.

[*After the catalogue, the deposition goes on as follows:*]

. . . That all the negroes slept upon deck, as is customary in this navigation, and none wore fetters, because the owner, his friend

Aranda, told him that they were all tractable; . . . that on the seventh day after leaving port, at three o'clock in the morning, all the Spaniards being asleep except the two officers on the watch, who were the boatswain, Juan Robles, and the carpenter, Juan Bautista Gayete, and the helmsman and his boy, the negroes revolted suddenly, wounded dangerously the boatswain and the carpenter, and successively killed eighteen men of those who were sleeping upon deck, some with handspikes and hatchets, and others by throwing them alive overboard, after tying them; that of the Spaniards upon deck, they left about seven, as he thinks, alive and tied, to manœuvre the ship and three or four more who hid themselves, remained also alive. Although in the act of revolt the negroes made themselves masters of the hatchway, six or seven wounded went through it to the cockpit, without any hindrance on their part; that in the act of revolt, the mate and another person, whose name he does not recollect, attempted to come up through the hatchway, but having been wounded at the onset, they were obliged to return to the cabin; that the deponent resolved at break of day to come up the companionway, where the negro Babo was, being the ringleader, and Atufal, who assisted him, and having spoken to them, exhorted them to cease committing such atrocities, asking them, at the same time, what they wanted and intended to do, offering, himself, to obey their commands; that, notwithstanding this, they threw, in his presence, three men, alive and tied, overboard; that they told the deponent to come up, and that they would not kill him; which having done, the negro Babo asked him whether there were in those seas any negro countries where they might be carried, and he answered them, no; that the negro Babo afterwards told him to carry them to Senegal, or to the neighbouring islands of St. Nicholas; and he answered, that this was impossible, on account of the great distance, the necessity involved of rounding Cape Horn, the bad condition of the vessel, the want of provisions, sails, and water; but that the negro Babo replied to him he must carry them in any way; that they would do and conform themselves to everything the deponent should require as to eating and drinking; that after a long conference, being absolutely compelled to please them, for they threatened him to kill all the whites if they were not, at all events, carried to Senegal, he told them that what was most wanting for the voyage was water; that they would go near the coast to take it, and hence they would proceed on their course; that the negro Babo agreed to it; and the deponent steered toward the intermediate ports, hoping to meet some Spanish or foreign vessel that would save them; that within ten or eleven days they saw the land, and continued their course by it in the vicinity of Nasca; that the deponent observed that the negroes were now restless and mutinous, because he did not effect the taking in of water, the negro Babo having required, with threats, that it should be done, without fail, the following day; he told him he saw plainly that the coast was steep, and the rivers designated in the maps were not to be found, with other reasons suitable to the circumstances; that the best way would be to go to the island of Santa Maria, where they might water and victual easily, it being a desert island, as the foreigners did; that the deponent did not go to Pisco, that was near, nor make any other port of the coast, because the negro Babo had intimated to him several times, that he would kill all the whites the very moment he should perceive any city, town, or settlement of any kind on the shores to which they should be carried: that having determined to go to the island of Santa Maria, as the deponent had planned, for the purpose of trying whether, in the passage or in the island itself, they could find any vessel that should favour them, or whether he could escape from it in a boat to the neighbouring coast of Arruco; to adopt the necessary means he immediately changed his course, steering for the island; that the negroes Babo and Atufal held daily conferences, in which they discussed what was necessary for their design of returning to Senegal, whether they were to kill all the Spaniards, and particularly the deponent; that eight days after parting from the coast of Nasca, the deponent being on the watch a little after day-break, and soon after the negroes had their meeting, the negro Babo came to the place where the deponent was, and told him that he had determined to kill his master, Don Alexandro Aranda, both because he and his companions could not otherwise be sure of their liberty, and that, to keep the seamen in subjection, he wanted to prepare a warning of what road they should be made to take did they or any of them oppose him; and that, by means of the death of Don Alexandro, that warning would best be given; but, that what this last meant, the deponent did not at the time comprehend, nor could not, further than that the death of Don Alexandro was intended; and moreover, the negro Babo proposed to the deponent to call the mate Raneds, who was sleeping in the cabin, before the thing was done, for fear, as the deponent understood it, that the mate, who was a good navigator, should be

killed with Don Alexandro and the rest; that the deponent, who
was the friend, from youth of Don Alexandro, prayed and conjured,
but all was useless; for the negro Babo answered him that the thing
could not be prevented, and that all the Spaniards risked their death
if they should attempt to frustrate his will in this matter, or any
other; that, in this conflict, the deponent called the mate, Raneds,
who was forced to go apart, and immediately the negro Babo commanded the Ashantee Martinqui and the Ashantee Lecbe to go and
commit the murder; that those two went down with hatchets to
the berth of Don Alexandro; that, yet half alive and mangled, they
dragged him on deck; that they were going to throw him overboard
in that state, but the negro Babo stopped them, bidding the murder
be completed on the deck before him, which was done, when, by his
orders, the body was carried below, forward; that nothing more was
seen of it by the deponent for three days; . . . that Don Alonzo
Sidonia, an old man, long resident at Valparaiso, and lately appointed
to a civil office in Peru, whither he had taken passage, was at the
time sleeping in the berth opposite Don Alexandro's; that, awakening at his cries, surprised by them, and at the sight of the negroes
with their bloody hatchets in their hands, he threw himself into the
sea through a window which was near him, and was drowned, without it being in the power of the deponent to assist or take him up;
. . . that, a short time after killing Aranda, they brought upon deck
his german-cousin, of middle-age, Don Francisco Masa, of Mendoza,
and the young Don Joaquin, Marques de Aramboalaza, then lately
from Spain, with his Spanish servant Ponce, and the three young
clerks of Aranda, José Mozairi, Lorenzo Bargas, and Hermenegildo
Gandix, all of Cadiz; that Don Joaquin and Hermenegildo Gandix,
the negro Babo for purposes hereafter to appear, preserved alive;
but Don Francisco Masa, José Mozairi, and Lorenzo Bargas, with
Ponce, the servant, beside the boatswain, Juan Robles, the boatswain's mates, Manuel Viscaya and Roderigo Hurta, and four of the
sailors, the negro Babo ordered to be thrown alive into the sea,
although they made no resistance, nor begged for anything else but
mercy; that the boatswain, Juan Robles, who knew how to swim, kept
the longest above water, making acts of contrition, and, in the last
words he uttered, charged this deponent to cause mass to be said
for his soul to our Lady of Succour: . . . that, during the three days
which followed, the deponent, uncertain what fate had befallen the
remains of Don Alexandro, frequently asked the negro Babo where

they were, and, if still on board, whether they were to be preserved for interment ashore, entreating him so to order it; that the negro Babo answered nothing till the fourth day, when at sunrise, the deponent coming on deck, the negro Babo showed him a skeleton, which had been substituted for the ship's proper figure-head, the image of Christopher Colon, the discoverer of the New World; that the negro Babo asked him whose skeleton that was, and whether, from its whiteness, he should not think it a white's; that, upon his covering his face, the negro Babo, coming close, said words to this effect: "Keep faith with the blacks from here to Senegal, or you shall in spirit, as now in body, follow your leader," pointing to the prow; . . . that the same morning the negro Babo took by succession each Spaniard forward, and asked him whose skeleton that was, and whether, from its whiteness, he should not think it a white's; that each Spaniard covered his face; that then to each the negro Babo repeated the words in the first place said to the deponent; . . . that they (the Spaniards), being then assembled aft, the negro Babo harangued them, saying that he had now done all; that the deponent (as navigator for the negroes) might pursue his course, warning him and all of them that they should, soul and body, go the way of Don Alexandro if he saw them (the Spaniards) speak or plot anything against them (the negroes)—a threat which was repeated every day; that, before the events last mentioned, they had tied the cook to throw him overboard, for it is not known what thing they heard him speak, but finally the negro Babo spared his life, at the request of the deponent; that a few days after, the deponent, endeavouring not to omit any means to preserve the lives of the remaining whites, spoke to the negroes peace and tranquillity, and agreed to draw up a paper, signed by the deponent and the sailors who could write, as also by the negro Babo, for himself and all the blacks, in which the deponent obliged himself to carry them to Senegal, and they not to kill any more, and he formally to make over to them the ship, with the cargo, with which they were for that time satisfied and quieted. . . . But the next day, the more surely to guard against the sailors' escape, the negro Babo commanded all the boats to be destroyed but the long-boat, which was unseaworthy, and another, a cutter in good condition, which, knowing it would yet be wanted for lowering the water casks, he had it lowered down into the hold.

[*Various particulars of the prolonged and perplexed navigation ensuing here follow, with incidents of a calamitous calm, from which portion one passage is extracted, to wit:*]

—That on the fifth day of the calm, all on board suffering much from the heat, and want of water, and five having died in fits, and mad, the negroes became irritable, and for a chance gesture, which they deemed suspicious—though it was harmless—made by the mate, Raneds, to the deponent, in the act of handing a quadrant, they killed him; but that for this they afterwards were sorry, the mate being the only remaining navigator on board, except the deponent.

.   .   .   .

—That omitting other events, which daily happened, and which can only serve uselessly to recall past misfortunes and conflicts, after seventy-three days' navigation, reckoned from the time they sailed from Nasca, during which they navigated under a scanty allowance of water, and were afflicted with the calms before mentioned, they at last arrived at the island of Santa Maria, on the seventeenth of the month of August, at about six o'clock in the afternoon, at which hour they cast anchor very near the American ship, *Bachelor's Delight*, which lay in the same bay, commanded by the generous Captain Amasa Delano; but at six o'clock in the morning, they had already descried the port, and the negroes became uneasy, as soon as at distance they saw the ship, not having expected to see one there; that the negro Babo pacified them, assuring them that no fear need be had; that straightway he ordered the figure on the bow to be covered with canvas, as for repairs, and had the decks a little set in order; that for a time the negro Babo and the negro Atufal conferred; that the negro Atufal was for sailing away, but the negro Babo would not, and, by himself, cast about what to do; that at last he came to the deponent, proposing to him to say and do all that the deponent declares to have said and done to the American captain; . . . that the negro Babo warned him that if he varied in the least, or uttered any word, or gave any look that should give the least intimation of the past events or present state, he would instantly kill him, with all his companions, showing a dagger, which he carried hid, saying something which, as he understood it, meant that that dagger would be alert as his eye; that the

negro Babo then announced the plan to all his companions, which
pleased them; that he then, the better to disguise the truth, devised
many expedients, in some of them uniting deceit and defence; that
of this sort was the device of the six Ashantees before named, who
were his bravos; that them he stationed on the break of the poop,
as if to clean certain hatchets (in cases, which were part of the
cargo), but in reality to use them, and distribute them at need, and
at a given word he told them that, among other devices, was the
device of presenting Atufal, his righthand man, as chained, though
in a moment the chains could be dropped; that in every particular
he informed the deponent what part he was expected to enact in
every device, and what story he was to tell on every occasion, always
threatening him with instant death if he varied in the least: that,
conscious that many of the negroes would be turbulent, the negro
Babo appointed the four aged negroes, who were caulkers, to keep
what domestic order they could on the decks; that again and again
he harangued the Spaniards and his companions, informing them
of his intent, and of his devices, and of the invented story that this
deponent was to tell, charging them lest any of them varied from
that story; that these arrangements were made and matured during
the interval of two or three hours, between their first sighting the
ship and the arrival on board of Captain Amasa Delano; that this
happened at about half-past seven in the morning, Captain Amasa
Delano coming in his boat, and all gladly receiving him; that the
deponent, as well as he could force himself, acting then the part
of principal owner, and a free captain of the ship, told Captain
Amasa Delano, when called upon, that he came from Buenos Ayres,
bound to Lima, with three hundred negroes; that off Cape Horn,
and in a subsequent fever, many negroes had died; that also, by
similar casualties, all the sea officers and the greatest part of the
crew had died.

. . . . .

[*And so the deposition goes on, circumstantially recounting the
fictitious story dictated to the deponent by Babo, and through the
deponent imposed upon Captain Delano; and also recounting the
friendly offers of Captain Delano, with other things, but all of which
is here omitted. After the fictitious, strange story, etc., the deposition
proceeds:*]

—That the generous Captain Amasa Delano remained on board all the day, till he left the ship anchored at six o'clock in the evening, deponent speaking to him always of his pretended misfortunes, under the fore-mentioned principles, without having had it in his power to tell a single word, or give him the least hint, that he might know the truth and state of things; because the negro Babo, performing the office of an officious servant with all the appearance of submission of the humble slave, did not leave the deponent one moment; that this was in order to observe the deponent's actions and words, for the negro Babo understands well the Spanish; and besides, there were thereabout some others who were constantly on the watch, and likewise understood the Spanish; . . . that upon one occasion, while deponent was standing on the deck conversing with Amasa Delano, by a secret sign the negro Babo drew him (the deponent) aside, the act appearing as if originating with the deponent; that then, he being drawn aside, the negro Babo proposed to him to gain from Amasa Delano full particulars about his ship, and crew, and arms; that the deponent asked "For what?" that the negro Babo answered he might conceive; that, grieved at the prospect of what might overtake the generous Captain Amasa Delano, the deponent at first refused to ask the desired questions, and used every argument to induce the negro Babo to give up this new design; that the negro Babo showed the point of his dagger; that, after the information had been obtained, the negro Babo again drew him aside, telling him that that very night he (the deponent) would be captain of two ships instead of one, for that, great part of the American's ship's crew being to be absent fishing, the six Ashantees, without any one else, would easily take it; that at this time he said other things to the same purpose; that no entreaties availed; that before Amasa Delano's coming on board, no hint had been given touching the capture of the American ship: that to prevent this project the deponent was powerless; . . . —that in some things his memory is confused, he cannot distinctly recall every event; . . . —that as soon as they had cast anchor at six of the clock in the evening, as has before been stated, the American captain took leave to return to his vessel; that upon a sudden impulse, which the deponent believes to have come from God and his angels, he, after the farewell had been said, followed the generous Captain Amasa Delano as far as the gunwale, where he stayed, under the pretence of taking leave, until Amasa Delano should have been seated in his boat; that on shoving off, the deponent sprang from the gunwale, into the boat, and fell into it, he knows not how, God guarding him; that—

. . . .

[Here, in the original, follows the account of what further happened at the escape, and how the "San Dominick" was retaken, and of the passage to the coast; including in the recital many expressions of "eternal gratitude" to the "generous Captain Amasa Delano." The deposition then proceeds with recapitulatory remarks, and a partial renumeration of the negroes, making record of their individual part in the past events, with a view to furnishing, according to command of the court, the data whereon to found the criminal sentences to be pronounced. From this portion is the following:]

—That he believes that all the negroes, though not in the first place knowing to the design of revolt, when it was accomplished, approved it. . . . That the negro, José, eighteen years old, and in the personal service of Don Alexandro, was the one who communicated the information to the negro Babo, about the state of things in the cabin, before the revolt; that this is known, because, in the preceding midnight, he used to come from his berth, which was under his master's, in the cabin, to the deck where the ringleader and his associates were, and had secret conversations with the negro Babo, in which he was several times seen by the mate; that, one night, the mate drove him away twice; . . . that this same negro José, was the one who, without being commanded to do so by the negro Babo, as Lecbe and Martinqui were, stabbed his master, Don Alexandro, after he had been dragged half-lifeless to the deck; . . . that the mulatto steward, Francesco, was of the first band of revolters, that he was, in all things, the creature and tool of the negro Babo; that, to make his court, he, just before a repast in the cabin, proposed, to the negro Babo, poisoning a dish for the generous Captain Amasa Delano; this is known and believed, because the negroes have said it; but that the negro Babo, having another design, forbade Francesco; . . . that the Ashantee Lecbe was one of the worst of them; for that, on the day the ship was retaken, he assisted in the defence of her, with a hatchet in each hand, with one of which he wounded, in the breast, the chief mate of Amasa Delano, in the first act of boarding; this all knew; that, in sight of the deponent,

Lecbe struck, with a hatchet, Don Francisco Masa when, by the negro Babo's orders, he was carrying him to throw him overboard, alive; beside participating in the murder, before mentioned, of Don Alexandro Aranda, and others of the cabin-passengers; that, owing to the fury with which the Ashantees fought in the engagement with the boats, but this Lecbe and Yan survived; that Yan was bad as Lecbe; that Yan was the man who, by Babo's command, willingly prepared the skeleton of Don Alexandro, in a way the negroes afterwards told the deponent, but which he, so long as reason is left him, can never divulge; that Yan and Lecbe were the two who, in a calm by night, riveted the skeleton to the bow; this also the negroes told him; that the negro Babo was he who traced the inscription below it; that the negro Babo was the plotter from first to last; he ordered every murder, and was the helm and keel of the revolt; that Atufal was his lieutenant in all; but Atufal, with his own hand, committed no murder; nor did the negro Babo; . . . that Atufal was shot, being killed in the fight with the boats, ere boarding; . . . that the negresses, of age, were knowing to the revolt, and testified themselves satisfied at the death of their master, Don Alexandro; that, had the negroes not restrained them, they would have tortured to death, instead of simply killing, the Spaniards slain by command of the negro Babo; that the negresses used their utmost influence to have the deponent made away with; that, in the various acts of murder, they sang songs and danced—not gaily, but solemnly; and before the engagement with the boats, as well as during the action, they sang melancholy songs to the negroes, and that this melancholy tone was more inflaming than a different one would have been, and was so intended; that all this is believed, because the negroes have said it. —That of the thirty-six men of the crew—exclusive of the passengers (all of whom are now dead), which the deponent had knowledge of —six only remained alive, with four cabin-boys and ship-boys, not included with the crew; . . .—that the negroes broke an arm of one of the cabin-boys and gave him strokes with hatchets.

[*Then follow various random disclosures referring to various periods of time. The following are extracted:*]

—That during the presence of Captain Amasa Delano on board, some attempts were made by the sailors, and one by Hermenegildo Gandix, to convey hints to him of the true state of affairs; but that these attempts were ineffectual, owing to fear of incurring death, and furthermore owing to the devices which offered contradictions to the true state of affairs; as well as owing to the generosity and piety of Amasa Delano, incapable of sounding such wickedness; . . . that Luys Galgo, a sailor about sixty years of age, and formerly of the king's navy, was one of those who sought to convey tokens to Captain Amasa Delano; but his intent, though undiscovered, being suspected, he was, on a pretence, made to retire out of sight, and at last into the hold, and there was made away with. This the negroes have since said; . . . that one of the ship-boys feeling, from Captain Amasa Delano's presence, some hopes of release, and not having enough prudence, dropped some chance-word respecting his expectations, which being overheard and understood by a slave-boy with whom he was eating at the time, the latter struck him on the head with a knife, inflicting a bad wound, but of which the boy is now healing; that likewise, not long before the ship was brought to anchor, one of the seamen, steering at the time, endangered himself by letting the blacks remark a certain unconscious hopeful expression in his countenance, arising from some cause similar to the above; but this sailor, by his heedful after conduct, escaped; . . . that these statements are made to show the court that from the beginning to the end of the revolt, it was impossible for the deponent and his men to act otherwise than they did; . . .—that the third clerk, Hermenegildo Gandix, who before had been forced to live among the seamen, wearing a seaman's habit, and in all respects appearing to be one for the time; he, Gandix, was killed by a musketball fired through a mistake from the American boats before boarding; having in his fright ran up the mizzen-rigging, calling to the boats—"don't board," lest upon their boarding the negroes should kill him; that this inducing the Americans to believe he some way favoured the cause of the negroes, they fired two balls at him, so that he fell wounded from the rigging, and was drowned in the sea; . . . — that the young Don Joaquin, Marques de Arambaolaza, like Hermenegildo Gandix, the third clerk, was degraded to the office and appearance of a common seaman; that upon one occasion, when Don Joaquin shrank, the negro Babo commanded the Ashantee Lecbe to take tar and heat it, and pour it upon Don Joaquin's hands; . . .—that Don Joaquin was killed owing to another mistake of the Americans, but one impossible to be avoided, as upon the approach of the boats, Don Joaquin, with a hatchet tied edge out and

upright to his hand, was made by the negroes to appear on the
bulwarks; whereupon, seen with arms in his hands and in a ques-
tionable attitude, he was shot for a renegade seaman; . . . —that on
the person of Don Joaquin was found secreted a jewel, which, by
papers that were discovered, proved to have been meant for the
shrine of our Lady of Mercy in Lima; a votive offering, beforehand
prepared and guarded, to attest his gratitude, when he should have
landed in Peru, his last destination, for the safe conclusion of his
entire voyage from Spain; . . . —that the jewel, with the other effects
of the late Don Joaquin, is in the custody of the brethren of the
Hospital de Sacerdotes, awaiting the decision of the honourable
court; . . . —that, owing to the condition of the deponent, as well
as the haste in which the boats departed for the attack, the Americans were not forewarned that there were, among the apparent
crew, a passenger and one of the clerks disguised by the negro
Babo; . . . —that, beside the negroes killed in the action, some were
killed after the capture and reanchoring at night, when shackled
to the ring-bolts on deck; that these deaths were committed by the
sailors, ere they could be prevented. That so soon as informed
of it, Captain Amasa Delano used all his authority, and, in particular with his own hand, struck down Martinez Gola, who, having
found a razor in the pocket of an old jacket of his, which one of the
shackled negroes had on, was aiming it at the negro's throat; that the
noble Captain Amasa Delano also wrenched from the hand of
Bartholomew Barlo, a dagger secreted at the time of the massacre
of the whites, with which he was in the act of stabbing a shackled
negro, who, the same day, with another negro, had thrown him down
and jumped upon him; . . . —that, for all the events, befalling
through so long a time, during which the ship was in the hands of
the negro Babo, he cannot here give account; but that, what he
has said is the most substantial of what occurs to him at present,
and is the truth under the oath which he has taken; which declaration he affirmed and ratified, after hearing it read to him.

He said that he is twenty-nine years of age, and broken in body
and mind; that when finally dismissed by the court, he shall not return home to Chili, but betake himself to the monastery on Mount
Agonia without; and signed with his honour, and crossed himself,
and, for the time, departed as he came, in his litter, with the monk
Infelez, to the Hospital de Sacerdotes.

BENITO CERENO.

DOCTOR ROZAS.

If the deposition of Benito Cereno has served as the key to fit into the lock of the complications which preceded it, then, as a vault whose door has been flung back, the *San Dominick's* hull lies open to-day.

Hitherto the nature of this narrative, besides rendering the intricacies in the beginning unavoidable, has more or less required that many things, instead of being set down in the order of occurrence, should be retrospectively, or irregularly given; this last is the case with the following passages, which will conclude the account:

During the long, mild voyage to Lima, there was, as before hinted, a period during which Don Benito, a little recovered his health, or, at least in some degree, his tranquillity. Ere the decided relapse which came, the two captains had many cordial conversations—their fraternal unreserve in singular contrast with former withdrawments.

Again and again, it was repeated, how hard it had been to enact the part forced on the Spaniard by Babo.

"Ah, my dear Don Amasa," Don Benito once said, "at those very times when you thought me so morose and ungrateful—nay when, as you now admit, you half thought me plotting your murder —at those very times my heart was frozen; I could not look at you, thinking of what, both on board this ship and your own, hung, from other hands, over my kind benefactor. And as God lives, Don Amasa, I know not whether desire for my own safety alone could have nerved me to that leap into your boat, had it not been for the thought that, did you, unenlightened, return to your ship, you, my best friend, with all who might be with you, stolen upon, that night, in your hammocks, would never in this world have wakened again. Do but think how you walked this deck, how you sat in this cabin, every inch of ground mined into honey-combs under you. Had I dropped the least hint, made the least advance toward an understanding between us, death, explosive death—yours as mine—would have ended the scene."

"True, true," cried Captain Delano, starting, "you saved my life, Don Benito, more than I yours; saved it, too, against my knowledge and will."

"Nay, my friend," rejoined the Spaniard, courteous even to the point of religion, "God charmed your life, but you saved mine. To think of some things you did—those smilings and chattings, rash pointings and gesturings. For less than these, they slew my mate,

Raneds; but you had the Prince of Heaven's safe conduct through all ambuscades."

"Yes, all is owing to Providence, I know; but the temper of my mind that morning was more than commonly pleasant, while the sight of so much suffering—more apparent than real—added to my good nature, compassion, and charity, happily interweaving the three. Had it been otherwise, doubtless, as you hint, some of my interferences with the blacks might have ended unhappily enough. Besides that, those feelings I spoke of enabled me to get the better of momentary distrust, at times when acuteness might have cost me my life, without saving another's. Only at the end did my suspicions get the better of me, and you know how wide of the mark they then proved."

"Wide, indeed," said Don Benito, sadly; "you were with me all day; stood with me, sat with me, talked with me, looked at me, ate with me, drank with me; and yet, your last act was to clutch for a villain, not only an innocent man, but the most pitiable of all men. To such degree may malign machinations and deceptions impose. So far may even the best men err, in judging the conduct of one with the recesses of whose condition he is not acquainted. But you were forced to it; and you were in time undeceived. Would that, in both respects, it was so ever, and with all men."

"I think I understand you; you generalize, Don Benito; and mournfully enough. But the past is passed; why moralize upon it? Forget it. See, yon bright sun has forgotten it all, and the blue sea, and the blue sky; these have turned over new leaves."

"Because they have no memory," he dejectedly replied; "because they are not human."

"But these mild trades that now fan your cheek, Don Benito, do they not come with a human-like healing to you? Warm friends, steadfast friends are the trades."

"With their steadfastness they but waft me to my tomb, Señor," was the foreboding response.

"You are saved, Don Benito," cried Captain Delano, more and more astonished and pained; "you are saved; what has cast such a shadow upon you?"

"The negro."

There was silence, while the moody man sat, slowly and unconsciously gathering his mantle about him, as if it were a pall.

There was no more conversation that day.

But if the Spaniard's melancholy sometimes ended in muteness upon topics like the above, there were others upon which he never spoke at all; on which, indeed, all his old reserves were piled. Pass over the worst and, only to elucidate, let an item or two of these be cited. The dress so precise and costly, worn by him on the day whose events have been narrated, had not willingly been put on. And that silver-mounted sword, apparent symbol of despotic command, was not, indeed, a sword, but the ghost of one. The scabbard, artificially stiffened, was empty.

As for the black—whose brain, not body, had schemed and led the revolt, with the plot—his slight frame, inadequate to that which it held, had at once yielded to the superior muscular strength of his captor, in the boat. Seeing all was over, he uttered no sound, and could not be forced to. His aspect seemed to say: since I cannot do deeds, I will not speak words. Put in irons in the hold, with the rest, he was carried to Lima. During the passage Don Benito did not visit him. Nor then, nor at any time after, would he look at him. Before the tribunal he refused. When pressed by the judges he fainted. On the testimony of the sailors alone rested the legal identity of Babo. And yet the Spaniard would, upon occasion, verbally refer to the negro, as has been shown; but look on him he would not, or could not.

Some months after, dragged to the gibbet at the tail of a mule, the black met his voiceless end. The body was burned to ashes; but for many days, the head, that hive of subtlety, fixed on a pole in the Plaza, met, unabashed, the gaze of the whites; and across the Plaza looked toward St. Bartholomew's church, in whose vaults slept then, as now, the recovered bones of Aranda; and across the Rimac bridge looked toward the monastery, on Mount Agonia without; where, three months after being dismissed by the court, Benito Cereno, borne on the bier, did, indeed, follow his leader.

Washington Square

1 8 9 4

❦❦❦❦❦❦❦❦❦❦❦❦❦❦❦❦❦❦❦❦❦❦❦❦❦❦❦

HENRY JAMES

Washington Square

I

DURING a portion of the first half of the present century, and more particularly during the latter part of it, there flourished and practised in the city of New York a physician who enjoyed perhaps an exceptional share of the consideration which, in the United States, has always been bestowed upon distinguished members of the medical profession. This profession in America has constantly been held in honor, and more successfully than elsewhere has put forward a claim to the epithet of "liberal." In a country in which, to play a social part, you must either earn your income or make believe that you earn it, the healing art has appeared in a high degree to combine two recognized sources of credit. It belongs to the realm of the practical, which in the United States is a great recommendation; and it is touched by the light of science—a merit appreciated in a community in which the love of knowledge has not always been accompanied by leisure and opportunity.

It was an element in Doctor Sloper's reputation that his learning and his skill were very evenly balanced; he was what you might call a scholarly doctor, and yet there was nothing abstract in his remedies —he always ordered you to take something. Though he was felt to be extremely thorough, he was not uncomfortably theoretic; and if he sometimes explained matters rather more minutely than might seem of use to the patient, he never went so far (like some practitioners one had heard of) as to trust to the explanation alone, but always left behind him an inscrutable prescription. There were some doctors that left the prescription without offering any explanation at all; and he did not belong to that class either, which was after all the most vulgar. It will be seen that I am describing a clever man; and this is really the reason why Doctor Sloper had become a local celebrity.

At the time at which we are chiefly concerned with him he was some fifty years of age, and his popularity was at its height. He was

very witty, and he passed in the best society of New York for a man
of the world—which, indeed, he was, in a very sufficient degree. I
hasten to add, to anticipate possible misconception, that he was not
the least of a charlatan. He was a thoroughly honest man—honest
in a degree of which he had perhaps lacked the opportunity to give
the complete measure; and, putting aside the great good-nature of
the circle in which he practised, which was rather fond of boasting
that it possessed the "brightest" doctor in the country, he daily
justified his claim to the talents attributed to him by the popular
voice. He was an observer, even a philosopher, and to be bright was
so natural to him, and (as the popular voice said) came so easily,
that he never aimed at mere effect, and had none of the little tricks
and pretensions of second-rate reputations. It must be confessed
that fortune had favored him, and that he had found the path to
prosperity very soft to his tread. He had married, at the age of
twenty-seven, for love, a very charming girl, Miss Catherine Harrington, of New York, who, in addition to her charms, had brought him
a solid dowry. Mrs. Sloper was amiable, graceful, accomplished,
elegant, and in 1820 she had been one of the pretty girls of the
small but promising capital which clustered about the Battery and
overlooked the Bay, and of which the uppermost boundary was
indicated by the grassy way-sides of Canal Street. Even at the age
of twenty-seven Austin Sloper had made his mark sufficiently to
mitigate the anomaly of his having been chosen among a dozen
suitors by a young woman of high fashion, who had ten thousand
dollars of income and the most charming eyes in the island of Man-
hattan. These eyes, and some of their accompaniments, were for
about five years a source of extreme satisfaction to the young
physician, who was both a devoted and a very happy husband.

The fact of his having married a rich woman made no difference
in the line he had traced for himself, and he cultivated his profession
with as definite a purpose as if he still had no other resources than
his fraction of the modest patrimony which, on his father's death,
he had shared with his brothers and sisters. This purpose had not
been preponderantly to make money—it had been rather to learn
something and to do something. To learn something interesting, and
to do something useful—this was, roughly speaking, the programme
he had sketched, and of which the accident of his wife having an
income appeared to him in no degree to modify the validity. He was
fond of his practice, and of exercising a skill of which he was agree-

ably conscious, and it was so patent a truth that if he were not a doctor there was nothing else he could be, that a doctor he persisted in being, in the best possible conditions. Of course his easy domestic situation saved him a good deal of drudgery, and his wife's affiliation to the "best people" brought him a good many of those patients whose symptoms are, if not more interesting in themselves than those of the lower orders, at least more consistently displayed. He desired experience, and in the course of twenty years he got a great deal. It must be added that it came to him in some forms which, whatever might have been their intrinsic value, made it the reverse of welcome. His first child, a little boy of extraordinary promise, as the Doctor, who was not addicted to easy enthusiasm, firmly believed, died at three years of age, in spite of everything that the mother's tenderness and the father's science could invent to save him. Two years later Mrs. Sloper gave birth to a second infant—an infant of a sex which rendered the poor child, to the Doctor's sense, an inadequate substitute for his lamented first-born, of whom he had promised himself to make an admirable man. The little girl was a disappointment; but this was not the worst. A week after her birth the young mother, who, as the phrase is, had been doing well, suddenly betrayed alarming symptoms, and before another week had elapsed Austin Sloper was a widower.

For a man whose trade was to keep people alive he had certainly done poorly in his own family; and a bright doctor who within three years loses his wife and his little boy should perhaps be prepared to see either his skill or his affection impugned. Our friend, however, escaped criticism; that is, he escaped all criticism but his own, which was much the most competent and most formidable. He walked under the weight of this very private censure for the rest of his days, and bore forever the scars of a castigation to which the strongest hand he knew had treated him on the night that followed his wife's death. The world, which, as I have said, appreciated him, pitied him too much to be ironical; his misfortune made him more interesting, and even helped him to be the fashion. It was observed that even medical families cannot escape the more insidious forms of disease, and that, after all, Doctor Sloper had lost other patients besides the two I have mentioned; which constituted an honorable precedent. His little girl remained to him; and though she was not what he had desired, he proposed to himself to make the best of her. He had on hand a stock of unexpended authority, by which the child, in its early years, profited largely. She had been named, as a matter of course, after her poor mother, and even in her most diminutive babyhood the Doctor never called her anything but Catherine. She grew up a very robust and healthy child, and her father, as he looked at her, often said to himself that, such as she was, he at least need have no fear of losing her. I say "such as she was," because, to tell the truth— But this is a truth of which I will defer the telling.

2

When the child was about ten years old, he invited his sister, Mrs. Penniman, to come and stay with him. The Miss Slopers had been but two in number, and both of them had married early in life. The younger, Mrs. Almond by name, was the wife of a prosperous merchant and the mother of a blooming family. She bloomed herself, indeed, and was a comely, comfortable, reasonable woman, and a favorite with her clever brother, who, in the matter of women, even when they were nearly related to him, was a man of distinct preferences. He preferred Mrs. Almond to his sister Lavinia, who had married a poor clergyman, of a sickly constitution and a flowery style of eloquence, and then, at the age of thirty-three, had been left a widow—without children, without fortune—with nothing but the memory of Mr. Penniman's flowers of speech, a certain vague aroma of which hovered about her own conversation. Nevertheless, he had offered her a home under his own roof, which Lavinia accepted with the alacrity of a woman who had spent the ten years of her married life in the town of Poughkeepsie. The Doctor had not proposed to Mrs. Penniman to come and live with him indefinitely; he had suggested that she should make an asylum of his house while she looked about for unfurnished lodgings. It is uncertain whether Mrs. Penniman ever instituted a search for unfurnished lodgings, but it is beyond dispute that she never found them. She settled herself with her brother and never went away and, when Catherine was twenty years old, her Aunt Lavinia was still one of the most striking features of her immediate *entourage*. Mrs. Penniman's own account of the matter was that she had remained to take charge of her niece's education. She had given this account, at least, to every one but the Doctor, who never asked for explanations which he could entertain himself any day with inventing. Mrs. Penniman, moreover, though she had a good deal of a certain sort of artificial assurance, shrunk, for indefinable reasons, from presenting herself to her brother as a fountain of instruction. She had not a high sense of humor, but she had enough to prevent her from making this mistake; and her brother, on his side, had enough to excuse her, in her situation, for laying him under contribution during a considerable part of a lifetime. He therefore assented tacitly to the proposition which Mrs. Penniman had tacitly laid down, that it was of importance that the poor motherless girl should have a brilliant woman near her. His assent could only be tacit, for he had never been dazzled by his sister's intellectual lustre. Save when he fell in love with Catherine Harrington, he had never been dazzled, indeed, by any feminine characteristics whatever; and though he was to a certain extent what is called a ladies' doctor, his private opinion of the more complicated sex was not exalted. He regarded its complications as more curious than edifying, and he had an idea of the beauty of *reason*, which was, on the whole, meagerly gratified by what he observed in his female patients. His wife had been a reasonable woman, but she was a bright exception; among several things that he was sure of, this was perhaps the principal. Such a conviction, of course, did little either to mitigate or to abbreviate his widowhood; and it set a limit to his recognition, at the best, of Catherine's possibilities and of Mrs. Penniman's ministrations. He nevertheless, at the end of six months, accepted his sister's permanent presence as an accomplished fact, and as Catherine grew older, perceived that there were in effect good reasons why she should have a companion of her own imperfect sex. He was extremely polite to Lavinia, scrupulously, formally polite; and she had never seen him in anger but once in her life, when he lost his temper in a theological discussion with her late husband. With her he never discussed theology, nor, indeed, discussed anything; he contented himself with making known, very distinctly, in the form of a lucid ultimatum, his wishes with regard to Catherine.

Once, when the girl was about twelve years old, he had said to her—

"Try and make a clever woman of her, Lavinia; I should like her to be a clever woman."

Mrs. Penniman, at this, looked thoughtful a moment. "My dear Austin," she then inquired, "do you think it is better to be clever than to be good?"

"Good for what?" asked the Doctor. "You are good for nothing unless you are clever."

From this assertion Mrs. Penniman saw no reason to dissent; she possibly reflected that her own great use in the world was owing to her aptitude for many things.

"Of course I wish Catherine to be good," the Doctor said next day; "but she won't be any the less virtuous for not being a fool. I am not afraid of her being wicked; she will never have the salt of malice in her character. She is 'as good as good bread,' as the French say; but six years hence I don't want to have to compare her to good bread-and-butter."

"Are you afraid she will be insipid? My dear brother, it is I who supply the butter; so you needn't fear!" said Mrs. Penniman, who had taken in hand the child's "accomplishments," overlooking her at the piano, where Catherine displayed a certain talent, and going with her to the dancing-class, where it must be confessed that she made but a modest figure.

Mrs. Penniman was a tall, thin, fair, rather faded woman, with a perfectly amiable disposition, a high standard of gentility, a taste for light literature, and a certain foolish indirectness and obliquity of character. She was romantic; she was sentimental; she had a passion for little secrets and mysteries—a very innocent passion, for her secrets had hitherto always been as unpractical as addled eggs. She was not absolutely veracious; but this defect was of no great consequence, for she had never had anything to conceal. She would have liked to have a lover, and to correspond with him under an assumed name, in letters left at a shop. I am bound to say that her imagination never carried the intimacy further than this. Mrs. Penniman had never had a lover, but her brother, who was very shrewd, understood her turn of mind. "When Catherine is about seventeen," he said to himself, "Lavinia will try and persuade her that some young man with a mustache is in love with her. It will be quite untrue; no young man, with a mustache or without, will ever be in love with Catherine. But Lavinia will take it up, and talk to her about it; perhaps, even, if her taste for clandestine operations doesn't prevail with her, she will talk to me about it. Catherine won't see it, and won't believe it, fortunately for her peace of mind; poor Catherine isn't romantic."

She was a healthy, well-grown child, without a trace of her mother's beauty. She was not ugly; she had simply a plain, dull, gentle countenance. The most that had ever been said for her was that she had a "nice" face; and, though she was an heiress, no one had ever thought of regarding her as a belle. Her father's opinion of her moral purity was abundantly justified; she was excellently, imperturbably good; affectionate, docile, obedient, and much addicted to speaking the truth. In her younger years she was a good deal of a romp, and, though it is an awkward confession to make about one's heroine, I must add that she was something of a glutton. She never, that I know of, stole raisins out of the pantry; but she devoted her pocket-money to the purchase of cream-cakes. As regards this, however, a critical attitude would be inconsistent with a candid reference to the early annals of any biographer. Catherine was decidedly not clever; she was not quick with her book, nor, indeed, with anything else. She was not abnormally deficient, and she mustered learning enough to acquit herself respectably in conversation with her contemporaries—among whom it must be avowed, however, that she occupied a secondary place. It is well known that in New York it is possible for a young girl to occupy a primary one. Catherine, who was extremely modest, had no desire to shine, and on most social occasions, as they are called, you would have found her lurking in the background. She was extremely fond of her father, and very much afraid of him; she thought him the cleverest and handsomest and most celebrated of men. The poor girl found her account so completely in the exercise of her affections that the little tremor of fear that mixed itself with her filial passion gave the thing an extra relish rather than blunted its edge. Her deepest desire was to please him, and her conception of happiness was to know that she had succeeded in pleasing him. She had never succeeded beyond a certain point. Though, on the whole, he was very kind to her, she was perfectly aware of this, and to go beyond the point in question seemed to her really something to live for. What she could not know, of course, was that she disappointed him, though on three or four occasions the Doctor had been almost frank about it. She grew up peacefully and prosperously; but at the age of eighteen Mrs. Penniman had not made a clever woman of her. Doctor Sloper would have liked to be proud of his daughter; but there was nothing to be proud of in poor Catherine. There was nothing, of course, to be ashamed of; but this was not enough for the Doctor, who was a proud man, and would have enjoyed being able to think of his daughter as an unusual girl. There would have been a fitness in her being pretty and graceful, intelligent and distinguished—for her mother had been the most charming woman of her little day—and as regards her father, of course he knew his own value. He had moments of irritation at having produced a commonplace child, and he even went so far at times as to take a certain satisfaction in the thought that his wife had not lived to find her out. He was naturally slow in making this discovery himself, and it was not till Catherine had become a young lady grown that he regarded the matter as settled. He gave her the benefit of a great many doubts; he was in no haste to conclude. Mrs. Penniman frequently assured him that his daughter had a delightful nature; but he knew how to interpret this assurance. It meant, to his sense, that Catherine was not wise enough to discover that her aunt was a goose—a limitation of mind that could not fail to be agreeable to Mrs. Penniman. Both she and her brother, however, exaggerated the young girl's limitations; for Catherine, though she was very fond of her aunt, and conscious of the gratitude she owed her, regarded her without a particle of that gentle dread which gave its stamp to her admiration of her father. To her mind there was nothing of the infinite about Mrs. Penniman; Catherine saw her all at once, as it were, and was not dazzled by the apparition; whereas her father's great faculties seemed, as they stretched away, to lose themselves in a sort of luminous vagueness, which indicated, not that they stopped, but that Catherine's own mind ceased to follow them.

It must not be supposed that Doctor Sloper visited his disappointment upon the poor girl, or ever let her suspect that she had played him a trick. On the contrary, for fear of being unjust to her, he did his duty with exemplary zeal, and recognized that she was a faithful and affectionate child. Besides, he was a philosopher: he smoked a good many cigars over his disappointment, and in the fulness of time he got used to it. He satisfied himself that he had expected nothing, though, indeed, with a certain oddity of reasoning. "I expect nothing," he said to himself; "so that, if she gives me a surprise, it will be all clear gain. If she doesn't, it will be no loss." This was about the time Catherine had reached her eighteenth year; so that it will be seen her father had not been precipitate. At this time she seemed not only incapable of giving surprises; it was almost a question whether she could have received one—she was so quiet and irresponsive. People who expressed themselves roughly called her stolid. But she was irresponsive because she was shy, uncomfortably, painfully shy. This was not always understood, and she sometimes produced an impression of insensibility. In reality, she was the softest creature in the world.

3

As a child she had promised to be tall; but when she was sixteen she ceased to grow, and her stature, like most other points in her composition, was not unusual. She was strong, however, and properly made, and, fortunately, her health was excellent. It has been noted that the Doctor was a philosopher, but I would not have answered for his philosophy if the poor girl had proved a sickly and suffering person. Her appearance of health constituted her principal claim to beauty; and her clear, fresh complexion, in which white and red were very equally distributed, was, indeed, an excellent thing to see. Her eye was small and quiet, her features were rather thick, her tresses brown and smooth. A dull, plain girl she was called by rigorous critics—a quiet, lady-like girl, by those of the more imaginative sort; but by neither class was she very elaborately discussed. When it had been duly impressed upon her that she was a young lady—it was a good while before she could believe it—she suddenly developed a lively taste for dress: a lively taste is quite the expression to use. I feel as if I ought to write it very small, her judgment in this matter was by no means infallible; it was liable to confusions and embarrassments. Her great indulgence of it was really the desire of a rather inarticulate nature to manifest itself; she sought to be eloquent in her garments, and to make up for her diffidence of speech by a fine frankness of costume. But if she expressed herself in her clothes, it is certain that people were not to blame for not thinking her a witty person. It must be added that, though she had the expectation of a fortune—Doctor Sloper for a long time had been making twenty thousand dollars a year by his profession, and laying aside the half of it—the amount of money at her disposal was not greater than the allowance made to many poorer girls. In those days, in New York, there were still a few altar-fires flickering in the temple of Republican simplicity, and Doctor Sloper would have been glad to see his daughter present herself, with a classic grace, as a priestess of this mild faith. It made him fairly grimace, in private, to think that a child of his should be both ugly and overdressed. For himself, he was fond of the good things of life, and he made a considerable use of them; but he had a dread of vulgarity, and even a theory that it was increasing in the society that surrounded him. Moreover, the standard of luxury in the United States thirty years ago was carried by no means so high as at present, and Catherine's clever father took the old-fashioned view of the education of young persons. He had no particular theory on the subject; it had scarcely as yet become a necessity of self-defence to have a collection of theories. It simply appeared to him proper and reasonable that a well-bred young woman should not carry half her fortune on her back. Catherine's back was a broad one, and would have carried a good deal; but to the weight of the paternal displeasure she never ventured to expose it, and our heroine was twenty years old before she treated herself, for evening wear, to a red satin gown trimmed with gold fringe; though this was an article which, for many years, she had coveted in secret. It made her look, when she sported it, like a woman of thirty; but oddly enough, in spite of her taste for fine clothes, she had not a grain of coquetry, and her anxiety when she put them on was as to whether they, and not she, would look well. It is a point on which history has not been explicit, but the assumption is warrantable; it was in the royal raiment just mentioned that she presented herself at a little entertainment given by her aunt, Mrs. Almond. The girl was at this time in her twenty-first year, and Mrs. Almond's party was the beginning of something very important.

Some three or four years before this, Doctor Sloper had moved his household goods up town, as they say in New York. He had been living ever since his marriage in an edifice of red brick, with granite copings and an enormous fan-light over the door, standing in a street within five minutes' walk of the City Hall, which saw its best days (from the social point of view) about 1820. After this, the tide of fashion began to set steadily northward, as, indeed, in New York, thanks to the narrow channel in which it flows, it is obliged to do, and the great hum of traffic rolled farther to the right and left of Broadway. By the time the Doctor changed his residence, the murmur of trade had become a mighty uproar, which was music in the ears of all good citizens interested in the commercial development, as they delighted to call it, of their fortunate isle. Doctor Sloper's interest in this phenomenon was only indirect—though, seeing that, as the years went on, half his patients came to be overworked men

of business, it might have been more immediate—and when most of
his neighbors' dwellings (also ornamented with granite copings
and large fan-lights) had been converted into offices, warehouses, and
shipping agencies, and otherwise applied to the base uses of com-
merce, he determined to look out for a quieter home. The ideal of
quiet and of genteel retirement, in 1835, was found in Washington
Square, where the Doctor built himself a handsome, modern, wide-
fronted house, with a big balcony before the drawing-room windows, and a flight of white marble steps ascending to a portal which
was also faced with white marble. This structure, and many of its
neighbors, which it exactly resembled, were supposed, forty years
ago, to embody the last results of architectural science, and they
remain to this day very solid and honorable dwellings. In front of
them was the square, containing a considerable quantity of inex-
pensive vegetation, enclosed by a wooden paling, which increased
its rural and accessible appearance; and round the corner was the
more august precinct of the Fifth Avenue, taking its origin at this
point with a spacious and confident air which already marked it
for high destinies. I know not whether it is owing to the tenderness
of early associations, but this portion of New York appears to many
persons the most delectable. It has a kind of established repose which
is not of frequent occurrence in other quarters of the long, shrill
city; it has a riper, richer, more honorable look than any of the
upper ramifications of the great longitudinal thoroughfare—the look
of having had something of a social history. It was here, as you might
have been informed on good authority, that you had come into a
world which appeared to offer a variety of sources of interest; it
was here that your grandmother lived, in venerable solitude, and dispensed a hospitality which commended itself alike to the infant
imagination and the infant palate; it was here that you took your
first walks abroad, following the nursery-maid with unequal step,
and sniffing up the strange odor of the ailanthus-trees which at that
time formed the principal umbrage of the Square, and diffused an
aroma that you were not yet critical enough to dislike as it deserved; it was here, finally, that your first school, kept by a broad-
bosomed, broad-based old lady with a ferule, who was always having
tea in a blue cup, with a saucer that didn't match, enlarged the
circle both of your observations and your sensations. It was here,
at any rate, that my heroine spent many years of her life; which is
my excuse for this topographical parenthesis.

Mrs. Almond lived much farther up town, in an embryonic street, with a high number—a region where the extension of the city began to assume a theoretic air, where poplars grew beside the pavement (when there was one), and mingled their shade with the steep roofs of desultory Dutch houses, and where pigs and chickens disported themselves in the gutter. These elements of rural picturesqueness have now wholly departed from New York street scenery; but they were to be found within the memory of middle-aged persons in quarters which now would blush to be reminded of them. Catherine had a great many cousins, and with her Aunt Almond's children, who ended by being nine in number, she lived on terms of considerable intimacy. When she was younger they had been rather afraid of her; she was believed, as the phrase is, to be highly educated, and a person who lived in the intimacy of their Aunt Penniman had something of reflected grandeur. Mrs. Penniman, among the little Almonds, was an object of more admiration than sympathy. Her manners were strange and formidable, and her mourning robes—she dressed in black for twenty years after her husband's death, and then suddenly appeared, one morning, with pink roses in her cap—were complicated in odd, unexpected places with buckles, bugles, and pins, which discouraged familiarity. She took children too hard, both for good and for evil, and had an oppressive air of expecting subtle things of them; so that going to see her was a good deal like being taken to church and made to sit in a front pew. It was discovered after awhile, however, that Aunt Penniman was but an accident in Catherine's existence, and not a part of its essence, and that when the girl came to spend a Saturday with her cousins, she was available for "follow-my-master," and even for leap-frog. On this basis an understanding was easily arrived at, and for several years Catherine fraternized with her young kinsmen. I say young kinsmen, because seven of the little Almonds were boys, and Catherine had a preference for those games which are most conveniently played in trousers. By degrees, however, the little Almonds' trousers began to lengthen, and the wearers to disperse and settle themselves in life. The elder children were older than Catherine, and the boys were sent to college or placed in counting-rooms. Of the girls, one married very punctually, and the other as punctually became engaged. It was to celebrate this latter event that Mrs. Almond gave the little party I have mentioned. Her daughter was to marry a stout young stock-broker, a boy of twenty: it was thought a very good thing.

4

Mrs. Penniman, with more buckles and bangles than ever, came, of course, to the entertainment, accompanied by her niece; the Doctor, too, had promised to look in later in the evening. There was to be a good deal of dancing, and before it had gone very far Marian Almond came up to Catherine, in company with a tall young man. She introduced the young man as a person who had a great desire to make our heroine's acquaintance, and as a cousin of Arthur Townsend, her own intended.

Marian Almond was a pretty little person of seventeen, with a very small figure and a very big sash, to the elegance of whose manners matrimony had nothing to add. She already had all the airs of a hostess, receiving the company, shaking her fan, saying that with so many people to attend to she should have no time to dance. She made a long speech about Mr. Townsend's cousin, to whom she administered a tap with her fan before turning away to other cares. Catherine had not understood all that she said; her attention was given to enjoying Marian's ease of manner and flow of ideas, and to looking at the young man, who was remarkably handsome. She had succeeded, however, as she often failed to do when people were presented to her, in catching his name, which appeared to be the same as that of Marian's little stock-broker. Catherine was always agitated by an introduction; it seemed a difficult moment, and she wondered that some people—her new acquaintance at this moment, for instance—should mind it so little. She wondered what she ought to say, and what would be the consequences of her saying nothing. The consequences at present were very agreeable. Mr. Townsend, leaving her no time for embarrassment, began to talk to her with an easy smile, as if he had known her for a year.

"What a delightful party! What a charming house! What an interesting family! What a pretty girl your cousin is!"

These observations, in themselves of no great profundity, Mr. Townsend seemed to offer for what they were worth, and as a contribution to an acquaintance. He looked straight into Catherine's eyes. She answered nothing; she only listened, and looked at him; and he, as if he expected no particular reply, went on to say many other things in the same comfortable and natural manner. Catherine, though she felt tongue-tied, was conscious of no embarrassment; it seemed proper that he should talk, and that she should simply look at him. What made it natural was that he was so handsome, or, rather, as she phrased it to herself, so beautiful. The music had been silent for awhile, but it suddenly began again; and then he asked her, with a deeper, intenser smile, if she would do him the honor of dancing with him. Even to this inquiry she gave no audible assent; she simply let him put his arm round her waist—as she did so, it occurred to her more vividly than it had ever done before that this was a singular place for a gentleman's arm to be—and in a moment he was guiding her round the room in the harmonious rotation of the polka. When they paused, she felt that she was red; and then, for some moments, she stopped looking at him. She fanned herself, and looked at the flowers that were painted on her fan. He asked her if she would begin again, and she hesitated to answer, still looking at the flowers.

"Does it make you dizzy?" he asked, in a tone of great kindness.

Then Catherine looked up at him; he was certainly beautiful, and not at all red. "Yes," she said; she hardly knew why, for dancing had never made her dizzy.

"Ah, well, in that case," said Mr. Townsend, "we will sit still and talk. I will find a good place to sit."

He found a good place—a charming place; a little sofa that seemed meant only for two persons. The rooms by this time were very full; the dancers increased in number, and people stood close in front of them, turning their backs, so that Catherine and her companion seemed secluded and unobserved. "*We* will talk," the young man had said; but he still did all the talking. Catherine leaned back in her place, with her eyes fixed upon him, smiling, and thinking him very clever. He had features like young men in pictures; Catherine had never seen such features—so delicate, so chiselled and finished—among the young New Yorkers whom she passed in the streets and met at dancing-parties. He was tall and slim, but he looked extremely strong. Catherine thought he looked like a statue. But a statue would not talk like that, and, above all, would not have eyes of so rare a color. He had never been at Mrs. Almond's before; he felt very much like a stranger; and it was very kind of Catherine to take pity on him. He was Arthur Townsend's cousin—not very near; several times removed—and Arthur had brought him to present him to the family. In fact, he was a great stranger in New York. It was his native place; but he had not been there for many years. He had been knocking about the world, and living in queer corners; he had only come back a month or two before. New York was very pleasant, only he felt lonely.

"You see, people forget you," he said, smiling at Catherine with his delightful gaze, while he leaned forward obliquely, turning toward her, with his elbows on his knees.

It seemed to Catherine that no one who had once seen him would ever forget him; but though she made this reflection she kept it to herself, almost as you would keep something precious.

They sat there for some time. He was very amusing. He asked her about the people that were near them; he tried to guess who some of them were, and he made the most laughable mistakes. He criticised them very freely, in a positive, off-hand way. Catherine had never heard any one—especially any young man—talk just like that. It was the way a young man might talk in a novel; or, better still, in a play, on the stage, close before the foot-lights, looking at the audience, and with every one looking at him, so that you wondered at his presence of mind. And yet Mr. Townsend was not like an actor; he seemed so sincere, so natural. This was very interesting; but in the midst of it Marian Almond came pushing through the crowd, with a little ironical cry, when she found these young people still together, which made every one turn round, and cost Catherine a conscious blush. Marian broke up their talk, and told Mr. Townsend—whom she treated as if she were already married, and he had become her cousin—to run away to her mother, who had been wishing for the last half hour to introduce him to Mr. Almond.

"We shall meet again," he said to Catherine as he left her, and Catherine thought it a very original speech.

Her cousin took her by the arm, and made her walk about. "I needn't ask you what you think of Morris," the young girl exclaimed.

"Is that his name?"

"I don't ask you what you think of his name, but what you think of himself," said Marian.

"Oh, nothing particular," Catherine answered, dissembling for the first time in her life.

"I have half a mind to tell him that!" cried Marian. "It will do him good; he's so terribly conceited."

"Conceited?" said Catherine, staring.

"So Arthur says, and Arthur knows about him."

"Oh, don't tell him!" Catherine murmured, imploringly.

"Don't tell him he's conceited! I have told him so a dozen times."

At this profession of audacity Catherine looked down at her little companion in amazement. She supposed it was because Marian was going to be married that she took so much on herself; but she wondered too, whether, when she herself should become engaged, such exploits would be expected of her.

Half an hour later she saw her aunt Penniman sitting in the embrasure of a window, with her head a little on one side, and her gold eye-glass raised to her eyes, which were wandering about the room. In front of her was a gentleman, bending forward a little, with his back turned to Catherine. She knew his back immediately, though she had never seen it; for when he left her, at Marian's instigation, he had retreated in the best order, without turning round. Morris Townsend—the name had already become very familiar to her, as if some one had been repeating it in her ear for the last half hour— Morris Townsend was giving his impressions of the company to her aunt, as he had done to herself; he was saying clever things, and Mrs. Penniman was smiling, as if she approved of them. As soon as Catherine had perceived this she moved away; she would not have liked him to turn round and see her. But it gave her pleasure—the whole thing. That he should talk with Mrs. Penniman, with whom she lived and whom she saw and talked with every day—that seemed to keep him near her, and to make him even easier to contemplate than if she herself had been the object of his civilities; and that Aunt Lavinia should like him, should not be shocked or startled by what he said, this also appeared to the girl a personal gain; for Aunt Lavinia's standard was extremely high, planted as it was over the grave of her late husband, in which, as she had convinced every one, the very genius of conversation was buried. One of the Almond boys, as Catherine called them, invited our heroine to dance a quadrille, and for a quarter of an hour her feet at least were occupied. This time she was not dizzy; her head was very clear. Just when the dance was over, she found herself in the crowd face to face with her father. Doctor Sloper had usually a little smile, never a very big one, and with this little smile playing in his clear eyes and on his neatly-shaved lips, he looked at his daughter's crimson gown.

"Is it possible that this magnificent person is my child?" he said.

You would have surprised him if you had told him so; but it is a literal fact that he almost never addressed his daughter save in the ironical form. Whenever he addressed her he gave her pleasure; but she had to cut her pleasure out of the piece, as it were. There were portions left over, light remnants and snippets of irony, which she never knew what to do with, which seemed too delicate for her own use; and yet Catherine, lamenting the limitations of her understanding, felt that they were too valuable to waste, and had a belief that if they passed over her head they yet contributed to the general sum of human wisdom.

"I am not magnificent," she said, mildly, wishing that she had put on another dress.

"You are sumptuous, opulent, expensive," her father rejoined. "You look as if you had eighty thousand a year."

"Well, so long as I haven't—" said Catherine, illogically. Her conception of her prospective wealth was as yet very indefinite.

"So long as you haven't you shouldn't look as if you had. Have you enjoyed your party?"

Catherine hesitated a moment; and then, looking away, "I am rather tired," she murmured. I have said that this entertainment was the beginning of something important for Catherine. For the second time in her life she made an indirect answer; and the beginning of a period of dissimulation is certainly a significant date. Catherine was not so easily tired as that.

Nevertheless, in the carriage, as they drove home, she was as quiet as if fatigue had been her portion. Doctor Sloper's manner of addressing his sister Lavinia had a good deal of resemblance to the tone he had adopted toward Catherine.

"Who was the young man that was making love to you?" he presently asked.

"Oh, my good brother!" murmured Mrs. Penniman, in deprecation.

"He seemed uncommonly tender. Whenever I looked at you for half an hour, he had the most devoted air."

"The devotion was not to me," said Mrs. Penniman. "It was to Catherine; he talked to me of her."

Catherine had been listening with all her ears. "Oh, Aunt Penniman!" she exclaimed, faintly.

"He is very handsome; he is very clever; he expressed himself with a great deal—a great deal of felicity," her aunt went on.

"He is in love with this regal creature, then?" the Doctor inquired, humorously.

"Oh, father!" cried the girl, still more faintly, devoutly thankful the carriage was dark.

"I don't know that; but he admired her dress."

Catherine did not say to herself in the dark, "My dress only?" Mrs. Penniman's announcement struck her by its richness, not by its meagreness.

"You see," said her father, "he thinks you have eighty thousand a year."

"I don't believe he thinks of that," said Mrs. Penniman; "he is too refined."

"He must be tremendously refined not to think of that!"

"Well, he is!" Catherine exclaimed, before she knew it.

"I thought you had gone to sleep," her father answered. "The hour has come!" he added to himself. "Lavinia is going to get up a romance for Catherine. It's a shame to play such tricks on the girl. What is the gentleman's name?" he went on, aloud.

"I didn't catch it, and I didn't like to ask him. He asked to be introduced to me," said Mrs. Penniman, with a certain grandeur; "but you know how indistinctly Jefferson speaks." Jefferson was Mr. Almond. "Catherine, dear, what was the gentleman's name?"

For a minute, if it had not been for the rumbling of the carriage, you might have heard a pin drop.

"I don't know, Aunt Lavinia," said Catherine, very softly. And, with all his irony, her father believed her.

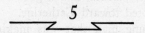

5

He learned what he had asked some three or four days later, after Morris Townsend, with his cousin, had called in Washington Square. Mrs. Penniman did not tell her brother, on the drive home, that she had intimated to this agreeable young man, whose name she did not know, that, with her niece, she should be very glad to see him; but she was greatly pleased, and even a little flattered, when, late on a Sunday afternoon, the two gentlemen made their appearance. His coming with Arthur Townsend made it more natural and easy; the latter young man was on the point of becoming connected with the family, and Mrs. Penniman had remarked to Catherine that, as he was going to marry Marian, it would be polite in him to call. These events came to pass late in the autumn, and Catherine and her aunt had been sitting together in the closing dusk, by the firelight, in the high back-parlor.

Arthur Townsend fell to Catherine's portion, while his companion placed himself on the sofa beside Mrs. Penniman. Catherine had hitherto not been a harsh critic; she was easy to please—she liked to talk with young men. But Marian's betrothed, this evening, made her feel vaguely fastidious; he sat looking at the fire and rubbing his knees with his hands. As for Catherine, she scarcely even pretended to keep up the conversation; her attention had fixed itself on the other side of the room; she was listening to what went on between the other Mr. Townsend and her aunt. Every now and then he looked over at Catherine herself and smiled, as if to show that what he said was for her benefit too. Catherine would have liked to change her place, to go and sit near them, where she might see and hear him better. But she was afraid of seeming bold— of looking eager; and, besides, it would not have been polite to Marian's little suitor. She wondered why the other gentleman had picked out her aunt—how he came to have so much to say to Mrs. Penniman, to whom, usually, young men were not especially devoted. She was not at all jealous of Aunt Lavinia, but she was a little envious, and, above all, she wondered; for Morris Townsend was an object on which she found that her imagination could exercise itself indefinitely. His cousin had been describing a house that he had taken in view of his union with Marian, and the domestic conveniences he meant to introduce into it; how Marian wanted a larger one, and Mrs. Almond recommended a smaller one, and how he himself was convinced that he had got the neatest house in New York.

"It doesn't matter," he said; "it's only for three or four years. At the end of three or four years we'll move. That's the way to live in New York—to move every three or four years. Then you always get the last thing. It's because the city's growing so quick—you've got to keep up with it. It's going straight up town—that's where New York's going. If I wasn't afraid Marian would be lonely, I'd go up there—right up to the top—and wait for it. Only have to wait ten years—they'll all come up after you. But Marian says she wants some neighbors—she doesn't want to be a pioneer. She says that if she's got to be the first settler she had better go out to Minnesota.

I guess we'll move up little by little; when we get tired of one street we'll go higher. So you see we'll always have a new house; it's a great advantage to have a new house; you get all the latest improvements. They invent everything all over again about every five years, and it's a great thing to keep up with the new things. I always try and keep up with the new things of every kind. Don't you think that's a good motto for a young couple—to keep 'going higher?' What's the name of that piece of poetry—what do they call it?—*Excelsior!*"

Catherine bestowed on her junior visitor only just enough attention to feel that this was not the way Mr. Morris Townsend had talked the other night, or that he was talking now to her fortunate aunt. But suddenly his aspiring kinsman became more interesting. He seemed to have become conscious that she was affected by his companion's presence, and he thought it proper to explain it.

"My cousin asked me to bring him, or I shouldn't have taken the liberty. He seemed to want very much to come; you know he's awfully sociable. I told him I wanted to ask you first, but he said Mrs. Penniman had invited him. He isn't particular what he says when he wants to come somewhere. But Mrs. Penniman seems to think it's all right."

"We are very glad to see him," said Catherine. And she wished to talk more about him, but she hardly knew what to say. "I never saw him before," she went on, presently.

Arthur Townsend stared.

"Why, he told me he talked with you for over half an hour the other night."

"I mean before the other night. That was the first time."

"Oh, he has been away from New York—he has been all round the world. He doesn't know many people here, but he's very sociable, and he wants to know every one."

"Every one?" said Catherine.

"Well, I mean all the good ones. All the pretty young ladies—like Mrs. Penniman!" And Arthur Townsend gave a private laugh.

"My aunt likes him very much," said Catherine.

"Most people like him—he's so brilliant."

"He's more like a foreigner," Catherine suggested.

"Well, I never knew a foreigner," said young Townsend, in a tone which seemed to indicate that his ignorance had been optional.

"Neither have I," Catherine confessed, with more humility. "They say they are generally brilliant," she added, vaguely.

"Well, the people of this city are clever enough for me. I know some of them that think they are too clever for me; but they ain't."

"I suppose you can't be too clever," said Catherine, still with humility.

"I don't know. I know some people that call my cousin too clever."

Catherine listened to this statement with extreme interest, and a feeling that if Morris Townsend had a fault it would naturally be that one. But she did not commit herself, and in a moment she asked, "Now that he has come back, will he stay here always?"

"Ah!" said Arthur, "if he can get something to do."

"Something to do?"

"Some place or other; some business."

"Hasn't he got any?" said Catherine, who had never heard of a young man—of the upper class—in this situation.

"No; he's looking round. But he can't find anything."

"I am very sorry," Catherine permitted herself to observe.

"Oh, he doesn't mind," said young Townsend. "He takes it easy—he isn't in a hurry. He is very particular."

Catherine thought he naturally would be, and gave herself up for some moments to the contemplation of this idea, in several of its bearings.

"Won't his father take him into his business—his office?" she at last inquired.

"He hasn't got any father—he has only got a sister. Your sister can't help you much."

It seemed to Catherine that if she were his sister she would disprove this axiom. "Is she—is she pleasant?" she asked in a moment.

"I don't know—I believe she's very respectable," said young Townsend. And then he looked across to his cousin and began to laugh. "I say, we are talking about you," he added.

Morris Townsend paused in his conversation with Mrs. Penniman, and stared, with a little smile. Then he got up, as if he were going.

"As far as you are concerned, I can't return the compliment," he said to Catherine's companion. "But as regards Miss Sloper, it's another affair."

Catherine thought this little speech wonderfully well turned;

but she was embarrassed by it, and she also got up. Morris Townsend stood looking at her and smiling; he put out his hand for farewell. He was going, without having said anything to her; but even on these terms she was glad to have seen him.

"I will tell her what you have said—when you go!" said Mrs. Penniman, with a little significant laugh.

Catherine blushed, for she felt almost as if they were making sport of her. What in the world could this beautiful young man have said? He looked at her still, in spite of her blush, but very kindly and respectfully.

"I have had no talk with you," he said, "and that was what I came for. But it will be a good reason for coming another time; a little pretext—if I am obliged to give one. I am not afraid of what your aunt will say when I go."

With this the two young men took their departure; after which Catherine, with her blush still lingering, directed a serious and interrogative eye to Mrs. Penniman. She was incapable of elaborate artifice, and she resorted to no jocular device—to no affectation of the belief that she had been maligned—to learn what she desired.

"What did you say you would tell me?" she asked.

Mrs. Penniman came up to her, smiling and nodding a little, looked at her all over, and gave a twist to the knot of ribbon in her neck. "It's a great secret, my dear child; but he is coming a-courting!"

Catherine was serious still. "Is that what he told you?"

"He didn't say so exactly; but he left me to guess it. I'm a good guesser."

"Do you mean a-courting me?"

"Not me, certainly, miss; though I must say he is a hundred times more polite to a person who has no longer extreme youth to recommend her than most of the young men. He is thinking of some one else." And Mrs. Penniman gave her niece a delicate little kiss. "You must be very gracious to him."

Catherine stared—she was bewildered. "I don't understand you," she said; "he doesn't know me."

"Oh yes, he does; more than you think. I have told him all about you."

"Oh, Aunt Penniman!" murmured Catherine, as if this had been a breach of trust. "He is a perfect stranger—we don't know him." There was infinite modesty in the poor girl's "we."

Aunt Penniman, however, took no account of it; she spoke even with a touch of acrimony. "My dear Catherine, you know very well that you admire him."

"Oh, Aunt Penniman!" Catherine could only murmur again. It might very well be that she admired him—though this did not seem to her a thing to talk about. But that this brilliant stranger—this sudden apparition, who had barely heard the sound of her voice—took that sort of interest in her that was expressed by the romantic phrase of which Mrs. Penniman had just made use—this could only be a figment of the restless brain of Aunt Lavinia, whom every one knew to be a woman of powerful imagination.

6

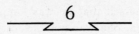

Mrs. Penniman even took for granted at times that other people had as much imagination as herself; so that when, half an hour later, her brother came in, she addressed him quite on this principle.

"He has just been here, Austin; it's such a pity you missed him."

"Whom in the world have I missed?" asked the Doctor.

"Mr. Morris Townsend; he has made us such a delightful visit."

"And who in the world is Mr. Morris Townsend?"

"Aunt Penniman means the gentleman—the gentleman whose name I couldn't remember," said Catherine.

"The gentleman at Elizabeth's party who was so struck with Catherine," Mrs. Penniman added.

"Oh, his name is Morris Townsend, is it? And did he come here to propose to you?"

"Oh, father!" murmured the girl for an answer, turning away to the window, where the dusk had deepened to darkness.

"I hope he won't do that without your permission," said Mrs. Penniman, very graciously.

"After all, my dear, he seems to have yours," her brother answered.

Lavinia simpered, as if this might not be quite enough, and Catherine, with her forehead touching the window-panes, listened to this exchange of epigrams as reservedly as if they had not each been a pin-prick in her own destiny.

"The next time he comes," the Doctor added, "you had better call me. He might like to see me."

Morris Townsend came again some five days afterward; but

Doctor Sloper was not called, as he was absent from home at the time. Catherine was with her aunt when the young man's name was brought in, and Mrs. Penniman, effacing herself and protesting, made a great point of her niece's going into the drawing-room alone.

"This time it's for you—for you only," she said. "Before, when he talked to me, it was only preliminary—it was to gain my confidence. Literally, my dear, I should not have the *courage* to show myself to-day."

And this was perfectly true. Mrs. Penniman was not a brave woman, and Morris Townsend had struck her as a young man of great force of character, and of remarkable powers of satire—a keen, resolute, brilliant nature, with which one must exercise a great deal of tact. She said to herself that he was "imperious," and she liked the word and the idea. She was not the least jealous of her niece, and she had been perfectly happy with Mr. Penniman, but in the bottom of her heart she permitted herself the observation, "That's the sort of husband I should have had!" He was certainly much more imperious—she ended by calling it imperial—than Mr. Penniman.

So Catherine saw Mr. Townsend alone, and her aunt did not come in even at the end of the visit. The visit was a long one; he sat there, in the front parlor, in the biggest arm-chair, for more than an hour. He seemed more at home this time—more familiar; lounging a little in the chair, slapping a cushion that was near him with his stick, and looking round the room a good deal, and at the objects it contained, as well as at Catherine; whom, however, he also contemplated freely. There was a smile of respectful devotion in his handsome eyes which seemed to Catherine almost solemnly beautiful; it made her think of a young knight in a poem. His talk, however, was not particularly knightly; it was light and easy and friendly; it took a practical turn, and he asked a number of questions about herself—what were her tastes—if she liked this and that —what were her habits. He said to her, with his charming smile, "Tell me about yourself; give me a little sketch." Catherine had very little to tell, and she had no talent for sketching; but before he went she had confided to him that she had a secret passion for the theatre, which had been but scantily gratified, and a taste for operatic music—that of Bellini and Donizetti, in especial (it must be remembered, in extenuation of this primitive young woman, that she held these opinions in an age of general darkness)—which she rarely had an occasion to hear, except on the hand-organ. She confessed that she was not particularly fond of literature. Morris Townsend agreed with her that books were tiresome things; only, as he said, you had to read a good many before you found it out. He had been to places that people had written books about, and they were not a bit like the descriptions. To see for yourself—that was the great thing; he always tried to see for himself. He had seen all the principal actors—he had been to all the best theatres in London and Paris. But the actors were always like the authors—they always exaggerated. He liked everything to be natural. Suddenly he stopped, looking at Catherine with his smile.

"That's what I like you for; you are so natural. Excuse me," he added; "you see I am natural myself."

And before she had time to think whether she excused him or not—which afterward, at leisure, she became conscious that she did —he began to talk about music, and to say that it was his greatest pleasure in life. He had heard all the great singers in Paris and London—Pasta and Rubini and Lablache—and when you had done that, you could say that you knew what singing was.

"I sing a little myself," he said; "some day I will show you. Not to-day, but some other time."

And then he got up to go. He had omitted, by accident, to say that he would sing to her if she would play to him. He thought of this after he got into the street; but he might have spared his compunction, for Catherine had not noticed the lapse. She was thinking only that "some other time" had a delightful sound; it seemed to spread itself over the future.

This was all the more reason, however, though she was ashamed and uncomfortable, why she should tell her father that Mr. Morris Townsend had called again. She announced the fact abruptly, almost violently, as soon as the Doctor came into the house; and having done so—it was her duty—she took measures to leave the room. But she could not leave it fast enough; her father stopped her just as she reached the door.

"Well, my dear, did he propose to you to-day?" the Doctor asked.

This was just what she had been afraid he would say; and yet she had no answer ready. Of course she would have liked to take it as a joke—as her father must have meant it; and yet she would have liked also, in denying it, to be a little positive, a little sharp, so that he would perhaps not ask the question again. She didn't like it—it made her unhappy. But Catherine could never be sharp; and for a moment she only stood, with her hand on the doorknob, looking at her satiric parent, and giving a little laugh.

"Decidedly," said the Doctor to himself, "my daughter is not brilliant!"

But he had no sooner made this reflection than Catherine found something; she had decided, on the whole, to take the thing as a joke.

"Perhaps he will do it the next time," she exclaimed, with a repetition of her laugh; and she quickly got out of the room.

The Doctor stood staring; he wondered whether his daughter were serious. Catherine went straight to her own room, and by the time she reached it she bethought herself that there was something else—something better—she might have said. She almost wished, now, that her father would ask his question again, so that she might reply, "Oh yes, Mr. Morris Townsend proposed to me, and I refused him."

The Doctor, however, began to put his questions elsewhere; it naturally having occurred to him that he ought to inform himself properly about this handsome young man, who had formed the habit of running in and out of his house. He addressed himself to the elder of his sisters, Mrs. Almond—not going to her for the purpose; there was no such hurry as that; but having made a note of the matter for the first opportunity. The Doctor was never eager, never impatient or nervous; but he made notes of everything, and he regularly consulted his notes. Among them the information he obtained from Mrs. Almond about Morris Townsend took its place.

"Lavinia has already been to ask me," she said. "Lavinia is most excited; I don't understand it. It's not, after all, Lavinia that the young man is supposed to have designs upon. She is very peculiar."

"Ah, my dear," the Doctor replied, "she has not lived with me these twelve years without my finding it out."

"She has got such an artificial mind," said Mrs. Almond, who always enjoyed an opportunity to discuss Lavinia's peculiarities with her brother. "She didn't want me to tell you that she had asked me about Mr. Townsend; but I told her I would. She always wants to conceal everything."

"And yet at moments no one blurts things out with such crudity. She is like a revolving lighthouse—pitch darkness alternating with a dazzling brilliancy! But what did you tell her?" the Doctor asked.

"What I tell you—that I know very little of him."

"Lavinia must have been disappointed at that," said the Doctor; "she would prefer him to have been guilty of some romantic crime. However, we must make the best of people. They tell me our gentleman is the cousin of the little boy to whom you are about to intrust the future of your little girl."

"Arthur is not a little boy; he is a very old man; you and I will never be so old! He is a distant relation of Lavinia's *protégé*. The name is the same, but I am given to understand that there are Townsends and Townsends. So Arthur's mother tells me; she talked about 'branches'—younger branches, elder branches, inferior branches—as if it were a royal house. Arthur, it appears, is of the reigning line, but poor Lavinia's young man is not. Beyond this, Arthur's mother knows very little about him; she has only a vague story that he has been 'wild.' But I know his sister a little, and she is a very nice woman. Her name is Mrs. Montgomery; she is a widow, with a little property and five children. She lives in the Second Avenue."

"What does Mrs. Montgomery say about him?"

"That he has talents by which he might distinguish himself."

"Only he is lazy, eh?"

"She doesn't say so."

"That's family pride," said the Doctor. "What is his profession?"

"He hasn't got any; he is looking for something. I believe he was once in the Navy."

"Once? What is his age?"

"I suppose he is upward of thirty. He must have gone into the Navy very young. I think Arthur told me that he inherited a small property—which was perhaps the cause of his leaving the Navy—and that he spent it all in a few years. He travelled all over the world, lived abroad, amused himself. I believe it was a kind of system, a theory he had. He has lately come back to America with the intention, as he tells Arthur, of beginning life in earnest."

"Is he in earnest about Catherine, then?"

"I don't see why you should be incredulous," said Mrs. Almond. "It seems to me that you have never done Catherine justice. You must remember that she has the prospect of thirty thousand a year."

The Doctor looked at his sister a moment, and then, with lightest touch of bitterness, "You at least appreciate her," he said.

Mrs. Almond blushed.

"I don't mean that is her only merit; I simply mean that it is a great one. A great many young men think so; and you appear to me never to have been properly aware of that. You have always had a little way of alluding to her as an unmarriageable girl."

"My allusions are as kind as yours, Elizabeth," said the Doctor, frankly. "How many suitors has Catherine had, with all her expectations—how much attention has she ever received? Catherine is not unmarriageable, but she is absolutely unattractive. What other reason is there for Lavinia being so charmed with the idea that there is a lover in the house? There has never been one before, and Lavinia, with her sensitive, sympathetic nature, is not used to the idea. It affects her imagination. I must do the young men of New York the justice to say that they strike me as very disinterested. They prefer pretty girls—lively girls—girls like your own. Catherine is neither pretty nor lively."

"Catherine does very well; she has a style of her own—which is more than my poor Marian has, who has no style at all," said Mrs. Almond. "The reason Catherine has received so little attention, is that she seems to all the young men to be older than themselves. She is so large, and she dresses so richly. They are rather afraid of her, I think; she looks as if she had been married already, and you know they don't like married women. And if our young men appear disinterested," the Doctor's wiser sister went on, "it is because they marry, as a general thing, so young—before twenty-five, at the age of innocence and sincerity—before the age of calculation. If they only waited a little, Catherine would fare better."

"As a calculation? Thank you very much," said the Doctor.

"Wait till some intelligent man of forty comes along, and he will be delighted with Catherine," Mrs. Almond continued.

"Mr. Townsend is not old enough, then? His motives may be pure."

"It is very possible that his motives are pure; I should be very sorry to take the contrary for granted. Lavinia is sure of it; and, as he is a very prepossessing youth, you might give him the benefit of the doubt."

Doctor Sloper reflected a moment.

"What are his present means of subsistence?"

"I have no idea. He lives, as I say, with his sister."

"A widow, with five children? Do you mean he lives *upon* her?"

Mrs. Almond got up, and with a certain impatience, "Had you not better ask Mrs. Montgomery herself?" she inquired.

"Perhaps I may come to that," said the Doctor. "Did you say the Second Avenue?" He made a note of the Second Avenue.

7

He was, however, by no means so much in earnest as this might seem to indicate; and, indeed, he was more than anything else amused with the whole situation. He was not in the least in a state of tension or of vigilance with regard to Catherine's prospects; he was even on his guard against the ridicule that might attach itself to the spectacle of a house thrown into agitation by its daughter and heiress receiving attentions unprecedented in its annals. More than this, he went so far as to promise himself some entertainment from the little drama—if drama it was—of which Mrs. Penniman desired to represent the ingenious Mr. Townsend as the hero. He had no intention, as yet, of regulating the *dénouement*. He was perfectly willing, as Elizabeth had suggested, to give the young man the benefit of every doubt. There was no great danger in it; for Catherine, at the age of twenty-two, was, after all, a rather mature blossom, such as could be plucked from the stem only by a vigorous jerk. The fact that Morris Townsend was poor, was not of necessity against him; the Doctor had never made up his mind that his daughter should marry a rich man. The fortune she would inherit struck him as a very sufficient provision for two reasonable persons, and if a penniless swain who could give a good account of himself should enter the lists, he should be judged quite upon his personal merits. There were other things besides. The Doctor thought it very vulgar to be precipitate in accusing people of mercenary motives, inasmuch as his door had as yet not been in the least besieged by fortune-hunters; and, lastly, he was very curious to see whether Catherine might really be loved for her moral worth. He smiled as he reflected that poor Mr. Townsend had been only twice to the house, and he said to Mrs. Penniman that the next time he should come she must ask him to dinner.

He came very soon again, and Mrs. Penniman had of course great pleasure in executing this mission. Morris Townsend accepted her invitation with equal good grace, and the dinner took place a few days later. The Doctor had said to himself, justly enough, that they must not have the young man alone; this would partake too much of the nature of encouragement. So two or three other persons were invited; but Morris Townsend, though he was by no means the ostensible, was the real occasion of the feast. There is every reason to suppose that he desired to make a good impression; and if he fell short of this result, it was not for want of a good deal of intelligent effort. The Doctor talked to him very little during dinner; but he observed him attentively, and after the ladies had gone out he pushed him the wine and asked him several questions. Morris was not a young man who needed to be pressed, and he found quite enough encouragement in the superior quality of the claret. The Doctor's wine was admirable, and it may be communicated to the reader that while he sipped it Morris reflected that a cellarful of good liquor—there was evidently a cellarful here—would be a most attractive idiosyncrasy in a father-in-law. The Doctor was struck with his appreciative guest; he saw that he was not a commonplace young man. "He has ability," said Catherine's father, "decided ability; he has a very good head if he chooses to use it. And he is uncommonly well turned out; quite the sort of figure that pleases the ladies; but I don't think I like him." The Doctor, however, kept his reflections to himself, and talked to his visitors about foreign lands, concerning which Morris offered him more information than he was ready, as he mentally phrased it, to swallow. Doctor Sloper had travelled but little, and he took the liberty of not believing everything that his talkative guest narrated. He prided himself on being something of a physiognomist; and while the young man, chatting with easy assurance, puffed his cigar and filled his glass again, the Doctor sat with his eyes quietly fixed on his bright, expressive face. "He has the assurance of the devil himself!" said Morris's host; "I don't think I ever saw such assurance. And his powers of invention are most remarkable. He is very knowing; they were not so knowing as that in my time. And a good head, did I say? I should think so—after a bottle of Madeira, and a bottle and a half of claret!"

After dinner Morris Townsend went and stood before Catherine, who was standing before the fire in her red satin gown.

"He doesn't like me—he doesn't like me at all," said the young man.

"Who doesn't like you?" asked Catherine.

"Your father; extraordinary man!"

"I don't see how you know," said Catherine, blushing.

"I feel; I am very quick to feel."

"Perhaps you are mistaken."

"Ah, well! you ask him, and you will see."

"I would rather not ask him, if there is any danger of his saying what you think."

Morris looked at her with an air of mock melancholy.

"It wouldn't give you any pleasure to contradict him?"

"I never contradict him," said Catherine.

"Will you hear me abused without opening your lips in my defence?"

"My father won't abuse you. He doesn't know you enough."

Morris Townsend gave a loud laugh, and Catherine began to blush again.

"I shall never mention you," she said, to take refuge from her confusion.

"That is very well; but it is not quite what I should have liked you to say. I should have liked you to say, 'If my father doesn't think well of you, what does it matter?'"

"Ah, but it would matter; I couldn't say that!" the girl exclaimed.

He looked at her for a moment, smiling a little; and the Doctor, if he had been watching him just then, would have seen a gleam of fine impatience in the sociable softness of his eye. But there was no impatience in his rejoinder—none, at least, save what was expressed in a little appealing sigh. "Ah, well! then I must not give up the hope of bringing him round."

He expressed it more frankly to Mrs. Penniman later in the evening. But before that he sung two or three songs at Catherine's timid request; not that he flattered himself that this would help to bring her father round. He had a sweet light tenor voice, and, when he had finished, every one made some exclamation—every one, that is, save Catherine, who remained intensely silent. Mrs. Penniman declared that his manner of singing was "most artistic," and Doctor Sloper said it was "very taking—very taking, indeed"; speaking loudly and distinctly, but with a certain dryness.

"He doesn't like me—he doesn't like me at all," said Morris Townsend, addressing the aunt in the same manner as he had done the niece. "He thinks I am all wrong."

Unlike her niece, Mrs. Penniman asked for no explanation. She only smiled very sweetly, as if she understood everything; and, unlike Catherine too, she made no attempt to contradict him. "Pray, what does it matter?" she murmured, softly.

"Ah, you say the right thing!" said Morris, greatly to the gratification of Mrs. Penniman, who prided herself on always saying the right thing.

The Doctor, the next time he saw his sister Elizabeth, let her know that he had made the acquaintance of Lavinia's *protégé*.

"Physically," he said, "he's uncommonly well set up. As an anatomist, it is really a pleasure to me to see such a beautiful structure; although, if people were all like him, I suppose there would be very little need for doctors."

"Don't you see anything in people but their bones?" Mrs. Almond rejoined. "What do you think of him as a father?"

"As a father? Thank Heaven, I am not his father!"

"No; but you are Catherine's. Lavinia tells me she is in love."

"She must get over it. He is not a gentleman."

"Ah, take care! Remember that he is a branch of the Townsends."

"He is not what I call a gentleman; he has not the soul of one. He is extremely insinuating; but it's a vulgar nature. I saw through it in a minute. He is altogether too familiar;—I hate familiarity. He is a plausible coxcomb."

"Ah, well," said Mrs. Almond, "if you make up your mind so easily, it's a great advantage."

"I don't make up my mind easily. What I tell you is the result of thirty years of observation; and in order to be able to form that judgment in a single evening, I have had to spend a lifetime in study."

"Very possibly you are right. But the thing is for Catherine to see it."

"I will present her with a pair of spectacles!" said the Doctor.

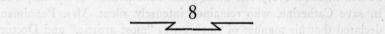

8

If it were true that she was in love, she was certainly very quiet about it; but the Doctor was of course prepared to admit that her quietness might mean volumes. She had told Morris Townsend that she would not mention him to her father, and she saw no reason to retract this vow of discretion. It was no more than decently civil, of course, that, after having dined in Washington Square, Morris should call there again; and it was no more than natural that, having been kindly received on this occasion, he should continue to present himself. He had had plenty of leisure on his hands;

and thirty years ago, in New York, a young man of leisure had reason to be thankful for aids to self-oblivion. Catherine said nothing to her father about these visits, though they had rapidly become the most important, the most absorbing thing in her life. The girl was very happy. She knew not as yet what would come of it; but the present had suddenly grown rich and solemn. If she had been told she was in love, she would have been a good deal surprised; for she had an idea that love was an eager and exacting passion, and her own heart was filled in these days with the impulse of self-effacement and sacrifice. Whenever Morris Townsend had left the house, her imagination projected itself, with all its strength, into the idea of his soon coming back; but if she had been told at such a moment that he would not return for a year, or even that he would never return, she would not have complained nor rebelled, but would have humbly accepted the decree, and sought for consolation in thinking over the times she had already seen him, the words he had spoken, the sound of his voice, of his tread, the expression of his face. Love demands certain things as a right; but Catherine had no sense of her rights; she had only a consciousness of immense and unexpected favors. Her very gratitude for these things had hushed itself; for it seemed to her that there would be something of impudence in making a festival of her secret. Her father suspected Morris Townsend's visits, and noted her reserve. She seemed to beg pardon for it; she looked at him constantly in silence, as if she meant to say that she said nothing because she was afraid of irritating him. But the poor girl's dumb eloquence irritated him more than anything else would have done, and he caught himself murmuring more than once that it was a grievous pity his only child was a simpleton. His murmurs, however, were inaudible; and for awhile he said nothing to any one. He would have liked to know exactly how often young Townsend came; but he had determined to ask no questions of the girl herself—to say nothing more to her that would show that he watched her. The Doctor had a great idea of being largely just: he wished to leave his daughter her liberty, and interfere only when the danger should be proved. It was not in his manner to obtain information by indirect methods, and it never even occurred to him to question the servants. As for Lavinia, he hated to talk to her about the matter; she annoyed him with her mock romanticism. But he had to come to this. Mrs. Penniman's convictions as regards the relations of her niece and the clever young visitor, who saved appearances by coming ostensibly for both the ladies—Mrs. Penniman's convictions had passed into a riper and richer phase. There was to be no crudity in Mrs. Penniman's treatment of the situation; she had become as uncommunicative as Catherine herself. She was tasting of the sweets of concealment; she had taken up the line of mystery. "She would be enchanted to be able to prove to herself that she is persecuted," said the Doctor; and when at last he questioned her, he was sure she would contrive to extract from his words a pretext for this belief.

"Be so good as to let me know what is going on in the house," he said to her, in a tone which, under the circumstances, he himself deemed genial.

"Going on, Austin?" Mrs. Penniman exclaimed. "Why, I am sure I don't know. I believe that last night the old gray cat had kittens."

"At her age?" said the Doctor. "The idea is startling—almost shocking. Be so good as to see that they are all drowned. But what else has happened?"

"Ah, the dear little kittens!" cried Mrs. Penniman. "I wouldn't have them drowned for the world!"

Her brother puffed his cigar a few moments in silence. "Your sympathy with kittens, Lavinia," he presently resumed, "arises from a feline element in your own character."

"Cats are very graceful, and very clean," said Mrs. Penniman, smiling.

"And very stealthy. You are the embodiment both of grace and of neatness; but you are wanting in frankness."

"You certainly are not, dear brother."

"I don't pretend to be graceful, though I try to be neat. Why haven't you let me know that Mr. Morris Townsend is coming to the house four times a week?"

Mrs. Penniman lifted her eyebrows. "Four times a week!"

"Three times, then, or five times, if you prefer it. I am away all day, and I see nothing. But when such things happen, you should let me know."

Mrs. Penniman, with her eyebrows still raised, reflected intently. "Dear Austin," she said at last, "I am incapable of betraying a confidence. I would rather suffer anything."

"Never fear; you shall not suffer. To whose confidence is it you allude? Has Catherine made you take a vow of eternal secrecy?"

"By no means. Catherine has not told me as much as she might. She has not been very trustful."

"It is the young man, then, who has made you his confidante? Allow me to say that it is extremely indiscreet of you to form secret alliances with young men; you don't know where they may lead you."

"I don't know what you mean by an alliance," said Mrs. Penniman. "I take a great interest in Mr. Townsend; I won't conceal that. But that's all."

"Under the circumstances, that is quite enough. What is the source of your interest in Mr. Townsend?"

"Why," said Mrs. Penniman, musing, and then breaking into her smile, "that he is so interesting!"

The Doctor felt that he had need of his patience. "And what makes him interesting?—his good looks?"

"His misfortunes, Austin."

"Ah, he has had misfortunes? That, of course, is always interesting. Are you at liberty to mention a few of Mr. Townsend's?"

"I don't know that he would like it," said Mrs. Penniman. "He has told me a great deal about himself—he has told me, in fact, his whole history. But I don't think I ought to repeat those things. He would tell them to you, I am sure, if he thought you would listen to him kindly. With kindness you may do anything with him."

The Doctor gave a laugh. "I shall request him very kindly, then, to leave Catherine alone."

"Ah!" said Mrs. Penniman, shaking her forefinger at her brother, with her little finger turned out, "Catherine has probably said something to him kinder than that!"

"Said that she loved him?—do you mean that?"

Mrs. Penniman fixed her eyes on the floor. "As I tell you, Austin, she doesn't confide in me."

"You have an opinion, I suppose, all the same. It is that I ask you for; though I don't conceal from you that I shall not regard it as conclusive."

Mrs. Penniman's gaze continued to rest on the carpet; but at last she lifted it, and then her brother thought it very expressive. "I think Catherine is very happy; that is all I can say."

"Townsend is trying to marry her—is that what you mean?"

"He is greatly interested in her."

"He finds her such an attractive girl?"

"Catherine has a lovely nature, Austin," said Mrs. Penniman, "and Mr. Townsend has had the intelligence to discover that."

"With a little help from you, I suppose. My dear Lavinia," cried the Doctor, "you are an admirable aunt!"

"So Mr. Townsend says," observed Lavinia, smiling.

"Do you think he is sincere?" asked her brother.

"In saying that?"

"No; that's of course. But in his admiration for Catherine?"

"Deeply sincere. He has said to me the most appreciative, the most charming things about her. He would say them to you, if he were sure you would listen to him—gently."

"I doubt whether I can undertake it. He appears to require a great deal of gentleness."

"He is a sympathetic, sensitive nature," said Mrs. Penniman.

Her brother puffed his cigar again in silence. "These delicate qualities have survived his vicissitudes, eh? All this while you haven't told me about his misfortunes."

"It is a long story," said Mrs. Penniman, "and I regard it as a sacred trust. But I suppose there is no objection to my saying that he has been wild—he frankly confesses that. But he has paid for it."

"That's what has impoverished him, eh?"

"I don't mean simply in money. He is very much alone in the world."

"Do you mean that he has behaved so badly that his friends have given him up?"

"He has had false friends, who have deceived and betrayed him."

"He seems to have some good ones too. He has a devoted sister, and half a dozen nephews and nieces."

Mrs. Penniman was silent a minute. "The nephews and nieces are children, and the sister is not a very attractive person."

"I hope he doesn't abuse her to you," said the Doctor; "for I am told he lives upon her."

"Lives upon her?"

"Lives with her, and does nothing for himself; it is about the same thing."

"He is looking for a position most earnestly," said Mrs. Penniman. "He hopes every day to find one."

"Precisely. He is looking for it here—over there in the front parlor. The position of husband of a weak-minded woman with a large fortune would suit him to perfection!"

Mrs. Penniman was truly amiable, but she now gave signs of temper. She rose with much animation, and stood for a moment looking at her brother. "My dear Austin," she remarked, "if you regard Catherine as a weak-minded woman you are particularly mistaken!" And with this she moved majestically away.

9

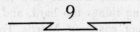

It was a regular custom with the family in Washington Square to go and spend Sunday evening at Mrs. Almond's. On the Sunday after the conversation I have just narrated this custom was not intermitted; and on this occasion, toward the middle of the evening, Doctor Sloper found reason to withdraw to the library with his brother-in-law, to talk over a matter of business. He was absent some twenty minutes, and when he came back into the circle, which was enlivened by the presence of several friends of the family, he saw that Morris Townsend had come in, and had lost as little time as possible in seating himself on a small sofa beside Catherine. In the large room, where several different groups had been formed, and the hum of voices and of laughter was loud, these two young persons might confabulate, as the Doctor phrased it to himself, without attracting attention. He saw in a moment, however, that his daughter was painfully conscious of his own observation. She sat motionless, with her eyes bent down, staring at her open fan, deeply flushed, shrinking together as if to minimize the indiscretion of which she confessed herself guilty.

The Doctor almost pitied her. Poor Catherine was not defiant; she had no genius for bravado, and as she felt that her father viewed her companion's attentions with an unsympathizing eye, there was nothing but discomfort for her in the accident of seeming to challenge him. The Doctor felt, indeed, so sorry for her that he turned away, to spare her the sense of being watched; and he was so intelligent a man that, in his thoughts, he rendered a sort of poetic justice to her situation.

"It must be deucedly pleasant for a plain, inanimate girl like that to have a beautiful young fellow come and sit down beside her, and whisper to her that he is her slave—if that is what this one whispers. No wonder she likes it, and that she thinks me a cruel tyrant; which of course she does, though she is afraid—she hasn't the animation necessary—to admit it to herself. Poor old Catherine!" mused the Doctor; "I verily believe she is capable of defending me when Townsend abuses me!"

And the force of this reflection, for the moment, was such in making him feel the natural opposition between his point of view and that of an infatuated child, that he said to himself that he was perhaps after all taking things too hard, and crying out before he was hurt. He must not condemn Morris Townsend unheard. He had a great aversion to taking things too hard; he thought that half the discomfort and many of the disappointments of life come from it; and for an instant he asked himself whether, possibly, he did not appear ridiculous to this intelligent young man, whose private perception of incongruities he suspected of being keen. At the end of a quarter of an hour Catherine had got rid of him, and Townsend was now standing before the fireplace in conversation with Mrs. Almond.

"We will try him again," said the Doctor. And he crossed the room and joined his sister and her companion, making her a sign that she should leave the young man to him. She presently did so, while Morris looked at him, smiling, without a sign of evasiveness in his affable eye.

"He's amazingly conceited!" thought the Doctor; and then he said, aloud, "I am told you are looking out for a position."

"Oh, a position is more than I should presume to call it," Morris Townsend answered. "That sounds so fine. I should like some quiet work—something to turn an honest penny."

"What sort of thing should you prefer?"

"Do you mean what am I fit for? Very little, I am afraid. I have nothing but my good right arm, as they say in the melodramas."

"You are too modest," said the Doctor. "In addition to your good right arm you have your subtle brain. I know nothing of you but what I see; but I see by your physiognomy that you are extremely intelligent."

"Ah," Townsend murmured, "I don't know what to answer when you say that. You advise me, then, not to despair?"

And he looked at his interlocutor as if the question might have a double meaning. The Doctor caught the look and weighed it a moment before he replied. "I should be very sorry to admit that a robust and well-disposed young man need ever despair. If he doesn't succeed in one thing, he can try another. Only, I should add, he should choose his line with discretion."

"Ah, yes, with discretion," Morris Townsend repeated, sympathetically. "Well, I have been indiscreet, formerly; but I think I have got over it. I am very steady now." And he stood a moment, looking down at his remarkably neat shoes. Then at last, "Were you kindly intending to propose something for my advantage?" he inquired, looking up and smiling.

"D—n his impudence!" the Doctor exclaimed, privately. But in a moment he reflected that he himself had, after all, touched first upon this delicate point, and that his words might have been construed as an offer of assistance. "I have no particular proposal to make," he presently said; "but it occurred to me to let you know that I have you in my mind. Sometimes one hears of opportunities. For instance, should you object to leaving New York—to going to a distance?"

"I am afraid I shouldn't be able to manage that. I must seek my fortune here or nowhere. You see," added Morris Townsend, "I have ties—I have responsibilities here. I have a sister, a widow, from whom I have been separated for a long time, and to whom I am almost everything. I shouldn't like to say to her that I must leave her. She rather depends upon me, you see."

"Ah, that's very proper; family feeling is very proper," said Doctor Sloper. "I often think there is not enough of it in our city. I think I have heard of your sister."

"It is possible, but I rather doubt it; she lives so very quietly."

"As quietly, you mean," the Doctor went on, with a short laugh, "as a lady may do who has several young children."

"Ah, my little nephews and nieces—that's the very point! I am helping to bring them up," said Morris Townsend. "I am a kind of amateur tutor; I give them lessons."

"That's very proper, as I say; but it is hardly a career."

"It won't make my fortune," the young man confessed.

"You must not be too much bent on a fortune," said the Doctor. "But I assure you I will keep you in mind; I won't lose sight of you."

"If my situation becomes desperate I shall perhaps take the liberty of reminding you," Morris rejoined, raising his voice a little, with a brighter smile, as his interlocutor turned away.

Before he left the house the Doctor had a few words with Mrs. Almond.

"I should like to see his sister," he said. "What do you call her— Mrs. Montgomery? I should like to have a little talk with her."

"I will try and manage it," Mrs. Almond responded. "I will take the first opportunity of inviting her, and you shall come and meet her; unless, indeed," Mrs. Almond added, "she first takes it into her head to be sick and to send for you."

"Ah no, not that; she must have trouble enough without that. But it would have its advantages, for then I should see the children. I should like very much to see the children."

"You are very thorough. Do you want to catechise them about their uncle?"

"Precisely. Their uncle tells me he has charge of their education, that he saves their mother the expense of school-bills. I should like to ask them a few questions in the commoner branches."

"He certainly has not the cut of a school-master," Mrs. Almond said to herself a short time afterward, as she saw Morris Townsend in a corner bending over her niece, who was seated.

And there was, indeed, nothing in the young man's discourse at this moment that savored of the pedagogue.

"Will you meet me somewhere to-morrow or next day?" he said, in a low tone, to Catherine.

"Meet you?" she asked, lifting her frightened eyes.

"I have something particular to say to you—very particular."

"Can't you come to the house? Can't you say it there?"

Townsend shook his head gloomily. "I can't enter your doors again."

"Oh, Mr. Townsend!" murmured Catherine. She trembled as she wondered what had happened—whether her father had forbidden it.

"I can't, in self-respect," said the young man. "Your father has insulted me."

"Insulted you?"

"He has taunted me with my poverty."

"Oh, you are mistaken—you misunderstood him!" Catherine spoke with energy, getting up from her chair.

"Perhaps I am too proud—too sensitive. But would you have me otherwise?" he asked, tenderly.

"Where my father is concerned, you must not be sure. He is full of goodness," said Catherine.

"He laughed at me for having no position. I took it quietly; but only because he belongs to you."

"I don't know," said Catherine—"I don't know what he thinks. I am sure he means to be kind. You must not be too proud."

"I will be proud only of you," Morris answered. "Will you meet me in the Square in the afternoon?"

A great blush on Catherine's part had been the answer to the declaration I have just quoted. She turned away, heedless of his question.

"Will you meet me?" he repeated. "It is very quiet there—no one need see us—toward dusk."

"It is you who are unkind, it is you who laugh, when you say such things as that."

"My dear girl!" the young man murmured.

"You know how little there is in me to be proud of. I am ugly and stupid."

Morris greeted this remark with an ardent murmur, in which she recognized nothing articulate but an assurance that she was his own dearest.

But she went on. "I am not even—I am not even—" And she paused a moment.

"You are not what?"

"I am not even brave."

"Ah, then, if you are afraid, what shall we do?"

She hesitated awhile; then at last— "You must come to the house," she said; "I am not afraid of that."

"I would rather it were in the Square," the young man urged. "You know how empty it is, often. No one will see us."

"I don't care who sees us. But leave me now."

He left her resignedly; he had got what he wanted. Fortunately he was ignorant that half an hour later, going home with her father, and feeling him near, the poor girl, in spite of her sudden declaration of courage, began to tremble again. Her father said nothing; but she had an idea his eyes were fixed upon her in the darkness. Mrs. Penniman also was silent; Morris Townsend had told her that her niece preferred, unromantically, an interview in a chintz-covered parlor to a sentimental tryst beside a fountain sheeted with dead leaves, and she was lost in wonderment at the oddity—almost the perversity—of the choice.

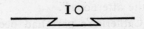

10

Catherine received the young man the next day on the ground she had chosen—amidst the chaste upholstery of a New York drawing-room furnished in the fashion of fifty years ago. Morris had swallowed his pride, and made the effort necessary to cross the threshold of her too derisive parent—an act of magnanimity which could not fail to render him doubly interesting.

"We must settle something—we must take a line," he declared, passing his hand through his hair and giving a glance at the long, narrow mirror which adorned the space between the two windows, and which had at its base a little gilded bracket covered by a thin slab of white marble, supporting in its turn a backgammon-board folded together in the shape of two volumes—two shining folios inscribed, in greenish-gilt letters, *History of England*. If Morris had been pleased to describe the master of the house as a heartless scoffer, it is because he thought him too much on his guard, and this was the easiest way to express his own dissatisfaction—a dissatisfaction which he had made a point of concealing from the Doctor. It will probably seem to the reader, however, that the Doctor's vigilance was by no means excessive, and that these two young people had an open field. Their intimacy was now considerable, and it may appear that, for a shrinking and retiring person, our heroine had been liberal of her favors. The young man, within a few days, had made her listen to things for which she had not supposed that she was prepared; having a lively foreboding of difficulties, he proceeded to gain as much ground as possible in the present. He remembered that fortune favors the brave, and even if he had forgotten it, Mrs. Penniman would have remembered it for him. Mrs. Penniman delighted of all things in a drama, and she flattered herself that a drama would now be enacted. Combining as she did the zeal of the prompter with the impatience of the spectator, she had long since done her utmost to pull up the curtain. She, too, expected to figure in the performance—to be the confidante, the Chorus, to speak the epilogue. It may even be said that there were times when she lost sight altogether of the modest heroine of the play in the contemplation of certain great scenes which would naturally occur between the hero and herself.

What Morris had told Catherine at last was simply that he loved her, or rather adored her. Virtually, he had made known as much already—his visits had been a series of eloquent intimations of it. But now he had affirmed it in lover's vows, and, as a memorable sign of it, he had passed his arm round the girl's waist and taken a kiss. This happy certitude had come sooner than Catherine expected, and she had regarded it, very naturally, as a priceless treasure. It may even be doubted whether she had ever definitely expected to possess it; she had not been waiting for it, and she had never said to herself that at a given moment it must come. As I have tried to explain, she was not eager and exacting; she took what was given her from day to day; and if the delightful custom of her lover's visits, which yielded her a happiness in which confidence and timidity were strangely blended, had suddenly come to an end, she would not only not have spoken of herself as one of the forsaken, but she would not have thought of herself as one of the disappointed. After Morris had kissed her, the last time he was with her, as a ripe assurance of his devotion, she begged him to go away, to leave her alone, to let her think. Morris went away, taking another kiss first. But Catherine's meditations had lacked a certain coherence. She felt his kisses on her lips and on her cheeks for a long time afterward; the sensation was rather an obstacle than an aid to reflection. She would have liked to see her situation all clearly before her, to make up her mind what she should do if, as she feared, her father should tell her that he disapproved of Morris Townsend. But all that she could see with any vividness was that it was terribly strange that any one should disapprove of him; that there must in that case be some mistake, some mystery, which in a little while would be set at rest. She put off deciding and choosing; before the vision of a conflict with her father she dropped her eyes and sat motionless, holding her breath and waiting. It made her heart beat; it was intensely painful. When Morris kissed her and said these things—that also made her heart beat; but this was worse, and it frightened her. Nevertheless, to-day when the young man spoke of settling something, taking a line, she felt that it was the truth, and she answered very simply and without hesitating. "We must do our duty," she said; "we must speak to my father. I will do it to-night; you must do it to-morrow."

"It is very good of you to do it first," Morris answered. "The young man—the happy lover—generally does that. But just as you please."

It pleased Catherine to think that she should be brave for his sake, and in her satisfaction she even gave a little smile. "Women have more tact," she said; "they ought to do it first. They are more conciliating; they can persuade better."

"You will need all your powers of persuasion. But, after all," Morris added, "you are irresistible."

"Please don't speak that way—and promise me this: To-morrow, when you talk with father, you will be very gentle and respectful."

"As much so as possible," Morris promised. "It won't be much use, but I shall try. I certainly would rather have you easily than have to fight for you."

"Don't talk about fighting; we shall not fight."

"Ah, we must be prepared," Morris rejoined; "you especially, because for you it must come hardest. Do you know the first thing your father will say to you?"

"No, Morris; please tell me."

"He will tell you I am mercenary."

"Mercenary!"

"It's a big word, but it means a low thing. It means that I am after your money."

"Oh!" murmured Catherine, softly.

The exclamation was so deprecating and touching that Morris indulged in another little demonstration of affection. "But he will be sure to say it," he added.

"It will be easy to be prepared for that," Catherine said. "I shall simply say that he is mistaken—that other men may be that way, but that you are not."

"You must make a great point of that, for it will be his own great point."

Catherine looked at her lover a minute, and then she said, "I shall persuade him. But I am glad we shall be rich," she added.

Morris turned away, looking into the crown of his hat. "No, it's a misfortune," he said at last. "It is from that our difficulty will come."

"Well, if it is the worst misfortune, we are not so unhappy. Many people would not think it so bad. I will persuade him, and after that we shall be very glad we have money."

Morris Townsend listened to this robust logic in silence. "I will leave my defence to you; it's a charge that a man has to stoop to defend himself from."

Catherine on her side was silent for awhile; she was looking at him while he looked, with a good deal of fixedness, out of the window. "Morris," she said, abruptly, "are you very sure you love me?"

He turned round, and in a moment he was bending over her. "My own dearest, can you doubt it?"

"I have only known it five days," she said; "but now it seems to me as if I could never do without it."

"You will never be called upon to try." And he gave a little tender, reassuring laugh. Then, in a moment, he added, "There is something you must tell me, too." She had closed her eyes after the last words she uttered, and kept them closed; and at this she nodded her head, without opening them. "You must tell me," he went on, "that if your father is dead against me, if he absolutely forbids our marriage, you will still be faithful."

Catherine opened her eyes, gazing at him, and she could give no better promise than what he read there.

"You will cleave to me?" said Morris. "You know you are your own mistress—you are of age."

"Ah, Morris!" she murmured, for all answer; or rather not for all, for she put her hand into his own. He kept it awhile, and presently he kissed her again. This is all that need be recorded of their conversation; but Mrs. Penniman, if she had been present, would probably have admitted that it was as well it had not taken place beside the fountain in Washington Square.

I I

Catherine listened for her father when he came in that evening, and she heard him go to his study. She sat quiet, though her heart was beating fast, for nearly half an hour; then she went and knocked at his door—a ceremony without which she never crossed the threshold of this apartment. On entering it now, she found him in his chair beside the fire, entertaining himself with a cigar and the evening paper.

"I have something to say to you," she began very gently; and she sat down in the first place that offered.

"I shall be very happy to hear it, my dear," said her father. He waited—waited, looking at her—while she stared, in a long silence, at the fire. He was curious and impatient, for he was sure she was going to speak of Morris Townsend; but he let her take her own time, for he was determined to be very mild.

"I am engaged to be married!" Catherine announced at last, still staring at the fire.

The Doctor was startled; the accomplished fact was more than he had expected; but he betrayed no surprise. "You do right to tell me," he simply said. "And who is the happy mortal whom you have honored with your choice?"

"Mr. Morris Townsend." And as she pronounced her lover's name Catherine looked at him. What she saw was her father's still gray eye and his clear-cut, definite smile. She contemplated these objects for a moment, and then she looked back at the fire; it was much warmer.

"When was this arrangement made?" the Doctor asked.

"This afternoon—two hours ago."

"Was Mr. Townsend here?"

"Yes, father; in the front-parlor." She was very glad that she was not obliged to tell him that the ceremony of their betrothal had taken place out there under the bare ailanthus-trees.

"Is it serious?" said the Doctor.

"Very serious, father."

Her father was silent a moment. "Mr. Townsend ought to have told me."

"He means to tell you to-morrow."

"After I know all about it from you? He ought to have told me before. Does he think I didn't care, because I left you so much liberty?"

"Oh no," said Catherine; "he knew you would care. And we have been so much obliged to you for—for the liberty."

The Doctor gave a short laugh. "You might have made a better use of it, Catherine."

"Please don't say that, father!" the girl urged, softly, fixing her dull and gentle eyes upon him.

He puffed his cigar awhile, meditatively. "You have gone very fast," he said, at last.

"Yes," Catherine answered, simply; "I think we have."

Her father glanced at her an instant, removing his eyes from the fire. "I don't wonder Mr. Townsend likes you; you are so simple and so good."

"I don't know why it is; but he *does* like me. I am sure of that."

"And are you very fond of Mr. Townsend?"

"I like him very much, of course, or I shouldn't consent to marry him."

"But you have known him a very short time, my dear."

"Oh," said Catherine, with some eagerness, "it doesn't take long to like a person—when once you begin."

"You must have begun very quickly. Was it the first time you saw him—that night at your aunt's party?"

"I don't know, father," the girl answered. "I can't tell you about that."

"Of course; that's your own affair. You will have observed that I have acted on that principle. I have not interfered; I have left you your liberty; I have remembered that you are no longer a little girl—that you have arrived at years of discretion."

"I feel very old—and very wise," said Catherine, smiling faintly.

"I am afraid that before long you will feel older and wiser yet. I don't like your engagement."

"Ah!" Catherine exclaimed, softly, getting up from her chair.

"No, my dear. I am sorry to give you pain; but I don't like it. You should have consulted me before you settled it. I have been too easy with you, and I feel as if you had taken advantage of my indulgence. Most decidedly you should have spoken to me first."

Catherine hesitated a moment, and then—"It was because I was afraid you wouldn't like it," she confessed.

"Ah, there it is! You had a bad conscience."

"No, I have not a bad conscience, father!" the girl cried out, with considerable energy. "Please don't accuse me of anything so dreadful!" These words, in fact, represented to her imagination something very terrible indeed, something base and cruel, which she associated with malefactors and prisoners. "It was because I was afraid—afraid—" she went on.

"If you were afraid, it was because you had been foolish."

"I was afraid you didn't like Mr. Townsend."

"You were quite right. I don't like him."

"Dear father, you don't know him," said Catherine, in a voice so timidly argumentative that it might have touched him.

"Very true; I don't know him intimately. But I know him enough; I have my impression of him. You don't know him either."

She stood before the fire with her hands lightly clasped in front of her; and her father, leaning back in his chair and looking up at her, made this remark with a placidity that might have been irritating.

I doubt, however, whether Catherine was irritated, though she broke into a vehement protest. "I don't know him?" she cried. "Why, I know him—better than I have ever known any one!"

"You know a part of him—what he has chosen to show you. But you don't know the rest."

"The rest? What is the rest?"

"Whatever it may be, there is sure to be plenty of it."

"I know what you mean," said Catherine, remembering how Morris had forewarned her. "You mean that he is mercenary."

Her father looked up at her still, with his cold, quiet, reasonable eye. "If I meant it, my dear, I should say it! But there is an error I wish particularly to avoid—that of rendering Mr. Townsend more interesting to you by saying hard things about him."

"I won't think them hard if they are true," said Catherine.

"If you don't, you will be a remarkably sensible young woman!"

"They will be your reasons, at any rate, and you will want me to hear your reasons."

The Doctor smiled a little. "Very true. You have a perfect right to ask for them." And he puffed his cigar a few moments. "Very well, then; without accusing Mr. Townsend of being in love only with your fortune—and with the fortune that you justly expect—I will say that there is every reason to suppose that these good things have entered into his calculation more largely than a tender solicitude for your happiness strictly requires. There is, of course, nothing impossible in an intelligent young man entertaining a disinterested affection for you. You are an honest, amiable girl, and an intelligent young man might easily find it out. But the principal thing that we know about this young man—who is, indeed, very intelligent—leads us to suppose that, however much he may value your personal merits, he values your money more. The principal thing we know about him is that he has led a life of dissipation, and has spent a fortune of his own in doing so. That is enough for me, my dear. I wish you to marry a young man with other antecedents—a young man who could give positive guarantees. If Morris Townsend has spent his own fortune in amusing himself, there is every reason to believe that he would spend yours."

The Doctor delivered himself of these remarks slowly, deliberately, with occasional pauses and prolongations of accent, which made no great allowance for poor Catherine's suspense as to his conclusion. She sat down at last, with her head bent and her eyes still fixed upon him; and strangely enough—I hardly know how to tell it—even while she felt that what he said went so terribly against her, she admired his neatness and nobleness of expression. There was something hopeless and oppressive in having to argue with her father; but she too, on her side, must try to be clear. He was so quiet; he was not at all angry; and she, too, must be quiet. But her very effort to be quiet made her tremble.

"That is not the principal thing we know about him," she said; and there was a touch of her tremor in her voice. "There are other things—many other things. He has very high abilities—he wants so much to do something. He is kind, and generous, and true," said poor Catherine, who had not suspected hitherto the resources of her eloquence. "And his fortune—his fortune that he spent—was very small."

"All the more reason he shouldn't have spent it," cried the Doctor, getting up with a laugh. Then, as Catherine, who had also risen to her feet again, stood there in her rather angular earnestness, wishing so much and expressing so little, he drew her toward him and kissed her. "You won't think me cruel?" he said, holding her a moment.

This question was not reassuring; it seemed to Catherine, on the contrary, to suggest possibilities which made her feel sick. But she answered coherently enough, "No, dear father; because if you knew how I feel—and you must know, you know everything—you would be so kind, so gentle."

"Yes, I think I know how you feel," the Doctor said. "I will be very kind—be sure of that. And I will see Mr. Townsend to-morrow. Meanwhile, and for the present, be so good as to mention to no one that you are engaged."

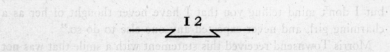

I 2

On the morrow, in the afternoon, he stayed at home, awaiting Mr. Townsend's call—a proceeding by which it appeared to him (justly perhaps, for he was a very busy man) that he paid Catherine's suitor great honor, and gave both these young people so much the less to complain of. Morris presented himself with a countenance sufficiently serene—he appeared to have forgotten the "insult" for which he had solicited Catherine's sympathy two evenings before—and Doctor Sloper lost no time in letting him know that he had been prepared for his visit.

"Catherine told me yesterday what has been going on between you," he said. "You must allow me to say that it would have been becoming of you to give me notice of your intentions before they had gone so far."

"I should have done so," Morris answered, "if you had not had so much the appearance of leaving your daughter at liberty. She seems to me quite her own mistress."

"Literally, she is. But she has not emancipated herself morally quite so far, I trust, as to choose a husband without consulting me. I have left her at liberty, but I have not been in the least indifferent. The truth is, that your little affair has come to a head with a rapidity that surprises me. It was only the other day that Catherine made your acquaintance."

"It was not long ago, certainly," said Morris, with great gravity. "I admit that we have not been slow to—to arrive at an understanding. But that was very natural, from the moment we were sure of ourselves—and of each other. My interest in Miss Sloper began the first time I saw her."

"Did it not by chance precede your first meeting?" the Doctor asked.

Morris looked at him an instant. "I certainly had already heard that she was a charming girl."

"A charming girl—that's what you think her?"

"Assuredly. Otherwise I should not be sitting here."

The Doctor meditated a moment. "My dear young man," he said at last, "you must be very susceptible. As Catherine's father I have, I trust, a just and tender appreciation of her many good qualities; but I don't mind telling you that I have never thought of her as a charming girl, and never expected any one else to do so."

Morris Townsend received this statement with a smile that was not wholly devoid of deference. "I don't know what I might think of her if I were her father. I can't put myself in that place. I speak from my own point of view."

"You speak very well," said the Doctor; "but that is not all that is necessary. I told Catherine yesterday that I disapproved of her engagement."

"She let me know as much, and I was very sorry to hear it. I am greatly disappointed." And Morris sat in silence awhile, looking at the floor.

"Did you really expect I would say I was delighted, and throw my daughter into your arms?"

"Oh no; I had an idea you didn't like me."

"What gave you the idea?"

"The fact that I am poor."

"That has a harsh sound," said the Doctor, "but it is about the truth—speaking of you strictly as a son-in-law. Your absence of means, of a profession, of visible resources or prospects, places you in a category from which it would be imprudent for me to select a husband for my daughter, who is a weak young woman with a large fortune. In any other capacity I am perfectly prepared to like you. As a son-in-law, I abominate you."

Morris Townsend listened respectfully. "I don't think Miss Sloper is a weak woman," he presently said.

"Of course you must defend her—it's the least you can do. But I have known my child twenty years, and you have known her six weeks. Even if she were not weak, however, you would still be a penniless man."

"Ah, yes; that is *my* weakness! And therefore, you mean, I am mercenary—I only want your daughter's money."

"I don't say that. I am not obliged to say it; and to say it, save under stress of compulsion, would be very bad taste. I say simply that you belong to the wrong category."

"But your daughter doesn't marry a category," Townsend urged, with his handsome smile. "She marries an individual—an individual whom she is so good as to say she loves."

"An individual who offers so little in return."

"Is it possible to offer more than the most tender affection and a life-long devotion?" the young man demanded.

"It depends how we take it. It is possible to offer a few other things besides, and not only is it possible, but it is the custom. A life-long devotion is measured after the fact; and meanwhile it is usual in these cases to give a few material securities. What are yours? A very handsome face and figure, and a very good manner. They are excellent as far as they go, but they don't go far enough."

"There is one thing you should add to them," said Morris—"the word of a gentleman."

"The word of a gentleman that you will always love Catherine? You must be a fine gentleman to be sure of that."

"The word of a gentleman that I am not mercenary; that my

affection for Miss Sloper is as pure and disinterested a sentiment as was ever lodged in a human breast. I care no more for her fortune than for the ashes in that grate."

"I take note—I take note," said the Doctor. "But, having done so, I turn to our category again. Even with that solemn vow on your lips, you take your place in it. There is nothing against you but an accident, if you will; but, with my thirty years' medical practice, I have seen that accidents may have far-reaching consequences."

Morris smoothed his hat—it was already remarkably glossy—and continued to display a self-control which, as the Doctor was obliged to admit, was extremely creditable to him. But his disappointment was evidently keen.

"Is there nothing I can do to make you believe in me?"

"If there were, I should be sorry to suggest it, for—don't you see?—I don't want to believe in you," said the Doctor, smiling.

"I would go and dig in the fields."

"That would be foolish."

"I will take the first work that offers to-morrow."

"Do so by all means—but for your own sake, not for mine."

"I see; you think I am an idler!" Morris exclaimed, a little too much in the tone of a man who has made a discovery. But he saw his error immediately and blushed.

"It doesn't matter what I think, when once I have told you I don't think of you as a son-in-law."

But Morris persisted: "You think I would squander her money?"

The Doctor smiled. "It doesn't matter, as I say; but I plead guilty to that."

"That's because I spent my own, I suppose," said Morris. "I frankly confess that. I have been wild; I have been foolish. I will tell you every crazy thing I ever did, if you like. There were some great follies among the number—I have never concealed that. But I have sown my wild-oats. Isn't there some proverb about a reformed rake? I was not a rake, but I assure you I have reformed. It is better to have amused one's self for awhile and have done with it. Your daughter would never care for a milksop; and I will take the liberty of saying that you would like one quite as little. Besides, between my money and hers there is a great difference. I spent my own; it was because it was my own that I spent it. And I made no debts; when it was gone I stopped. I don't owe a penny in the world."

"Allow me to inquire what you are living on now—though I

admit," the Doctor added, "that the question, on my part, is inconsistent."

"I am living on the remnants of my property," said Morris Townsend.

"Thank you," the Doctor gravely replied.

Yes, certainly, Morris's self-control was laudable. "Even admitting I attach an undue importance to Miss Sloper's fortune," he went on, "would not that be in itself an assurance that I would take good care of it?"

"That you should take too much care would be quite as bad as that you should take too little. Catherine might suffer as much by your economy as by your extravagance."

"I think you are very unjust!" The young man made this declaration decently, civilly, without violence.

"It is your privilege to think so, and I surrender my reputation to you! I certainly don't flatter myself, I gratify you."

"Don't you care a little to gratify your daughter? Do you enjoy the idea of making her miserable?"

"I am perfectly resigned to her thinking me a tyrant for a twelvemonth."

"For a twelvemonth!" exclaimed Morris, with a laugh.

"For a lifetime, then. She may as well be miserable in that way as in the other.'"

Here at last Morris lost his temper. "Ah, you are not polite, sir!" he cried.

"You push me to it—you argue too much."

"I have a great deal at stake."

"Well, whatever it is," said the Doctor, "you have lost it."

"Are you sure of that?" asked Morris; "are you sure your daughter will give me up?"

"I mean, of course, you have lost it as far as I am concerned. As for Catherine's giving you up—no, I am not sure of it. But as I shall strongly recommend it, as I have a great fund of respect and affection in my daughter's mind to draw upon, and as she has the sentiment of duty developed in a very high degree, I think it extremely possible."

Morris Townsend began to smooth his hat again. "I, too, have a fund of affection to draw upon," he observed, at last.

The Doctor at this point showed his own first symptoms of irritation. "Do you mean to defy me?"

"Call it what you please, sir. I mean not to give your daughter up."

The Doctor shook his head. "I haven't the least fear of your pining away your life. You are made to enjoy it."

Morris gave a laugh. "Your opposition to my marriage is all the more cruel, then. Do you intend to forbid your daughter to see me again?"

"She is past the age at which people are forbidden, and I am not a father in an old-fashioned novel. But I shall strongly urge her to break with you."

"I don't think she will," said Morris Townsend.

"Perhaps not; but I shall have done what I could."

"She has gone too far—" Morris went on.

"To retreat? Then let her stop where she is."

"Too far to stop, I mean."

The Doctor looked at him a moment; Morris had his hand on the door. "There is a great deal of impertinence in your saying it."

"I will say no more, sir," Morris answered; and, making his bow, he left the room.

13

It may be thought the Doctor was too positive, and Mrs. Almond intimated as much. But, as he said, he had his impression; it seemed to him sufficient, and he had no wish to modify it. He had passed his life in estimating people (it was part of the medical trade), and in nineteen cases out of twenty he was right.

"Perhaps Mr. Townsend is the twentieth case," said Mrs. Almond.

"Perhaps he is, though he doesn't look to me at all like a twentieth case. But I will give him the benefit of the doubt, and, to make sure, I will go and talk with Mrs. Montgomery. She will almost certainly tell me I have done right; but it is just possible that she will prove to me that I have made the greatest mistake of my life. If she does, I will beg Mr. Townsend's pardon. You needn't invite her to meet me, as you kindly proposed; I will write her a frank letter, telling her how matters stand, and asking leave to come and see her."

"I am afraid the frankness will be chiefly on your side. The poor little woman will stand up for her brother, whatever he may be."

"Whatever he may be! I doubt that. People are not always so fond of their brothers."

"Ah," said Mrs. Almond, "when it's a question of thirty thousand a year coming into a family—"

"If she stands up for him on account of the money, she will be a humbug. If she is a humbug, I shall see it. If I see it, I won't waste time with her."

"She is not a humbug—she is an exemplary woman. She will not wish to play her brother a trick simply because he is selfish."

"If she is worth talking to, she will sooner play him a trick than that he should play Catherine one. Has she seen Catherine, by-the-way—does she know her?"

"Not to my knowledge. Mr. Townsend can have had no particular interest in bringing them together."

"If she is an exemplary woman, no. But we shall see to what extent she answers your description."

"I shall be curious to hear her description of you," said Mrs. Almond, with a laugh. "And, meanwhile, how is Catherine taking it?"

"As she takes everything—as a matter of course."

"Doesn't she make a noise? Hasn't she made a scene?"

"She is not scenic."

"I thought a lovelorn maiden was always scenic."

"A ridiculous widow is more so. Lavinia has made me a speech; she thinks me very arbitrary."

"She has a talent for being in the wrong," said Mrs. Almond. "But I am very sorry for Catherine, all the same."

"So am I. But she will get over it."

"You believe she will give him up?"

"I count upon it. She has such an admiration for her father."

"Oh, we know all about that. But it only makes me pity her the more. It makes her dilemma the more painful, and the effort of choosing between you and her lover almost impossible."

"If she can't choose, all the better."

"Yes; but he will stand there entreating her to choose, and Lavinia will pull on that side."

"I am glad she is not on my side; she is capable of ruining an excellent cause. The day Lavinia gets into your boat it capsizes. But she had better be careful," said the Doctor. "I will have no treason in my house."

"I suspect she will be careful; for she is at bottom very much afraid of you."

"They are both afraid of me, harmless as I am," the Doctor

answered. "And it is on that that I build—on the salutary terror I inspire."

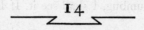

He wrote his frank letter to Mrs. Montgomery, who punctually answered it, mentioning an hour at which he might present himself in the Second Avenue. She lived in a neat little house of red brick, which had been freshly painted, with the edges of the bricks very sharply marked out in white. It has now disappeared, with its companions, to make room for a row of structures more majestic. There were green shutters upon the windows without slats, but pierced with little holes, arranged in groups; and before the house was a diminutive "yard," ornamented with a bush of mysterious character, and surrounded by a low wooden paling, painted in the same green as the shutters. The place looked like a magnified baby-house, and might have been taken down from a shelf in a toy-shop. Doctor Sloper, when he went to call, said to himself, as he glanced at the objects I have enumerated, that Mrs. Montgomery was evidently a thrifty and self-respecting little person—the modest proportions of her dwelling seemed to indicate that she was of small stature— who took a virtuous satisfaction in keeping herself tidy, and had resolved that, since she might not be splendid, she would at least be immaculate. She received him in a little parlor, which was precisely the parlor he had expected: a small unspeckled bower, ornamented with a desultory foliage of tissue-paper, and with clusters of glass drops, amidst which—to carry out the analogy—the temperature of the leafy season was maintained by means of a cast-iron stove, emitting a dry blue flame, and smelling strongly of varnish. The walls were embellished with engravings swathed in pink gauze, and the tables ornamented with volumes of extracts from the poets, usually bound in black cloth stamped with florid designs in jaundiced gilt. The Doctor had time to take cognizance of these details; for Mrs. Montgomery, whose conduct he pronounced under the circumstances inexcusable, kept him waiting some ten minutes before she appeared. At last, however, she rustled in, smoothing down a stiff poplin dress, with a little frightened flush in a gracefully rounded cheek.

She was a small, plump, fair woman, with a bright, clear eye, and an extraordinary air of neatness and briskness. But these qualities were evidently combined with an unaffected humility, and the Doctor gave her his esteem as soon as he had looked at her. A brave little person, with lively perceptions, and yet a disbelief in her own talent for social, as distinguished from practical, affairs—this was his rapid mental *résumé* of Mrs. Montgomery; who, as he saw, was flattered by what she regarded as the honor of his visit. Mrs. Montgomery, in her little red house in the Second Avenue, was a person for whom Dr. Sloper was one of the great men—one of the fine gentlemen of New York; and while she fixed her agitated eyes upon him, while she clasped her mittened hands together in her glossy poplin lap, she had the appearance of saying to herself that he quite answered her idea of what a distinguished guest would naturally be. She apologized for being late; but he interrupted her.

"It doesn't matter," he said; "for while I sat here I had time to think over what I wish to say to you, and to make up my mind how to begin."

"Oh, do begin!" murmured Mrs. Montgomery.

"It is not so easy," said the Doctor, smiling. "You will have gathered from my letter that I wish to ask you a few questions, and you may not find it very comfortable to answer them."

"Yes; I have thought what I should say. It is not very easy."

"But you must understand my situation—my state of mind. Your brother wishes to marry my daughter, and I wish to find out what sort of a young man he is. A good way to do so seemed to be to come and ask you, which I have proceeded to do."

Mrs. Montgomery evidently took the situation very seriously; she was in a state of extreme moral concentration. She kept her pretty eyes, which were illumined by a sort of brilliant modesty, attached to his own countenance, and evidently paid the most earnest attention to each of his words. Her expression indicated that she thought his idea of coming to see her a very superior conception, but that she was really afraid to have opinions on strange subjects.

"I am extremely glad to see you," she said, in a tone which seemed to admit, at the same time, that this had nothing to do with the question.

The Doctor took advantage of this admission. "I didn't come to see you for your pleasure; I came to make you say disagreeable things—and you can't like that. What sort of a gentleman is your brother?"

Mrs. Montgomery's illuminated gaze grew vague, and began to

wander. She smiled a little, and for some time made no answer, so that the Doctor at last became impatient. And her answer, when it came, was not satisfactory. "It is difficult to talk about one's brother."

"Not when one is fond of him, and when one has plenty of good to say."

"Yes, even then, when a good deal depends on it," said Mrs. Montgomery.

"Nothing depends on it for you."

"I mean for—for—" and she hesitated.

"For your brother himself. I see."

"I mean for Miss Sloper," said Mrs. Montgomery.

The Doctor liked this; it had the accent of sincerity. "Exactly; that's the point. If my poor girl should marry your brother, everything—as regards her happiness—would depend on his being a good fellow. She is the best creature in the world, and she could never do him a grain of injury. He, on the other hand, if he should not be all that we desire, might make her very miserable. That is why I want you to throw some light upon his character, you know. Of course, you are not bound to do it. My daughter, whom you have never seen, is nothing to you; and I, possibly, am only an indiscreet and impertinent old man. It is perfectly open to you to tell me that my visit is in very bad taste, and that I had better go about my business. But I don't think you will do this; because I think we shall interest you— my poor girl and I. I am sure that if you were to see Catherine she would interest you very much. I don't mean because she is interesting in the usual sense of the word, but because you would feel sorry for her. She is so soft, so simple-minded, she would be such an easy victim! A bad husband would have remarkable facilities for making her miserable; for she would have neither the intelligence nor the resolution to get the better of him, and yet she would have an exaggerated power of suffering. I see," added the Doctor, with his most insinuating, his most professional laugh, "you are already interested."

"I have been interested from the moment he told me he was engaged," said Mrs. Montgomery.

"Ah! he says that—he calls it an engagement?"

"Oh, he has told me you didn't like it."

"Did he tell you that I don't like him?"

"Yes, he told me that too. I said I couldn't help it," added Mrs. Montgomery.

"Of course you can't. But what you can do is to tell me I am right

—to give me an attestation, as it were." And the Doctor accompanied this remark with another professional smile.

Mrs. Montgomery, however, smiled not at all; it was obvious that she could not take the humorous view of his appeal. "That is a good deal to ask," she said, at last.

"There can be no doubt of that; and I must, in conscience, remind you of the advantages a young man marrying my daughter would enjoy. She has an income of ten thousand dollars in her own right, left her by her mother; if she marries a husband I approve, she will come into almost twice as much more at my death."

Mrs. Montgomery listened in great earnestness to this splendid financial statement; she had never heard thousands of dollars so familiarly talked about. She flushed a little with excitement. "Your daughter will be immensely rich," she said, softly.

"Precisely—that's the bother of it."

"And if Morris should marry her, he—he—" And she hesitated, timidly.

"He would be master of all that money? By no means. He would be master of the ten thousand a year that she has from her mother; but I should leave every penny of my own fortune, earned in the laborious exercise of my profession, to my nephews and nieces."

Mrs. Montgomery dropped her eyes at this, and sat for some time gazing at the straw matting which covered her floor.

"I suppose it seems to you," said the Doctor, laughing, "that in so doing I should play your brother a very shabby trick."

"Not at all. That is too much money to get possession of so easily by marrying. I don't think it would be right."

"It's right to get all one can. But in this case your brother wouldn't be able. If Catherine marries without my consent, she doesn't get a penny from my own pocket."

"Is that certain?" asked Mrs. Montgomery, looking up.

"As certain as that I sit here."

"Even if she should pine away?"

"Even if she should pine to a shadow, which isn't probable."

"Does Morris know this?"

"I shall be most happy to inform him," the Doctor exclaimed.

Mrs. Montgomery resumed her meditations; and her visitor, who was prepared to give time to the affair, asked himself whether, in spite of her little conscientious air, she was not playing into her brother's hands. At the same time he was half ashamed of the ordeal to which he had subjected her, and was touched by the gentleness with which she bore it. "If she were a humbug," he said, "she would get angry, unless she be very deep indeed. It is not probable that she is as deep as that."

"What makes you dislike Morris so much?" she presently asked, emerging from her reflections.

"I don't dislike him in the least as a friend, as a companion. He seems to me a charming fellow, and I should think he would be excellent company. I dislike him exclusively as a son-in-law. If the only office of a son-in-law were to dine at the paternal table, I should set a high value upon your brother: he dines capitally. But that is a small part of his function, which, in general, is to be a protector and care-taker of my child, who is singularly ill-adapted to take care of herself. It is there that he doesn't satisfy me. I confess I have nothing but my impression to go by; but I am in the habit of trusting my impression. Of course you are at liberty to contradict it flat. He strikes me as selfish and shallow."

Mrs. Montgomery's eyes expanded a little, and the Doctor fancied he saw the light of admiration in them. "I wonder you have discovered he is selfish," she exclaimed.

"Do you think he hides it so well?"

"Very well indeed," said Mrs. Montgomery. "And I think we are all rather selfish," she added, quickly.

"I think so too; but I have seen people hide it better than he. You see I am helped by a habit I have of dividing people into classes, into types. I may easily be mistaken about your brother as an individual, but his type is written on his whole person."

"He is very good-looking," said Mrs. Montgomery.

The Doctor eyed her a moment. "You women are all the same! But the type to which your brother belongs was made to be the ruin of you, and you were made to be its handmaids and victims. The sign of the type in question is the determination—sometimes terrible in its quiet intensity—to accept nothing of life but its pleasures, and to secure these pleasures chiefly by the aid of your complaisant sex. Young men of this class never do anything for themselves that they can get other people to do for them, and it is the infatuation, the devotion, the superstition of others that keeps them going. These others, in ninety-nine cases out of a hundred, are women. What our young friends chiefly insist upon is that some one else shall suffer for them; and women do that sort of thing, as you must know, wonderfully well." The Doctor paused a moment, and then he added, abruptly, "You have suffered immensely for your brother!"

This exclamation was abrupt, as I say, but it was also perfectly calculated. The Doctor had been rather disappointed at not finding his compact and comfortable little hostess surrounded in a more visible degree by the ravages of Morris Townsend's immorality; but he had said to himself that this was not because the young man had spared her, but because she had contrived to plaster up her wounds. They were aching there behind the varnished stove, the festooned engravings, beneath her own neat little poplin bosom; and if he could only touch the tender spot, she would make a movement that would betray her. The words I have just quoted were an attempt to put his finger suddenly upon the place, and they had some of the success that he looked for. The tears sprung for a moment to Mrs. Montgomery's eyes, and she indulged in a proud little jerk of the head.

"I don't know how you have found that out!" she exclaimed.

"By a philosophic trick—by what they call induction. You know you have always your option of contradicting me. But kindly answer me a question: Don't you give your brother money? I think you ought to answer that."

"Yes, I have given him money," said Mrs. Montgomery.

"And you have not had much to give him?"

She was silent a moment. "If you ask me for a confession of poverty, that is easily made. I am very poor."

"One would never suppose it from your—your charming house," said the Doctor. "I learned from my sister that your income was moderate, and your family numerous."

"I have five children," Mrs. Montgomery observed; "but I am happy to say I can bring them up decently."

"Of course you can—accomplished and devoted as you are. But your brother has counted them over, I suppose?"

"Counted them over?"

"He knows there are five, I mean. He tells me it is he that brings them up."

Mrs. Montgomery stared a moment, and then quickly—"Oh yes; he teaches them—Spanish."

The Doctor laughed out. "That must take a great deal off your hands! Your brother also knows, of course, that you have very little money?"

"I have often told him so," Mrs. Montgomery exclaimed, more unreservedly than she had yet spoken. She was apparently taking some comfort in the Doctor's clairvoyance.

"Which means that you have often occasion to, and that he often sponges on you. Excuse the crudity of my language; I simply express a fact. I don't ask you how much of your money he has had, it is none of my business. I have ascertained what I suspected—what I wished." And the Doctor got up, gently smoothing his hat. "Your brother lives on you," he said, as he stood there.

Mrs. Montgomery quickly rose from her chair, following her visitor's movements with a look of fascination. But then, with a certain inconsequence—"I have never complained of him," she said.

"You needn't protest—you have not betrayed him. But I advise you not to give him any more money."

"Don't you see it is in my interest that he should marry a rich person?" she asked. "If, as you say, he lives on me, I can only wish to get rid of him; and to put obstacles in the way of his marrying is to increase my own difficulties."

"I wish very much you would come to me with your difficulties," said the Doctor. "Certainly, if I throw him back on your hands, the least I can do is to help you to bear the burden. If you will allow me to say so, then, I shall take the liberty of placing in your hands, for the present, a certain fund for your brother's support."

Mrs. Montgomery stared; she evidently thought he was jesting; but she presently saw that he was not, and the complication of her feelings became painful. "It seems to me that I ought to be very much offended with you," she murmured.

"Because I have offered you money? That's a superstition," said the Doctor. "You must let me come and see you again, and we will talk about these things. I suppose that some of your children are girls?"

"I have two little girls," said Mrs. Montgomery.

"Well, when they grow up, and begin to think of taking husbands, you will see how anxious you will be about the moral character of these husbands. Then you will understand this visit of mine."

"Ah, you are not to believe that Morris's moral character is bad."

The Doctor looked at her a little, with folded arms. "There is something I should greatly like, as a moral satisfaction. I should like to hear you say, 'He is abominably selfish.'"

The words came out with the grave distinctness of his voice, and they seemed for an instant to create, to poor Mrs. Montgomery's troubled vision, a material image. She gazed at it an instant, and then she turned away. "You distress me, sir!" she exclaimed. "He is, after all, my brother; and his talents, his talents—" On these last words her voice quavered, and before he knew it she had burst into tears.

"His talents are first-rate," said the Doctor. "We must find the proper field for them." And he assured her most respectfully of his regret at having so greatly discomposed her. "It's all for my poor Catherine," he went on. "You must know her, and you will see."

Mrs. Montgomery brushed away her tears, and blushed at having shed them. "I should like to know your daughter," she answered; and then, in an instant— "Don't let her marry him!"

Doctor Sloper went away with the words gently humming in his ears—"Don't let her marry him!" They gave him the moral satisfaction of which he had just spoken, and their value was the greater that they had evidently cost a pang to poor little Mrs. Montgomery's family pride.

15

He had been puzzled by the way that Catherine carried herself; her attitude at this sentimental crisis seemed to him unnaturally passive. She had not spoken to him again after that scene in the library, the day before his interview with Morris; and a week had elapsed without making any change in her manner. There was nothing in it that appealed for pity, and he was even a little disappointed at her not giving him an opportunity to make up for his harshness by some manifestation of liberality which should operate as a compensation. He thought a little of offering to take her for a tour in Europe; but he was determined to do this only in case she should seem mutely to reproach him. He had an idea that she would display a talent for mute reproaches, and he was surprised at not finding himself exposed to these silent batteries. She said nothing, either tacitly or explicitly, and as she was never very talkative, there was now no especial eloquence in her reserve. And poor Catherine was not sulky —a style of behavior for which she had too little histrionic talent— she was simply very patient. Of course she was thinking over her situation, and she was apparently doing so in a deliberate and unimpassioned manner, with a view of making the best of it.

"She will do as I have bidden her," said the Doctor; and he made the further reflection that his daughter was not a woman of a great spirit.

I know not whether he had hoped for a little more resistance for the sake of a little more entertainment; but he said to himself, as he had said before, that though it might have its momentary alarms, paternity was, after all, not an exciting vocation.

Catherine meanwhile had made a discovery of a very different sort; it had become vivid to her that there was a great excitement in trying to be a good daughter. She had an entirely new feeling, which may be described as a state of expectant suspense about her own actions. She watched herself as she would have watched another person, and wondered what she would do. It was as if this other person, who was both herself and not herself, had suddenly sprung into being, inspiring her with a natural curiosity as to the performance of untested functions.

"I am glad I have such a good daughter," said her father, kissing her, after the lapse of several days.

"I am trying to be good," she answered, turning away, with a conscience not altogether clear.

"If there is anything you would like to say to me, you know you must not hesitate. You needn't feel obliged to be so quiet. I shouldn't care that Mr. Townsend should be a frequent topic of conversation, but whenever you have anything particular to say about him I shall be very glad to hear it."

"Thank you," said Catherine; "I have nothing particular at present."

He never asked her whether she had seen Morris again, because he was sure that if this had been the case she would tell him. She had, in fact, not seen him; she had only written him a long letter. The letter, at least, was long for her; and, it may be added, that it was long for Morris; it consisted of five pages, in a remarkably neat and handsome hand. Catherine's handwriting was beautiful, and she was even a little proud of it: she was extremely fond of copying, and possessed volumes of extracts which testified to this accomplishment; volumes which she had exhibited one day to her lover, when the bliss of feeling that she was important in his eyes was exceptionally keen. She told Morris, in writing, that her father had expressed the wish that she should not see him again, and that she begged he would not come to the house until she should have "made up her mind." Morris replied with a passionate epistle, in which he asked to what, in Heaven's name, she wished to make up her mind. Had not her mind been made up two weeks before, and could it be possible that she entertained the idea of throwing him off? Did she mean to break down at the very beginning of their ordeal, after all the promises of fidelity she had both given and extracted? And he gave an account of his own interview with her father—an account not identical at all points with that offered in these pages. "He was terribly violent," Morris wrote, "but you know my self-control. I have need of it all when I remember that I have it in my power to break in upon your cruel captivity." Catherine sent him, in answer to this, a note of three lines. "I am in great trouble; do not doubt of my affection, but let me wait a little and think." The idea of a struggle with her father, of setting up her will against his own, was heavy on her soul, and it kept her quiet, as a great physical weight keeps us motionless. It never entered into her mind to throw her lover off; but from the first she tried to assure herself that there would be a peaceful way out of their difficulty. The assurance was vague, for it contained no element of positive conviction that her father would change his mind. She only had an idea that if she should be very good, the situation would in some mysterious manner improve. To be good she must be patient, outwardly submissive, abstain from judging her father too harshly, and from committing any act of open defiance. He was perhaps right, after all, to think as he did; by which Catherine meant not in the least that his judgment of Morris's motives in seeking to marry her was perhaps a just one, but that it was probably natural and proper that conscientious parents should be suspicious and even unjust. There were probably people in the world as bad as her father supposed Morris to be, and if there were the slightest chance of Morris being one of these sinister persons, the Doctor was right in taking it into account. Of course he could not know what she knew—how the purest love and truth were seated in the young man's eyes; but Heaven, in its time, might appoint a way of bringing him to such knowledge. Catherine expected a good deal of Heaven, and referred to the skies the initiative, as the French say, in dealing with her dilemma. She could not imagine herself imparting any kind of knowledge to her father; there was something superior even in his injustice, and absolute in his mistakes. But she could at least be good, and if she were only good enough, Heaven would invent some way of reconciling all things—the dignity of her father's errors and the sweetness of her own confidence, the strict performance of her filial duties, and the enjoyment of Morris Townsend's affection.

Poor Catherine would have been glad to regard Mrs. Penniman as an illuminating agent, a part which this lady herself, indeed, was but imperfectly prepared to play. Mrs. Penniman took too much satisfaction in the sentimental shadows of this little drama to have, for the moment, any great interest in dissipating them. She wished the plot to thicken, and the advice that she gave her niece tended, in her own imagination, to produce this result. It was rather incoherent counsel, and from one day to another it contradicted itself; but it was pervaded by an earnest desire that Catherine should do something striking. "You must *act*, my dear; in your situation the great thing is to act," said Mrs. Penniman, who found her niece altogether beneath her opportunities. Mrs. Penniman's real hope was that the girl would make a secret marriage, at which she should officiate as bride'swoman or duenna. She had a vision of this ceremony being performed in some subterranean chapel; subterranean chapels in New York were not frequent, but Mrs. Penniman's imagination was not chilled by trifles; and of the guilty couple—she liked to think of poor Catherine and her suitor as the guilty couple—being shuffled away in a fast-whirling vehicle to some obscure lodging in the suburbs, where she would pay them (in a thick veil) clandestine visits; where they would endure a period of romantic privation; and when ultimately, after she should have been their earthly providence, their intercessor, their advocate, and their medium of communication with the world, they would be reconciled to her brother in an artistic tableau, in which she herself should be somehow the central figure. She hesitated as yet to recommend this course to Catherine, but she attempted to draw an attractive picture of it to Morris Townsend. She was in daily communication with the young man, whom she kept informed by letters of the state of affairs in Washington Square. As he had been banished, as she said, from the house, she no longer saw him; but she ended by writing to him that she longed for an interview. This interview could take place only on neutral ground, and she bethought herself greatly before selecting a place of meeting. She had an inclination for Greenwood Cemetery, but she gave it up as too distant; she could not absent herself for so long, as she said, without exciting suspicion. Then she thought of the Battery, but that was rather cold and windy, besides one's being exposed to intrusion from the Irish emigrants who at this point alight, with large appetites, in the New World; and at last she fixed upon an oyster saloon in the Seventh Avenue, kept by a negro—an establishment of which she knew nothing save that she had noticed it in passing. She made an appointment with Morris Townsend to meet him there, and she went to the tryst at dusk, enveloped in an impenetrable veil. He kept her waiting for half an hour—he had almost the whole width of the city to traverse—but she liked to wait, it seemed, to intensify the situation. She ordered a cup of tea, which proved excessively bad, and this gave her a sense that she was suffering in a romantic cause. When Morris at last arrived, they sat together for half an hour in the duskiest corner of the back shop; and it is hardly too much to say that this was the happiest half-hour that Mrs. Penniman had known for years. The situation was really thrilling, and it scarcely seemed to her a false note when her companion asked for an oyster stew, and proceeded to consume it before her eyes. Morris, indeed, needed all the satisfaction that stewed oysters could give him, for it may be intimated to the reader that he regarded Mrs. Penniman in the light of a fifth wheel to his coach. He was in a state of irritation natural to a gentleman of fine parts who had been snubbed in a benevolent attempt to confer a distinction upon a young woman of inferior characteristics, and the insinuating sympathy of this somewhat desiccated matron appeared to offer him no practical relief. He thought her a humbug, and he judged of humbugs with a good deal of confidence. He had listened and made himself agreeable to her at first, in order to get a footing in Washington Square; and at present he needed all his self-command to be decently civil. It would have gratified him to tell her that she was a fantastic old woman, and that he would like to put her into an omnibus and send her home. We know, however, that Morris possessed the virtue of self-control, and he had moreover the constant habit of seeking to be agreeable; so that, although Mrs. Penniman's demeanor only exasperated his already unquiet nerves, he listened to her with a sombre deference in which she found much to admire.

16

They had of course immediately spoken of Catherine. "Did she send me a message, or—or anything?" Morris asked. He appeared to think that she might have sent him a trinket or a lock of her hair.

Mrs. Penniman was slightly embarrassed, for she had not told her niece of her intended expedition. "Not exactly a message," she said; "I didn't ask her for one, because I was afraid to—to excite her."

"I am afraid she is not very excitable." And Morris gave a smile of some bitterness.

"She is better than that—she is steadfast, she is true."

"Do you think she will hold fast, then?"

"To the death!"

"Oh, I hope it won't come to that," said Morris.

"We must be prepared for the worst, and that is what I wish to speak to you about."

"What do you call the worst?"

"Well," said Mrs. Penniman, "my brother's hard, intellectual nature."

"Oh, the devil!"

"He is impervious to pity," Mrs. Penniman added, by way of explanation.

"Do you mean that he won't come round?"

"He will never be vanquished by argument. I have studied him. He will be vanquished only by the accomplished fact."

"The accomplished fact?"

"He will come round afterward," said Mrs. Penniman, with extreme significance. "He cares for nothing but facts—he must be met by facts."

"Well," rejoined Morris, "it is a fact that I wish to marry his daughter. I met him with that the other day, but he was not at all vanquished."

Mrs. Penniman was silent a little, and her smile beneath the shadow of her capacious bonnet, on the edge of which her black veil was arranged curtainwise, fixed itself upon Morris's face with a still more tender brilliancy. "Marry Catherine first, and meet him afterward!" she exclaimed.

"Do you recommend that?" asked the young man, frowning heavily.

She was a little frightened, but she went on with considerable boldness. "That is the way I see it: a private marriage—a private marriage." She repeated the phrase because she liked it.

"Do you mean that I should carry Catherine off? What do they call it—elope with her?"

"It is not a crime when you are driven to it," said Mrs. Penniman. "My husband, as I have told you, was a distinguished clergyman— one of the most eloquent men of his day. He once married a young couple that had fled from the house of the young lady's father; he was so interested in their story. He had no hesitation, and every-thing came out beautifully. The father was afterward reconciled, and thought everything of the young man. Mr. Penniman married them in the evening, about seven o'clock. The church was so dark you could scarcely see, and Mr. Penniman was intensely agitated—he was so sympathetic. I don't believe he could have done it again."

"Unfortunately, Catherine and I have not Mr. Penniman to marry us," said Morris.

"No, but you have me!" rejoined Mrs. Penniman, expressively. "I can't perform the ceremony, but I can help you; I can watch!"

"The woman's an idiot!" thought Morris; but he was obliged to say something different. It was not, however, materially more civil. "Was it in order to tell me this that you requested I would meet you here?"

Mrs. Penniman had been conscious of a certain vagueness in her errand, and of not being able to offer him any very tangible reward for his long walk. "I thought perhaps you would like to see one who is so near to Catherine," she observed, with considerable majesty; "and also," she added, "that you would value an oppor-tunity of sending her something."

Morris extended his empty hands with a melancholy smile. "I am greatly obliged to you, but I have nothing to send."

"Haven't you a *word*?" asked his companion, with her sug-gestive smile coming back.

Morris frowned again. "Tell her to hold fast," he said, rather curtly.

"That is a good word—a noble word: it will make her happy for many days. She is very touching, very brave," Mrs. Penniman went on, arranging her mantle and preparing to depart. While she was so engaged she had an inspiration; she found the phrase that she could boldly offer as a vindication of the step she had taken. "If you marry Catherine at all risks," she said, "you will give my brother a proof of your being what he pretends to doubt."

"What he pretends to doubt?"

"Don't you know what that is?" Mrs. Penniman asked, almost playfully.

"It does not concern me to know," said Morris, grandly.

"Of course it makes you angry."

"I despise it," Morris declared.

"Ah, you know what it is, then?" said Mrs. Penniman, shaking her finger at him. "He pretends that you like—you like the money."

Morris hesitated a moment; and then, as if he spoke advisedly, "I *do* like the money!"

"Ah, but not—but not as he means it. You don't like it more than Catherine?"

He leaned his elbows on the table and buried his head in his hands. "You torture me!" he murmured. And, indeed, this was almost the effect of the poor lady's too importunate interest in his situation.

But she insisted in making her point. "If you marry her in spite of him, he will take for granted that you expect nothing of him, and are prepared to do without it; and so he will see that you are disinterested."

Morris raised his head a little, following this argument. "And what shall I gain by that?"

"Why, that he will see that he has been wrong in thinking that you wished to get his money."

"And seeing that I wish he would go to the deuce with it, he will leave it to a hospital. Is that what you mean?" asked Morris.

"No, I don't mean that; though that would be very grand," Mrs. Penniman quickly added. "I mean that, having done you such an injustice, he will think it his duty, at the end, to make some amends."

Morris shook his head, though it must be confessed he was a little struck with this idea. "Do you think he is so sentimental?"

"He is not sentimental," said Mrs. Penniman; "but, to be perfectly fair to him, I think he has, in his own narrow way, a certain sense of duty."

There passed through Morris Townsend's mind a rapid wonder as to what he might, even under a remote contingency, be indebted to from the action of this principle in Doctor Sloper's breast, and the inquiry exhausted itself in his sense of the ludicrous. "Your brother has no duties to me," he said presently, "and I none to him."

"Ah, but he has duties to Catherine."

"Yes; but you see, on that principle Catherine has duties to him as well."

Mrs. Penniman got up with a melancholy sigh, as if she thought him very unimaginative. "She has always performed them faithfully; and now do you think she has no duties to *you?*" Mrs. Penniman always, even in conversation, italicized her personal pronouns.

"It would sound harsh to say so. I am so grateful for her love," Morris added.

"I will tell her you said that. And now, remember that if you need me I am there." And Mrs. Penniman, who could think of nothing more to say, nodded vaguely in the direction of Washington Square.

Morris looked some moments at the sanded floor of the shop; he seemed to be disposed to linger a moment. At last, looking up with a certain abruptness, "It is your belief that if she marries me he will cut her off?" he asked.

Mrs. Penniman stared a little, and smiled. "Why, I have explained to you what I think would happen—that in the end it would be the best thing to do."

"You mean that, whatever she does, in the long run she will get the money?"

"It doesn't depend upon her, but upon you. Venture to appear as disinterested as you are," said Mrs. Penniman, ingeniously. Morris dropped his eyes on the sanded floor again, pondering this, and she pursued: "Mr. Penniman and I had nothing, and we were very happy. Catherine, moreover, has her mother's fortune, which, at the time my sister-in-law married, was considered a very handsome one."

"Oh, don't speak of that!" said Morris; and indeed it was quite superfluous, for he had contemplated the fact in all its lights.

"Austin married a wife with money—why shouldn't you?"

"Ah! but your brother was a doctor," Morris objected.

"Well, all young men can't be doctors."

"I should think it an extremely loathsome profession," said Morris, with an air of intellectual independence; then, in a moment, he went on rather inconsequently, "Do you suppose there is a will already made in Catherine's favor?"

"I suppose so—even doctors must die; and perhaps a little in mine," Mrs. Penniman frankly added.

"And you believe he would certainly change it—as regards Catherine?"

"Yes, and then change it back again."

"Ah, but one can't depend on that," said Morris.

"Do you want to *depend* on it?" Mrs. Penniman asked.

Morris blushed a little. "Well, I am certainly afraid of being the cause of an injury to Catherine."

"Ah! you must not be afraid. Be afraid of nothing, and everything will go well."

And then Mrs. Penniman paid for her cup of tea, and Morris paid for his oyster stew, and they went out together into the dimly-lighted wilderness of the Seventh Avenue. The dusk had closed in completely, and the street lamps were separated by wide intervals of a pavement in which cavities and fissures played a disproportionate part. An omnibus, emblazoned with strange pictures, went tumbling over the dislocated cobble-stones.

"How will you go home?" Morris asked, following this vehicle with an interested eye. Mrs. Penniman had taken his arm.

She hesitated a moment. "I think this manner would be pleasant," she said; and she continued to let him feel the value of his support.

So he walked with her through the devious ways of the west side of the town, and through the bustle of gathering nightfall in populous streets, to the quiet precinct of Washington Square. They lingered a moment at the foot of Doctor Sloper's white marble steps, above which a spotless white door, adorned with a glittering silver plate, seemed to figure for Morris the closed portal of happiness; and then Mrs. Penniman's companion rested a melancholy eye upon a lighted window in the upper part of the house.

"That is my room—my dear little room!" Mrs. Penniman remarked.

Morris started. "Then I needn't come walking round the Square to gaze at it."

"That's as you please. But Catherine's is behind; two noble windows on the second floor. I think you can see them from the other street."

"I don't want to see them, ma'am." And Morris turned his back to the house.

"I will tell her you have been *here*, at any rate," said Mrs. Penniman, pointing to the spot where they stood; "and I will give her your message—that she is to hold fast."

"Oh yes; of course. You know I write her all that."

"It seems to say more when it is spoken. And remember, if you need me, that I am *there*," and Mrs. Penniman glanced at the third floor.

On this they separated, and Morris, left to himself, stood looking at the house a moment; after which he turned away, and took a gloomy walk round the Square, on the opposite side, close to the wooden fence. Then he came back, and paused for a minute in front of Doctor Sloper's dwelling. His eyes travelled over it; they even rested on the ruddy windows of Mrs. Penniman's apartment. He thought it a devilish comfortable house.

17

Mrs. Penniman told Catherine that evening—the two ladies were sitting in the back-parlor—that she had had an interview with Morris Townsend; and on receiving this news the girl started with a sense of pain. She felt angry for the moment; it was almost the first time she had ever felt angry. It seemed to her that her aunt was meddlesome; and from this came a vague apprehension that she would spoil something.

"I don't see why you should have seen him. I don't think it was right," Catherine said.

"I was so sorry for him—it seemed to me some one ought to see him."

"No one but I," said Catherine, who felt as if she were making the most presumptuous speech of her life, and yet at the same time had an instinct that she was right in doing so.

"But you wouldn't, my dear," Aunt Lavinia rejoined; "and I didn't know what might have become of him."

"I have not seen him because my father has forbidden it," Catherine said, very simply.

There was a simplicity in this, indeed, which fairly vexed Mrs. Penniman. "If your father forbade you to go to sleep, I suppose you would keep awake!" she commented.

Catherine looked at her. "I don't understand you. You seem to me very strange."

"Well, my dear, you will understand me some day!" And Mrs. Penniman, who was reading the evening paper, which she perused daily from the first line to the last, resumed her occupation. She wrapped herself in silence; she was determined Catherine should ask her for an account of her interview with Morris. But Catherine was silent for so long that she almost lost patience; and she was on the point of remarking to her that she was very heartless, when the girl at last spoke.

"What did he say?" she asked.

"He said he is ready to marry you any day, in spite of everything."

Catherine made no answer to this, and Mrs. Penniman almost lost patience again; owing to which she at last volunteered the information that Morris looked very handsome, but terribly haggard.

"Did he seem sad?" asked her niece.

"He was dark under the eyes," said Mrs. Penniman. "So different from when I first saw him; though I am not sure that if I had seen him in this condition the first time, I should not have been even more struck with him. There is something brilliant in his very misery."

This was, to Catherine's sense, a vivid picture, and though she disapproved, she felt herself gazing at it. "Where did you see him?" she asked, presently.

"In—in the Bowery; at a confectioner's," said Mrs. Penniman, who had a general idea that she ought to dissemble a little.

"Whereabouts is the place?" Catherine inquired, after another pause.

"Do you wish to go there, my dear?" said her aunt.

"Oh no." And Catherine got up from her seat and went to the fire, where she stood looking awhile at the glowing coals.

"Why are you so dry, Catherine?" Mrs. Penniman said at last.

"So dry?"

"So cold—so irresponsive."

The girl turned very quickly. "Did *he* say that?"

Mrs. Penniman hesitated a moment. "I will tell you what he said. He said he feared only one thing—that you would be afraid."

"Afraid of what?"

"Afraid of your father."

Catherine turned back to the fire again, and then, after a pause, she said, "I *am* afraid of my father."

Mrs. Penniman got quickly up from her chair and approached her niece. "Do you mean to give him up, then?"

Catherine for some time never moved; she kept her eyes on the coals. At last she raised her head and looked at her aunt. "Why do you push me so?" she asked.

"I don't push you. When have I spoken to you before?"

"It seems to me that you have spoken to me several times."

"I am afraid it is necessary, then, Catherine," said Mrs. Penniman, with a good deal of solemnity. "I am afraid you don't feel the importance"—she paused a little; Catherine was looking at her—"the importance of not disappointing that gallant young heart!" And Mrs. Penniman went back to her chair by the lamp, and, with a little jerk, picked up the evening paper again.

Catherine stood there before the fire, with her hands behind her, looking at her aunt, to whom it seemed that the girl had never had just this dark fixedness in her gaze. "I don't think you understand or that you know me," she said.

"If I don't, it is not wonderful; you trust me so little."

Catherine made no attempt to deny this charge, and for some time more nothing was said. But Mrs. Penniman's imagination was restless, and the evening paper failed on this occasion to enchain it.

"If you succumb to the dread of your father's wrath," she said, "I don't know what will become of us."

"Did *he* tell you to say these things to me?"

"He told me to use my influence."

"You must be mistaken," said Catherine. "He trusts me."

"I hope he may never repent of it!" And Mrs. Penniman gave a little sharp slap to her newspaper. She knew not what to make of her niece, who had suddenly become stern and contradictious.

This tendency on Catherine's part was presently even more apparent. "You had much better not make any more appointments with Mr. Townsend," she said. "I don't think it is right."

Mrs. Penniman rose with considerable majesty. "My poor child, are you jealous of me?" she inquired.

"Oh, Aunt Lavinia!" murmured Catherine, blushing.

"I don't think it is your place to teach me what is right."

On this point Catherine made no concession. "It can't be right to deceive."

"I certainly have not deceived *you*!"

"Yes; but I promised my father—"

"I have no doubt you promised your father. But I have promised him nothing."

Catherine had to admit this, and she did so in silence. "I don't believe Mr. Townsend himself likes it," she said, at last.

"Doesn't like meeting me?"

"Not in secret."

"It was not in secret; the place was full of people."

"But it was a secret place—away off in the Bowery."

Mrs. Penniman flinched a little. "Gentlemen enjoy such things," she remarked, presently. "I know what gentlemen like."

"My father wouldn't like it, if he knew."

"Pray, do you propose to inform him?" Mrs. Penniman inquired.

"No, Aunt Lavinia. But please don't do it again."

"If I do it again you will inform him—is that what you mean? I do not share your dread of my brother; I have always known how to defend my own position. But I shall certainly never again take any step on your behalf; you are much too thankless. I knew you were not a spontaneous nature, but I believed you were firm, and I told your father that he would find you so. I am disappointed, but your father will not be." And with this Mrs. Penniman offered her niece a brief good-night, and withdrew to her own apartment.

18

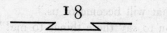

Catherine sat alone by the parlor fire—sat there for more than an hour, lost in her meditations. Her aunt seemed to her aggressive and foolish; and to see it so clearly—to judge Mrs. Penniman so positively—made her feel old and grave. She did not resent the imputation of weakness; it made no impression on her, for she had not the sense of weakness, and she was not hurt at not being appreciated. She had an immense respect for her father, and she felt that to displease him would be a misdemeanor analogous to an act of profanity in a great temple: but her purpose had slowly ripened, and she believed that her prayers had purified it of its violence. The evening advanced, and the lamp burnt dim without her noticing it; her eyes were fixed upon her terrible plan. She knew her father was in his study—that he had been there all the evening; from time to time she expected to hear him move. She thought he would perhaps come, as he sometimes came, into the parlor. At last the clock struck eleven, and the house was wrapped in silence; the servants had gone to bed. Catherine got up and went slowly to the door of the library, where she waited a moment, motionless. Then she knocked, and then she waited again. Her father had answered her, but she had not the courage to turn the latch. What she had said to her aunt was true enough—she was afraid of him; and in saying that she had no sense of weakness, she meant that she was not afraid of herself. She heard him move within, and he came and opened the door for her.

"What is the matter?" asked the Doctor. "You are standing there like a ghost!"

She went into the room, but it was some time before she contrived to say what she had come to say. Her father, who was in his dressing-gown and slippers, had been busy at his writing-table, and after looking at her for some moments, and waiting for her to speak, he went and seated himself at his papers again. His back was turned to her—she began to hear the scratching of his pen. She remained near the door, with her heart thumping beneath her bodice; and she was very glad that his back was turned, for it seemed to her that she could more easily address herself to this portion of his person than to his face. At last she began, watching it while she spoke:

"You told me that if I should have anything more to say about Mr. Townsend you would be glad to listen to it."

"Exactly, my dear," said the Doctor, not turning round, but stopping his pen.

Catherine wished it would go on, but she herself continued: "I thought I would tell you that I have not seen him again, but that I should like to do so."

"To bid him good-bye?" asked the Doctor.

The girl hesitated a moment. "He is not going away."

The Doctor wheeled slowly round in his chair, with a smile that seemed to accuse her of an epigram; but extremes meet, and Catherine had not intended one. "It is not to bid him good-bye, then?" her father said.

"No, father, not that; at least not forever. I have not seen him again, but I should like to see him," Catherine repeated.

The Doctor slowly rubbed his underlip with the feather of his quill.

"Have you written to him?"

"Yes, four times."

"You have not dismissed him, then. Once would have done that."

"No," said Catherine; "I have asked him—asked him to wait."

Her father sat looking at her, and she was afraid he was going to break out into wrath, his eyes were so fine and cold.

"You are a dear, faithful child," he said, at last. "Come here to your father." And he got up, holding out his hands toward her.

The words were a surprise, and they gave her an exquisite joy. She went to him, and he put his arm round her tenderly, soothingly; and then he kissed her. After this he said,

"Do you wish to make me very happy?"

"I should like to—but I am afraid I can't," Catherine answered.

"You can if you will. It all depends on your will."

"Is it to give him up?" said Catherine.

"Yes, it is to give him up."

And he held her still, with the same tenderness, looking into her face and resting his eyes on her averted eyes. There was a long silence; she wished he would release her.

"You are happier than I, father," she said, at last.

"I have no doubt you are unhappy just now. But it is better to be unhappy for three months and get over it, than for many years and never get over it."

"Yes, if that were so," said Catherine.

"It would be so; I am sure of that." She answered nothing, and he went on: "Have you no faith in my wisdom, in my tenderness, in my solicitude for your future?"

"Oh, father!" murmured the girl.

"Don't you suppose that I know something of men—their vices, their follies, their falsities?"

She detached herself, and turned upon him. "He is not vicious—he is not false!"

Her father kept looking at her with his sharp, pure eye. "You make nothing of my judgment, then?"

"I can't believe that!"

"I don't ask you to believe it, but to take it on trust."

Catherine was far from saying to herself that this was an ingenious sophism; but she met the appeal none the less squarely. "What has he done—what do you know?"

"He has never done anything—he is a selfish idler."

"Oh, father, don't abuse him!" she exclaimed, pleadingly.

"I don't mean to abuse him; it would be a great mistake. You may do as you choose," he added, turning away.

"I may see him again?"

"Just as you choose."

"Will you forgive me?"

"By no means."

"It will only be for once."

"I don't know what you mean by once. You must either give him up or continue the acquaintance."

"I wish to explain—to tell him to wait."

"To wait for what?"

"Till you know him better—till you consent."

"Don't tell him any such nonsense as that. I know him well enough, and I shall never consent."

"But we can wait a long time," said poor Catherine, in a tone which was meant to express the humblest conciliation, but which had upon her father's nerves the effect of an iteration not characterized by tact.

The Doctor answered, however, quietly enough: "Of course; you can wait till I die, if you like."

Catherine gave a cry of natural horror.

"Your engagement will have one delightful effect upon you; it will make you extremely impatient for that event."

Catherine stood staring, and the Doctor enjoyed the point he had made. It came to Catherine with the force—or rather with the vague impressiveness—of a logical axiom which it was not in her province to controvert; and yet, though it was a scientific truth, she felt wholly unable to accept it.

"I would rather not marry, if that were true," she said.

"Give me a proof of it, then; for it is beyond a question that by engaging yourself to Morris Townsend you simply wait for my death."

She turned away, feeling sick and faint; and the Doctor went on: "And if you wait for it with impatience, judge, if you please, what *his* eagerness will be."

Catherine turned it over—her father's words had such an authority for her that her very thoughts were capable of obeying him. There was a dreadful ugliness in it, which seemed to glare at her through the interposing medium of her own feebler reason. Suddenly, however, she had an inspiration—she almost knew it to be an inspiration.

"If I don't marry before your death, I will not after," she said.

To her father, it must be admitted, this seemed only another epigram; and as obstinacy, in unaccomplished minds, does not usually select such a mode of expression, he was the more surprised at this wanton play of a fixed idea.

"Do you mean that for an impertinence?" he inquired; an inquiry of which, as he made it, he quite perceived the grossness.

"An impertinence? Oh, father, what terrible things you say!"

"If you don't wait for my death, you might as well marry immediately; there is nothing else to wait for."

For some time Catherine made no answer; but finally she said, "I think Morris—little by little—might persuade you."

"I shall never let him speak to me again. I dislike him too much."

Catherine gave a long, low sigh; she tried to stifle it, for she had made up her mind that it was wrong to make a parade of her trouble, and to endeavor to act upon her father by the meretricious aid of emotion. Indeed, she even thought it wrong—in the sense of being inconsiderate—to attempt to act upon his feelings at all; her part was to effect some gentle, gradual change in his intellectual perception of poor Morris's character. But the means of effecting such a change were at present shrouded in mystery, and she felt miserably helpless and hopeless. She had exhausted all arguments, all replies. Her father might have pitied her, and in fact he did so; but he was sure he was right.

"There is one thing you can tell Mr. Townsend when you see him again," he said, "that if you marry without my consent, I don't leave you a farthing of money. That will interest him more than anything else you can tell him."

"That would be very right," Catherine answered. "I ought not in that case to have a farthing of your money."

"My dear child," the Doctor observed, laughing, "your simplicity is touching. Make that remark, in that tone, and with that expression of countenance, to Mr. Townsend, and take a note of his answer. It won't be polite—it will express irritation; and I shall be glad of that, as it will put me in the right; unless, indeed—which is perfectly possible—you should like him the better for being rude to you."

"He will never be rude to me," said Catherine, gently.

"Tell him what I say, all the same."

She looked at her father, and her quiet eyes filled with tears.

"I think I will see him, then," she murmured, in her timid voice.

"Exactly as you choose." And he went to the door and opened it for her to go out. The movement gave her a terrible sense of his turning her off.

"It will be only once, for the present," she added, lingering a moment.

"Exactly as you choose," he repeated, standing there with his hand on the door. "I have told you what I think. If you see him, you will be an ungrateful, cruel child; you will have given your old father the greatest pain of his life."

This was more than the poor girl could bear; her tears over-flowed, and she moved toward her grimly consistent parent with a pitiful cry. Her hands were raised in supplication, but he sternly evaded this appeal. Instead of letting her sob out her misery on his shoulder, he simply took her by the arm and directed her course across the threshold, closing the door gently but firmly behind her. After he had done so, he remained listening. For a long time there was no sound; he knew that she was standing outside. He was sorry for her, as I have said; but he was so sure he was right. At last he heard her move away, and then her footstep creaked faintly upon the stairs.

The Doctor took several turns round his study, with his hands in his pockets, and a thin sparkle, possibly of irritation, but partly also of something like humor, in his eye. "By Jove," he said to himself, "I believe she will stick—I believe she will stick!" And this idea of Catherine "sticking" appeared to have a comical side, and to offer a prospect of entertainment. He determined, as he said to himself, to see it out.

19

It was for reasons connected with this determination that on the morrow he sought a few words of private conversation with Mrs. Penniman. He sent for her to the library, and he there informed her that he hoped very much that, as regarded this affair of Cathe-rine's, she would mind her *p's* and *q's*.

"I don't know what you mean by such an expression," said his sister. "You speak as if I were learning the alphabet."

"The alphabet of common-sense is something you will never learn," the Doctor permitted himself to respond.

"Have you called me here to insult me?" Mrs. Penniman inquired.

"Not at all. Simply to advise you. You have taken up young Townsend; that's your own affair. I have nothing to do with your sentiments, your fancies, your affections, your delusions; but what I request of you is that you will keep these things to yourself. I have explained my views to Catherine; she understands them perfectly, and anything that she does further in the way of encouraging Mr. Townsend's attentions will be in deliberate opposition to my wishes. Anything that you should do in the way of giving her aid and comfort will be—permit me the expression—distinctly treasonable. You know high-treason is a capital offence: take care how you incur the penalty."

Mrs. Penniman threw back her head, with a certain expansion of the eye which she occasionally practiced. "It seems to me that you talk like a great autocrat."

"I talk like my daughter's father."

"Not like your sister's brother," cried Lavinia.

"My dear Lavinia," said the Doctor, "I sometimes wonder whether I *am* your brother, we are so extremely different. In spite of differences, however, we can, at a pinch, understand each other; and that is the essential thing just now. Walk straight with regard to Mr. Townsend; that's all I ask. It is highly probable you have been corresponding with him for the last three weeks—perhaps even seeing him. I don't ask you—you needn't tell me." He had a moral conviction that she would contrive to tell a fib about the matter, which it would disgust him to listen to. "Whatever you have done, stop doing it; that's all I wish."

"Don't you wish also by chance to murder your child?" Mrs. Penniman inquired.

"On the contrary, I wish to make her live and be happy."

"You will kill her: she passed a dreadful night."

"She won't die of one dreadful night, nor of a dozen. Remember that I am a distinguished physician."

Mrs. Penniman hesitated a moment; then she risked her retort. "Your being a distinguished physician has not prevented you from already losing *two members* of your family."

She had risked it, but her brother gave her such a terribly incisive look—a look so like a surgeon's lancet—that she was frightened at her courage. And he answered her, in words that corresponded to the look, "It may not prevent me, either, from losing the society of still another."

Mrs. Penniman took herself off with whatever air of depreciated merit was at her command, and repaired to Catherine's room, where the poor girl was closeted. She knew all about her dreadful night, for the two had met again, the evening before, after Catherine left her father. Mrs. Penniman was on the landing of the second floor when her niece came up-stairs; it was not remarkable that a person of so much subtlety should have discovered that Catherine had been shut up with the Doctor. It was still less remarkable that she should have felt an extreme curiosity to learn the result of this interview, and that this sentiment, combined with her great amiability and generosity, should have prompted her to regret the sharp words lately exchanged between her niece and herself. As the unhappy girl came into sight in the dusky corridor, she made a lively demonstration of sympathy. Catherine's bursting heart was equally oblivious; she only knew that her aunt was taking her into her arms. Mrs. Penniman drew her into Catherine's own room, and the two women sat there together far into the small hours, the younger one with her head on the other's lap, sobbing, and sobbing at first in a soundless, stifled manner, and then at last perfectly still. It gratified Mrs. Penniman to be able to feel conscientiously that this scene virtually removed the interdict which Catherine had placed upon her indulging in further communion with Morris Townsend. She was not gratified, however, when, in coming back to her niece's room before breakfast, she found that Catherine had risen and was preparing herself for this meal.

"You should not go to breakfast," she said; "you are not well enough, after your fearful night."

"Yes, I am very well, and I am only afraid of being late."

"I can't understand you," Mrs. Penniman cried. "You should stay in bed for three days."

"Oh, I could never do that," said Catherine, to whom this idea presented no attractions.

Mrs. Penniman was in despair; and she noted, with extreme annoyance, that the trace of the night's tears had completely vanished from Catherine's eyes. She had a most impracticable physique. "What effect do you expect to have upon your father," her aunt demanded, "if you come plumping down, without a vestige of any sort of feeling, as if nothing in the world had happened?"

"He would not like me to lie in bed," said Catherine, simply.

"All the more reason for your doing it. How else do you expect to move him?"

Catherine thought a little. "I don't know how; but not in that way. I wish to be just as usual." And she finished dressing—and, according to her aunt's expression, went plumping down into the paternal presence. She was really too modest for consistent pathos.

And yet it was perfectly true that she had had a dreadful night. Even after Mrs. Penniman left her she had had no sleep; she lay staring at the uncomforting gloom, with her eyes and ears filled with the movement with which her father had turned her out of his room, and of the words in which he had told her that she was a heartless daughter. Her heart was breaking; she had heart enough for that. At moments it seemed to her that she believed him, and that to do what she was doing a girl must indeed be bad. She *was* bad; but she couldn't help it. She would try to appear good, even if her heart were perverted; and from time to time she had a fancy that she might accomplish something by ingenious concessions to form, though she should persist in caring for Morris. Catherine's ingenuities were indefinite, and we are not called upon to expose their hollowness. The best of them, perhaps, showed itself in that freshness of aspect which was so discouraging to Mrs. Penniman, who was amazed at the absence of haggardness in a young woman who for a whole night had lain quivering beneath a father's curse. Poor Catherine was conscious of her freshness; it gave her a feeling about the future which rather added to the weight upon her mind. It seemed a proof that she was strong and solid and dense, and would live to a great age—longer than might be generally convenient; and this idea was pressing, for it appeared to saddle her with a pretension the more, just when the cultivation of any pretension was inconsistent with her doing right. She wrote that day to Morris Townsend, requesting him to come and see her on the morrow, using very few words, and explaining nothing. She would explain everything face to face.

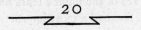

20

On the morrow, in the afternoon, she heard his voice at the door, and his step in the hall. She received him in the big, bright front-parlor, and she instructed the servant that, if any one should call, she was particularly engaged. She was not afraid of her father's coming in, for at that hour he was always driving about town. When Morris stood there before her, the first thing that she was conscious of was that he was even more beautiful to look at than fond recollection had painted him; the next was that he had pressed her in his arms. When she was free again it appeared to her that she had now indeed thrown herself into the gulf of defiance, and even, for an instant, that she had been married to him.

He told her that she had been very cruel, and had made him very unhappy; and Catherine felt acutely the difficulty of her destiny, which forced her to give pain in such opposite quarters. But she wished that, instead of reproaches, however tender, he would give her help; he was certainly wise enough and clever enough to invent some issue from their troubles. She expressed this belief, and Morris received the assurance as if he thought it natural; but he interrogated at first—as was natural too—rather than committed himself to marking out a course.

"You should not have made me wait so long," he said. "I don't know how I have been living; every hour seemed like years. You should have decided sooner."

"Decided?" Catherine asked.

"Decided whether you would keep me or give me up."

"Oh, Morris," she cried, with a long, tender murmur, "I never thought of giving you up!"

"What, then, were you waiting for?" The young man was ardently logical.

"I thought my father might—might—" and she hesitated.

"Might see how unhappy you were?"

"Oh no. But that he might look at it differently."

"And now you have sent for me to tell me that at last he does so. Is that it?"

This hypothetical optimism gave the poor girl a pang. "No, Morris," she said, solemnly, "he looks at it still in the same way."

"Then why have you sent for me?"

"Because I wanted to see you," cried Catherine, piteously.

"That's an excellent reason, surely. But did you want to look at me only? Have you nothing to tell me?"

His beautiful persuasive eyes were fixed upon her face, and she wondered what answer would be noble enough to make to such a gaze as that. For a moment her own eyes took it in, and then—"I *did* want to look at you," she said, gently. But after this speech, most inconsistently, she hid her face.

Morris watched her for a moment attentively. "Will you marry me to-morrow?" he asked, suddenly.

"To-morrow?"

"Next week, then—any time within a month?"

"Isn't it better to wait?" said Catherine.

"To wait for what?"

She hardly knew for what; but this tremendous leap alarmed her. "Till we have thought about it a little more."

He shook his head sadly and reproachfully. "I thought you had been thinking about it these three weeks. Do you want to turn it over in your mind for five years? You have given me more than time enough. My poor girl," he added, in a moment, "you are not sincere."

Catherine colored from brow to chin, and her eyes filled with tears. "Oh, how can you say that?" she murmured.

"Why, you must take me or leave me," said Morris, very reasonably. "You can't please your father and me both; you must choose between us."

"I have chosen you," she said, passionately.

"Then marry me next week!"

She stood gazing at him. "Isn't there any other way?"

"None that I know of for arriving at the same result. If there is, I should be happy to hear of it."

Catherine could think of nothing of the kind, and Morris's luminosity seemed almost pitiless. The only thing she could think of was that her father might, after all, come round; and she articulated, with an awkward sense of her helplessness in doing so, a wish that this miracle might happen.

"Do you think it is in the least degree likely?" Morris asked.

"It would be, if he could only know you."

"He can know me if he will. What is to prevent it?"

"His ideas, his reasons," said Catherine. "They are so—so terribly strong." She trembled with the recollection of them yet.

"Strong!" cried Morris. "I would rather you should think them weak."

"Oh, nothing about my father is weak," said the girl.

Morris turned away, walking to the window, where he stood looking out. "You are terribly afraid of him," he remarked at last.

She felt no impulse to deny it, because she had no shame in it; for, if it was no honor to herself, at least it was an honor to him. "I suppose I must be," she said, simply.

"Then you don't love me—not as I love you. If you fear your father more than you love me, then your love is not what I hoped it was."

"Ah, my friend!" she said, going to him.

"Do *I* fear anything?" he demanded, turning round on her. "For your sake what am I not ready to face?"

"You are noble—you are brave!" she answered, stopping short at a distance that was almost respectful.

"Small good it does me, if you are so timid."

"I don't think I am—*really*," said Catherine.

"I don't know what you mean by 'really.' It is really enough to make us miserable."

"I should be strong enough to wait—to wait a long time."

"And suppose after a long time your father should hate me worse than ever?"

"He wouldn't—he couldn't."

"He would be touched by my fidelity; is that what you mean? If he is so easily touched, then why should you be afraid of him?"

This was much to the point, and Catherine was struck by it. "I will try not to be," she said. And she stood there submissively, the image, in advance, of a dutiful and responsible wife. This image could not fail to recommend itself to Morris Townsend, and he continued to give proof of the high estimation in which he held her. It could only have been at the prompting of such a sentiment that he presently mentioned to her that the course recommended by Mrs. Penniman was an immediate union, regardless of consequences.

"Yes, Aunt Penniman would like that," Catherine said, simply, and yet with a certain shrewdness. It must, however, have been in pure simplicity, and from motives quite untouched by sarcasm, that a few moments after she went on to say to Morris that her father had given her a message for him. It was quite on her conscience to deliver this message, and had the mission been ten times more painful, she would have as scrupulously performed it. "He told me to tell you—to tell you very distinctly, and directly from himself—that if I marry without his consent, I shall not inherit a penny of his fortune. He made a great point of this. He seemed to think—he seemed to think—"

Morris flushed, as any young man of spirit might have flushed at an imputation of baseness. "What did he seem to think?"

"That it would make a difference."

"It *will* make a difference—in many things. We shall be by many thousands of dollars the poorer; and that is a great difference. But it will make none in my affection."

"We shall not want the money," said Catherine; "for you know I have a good deal myself."

"Yes, my dear girl, I know you have something. And he can't touch that."

"He would never," said Catherine. "My mother left it to me."

Morris was silent awhile. "He was very positive about this, was he?" he asked at last. "He thought such a message would annoy me terribly, and make me throw off the mask, eh?"

"I don't know what he thought," said Catherine, sadly.

"Please tell him that I care for his message as much as for that!" and Morris snapped his fingers sonorously.

"I don't think I could tell him that."

"Do you know you sometimes disappoint me," said Morris.

"I should think I might. I disappoint every one—father and Aunt Penniman."

"Well, it doesn't matter with me, because I am fonder of you than they are."

"Yes, Morris," said the girl, with her imagination—what there was of it—swimming in this happy truth, which seemed, after all, invidious to no one.

"Is it your belief that he will stick to it—stick to it forever—to this idea of disinheriting you?—that your goodness and patience will never wear out his cruelty?"

"The trouble is that if I marry you he will think I am not good. He will think that a proof."

"Ah, then he will never forgive you!"

This idea, sharply expressed by Morris's handsome lips, renewed for a moment to the poor girl's temporarily pacified conscience all its dreadful vividness. "Oh, you must love me very much!" she cried.

"There is no doubt of that, my dear," her lover rejoined. "You don't like that word 'disinherited,' " he added, in a moment.

"It isn't the money; it is that he should—that he should feel so."

"I suppose it seems to you a kind of curse?" said Morris. "It must be very dismal. But don't you think," he went on, presently, "that if you were to try to be very clever, and to set rightly about it, you might in the end conjure it away? Don't you think," he continued further, in a tone of sympathetic speculation, "that a really clever woman, in your place, might bring him round at last? Don't you think—"

Here, suddenly, Morris was interrupted; these ingenious inquiries had not reached Catherine's ears. The terrible word disinheritance, with all its impressive moral reprobation, was still ringing there— seemed, indeed, to gather force as it lingered. The mortal chill of her situation struck more deeply into her childlike heart, and she was overwhelmed by a feeling of loneliness and danger. But her refuge was there, close to her, and she put out her hands to grasp it. "Ah, Morris," she said, with a shudder, "I will marry you as soon as you please!" and she surrendered herself, leaning her head on his shoulder.

"My dear good girl!" he exclaimed, looking down at his prize. And then he looked up again, rather vaguely, with parted lips and lifted eyebrows.

2 1

Doctor Sloper very soon imparted his conviction to Mrs. Almond in the same terms in which he had announced it to himself. "She's going to stick, by Jove! she's going to stick."

"Do you mean that she is going to marry him?" Mrs. Almond inquired.

"I don't know that; but she is not going to break down. She is going to drag out the engagement, in the hope of making me relent."

"And shall you not relent?"

"Shall a geometrical proposition relent? I am not so superficial."

"Doesn't geometry treat of surfaces?" asked Mrs. Almond, who, as we know, was clever, smiling.

"Yes, but it treats of them profoundly. Catherine and her young man are my surfaces; I have taken their measure."

"You speak as if it surprised you."

"It is immense; there will be a great deal to observe."

"You are shockingly cold-blooded!" said Mrs. Almond.

"I need to be, with all this hot blood about me. Young Townsend, indeed, is cool; I must allow him that merit."

"I can't judge him," Mrs. Almond answered; "but I am not at all surprised at Catherine."

"I confess I am a little; she must have been so deucedly divided and bothered."

"Say it amuses you outright. I don't see why it should be such a joke that your daughter adores you."

"It is the point where the adoration stops that I find it interesting to fix."

"It stops where the other sentiment begins."

"Not at all; that would be simple enough. The two things are extremely mixed up, and the mixture is extremely odd. It will produce some third element, and that's what I'm waiting to see. I wait with suspense—with positive excitement; and that is a sort of emotion that I didn't suppose Catherine would ever provide for me. I am really very much obliged to her."

"She will cling," said Mrs. Almond; "she will certainly cling."

"Yes, as I say, she will stick."

"Cling is prettier. That's what those very simple natures always do, and nothing could be simpler than Catherine. She doesn't take many impressions; but when she takes one, she keeps it. She is like a copper kettle that receives a dent: you may polish up the kettle, but you can't efface the mark."

"We must try and polish up Catherine," said the Doctor. "I will take her to Europe!"

"She won't forget him in Europe."

"He will forget her, then."

Mrs. Almond looked grave. "Should you really like that?"

"Extremely," said the Doctor.

Mrs. Penniman, meanwhile, lost little time in putting herself again in communication with Morris Townsend. She requested him to favor her with another interview, but she did not on this occasion select an oyster saloon as the scene of their meeting. She proposed that he should join her at the door of a certain church after service on Sunday afternoon; and she was careful not to appoint the place of worship which she usually visited, and where, as she said, the congregation would have spied upon her. She picked out a less elegant resort, and on issuing from its portal at the hour she had fixed she saw the young man standing apart. She offered him no recognition until she had crossed the street, and he had followed her to some distance. Here, with a smile, "Excuse my apparent want of cordiality," she said. "You know what to believe about that. Prudence before everything." And on his asking her in what direction they should walk, "Where we shall be least observed," she murmured.

Morris was not in high good-humor, and his response to this speech was not particularly gallant. "I don't flatter myself we shall be much observed anywhere." Then he turned recklessly toward the centre of the town. "I hope you have come to tell me that he has knocked under," he went on.

"I am afraid I am not altogether a harbinger of good; and yet, too, I am to a certain extent a messenger of peace. I have been thinking a great deal, Mr. Townsend," said Mrs. Penniman.

"You think too much."

"I suppose I do; but I can't help it, my mind is so terribly active. When I give myself, I give myself. I pay the penalty in my head-aches, my famous headaches—a perfect circlet of pain! But I carry it as a queen carries her crown. Would you believe that I have one now? I wouldn't, however, have missed our rendezvous for anything. I have something very important to tell you."

"Well, let's have it," said Morris.

"I was perhaps a little headlong the other day in advising you to marry immediately. I have been thinking it over, and now I see it just a little differently."

"You seem to have a great many different ways of seeing the same object."

"Their number is infinite!" said Mrs. Penniman, in a tone which seemed to suggest that this convenient faculty was one of her brightest attributes.

"I recommend you to take one way, and stick to it," Morris replied.

"Ah, but it isn't easy to choose. My imagination is never quiet, never satisfied. It makes me a bad adviser, perhaps, but it makes me a capital friend."

"A capital friend who gives bad advice!" said Morris.

"Not intentionally—and who hurries off, at every risk, to make the most humble excuses."

"Well, what do you advise me now?"

"To be very patient; to watch and wait."

"And is that bad advice or good?"

"That is not for me to say," Mrs. Penniman rejoined, with some dignity. "I only claim it is sincere."

"And will you come to me next week and recommend something different and equally sincere?"

"I may come to you next week, and tell you that I am in the streets."

"In the streets?"

"I have had a terrible scene with my brother, and he threatens, if anything happens, to turn me out of the house. You know I am a poor woman."

Morris had a speculative idea that she had a little property; but he naturally did not press this.

"I should be very sorry to see you suffer martyrdom for me," he said. "But you make your brother out a regular Turk."

Mrs. Penniman hesitated a little.

"I certainly do not regard Austin as an orthodox Christian."

"And am I to wait till he is converted?"

"Wait at any rate till he is less violent. Bide your time, Mr. Townsend; remember the prize is great."

Morris walked along some time in silence, tapping the railings and gate-posts very sharply with his stick.

"You certainly are devilish inconsistent!" he broke out at last. "I have already got Catherine to consent to a private marriage."

Mrs. Penniman was indeed inconsistent, for at this news she gave a little jump of gratification.

"Oh, when and where?" she cried. And then she stopped short.

Morris was a little vague about this.

"That isn't fixed; but she consents. It's deuced awkward now to back out."

Mrs. Penniman, as I say, had stopped short; and she stood there with her eyes fixed brilliantly on her companion.

"Mr. Townsend," she proceeded, "shall I tell you something? Catherine loves you so much that you may do anything."

This declaration was slightly ambiguous, and Morris opened his eyes.

"I am happy to hear it. But what do you mean by 'anything'?"

"You may postpone—you may change about; she won't think the worse of you."

Morris stood there still, with his raised eyebrows; then he said, simply and rather dryly, "Ah!" After this he remarked to Mrs.

Penniman that if she walked so slowly she would attract notice, and he succeeded, after a fashion, in hurrying her back to the domicile of which her tenure had become so insecure.

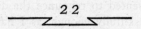

He had slightly misrepresented the matter in saying that Catherine had consented to take the great step. We left her just now declaring that she would burn her ships behind her; but Morris, after having elicited this declaration, had become conscious of good reasons for not taking it up. He avoided, gracefully enough, fixing a day, though he left her under the impression that he had his eye on one. Catherine may have had her difficulties; but those of her circumspect suitor are also worthy of consideration. The prize was certainly great; but it was only to be won by striking the happy mean between precipitancy and caution. It would be all very well to take one's jump and trust to Providence; Providence was more especially on the side of clever people, and clever people were known by an indisposition to risk their bones.

The ultimate reward of a union with a young woman who was both unattractive and impoverished ought to be connected with immediate disadvantages by some very palpable chain. Between the fear of losing Catherine and her possible fortune altogether, and the fear of taking her too soon and finding this possible fortune as void of actuality as a collection of emptied bottles, it was not comfortable for Morris Townsend to choose—a fact that should be remembered by readers disposed to judge harshly of a young man who may have struck them as making but an indifferently successful use of fine natural parts. He had not forgotten that in any event Catherine had her own ten thousand a year; he had devoted an abundance of meditation to this circumstance. But with his fine parts he rated himself high, and he had a perfectly definite appreciation of his value, which seemed to him inadequately represented by the sum I have mentioned. At the same time he reminded himself that this sum was considerable, that everything is relative, and that if a modest income is less desirable than a large one, the complete absence of revenue is nowhere accounted an advantage.

These reflections gave him plenty of occupation, and made it necessary that he should trim his sail. Doctor Sloper's opposition was the unknown quantity in the problem he had to work out. The natural way to work it out was by marrying Catherine; but in mathematics there are many short cuts, and Morris was not without a hope that he should yet discover one. When Catherine took him at his word, and consented to renounce the attempt to mollify her father, he drew back skilfully enough, as I have said, and kept the wedding-day still an open question. Her faith in his sincerity was so complete that she was incapable of suspecting that he was playing with her; her trouble just now was of another kind. The poor girl had an admirable sense of honor, and from the moment she had brought herself to the point of violating her father's wish, it seemed to her that she had no right to enjoy his protection. It was on her conscience that she ought to live under his roof only so long as she conformed to his wisdom. There was a great deal of glory in such a position, but poor Catherine felt that she had forfeited her claim to it. She had cast her lot with a young man against whom he had solemnly warned her, and broken the contract under which he provided her with a happy home. She could not give up the young man, so she must leave the home; and the sooner the object of her preference offered her another, the sooner her situation would lose its awkward twist. This was close reasoning; but it was commingled with an infinite amount of merely instinctive penitence. Catherine's days, at this time, were dismal, and the weight of some of her hours was almost more than she could bear. Her father never looked at her, never spoke to her. He knew perfectly what he was about, and this was part of a plan. She looked at him as much as she dared (for she was afraid of seeming to offer herself to his observation), and she pitied him for the sorrow she had brought upon him. She held up her head and busied her hands, and went about her daily occupations; and when the state of things in Washington Square seemed intolerable, she closed her eyes and indulged herself with an intellectual vision of the man for whose sake she had broken a sacred law.

Mrs. Penniman, of the three persons in Washington Square, had much the most of the manner that belongs to a great crisis. If Catherine was quiet, she was quietly quiet, as I may say, and her pathetic effects, which there was no one to notice, were entirely unstudied and unintended. If the Doctor was stiff and dry, and absolutely indifferent to the presence of his companions, it was so lightly, neatly, easily done, that you would have had to know him well to discover that, on the whole, he rather enjoyed having to be so disagreeable. But Mrs. Penniman was elaborately reserved and significantly silent; there was a richer rustle in the very deliberate movements to which she confined herself, and when she occasionally spoke, in connection with some very trivial event, she had the air of meaning something deeper than what she said. Between Catherine and her father nothing had passed since the evening she went to speak to him in his study. She had something to say to him—it seemed to her she ought to say it—but she kept it back for fear of irritating him. He also had something to say to her; but he was determined not to speak first. He was interested, as we know, in seeing how, if she were left to herself, she would "stick." At last she told him she had seen Morris Townsend again, and that their relations remained quite the same.

"I think we shall marry—before very long. And probably, meanwhile, I shall see him rather often; about once a week—not more."

The Doctor looked at her coldly from head to foot, as if she had been a stranger. It was the first time his eyes had rested on her for a week, which was fortunate, if that was to be their expression. "Why not three times a day?" he asked. "What prevents your meeting as often as you choose?"

She turned away a moment; there were tears in her eyes. Then she said, "It is better once a week."

"I don't see how it is better. It is as bad as it can be. If you flatter yourself that I care for little modifications of that sort, you are very much mistaken. It is as wrong of you to see him once a week as it would be to see him all day long. Not that it matters to me, however."

Catherine tried to follow these words, but they seemed to lead toward a vague horror from which she recoiled. "I think we shall marry pretty soon," she repeated, at last.

Her father gave her his dreadful look again, as if she were some one else. "Why do you tell me that? It's no concern of mine."

"Oh, father," she broke out, "don't you care, even if you do feel so?"

"Not a button. Once you marry, it's quite the same to me when, or where, or why you do it; and if you think to compound for your folly by hoisting your fly in this way, you may spare yourself the trouble."

With this he turned away. But the next day he spoke to her of his own accord, and his manner was somewhat changed. "Shall you be married within the next four or five months?" he asked.

"I don't know, father," said Catherine. "It is not very easy for us to make up our minds."

"Put it off, then, for six months, and in the meantime I will take you to Europe. I should like you very much to go."

It gave her such delight, after his words of the day before, to hear that he should "like" her to do something, and that he still had in his heart any of the tenderness of preference, that she gave a little exclamation of joy. But then she became conscious that Morris was not included in this proposal, and that—as regards really going—she would greatly prefer to remain at home with him. But she blushed none the less more comfortably than she had done of late. "It would be delightful to go to Europe," she remarked, with a sense that the idea was not original, and that her tone was not all it might be.

"Very well, then, we will go. Pack up your clothes."

"I had better tell Mr. Townsend," said Catherine.

Her father fixed his cold eyes upon her. "If you mean that you had better ask his leave, all that remains to me is to hope he will give it."

The girl was sharply touched by the pathetic ring of the words; it was the most calculated, the most dramatic little speech the Doctor had ever uttered. She felt that it was a great thing for her, under the circumstances, to have this fine opportunity of showing him her respect; and yet there was something else that she felt as well, and that she presently expressed. "I sometimes think that if I do what you dislike so much, I ought not to stay with you."

"To stay with me?"

"If I live with you, I ought to obey you."

"If that's your theory, it's certainly mine," said the Doctor, with a dry laugh.

"But if I don't obey you, I ought not to live with you—to enjoy your kindness and protection."

This striking argument gave the Doctor a sudden sense of having underestimated his daughter; it seemed even more than worthy of a young woman who had revealed the quality of unaggressive obstinacy. But it displeased him—displeased him deeply, and he signified as much. "That idea is in very bad taste," he said. "Did you get it from Mr. Townsend?"

"Oh no; it's my own," said Catherine, eagerly.

"Keep it to yourself, then," her father answered, more than ever determined she should go to Europe.

23

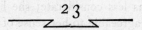

If Morris Townsend was not to be included in this journey, no more was Mrs. Penniman, who would have been thankful for an invitation, but who (to do her justice) bore her disappointment in a perfectly lady-like manner. "I should enjoy seeing the works of Raphael and the ruins—the ruins of the Pantheon," she said to Mrs. Almond; "but, on the other hand, I shall not be sorry to be alone and at peace for the next few months in Washington Square. I want rest; I have been through so much in the last four months." Mrs. Almond thought it rather cruel that her brother should not take poor Lavinia abroad; but she easily understood that, if the purpose of his expedition was to make Catherine forget her lover, it was not in his interest to give his daughter this young man's best friend as a companion. "If Lavinia had not been so foolish, she might visit the ruins of the Pantheon," she said to herself; and she continued to regret her sister's folly, even though the latter assured her that she had often heard the relics in question most satisfactorily described by Mr. Penniman. Mrs. Penniman was perfectly aware that her brother's motive in undertaking a foreign tour was to lay a trap for Catherine's constancy; and she imparted this conviction very frankly to her niece.

"He thinks it will make you forget Morris," she said (she always called the young man "Morris" now): "out of sight, out of mind, you know. He thinks that all the things you will see over there will drive him out of your thoughts."

Catherine looked greatly alarmed. "If he thinks that, I ought to tell him beforehand."

Mrs. Penniman shook her head. "Tell him afterward, my dear—after he has had all the trouble and expense. That's the way to serve him." And she added, in a softer key, that it must be delightful to think of those who love us among the ruins of the Pantheon.

Her father's displeasure had cost the girl, as we know, a great deal of deep-welling sorrow—sorrow of the purest and most generous kind, without a touch of resentment or rancor; but for the first time, after he had dismissed with such contemptuous brevity her apology for being a charge upon him, there was a spark of anger in her grief. She had felt his contempt; it had scorched her; that speech about her bad taste had made her ears burn for three days. During this period she was less considerate; she had an idea—a rather vague one, but it was agreeable to her sense of injury—that now she was absolved from penance, and might do what she chose. She chose to write to Morris Townsend to meet her in the Square and take her to walk about the town. If she were going to Europe out of respect to her father, she might at least give herself this satisfaction. She felt in every way at present more free and more resolute; there was a force that urged her. Now at last, completely and unreservedly, her passion possessed her.

Morris met her at last, and they took a long walk. She told him immediately what had happened; that her father wished to take her away—it would be for six months—to Europe; she would do absolutely what Morris should think best. She hoped inexpressibly that he would think it best she should stay at home. It was some time before he said what he thought; he asked, as they walked along, a great many questions. There was one that especially struck her; it seemed so incongruous.

"Should you like to see all those celebrated things over there?"

"Oh no, Morris!" said Catherine, quite deprecatingly.

"Gracious Heaven, what a dull woman!" Morris exclaimed to himself.

"He thinks I will forget you," said Catherine; "that all these things will drive you out of my mind."

"Well, my dear, perhaps they will."

"Please don't say that," Catherine answered, gently, as they walked along. "Poor father will be disappointed."

Morris gave a little laugh. "Yes, I verily believe that your poor father will be disappointed. But you will have seen Europe," he added, humorously. "What a take-in!"

"I don't care for seeing Europe," Catherine said.

"You ought to care, my dear; and it may mollify your father."

Catherine, conscious of her obstinacy, expected little of this, and could not rid herself of the idea that in going abroad and yet remaining firm, she should play her father a trick. "Don't you think it would be a kind of deception?" she asked.

"Doesn't he want to deceive you?" cried Morris. "It will serve him right. I really think you had better go."

"And not be married for so long?"

"Be married when you come back. You can buy your wedding clothes in Paris." And then Morris, with great kindness of tone, explained his view of the matter. It would be a good thing that she should go; it would put them completely in the right. It would show they were reasonable, and willing to wait. Once they were so sure of each other, they could afford to wait—what had they to fear? If there was a particle of chance that her father would be favorably affected by her going, that ought to settle it; for, after all, Morris was very unwilling to be the cause of her being disinherited. It was not for himself, it was for her and for her children. He was willing to wait for her; it would be hard, but he could do it. And over there, among beautiful scenes and noble monuments, perhaps the old gentleman would be softened; such things were supposed to exert a humanizing influence. He might be touched by her gentleness, her patience, her willingness to make any sacrifice but *that* one; and if she should appeal to him some day, in some celebrated spot—in Italy, say, in the evening; in Venice, in a gondola, by moonlight—if she should be a little clever about it, and touch the right chord, perhaps he would fold her in his arms, and tell her that he forgave her. Catherine was immensely struck with this conception of the affair, which seemed eminently worthy of her lover's brilliant intellect, though she viewed it askance in so far as it depended upon her own powers of execution. The idea of being "clever" in a gondola by moonlight appeared to her to involve elements of which her grasp was not active. But it was settled between them that she should tell her father that she was ready to follow him obediently anywhere, making the mental reservation that she loved Morris Townsend more than ever.

She informed the Doctor she was ready to embark, and he made rapid arrangements for this event. Catherine had many farewells to make, but with only two of them are we actively concerned. Mrs. Penniman took a discriminating view of her niece's journey; it seemed to her very proper that Mr. Townsend's destined bride should wish to embellish her mind by a foreign tour.

"You leave him in good hands," she said, pressing her lips to Catherine's forehead. (She was very fond of kissing people's foreheads; it was an involuntary expressing of sympathy with the intellectual part.) "I shall see him often; I shall feel like one of the vestals of old tending the sacred flame."

"You behave beautifully about not going with us," Catherine answered, not presuming to examine this analogy.

"It is my pride that keeps me up," said Mrs. Penniman, tapping the body of her dress, which always gave forth a sort of metallic ring.

Catherine's parting with her lover was short, and few words were exchanged.

"Shall I find you just the same when I come back?" she asked; though the question was not the fruit of scepticism.

"The same—only more so," said Morris, smiling.

It does not enter into our scheme to narrate in detail Doctor Sloper's proceedings in the Eastern hemisphere. He made the grand tour of Europe, travelled in considerable splendor, and (as was to have been expected in a man of his high cultivation) found so much in art and antiquity to interest him, that he remained abroad, not for six months, but for twelve. Mrs. Penniman, in Washington Square, accommodated herself to his absence. She enjoyed her uncontested dominion in the empty house, and flattered herself that she made it more attractive to their friends than when her brother was at home. To Morris Townsend, at least, it would have appeared that she made it singularly attractive. He was altogether her most frequent visitor, and Mrs. Penniman was very fond of asking him to tea. He had his chair—a very easy one—at the fireside in the back parlor (when the great mahogany sliding doors, with silver knobs and hinges, which divided this apartment from its more formal neighbor, were closed), and he used to smoke cigars in the Doctor's study, where he often spent an hour in turning over the curious collections of its absent proprietor. He thought Mrs. Penniman a goose, as we know; but he was no goose himself, and, as a young man of luxurious tastes and scanty resources, he found the house a perfect castle of indolence. It became for him a club with a single member. Mrs. Penniman saw much less of her sister than while the Doctor was at home; for Mrs. Almond had felt moved to tell her that she disapproved of her relations with Mr. Townsend. She had no business to be so friendly to a young man of whom their brother thought so meanly, and Mrs. Almond was surprised at her levity in foisting a most deplorable engagement upon Catherine.

"Deplorable!" cried Lavinia. "He will make her a lovely husband."

"I don't believe in lovely husbands," said Mrs. Almond; "I only believe in good ones. If he marries her, and she comes into Austin's money, they may get on. He will be an idle, amiable, selfish, and, doubtless, tolerably good-natured fellow. But if she doesn't get the money, and he finds himself tied to her, Heaven have mercy on her! He will have none. He will hate her for his disappointment, and take his revenge; he will be pitiless and cruel. Woe betide poor Catherine! I recommend you to talk a little with his sister; it's a pity Catherine can't marry *her*!"

Mrs. Penniman had no appetite whatever for conversation with Mrs. Montgomery, whose acquaintance she made no trouble to cultivate; and the effect of this alarming forecast of her niece's destiny was to make her think it indeed a thousand pities that Mr. Townsend's generous nature should be embittered. Bright enjoyment was his natural element, and how could he be comfortable if there should prove to be nothing to enjoy? It became a fixed idea with Mrs. Penniman that he should yet enjoy her brother's fortune, on which she had acuteness enough to perceive that her own claim was small.

"If he doesn't leave it to Catherine, it certainly won't be to leave it to me," she said.

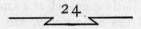

24

The Doctor, during the first six months he was abroad, never spoke to his daughter of their little difference, partly on system, and partly because he had a great many other things to think about. It was idle to attempt to ascertain the state of her affections without direct inquiry, because if she had not had an expressive manner among the familiar influences of home, she failed to gather animation from the mountains of Switzerland or the monuments of Italy. She was always her father's docile and reasonable associate—going through their sightseeing in deferential silence, never complaining of fatigue, always ready to start at the hour he had appointed overnight, making no foolish criticisms, and indulging in no refinements of appreciation. "She is about as intelligent as the bundle of shawls," the Doctor said, her main superiority being that, while the bundle of shawls sometimes got lost, or tumbled out of the carriage, Catherine was always at her post, and had a firm and ample seat. But her father had expected this, and he was not constrained to set down her intellectual limitations as a tourist to sentimental depression; she had completely divested herself of the characteristics of a victim, and during the whole time that they were abroad she never uttered an audible sigh.

He supposed she was in correspondence with Morris Townsend, but he held his peace about it, for he never saw the young man's letters, and Catherine's own missives were always given to the courier to post. She heard from her lover with considerable regularity, but his letters came enclosed in Mrs. Penniman's; so that, whenever the Doctor handed her a packet addressed in his sister's hand, he was an involuntary instrument of the passion he condemned. Catherine made this reflection, and six months earlier she would have felt bound to give him warning; but now she deemed herself absolved. There was a sore spot in her heart that his own words had made when once she spoke to him as she thought honor prompted; she would try and please him as far as she could, but she would never speak that way again. She read her lover's letters in secret.

One day, at the end of the summer, the two travellers found themselves in a lonely valley of the Alps. They were crossing one of the passes, and on the long ascent they had got out of the carriage and had wandered much in advance. After awhile the Doctor descried a foot-path which, leading through a transverse valley, would bring them out, as he justly supposed, at a much higher point of the ascent. They followed this devious way, and finally lost the path; the valley proved very wild and rough, and their walk became rather a scramble. They were good walkers, however, and they took their adventure easily; from time to time they stopped, that Catherine might rest; and then she sat upon a stone and looked about her at the hard-featured rocks and the glowing sky. It was late in the afternoon, in the last of August; night was coming on, and as they had reached a great elevation, the air was cold and sharp. In the west there was a great suffusion of cold red light, which made the sides of the little valley look only the more rugged and dusky. During one of their pauses her father left her and wandered away to some high place, at a distance, to get a view. He was out of sight; she sat there alone in the stillness, which was just touched by the vague murmur somewhere of a mountain brook. She thought of Morris Townsend, and the place was so desolate and lonely that he seemed very far away. Her father remained absent a long time; she began to wonder what had become of him. But at last he reappeared, coming toward her in the clear twilight, and she got up to go on. He made no motion to proceed, however, but came close to her, as if he had something to say. He stopped in front of her, and stood looking at her with eyes that had kept the light of the flushing snow-summits on which they had just been fixed. Then, abruptly, in a low tone, he asked her an unexpected question,

"Have you given him up?"

The question was unexpected, but Catherine was only superficially unprepared.

"No, father," she answered.

He looked at her again for some moments without speaking.

"Does he write to you?" he asked.

"Yes, about twice a month."

The Doctor looked up and down the valley, swinging his stick; then he said to her, in the same low tone,

"I am very angry."

She wondered what he meant—whether he wished to frighten her. If he did, the place was well chosen: this hard, melancholy dell, abandoned by the summer light, made her feel her loneliness. She looked around her, and her heart grew cold; for a moment her fear was great. But she could think of nothing to say, save to murmur, gently, "I am sorry."

"You try my patience," her father went on, "and you ought to know what I am. I am not a very good man. Though I am very smooth externally, at bottom I am very passionate; and I assure you I can be very hard."

She could not think why he told her these things. Had he brought her there on purpose, and was it part of a plan? What was the plan? Catherine asked herself. Was it to startle her suddenly into a retraction—to take an advantage of her by dread? Dread of what? The place was ugly and lonely, but the place could do her no harm. There was a kind of still intensity about her father which made him dangerous, but Catherine hardly went so far as to say to herself that it might be part of his plan to fasten his hand—the neat, fine, supple hand of a distinguished physician—in her throat. Nevertheless, she receded a step. "I am sure you can be anything you please," she said; and it was her simple belief.

"I am very angry," he replied, more sharply.

"Why has it taken you so suddenly?"

"It has not taken me suddenly. I have been raging inwardly for the last six months. But just now this seemed a good place to flare out. It's so quiet, and we are alone."

"Yes, it's very quiet," said Catherine, vaguely looking about her. "Won't you come back to the carriage?"

"In a moment. Do you mean that in all this time you have not yielded an inch?"

"I would if I could, father; but I can't."

The Doctor looked round him too. "Should you like to be left in such a place as this, to starve?"

"What do you mean?" cried the girl.

"That will be your fate—that's how he will leave you."

He would not touch her, but he had touched Morris. The warmth came back to her heart. "That is not true, father," she broke out, "and you ought not to say it. It is not right, and it's not true."

He shook his head slowly. "No, it's not right, because you won't believe it. But it *is* true. Come back to the carriage."

He turned away, and she followed him; he went faster, and was presently much in advance. But from time to time he stopped, without turning round, to let her keep up with him, and she made her way forward with difficulty, her heart beating with the excitement of having for the first time spoken to him in violence. By this time it had grown almost dark, and she ended by losing sight of him. But she kept her course, and after a little, the valley making a sudden turn, she gained the road, where the carriage stood waiting. In it sat her father, rigid and silent; in silence, too, she took her place beside him.

It seemed to her, later, in looking back upon all this, that for days afterward not a word had been exchanged between them. The scene had been a strange one, but it had not permanently affected her feeling toward her father, for it was natural, after all, that he should occasionally make a scene of some kind, and he had let her alone for six months. The strangest part of it was that he had said he was not a good man; Catherine wondered a good deal what he had meant by that. The statement failed to appeal to her credence, and it was not grateful to any resentment that she entertained. Even in the utmost bitterness that she might feel, it would give her no satisfaction to think him less complete. Such a saying as that was a part of his great subtlety—men so clever as he might say anything and mean anything; and as to his being hard, that surely, in a man, was a virtue.

He let her alone for six months more—six months during which she accommodated herself without a protest to the extension of their tour. But he spoke again at the end of this time: it was at the very last, the night before they embarked for New York, in the hotel at

Liverpool. They had been dining together in a great, dim, musty sitting-room; and then the cloth had been removed, and the Doctor walked slowly up and down. Catherine at last took her candle to go to bed, but her father motioned her to stay.

"What do you mean to do when you get home?" he asked, while she stood there with her candle in her hand.

"Do you mean about Mr. Townsend?"

"About Mr. Townsend."

"We shall probably marry."

The Doctor took several turns again while she waited. "Do you hear from him as much as ever?"

"Yes, twice a month," said Catherine, promptly.

"And does he always talk about marriage?"

"Oh yes; that is, he talks about other things too, but he always says something about that."

"I am glad to hear he varies his subjects; his letters might otherwise be monotoncus."

"He writes beautifully," said Catherine, who was very glad of a chance to say it.

"They always write beautifully. However, in a given case that doesn't diminish the merit. So, as soon as you arrive, you are going off with him?"

This seemed a rather gross way of putting it, and something that there was of dignity in Catherine resented it. "I cannot tell you till we arrive," she said.

"That's reasonable enough," her father answered. "That's all I ask of you—that you *do* tell me, that you give me definite notice. When a poor man is to lose his only child, he likes to have an inkling of it beforehand."

"Oh, father! you will not lose me," Catherine said, spilling her candle wax.

"Three days before will do," he went on, "if you are in a position to be positive then. He ought to be very thankful to me, do you know. I have done a mighty good thing for him in taking you abroad; your value is twice as great, with all the knowledge and taste that you have acquired. A year ago, you were perhaps a little limited—a little rustic; but now you have seen everything, and appreciated everything, and you will be a most entertaining companion. We have fattened the sheep for him before he kills it." Catherine turned away, and stood staring at the blank door. "Go to bed," said her father; "and as we don't go aboard till noon, you may sleep late. We shall probably have a most uncomfortable voyage."

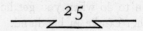

The voyage was indeed uncomfortable, and Catherine, on arriving in New York, had not the compensation of "going off," in her father's phrase, with Morris Townsend. She saw him, however, the day after she landed; and in the meantime he formed a natural subject of conversation between our heroine and her aunt Lavinia, with whom, the night she disembarked, the girl was closeted for a long time before either lady retired to rest.

"I have seen a great deal of him," said Mrs. Penniman. "He is not very easy to know. I suppose you think you know him; but you don't, my dear. You will some day; but it will only be after you have lived with him. I may almost say *I* have lived with him," Mrs. Penniman proceeded, while Catherine stared. "I think I know him now; I have had such remarkable opportunities. You will have the same—or, rather, you will have better"; and Aunt Lavinia smiled. "Then you will see what I mean. It's a wonderful character, full of passion and energy, and just as true."

Catherine listened with a mixture of interest and apprehension. Aunt Lavinia was intensely sympathetic, and Catherine, for the past year, while she wandered through foreign galleries and churches, and rolled over the smoothness of posting roads, nursing the thoughts that never passed her lips, had often longed for the company of some intelligent person of her own sex. To tell her story to some kind woman—at moments it seemed to her that this would give her comfort, and she had more than once been on the point of taking the landlady, or the nice young person from the dress-maker's, into her confidence. If a woman had been near her, she would on certain occasions have treated such a companion to a fit of weeping; and she had an apprehension that, on her return, this would form her response to Aunt Lavinia's first embrace. In fact, however, the two ladies had met, in Washington Square, without tears; and when they found themselves alone together a certain dryness fell upon the girl's emotion. It came over her with a greater force that Mrs. Penniman had enjoyed a whole year of her lover's society, and it was not a pleasure to her to hear her aunt explain and interpret the young man, speaking of him as if her own knowledge of him were supreme. It was not that Catherine was jealous; but her sense of Mrs. Penniman's innocent falsity, which had lain dormant, began to haunt her again, and she was glad that she was safely at home. With this, however, it was a blessing to be able to talk of Morris, to sound his name, to be with a person who was not unjust to him.

"You have been very kind to him," said Catherine. "He has written me that, often. I shall never forget that, Aunt Lavinia."

"I have done what I could; it has been very little. To let him come and talk to me, and give him his cup of tea—that was all. Your aunt Almond thought it was too much, and used to scold me terribly; but she promised me, at least, not to betray me."

"To betray you?"

"Not to tell your father. He used to sit in your father's study," said Mrs. Penniman, with a little laugh.

Catherine was silent a moment. This idea was disagreeable to her, and she was reminded again, with pain, of her aunt's secretive habits. Morris, the reader may be informed, had had the tact not to tell her that he sat in her father's study. He had known her but for a few months, and her aunt had known her for fifteen years; and yet he would not have made the mistake of thinking that Catherine would see the joke of the thing. "I am sorry you made him go into father's room," she said, after awhile.

"I didn't send him; he went himself. He liked to look at the books, and at all those things in the glass cases. He knows all about them; he knows all about everything."

Catherine was silent again; then, "I wish he had found some employment," she said.

"He has found some employment. It's beautiful news, and he told me to tell you as soon as you arrived. He has gone into partnership with a commission merchant. It was all settled, quite suddenly, a week ago."

This seemed to Catherine indeed beautiful news; it had a fine prosperous air. "Oh, I'm so glad!" she said; and now, for a moment, she was disposed to throw herself on Aunt Lavinia's neck.

"It's much better than being under some one; and he has never been used to that," Mrs. Penniman went on. "He is just as good as his partner—they are perfectly equal. You see how right he was to wait. I should like to know what your father can say now! They have got an office in Duane Street, and little printed cards; he brought me one to show me. I have got it in my room, and you shall see it tomorrow. That's what he said to me the last time he was here—'You see how right I was to wait.' He has got other people under him instead of being a subordinate. He could never be a subordinate; I have often told him I could never think of him in that way."

Catherine assented to this proposition, and was very happy to know that Morris was his own master; but she was deprived of the satisfaction of thinking that she might communicate this news in triumph to her father. Her father would care equally little whether Morris were established in business or transported for life. Her trunks had been brought into her room, and further reference to her lover was for a short time suspended, while she opened them and displayed to her aunt some of the spoils of foreign travel. These were rich and abundant; and Catherine had brought home a present to every one—to every one save Morris, to whom she had brought simply her undiverted heart. To Mrs. Penniman she had been lavishly generous, and Aunt Lavinia spent half an hour in unfolding and folding again, with little ejaculations of gratitude and taste. She marched about for some time in a splendid cashmere shawl, which Catherine had begged her to accept, settling it on her shoulders, and twisting down her head to see how low the point descended behind.

"I shall regard it only as a loan," she said. "I will leave it to you again when I die; or, rather," she added, kissing her niece again, "I will leave it to your first-born little girl." And draped in her shawl, she stood there smiling.

"You had better wait till she comes," said Catherine.

"I don't like the way you say that," Mrs. Penniman rejoined, in a moment. "Catherine, are you changed?"

"No; I am the same."

"You have not swerved a line?"

"I am exactly the same," Catherine repeated, wishing her aunt were a little less sympathetic.

"Well, I am glad"; and Mrs. Penniman surveyed her cashmere in the glass. Then, "How is your father?" she asked, in a moment, with her eyes on her niece. "Your letters were so meagre—I could never tell."

"Father is very well."

"Ah, you know what I mean," said Mrs. Penniman, with a dignity to which the cashmere gave a richer effect. "Is he still implacable?"

"Oh yes!"

"Quite unchanged?"

"He is, if possible, more firm."

Mrs. Penniman took off her great shawl, and slowly folded it up. "That is very bad. You had no success with your little project."

"What little project?"

"Morris told me all about it. The idea of turning the tables on him, in Europe; of watching him, when he was agreeably impressed by some celebrated sight—he pretends to be so artistic, you know—and then just pleading with him and bringing him round."

"I never tried it. It was Morris's idea; but if he had been with us in Europe, he would have seen that father was never impressed in that way. He *is* artistic—tremendously artistic; but the more celebrated places we visited, and the more he admired them, the less use it would have been to plead with him. They seemed only to make him more determined—more terrible," said poor Catherine. "I shall never bring him round, and I expect nothing now."

"Well, I must say," Mrs. Penniman answered, "I never supposed you were going to give it up."

"I have given it up. I don't care now."

"You have grown very brave," said Mrs. Penniman, with a short laugh. "I didn't advise you to sacrifice your property."

"Yes, I am braver than I was. You asked me if I had changed; I have changed in that way. Oh," the girl went on, "I have changed very much. And it isn't my property. If *he* doesn't care for it, why should I?"

Mrs. Penniman hesitated. "Perhaps he does care for it."

"He cares for it for my sake, because he doesn't want to injure me. But he will know—he knows already—how little he need be afraid about that. Besides," said Catherine, "I have got plenty of money of my own. We shall be very well off; and now hasn't he got his business? I am delighted about that business." She went on talking, showing a good deal of excitement as she proceeded. Her aunt had never seen her with just this manner, and Mrs. Penniman, observing her, set it down to foreign travel, which had made her more positive, more mature. She thought also that Catherine had improved in appearance; she looked rather handsome. Mrs. Penniman wondered whether Morris Townsend would be struck with that. While she was engaged in this speculation, Catherine broke out, with a certain sharpness, "Why are you so contradictory, Aunt Penniman? You seem to think one thing at one time, and another at another. A year ago, before you went away, you wished me not to mind about displeasing father, and now you seem to recommend me to take another line. You change about so."

This attack was unexpected, for Mrs. Penniman was not used, in any discussion, to seeing the war carried into her own country—possibly because the enemy generally had doubts of finding subsistence there. To her own consciousness, the flowery fields of her reason had rarely been ravaged by a hostile force. It was perhaps on this account that in defending them she was majestic rather than agile.

"I don't know what you accuse me of, save of being too deeply interested in your happiness. It is the first time I have been told I am capricious. That fault is not what I am usually reproached with."

"You were angry last year that I wouldn't marry immediately, and now you talk about my winning my father over. You told me it would serve him right if he should take me to Europe for nothing. Well, he has taken me for nothing, and you ought to be satisfied. Nothing is changed—nothing but my feeling about father. I don't mind nearly so much now. I have been as good as I could, but he doesn't care. Now I don't care either. I don't know whether I have grown bad; perhaps I have. But I don't care for that. I have come home to be married—that's all I know. That ought to please you, unless you have taken up some new idea; you are so strange. You may do as you please, but you must never speak to me again about pleading with father. I shall never plead with him for anything; that is all over. He has put me off. I am come home to be married."

This was a more authoritative speech than she had ever heard on her niece's lips, and Mrs. Penniman was proportionately startled. She was, indeed, a little awe-struck, and the force of the girl's emotion and resolution left her nothing to reply. She was easily frightened, and she always carried off her discomfiture by a concession—a concession which was often accompanied, as in the present case, by a little nervous laugh.

26

If she had disturbed her niece's temper—she began from this moment forward to talk a good deal about Catherine's temper, an article which up to that time had never been mentioned in connection with our heroine—Catherine had opportunity on the morrow to recover her serenity. Mrs. Penniman had given her a message from Morris Townsend to the effect that he would come and welcome her home on the day after her arrival. He came in the afternoon; but, as may be imagined, he was not on this occasion made free of Doctor Sloper's study. He had been coming and going, for the past year, so comfortably and irresponsibly, that he had a certain sense of being wronged by finding himself reminded that he must now limit his horizon to the front parlor, which was Catherine's particular province.

"I am very glad you have come back," he said; "it makes me very happy to see you again." And he looked at her, smiling, from head to foot, though it did not appear afterward that he agreed with Mrs. Penniman (who, woman-like, went more into details) in thinking her embellished.

To Catherine he appeared resplendent; it was some time before she could believe again that this beautiful young man was her own exclusive property. They had a great deal of characteristic lovers' talk—a soft exchange of inquiries and assurances. In these matters Morris had an excellent grace, which flung a picturesque interest even over the account of his début in the commission business—a subject as to which his companion earnestly questioned him. From time to time he got up from the sofa where they sat together, and walked about the room; after which he came back, smiling and passing his hand through his hair. He was unquiet, as was natural in a young man who has just been reunited to a long-absent mistress, and Catherine made the reflection that she had never seen him so excited. It gave her pleasure, somehow, to note this fact. He asked her questions about her travels, to some of which she was unable to reply, for she had forgotten the names of places and the order of her father's journey. But for the moment she was so happy, so lifted up by the belief that her troubles at last were over, that she forgot to be ashamed of her meagre answers. It seemed to her now that she could marry him without the remnant of a scruple, or a single tremor save those that belonged to joy. Without waiting for him to ask, she told him that her father had come back in exactly the same state of mind—that he had not yielded an inch.

"We must not expect it now," she said, "and we must do without it."

Morris sat looking and smiling. "My poor, dear girl!" he exclaimed.

"You mustn't pity me," said Catherine. "I don't mind it now; I am used to it."

Morris continued to smile, and then he got up and walked about again. "You had better let me try him."

"Try to bring him over? You would only make him worse," Catherine answered, resolutely.

"You say that because I managed it so badly before. But I should manage it differently now. I am much wiser; I have had a year to think of it. I have more tact."

"Is that what you have been thinking of for a year?"

"Much of the time. You see, the idea sticks in my crop. I don't like to be beaten."

"How are you beaten if we marry?"

"If course I am not beaten on the main issue; but I am, don't you see? on all the rest of it—on the question of my reputation, of my relations with your father, of my relations with my own children, if we should have any."

"We shall have enough for our children; we shall have enough for everything. Don't you expect to succeed in business?"

"Brilliantly, and we shall certainly be very comfortable. But it isn't of the mere material comfort I speak; it is of the moral comfort," said Morris—"of the intellectual satisfaction."

"I have great moral comfort now," Catherine declared, very simply.

"Of course you have. But with me it is different. I have staked my pride on proving to your father that he is wrong, and now that I am at the head of a flourishing business, I can deal with him as an equal. I have a capital plan—do let me go at him!"

He stood before her with his bright face, his jaunty air, his hands in his pockets; and she got up, with her eyes resting on his own. "Please don't, Morris; please don't," she said; and there was a certain mild, sad firmness in her tone which he heard for the first time. "We must ask no favors of him—we must ask nothing more. He won't relent, and nothing good will come of it. I know it now—I have a very good reason."

"And pray what is your reason?"

She hesitated to bring it out, but at last it came. "He is not very fond of me."

"Oh, bother!" cried Morris, angrily.

"I wouldn't say such a thing without being sure. I saw it, I felt it, in England, just before he came away. He talked to me one night— the last night—and then it came over me. You can tell when a person feels that way. I wouldn't accuse him if he hadn't made me feel that way. I don't accuse him; I just tell you that that's how it is. He can't help it; we can't govern our affections. Do I govern mine? Mightn't he say that to me? It's because he is so fond of my mother, whom we lost so long ago. She was beautiful, and very, very brilliant; he is always thinking of her. I am not at all like her; Aunt Penniman has told me that. Of course it isn't my fault; but neither is it his fault. All I mean is, it's true; and it's a stronger reason for his never being reconciled than simply his dislike for you."

" 'Simply?' " cried Morris, with a laugh. "I am much obliged for that."

"I don't mind about his disliking you now; I mind everything less. I feel differently; I feel separated from my father."

"Upon my word," said Morris, "you are a queer family."

"Don't say that—don't say anything unkind," the girl entreated. "You must be very kind to me now, because, Morris, because"— and she hesitated a moment—"because I have done a great deal for you."

"Oh, I know that, my dear."

She had spoken up to this moment without vehemence or outward sign of emotion, gently, reasoningly, only trying to explain. But her emotion had been ineffectually smothered, and it betrayed itself at last in the trembling of her voice. "It is a great thing to be separated like that from your father, when you have worshipped him before. It has made me very unhappy; or it would have made me so if I didn't love you. You can tell when a person speaks to you as if— as if—"

"As if what?"

"As if they despised you!" said Catherine, passionately. "He spoke that way the night before we sailed. It wasn't much, but it was enough, and I thought of it on the voyage all the time. Then I made up my mind. I will never ask him for anything again, or expect anything from him. It would not be natural now. We must be very happy together, and we must not seem to depend upon his forgiveness. And, Morris, Morris, you must never despise me!"

This was an easy promise to make, and Morris made it with fine effect. But for the moment he undertook nothing more onerous.

27

The Doctor, of course, on his return, had a good deal of talk with his sisters. He was at no great pains to narrate his travels or to communicate his impressions of distant lands to Mrs. Penniman, upon whom he contented himself with bestowing a memento of his enviable experience in the shape of a velvet gown. But he conversed with her at some length about matters nearer home, and lost no time in assuring her that he was still an inflexible father.

"I have no doubt you have seen a great deal of Mr. Townsend, and done your best to console him for Catherine's absence," he said. "I don't ask you, and you needn't deny it. I wouldn't put the question to you for the world, and expose you to the inconvenience of having to—a—excogitate an answer. No one has betrayed you, and there has been no spy upon your proceedings. Elizabeth has told no tales, and has never mentioned you except to praise your good looks and good spirits. The thing is simply an inference of my own—an induction, as the philosophers say. It seems to me likely that you would have offered an asylum to an interesting sufferer. Mr. Townsend has been a good deal in the house; there is something in the house that tells me so. We doctors, you know, end by acquiring fine perceptions, and it is impressed upon my sensorium that he has sat in these chairs, in a very easy attitude, and warmed himself at that fire. I don't grudge him the comfort of it; it is the only one he will ever enjoy at my expense. It seems likely, indeed, that I shall be able to economize at his own. I don't know what you may have said to him, or what you may say hereafter; but I should like you to know that if you have encouraged him to believe that he will gain anything by hanging on, or that I have budged a hair-breadth from the position I took up a year ago, you have played him a trick for which he may exact reparation. I'm not sure that he may not bring a suit against you. Of course you have done it conscientiously; you have made yourself believe that I can be tired out. This is the most baseless hallucination that ever visited the brain of a genial optimist. I am not in the least tired; I am as fresh as when I started; I am good for fifty years yet. Catherine appears not to have budged an inch either; she is equally fresh; so we are about where we were before. This, however, you know as well as I. What I wish is simply to give you notice of my own state of mind. Take it to heart, dear Lavinia. Beware of the just resentment of a deluded fortune-hunter!"

"I can't say I expected it," said Mrs. Penniman. "And I had a sort of foolish hope that you would come home without that odious ironical tone with which you treat the most sacred subjects."

"Don't undervalue irony; it is often of great use. It is not, however, always necessary, and I will show you how gracefully I can lay it aside. I should like to know whether you think Morris Townsend will hang on?"

"I will answer you with your own weapons," said Mrs. Penniman. "You had better wait and see."

"Do you call such a speech as that one of my own weapons? I never said anything so rough."

"He will hang on long enough to make you very uncomfortable, then."

"My dear Lavinia," exclaimed the Doctor, "do you call that irony? I call it pugilism."

Mrs. Penniman, however, in spite of her pugilism, was a good deal frightened, and she took counsel of her fears. Her brother meanwhile took counsel, with many reservations, of Mrs. Almond, to whom he was no less generous than to Lavinia, and a good deal more communicative.

"I suppose she has had him there all the while," he said. "I must look into the state of my wine. You needn't mind telling me now; I have already said all I mean to say to her on the subject."

"I believe he was in the house a good deal," Mrs. Almond answered. "But you must admit that your leaving Lavinia quite alone was a great change for her, and that it was natural she should want some society."

"I do admit that, and that is why I shall make no row about the wine; I shall set it down as compensation to Lavinia. She is capable of telling me that she drank it all herself. Think of the inconceivable bad taste, in the circumstances, of that fellow making free with the house—or coming there at all! If that doesn't describe him, he is indescribable."

"His plan is to get what he can. Lavinia will have supported him for a year," said Mrs. Almond. "It's so much gained."

"She will have to support him for the rest of his life, then," cried the Doctor; "but without wine, as they say at the *tables d'hôte*."

"Catherine tells me he has set up a business, and is making a great deal of money."

The Doctor stared. "She has not told me that—and Lavinia didn't deign. Ah!" he cried, "Catherine has given me up. Not that it matters, for all that the business amounts to."

"She has not given up Mr. Townsend," said Mrs. Almond; "I saw that in the first half-minute. She has come home exactly the same."

"Exactly the same; not a grain more intelligent. She didn't notice a stick or a stone all the while we were away—not a picture nor a view, not a statue nor a cathedral."

"How could she notice? She had other things to think of; they are never for an instant out of her mind. She touches me very much."

"She would touch me if she didn't irritate me. That's the effect she has upon me now. I have tried everything upon her; I really have been quite merciless. But it is of no use whatever; she is absolutely *glued*. I have passed, in consequence, into the exasperated stage. At first I had a good deal of a certain genial curiosity about it; I wanted to see if she really would stick. But, good Lord, one's curiosity is satisfied! I see she is capable of it, and now she can let go."

"She will never let go," said Mrs. Almond.

"Take care, or you will exasperate me too. If she doesn't let go, she will be shaken off—sent tumbling into the dust. That's a nice position for my daughter. She can't see that if you are going to be pushed, you had better jump. And then she will complain of her bruises."

"She will never complain," said Mrs. Almond.

"That I shall object to even more. But the deuce will be that I can't prevent anything."

"If she is to have a fall," said Mrs. Almond, with a gentle laugh, "we must spread as many carpets as we can." And she carried out this idea by showing a great deal of motherly kindness to the girl.

Mrs. Penniman immediately wrote to Morris Townsend. The intimacy between these two was by this time consummate, but I must content myself with noting but a few of its features. Mrs. Penniman's own share in it was a singular sentiment, which might have been misinterpreted, but which in itself was not discreditable to the poor lady. It was a romantic interest in this attractive and unfortunate young man, and yet it was not such an interest as Catherine might have been jealous of. Mrs. Penniman had not a particle of jealousy of her niece. For herself, she felt as if she were Morris's mother or sister

—a mother or sister of an emotional temperament—and she had an absorbing desire to make him comfortable and happy. She had striven to do so during the year that her brother left her an open field, and her efforts had been attended with the success that has been pointed out. She had never had a child of her own, and Catherine, whom she had done her best to invest with the importance that would naturally belong to a youthful Penniman, had only partly rewarded her zeal. Catherine, as an object of affection and solicitude, had never had that picturesque charm which (as it seemed to her) would have been a natural attribute of her own progeny. Even the maternal passion in Mrs. Penniman would have been romantic and factitious, and Catherine was not constituted to inspire a romantic passion. Mrs. Penniman was as fond of her as ever, but she had grown to feel that with Catherine she lacked opportunity. Sentimentally speaking, therefore, she had (though she had not disinherited her niece) adopted Morris Townsend, who gave her opportunity in abundance. She would have been very happy to have a handsome and tyrannical son, and would have taken an extreme interest in his love affairs. This was the light in which she had come to regard Morris, who had conciliated her at first, and made his impression by his delicate and calculated deference—a sort of exhibition to which Mrs. Penniman was particularly sensitive. He had largely abated his deference afterward, for he economized his resources, but the impression was made, and the young man's very brutality came to have a sort of filial value. If Mrs. Penniman had had a son, she would probably have been afraid of him, and at this stage of our narrative she was certainly afraid of Morris Townsend. This was one of the results of his domestication in Washington Square. He took his ease with her—as, for that matter, he would certainly have done with his own mother.

28

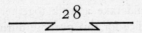

The letter was a word of warning; it informed him that the Doctor had come home more impracticable than ever. She might have reflected that Catherine would supply him with all the information he needed on this point; but we know that Mrs. Penniman's reflections were rarely just; and, moreover, she felt that it was not for her to depend on what Catherine might do. She was to do her duty, quite irrespective of Catherine. I have said that her young friend took his ease with her, and it is an illustration of the fact that he made no answer to her letter. He took note of it amply; but he lighted his cigar with it, and he waited, in tranquil confidence that he should receive another. "His state of mind really freezes my blood," Mrs. Penniman had written, alluding to her brother; and it would have seemed that upon this statement she could hardly improve. Nevertheless, she wrote again, expressing herself with the aid of a different figure. "His hatred of you burns with a lurid flame—the flame that never dies," she wrote. "But it doesn't light up the darkness of your future. If my affection could do so, all the years of your life would be an eternal sunshine. I can extract nothing from C.; she is so terribly secretive, like her father. She seems to expect to be married very soon, and has evidently made preparations in Europe—quantities of clothing, ten pairs of shoes, etc. My dear friend, you cannot set up in married life simply with a few pairs of shoes, can you? Tell me what you think of this. I am intensely anxious to see you, I have so much to say. I miss you dreadfully; the house seems so empty without you. What is the news down town? Is the business extending?—that dear little business: I think it's so brave of you! Couldn't I come to your office?—just for three minutes? I might pass for a customer—is that what you call them? I might come in to buy something—some shares or some railroad things. *Tell me what you think of this plan.* I would carry a little reticule, like a woman of the people."

In spite of the suggestion about the reticule, Morris appeared to think poorly of the plan, for he gave Mrs. Penniman no encouragement whatever to visit his office, which he had already represented to her as a place peculiarly and unnaturally difficult to find. But as she persisted in desiring an interview—up to the last, after months of intimate colloquy, she called these meetings "interviews"—he agreed that they should take a walk together, and was even kind enough to leave his office for this purpose during the hours at which business might have been supposed to be liveliest. It was no surprise to him, when they met at a street corner, in a region of empty lots and undeveloped pavements (Mrs. Penniman being attired as much as possible like a "woman of the people"), to find that, in spite of her urgency, what she chiefly had to convey to him was the assurance of her sympathy. Of such assurances, however, he had already a voluminous collection, and it would not have been worth his while to forsake a fruitful avocation merely to hear Mrs. Penniman say, for the thousandth time, that she had made his cause her own. Morris had something of his own to say. It was not an easy thing to bring out, and while he turned it over, the difficulty made him acrimonious.

"Oh yes, I know perfectly that he combines the properties of a lump of ice and red-hot coal," he observed. "Catherine had made it thoroughly clear, and you have told me so till I am sick of it. You needn't tell me again; I am perfectly satisfied. He will never give us a penny; I regard that as mathematically proved."

Mrs. Penniman at this point had an inspiration.

"Couldn't you bring a lawsuit against him?" She wondered that this simple expedient had never occurred to her before.

"I will bring a lawsuit against *you*," said Morris, "if you ask me any more such aggravating questions. A man should know when he is beaten," he added, in a moment. "I must give her up!"

Mrs. Penniman received this declaration in silence, though it made her heart beat a little. It found her by no means unprepared, for she had accustomed herself to the thought that, if Morris should decidedly not be able to get her brother's money, it would not do for him to marry Catherine without it. "It would not do," was a vague way of putting the thing; but Mrs. Penniman's natural affection completed the idea, which, though it had not as yet been so crudely expressed between them as in the form that Morris had just given it, had nevertheless been implied so often, in certain easy intervals of talk, as he sat stretching his legs in the Doctor's well-stuffed armchairs, that she had grown first to regard it with an emotion which she flattered herself was philosophic, and then to have a secret tenderness for it. The fact that she kept her tenderness secret proves, of course, that she was ashamed of it; but she managed to blink her shame by reminding herself that she was, after all, the official protector of her niece's marriage. Her logic would scarcely have passed muster with the Doctor. In the first place, Morris *must* get the money, and she would help him to it. In the second, it was plain it would never come to him, and it would be a grievous pity he should marry without it—a young man who might so easily find something better. After her brother had delivered himself, on his return from Europe, of that incisive little address that has been quoted, Morris's cause seemed so hopeless that Mrs. Penniman fixed her attention exclusively upon the latter branch of her argument. If Morris had been her son, she would certainly have sacrificed Catherine to a superior conception of his future; and to be ready to do so, as the

case stood, was therefore even a finer degree of devotion. Nevertheless, it checked her breath a little to have the sacrificial knife, as
it were, suddenly thrust into her hand.

Morris walked along a moment, and then he repeated, harshly,
"I must give her up!"

"I think I understand you," said Mrs. Penniman, gently.

"I certainly say it distinctly enough—brutally and vulgarly
enough."

He was ashamed of himself, and his shame was uncomfortable;
and as he was extremely intolerant of discomfort, he felt vicious and
cruel. He wanted to abuse somebody, and he began, cautiously—for
he was always cautious—with himself.

"Couldn't you take her down a little?" he asked.

"Take her down?"

"Prepare her—try and ease me off."

Mrs. Penniman stopped, looking at him very solemnly.

"My poor Morris, do you know how much she loves you?"

"No, I don't. I don't want to know. I have always tried to keep
from knowing. It would be too painful."

"She will suffer much," said Mrs. Penniman.

"You must console her. If you are as good a friend to me as you
pretend to be, you will manage it."

Mrs. Penniman shook her head sadly.

"You talk of my 'pretending' to like you; but I can't pretend to
hate you. I can only tell her I think very highly of you; and how will
that console her for losing you?"

"The Doctor will help you. He will be delighted at the thing being
broken off; and as he is a knowing fellow, he will invent something
to comfort her."

"He will invent a new torture," cried Mrs. Penniman. "Heaven
deliver her from her father's comfort! It will consist of his crowing
over her, and saying, 'I always told you so!'"

Morris colored a most uncomfortable red.

"If you don't console her any better than you console me, you
certainly won't be of much use. It's a damned disagreeable necessity;
I feel it extremely, and you ought to make it easy for me."

"I will be your friend for life," Mrs. Penniman declared.

"Be my friend now!" and Morris walked on.

She went with him; she was almost trembling.

"Should you like me to tell her?" she asked.

"You mustn't tell her, but you can—you can—" And he hesitated, trying to think what Mrs. Penniman could do. "You can explain to her why it is. It's because I can't bring myself to step in between her and her father—to give him the pretext he grasps at so eagerly (it's a hideous sight!) for depriving her of her rights."

Mrs. Penniman felt with remarkable promptitude the charm of this formula.

"That's so like you," she said; "it's so finely felt."

Morris gave his stick an angry swing.

"Oh damnation!" he exclaimed, perversely.

Mrs. Penniman, however, was not discouraged.

"It may turn out better than you think. Catherine is, after all, so very peculiar." And she thought she might take it upon herself to assure him that, whatever happened, the girl would be very quiet— she wouldn't make a noise. They extended their walk, and while they proceeded Mrs. Penniman took upon herself other things besides, and ended by having assumed a considerable burden; Morris being ready enough, as may be imagined, to put everything off upon her. But he was not for a single instant the dupe of her blundering alacrity; he knew that of what she promised she was competent to perform but an insignificant fraction, and the more she professed her willingness to serve him, the greater fool he thought her.

"What will you do if you don't marry her?" she ventured to inquire in the course of this conversation.

"Something brilliant," said Morris. "Shouldn't you like me to do something brilliant?"

The idea gave Mrs. Penniman exceeding pleasure.

"I shall feel sadly taken in if you don't."

"I shall have to, to make up for this. This isn't at all brilliant, you know."

Mrs. Penniman mused a little, as if there might be some way of making out that it was; but she had to give up the attempt, and, to carry off the awkwardness of failure, she risked a new inquiry.

"Do you mean—do you mean another marriage?"

Morris greeted this question with a reflection which was hardly the less impudent from being inaudible. "Surely women are more crude than men!" And then he answered, audibly,

"Never in the world!"

Mrs. Penniman felt disappointed and snubbed, and she relieved herself in a little vaguely sarcastic cry. He was certainly perverse.

"I give her up, not for another woman, but for a wider career," Morris announced.

This was very grand; but still Mrs. Penniman, who felt that she had exposed herself, was faintly rancorous.

"Do you mean never to come to see her again?" she asked, with some sharpness.

"Oh no, I shall come again; but what is the use of dragging it out? I have been four times since she came back, and it's terribly awkward work. I can't keep it up indefinitely; she oughtn't to expect that, you know. A woman should never keep a man dangling," he added, finely.

"Ah, but you must have your last parting!" urged his companion, in whose imagination the idea of last partings occupied a place inferior in dignity only to that of first meetings.

29

He came again, without managing the last parting; and again and again, without finding that Mrs. Penniman had as yet done much to pave the path of retreat with flowers. It was devilish awkward, as he said, and he felt a lively animosity for Catherine's aunt, who, as he had now quite formed the habit of saying to himself, had dragged him into the mess, and was bound in common charity to get him out of it. Mrs. Penniman, to tell the truth, had, in the seclusion of her own apartment—and, I may add, amid the suggestiveness of Catherine's, which wore in those days the appearance of that of a young lady laying out her *trousseau*—Mrs. Penniman had measured her responsibilities, and taken fright at their magnitude. The task of preparing Catherine and easing off Morris presented difficulties which increased in the execution, and even led the impulsive Lavinia to ask herself whether the modification of the young man's original project had been conceived in a happy spirit. A brilliant future, a wider career, a conscience exempt from the reproach of interference between a young lady and her natural rights —these excellent things might be too troublesomely purchased. From Catherine herself Mrs. Penniman received no assistance whatever; the poor girl was apparently without suspicion of her danger. She looked at her lover with eyes of undiminished trust, and though she had less confidence in her aunt than in a young man with whom she had exchanged so many tender vows, she gave her no handle for explaining or confessing. Mrs. Penniman, faltering and wavering, declared Catherine was very stupid, put off the great scene, as she would have called it, from day to day, and wandered about, very uncomfortably, with her unexploded bomb in her hands. Morris's own scenes were very small ones just now; but even these were beyond his strength. He made his visits as brief as possible, and, while he sat with his mistress, found terribly little to talk about. She was waiting for him, in vulgar parlance, to name the day; and so long as he was unprepared to be explicit on this point, it seemed a mockery to pretend to talk about matters more abstract. She had no airs and no arts; she never attempted to disguise her expectancy. She was waiting on his good pleasure, and would wait modestly and patiently; his hanging back at this supreme time might appear strange, but of course he must have a good reason for it. Catherine would have made a wife of the gentle, old-fashioned pattern—regarding reasons as favors and windfalls, but no more expecting one every day than she would have expected a bouquet of camellias. During the period of her engagement, however, a young lady even of the most slender pretensions counts upon more bouquets than at other times; and there was a want of perfume in the air at this moment which at last excited the girl's alarm.

"Are you sick?" she asked of Morris. "You seem so restless, and you look pale."

"I am not at all well," said Morris; and it occurred to him that, if he could only make her pity him enough, he might get off.

"I am afraid you are overworked; you oughtn't to work so much."

"I must do that." And then he added, with a sort of calculated brutality, "I don't want to owe you everything."

"Ah, how can you say that?"

"I am too proud," said Morris.

"Yes—you are too proud."

"Well, you must take me as I am," he went on; "you can never change me."

"I don't want to change you," she said, gently; "I will take you as you are." And she stood looking at him.

"You know people talk tremendously about a man's marrying a rich girl," Morris remarked. "It's excessively disagreeable."

"But I am not rich," said Catherine.

"You are rich enough to make me talked about."

"Of course you are talked about. It's an honor."

"It's an honor I could easily dispense with."

She was on the point of asking him whether it was not a compensation for this annoyance that the poor girl who had the misfortune to bring it upon him loved him so dearly and believed in him so truly; but she hesitated, thinking that this would perhaps seem an exacting speech, and while she hesitated, he suddenly left her.

The next time he came, however, she brought it out, and she told him again that he was too proud. He repeated that he couldn't change, and this time she felt the impulse to say that with a little effort he might change.

Sometimes he thought that if he could only make a quarrel with her it might help him; but the question was how to quarrel with a young woman who had such treasures of concession. "I suppose you think the effort is all on your side," he broke out. "Don't you believe that I have my own effort to make?"

"It's all yours now," she said; "my effort is finished and done with."

"Well, mine is not."

"We must bear things together," said Catherine. "That's what we ought to do."

Morris attempted a natural smile. "There are some things which we can't very well bear together—for instance, separation."

"Why do you speak of separation?"

"Ah! you don't like it; I knew you wouldn't."

"Where are you going, Morris?" she suddenly asked.

He fixed his eye on her a moment, and for a part of that moment she was afraid of it. "Will you promise not to make a scene?"

"A scene!—do I make scenes?"

"All women do!" said Morris, with the tone of large experience.

"I don't. Where are you going?"

"If I should say I was going away on business, should you think it very strange?"

She wondered a moment, gazing at him. "Yes—no. Not if you will take me with you."

"Take you with me—on business?"

"What is your business? Your business is to be with me."

"I don't earn my living with you," said Morris. "Or, rather," he cried, with a sudden inspiration, "that's just what I do—or what the world says I do!"

This ought perhaps to have been a great stroke, but it miscarried. "Where are you going?" Catherine simply repeated.

"To New Orleans—about buying some cotton."

"I am perfectly willing to go to New Orleans," Catherine said.

"Do you suppose I would take you to a nest of yellow-fever?" cried Morris. "Do you suppose I would expose you at such a time as this?"

"If there is yellow-fever, why should you go? Morris, you must not go."

"It is to make six thousand dollars," said Morris. "Do you grudge me that satisfaction?"

"We have no need of six thousand dollars. You think too much about money."

"You can afford to say that. This is a great chance; we heard of it last night." And he explained to her in what the chance consisted; and told her a long story, going over more than once several of the details, about the remarkable stroke of business which he and his partner had planned between them.

But Catherine's imagination, for reasons best known to herself, absolutely refused to be fired. "If you can go to New Orleans, I can go," she said. "Why shouldn't you catch yellow-fever quite as easily as I? I am every bit as strong as you, and not in the least afraid of any fever. When we were in Europe we were in very unhealthy places; my father used to make me take some pills. I never caught anything, and I never was nervous. What will be the use of six thousand dollars if you die of a fever? When persons are going to be married they oughtn't to think so much about business. You shouldn't think about cotton; you should think about me. You can go to New Orleans some other time—there will always be plenty of cotton. It isn't the moment to choose: we have waited too long already." She spoke more forcibly and volubly than he had ever heard her, and she held his arm in her two hands.

"You said you wouldn't make a scene," cried Morris. "I call this a scene."

"It's you that are making it. I have never asked you anything before. We have waited too long already." And it was a comfort to her to think that she had hitherto asked so little; it seemed to make her right to insist the greater now.

Morris bethought himself a little. "Very well, then; we won't talk about it any more. I will transact my business by letter." And he began to smooth his hat, as if to take leave.

"You won't go?" and she stood looking up at him.

He could not give up his idea of provoking a quarrel; it was so much the simplest way. He bent his eyes on her upturned face with the darkest frown he could achieve. "You are not discreet; you mustn't bully me."

But, as usual, she conceded everything. "No, I am not discreet; I know I am too pressing. But isn't it natural? It is only for a moment."

"In a moment you may do a great deal of harm. Try and be calmer the next time I come."

"When will you come?"

"Do you want to make conditions?" Morris asked. "I will come next Saturday."

"Come to-morrow," Catherine begged; "I want you to come to-morrow. I will be very quiet," she added; and her agitation had by this time become so great that the assurance was not unbecoming. A sudden fear had come over her; it was like the solid conjunction of a dozen disembodied doubts, and her imagination, at a single bound, had traversed an enormous distance. All her being, for the moment, was centred in the wish to keep him in the room.

Morris bent his head and kissed her forehead. "When you are quiet, you are perfection," he said; "but when you are violent, you are not in character."

It was Catherine's wish that there should be no violence about her save the beating of her heart, which she could not help; and she went on, as gently as possible, "Will you promise to come to-morrow?"

"I said Saturday!" Morris answered, smiling. He tried a frown at one moment, a smile at another; he was at his wit's end.

"Yes, Saturday too," she answered, trying to smile. "But to-morrow first." He was going to the door, and she went with him quickly. She leaned her shoulder against it; it seemed to her that she would do anything to keep him.

"If I am prevented from coming to-morrow, you will say I have deceived you," he said.

"How can you be prevented? You can come if you will."

"I am a busy man—I am not a dangler!" cried Morris, sternly.

His voice was so hard and unnatural that, with a helpless look at him, she turned away; and then he quickly laid his hand on the doorknob. He felt as if he were absolutely running away from her. But in an instant she was close to him again, and murmuring in a tone none the less penetrating for being low, "Morris, you are going to leave me."

"Yes, for a little while."

"For how long?"

"Till you are reasonable again."

"I shall never be reasonable, in that way." And she tried to keep him longer; it was almost a struggle. "Think of what I have done!" she broke out. "Morris, I have given up everything."

"You shall have everything back."

"You wouldn't say that if you didn't mean something. What is it? —what has happened?—what have I done?—what has changed you?"

"I will write to you—that is better," Morris stammered.

"Ah, you won't come back!" she cried, bursting into tears.

"Dear Catherine," he said, "don't believe that. I promise you that you shall see me again." And he managed to get away, and to close the door behind him.

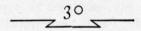

30

It was almost the last outbreak of passion of her life; at least, she never indulged in another that the world knew anything about. But this one was long and terrible; she flung herself on the sofa and gave herself up to her grief. She hardly knew what had happened; ostensibly she had only had a difference with her lover, as other girls had had before, and the thing was not only not a rupture, but she was under no obligation to regard it even as a menace. Nevertheless, she felt a wound, even if he had not dealt it; it seemed to her that a mask had suddenly fallen from his face. He had wished to get away from her; he had been angry and cruel, and said strange things, with strange looks. She was smothered and stunned; she buried her head in the cushions, sobbing and talking to herself. But at last she raised herself, with the fear that either her father or Mrs. Penniman would come in; and then she sat there, staring before her, while the room grew darker. She said to herself that perhaps he would come back to tell her he had not meant what he said; and she listened for his ring at the door, trying to believe that this was probable. A long time passed, but Morris remained absent; the shadows gathered; the evening settled down on the meagre elegance of the light, clear-colored room; the fire went out. When it had grown dark, Catherine went to the window and looked out; she stood there for half an hour, on the mere chance that he would come up the steps. At last she turned away, for she saw her father come in. He had seen her at the window looking out, and he stopped a moment at the bottom of the white steps, and gravely, with an air of exaggerated courtesy, lifted his hat to her. The gesture was so incongruous to the condition she was in, this stately tribute of respect to a poor girl despised and forsaken was so out of place, that the thing gave her a kind of horror, and she hurried away to her room. It seemed to her that she had given Morris up.

She had to show herself half an hour later, and she was sustained at table by the immensity of her desire that her father should not perceive that anything had happened. This was a great help to her afterward, and it served her (though never as much as she supposed) from the first. On this occasion Doctor Sloper was rather talkative. He told a great many stories about a wonderful poodle that he had seen at the house of an old lady whom he visited professionally. Catherine not only tried to appear to listen to the anecdotes of the poodle, but she endeavored to interest herself in them, so as not to think of her scene with Morris. That perhaps was an hallucination; he was mistaken, she was jealous; people didn't change like that from one day to another. Then she knew that she had had doubts before—strange suspicions, that were at once vague and acute—and that he had been different ever since her return from Europe: whereupon she tried again to listen to her father, who told a story so remarkably well. Afterward she went straight to her own room; it was beyond her strength to undertake to spend the evening with her aunt. All the evening, alone, she questioned herself. Her trouble was terrible; but was it a thing of her imagination, engendered by an extravagant sensibility, or did it represent a clear-cut reality, and had the worst that was possible actually come to pass? Mrs. Penniman, with a degree of tact that was as unusual as it was commendable, took the line of leaving her alone. The truth is, that her suspicions having been aroused, she indulged a desire, natural to a timid person, that the explosion should be localized. So long as the air still vibrated she kept out of the way.

She passed and repassed Catherine's door several times in the course of the evening, as if she expected to hear a plaintive moan behind it. But the room remained perfectly still; and accordingly, the last thing before retiring to her own couch, she applied for admittance. Catherine was sitting up, and had a book that she pretended to be reading. She had no wish to go to bed, for she had no expectation of sleeping. After Mrs. Penniman had left her she sat up half the night, and she offered her visitor no inducement to remain. Her aunt came stealing in very gently, and approached her with great solemnity.

"I am afraid you are in trouble, my dear. Can I do anything to help you?"

"I am not in any trouble whatever, and do not need any help," said Catherine, fibbing roundly, and proving thereby that not only our faults, but our most involuntary misfortunes, tend to corrupt our morals.

"Has nothing happened to you?"

"Nothing whatever."

"Are you very sure, dear?"

"Perfectly sure."

"And can I really do nothing for you?"

"Nothing, aunt, but kindly leave me alone," said Catherine.

Mrs. Penniman, though she had been afraid of too warm a welcome before, was now disappointed at so cold a one; and in relating afterward, as she did to many persons, and with considerable variations of detail, the history of the termination of her niece's engagement, she was usually careful to mention that the young lady, on a certain occasion, had "hustled" her out of the room It was characteristic of Mrs. Penniman that she related this fact, not in the least out of malignity to Catherine, whom she very sufficiently pitied, but simply from a natural disposition to embellish any subject that she touched.

Catherine, as I have said, sat up half the night, as if she still expected to hear Morris Townsend ring at the door. On the morrow this expectation was less unreasonable; but it was not gratified by the reappearance of the young man. Neither had he written; there was not a word of explanation or reassurance. Fortunately for Catherine, she could take refuge from her excitement, which had now become intense, in her determination that her father should see nothing of it. How well she deceived her father we shall have occasion to learn; but her innocent arts were of little avail before a person of the rare perspicacity of Mrs. Penniman. This lady easily saw that she was agitated, and if there was any agitation going forward, Mrs. Penniman was not a person to forfeit her natural share in it. She returned to the charge the next evening, and requested her niece to confide in her—to unburden her heart. Perhaps she should be able to explain certain things that now seemed dark, and that she knew more about than Catherine supposed. If Catherine had been frigid the night before, to-day she was haughty.

"You are completely mistaken, and I have not the least idea what you mean. I don't know what you are trying to fasten on me, and I have never had less need of any one's explanations in my life."

In this way the girl delivered herself, and from hour to hour kept her aunt at bay. From hour to hour Mrs. Penniman's curiosity grew. She would have given her little finger to know what Morris had said and done, what tone he had taken, what pretext he had found. She wrote to him, naturally, to request an interview; but she received, as naturally, no answer to her petition. Morris was not in a writing mood; for Catherine had addressed him two short notes which met with no acknowledgment. These notes were so brief that I may give them entire. "Won't you give me some sign that you didn't mean to be so cruel as you seemed on Tuesday?"—that was the first; the other was a little longer. "If I was unreasonable or suspicious on Tuesday—if I annoyed you or troubled you in any way—I beg your forgiveness, and I promise never again to be so foolish. I am punished enough, and I don't understand. Dear Morris, you are killing me!" These notes were despatched on the Friday and Saturday; but Saturday and Sunday passed without bringing the poor girl the satisfaction she desired. Her punishment accumulated; she continued to bear it, however, with a good deal of superficial fortitude. On Saturday morning, the Doctor, who had been watching in silence, spoke to his sister Lavinia.

"The thing has happened—the scoundrel has backed out!"

"Never!" cried Mrs. Penniman, who had bethought herself what she should say to Catherine, but was not provided with a line of defence against her brother, so that indignant negation was the only weapon in her hands.

"He has begged for a reprieve, then, if you like that better!"

"It seems to make you very happy that your daughter's affections have been trifled with."

"It does," said the Doctor; "for I had foretold it! It's a great pleasure to be in the right."

"Your pleasures make one shudder!" his sister exclaimed.

Catherine went rigidly through her usual occupations; that is, up to the point of going with her aunt to church on Sunday morning. She generally went to afternoon service as well; but on this occasion her courage faltered, and she begged of Mrs. Penniman to go without her.

"I am sure you have a secret," said Mrs. Penniman, with great significance, looking at her rather grimly.

"If I have, I shall keep it!" Catherine answered, turning away.

Mrs. Penniman started for church; but before she had arrived, she stopped and turned back, and before twenty minutes had elapsed she re-entered the house, looked into the empty parlors, and then went up-stairs and knocked at Catherine's door. She got no answer; Catherine was not in her room, and Mrs. Penniman presently ascertained that she was not in the house. "She has gone to him! she has fled!" Lavinia cried, clasping her hands with admiration and envy. But she soon perceived that Catherine had taken nothing with her—all her personal property in her room was intact—and then she jumped at the hypothesis that the girl had gone forth, not in tenderness, but in resentment. "She has followed him to his own door! she has burst upon him in his own apartment!" It was in these terms that Mrs. Penniman depicted to herself her niece's errand, which, viewed in this light, gratified her sense of the picturesque only a shade less strongly than the idea of a clandestine marriage. To visit one's lover, with tears and reproaches, at his own residence, was an image so agreeable to Mrs. Penniman's mind that she felt a sort of æsthetic disappointment at its lacking, in this case, the harmonious accompaniments of darkness and storm. A quiet Sunday afternoon appeared an inadequate setting for it; and, indeed, Mrs. Penniman was quite out of humor with the conditions of the time, which passed very slowly as she sat in the front parlor, in her bonnet and her cashmere shawl, awaiting Catherine's return.

This event at last took place. She saw her—at the window— mount the steps, and she went to await her in the hall, where she pounced upon her as soon as she had entered the house, and drew her into the parlor, closing the door with solemnity. Catherine was flushed, and her eye was bright. Mrs. Penniman hardly knew what to think.

"May I venture to ask where you have been?" she demanded.

"I have been to take a walk," said Catherine. "I thought you had gone to church."

"I did go to church; but the service was shorter than usual. And pray where did you walk?"

"I don't know!" said Catherine.

"Your ignorance is most extraordinary! Dear Catherine, you can trust me."

"What am I to trust you with?"

"With your secret—your sorrow."

"I have no sorrow!" said Catherine, fiercely.

"My poor child," Mrs. Penniman insisted, "you can't deceive me. I know everything. I have been requested to—a—to converse with you."

"I don't want to converse!"

"It will relieve you. Don't you know Shakespeare's lines?—'The grief that does not speak!' My dear girl, it is better as it is!"

"What is better?" Catherine asked.

She was really too perverse. A certain amount of perversity was to be allowed for in a young lady whose lover had thrown her over; but not such an amount as would prove inconvenient to his apologists. "That you should be reasonable," said Mrs. Penniman, with some sternness; "that you should take counsel of worldly prudence, and submit to practical considerations; that you should agree to—a—separate."

Catherine had been ice up to this moment, but at this word she flamed up. "Separate? What do you know about our separating?"

Mrs. Penniman shook her head with a sadness in which there was almost a sense of injury. "Your pride is my pride, and your susceptibilities are mine. I see your side perfectly, but I also—" and she smiled with melancholy suggestiveness—"I also see the situation as a whole!"

This suggestiveness was lost upon Catherine, who repeated her violent inquiry. "Why do you talk about separation; what do you know about it?"

"We must study resignation," said Mrs. Penniman, hesitating, but sententious at a venture.

"Resignation to what?"

"To a change of—of our plans."

"My plans have not changed!" said Catherine, with a little laugh.

"Ah, but Mr. Townsend's have," her aunt answered, very gently. "What do you mean?"

There was an imperious brevity in the tone of this inquiry, against which Mrs. Penniman felt bound to protest; the information with which she had undertaken to supply her niece was after all a favor. She had tried sharpness, and she had tried sternness; but neither would do; she was shocked at the girl's obstinacy. "Ah well," she said, "if he hasn't told you! . . ." and she turned away.

Catherine watched her a moment in silence; then she hurried after her, stopping her before she reached the door. "Told me what? What do you mean? What are you hinting at and threatening me with?"

"Isn't it broken off?" asked Mrs. Penniman.

"My engagement? Not in the least!"

"I beg your pardon in that case. I have spoken too soon!"

"Too soon? Soon or late," Catherine broke out, "you speak foolishly and cruelly!"

"What has happened between you then?" asked her aunt, struck by the sincerity of this cry; "for something certainly has happened."

"Nothing has happened but that I love him more and more!"

Mrs. Penniman was silent an instant. "I suppose that's the reason you went to see him this afternoon."

Catherine flushed as if she had been struck. "Yes, I did go to see him! But that's my own business."

"Very well, then; we won't talk about it." And Mrs. Penniman moved toward the door again; but she was stopped by a sudden imploring cry from the girl.

"Aunt Lavinia, *where* has he gone?"

"Ah, you admit then that he has gone away! Didn't they know at his house?"

"They said he had left town. I asked no more questions; I was ashamed," said Catherine, simply enough.

"You needn't have taken so compromising a step if you had had a little more confidence in me," Mrs. Penniman observed, with a good deal of grandeur.

"Is it to New Orleans?" Catherine went on, irrelevantly.

It was the first time Mrs. Penniman had heard of New Orleans in this connection; but she was averse to letting Catherine know that she was in the dark. She attempted to strike an illumination from the instructions she had received from Morris. "My dear

Catherine," she said, "when a separation has been agreed upon, the farther he goes away the better."

"Agreed upon? Has he agreed upon it with you?" A consummate sense of her aunt's meddlesome folly had come over her during the last five minutes, and she was sickened at the thought that Mrs. Penniman had been let loose, as it were, upon her happiness.

"He certainly has sometimes advised with me," said Mrs. Penniman.

"Is it you, then, that has changed him and made him so unnatural?" Catherine cried. "Is it you that have worked on him and taken him from me? He doesn't belong to you, and I don't see how you have anything to do with what is between us! Is it you that have made this plot, and told him to leave me? How could you be so wicked, so cruel? What have I ever done to you? Why can't you leave me alone? I was afraid you would spoil everything; for you *do* spoil everything you touch! I was afraid of you all the time we were abroad; I had no rest when I thought that you were always talking to him." Catherine went on with growing vehemence, pouring out, in her bitterness and in the clairvoyance of her passion (which suddenly, jumping all processes, made her judge her aunt finally and without appeal), the uneasiness which had lain for so many months upon her heart.

Mrs. Penniman was scared and bewildered; she saw no prospect of introducing her little account of the purity of Morris's motives. "You are a most ungrateful girl!" she cried. "Do you scold me for talking with him? I'm sure we never talked of anything but you!"

"Yes; and that was the way you worried him; you made him tired of my very name! I wish you had never spoken of me to him; I never asked your help!"

"I am sure if it hadn't been for me he would never have come to the house, and you would never have known that he thought of you," Mrs. Penniman rejoined, with a good deal of justice.

"I wish he never had come to the house, and that I never had known it! That's better than this," said poor Catherine.

"You are a very ungrateful girl," Aunt Lavinia repeated.

Catherine's outbreak of anger and the sense of wrong gave her, while they lasted, the satisfaction that comes from all assertion of force; they hurried her along, and there is always a sort of pleasure in cleaving the air. But at bottom she hated to be violent, and she was conscious of no aptitude for organized resentment. She calmed herself with a great effort, but with great rapidity, and walked about the room a few moments, trying to say to herself that her aunt had meant everything for the best. She did not succeed in saying it with much conviction, but after a little she was able to speak quietly enough.

"I am not ungrateful, but I am very unhappy. It's hard to be grateful for that," she said. "Will you please tell me where he is?"

"I haven't the least idea; I am not in secret correspondence with him!" And Mrs. Penniman wished, indeed, that she were, so that she might let him know how Catherine abused her, after all she had done.

"Was it a plan of his, then, to break off—?" By this time Catherine had become completely quiet.

Mrs. Penniman began again to have a glimpse of her chance for explaining. "He shrunk—he shrunk," she said; "he lacked courage, but it was the courage to injure you! He couldn't bear to bring down on you your father's curse."

Catherine listened to this with her eyes fixed upon her aunt, and continued to gaze at her for some time afterward. "Did he tell you to say that?"

"He told me to say many things—all so delicate, so discriminating; and he told me to tell you he hoped you wouldn't despise him."

"I don't," said Catherine; and then she added, "And will he stay away forever?"

"Oh, forever is a long time. Your father, perhaps, won't live forever."

"Perhaps not."

"I am sure you appreciate—you understand—even though your heart bleeds," said Mrs. Penniman. "You doubtless think him too scrupulous. So do I, but I respect his scruples. What he asks of you is that you should do the same."

Catherine was still gazing at her aunt, but she spoke at last as if she had not heard or not understood her. "It has been a regular plan, then. He has broken it off deliberately; he has given me up."

"For the present, dear Catherine; he has put it off, only."

"He has left me alone," Catherine went on.

"Haven't you *me*?" asked Mrs. Penniman, with some solemnity.

Catherine shook her head slowly. "I don't believe it!" and she left the room.

31

Though she had forced herself to be calm, she preferred practising this virtue in private, and she forbore to show herself at tea—a repast which, on Sundays, at six o'clock, took the place of dinner. Doctor Sloper and his sister sat face to face, but Mrs. Penniman never met her brother's eye. Late in the evening she went with him, but without Catherine, to their sister Almond's, where, between the two ladies, Catherine's unhappy situation was discussed with a frankness that was conditioned by a good deal of mysterious reticence on Mrs. Penniman's part.

"I am delighted he is not to marry her," said Mrs. Almond, "but he ought to be horsewhipped all the same."

Mrs. Penniman, who was shocked at her sister's coarseness, replied that he had been actuated by the noblest of motives—the desire not to impoverish Catherine.

"I am very happy that Catherine is not to be impoverished—but I hope he may never have a penny too much! And what does the poor girl say to *you*?" Mrs. Almond asked.

"She says I have a genius for consolation," said Mrs. Penniman.

This was the account of the matter that she gave to her sister, and it was perhaps with the consciousness of genius that, on her return that evening to Washington Square, she again presented herself for admittance at Catherine's door. Catherine came and opened it; she was apparently very quiet.

"I only want to give you a little word of advice," she said. "If your father asks you, say that everything is going on."

Catherine stood there, with her hand on the knob, looking at her aunt, but not asking her to come in. "Do you think he will ask me?"

"I am sure he will. He asked me just now, on our way home from your aunt Elizabeth's. I explained the whole thing to your aunt Elizabeth. I said to your father I knew nothing about it."

"Do you think he will ask me, when he sees—when he sees—?" But here Catherine stopped.

"The more he sees, the more disagreeable he will be," said her aunt.

"He shall see as little as possible!" Catherine declared.

"Tell him you are to be married."

"So I am," said Catherine, softly; and she closed the door upon her aunt.

She could not have said this two days later—for instance, on Tuesday, when she at last received a letter from Morris Townsend. It was an epistle of considerable length, measuring five large square pages, and written at Philadelphia. It was an explanatory document, and it explained a great many things, chief among which were the considerations that had led the writer to take advantage of an urgent "professional" absence to try and banish from his mind the image of one whose path he had crossed only to scatter it with ruins. He ventured to expect but partial success in this attempt, but he could promise her that, whatever his failure, he would never again interpose between her generous heart and her brilliant prospects and filial duties. He closed with an intimation that his professional pursuits might compel him to travel for some months, and with the hope that when they should each have accommodated themselves to what was sternly involved in their respective positions—even should this result not be reached for years—they should meet as friends, as fellow-sufferers, as innocent but philosophic victims of a great social law. That her life should be peaceful and happy was the dearest wish of him who ventured still to subscribe himself her most obedient servant. The letter was beautifully written, and Catherine, who kept it for many years after this, was able, when her sense of the bitterness of its meaning and the hollowness of its tone had grown less acute, to admire its grace of expression. At present, for a long time after she received it, all she had to help her was the determination, daily more rigid, to make no appeal to the compassion of her father.

He suffered a week to elapse, and then one day, in the morning, at an hour at which she rarely saw him, he strolled into the back parlor. He had watched his time, and he found her alone. She was sitting with some work, and he came and stood in front of her. He was going out; he had on his hat, and was drawing on his gloves.

"It doesn't seem to me that you are treating me just now with all the consideration I deserve," he said in a moment.

"I don't know what I have done," Catherine answered, with her eyes on her work.

"You have apparently quite banished from your mind the request I made you at Liverpool before we sailed—the request that you would notify me in advance before leaving my house."

"I have not left your house," said Catherine.

"But you intend to leave it, and, by what you gave me to understand, your departure must be impending. In fact, though you are still here in body, you are already absent in spirit. Your mind has taken up its residence with your prospective husband, and you might quite as well be lodged under the conjugal roof for all the benefit we get from your society."

"I will try and be more cheerful," said Catherine.

"You certainly ought to be cheerful; you ask a great deal if you are not. To the pleasure of marrying a charming young man you add that of having your own way; you strike me as a very lucky young lady!"

Catherine got up; she was suffocating. But she folded her work deliberately and correctly, bending her burning face upon it. Her father stood where he had planted himself; she hoped he would go, but he smoothed and buttoned his gloves, and then he rested his hands upon his hips.

"It would be a convenience to me to know when I may expect to have an empty house," he went on. "When you go, your aunt marches."

She looked at him at last, with a long, silent gaze, which, in spite of her pride and her resolution, uttered part of the appeal she had tried not to make. Her father's cold gray eye sounded her own, and he insisted on his point.

"Is it to-morrow? Is it next week, or the week after?"

"I shall not go away!" said Catherine.

The Doctor raised his eyebrows. "Has he backed out?"

"I have broken off my engagement."

"Broken it off?"

"I have asked him to leave New York, and he has gone away for a long time."

The Doctor was both puzzled and disappointed, but he solved his perplexity by saying to himself that his daughter simply misrepresented—justifiably, if one would, but nevertheless, misrepresented—the facts; and he eased off his disappointment, which was that of a man losing a chance for a little triumph that he had rather counted on, by a few words that he uttered aloud.

"How does he take his dismissal?"

"I don't know!" said Catherine, less ingeniously than she had hitherto spoken.

"You mean you don't care? You are rather cruel, after encouraging him and playing with him for so long!"

The Doctor had his revenge, after all.

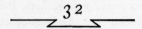

Our story has hitherto moved with very short steps, but as it approaches its termination it must take a long stride. As time went on, it might have appeared to the Doctor that his daughter's account of her rupture with Morris Townsend, mere bravado as he had deemed it, was in some degree justified by the sequel. Morris remained as rigidly and unremittingly absent as if he had died of a broken heart, and Catherine had apparently buried the memory of this fruitless episode as deep as if it had terminated by her own choice. We know that she had been deeply and incurably wounded, but the Doctor had no means of knowing it. He was certainly curious about it, and would have given a good deal to discover the exact truth; but it was his punishment that he never knew—his punishment, I mean, for the abuse of sarcasm in his relations with his daughter. There was a good deal of effective sarcasm in her keeping him in the dark, and the rest of the world conspired with her, in this sense, to be sarcastic. Mrs. Penniman told him nothing, partly because he never questioned her —he made too light of Mrs. Penniman for that—and partly because she flattered herself that a tormenting reserve, and a serene profession of ignorance, would avenge her for his theory that she had meddled in the matter. He went two or three times to see Mrs. Montgomery, but Mrs. Montgomery had nothing to impart. She simply knew that her brother's engagement was broken off; and now that Miss Sloper was out of danger, she preferred not to bear witness in any way against Morris. She had done so before—however unwillingly—because she was sorry for Miss Sloper; but she was not sorry for Miss Sloper now—not at all sorry. Morris had told her nothing about his relations with Miss Sloper at the time, and he had told her nothing since. He was always away, and he very seldom wrote to her; she believed he had gone to California. Mrs. Almond had, in her sister's phrase, "taken up" Catherine violently since the recent catastrophe; but, though the girl was very grateful to her for her kindness, she revealed no secrets, and the good lady could give the Doctor no satisfaction. Even, however, had she been able to narrate to him the private history of his daughter's unhappy love affair, it would have given her a certain comfort to leave him in ignorance; for Mrs. Almond was at this time not altogether in sympathy with her brother. She had guessed for herself that Catherine had been cruelly jilted—she knew nothing from Mrs. Penniman, for Mrs. Penniman had not ventured to lay the famous explanation of Morris's motives before Mrs. Almond, though she had thought it good enough for Catherine—and she pronounced her brother too consistently indifferent to what the poor creature must have suffered and must still be suffering. Doctor Sloper had his theory, and he rarely altered his theories. The marriage would have been an abominable one, and the girl had had a blessed escape. She was not to be pitied for that, and to pretend to condole with her would have been to make concessions to the idea that she had ever had a right to think of Morris.

"I put my foot on this idea from the first, and I keep it there now," said the Doctor. "I don't see anything cruel in that; one can't keep it there too long." To this Mrs. Almond more than once replied that, if Catherine had got rid of her incongruous lover, she deserved the credit of it, and that to bring herself to her father's enlightened view of the matter must have cost her an effort that he was bound to appreciate.

"I am by no means sure she has got rid of him," the Doctor said. "There is not the smallest probability that, after having been as obstinate as a mule for two years, she suddenly became amenable to reason. It is infinitely more probable that he got rid of her."

"All the more reason you should be gentle with her."

"I *am* gentle with her. But I can't do the pathetic; I can't pump up tears, to look graceful, over the most fortunate thing that ever happened to her."

"You have no sympathy," said Mrs. Almond; "that was never your strong point. You have only to look at her to see that, right or wrong, and whether the rupture came from herself or from him, her poor little heart is grievously bruised."

"Handling bruises, and even dropping tears on them, doesn't make them any better! My business is to see she gets no more knocks, and that I shall carefully attend to. But I don't at all recognize your description of Catherine. She doesn't strike me in the least as a young woman going about in search of a moral poultice. In fact, she seems to me much better than while the fellow was hanging about. She is perfectly comfortable and blooming; she eats and sleeps, takes her usual exercise, and overloads herself, as usual, with finery. She is always knitting some purse or embroidering some handkerchief, and it seems to me she turns these articles out about as fast as ever. She hasn't much to say; but when had she anything to say? She had her little dance, and now she is sitting down to rest. I suspect that, on the whole, she enjoys it."

"She enjoys it as people enjoy getting rid of a leg that has been crushed. The state of mind after amputation is doubtless one of comparative repose."

"If your leg is a metaphor for young Townsend, I can assure you he has never been crushed. Crushed? Not he! He is alive and perfectly intact; and that's why I am not satisfied."

"Should you have liked to kill him?" asked Mrs. Almond.

"Yes, very much. I think it is quite possible that it is all a blind."

"A blind?"

"An arrangement between them. *Il fait le mort*, as they say in France; but he is looking out of the corner of his eye. You can depend upon it, he has not burnt his ships; he has kept one to come back in. When I am dead, he will set sail again, and then she will marry him."

"It is interesting to know that you accuse your only daughter of being the vilest of hypocrites," said Mrs. Almond.

"I don't see what difference her being my only daughter makes. It is better to accuse one than a dozen. But I don't accuse any one. There is not the smallest hypocrisy about Catherine, and I deny that she even pretends to be miserable."

The Doctor's idea that the thing was a "blind" had its intermissions and revivals; but it may be said, on the whole, to have increased as he grew older; together with his impressions of Catherine's blooming and comfortable condition. Naturally, if he had not found grounds for viewing her as a lovelorn maiden during the year or two that followed her great trouble, he found none at a time when she had completely recovered her self-possession. He was obliged to recognize the fact that, if the two young people were waiting for him to get out of the way, they were at least waiting very patiently. He had heard from time to time that Morris was in New York; but he never remained there long, and, to the best of the Doctor's belief, had no communication with Catherine. He was sure they never met, and he had reason to suspect that Morris never wrote to her. After the letter that has been mentioned, she heard from him twice again, at con-

siderable intervals; but on none of these occasions did she write herself. On the other hand, as the Doctor observed, she averted herself
rigidly from the idea of marrying other people. Her opportunities for
doing so were not numerous, but they occurred often enough to test
her disposition. She refused a widower, a man with a genial temperament, a handsome fortune, and three little girls (he had heard that
she was very fond of children, and he pointed to his own with some
confidence); and she turned a deaf ear to the solicitations of a clever
young lawyer, who, with the prospect of a great practice, and the
reputation of a most agreeable man, had had the shrewdness, when
he came to look about him for a wife, to believe that she would suit
him better than several younger and prettier girls. Mr. Macalister,
the widower, had desired to make a marriage of reason, and had
chosen Catherine for what he supposed to be her latent matronly
qualities; but John Ludlow, who was a year the girl's junior, and
spoken of always as a young man who might have his "pick," was
seriously in love with her. Catherine, however, would never look at
him; she made it plain to him that she thought he came to see her too
often. He afterward consoled himself, and married a very different
person, little Miss Sturtevant, whose attractions were obvious to the
dullest comprehension. Catherine, at the time of these events, had
left her thirtieth year well behind her, and had quite taken her place
as an old maid. Her father would have preferred she should marry,
and he once told her that he hoped she would not be too fastidious.
"I should like to see you an honest man's wife before I die," he said.
This was after John Ludlow had been compelled to give it up, though
the Doctor had advised him to persevere. The Doctor exercised no
further pressure, and had the credit of not "worrying" at all over his
daughter's singleness; in fact, he worried rather more than appeared,
and there were considerable periods during which he felt sure that
Morris Townsend was hidden behind some door. "If he is not, why
doesn't she marry?" he asked himself. "Limited as her intelligence
may be, she must understand perfectly well that she is made to do
the usual thing." Catherine, however, became an admirable old maid.
She formed habits, regulated her days upon a system of her own,
interested herself in charitable institutions, asylums, hospitals, and
aid societies; and went generally, with an even and noiseless step,
about the rigid business of her life. This life had, however, a secret
history as well as a public one—if I may talk of the public history
of a mature and diffident spinster for whom publicity had always a

combination of terrors. From her own point of view the great facts
of her career were that Morris Townsend had trifled with her affection, and that her father had broken its spring. Nothing could ever
alter these facts; they were always there, like her name, her age,
her plain face. Nothing could ever undo the wrong or cure the pain
that Morris had inflicted on her, and nothing could ever make her
feel toward her father as she felt in her younger years. There was
something dead in her life, and her duty was to try and fill the void.
Catherine recognized this duty to the utmost; she had a great disapproval of brooding and moping. She had, of course, no faculty for
quenching memory in dissipation; but she mingled freely in the
usual gayeties of the town, and she became at last an inevitable figure at all respectable entertainments. She was greatly liked, and as
time went on she grew to be a sort of kindly maiden-aunt to the
younger portion of society. Young girls were apt to confide to her
their love affairs (which they never did to Mrs. Penniman), and
young men to be fond of her without knowing why. She developed a
few harmless eccentricities; her habits, once formed, were rather
stiffly maintained; her opinions, on all moral and social matters,
were extremely conservative; and before she was forty she was regarded as an old-fashioned person, and an authority on customs that
had passed away. Mrs. Penniman, in comparison, was quite a girlish
figure; she grew younger as she advanced in life. She lost none of her
relish for beauty and mystery, but she had little opportunity to
exercise it. With Catherine's later wooers she failed to establish relations as intimate as those which had given her so many interesting
hours in the society of Morris Townsend. These gentlemen had an
indefinable mistrust of her good offices, and they never talked to her
about Catherine's charms. Her ringlets, her buckles and bangles
glistened more brightly with each succeeding year, and she remained
quite the same officious and imaginative Mrs. Penniman, and the
odd mixture of impetuosity and circumspection, that we have hitherto
known. As regards one point, however, her circumspection prevailed,
and she must be given due credit for it. For upward of seventeen
years she never mentioned Morris Townsend's name to her niece.
Catherine was grateful to her, but this consistent silence, so little in
accord with her aunt's character, gave her a certain alarm, and she
could never wholly rid herself of a suspicion that Mrs. Penniman
sometimes had news of him.

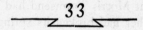

Little by little Doctor Sloper had retired from his profession; he visited only those patients in whose symptoms he recognized a certain originality. He went again to Europe, and remained two years; Catherine went with him, and on this occasion Mrs. Penniman was of the party. Europe apparently had few surprises for Mrs. Penniman, who frequently remarked, in the most romantic sites, "You know I am very familiar with all this." It should be added that such remarks were usually not addressed to her brother, or yet to her niece, but to fellow-tourists who happened to be at hand, or even to the cicerone or the goatherd in the foreground.

One day, after his return from Europe, the Doctor said something to his daughter that made her start—it seemed to come from so far out of the past.

"I should like you to promise me something before I die."

"Why do you talk about your dying?" she asked.

"Because I am sixty-eight years old."

"I hope you will live a long time," said Catherine.

"I hope I shall! But some day I shall take a bad cold, and then it will not matter much what any one hopes. That will be the manner of my exit, and when it takes place, remember I told you so. Promise me not to marry Morris Townsend after I am gone."

This was what made Catherine start, as I have said; but her start was a silent one, and for some moments she said nothing. "Why do you speak of him?" she asked at last.

"You challenge everything I say. I speak of him because he's a topic, like any other. He's to be seen, like any one else, and he is still looking for a wife—having had one and got rid of her, I don't know by what means. He has lately been in New York, and at your cousin Marian's house; your aunt Elizabeth saw him there."

"They neither of them told me," said Catherine.

"That's their merit; it's not yours. He has grown fat and bald, and he has not made his fortune. But I can't trust those facts alone to steel your heart against him, and that's why I ask you to promise."

"Fat and bald"; these words presented a strange image to Catherine's mind, out of which the memory of the most beautiful young man in the world had never faded. "I don't think you understand," she said. "I very seldom think of Mr. Townsend."

"It will be very easy for you to go on, then. Promise me, after my death, to do the same."

Again, for some moments, Catherine was silent; her father's request deeply amazed her; it opened an old wound, and made it ache afresh. "I don't think I can promise that," she answered.

"It would be a great satisfaction," said her father.

"You don't understand. I can't promise that."

The Doctor was silent a minute. "I ask you for a particular reason. I am altering my will."

This reason failed to strike Catherine; and indeed she scarcely understood it. All her feelings were merged in the sense that he was trying to treat her as he had treated her years before. She had suffered from it then; and now all her experience, all her acquired tranquillity and rigidity protested. She had been so humble in her youth that she could now afford to have a little pride, and there was something in this request, and in her father's thinking himself so free to make it, that seemed an injury to her dignity. Poor Catherine's dignity was not aggressive; it never sat in state; but if you pushed far enough you could find it. Her father had pushed very far.

"I can't promise," she simply repeated.

"You are very obstinate," said the Doctor.

"I don't think you understand."

"Please explain, then."

"I can't explain," said Catherine; "and I can't promise."

"Upon my word," her father exclaimed, "I had no idea how obstinate you are!"

She knew herself that she was obstinate, and it gave her a certain joy. She was now a middle-aged woman.

About a year after this, the accident that the Doctor had spoken of occurred: he took a violent cold. Driving out to Bloomingdale one April day to see a patient of unsound mind, who was confined in a private asylum for the insane, and whose family greatly desired a medical opinion from an eminent source, he was caught in a spring shower, and being in a buggy, without a hood, he found himself soaked to the skin. He came home with an ominous chill, and on the morrow he was seriously ill. "It is congestion of the lungs," he said to Catherine; "I shall need very good nursing. It will make no difference, for I shall not recover; but I wish everything to be done, to the smallest detail, as if I should. I hate an ill-conducted sick-room, and you will be so good as to nurse me, on the hypothesis that I shall get well." He told her which of his fellow-physicians to send for, and gave her a multitude of minute directions; it was quite on the optimistic hypothesis that she nursed him. But he had never been wrong in his life, and he was not wrong now. He was touching his seventieth year, and though he had a very well-tempered constitution, his hold upon life had lost its firmness. He died after three weeks' illness, during which Mrs. Penniman, as well as his daughter, had been assiduous at his bedside.

On his will being opened, after a decent interval, it was found to consist of two portions. The first of these dated from ten years back, and consisted of a series of dispositions by which he left the great mass of his property to his daughter, with becoming legacies to his two sisters. The second was a codicil, of recent origin, maintaining the annuities to Mrs. Penniman and Mrs. Almond, but reducing Catherine's share to a fifth of what he had first bequeathed her. "She is amply provided for from her mother's side," the document ran, "never having spent more than a fraction of her income from this source; so that her fortune is already more than sufficient to attract those unscrupulous adventurers whom she has given me reason to believe that she persists in regarding as an interesting class." The large remainder of his property, therefore, Doctor Sloper had divided into seven unequal parts, which he left, as endowments, to as many different hospitals and schools of medicine in various cities of the Union.

To Mrs. Penniman it seemed monstrous that a man should play such tricks with other people's money; for after his death, of course, as she said, it was other people's. "Of course, you will immediately break the will," she remarked to Catherine.

"Oh no," Catherine answered, "I like it very much. Only I wish it had been expressed a little differently!"

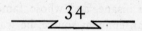

34

It was her habit to remain in town very late in the summer; she preferred the house in Washington Square to any other habitation whatever, and it was under protest that she used to go to the seaside for the month of August. At the sea she spent her month at an hotel. The year that her father died she intermitted this custom altogether, not thinking it consistent with deep mourning; and the year after that she put off her departure till so late that the middle of August found her still in the heated solitude of Washington Square. Mrs. Penniman, who was fond of a change, was usually eager for a visit to the country; but this year she appeared quite content with such rural impressions as she could gather at the parlor-window from the ailanthus-trees behind the wooden paling. The peculiar fragrance of this vegetation used to diffuse itself in the evening air, and Mrs. Penniman, on the warm nights of July, often sat at the open window and inhaled it. This was a happy moment for Mrs. Penniman; after the death of her brother she felt more free to obey her impulses. A vague oppression had disappeared from her life, and she enjoyed a sense of freedom of which she had not been conscious since the memorable time, so long ago, when the Doctor went abroad with Catherine and left her at home to entertain Morris Townsend. The year that had elapsed since her brother's death reminded her of that happy time, because, although Catherine, in growing older, had become a person to be reckoned with, yet her society was a very different thing, as Mrs. Penniman said, from that of a tank of cold water. The elder lady hardly knew what use to make of this larger margin of her life; she sat and looked at it very much as she had often sat, with her poised needle in her hand, before her tapestry-frame. She had a confident hope, however, that her rich impulses, her talent for embroidery, would still find their application, and this confidence was justified before many months had elapsed.

Catherine continued to live in her father's house, in spite of its being represented to her that a maiden lady of quiet habits might find a more convenient abode in one of the smaller dwellings, with brown stone fronts, which had at this time begun to adorn the transverse thoroughfares in the upper part of the town. She liked the earlier structure—it had begun by this time to be called an "old" house—and proposed to herself to end her days in it. If it was too large for a pair of unpretending gentlewomen, this was better than the opposite fault; for Catherine had no desire to find herself in closer quarters with her aunt. She expected to spend the rest of her life in Washington Square, and to enjoy Mrs. Penniman's society for the whole of this period; as she had a conviction that, long as she might live, her aunt would live at least as long, and always retain her brilliancy and activity. Mrs. Penniman suggested to her the idea of a rich vitality.

On one of those warm evenings in July of which mention has been made, the two ladies sat together at an open window, looking out on the quiet Square. It was too hot for lighted lamps, for reading, or for work; it might have appeared too hot even for conversation, Mrs. Penniman having long been speechless. She sat forward in the window, half on the balcony, humming a little song. Catherine was within the room, in a low rocking-chair, dressed in white, and slowly using a large palmetto fan. It was in this way, at this season, that the aunt and niece, after they had had tea, habitually spent their evenings.

"Catherine," said Mrs. Penniman at last, "I am going to say something that will surprise you."

"Pray do," Catherine answered; "I like surprises. And it is so quiet now."

"Well, then, I have seen Morris Townsend."

If Catherine was surprised, she checked the expression of it; she gave neither a start nor an exclamation. She remained, indeed, for some moments intensely still, and this may very well have been a symptom of emotion. "I hope he was well," she said at last.

"I don't know; he is a great deal changed. He would like very much to see you."

"I would rather not see him," said Catherine, quickly.

"I was afraid you would say that. But you don't seem surprised!"

"I am—very much."

"I met him at Marian's," said Mrs. Penniman. "He goes to Marian's, and they are so afraid you will meet him there. It's my belief that that's why he goes. He wants so much to see you." Catherine made no response to this, and Mrs. Penniman went on. "I didn't know him at first, he is so remarkably changed; but he knew me in a minute. He says I am not in the least changed. You know how polite he always was. He was coming away when I came, and we walked a little distance together. He is still very handsome, only of course he looks older, and he is not so—so animated as he used to be. There was a touch of sadness about him; but there was a touch of sadness about him before, especially when he went away. I am afraid he has not been very successful—that he has never got thoroughly established. I don't suppose he is sufficiently plodding, and that, after all, is what succeeds in this world." Mrs. Penniman had not mentioned Morris Townsend's name to her niece for upwards of the fifth of a century; but now that she had broken the spell, she seemed to wish to make up for lost time, as if there had been a sort of exhilaration in hearing herself talk to him. She proceeded, however, with considerable caution, pausing occasionally to let Catherine give some sign. Catherine gave no other sign than to stop the rocking of her chair and the swaying of her fan; she sat motionless and silent. "It was on Tuesday last," said Mrs. Penniman, "and I have been hesitating ever since about telling you. I didn't know how you might like it. At last I thought that it was so long ago that you would probably not have any particular feeling. I saw him again after meeting him at Marian's. I met him in the street, and he went a few steps with me. The first thing he said was about you; he asked ever so many questions. Marian didn't want me to speak to you; she didn't want you to know that they receive him. I told him I was sure that after all these years you couldn't have any feeling about that; you couldn't grudge him the hospitality of his own cousin's house. I said you would be bitter indeed if you did that. Marian has the most extraordinary ideas about what happened between you; she seems to think he behaved in some very unusual manner. I took the liberty of reminding her of the real facts, and placing the story in its true light. *He* has no bitterness, Catherine, I can assure you; and he might be excused for it, for things have not gone well with him. He has been all over the world, and tried to establish himself everywhere; but his evil star was against him. It is most interesting to hear him talk of his evil star. Everything failed; everything but his—you know, you remember—his proud, high spirit. I believe he married some lady somewhere in Europe. You know they marry in such a peculiar matter-of-course way in Europe; a marriage of reason they call it. She died soon afterward; as he said to me, she only flitted across his life. He has not been in New York for ten years; he came back a few days ago. The first thing he did was to ask me about you. He had heard you had never married; he seemed very much interested about that. He said you had been the real romance of his life."

Catherine had suffered her companion to proceed from point to point, and pause to pause, without interrupting her; she fixed her eyes on the ground and listened. But the last phrase I have quoted was followed by a pause of peculiar significance, and then, at last, Catherine spoke. It will be observed that before doing so she had received a good deal of information about Morris Townsend. "Please say no more; please don't follow up that subject."

"Doesn't it interest you?" asked Mrs. Penniman, with a certain timorous archness.

"It pains me," said Catherine.

"I was afraid you would say that. But don't you think you could get used to it? He wants so much to see you."

"Please don't, Aunt Lavinia," said Catherine, getting up from her seat. She moved quickly away, and went to the other window, which stood open to the balcony; and here, in the embrasure, concealed from her aunt by the white curtains, she remained a long time, looking out into the warm darkness. She had had a great shock; it was as if the gulf of the past had suddenly opened, and a spectral figure had risen out of it. There were some things she believed she had got over, some feelings that she had thought of as dead; but apparently there was a certain vitality in them still. Mrs. Penniman had made them stir themselves. It was but a momentary agitation, Catherine said to herself; it would presently pass away. She was trembling, and her heart was beating so that she could feel it; but this also would subside. Then suddenly, while she waited for a return of her calmness, she burst into tears. But her tears flowed very silently, so that Mrs. Penniman had no observation of them. It was perhaps, however, because Mrs. Penniman suspected them that she said no more that evening about Morris Townsend.

35

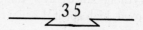

Her refreshed attention to this gentleman had not those limits of which Catherine desired, for herself, to be conscious; it lasted long enough to enable her to wait another week before speaking of him again. It was under the same circumstances that she once more attacked the subject. She had been sitting with her niece in the evening; only on this occasion, as the night was not so warm, the lamp had been lighted, and Catherine had placed herself near it with a morsel of fancy-work. Mrs. Penniman went and sat alone for half an hour on the balcony; then she came in, moving vaguely about the room. At last she sank into a seat near Catherine, with clasped hands, and a little look of excitement.

"Shall you be angry if I speak to you again about *him?*" she asked.

Catherine looked up at her quietly. "Who is *he?*"

"He whom you once loved."

"I shall not be angry, but I shall not like it."

"He sent you a message," said Mrs. Penniman. "I promised him to deliver it, and I must keep my promise."

In all these years Catherine had had time to forget how little she had to thank her aunt for in the season of her misery; she had long ago forgiven Mrs. Penniman for taking too much upon herself. But for a moment this attitude of interposition and disinterestedness, this carrying of messages and redeeming of promises, brought back the sense that her companion was a dangerous woman. She had said she would not be angry; but for an instant she felt sore. "I don't care what you do with your promise!" she answered.

Mrs. Penniman, however, with her high conception of the sanctity of pledges, carried her point. "I have gone too far to retreat," she said, though precisely what this meant she was not at pains to explain. "Mr. Townsend wishes most particularly to see you, Catherine; he believes that if you knew how much, and why, he wishes it, you would consent to do so."

"There can be no reason," said Catherine; "no good reason."

"His happiness depends upon it. Is not that a good reason?" asked Mrs. Penniman, impressively.

"Not for me. My happiness does not."

"I think you will be happier after you have seen him. He is going away again—going to resume his wanderings. It is a very lonely, restless, joyless life. Before he goes he wishes to speak to you; it is a fixed idea with him—he is always thinking of it. He has something very important to say to you. He believes that you never understood him—that you never judged him rightly, and the belief has always weighed upon him terribly. He wishes to justify himself; he believes that in a very few words he could do so. He wishes to meet you as a friend."

Catherine listened to this wonderful speech without pausing in her work; she had now had several days to accustom herself to think of Morris Townsend again as an actuality. When it was over she said simply, "Please say to Mr. Townsend that I wish he would leave me alone."

She had hardly spoken when a sharp, firm ring at the door

vibrated through the summer night. Catherine looked up at the clock; it marked a quarter past nine—a very late hour for visitors, especially in the empty condition of the town. Mrs. Penniman at the same moment gave a little start, and then Catherine's eyes turned quickly to her aunt. They met Mrs. Penniman's, and sounded them for a moment sharply. Mrs. Penniman was blushing; her look was a conscious one; it seemed to confess something. Catherine guessed its meaning, and rose quickly from her chair.

"Aunt Penniman," she said, in a tone that scared her companion, "have you taken *the liberty* . . . ?"

"My dearest Catherine," stammered Mrs. Penniman, "just wait till you see him!"

Catherine had frightened her aunt, but she was also frightened herself; she was on the point of rushing to give orders to the servant, who was passing to the door, to admit no one; but the fear of meeting her visitor checked her.

"Mr. Morris Townsend."

This was what she heard, vaguely but recognizably, articulated by the domestic, while she hesitated. She had her back turned to the door of the parlor, and for some moments she kept it turned, feeling that he had come in. He had not spoken, however, and at last she faced about. Then she saw a gentleman standing in the middle of the room, from which her aunt had discreetly retired.

She would never have known him. He was forty-five years old, and his figure was not that of the straight, slim young man she remembered. But it was a very fine presence, and a fair and lustrous beard, spreading itself upon a well-presented chest, contributed to its effect. After a moment Catherine recognized the upper half of the face, which, though her visitor's clustering locks had grown thin, was still remarkably handsome. He stood in a deeply deferential attitude, with his eyes on her face. "I have ventured—I have ventured"; he said, and then he paused, looking about him, as if he expected her to ask him to sit down. It was the old voice; but it had not the old charm. Catherine, for a minute, was conscious of a distinct determination not to invite him to take a seat. Why had he come? It was wrong for him to come. Morris was embarrassed, but Catherine gave him no help. It was not that she was glad of his embarrassment; on the contrary, it excited all her own liabilities of this kind, and gave her great pain. But how could she welcome him when she felt so vividly that he ought not to have come? "I wanted

so much—I was determined," Morris went on. But he stopped
again; it was not easy. Catherine still said nothing, and he may well
have recalled with apprehension her ancient faculty of silence. She
continued to look at him, however, and as she did so she made the
strangest observation. It seemed to be he, and yet not he; it was the
man who had been everything, and yet this person was nothing. How
long ago it was—how old she had grown—how much she had lived!
She had lived on something that was connected with *him*, and she
had consumed it in doing so. This person did not look unhappy. He
was fair and well-preserved, perfectly dressed, mature and complete. As Catherine looked at him, the story of his life defined itself
in his eyes; he had made himself comfortable, and he had never been
caught. But even while her perception opened itself to this, she had
no desire to catch him; his presence was painful to her, and she only
wished he would go.

"Will you not sit down?" he asked.

"I think we had better not," said Catherine.

"I offend you by coming?" He was **very grave**; he spoke in a
tone of the richest respect.

"I don't think you ought to have come."

"Did not Mrs. Penniman tell you—did she not give you my
message?"

"She told me something, but I did not understand."

"I wish you would let *me* tell you—let me speak for myself."

"I don't think it is necessary," said Catherine.

"Not for you, perhaps, but for me. It would be a great satisfaction—and I have not many." He seemed to be coming nearer; Catherine turned away. "Can we not be friends again?" he asked.

"We are not enemies," said Catherine. "I have none but friendly
feelings to you."

"Ah, I wonder whether you know the happiness it gives me to
hear you say that!" Catherine uttered no intimation that she measured the influence of her words; and he presently went on, "You
have not changed—the years have passed happily for you."

"They have passed very quietly," said Catherine.

"They have left no marks; you are admirably young." This time
he succeeded in coming nearer—he was close to her; she saw his
glossy perfumed beard, and his eyes above it looking strange and
hard. It was very different from his old—from his young—face. If
she had first seen him this way she would not have liked him. It

seemed to her that he was smiling, or trying to smile. "Catherine," he said, lowering his voice, "I have never ceased to think of you."

"Please don't say these things," she answered.

"Do you hate me?"

"Oh no," said Catherine.

Something in her tone discouraged him, but in a moment he recovered himself. "Have you still some kindness for me, then?"

"I don't know why you have come here to ask me such things!" Catherine exclaimed.

"Because for many years it has been the desire of my life that we should be friends again."

"That is impossible."

"Why so? Not if you will allow it."

"I will not allow it," said Catherine.

He looked at her again in silence. "I see; my presence troubles you and pains you. I will go away; but you must give me leave to come again."

"Please don't come again," she said.

"Never?—never?"

She made a great effort; she wished to say something that would make it impossible he should ever again cross her threshold. "It is wrong of you. There is no propriety in it—no reason for it."

"Ah, dearest lady, you do me injustice!" cried Morris Townsend. "We have only waited, and now we are free."

"You treated me badly," said Catherine.

"Not if you think of it rightly. You had your quiet life with your father—which was just what I could not make up my mind to rob you of."

"Yes; I had that."

Morris felt it to be a considerable damage to his cause that he could not add that she had had something more besides; for it is needless to say that he had learned the contents of Doctor Sloper's will. He was, nevertheless, not at a loss. "There are worse fates than that!" he exclaimed, with expression; and he might have been supposed to refer to his own unprotected situation. Then he added, with a deeper tenderness, "Catherine, have you never forgiven me?"

"I forgave you years ago, but it is useless for us to attempt to be friends."

"Not if we forget the past. We have still a future, thank God!"

"I can't forget—I don't forget," said Catherine. "You treated me too badly. I felt it very much; I felt it for years. And then she went on, with her wish to show him that he must not come to her this way, "I can't begin again—I can't take it up. Everything is dead and buried. It was too serious; it made a great change in my life. I never expected to see you here."

"Ah, you are angry!" cried Morris, who wished immensely that he could extort some flash of passion from her calmness. In that case he might hope.

"No, I am not angry. Anger does not last that way for years. But there are other things. Impressions last, when they have been strong. But I can't talk."

Morris stood stroking his beard, with a clouded eye. "Why have you never married?" he asked, abruptly. "You have had opportunities."

"I didn't wish to marry."

"Yes, you are rich, you are free; you had nothing to gain."

"I had nothing to gain," said Catherine.

Morris looked vaguely round him, and gave a deep sigh. "Well, I was in hopes that we might still have been friends."

"I meant to tell you, by my aunt, in answer to your message—if you had waited for an answer—that it was unnecessary for you to come in that hope."

"Good-bye, then," said Morris. "Excuse my indiscretion."

He bowed, and she turned away—standing there, averted, with her eyes on the ground, for some moments after she had heard him close the door of the room.

In the hall he found Mrs. Penniman, fluttered and eager; she appeared to have been hovering there under the irreconcilable promptings of her curiosity and her dignity.

"That was a precious plan of yours!" said Morris, clapping on his hat.

"Is she so hard?" asked Mrs. Penniman.

"She doesn't care a button for me—with her confounded little dry manner."

"Was it very dry?" pursued Mrs. Penniman, with solicitude.

Morris took no notice of her question; he stood musing an instant, with his hat on. "But why the deuce, then, would she never marry?"

"Yes—why indeed?" sighed Mrs. Penniman. And then, as if from a sense of the inadequacy of this explanation, "But you will not despair—you will come back?"

"Come back? Damnation!" And Morris Townsend strode out of the house, leaving Mrs. Penniman staring.

Catherine, meanwhile, in the parlor, picking up her morsel of fancy-work, had seated herself with it again—for life, as it were.

Maggie

1893

STEPHEN CRANE

Maggie

I

A VERY little boy stood upon a heap of gravel for the honour
of Rum Alley. He was throwing stones at howling urchins
from Devil's Row, who were circling madly about the heap
and pelting him. His infantile countenance was livid with the fury of
battle. His small body was writhing in the delivery of oaths.

"Run, Jimmie, run! Dey'll git yehs!" screamed a retreating Rum
Alley child.

"Naw," responded Jimmie with a valiant roar, "dese mugs can't
make me run."

Howls of renewed wrath went up from Devil's Row throats. Tattered gamins on the right made a furious assault on the gravel-heap.
On their small convulsed faces shone the grins of true assassins. As
they charged, they threw stones and cursed in shrill chorus.

The little champion of Rum Alley stumbled precipitately down
the other side. His coat had been torn to shreds in a scuffle, and his
hat was gone. He had bruises on twenty parts of his body, and
blood was dripping from a cut in his head. His wan features looked
like those of a tiny insane demon. On the ground, children from
Devil's Row closed in on their antagonist. He crooked his left arm
defensively about his head and fought with madness. The little boys
ran to and fro, dodging, hurling stones, and swearing in barbaric
trebles.

From a window of an apartment-house that uprose from amid
squat ignorant stables there leaned a curious woman. Some
labourers, unloading a scow at a dock at the river, paused for a
moment and regarded the fight. The engineer of a passive tugboat
hung lazily over a railing and watched. Over on the island a worm
of yellow convicts came from the shadow of a grey ominous building
and crawled slowly along the river's bank.

A stone had smashed in Jimmie's mouth. Blood was bubbling
over his chin and down upon his ragged shirt. Tears made furrows

on his dirt-stained cheeks. His thin legs had begun to tremble and
turn weak, causing his small body to reel. His roaring curses of the
first part of the fight had changed to a blasphemous chatter. In the
yells of the whirling mob of Devil's Row children there were notes
of joy like songs of triumphant savagery. The little boys seemed to
leer gloatingly at the blood upon the other child's face.

Down the avenue came boastfully sauntering a lad of sixteen
years, although the chronic sneer of an ideal manhood already sat
upon his lips. His hat was tipped over his eye with an air of challenge. Between his teeth a cigar-stump was tilted at the angle of
defiance. He walked with a certain swing of the shoulders which
appalled the timid. He glanced over into the vacant lot in which the
little raving boys from Devil's Row seethed about the shrieking and
tearful child from Rum Alley.

"Gee!" he murmured with interest, "a scrap. Gee!" He strode
over to the cursing circle, swinging his shoulders in a manner which
denoted that he held victory in his fists. He approached at the back
of one of the most deeply engaged of the Devil's Row children.
"Ah, what d' hell," he said, and smote the deeply engaged one on
the back of the head.

The little boy fell to the ground and gave a tremendous howl.
He scrambled to his feet, and perceiving, evidently, the size of his
assailant, ran quickly off, shouting alarms. The entire Devil's Row
party followed him. They came to a stand a short distance away and
yelled taunting oaths at the boy with the chronic sneer.

The latter, momentarily, paid no attention to them. "What's wrong
wi'che, Jimmie?" he asked of the small champion.

Jimmie wiped his blood-wet features with his sleeve. "Well, it was
dis way, Pete, see? I was goin' teh lick dat Riley kid, an' dey all
pitched on me."

Some Rum Alley children now came forward. The party stood
for a moment exchanging vainglorious remarks with Devil's Row.
A few stones were thrown at long distances, and words of challenge
passed between small warriors. Then the Rum Alley contingent
turned slowly in the direction of their home street. They began to
give, each to each, distorted versions of the fight. Causes of retreat
in particular cases were magnified. Blows dealt in the fight were
enlarged to catapultian power, and stones thrown were alleged to
have hurtled with infinite accuracy. Valour grew strong again, and
the little boys began to brag with great spirit. "Ah, we blokies kin
lick d' hull damn Row," said a child, swaggering.

Little Jimmie was trying to stanch the flow of blood from his cut lips. Scowling, he turned upon the speaker. "Ah, where was yehs when I was doin' all deh fightin'?" he demanded. "Youse kids makes me tired."

"Ah, go ahn!" replied the other argumentatively.

Jimmie replied with heavy contempt. "Ah, youse can't fight, Blue Billie! I kin lick yeh wid one han'."

"Ah, go ahn!" replied Billie again.

"Ah!" said Jimmie threateningly.

"Ah!" said the other in the same tone.

They struck at each other, clinched, and rolled over on the cobble-stones.

"Smash 'im, Jimmie, kick d' face off 'im!" yelled Pete, the lad with the chronic sneer, in tones of delight.

The small combatants pounded and kicked, scratched and tore. They began to weep, and their curses struggled in their throats with sobs. The other little boys clasped their hands and wriggled their legs in excitement. They formed a bobbing circle about the pair.

A tiny spectator was suddenly agitated. "Cheese it, Jimmie, cheese it! Here comes yer fader," he yelled.

The circle of little boys instantly parted. They drew away and waited in ecstatic awe for that which was about to happen. The two little boys, fighting in the modes of four thousand years ago, did not hear the warning.

Up the avenue there plodded slowly a man with sullen eyes. He was carrying a dinner-pail and smoking an apple-wood pipe. As he neared the spot where the little boys strove, he regarded them listlessly. But suddenly he roared an oath and advanced upon the rolling fighters. "Here, you Jim, git up, now, while I belt yer life out, yeh disorderly brat." He began to kick into the chaotic mass on the ground. The boy Billie felt a heavy boot strike his head. He made a furious effort and disentangled himself from Jimmie. He tottered away.

Jimmie arose painfully from the ground and, confronting his father, began to curse him. His parent kicked him. "Come home, now," he cried, "an' stop yer jawin', er I'll lam the everlasting head off yehs."

They departed. The man paced placidly along with the apple-wood emblem of serenity between his teeth. The boy followed a dozen feet in the rear. He swore luridly, for he felt that it was degradation for one who aimed to be some vague kind of soldier, or a man of blood with a sort of sublime licence, to be taken home by a father.

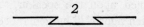

Eventually they entered a dark region where, from a careening building, a dozen gruesome doorways gave up loads of babies to the street and the gutter. A wind of early autumn raised yellow dust from cobbles and swirled it against a hundred windows. Long streamers of garments fluttered from fire-escapes. In all unhandy places there were buckets, brooms, rags, and bottles. In the street infants played or fought with other infants or sat stupidly in the way of vehicles. Formidable women, with uncombed hair and disordered dress, gossiped while leaning on railings, or screamed in frantic quarrels. Withered persons, in curious postures of submission to something, sat smoking pipes in obscure corners. A thousand odours of cooking food came forth to the street. The building quivered and creaked from the weight of humanity stamping about in its bowels.

A small ragged girl dragged a red, bawling infant along the crowded ways. He was hanging back, baby-like, bracing his wrinkled, bare legs. The little girl cried out: "Ah, Tommie, come ahn. Dere's Jimmie and fader. Don't be a-pullin' me back." She jerked the baby's arm impatiently. He fell on his face, roaring. With a second jerk she pulled him to his feet, and they went on. With the obstinacy of his order, he protested against being dragged in a chosen direction. He made heroic endeavours to keep on his legs, denounced his sister, and consumed a bit of orange-peeling which he chewed between the times of his infantile orations.

As the sullen-eyed man, followed by the blood-covered boy, drew near, the little girl burst into reproachful cries. "Ah, Jimmie, youse bin fightin' agin."

The urchin swelled disdainfully. "Ah, what d' hell, Mag. See?"

The little girl upbraided him. "Youse allus fightin', Jimmie, an' yeh knows it puts mudder out when yehs come home half dead, an it's like we'll all get a poundin'." She began to weep. The babe threw back his head and roared at his prospects.

"Ah," cried Jimmie, "shut up er I'll smack yer mout'. See?" As his sister continued her lamentations, he suddenly struck her. The little girl reeled, and, recovering herself, burst into tears and quaveringly cursed him. As she slowly retreated, her brother advanced, dealing her cuffs.

The father heard, and turned about. "Stop that, Jim, d'yeh hear? Leave yer sister alone on the street. It's like I can never beat any sense into yer wooden head."

The urchin raised his voice in defiance to his parent, and continued his attacks. The babe bawled tremendously, protesting with great violence. During his sister's hasty manœuvres he was dragged by the arm.

Finally the procession plunged into one of the gruesome doorways. They crawled up dark stairways and along cold, gloomy halls. At last the father pushed open a door, and they entered a lighted room in which a large woman was rampant.

She stopped in a career from a seething stove to a pan-covered table. As the father and children filed in she peered at them. "Eh, what? Been fightin' again!" She threw herself upon Jimmie. The urchin tried to dart behind the others, and in the scuffle the babe, Tommie, was knocked down. He protested with his usual vehemence because they had bruised his tender shins against a table leg.

The mother's massive shoulders heaved with anger. Grasping the urchin by the neck and shoulder she shook him until he rattled. She dragged him to an unholy sink, and, soaking a rag in water, began to scrub his lacerated face with it. Jimmie screamed in pain, and tried to twist his shoulders out of the clasp of the huge arms.

The babe sat on the floor watching the scene, his face in contortions like that of a woman at a tragedy. The father, with a newly ladened pipe in his mouth, sat in a backless chair near the stove. Jimmie's cries annoyed him. He turned about and bellowed at his wife. "Let the kid alone for a minute, will yeh, Mary? Yer allus poundin' 'im. When I come nights I can't get no rest 'cause yer allus poundin' a kid. Let up, d'yeh hear? Don't be allus poundin' a kid." The woman's operations on the urchin instantly increased in violence. At last she tossed him to a corner, where he limply lay weeping.

The wife put her immense hands on her hips, and with a chieftain-like stride approached her husband. "Ho!" she said, with a great grunt of contempt. "An' what in the devil are you stickin' your nose for?" The babe crawled under the table, and, turning, peered out cautiously. The ragged girl retreated, and the urchin in the corner drew his legs carefully beneath him.

The man puffed his pipe calmly and put his great muddied boots on the back part of the stove. "Go t' hell," he said tranquilly.

The woman screamed, and shook her fists before her husband's eyes. The rough yellow of her face and neck flared suddenly crimson. She began to howl.

He puffed imperturbably at his pipe for a time, but finally arose and went to look out the window into the darkening chaos of back yards. "You've been drinkin', Mary," he said. "You'd better let up on the bot', ol' woman, or you'll git done."

"You're a liar. I ain't had a drop," she roared in reply. They had a lurid altercation.

The babe was staring out from under the table, his small face working in his excitement. The ragged girl went stealthily over to the corner where the urchin lay. "Are yehs hurted much, Jimmie?" she whispered timidly.

"Not a little bit. See?" growled the little boy.

"Will I wash d' blood?"

"Naw!"

"Will I——"

"When I catch dat Riley kid I'll break 'is face! Dat's right! See?" He turned his face to the wall as if resolved grimly to bide his time.

In the quarrel between husband and wife the woman was victor. The man seized his hat and rushed from the room, apparently determined upon a vengeful drunk. She followed to the door and thundered at him as he made his way downstairs.

She returned and stirred up the room until her children were bobbing about like bubbles. "Git outa d' way," she bawled persistently, waving feet with their dishevelled shoes near the heads of her children. She shrouded herself, puffing and snorting, in a cloud of steam at the stove, and eventually extracted a frying-pan full of potatoes that hissed. She flourished it. "Come t' yer suppers, now," she cried with sudden exasperation. "Hurry up, now, er I'll help yeh!"

The children scrambled hastily. With prodigious clatter they arranged themselves at table. The babe sat with his feet dangling high from a precarious infant's chair and gorged his small stomach. Jimmie forced, with feverish rapidity, the grease-enveloped pieces between his wounded lips. Maggie, with side glances of fear of interruption, ate like a small pursued tigress.

The mother sat blinking at them. She delivered reproaches, swallowed potatoes, and drank from a yellow-brown bottle. After a time her mood changed, and she wept as she carried little Tommie into another room and laid him to sleep, with his fists doubled, in an old quilt of faded red-and-green grandeur. Then she came and moaned by the stove. She rocked to and fro upon a chair, shedding tears and crooning miserably to the two children about their "poor mother" and "yer fader, damn 'is soul."

The little girl plodded between the table and the chair with a dishpan on it. She tottered on her small legs beneath burdens of dishes. Jimmie sat nursing his various wounds. He cast furtive glances at his mother. His practised eye perceived her gradually emerge from a mist of muddled sentiment until her brain burned in drunken heat. He sat breathless.

Maggie broke a plate.

The mother started to her feet as if propelled. "Good Gawd!" she howled. Her glittering eyes fastened on her child with sudden hatred. The fervent red of her face turned almost to purple. The little boy ran to the halls, shrieking like a monk in an earthquake. He floundered about in darkness until he found the stairs. He stumbled, panic-stricken, to the next floor.

An old woman opened a door. A light behind her threw a flare on the urchin's face. "Eh, child, what is it dis time? Is yer fader beatin' yer mudder, or yer mudder beatin' ye fader?"

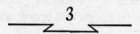

3

Jimmie and the old woman listened long in the hall. Above the muffled roar of conversation, the dismal wailings of babies at night, the thumping of feet in unseen corridors and rooms, and the sound of varied hoarse shoutings in the street and the rattling of wheels over cobbles, they heard the screams of the child and the roars of the mother die away to a feeble moaning and a subdued bass muttering.

The old woman was a gnarled and leathery personage who could don at will an expression of great virtue. She possessed a small music-box capable of one tune, and a collection of "God bless yeh's" pitched in assorted keys of fervency. Each day she took a position upon the stones of Fifth Avenue, where she crooked her legs under her and crouched, immovable and hideous, like an idol. She received daily a small sum in pennies. It was contributed, for the most part, by persons who did not make their homes in that vicinity. Once, when a lady had dropped her purse on the sidewalk, the gnarled woman had grabbed it and smuggled it with great dexterity beneath her cloak. When she was arrested she had cursed the lady into a partial swoon, and with her aged limbs, twisted from rheumatism, had kicked the breath out of a huge policeman whose conduct upon that occasion she referred to when she said, "The police, damn 'em!"

"Eh, Jimmie, it's a shame," she said. "Go, now, like a dear, an' buy me a can, an' if yer mudder raises 'ell all night yehs can sleep here." Jimmie took a tendered tin pail and seven pennies and departed. He passed into the side door of a saloon and went to the bar. Straining up on his toes he raised the pail and pennies as high as his arms would let him. He saw two hands thrust down to take them. Directly the same hands let down the filled pail, and he left.

In front of the gruesome doorway he met a lurching figure. It was his father, swaying about on uncertain legs. "Give me deh can. See?" said the man.

"Ah, come off! I got dis can fer dat ol' woman, an' it 'ud be dirt teh swipe it. See?" cried Jimmie.

The father wrenched the pail from the urchin. He grasped it in both hands and lifted it to his mouth. He glued his lips to the under edge and tilted his head. His throat swelled until it seemed to grow near his chin. There was a tremendous gulping movement and the beer was gone. The man caught his breath and laughed. He hit his son on the head with the empty pail.

As it rolled clanging into the street, Jimmie began to scream, and kicked repeatedly at his father's shins. "Look at deh dirt what yeh done me," he yelled. "Deh ol' woman 'll be t'rowin' fits." He retreated to the middle of the street, but the old man did not pursue. He staggered toward the door. "I'll paste yeh when I ketch yeh!" he shouted, and disappeared.

During the evening he had been standing against a bar drinking whiskies, and declaring to all comers confidentially: "My home reg'lar livin' hell! Why do I come an' drin' whisk' here thish way? 'Cause home reg'lar livin' hell!"

Jimmie waited a long time in the street and then crept warily up through the building. He passed with great caution the door of the gnarled woman, and finally stopped outside his home and listened. He could hear his mother moving heavily about among the furniture of the room. She was chanting in a mournful voice, occasionally interjecting bursts of volcanic wrath at the father, who, Jimmie judged, had sunk down on the floor or in a corner.

"Why deh blazes don'cher try teh keep Jim from fightin'? I'll break yer jaw!" she suddenly bellowed.

The man mumbled with drunken indifference. "Ah, w'at's bitin' yeh? W'a' 's odds? W'a' makes kick?"

"Because he tears 'is clothes, yeh fool!" cried the woman in supreme wrath.

The husband seemed to become aroused. "Go chase yerself!" he thundered fiercely in reply. There was a crash against the door, and something broke into clattering fragments. Jimmie partially suppressed a yell and darted down the stairway. Below he paused and listened. He heard howls and curses, groans and shrieks—a confused chorus as if a battle were raging. With it all there was the crash of splintering furniture. The eyes of the urchin glared in his fear that one of them would discover him.

Curious faces appeared in doorways, and whispered comments passed to and fro. "Ol' Johnson's playin' horse agin."

Jimmie stood until the noises ceased and the other inhabitants of the tenement had all yawned and shut their doors. Then he crawled upstairs with the caution of an invader of a panther's den. Sounds of laboured breathing came through the broken door-panels. He pushed the door open and entered, quaking.

A glow from the fire threw red hues over the bare floor, the cracked and soiled plastering, and the overturned and broken furniture. In the middle of the floor lay his mother asleep. In one corner of the room his father's limp body hung across the seat of a chair.

The urchin stole forward. He began to shiver in dread of awakening his parents. His mother's great chest was heaving painfully. Jimmie paused and looked down at her. Her face was inflamed and swollen from drinking. Her yellow brows shaded eyelids that had grown blue. Her tangled hair tossed in waves over her forehead. Her mouth was set in the same lines of vindictive hatred that it had, perhaps, borne during the fight. Her bare red arms were thrown out above her head in an attitude of exhaustion, something, mayhap, like that of a sated villain.

The urchin bent over his mother. He was fearful lest she should open her eyes, and the dread within him was so strong that he could not forbear to stare, but hung as if fascinated over the woman's grim face. Suddenly her eyes opened. The urchin found himself looking straight into an expression which, it would seem, had the power to change his blood to salt. He howled piercingly and fell backward.

The woman floundered for a moment, tossed her arms about her head as if in combat, and again began to snore. Jimmie crawled back into the shadows and waited. A noise in the next room had followed his cry at the discovery that his mother was awake. He grovelled in the gloom, his eyes riveted upon the intervening door. He heard it creak, and then the sound of a small voice came to him. "Jimmie! Jimmie! Are yehs dere?" it whispered. The urchin started. The thin white face of his sister looked at him from the doorway of the other room. She crept to him across the floor.

The father had not moved, but lay in the same deathlike sleep. The mother writhed in an uneasy slumber, her chest wheezing as if she were in the agonies of strangulation. Out at the window a florid moon was peering over dark roofs, and in the distance the waters of a river glimmered pallidly.

The small frame of the ragged girl was quivering. Her features were haggard from weeping, and her eyes gleamed with fear. She grasped the urchin's arm in her little trembling hands and they huddled in a corner. The eyes of both were drawn, by some force, to stare at the woman's face, for they thought she need only to awake and all the fiends would come from below. They crouched until the ghost mists of dawn appeared at the window, drawing close to the panes, and looking in at the prostrate, heaving body of the mother.

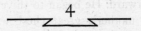

4

The babe, Tommie, died. He went away in an insignificant coffin, his small waxen hand clutching a flower that the girl, Maggie, had stolen from an Italian.

She and Jimmie lived.

The inexperienced fibres of the boy's eyes were hardened at an early age. He became a young man of leather. He lived some red years without labouring. During that time his sneer became chronic. He studied human nature in the gutter, and found it no worse than he thought he had reason to believe it. He never conceived a respect for the world, because he had begun with no idols that it had smashed.

He clad his soul in armour by means of happening hilariously in at a mission church where a man composed his sermons of "you's." Once a philosopher asked this man why he did not say "we" instead of "you." The man replied, "What?" While they got warm at the stove he told his hearers just where he calculated they stood with the Lord. Many of the sinners were impatient over the pictured depths of their degradation. They were waiting for soup-tickets. A reader of the words of wind-demons might have been able to see the portions of a dialogue pass to and fro between the exhorter and his hearers. "You are damned," said the preacher. And the reader of sounds might have seen the reply go forth from the ragged people: "Where's our soup?" Jimmie and a companion sat in a rear seat and commented upon the things that didn't concern them, with all the freedom of English tourists. When they grew thirsty and went out, their minds confused the speaker with Christ.

Momentarily, Jimmie was sullen with thoughts of a hopeless altitude where grew fruit. His companion said that if he should ever go to heaven he would ask for a million dollars and a bottle of beer. Jimmie's occupation for a long time was to stand at street corners and watch the world go by, dreaming blood-red dreams at the passing of pretty women. He menaced mankind at the intersections of streets. At the corners he was in life and of life. The world was going on and he was there to perceive it.

He maintained a belligerent attitude toward all well-dressed men. To him fine raiment was allied to weakness, and all good coats covered faint hearts. He and his orders were kings, to a certain extent, over the men of untarnished clothes, because these latter dreaded, perhaps, to be either killed or laughed at. Above all things he despised obvious Christians and ciphers with the chrysanthemums of aristocracy in their buttonholes. He considered himself above both of these classes. He was afraid of nothing.

When he had a dollar in his pocket his satisfaction with existence was the greatest thing in the world. So, eventually, he felt obliged to work. His father died, and his mother's years were divided up into periods of thirty days.

He became a truck-driver. There was given to him the charge of a painstaking pair of horses and a large rattling truck. He invaded the turmoil and tumble of the downtown streets, and learned to breathe maledictory defiance at the police, who occasionally used to climb up, drag him from his perch, and punch him. In the lower part of the city he daily involved himself in hideous tangles. If he and his team chanced to be in the rear he preserved a demeanour of serenity, crossing his legs and bursting forth into yells when foot passengers took dangerous dives beneath the noses of his champing horses. He smoked his pipe calmly, for he knew that his pay was marching on. If his charge was in the front, and if it became the key-truck of chaos, he entered terrifically into the quarrel that was raging to and fro among the drivers on their high seats, and sometimes roared oaths and violently got himself arrested.

After a time his sneer grew so that it turned its glare upon all things. He became so sharp that he believed in nothing. To him the police were always actuated by malignant impulses, and the rest of the world was composed, for the most part, of despicable creatures who were all trying to take advantage of him, and with whom, in defence, he was obliged to quarrel on all possible occasions. He himself occupied a down-trodden position, which had a private but distinct element of grandeur in its isolation.

The greatest cases of aggravated idiocy were, to his mind, rampant upon the front platforms of all the street-cars. At first his tongue strove with these beings, but he eventually became superior. In him grew a majestic contempt for those strings of street-cars that followed him like intent bugs. He fell into the habit, when starting on a long journey, of fixing his eye on a high and distant object, commanding his horses to start, and then going into a trance of oblivion. Multitudes of drivers might howl in his rear, and passengers might load him with opprobrium, but he would not awaken until some blue policeman turned red and began frenziedly to seize bridles and beat the soft noses of the responsible horses.

When he paused to contemplate the attitude of the police toward himself and his fellows, he believed that they were the only men in the city who had no rights. When driving about, he felt that he was held liable by the police for anything that might occur in the streets, and that he was the common prey of all energetic officials. In revenge, he resolved never to move out of the way of anything, until formidable circumstances or a much larger man than himself forced him to it.

Foot passengers were mere pestering flies with an insane disregard for their legs and his convenience. He could not comprehend their desire to cross the streets. Their madness smote him with eternal amazement. He was continually storming at them from his throne. He sat aloft and denounced their frantic leaps, plunges, dives, and straddles. When they would thrust at, or parry, the noses of his champing horses, making them swing their heads and move their feet, and thus disturbing a stolid, dreamy repose, he swore at the men as fools, for he himself could perceive that Providence had caused it to be clearly written that he and his team had the inalienable right to stand in the proper path of the sun-chariot and, if they so minded, to obstruct its mission or take a wheel off. And if the good driver had had a desire to step down, put up his flame-coloured fists, and manfully dispute the right of way, he would have probably been immediately opposed by a scowling mortal with two sets of hard knuckles.

It is possible, perhaps, that this young man would have derided, in an axle-wide alley, the approach of a flying ferryboat. Yet he achieved a respect for a fire-engine. As one charged toward his truck, he would drive fearfully upon a sidewalk, threatening untold people with annihilation. When an engine struck a mass of blocked trucks, splitting it into fragments as a blow annihilates a cake of ice, Jimmie's team could usually be observed high and safe, with whole wheels, on the sidewalk. The fearful coming of the engine could break up the most intricate muddle of heavy vehicles at which the police had been storming for half an hour. A fire-engine was enshrined in his heart as an appalling thing that he loved with a distant, dog-like devotion. It had been known to overturn a street-car. Those leaping horses, striking sparks from the cobbles in their forward lunge, were creatures to be ineffably admired. The clang of the gong pierced his breast like a noise of remembered war.

When Jimmie was a little boy he began to be arrested. Before he reached a great age, he had a fair record. He developed too great a tendency to climb down from his truck and fight with other drivers. He had been in quite a number of miscellaneous fights, and in some general barroom rows that had become known to the police. Once he had been arrested for assaulting a Chinaman. Two women in different parts of the city, and entirely unknown to each other, caused him considerable annoyance by breaking forth, simultaneously, at fateful intervals, into wailings about marriage and support and infants.

Nevertheless, he had, on a certain star-lit evening, said wonderingly and quite reverently, "Deh moon looks like hell, don't it?"

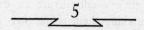

5

The girl, Maggie, blossomed in a mud-puddle. She grew to be a most rare and wonderful production of a tenement district, a pretty girl. None of the dirt of Rum Alley seemed to be in her veins. The philosophers, upstairs, downstairs, and on the same floor, puzzled over it. When a child, playing and fighting with gamins in the street, dirt disgusted her. Attired in tatters and grime, she went unseen.

There came a time, however, when the young men of the vicinity said, "Dat Johnson goil is a putty good looker." About this period her brother remarked to her: "Mag, I'll tell yeh dis! See? Yeh've eeder got t' go on d' toif er go t' work!" Whereupon she went to work, having the feminine aversion to the alternative. By a chance, she got a position in an establishment where they made collars and cuffs. She received a stool and a machine in a room where sat twenty girls of various shades of yellow discontent. She perched on the stool and treadled at her machine all day, turning out collars with a name which might have been noted for its irrelevancy to anything connected with collars. At night she returned home to her mother.

Jimmie grew large enough to take the vague position of head of the family. As incumbent of that office, he stumbled upstairs late at night, as his father had done before him. He reeled about the room, swearing at his relations, or went to sleep on the floor.

The mother had gradually risen to such a degree of fame that she could bandy words with her acquaintances among the police justices. Court officials called her by her first name. When she appeared they pursued a course which had been theirs for months. They invariably grinned, and cried out, "Hello, Mary, you here again?" Her grey head wagged in many courts. She always besieged the bench with voluble excuses, explanations, apologies, and prayers. Her flaming face and rolling eyes were a familiar sight on the island. She measured time by means of sprees, and was swollen and dishevelled.

One day the young man Pete, who as a lad had smitten the Devil's Row urchin in the back of the head and put to flight the antagonists of his friend Jimmie, strutted upon the scene. He met Jimmie one day on the street, promised to take him to a boxing match in Williamsburg, and called for him in the evening.

Maggie observed Pete.

He sat on a table in the Johnson home, and dangled his checked legs with an enticing nonchalance. His hair was curled down over his forehead in an oiled bang. His pugged nose seemed to revolt from contact with a bristling moustache of short, wire-like hairs. His blue double-breasted coat, edged with black braid, was buttoned close to a red puff tie, and his patent leather shoes looked like weapons. His mannerisms stamped him as a man who had a correct sense of his personal superiority. There were valour and contempt for circumstances in the glance of his eye. He waved his hands like a man of the world who dismisses religion and philosophy, and says "Rats!" He had certainly seen everything, and with each curl of his lip he declared that it amounted to nothing. Maggie thought he must be a very "elegant" bartender.

He was telling tales to Jimmie. Maggie watched him furtively, with half-closed eyes lit with a vague interest.

"Hully gee! Dey makes me tired," he said. "Mos' e'ry day some farmer comes in an' tries t' run d' shop. See? But d' gits t'rowed right out. I jolt dem right out in d' street before dey knows where dey is. See?"

"Sure," said Jimmie.

"Dere was a mug come in d' place d' odder day wid an idear he was goin' t' own d' place. Hully gee! he was goin' t' own d' place. I see he had a still on, an' I didn' wanna giv' 'im no stuff, so I says, 'Git outa here an' don' make no trouble,' I says like dat. See? 'Git outa here an' don' make no trouble'; like dat. 'Git outa here,' I says. See?"

Jimmie nodded understandingly. Over his features played an eager desire to state the amount of his valour in a similar crisis, but the narrator proceeded.

"Well, deh blokie he says: 'T' blazes wid it! I ain' lookin' for no scrap,' he says—see?—'but,' he says, 'I'm 'spectable cit'zen an' I wanna drink, an' quick, too.' See? 'Aw, go ahn!' I says, like dat. 'Aw, go ahn,' I says. See? 'Don' make no trouble,' I says, like dat. 'Don make no trouble.' See? Den d' mug, he squared off an' said he was fine as silk wid his dukes—see?—an' he wan'ed a drink—quick. Dat's what he said. See?"

"Sure," repeated Jimmie.

Pete continued. "Say, I jes' jumped d' bar, an' d' way I plunked dat blokie was outa sight. See? Dat's right! In d' jaw! See? Hully gee! he t'rowed a spittoon t'rough d' front windee. Say, I t'ought I'd drop dead. But d' boss, he comes in after, an' he says: 'Pete, yehs done jes' right! Yeh've gotta keep order, an' it's all right.' See? 'It's all right,' he says. Dat's what he said."

The two held a technical discussion.

"Dat bloke was a dandy," said Pete, in conclusion, "but he hadn' oughta made no trouble. Dat's what I says t' dem: 'Don' come in here an' make no trouble,' I says, like dat. 'Don' make no trouble.' See?"

As Jimmie and his friend exchanged tales descriptive of their prowess, Maggie leaned back in the shadow. Her eyes dwelt wonderingly and rather wistfully upon Pete's face. The broken furniture, grimy walls, and general disorder and dirt of her home of a sudden appeared before her and began to take a potential aspect. Pete's aristocratic person looked as if it might soil. She looked keenly at him, occasionally wondering if he was feeling contempt. But Pete seemed to be enveloped in reminiscence.

"Hully gee!" said he, "dose mugs can't feaze me. Dey knows I kin wipe up d' street wid any t'ree of dem."

When he said, "Ah, what d' hell!" his voice was burdened with disdain for the inevitable and contempt for anything that fate might compel him to endure.

Maggie perceived that here was the ideal man. Her dim thoughts were often searching for far-away lands where the little hills sing together in the morning. Under the trees of her dream-gardens there had always walked a lover.

6

Pete took note of Maggie. "Say, Mag, I'm stuck on yer shape. It's outa sight," he said parenthetically, with an affable grin.

As he became aware that she was listening closely, he grew still more eloquent in his descriptions of various happenings in his career. It appeared that he was invincible in fights. "Why," he said, referring to a man with whom he had had a misunderstanding, "dat mug scrapped like a dago. Dat's right. He was dead easy. See? He t'ought he was a scrapper. But he foun' out diff'ent. Hully gee!"

He walked to and fro in the small room, which seemed then to grow even smaller and unfit to hold his dignity, the attribute of a supreme warrior. That swing of the shoulders which had frozen the timid when he was but a lad had increased with his growth and education in the ratio of ten to one. It, combined with the sneer upon his mouth, told mankind that there was nothing in space which could appal him. Maggie marvelled at him and surrounded him with greatness. She vaguely tried to calculate the altitude of the pinnacle from which he must have looked down upon her.

"I met a chump deh odder day way up in deh city," he said. "I was goin' teh see a frien' of mine. When I was a-crossin' deh street deh chump runned plump inteh me, an' den he turns aroun' an' says, 'Yer insolen' ruffin!' he says, like dat. 'Oh, gee!' I says, 'oh, gee! git off d' eart'!' I says, like dat. See? 'Git off d' eart'!' like dat. Den deh blokie he got wild. He says I was a contempt'ble scoun'el, er somethin' like dat, an' he says I was doom' teh everlastin' pe'dition, er somethin' like dat. 'Gee!' I says, 'gee! Yer joshin' me,' I says. 'Yer joshin' me.' An' den I slugged 'im. See?"

With Jimmie in his company, Pete departed in a sort of blaze of glory from the Johnson home. Maggie, leaning from the window, watched him as he walked down the street. Here was a formidable man who disdained the strength of a world full of fists. Here was one who had contempt for brass-clothed power; one whose knuckles could ring defiantly against the granite of law. He was a knight.

The two men went from under the glimmering street lamp and passed into shadows. Turning, Maggie contemplated the dark, dust-stained walls, and the scant and crude furniture of her home. A clock, in a splintered and battered oblong box of varnished wood, she suddenly regarded as an abomination. She noted that it ticked raspingly. The almost vanished flowers in the carpet pattern, she conceived to be newly hideous. Some faint attempts which she had made with blue ribbon to freshen the appearance of a dingy curtain, she now saw to be piteous.

She wondered what Peter dined on.

She reflected upon the collar-and-cuff factory. It began to appear to her mind as a dreary place of endless grinding. Pete's elegant occupation brought him, no doubt, into contact with people who had money and manners. It was probable that he had a large acquaintance with pretty girls. He must have great sums of money to spend.

To her the earth was composed of hardships and insults. She felt instant admiration for a man who openly defied it. She thought that if the grim angel of death should clutch his heart, Pete would shrug his shoulders and say, "Oh, ev'ryt'ing goes."

She anticipated that he would come again shortly. She spent some of her week's pay in the purchase of flowered cretonne for a lambrequin. She made it with infinite care, and hung it to the slightly careening mantel over the stove in the kitchen. She studied it with painful anxiety from different points in the room. She wanted it to look well on Sunday night when, perhaps, Jimmie's friend would come. On Sunday night, however, Pete did not appear. Afterward the girl looked at it with a sense of humiliation. She was now convinced that Pete was superior to admiration for lambrequins.

A few evenings later Pete entered with fascinating innovations in his apparel. As she had seen him twice and he wore a different suit each time, Maggie had a dim impression that his wardrobe was prodigious.

"Say, Mag," he said, "put on yer bes' duds Friday night an' I'll take yehs t' d' show. See?" He spent a few moments in flourishing his clothes, and then vanished without having glanced at the lambrequin.

Over the eternal collars and cuffs in the factory Maggie spent the most of three days in making imaginary sketches of Pete and his daily environment. She imagined some half-dozen women in love with him, and thought he must lean dangerously toward an indefinite one whom she pictured as endowed with great charms of person, but with an altogether contemptible disposition. She thought he must live in a blare of pleasure. He had friends and people who were afraid of him. She saw the golden glitter of the place where Pete was to take her. It would be an entertainment of many hues and many melodies, where she was afraid she might appear small and mouse-coloured.

Her mother drank whisky all Friday morning. With lurid face and tossing hair she cursed and destroyed furniture all Friday afternoon. When Maggie came home at half-past six her mother lay asleep amid the wreck of chairs and a table. Fragments of various household utensils were scattered about the floor. She had vented some phase of drunken fury upon the lambrequin. It lay in a bedraggled heap in the corner.

"Hah!" she snorted, sitting up suddenly, "where yeh been? Why don' yeh come home earlier? Been loafin' round d' streets. Yer gettin' t' be a reg'lar devil."

When Pete arrived, Maggie, in a worn black dress, was waiting
for him in the midst of a floor strewn with wreckage. The curtain
at the window had been pulled by a heavy hand and hung by one
tack, dangling to and fro in the draught through the cracks at the
sash. The knots of blue ribbons appeared like violated flowers. The
fire in the stove had gone out. The displaced lids and open doors
showed heaps of sullen grey ashes. The remnants of a meal, ghastly,
lay in a corner. Maggie's mother, stretched on the floor, blasphemed,
and gave her daughter a bad name.

7

An orchestra of yellow silk women and bald-headed men, on an
elevated stage near the centre of a great green-hued hall, played
a popular waltz. The place was crowded with people grouped about
little tables. A battalion of waiters slid among the throng, carrying
trays of beer-glasses, and making change from the inexhaustible
vaults of their trousers pockets. Little boys, in the costumes of
French chefs, paraded up and down the irregular aisles vending
fancy cakes. There was a low rumble of conversation and a subdued
clinking of glasses. Clouds of tobacco smoke rolled and wavered
high in air above the dull gilt of the chandeliers.

The vast crowd had an air throughout of having just quitted
labour. Men with calloused hands, and attired in garments that
showed the wear of an endless drudging for a living, smoked their
pipes contentedly and spent five, ten, or perhaps fifteen cents for
beer. There was a mere sprinkling of men who smoked cigars
purchased elsewhere. The great body of the crowd was composed
of people who showed that all day they strove with their hands.
Quiet Germans, with maybe their wives and two or three children,
sat listening to the music, with the expressions of happy cows. An
occasional party of sailors from a war-ship, their faces pictures of
sturdy health, spent the earlier hours of the evening at the small
round tables. Very infrequent tipsy men, swollen with the value of
their opinions, engaged their companions in earnest and confidential
conversation. In the balcony, and here and there below, shone the
impassive faces of women. The nationalities of the Bowery beamed
upon the stage from all directions.

Pete walked aggressively up a side aisle and took seats with

Maggie at a table beneath the balcony. "Two beehs!" Leaning back, he regarded with eyes of superiority the scene before him. This attitude affected Maggie strongly. A man who could regard such a sight with indifference must be accustomed to very great things. It was obvious that Pete had visited this place many times before, and was very familiar with it. A knowledge of this fact made Maggie feel little and new.

He was extremely gracious and attentive. He displayed the consideration of a cultured gentleman who knew what was due. "Say, what's eatin' yeh? Bring d' lady a big glass! What use is dat pony?"

"Don't be fresh, now," said the waiter, with some warmth, as he departed.

"Ah, git off d' eart'!" said Pete, after the other's retreating form.

Maggie perceived that Pete brought forth all his elegance and all his knowledge of high-class customs for her benefit. Her heart warmed as she reflected upon his condescension.

The orchestra of yellow silk women and bald-headed men gave vent to a few bars of anticipatory music, and a girl, in a pink dress with short skirts, galloped upon the stage. She smiled upon the throng as if in acknowledgment of a warm welcome, and began to walk to and fro, making profuse gesticulations, and singing, in brazen soprano tones, a song the words of which were inaudible. When she broke into the swift rattling measures of a chorus some half-tipsy men near the stage joined in the rollicking refrain, and glasses were pounded rhythmically upon the tables. People leaned forward to watch her and to try to catch the words of the song. When she vanished there were long rollings of applause. Obedient to more anticipatory bars, she reappeared among the half-suppressed cheering of the tipsy men. The orchestra plunged into dance music, and the laces of the dancer fluttered and flew in the glare of gas-jets. She divulged the fact that she was attired in some half-dozen skirts. It was patent that any one of them would have proved adequate for the purpose for which skirts are intended. An occasional man bent forward, intent upon the pink stockings. Maggie wondered at the splendour of the costume and lost herself in calculations of the cost of the silks and laces.

The dancer's smile of enthusiasm was turned for ten minutes upon the faces of her audience. In the finale she fell into some of those grotesque attitudes which were at the time popular among the dancers in the theatres up-town, giving to the Bowery public the diversions of the aristocratic theatre-going public at reduced rates.

"Say, Pete," said Maggie, leaning forward, "dis is great."

"Sure!" said Pete, with proper complacence.

A ventriloquist followed the dancer. He held two fantastic dolls on his knees. He made them sing mournful ditties and say funny things about geography and Ireland.

"Do dose little men talk?" asked Maggie.

"Naw," said Pete, "It's some big jolly. See?"

Two girls, set down on the bills as sisters, came forth and sang a duet which is heard occasionally at concerts given under church auspices. They supplemented it with a dance, which, of course, can never be seen at concerts given under church auspices.

After they had retired, a woman of debatable age sang a negro melody. The chorus necessitated some grotesque waddlings supposed to be an imitation of a plantation darky, under the influence, probably, of music and the moon. The audience was just enthusiastic enough over it to make her return and sing a sorrowful lay, whose lines told of a mother's love, and a sweetheart who waited, and a young man who was lost at sea under harrowing circumstances. From the faces of a score or so in the crowd the self-contained look faded. Many heads were bent forward with eagerness and sympathy. As the last distressing sentiment of the piece was brought forth, it was greeted by the kind of applause which rings as sincere.

As a final effort, the singer rendered some verses which described a vision of Britain annihilated by America, and Ireland bursting her bonds. A carefully prepared climax was reached in the last line of the last verse, when the singer threw out her arms and cried, "The star-spangled banner." Instantly a great cheer swelled from the throats of this assemblage of the masses, most of them of foreign birth. There was a heavy rumble of booted feet thumping the floor. Eyes gleamed with sudden fire, and calloused hands waved frantically in the air.

After a few moments' rest, the orchestra played noisily, and a small fat man burst out upon the stage. He began to roar a song and to stamp back and forth before the footlights, wildly waving a silk hat and throwing leers broadcast. He made his face into fantastic grimaces until he looked like a devil on a Japanese kite. The crowd laughed gleefully. His short, fat legs were never still a moment. He shouted and roared and bobbed his shock of red wig until the audience broke out in excited applause.

Pete did not pay much attention to the progress of events upon the stage. He was drinking beer and watching Maggie. Her cheeks were blushing with excitement and her eyes were glistening. She drew deep breaths of pleasure. No thoughts of the atmosphere of the collar-and-cuff factory came to her.

With the final crash of the orchestra they jostled their way to the sidewalk in the crowd. Pete took Maggie's arm and pushed a way for her, offering to fight with a man or two. They reached Maggie's home at a late hour and stood for a moment in front of the gruesome doorway.

"Say, Mag," said Pete, "give us a kiss for takin' yeh t' d' show, will yer?"

Maggie laughed, as if startled, and drew away from him. "Naw, Pete," she said, "dat wasn't in it."

"Ah, why wasn't it?" urged Pete.

The girl retreated nervously.

"Ah, go ahn!" repeated he.

Maggie darted into the hall and up the stairs. She turned and smiled at him, then disappeared.

Pete walked slowly down the street. He had something of an astonished expression upon his features. He paused under a lamp-post and breathed a low breath of surprise. "Gee!" he said, "I wonner if I've been played fer a duffer."

8

As thoughts of Pete came to Maggie's mind, she began to have an intense dislike for all of her dresses. "What ails yeh? What makes ye be allus fixin' and fussin'?" her mother would frequently roar at her. She began to note with more interest the well-dressed women she met on the avenues. She envied elegance and soft palms. She craved those adornments of person which she saw every day on the street, conceiving them to be allies of vast importance to women. Studying faces, she thought many of the women and girls she chanced to meet smiled with serenity as though for ever cherished and watched over by those they loved.

The air in the collar-and-cuff establishment strangled her. She knew she was gradually and surely shrivelling in the hot, stuffy room. The begrimed windows rattled incessantly from the passing of elevated trains. The place was filled with a whirl of noises and odours. She became lost in thought as she looked at some of the grizzled women in the room, mere mechanical contrivances sewing seams and grinding out, with heads bent over their work, tales of imagined or real girlhood happiness, or of past drunks, or the baby at home, and unpaid wages. She wondered how long her youth would endure. She began to see the bloom upon her cheeks as something of value. She imagined herself, in an exasperating future, as a scrawny woman with an eternal grievance. She thought Pete to be a very fastidious person concerning the appearance of women.

She felt that she should love to see somebody entangle their fingers in the oily beard of the fat foreigner who owned the establishment. He was a detestable creature. He wore white socks with low shoes. He sat all day delivering orations in the depths of a cushioned chair. His pocket-book deprived them of the power of retort. "What do you sink I pie fife dolla a week for? Play? No, py tamn!"

Maggie was anxious for a friend to whom she could talk about Pete. She would have liked to discuss his admirable mannerisms with a reliable mutual friend. At home, she found her mother often drunk and always raving. It seemed that the world had treated this woman very badly, and she took a deep revenge upon such portions of it as came within her reach. She broke furniture as if she were at last getting her rights. She swelled with virtuous indignation as she carried the lighter articles of household use, one by one, under the shadows of the three gilt balls, where Hebrews chained them with chains of interest.

Jimmie came when he was obliged to by circumstances over which he had no control. His well-trained legs brought him staggering home and put him to bed some nights when he would rather have gone elsewhere.

Swaggering Pete loomed like a golden sun to Maggie. He took her to a dime museum, where rows of meek freaks astonished her. She contemplated their deformities with awe, and thought them a sort of chosen tribe. Pete, racking his brains for amusement, discovered the Central Park Menagerie and the Museum of Arts. Sunday afternoons would sometimes find them at these places. Pete did not appear to be particularly interested in what he saw. He stood around looking heavy, while Maggie giggled in glee.

Once at the menagerie he went into a trance of admiration before the spectacle of a very small monkey threatening to thrash a cageful because one of them had pulled his tail and he had not wheeled about quickly enough to discover who did it. Ever after Pete knew that monkey by sight, and winked at him, trying to induce him to fight with other and larger monkeys.

At the museum, Maggie said, "Dis is outa sight!"

"Aw, rats!" said Pete; "wait till next summer an' I'll take yehs to a picnic."

While the girl wandered in the vaulted rooms, Pete occupied himself in returning, stony stare for stony stare, the appalling scrutiny of the watch-dogs of the treasures. Occasionally he would remark in loud tones, "Dat jay has got glass eyes," and sentences of the sort. When he tired of this amusement he would go to the mummies and moralize over them.

Usually he submitted with silent dignity to all that he had to go through, but at times he was goaded into comment. "Aw!" he demanded once. "Look at all dese little jugs! Hundred jugs in a row! Ten rows in a case, an' 'bout a t'ousand cases! What d' blazes use is dem?"

In the evenings of week days he often took her to see plays in which the dazzling heroine was rescued from the palatial home of her treacherous guardian by the hero with the beautiful sentiments. The latter spent most of his time out at soak in pale-green snow-storms, busy with a nickel-plated revolver rescuing aged strangers from villains. Maggie lost herself in sympathy with the wanderers swooning in snow-storms beneath happy-hued church windows, while a choir within sang "Joy to the World." To Maggie and the rest of the audience this was transcendental realism. Joy always within, and they, like the actor, inevitably without. Viewing it, they hugged themselves in ecstatic pity of their imagined or real condition. The girl thought the arrogance and granite-heartedness of the magnate of the play were very accurately drawn. She echoed the maledictions that the occupants of the gallery showered on this individual when his lines compelled him to expose his extreme selfishness.

Shady persons in the audience revolted from the pictured villainy of the drama. With untiring zeal they hissed vice and applauded virtue. Unmistakably bad men evinced an apparently sincere admiration for virtue. The loud gallery was overwhelmingly with the unfortunate and the oppressed. They encouraged the struggling hero with cries, and jeered the villain, hooting and calling attention to his whiskers. When anybody died in the pale-green snow-storms, the gallery mourned. They sought out the painted misery and hugged it as akin.

In the hero's erratic march from poverty in the first act to wealth and triumph in the final one, in which he forgives all the enemies that he has left, he was assisted by the gallery, which applauded his generous and noble sentiments and confounded the speeches of his opponents by making irrelevant but very sharp remarks. Those actors who were cursed with the parts of villains were confronted at every turn by the gallery. If one of them rendered lines containing the most subtle distinctions between right and wrong, the gallery was immediately aware that the actor meant wickedness, and denounced him accordingly. The last act was a triumph for the hero, poor and of the masses, the representative of the audience, over the villain and the rich man, his pockets stuffed with bonds, his heart packed with tyrannical purposes, imperturbable amid suffering.

Maggie always departed with raised spirits from these melodramas. She rejoiced at the way in which the poor and virtuous eventually overcame the wealthy and wicked. The theatre made her think. She wondered if the culture and refinement she had seen imitated, perhaps grotesquely, by the heroine on the stage, could be acquired by a girl who lived in a tenement house and worked in a shirt factory.

9

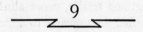

A group of urchins were intent upon the side door of a saloon. Expectancy gleamed from their eyes. They were twisting their fingers in excitement. "Here she comes!" yelled one of them suddenly. The group of urchins burst instantly asunder and its individual fragments were spread in a wide, respectable half-circle about the point of interest. The saloon door opened with a crash, and the figure of a woman appeared upon the threshold. Her grey hair fell in knotted masses about her shoulders. Her face was crimsoned and wet with perspiration. Her eyes had a rolling glare. "Not a cent more of me money will yehs ever get—not a red! I spent me money here fer t'ree years, an' now yehs tells me yeh'll sell me no more stuff! Go fall on yerself, Johnnie Murckre! 'Disturbance'? Disturbance be blowed! Go fall on yerself, Johnnie——"

The door received a kick of exasperation from within, and the woman lurched heavily out on the sidewalk. The gamins in the half-circle became violently agitated. They began to dance about and hoot and yell and jeer. A wide dirty grin spread over each face.

The woman made a furious dash at a particularly outrageous cluster of little boys. They laughed delightedly, and scampered off a short distance, calling out to her over their shoulders. She stood tottering on the kerb-stone and thundered at them. "Yeh devil's kids!" she howled, shaking her fists. The little boys whooped in glee. As she started up the street they fell in behind and marched uproariously. Occasionally she wheeled about and made charges on them. They ran nimbly out of reach and taunted her.

In the frame of a gruesome doorway she stood for a moment cursing them. Her hair straggled, giving her red features a look of insanity. Her great fists quivered as she shook them madly in the air. The urchins made terrific noises until she turned and disappeared. Then they filed off quietly in the way they had come.

The woman floundered about in the lower hall of the tenement house, and finally stumbled up the stairs. On an upper hall a door was opened and a collection of heads peered curiously out, watching her. With a wrathful snort the woman confronted the door, but it was slammed hastily in her face and the key was turned.

She stood for a few minutes, delivering a frenzied challenge at the panels. "Come out in deh hall, Mary Murphy, if yehs want a scrap! Come ahn! yeh over-grown terrier, come ahn!" She began to kick the door. She shrilly defied the universe to appear and do battle. Her cursing trebles brought heads from all doors save the one she threatened. Her eyes glared in every direction. The air was full of her tossing fists. "Come ahn! deh hull gang of yehs, come ahn!" she roared at the spectators. An oath or two, catcalls, jeers, and bits of facetious advice were given in reply. Missiles clattered about her feet.

"What's wrong wi'che?" said a voice in the gathered gloom, and Jimmie came forward. He carried a tin dinner-pail in his hand and under his arm a truckman's brown apron done in a bundle. "What's wrong?" he demanded.

"Come out! all of yehs, come out," his mother was howling. "Come ahn an' I'll stamp yer faces t'rough d' floor."

"Shet yer face, an' come home, yeh old fool!" roared Jimmie at her. She strode up to him and twirled her fingers in his face. Her eyes were darting flames of unreasoning rage, and her frame trembled with eagerness for a fight.

"An' who are youse? I ain't givin' a snap of me fingers fer youse!" she bawled at him. She turned her huge back in tremendous disdain and climbed the stairs to the next floor.

Jimmie followed, and at the top of the flight he seized his mother's arm and started to drag her toward the door of their room. "Come home!" he gritted between his teeth.

"Take yer hands off me! Take yer hands off me!" shrieked his mother. She raised her arm and whirled her great fist at her son's face. Jimmie dodged his head, and the blow struck him in the back of the neck. "Come home!" he gritted again. He threw out his left hand and writhed his fingers about her middle arm. The mother and the son began to sway and struggle like gladiators.

"Whoop!" said the Rum Alley tenement house. The hall filled with interested spectators. "Hi, ol' lady, dat was a dandy!" "T'ree t' one on d' red!" "Ah, quit yer scrappin'!"

The door of the Johnson home opened and Maggie looked out. Jimmie made a supreme cursing effort and hurled his mother into the room. He quickly followed and closed the door. The Rum Alley tenement swore disappointedly and retired.

The mother slowly gathered herself up from the floor. Her eyes glittered menacingly upon her children.

"Here now," said Jimmie, "we've had enough of dis. Sit down, an' don' make no trouble."

He grasped her arm and, twisting it, forced her into a creaking chair.

"Keep yer hands off me!" roared his mother again.

"Say, yeh ol' bat! Quit dat!" yelled Jimmie, madly. Maggie shrieked and ran into the other room. To her there came the sound of a storm of crashes and curses. There was a great final thump and Jimmie's voice cried: "Dere, now! Stay still." Maggie opened the door now, and went warily out. "Oh, Jimmie!"

He was leaning against the wall and swearing. Blood stood upon bruises on his knotty forearms where they had scraped against the floor or the walls in the scuffle. The mother lay screeching on the floor, the tears running down her furrowed face.

Maggie, standing in the middle of the room, gazed about her. The usual upheaval of the tables and chairs had taken place. Crockery was strewn broadcast in fragments. The stove had been disturbed on its legs, and now leaned idiotically to one side. A pail had been upset and water spread in all directions.

The door opened and Pete appeared. He shrugged his shoulders. "Oh, gee!" he observed. He walked over to Maggie and whispered in her ear: "Ah, what d' hell, Mag? Come ahn and we'll have a outa-sight time."

The mother in the corner upreared her head and shook her tangled locks. "Aw, yer bote no good, needer of yehs," she said, glowering at her daughter in the gloom. Her eyes seemed to burn balefully. "Yeh've gone t' d' devil, Mag Johnson, yehs knows yehs have gone t' d' devil. Yer a disgrace t' yer people. An' now, git out an' go ahn wid dat doe-faced jude of yours. Go wid him, curse yeh, an' a good riddance. Go, an' see how yeh likes it."

Maggie gazed long at her mother.

"Go now, an' see how yeh likes it. Git out. I won't have sech as youse in me house! Git out, d' yeh hear! Damn yeh, git out!"

The girl began to tremble.

At this instant Pete came forward. "Oh, what d' hell, Mag, see?" whispered he softly in her ear. "Dis all blows over. See? D' ol' woman'ill be all right in d' mornin'. Come ahn out wid me! We'll have a outa-sight time."

The woman on the floor cursed. Jimmie was intent upon his bruised forearms. The girl cast a glance about the room filled with a chaotic mass of *débris*, and at the writhing body of her mother.

"Git th' devil outa here."

Maggie went.

10

Jimmie had an idea it wasn't common courtesy for a friend to come to one's home and ruin one's sister. But he was not sure how much Pete knew about the rules of politeness.

The following night he returned home from work at a rather late hour in the evening. In passing through the halls he came upon the gnarled and leathery old woman who possessed the music-box. She was grinning in the dim light that drifted through dust-stained panes. She beckoned to him with a smudged forefinger.

"Ah, Jimmie, what do yehs t'ink I tumbled to, las' night! It was deh funnies' t'ing I ever saw," she cried, coming close to him and leering. She was trembling with eagerness to tell her tale. "I was by me door las' night when yer sister and her jude feller came in late, oh, very late. An' she, the dear, she was a-cryin' as if her heart would break, she was. It was deh funnies' t'ing I ever saw. An' right out here by me door she asked him did he love her, did he. An' she was a-crying as if her heart would break, poor t'ing. An' him, I could see be deh way what he said it dat she had been askin' orften; he says, 'Oh, gee, yes,' he says, says he. 'Oh, gee, yes.'"

Storm-clouds swept over Jimmie's face, but he turned from the leathery old woman and plodded on upstairs.

"'Oh, gee, yes,'" she called after him. She laughed a laugh that was like a prophetic croak.

There was no one in at home. The rooms showed that attempts had been made at tidying them. Parts of the wreckage of the day before had been repaired by an unskilled hand A chair or two and the table stood uncertainly upon legs. The floor had been newly swept. The blue ribbons had been restored to the curtains, and the lambrequin, with its immense sheaves of yellow wheat and red roses of equal size, had been returned, in a worn and sorry state, to its place at the mantel. Maggie's jacket and hat were gone from the nail behind the door.

Jimmie walked to the window and began to look through the blurred glass. It occurred to him to wonder vaguely, for an instant, if some of the women of his acquaintance had brothers.

Suddenly, however, he began to swear. "But he was me frien'! I brought 'im here! Dat's d' devil of it!" He fumed about the room, his anger gradually rising to the furious pitch. "I'll kill deh jay! Dat's what I'll do! I'll kill deh jay!"

He clutched his hat and sprang toward the door. But it opened, and his mother's great form blocked the passage. "What's d' matter wid yeh?" exclaimed she, coming into the rooms.

Jimmie gave vent to a sardonic curse and then laughed heavily, "Well, Maggie's gone teh d' devil! Dat's what! See?"

"Eh?" said his mother.

"Maggie's gone teh d' devil! Are yehs deaf?" roared Jimmie, impatiently.

"Aw, git out!" murmured the mother, astounded.

Jimmie grunted, and then began to stare out the window. His mother sat down in a chair, but a moment late sprang erect and delivered a maddened whirl of oaths. Her son turned to look at her as she reeled and swayed in the middle of the room, her fierce face convulsed with passion, her blotched arms raised high in imprecation.

"May she be cursed for ever!" she shrieked. "May she eat nothin' but stones and deh dirt in deh street. May she sleep in deh gutter an' never see deh sun shine again. D' bloomin'——"

"Here now," said her son. "Go fall on yerself, an' quit dat."

The mother raised lamenting eyes to the ceiling. "She's d' devil's own chil', Jimmie," she whispered. "Ah, who would t'ink such a bad girl could grow up in our fambly, Jimmie, me son. Many d' hour I've spent in talk wid dat girl an' tol' her if she ever went on d' streets I'd see her damned. An' after all her bringin'-up an' what I tol' her and talked wid her, she goes teh d' bad, like a duck teh water."

The tears rolled down her furrowed face. Her hands trembled. "An' den when dat Sadie MacMallister next door to us was sent teh d' devil by dat feller what worked in d' soap factory, didn't I tell our Mag dat if she——"

"Ah, dat's anudder story," interrupted the brother. "Of course, dat Sadie was nice an' all dat—but—see?—it ain't dessame as if—well, Maggie was diff'ent—see?—she was diff'ent." He was trying to formulate a theory that he had always unconsciously held, that all sisters excepting his own could, advisedly, be ruined.

He suddenly broke out again. "I'll go t'ump d' mug what done her d' harm. I'll kill 'im! He t'inks he kin scrap, but when he gits me a-chasin' 'im he'll fin' out where he's wrong, d' big stiff! I'll wipe up d' street wid 'im." In a fury he plunged out the doorway.

As he vanished the mother raised her head and lifted both hands, entreating. "May she be cursed for ever!" she cried.

In the darkness of the hallway Jimmie discerned a knot of women talking volubly. When he strode by they paid no attention to him. "She allus was a bold thing," he heard one of them cry in an eager voice. "Dere wasn't a feller come teh deh house but she'd try teh mash 'im. My Annie says deh shameless t'ing tried teh ketch her feller, her own feller, what we useter know his fader."

"I could 'a' tol' yehs dis two years ago," said a woman, in a key of triumph. "Yes, sir, it was over two years ago dat I says teh my ol' man, I says, 'Dat Johnson girl ain't straight,' I says. 'Oh, rats!' he says. 'Oh, hell!' 'Dat's all right,' I says, 'but I know what I knows,' I says, 'an' it'll come out later. You wait an' see,' I says, 'you see.'"

"Anybody what had eyes could see dat dere was somethin' wrong wid dat girl. I didn't like her actions."

On the street Jimmie met a friend. "What's wrong?" asked the latter.

Jimmie explained. "An' I'll t'ump 'im till he can't stand."

"Oh, go ahn!" said the friend. "What's deh use! Yeh'll git pulled in! Everybody 'ill be on to it! An' ten plunks! Gee!"

Jimmie was determined. "He t'inks he kin scrap, but he'll fin' out diff'ent."

"Gee!" remonstrated the friend, "what's d' use?"

I I

On a corner a glass-fronted building shed a yellow glare upon the pavements. The open mouth of a saloon called seductively to passengers to enter and annihilate sorrow or create rage.

The interior of the place was papered in olive and bronze tints of imitation leather. A shining bar of counterfeit massiveness extended down the side of the room. Behind it a great mahogany-imitation sideboard reached the ceiling. Upon its shelves rested pyramids of shimmering glasses that were never disturbed. Mirrors set in the face of the sideboard multiplied them. Lemons, oranges, and paper napkins, arranged with mathematical precision, sat among the glasses. Many-hued decanters of liquor perched at regular intervals on the lower shelves. A nickel-plated cash-register occupied a place in the exact centre of the general effect. The elementary senses of it all seemed to be opulence and geometrical accuracy.

Across from the bar a smaller counter held a collection of plates upon which swarmed frayed fragments of crackers, slices of boiled ham, dishevelled bits of cheese, and pickles swimming in vinegar. An odour of grasping, begrimed hands and munching mouths pervaded all.

Pete, in a white jacket, was behind the bar bending expectantly toward a quiet stranger. "A beeh," said the man. Pete drew a foam-topped glassful, and set it dripping upon the bar.

At this moment the light bamboo doors at the entrance swung open and crashed against the wall. Jimmie and a companion entered. They swaggered unsteadily but belligerently toward the bar, and looked at Pete with bleared and blinking eyes.

"Gin," said Jimmie.

"Gin," said the companion.

Pete slid a bottle and two glasses along the bar. He bent his head sideways as he assiduously polished away with a napkin at the gleaming wood. He wore a look of watchfulness.

Jimmie and his companion kept their eyes upon the bartender and conversed loudly in tones of contempt.

"He's a dandy masher, ain't he?" laughed Jimmie.

"Well, ain't he!" said the companion, sneering. "He's great, he is. Git on to deh mug on deh blokie. Dat's enough to make a feller turn handsprings in 'is sleep."

The quiet stranger moved himself and his glass a trifle farther away and maintained an attitude of obliviousness.

"Gee! ain't he hot stuff?"

"Git on to his shape!"

"Hey!" cried Jimmie, in tones of command. Pete came along slowly, with a sullen dropping of the under lip.

"Well," he growled, "what's eatin' yehs?"

"Gin," said Jimmie.

"Gin," said the companion.

As Pete confronted them with the bottle and the glasses they laughed in his face. Jimmie's companion, evidently overcome with merriment, pointed a grimy forefinger in Pete's direction. "Say, Jimmie," demanded he, "what's dat behind d' bar?"

"Looks like some chump," replied Jimmie. They laughed loudly.

Pete put down a bottle with a bang and turned a formidable face toward them. He disclosed his teeth, and his shoulders heaved restlessly. "You fellers can't guy me," he said. "Drink yer stuff an' git out an' don' make no trouble."

Instantly the laughter faded from the faces of the two men, and expressions of offended dignity immediately came. "Aw, who has said anyt'ing t' you?" cried they in the same breath.

The quiet stranger looked at the door calculatingly.

"Ah, come off," said Pete to the two men. "Don't pick me up fer no jay. Drink yer rum an' git out an' don' make no trouble."

"Aw, go ahn!" airily cried Jimmie.

"Aw, go ahn!" airily repeated his companion.

"We goes when we git ready! See?" continued Jimmie.

"Well," said Pete in a threatening voice, "don' make no trouble."

Jimmie suddenly leaned forward with his head on one side. He snarled like a wild animal. "Well, what if we does? See?" said he.

Hot blood flushed into Pete's face, and he shot a lurid glance at Jimmie. "Well, den we'll see who's d' bes' man, you or me," he said.

The quiet stranger moved modestly toward the door.

Jimmie began to swell with valour. "Don' pick me up fer no tenderfoot. When yeh tackles me yeh tackles one of d' bes' men in d' city. See? I'm a scrapper, I am. Ain't dat right, Billie?"

"Sure, Mike," responded his companion in tones of conviction.

"Aw!" said Pete, easily. "Go fall on yerself."

The two men again began to laugh.

"What is dat talking?" cried the companion.

"Don' ast me," replied Jimmie with exaggerated contempt.

Pete made a furious gesture. "Git outa here now, an' don' make no trouble. See? Youse fellers er lookin' fer a scrap, an' it's like yeh'll fin' one if yeh keeps on shootin' off yer mout's. I know yehs! See? I kin lick better men dan yehs ever saw in yer lifes. Dat's right! See? Don' pick me up fer no stiff, er yeh might be jolted out in d' street before yeh knows where yeh is. When I comes from behind dis bar, I t'rows yehs bote inteh d' street. See?"

"Ah, go ahn!" cried the two men in chorus.

The glare of a panther came into Pete's eyes. "Dat's what I said! Unnerstan'?"

He came through a passage at the end of the bar and swelled down upon the two men. They stepped promptly forward and crowded close to him. They bristled like three roosters. They moved their heads pugnaciously and kept their shoulders braced. The nervous muscles about each mouth twitched with a forced smile of mockery.

"Well, what yer goin' t' do?" gritted Jimmie.

Pete stepped warily back, waving his hands before him to keep the men from coming too near.

"Well, what yer goin' t' do?" repeated Jimmie's ally. They kept close to him, taunting and leering. They strove to make him attempt the initial blow.

"Keep back now! Don' crowd me," said Pete ominously.

Again they chorused in contempt. "Aw, go ahn!"

In a small, tossing group, the three men edged for positions like frigates contemplating battle.

"Well, why don' yeh try t' t'row us out?" cried Jimmie and his ally with copious sneers.

The bravery of bulldogs sat upon the faces of the men. Their clenched fists moved like eager weapons. The allied two jostled the bartender's elbows, glaring at him with feverish eyes and forcing him toward the wall.

Suddenly Pete swore furiously. The flash of action gleamed from his eyes. He threw back his arm and aimed a tremendous, lightning-like blow at Jimmie's face. His foot swung a step forward and the weight of his body was behind his fist. Jimmie ducked his head, Bowery-like, with the quickness of a cat. The fierce answering blows of Jimmie and his ally crushed on Pete's bowed head.

The quiet stranger vanished.

The arms of the combatants whirled in the air like flails. The faces of the men, at first flushed to flame-coloured anger, now began to fade to the pallor of warriors in the blood and heat of a battle. Their lips curled back and stretched tightly over the gums in ghoul-like grins. Through their white, gripped teeth struggled hoarse whisperings of oaths. Their eyes glittered with murderous fire.

Each head was huddled between its owner's shoulders, and arms were swinging with marvellous rapidity. Feet scraped to and fro with a loud scratching sound upon the sanded floor. Blows left crimson blotches upon the pale skin. The curses of the first quarter-minute of the fight died away. The breaths of the fighters came wheezing from their lips and the three chests were straining and heaving. Pete at intervals gave vent to low, laboured hisses, that sounded like a desire to kill. Jimmie's ally gibbered at times like a wounded maniac. Jimmie was silent, fighting with the face of a sacrificial priest. The rage of fear shone in all their eyes, and their blood-coloured fists whirled.

At a critical moment a blow from Pete's hand struck the ally, and he crashed to the floor. He wriggled instantly to his feet and, grasping the quiet stranger's beer-glass from the bar, hurled it at Pete's head.

High on the wall it burst like a bomb, shivering fragments flying in all directions. Then missiles came to every man's hand. The place had heretofore appeared free of things to throw, but suddenly glasses and bottles went singing through the air. They were thrown point-blank at bobbing heads. The pyramids of shimmering glasses, that had never been disturbed, changed to cascades as heavy bottles were flung into them. Mirrors splintered to nothing.

The three frothing creatures on the floor buried themselves in a frenzy for blood. There followed in the wake of missiles and fists some unknown prayers, perhaps for death.

The quiet stranger had sprawled very pyrotechnically out on the sidewalk. A laugh ran up and down the avenue for the half of a block. "Dey've t'rowed a bloke inteh deh street."

People heard the sound of breaking glass and shuffling feet within the saloon and came running. A small group, bending down to look under the bamboo doors, and watching the fall of glass and three pairs of violent legs, changed in a moment to a crowd. A policeman came charging down the sidewalk and bounced through the doors into the saloon. The crowd bent and surged in absorbing anxiety to see.

Jimmie caught the first sight of the oncoming interruption. On his feet he had the same regard for a policeman that, when on his truck, he had for a fire-engine. He howled and ran for the side door.

The officer made a terrific advance, club in hand. One comprehensive sweep of the long night-stick threw the ally to the floor and forced Pete to a corner. With his disengaged hand he made a furious effort at Jimmie's coat-tails. Then he regained his balance and paused. "Well, well, you are a pair of pictures. What have ye been up to?"

Jimmie, with his face drenched in blood, escaped up a side street, pursued a short distance by some of the more law-loving or excited individuals of the crowd.

Later, from a safe dark corner, he saw the policeman, the ally, and the bartender emerge from the saloon. Pete locked the doors and then followed up the avenue in the rear of the crowd-encompassed policeman and his charge.

At first Jimmie, with his heart throbbing at battle heat, started to go desperately to the rescue of his friend, but he halted. "Ah, what's d' use?" he demanded of himself.

12

In a hall of irregular shape sat Pete and Maggie drinking beer. A submissive orchestra dictated to by a spectacled man with frowsy hair and in soiled evening dress, industriously followed the bobs of his head and the waves of his baton. A ballad-singer, in a gown of flaming scarlet, sang in the inevitable voice of brass. When she vanished, men seated at the tables near the front applauded loudly, pounding the polished wood with their beer-glasses. She returned attired in less gown, and sang again. She received another enthusiastic encore. She reappeared in still less gown and danced. The deafening rumble of glasses and clapping of hands that followed her exit indicated an overwhelming desire to have her come on for the fourth time, but the curiosity of the audience was not gratified.

Maggie was pale. From her eyes had been plucked all look of self-reliance. She leaned with a dependent air toward her companion. She was timid, as if fearing his anger or displeasure. She seemed to beseech tenderness of him.

Pete's air of distinguished valour had grown upon him until it threatened to reach stupendous dimensions. He was infinitely gracious to the girl. It was apparent to her that his condescension was a marvel. He could appear to strut even while sitting still, and he showed that he was a lion of lordly characteristics by the air with which he spat.

With Maggie gazing at him wonderingly, he took pride in commanding the waiters, who were, however, indifferent or deaf. "Hi, you, git a russle on yehs! What yehs lookin' at? Two more beehs, d' yeh hear?" He leaned back and critically regarded the person of a girl with a straw-coloured wig who was flinging her heels about upon the stage in somewhat awkward imitation of a well-known *danseuse*.

At times Maggie told Pete long confidential tales of her former home life, dwelling upon the escapades of the other members of the family and the difficulties she had had to combat in order to obtain a degree of comfort. He responded in the accents of philanthropy. He pressed her arm with an air of reassuring proprietorship.

"Dey was cursed jays," he said, denouncing the mother and brother.

The sound of the music which, through the efforts of the frowsy-headed leader, drifted to her ears in the smoke-filled atmosphere, made the girl dream. She thought of her former Rum Alley environment and turned to regard Pete's strong protecting fists. She thought of a collar-and-cuff manufactory and the eternal moan of the proprietor: "What een hale do you sink I pie fife dolla a week for? Play? No, py tamn!" She contemplated Pete's man-subduing eyes and noted that wealth and prosperity were indicated by his clothes. She imagined a future rose-tinted because of its distance from all that she had experienced before.

As to the present she perceived only vague reasons to be miserable. Her life was Pete's, and she considered him worthy of the charge. She would be disturbed by no particular apprehensions so long as Pete adored her as he now said he did. She did not feel like a bad woman. To her knowledge she had never seen any better.

At times men at other tables regarded the girl furtively. Pete, aware of it, nodded at her and grinned. He felt proud. "Mag, yer a bloomin' good looker," he remarked, studying her face through the haze. The men made Maggie fear, but she blushed at Pete's words as it became apparent to her that she was the apple of his eye.

Grey-headed men, wonderfully pathetic in their dissipation, stared at her through clouds. Smooth-cheeked boys, some of them with faces of stone and mouths of sin, not nearly so pathetic as the grey heads, tried to find the girl's eyes in the smoke-wreaths. Maggie considered she was not what they thought her. She confined her glances to Pete and the stage.

The orchestra played negro melodies, and a versatile drummer pounded, whacked, clattered, and scratched on a dozen machines to make noise.

Those glances of the men, shot at Maggie from under half-closed lids, made her tremble. She thought them all to be worse men than Pete. "Come, let's go," she said.

As they went out Maggie perceived two women seated at a table with some men. They were painted, and their cheeks had lost their roundness. As she passed them the girl, with a shrinking movement, drew back her skirts.

13

Jimmie did not return home for a number of days after the fight with Pete in the saloon. When he did, he approached with extreme caution.

He found his mother raving. Maggie had not returned home. The parent continually wondered how her daughter could come to such a pass. She had never considered Maggie as a pearl dropped unstained into Rum Alley from Heaven, but she could not conceive how it was possible for her daughter to fall so low as to bring disgrace upon her family. She was terrific in denunciation of the girl's wickedness.

The fact that the neighbours talked of it maddened her. When women came in, and in the course of their conversation casually asked, "Where's Maggie dese days?" the mother shook her fuzzy head at them and appalled them with curses. Cunning hints inviting confidence she rebuffed with violence.

"An' wid all d' bringin'-up she had, how could she?" moaningly she asked of her son. "Wid all d' talkin' wid her I did an' d' t'ings I tol' her to remember. When a girl is bringed up d' way I bringed up Maggie, how kin she go teh d' devil?"

Jimmie was transfixed by these questions. He could not conceive how, under the circumstances, his mother's daughter and his sister could have been so wicked.

His mother took a drink from a bottle that sat on the table. She continued her lament. "She had a bad heart, dat girl did, Jimmie. She was wicked t' d' heart an' we never knowed it."

Jimmie nodded, admitting the fact.

"We lived in d' same house wid her an' I brought her up, an' we never knowed how bad she was."

Jimmie nodded again.

"Wid a home like dis an' a mudder like me, she went teh d' bad," cried the mother, raising her eyes.

One day Jimmie came home, sat down in a chair, and began to wriggle about with a new and strange nervousness. At last he spoke shamefacedly. "Well, look-a-here, dis t'ing queers us! See? We're queered! An' maybe it 'ud be better if I—well, I t'ink I kin look 'er up an'—maybe it 'ud be better if I fetched her home an'——"

The mother started from her chair and broke forth into a storm of passionate anger. "What! Let 'er come an' sleep under deh same roof wid her mudder agin? Oh, yes, I will, won't I! Sure! Shame on yehs, Jimmie Johnson, fer sayin' such a t'ing teh yer own mudder! Little did I t'ink when yehs was a babby playin' about me feet dat ye'd grow up teh say sech a t'ing teh yer mudder—yer own mudder. I never t'ought——"

Sobs choked her and interrupted her reproaches.

"Dere ain't nottin' teh make sech trouble about," said Jimmie. "I on'y says it 'ud be better if we keep dis t'ing dark, see? It queers us! See?"

His mother laughed a laugh that seemed to ring through the city and be echoed and re-echoed by countless other laughs. "Oh, yes, I will, won't I? Sure!"

"Well, yeh must take me fer a damn fool," said Jimmie, indignant at his mother for mocking him. "I didn't say we'd make 'er inteh a little tin angel, ner nottin', but deh way it is now she can queer us! Don'che see?"

"Ay, she'll git tired of deh life atter a while, an' den she'll wanna be a-comin' home, won' she, deh beast! I'll let 'er in den, won't I?"

"Well, I didn't mean none of dis prod'gal bus'ness anyway," explained Jimmie.

"It wa'n't no prod'gal daughter, yeh fool," said the mother. "It was prod'gal son, anyhow."

"I know dat," said Jimmie.

For a time they sat in silence. The mother's eyes gloated on the scene which her imagination called before her. Her lips were set in a vindictive smile. "Ay, she'll cry, won' she, an' carry on, an' tell how Pete, or some odder feller, beats 'er, an' she'll say she's sorry an' all dat, an' she ain't happy, she ain't, an' she wants to come home agin, she does." With grim humour the mother imitated the possible wailing notes of the daughter's voice. "Den I'll take 'er in, won't I? She kin cry 'er two eyes out on deh stones of deh street before I'll dirty d' place wid her. She abused an' ill-treated her own mudder—her own mudder what loved her, an' she'll never git anodder chance."

Jimmie thought he had a great idea of women's frailty, but he could not understand why any of his kin should be victims. "Curse her!" he said fervidly. Again he wondered vaguely if some of the women of his acquaintance had brothers. Nevertheless, his mind did not for an instant confuse himself with those brothers nor his sister with theirs.

After the mother had, with great difficulty, suppressed the neighbours, she went among them and proclaimed her grief. "May Heaven forgive dat girl," was her continual cry. To attentive ears she recited the whole length and breadth of her woes. "I bringed 'er up deh way a daughter oughta be bringed up, an' dis is how she served me! She went teh deh devil deh first chance she got! May Heaven forgive her."

When arrested for drunkenness she used the story of her daughter's downfall with telling effect upon the police justices. Finally one of them said to her, peering down over his spectacles: "Mary, the records of this and other courts show that you are the mother of forty-two daughters who have been ruined. The case is unparalleled in the annals of this court, and this court thinks——"

The mother went through life shedding large tears of sorrow. Her red face was a picture of agony.

Of course Jimmie publicly damned his sister that he might appear on a higher social plane. But, arguing with himself, stumbling about in ways that he knew not, he, once, almost came to a conclusion that his sister would have been more firmly good had she better known how. However, he felt that he could not hold such a view. He threw it hastily aside.

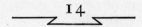

In a hilarious hall there were twenty-eight tables and twenty-eight women and a crowd of smoking men. Valiant noise was made on a stage at the end of the hall by an orchestra composed of men who looked as if they had just happened in. Soiled waiters ran to and fro, swooping down like hawks on the unwary in the throng; clattering along the aisles with trays covered with glasses; stumbling over women's skirts and charging two prices for everything but beer, all with a swiftness that blurred the view of the coconut palms and dusty monstrosities painted upon the walls of the room. A "bouncer," with an immense load of business upon his hands, plunged about in the crowd, dragging bashful strangers to prominent chairs, ordering waiters here and there, and quarrelling furiously with men who wanted to sing with the orchestra.

The usual smoke-cloud was present, but so dense that heads and arms seemed entangled in it. The rumble of conversation was replaced by a roar. Plenteous oaths heaved through the air. The room rang with the shrill voices of women bubbling over with drink-laughter. The chief element in the music of the orchestra was speed. The musicians played in intent fury. A woman was singing and smiling upon the stage, but no one took notice of her. The rate at which the piano, cornet, and violins were going seemed to impart wildness to the half-drunken crowd. Beer-glasses were emptied at a gulp and conversation became a rapid chatter. The smoke eddied and swirled like a shadowy river hurrying toward some unseen falls. Pete and Maggie entered the hall and took chairs at a table near the door. The woman who was seated there made an attempt to occupy Pete's attention, and, failing, went away.

Three weeks had passed since the girl had left home. The air of spaniel-like dependence had been magnified and showed its direct effect in the peculiar off-handedness and ease of Pete's ways toward her. She followed Pete's eyes with hers, anticipating with smiles gracious looks from him.

A woman of brilliance and audacity, accompanied by a mere boy, came into the place and took a seat near them. At once Pete sprang to his feet, his face beaming with glad surprise. "Hully gee, dere's Nellie!" he cried. He went over to the table and held out an eager hand to the woman.

"Why, hello, Pete, me boy, how are you?" said she, giving him her fingers.

Maggie took instant note of the woman. She perceived that her black dress fitted her to perfection. Her linen collar and cuffs were spotless. Tan gloves were stretched over her well-shaped hands. A hat of a prevailing fashion perched jauntily upon her dark hair. She wore no jewelry and was painted with no apparent paint. She looked clear-eyed through the stares of the men.

"Sit down, and call your lady friend over," she said to Pete. At his beckoning Maggie came and sat between Pete and the mere boy.

"I t'ought yeh was gone away fer good," began Pete, at once. "When did yeh git back? How did dat Buff'lo business turn out?"

The woman shrugged her shoulders. "Well, he didn't have as many stamps as he tried to make out, so I shook him, that's all."

"Well, I'm glad teh see yehs back in deh city," said Pete, with gallantry. He and the woman entered into a long conversation, exchanging reminiscences of days together. Maggie sat still, unable to formulate an intelligent sentence as her addition to the conversation, and painfully aware of it.

She saw Pete's eyes sparkle as he gazed upon the handsome stranger. He listened smilingly to all she said. The woman was familiar with all his affairs, asked him about mutual friends, and knew the amount of his salary. She paid no attention to Maggie, looking toward her once or twice and apparently seeing the wall beyond.

The mere boy was sulky. In the beginning he had welcomed the additions with acclamations. "Let's all have a drink! What'll you take, Nell? And you, Miss What's-your-name. Have a drink, Mr.—— you, I mean." He had shown a sprightly desire to do the talking for the company and tell all about his family. In a loud voice he declaimed on various topics. He assumed a patronizing air toward Pete. As Maggie was silent, he paid no attention to her. He made a great show of lavishing wealth upon the woman of brilliance and audacity.

"Do keep still, Freddie! You talk like a clock," said the woman to him. She turned away and devoted her attention to Pete. "We'll have many a good time together again, eh?"

"Sure, Mike," said Pete, enthusiastic at once.

"Say," whispered she, leaning forward, "let's go over to Billie's and have a time."

"Well, it's dis way! See?" said Pete. "I got dis lady frien' here."

"Oh, g'way with her," argued the woman.

Pete appeared disturbed.

"All right," said she, nodding her head at him. "All right for you! We'll see the next time you ask me to go anywheres with you."

Pete squirmed. "Say," he said, beseechingly, "come wid me a minute an' I'll tell yer why."

The woman waved her hand. "Oh, that's all right, you needn't explain, you know. You wouldn't come merely because you wouldn't come, that's all." To Pete's visible distress she turned to the mere boy, bringing him speedily out of a terrific rage. He had been debating whether it would be the part of a man to pick a quarrel with Pete, or would he be justified in striking him savagely with his beer-glass without warning. But he recovered himself when the woman turned to renew her smilings. He beamed upon her with an expression that was somewhat tipsy and inexpressibly tender.

"Say, shake that Bowery jay," requested he, in a loud whisper.

"Freddie, you are so funny," she replied.

Pete reached forward and touched the woman on the arm. "Come out a minute while I tells yeh why I can't go wid yer. Yer doin' me dirt, Nell! I never t'ought ye'd do me dirt, Nell. Come on, will yer?" He spoke in tones of injury.

"Why, I don't see why I should be interested in your explanations," said the woman, with a coldness that seemed to reduce Pete to a pulp.

His eyes pleaded with her. "Come out a minute while I tells yeh. On d' level, now."

The woman nodded slightly at Maggie and the mere boy, saying, " 'Scuse me."

The mere boy interrupted his loving smile and turned a shrivelling glare upon Pete. His boyish countenance flushed and he spoke in a whine to the woman: "Oh, I say, Nellie, this ain't a square deal, you know. You aren't going' to leave me and go off with that duffer, are you? I should think——"

"Why, you dear boy, of course I'm not," cried the woman, affectionately. She bent over and whispered in his ear. He smiled again and settled in his chair as if resolved to wait patiently.

As the woman walked down between the rows of tables, Pete was at her shoulder talking earnestly, apparently in explanation. The woman waved her hands with studied airs of indifference. The doors swung behind them, leaving Maggie and the mere boy seated at the table.

Maggie was dazed. She could dimly perceive that something stupendous had happened. She wondered why Pete saw fit to remonstrate with the woman, pleading forgiveness with his eyes. She thought she noted an air of submission about her leonine Pete. She was astounded.

The mere boy occupied himself with cocktails and a cigar. He was tranquilly silent for half an hour. Then he bestirred himself and spoke. "Well," he said, sighing, "I knew this was the way it would be. They got cold feet." There was another stillness. The mere boy seemed to be musing. "She was pulling m' leg. That's the whole amount of it," he said, suddenly. "It's a bloomin' shame the way that girl does. Why, I've spent over two dollars in drinks to-night. And she goes off with that plug-ugly, who looks as if he had been hit in the face with a coin die. I call it rocky treatment for a fellah like me. Here, waiter, bring me a cocktail, and make it strong."

Maggie made no reply. She was watching the doors.

"It's a mean piece of business," complained the mere boy. He explained to her how amazing it was that anybody should treat him in such a manner. "But I'll get square with her, you bet. She won't get far ahead of yours truly, you know," he added, winking. "I'll tell her plainly that it was bloomin' mean business. And she won't come it over me with any of her 'now-Freddie-dear's.' She thinks my name is Freddie, you know, but of course it ain't. I always tell these people some name like that, because if they got on to your right name they might use it sometime. Understand? Oh, they don't fool me much."

Maggie was paying no attention, being intent upon the doors. The mere boy relapsed into a period of gloom, during which he exterminated a number of cocktails with a determined air, as if replying defiantly to fate. He occasionally broke forth into sentences composed of invectives joined together in a long chain.

The girl was still staring at the doors. After a time the mere boy began to see cobwebs just in front of his nose. He spurred himself into being agreeable and insisted upon her having a Charlotte Russe and a glass of beer.

"They's gone," he remarked, "they's gone." He looked at her through the smoke-wreaths. "Shay, lil' girl, we mightish well make bes' of it. You ain't such bad-lookin' girl, y' know. Not half bad. Can't come up to Nell, though. No, can't do it! Well, I should shay not! Nell fine-lookin' girl! F-i-n-ine. You look bad longsider her, but by y'self ain't so bad. Have to do, anyhow. Nell gone. O'ny you left. Not half bad, though."

Maggie stood up. "I'm going home," she said.

The mere boy started. "Eh? What? Home!" he cried, struck with amazement. "I beg pardon, did hear say home?"

"I'm going home," she repeated.

"Great heavens! what hav' a struck?" demanded the mere boy of himself, stupefied. In a semi-comatose state he conducted her on board an up-town car, ostentatiously paid her fare, leered kindly at her through the rear window, and fell off the steps.

15

A forlorn woman went along a lighted avenue. The street was filled with people desperately bound on missions. An endless crowd darted at the elevated station stairs, and the horse-cars were thronged with owners of bundles.

The pace of the forlorn woman was slow. She was apparently searching for some one. She loitered near the doors of saloons and watched men emerge from them. She furtively scanned the faces in the rushing stream of pedestrians. Hurrying men, bent on catching some boat or train, jostled her elbows, failing to notice her, their thoughts fixed on distant dinners.

The forlorn woman had a peculiar face. Her smile was no smile. But when in repose her features had a shadowy look that was like a sardonic grin, as if some one had sketched with cruel forefinger indelible lines about her mouth.

Jimmie came strolling up the avenue. The woman encountered him with an aggrieved air. "Oh, Jimmie, I've been lookin' all over for yehs——" she began.

Jimmie made an impatient gesture and quickened his pace. "Ah, don't bodder me!" he said, with the savageness of a man whose life is pestered.

The woman followed him along the sidewalk in somewhat the manner of a suppliant. "But, Jimmie," she said, "yehs told me yehs——"

Jimmie turned upon her fiercely as if resolved to make a last stand for comfort and peace. "Say, Hattie, don' foller me from one end of deh city teh deh odder. Let up, will yehs! Give me a minute's res', can't yehs? Yehs makes me tired, allus taggin' me. See? Ain' yehs got no sense? Do yehs want people teh get on to me? Go chase yerself."

The woman stepped closer and laid her fingers on his arm. "But, look a' here——"

Jimmie snarled. "Oh, go teh blazes!" He darted into the front door of a convenient saloon and a moment later came out into the shadows that surrounded the side door. On the brilliantly lighted avenue he perceived the forlorn woman dodging about like a scout. Jimmie laughed with an air of relief and went away.

When he returned home he found his mother clamouring. Maggie had returned. She stood shivering beneath the torrent of her mother's wrath.

"Well, I'm damned!" said Jimmie in greeting.

His mother, tottering about the room, pointed a quivering forefinger. "Look ut her, Jimmie, look ut her. Dere's yer sister, boy. Dere's yer sister. Look ut her! Look ut her!" She screamed at Maggie with scoffing laughter.

The girl stood in the middle of the room. She edged about as if unable to find a place on the floor to put her feet.

"Ha ha, ha!" bellowed the mother. "Dere she stands! Ain't she purty? Look ut her! Ain' she sweet, deh beast? Look ut her! Ha, ha! look ut her!" She lurched forward and put her red and seamed hands upon her daughter's face. She bent down and peered keenly up into the eyes of the girl. "Oh, she's jes' dessame as she ever was, ain' she? She's her mudder's putty darlin' yit, ain' she? Look ut her, Jimmie. Come here and look ut her."

The loud, tremendous railing of the mother brought the denizens of the Rum Alley tenement to their doors. Women came in the hallways. Children scurried to and fro.

"What's up? Dat Johnson party on anudder tear?"

"Naw! Young Mag's come home!"

"Git out!"

Through the open doors curious eyes stared in at Maggie. Children ventured into the room and ogled her as if they formed the front row at a theatre. Women, without, bent toward each other and whispered, nodding their heads with airs of profound philosophy.

A baby, overcome with curiosity concerning this object at which all were looking, sidled forward and touched her dress, cautiously, as if investigating a red-hot stove. Its mother's voice rang out like a warning trumpet. She rushed forward and grabbed her child, casting a terrible look of indignation at the girl.

Maggie's mother paced to and fro, addressing the doorful of eyes, expounding like a glib showman. Her voice rang through the building. "Dere she stands," she cried, wheeling suddenly and pointing with dramatic finger. "Dere she stands! Look ut her! Ain' she a dandy? An' she was so good as to come home teh her mudder, she was! Ain' she a beaut'? Ain' she a dandy?"

The jeering cries ended in another burst of shrill laughter.

The girl seemed to awaken. "Jimmie——"

He drew hastily back from her. "Well, now, yer a t'ing, ain' yeh?" he said, his lips curling in scorn. Radiant virtue sat upon his brow, and his repelling hands expressed horror of contamination.

Maggie turned and went.

The crowd at the door fell back precipitately. A baby falling down in front of the door wrenched a scream like that of a wounded animal from its mother. Another woman sprang forward and picked it up with a chivalrous air, as if rescuing a human being from an oncoming express train.

As the girl passed down through the hall, she went before open doors framing more eyes strangely microscopic, and sending broad beams of inquisitive light into the darkness of her path. On the second floor she met the gnarled old woman who possessed the music-box.

"So," she cried, " 'ere yehs are back again, are yehs? An' dey've kicked yehs out? Well, come in an' stay wid me t'-night. I ain' got no moral standin'."

From above came an unceasing babble of tongues, over all of which rang the mother's derisive laughter.

16

Pete did not consider that he had ruined Maggie. If he had thought that her soul could never smile again, he would have believed the mother and brother, who were pyrotechnic over the affair, to be responsible for it. Besides, in his world, souls did not insist upon being able to smile. "What d' hell?"

He felt a trifle entangled. It distressed him. Revelations and scenes might bring upon him the wrath of the owner of the saloon, who insisted upon respectability of an advanced type. "What do dey wanna raise such a smoke about it fer?" demanded he of himself, disgusted with the attitude of the family. He saw no necessity that people should lose their equilibrium merely because their sister or their daughter had stayed away from home. Searching about in his mind for possible reasons for their conduct, he came upon the conclusion that Maggie's motives were correct, but that the two others wished to snare him. He felt pursued.

The woman whom he had met in the hilarious hall showed a disposition to ridicule him. "A little pale thing with no spirit," she said. "Did you note the expression of her eyes? There was something in them about pumpkin pie and virtue. That is a peculiar way the left corner of her mouth has of twitching, isn't it? Dear, dear, Pete, what are you coming to?"

Pete asserted at once that he never was very much interested in the girl. The woman interrupted him, laughing. "Oh, it's not of the slightest consequence to me, my dear young man. You needn't draw maps for my benefit. Why should I be concerned about it?" But Pete continued with his explanations. If he was laughed at for his tastes in women, he felt obliged to say that they were only temporary or indifferent ones.

The morning after Maggie had departed from home Pete stood behind the bar. He was immaculate in white jacket and apron, and his hair was plastered over his brow with infinite correctness. No customers were in the place. Pete was twisting his napkined fist slowly in a beer-glass, softly whistling to himself, and occasionally holding the object of his attention between his eyes and a few weak beams of sunlight that found their way over the thick screens and into the shaded rooms.

With lingering thoughts of the woman of brilliance and audacity, the bartender raised his head and stared through the varying cracks between the swaying bamboo doors. Suddenly the whistling pucker faded from his lips. He saw Maggie walking slowly past. He gave a great start, fearing for the previously mentioned eminent respectability of the place.

He threw a swift, nervous glance about him, all at once feeling guilty. No one was in the room. He went hastily over to the side door. Opening it and looking out, he perceived Maggie standing, as if undecided, at the corner. She was searching the place with her eyes. As she turned her face toward him, Pete beckoned to her hurriedly, intent upon returning with speed to a position behind the bar, and to the atmosphere of respectability upon which the proprietor insisted.

Maggie came to him, the anxious look disappearing from her face and a smile wreathing her lips. "Oh, Pete——" she began brightly.

The bartender made a violent gesture of impatience. "Oh, say," cried he vehemently. "What d' yeh wanna hang aroun' here fer? Do yer wanna git me inteh trouble?" he demanded with an air of injury.

Astonishment swept over the girl's features. "Why, Pete! yehs tol' me——"

Pete's glance expressed profound irritation. His countenance reddened with the anger of a man whose respectability is being threatened. "Say, yehs makes me tired! See? What d' yeh wanna tag aroun' atter me fer? Yeh'll do me dirt wid d' ol man an' dey'll be trouble! If he sees a woman roun' here he'll go crazy an' I'll lose me job! See? Ain' yehs got no sense? Don' be allus bodderin' me. See? Yer brudder came in here an' made trouble an' d' ol' man hadda put up fer it! An' now I'm done! See? I'm done."

The girl's eyes stared into his face. "Pete, don' yeh remem——"

"Oh, go ahn!" interrupted Pete, anticipating.

The girl seemed to have a struggle with herself. She was apparently bewildered and could not find speech. Finally she asked in a low voice, "But where kin I go?"

The question exasperated Pete beyond the powers of endurance. It was a direct attempt to give him some responsibility in a matter that did not concern him. In his indignation he volunteered information. "Oh, go to hell!" cried he. He slammed the door furiously and returned, with an air of relief, to his respectability.

Maggie went away. She wandered aimlessly for several blocks. She stopped once and asked aloud a question of herself: "Who?" A man who was passing near her shoulder humorously took the questioning word as intended for him. "Eh! What? Who? Nobody! I didn't say anything," he laughingly said, and continued his way.

Soon the girl discovered that if she walked with such apparent aimlessness, some men looked at her with calculating eyes. She quickened her step, frightened. As a protection, she adopted a demeanour of intentness as if going somewhere.

After a time she left rattling avenues and passed between rows of houses with sternness and stolidity stamped upon their features. She hung her head, for she felt their eyes grimly upon her.

Suddenly she came upon a stout gentleman in a silk hat and a chaste black coat, whose decorous row of buttons reached from his chin to his knees. The girl had heard of the grace of God and she decided to approach this man. His beaming, chubby face was a picture of benevolence and kind-heartedness. His eyes shone good will.

But as the girl timidly accosted him he made a convulsive movement and saved his respectability by a vigorous side-step. He did not risk it to save a soul. For how was he to know that there was a soul before him that needed saving?

17

Upon a wet evening, several months later, two interminable rows of cars, pulled by slipping horses, jangled along a prominent side street. A dozen cabs, with coat-enshrouded drivers, clattered to and fro. Electric lights, whirring softly, shed a blurred radiance. A flower-dealer, his feet tapping impatiently, his nose and his wares glistening with raindrops, stood behind an array of roses and chrysanthemums. Two or three theatres emptied a crowd upon the storm-swept sidewalks. Men pulled their hats over their eyebrows and raised their collars to their ears. Women shrugged impatient shoulders in their warm cloaks and stopped to arrange their skirts for a walk through the storm. People who had been constrained to comparative silence for two hours burst into a roar of conversation, their hearts still kindling from the glowings of the stage.

The sidewalks became tossing seas of umbrellas. Men stepped forth to hail cabs or cars, raising their fingers in varied forms of polite request or imperative demand. An endless procession wended toward elevated stations. An atmosphere of pleasure and prosperity seemed to hang over the throng, born, perhaps, of good clothes and of two hours in a place of forgetfulness.

In the mingled light and gloom of an adjacent park, a handful of wet wanderers, in attitudes of chronic dejection, were scattered among the benches.

A girl of the painted cohorts of the city went along the street. She threw changing glances at men who passed her, giving smiling invitations to those of rural or untaught pattern and usually seeming sedately unconscious of the men with a metropolitan seal upon their faces. Crossing glittering avenues, she went into the throng emerging from the places of forgetfulness. She hurried forward through the crowd as if intent upon reaching a distant home, bending forward in her handsome cloak, daintily lifting her skirts, and picking for her well-shod feet the dryer spots upon the sidewalks.

The restless doors of saloons, clashing to and fro, disclosed animated rows of men before bars and hurrying barkeepers. A concert-hall gave to the street faint sounds of swift, machine-like music, as if a group of phantom musicians were hastening.

A tall young man, smoking a cigarette with a sublime air, strolled near the girl. He had on evening dress, a moustache, a chrysanthemum, and a look of *ennui*, all of which he kept carefully under his eye. Seeing the girl walk on as if such a young man as he was not in existence, he looked back transfixed with interest. He stared glassily for a moment, but gave a slight convulsive start when he discerned that she was neither new, Parisian, nor theatrical. He wheeled about hastily and turned his stare into the air, like a sailor with a searchlight.

A stout gentleman, with pompous and philanthropic whiskers, went stolidly by, the broad of his back sneering at the girl. A belated man in business clothes, and in haste to catch a car, bounced against her shoulder. "Hi, there, Mary, I beg your pardon! Brace up, old girl." He grasped her arm to steady her, and then was away running down the middle of the street.

The girl walked on out of the realm of restaurants and saloons. She passed more glittering avenues and went into darker blocks than those where the crowd travelled.

A young man in light overcoat and Derby hat received a glance shot keenly from the eyes of the girl. He stopped and looked at her, thrusting his hands into his pockets and making a mocking smile curl his lips. "Come, now, old lady," he said, "you don't mean to tell me that you sized me up for a farmer?"

A labouring man marched along with bundles under his arms. To her remarks he replied, "It's a fine evenin', ain't it?"

She smiled squarely into the face of a boy who was hurrying by with his hands buried in his overcoat pockets, his blond locks bobbing on his youthful temples, and a cheery smile of unconcern upon his lips. He turned his head and smiled back at her, waving his hands. "Not this eve—some other eve."

A drunken man, reeling in her pathway, began to roar at her. "I ain' go' no money!" he shouted, in a dismal voice. He lurched on up the street, wailing to himself: "I ain' go' no money. Ba' luck. Ain' go' no more money."

The girl went into gloomy districts near the river, where the tall black factories shut in the street and only occasional broad beams of light fell across the sidewalks from saloons. In front of one of these places, whence came the sound of a violin vigorously scraped, the patter of feet on boards, and the ring of loud laughter, there stood a man with blotched features.

Farther on in the darkness she met a ragged being with shifting, bloodshot eyes and grimy hands.

She went into the blackness of the final block. The shutters of the tall buildings were closed like grim lips. The structure seemed to have eyes that looked over them, beyond them, at other things. Afar off the lights of the avenues glittered as if from an impossible distance. Street-car bells jingled with a sound of merriment.

At the feet of the tall buildings appeared the deathly black hue of the river. Some hidden factory sent up a yellow glare, that lit for a moment the waters lapping oilily against timbers. The varied sounds of life, made joyous by distance and seeming unapproachableness, came faintly and died away to a silence.

18

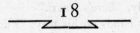

In a partitioned-off section of a saloon sat a man with a half-dozen women, gleefully laughing, hovering about him. The man had arrived at that stage of drunkenness where affection is felt for the universe. "I'm good f'ler, girls," he said, convincingly. "I'm good f'ler. An'body trea's me right, I allus trea's zem right! See?"

The women nodded their heads approvingly. "To be sure," they cried in hearty chorus. "You're the kind of a man we like, Pete. You're outa sight! What yeh goin' to buy this time, dear?"

"An't'ing yehs wants!" said the man in an abandonment of good will. His countenance shone with the true spirit of benevolence. He was in the proper mood of missionaries. He would have fraternized with obscure Hottentots. And above all he was overwhelmed in tenderness for his friends, who were all illustrious. "An't'ing yehs wants!" repeated he, waving his hands with beneficent recklessness.

"I'm good f'ler, girls, an' if an'body trea's me right I——Here," called he through an open door to a waiter, "bring girls drinks. What 'ill yehs have, girls? An't'ing yehs want."

The waiter glanced in with the disgusted look of the man who serves intoxicants for the man who takes too much of them. He nodded his head shortly at the order from each individual, and went.

"W' 're havin' great time," said the man. "I like you girls! Yer right sort! See?" He spoke at length and with feeling concerning the excellences of his assembled friends. "Don' try pull man's leg, but have a good time! Dass right! Dass way teh do! Now, if I s'ought yehs tryin' work me for drinks, wouldn' buy notting! But yer right sort! Yehs know how ter treat a f'ler, an' I stays by yehs till spen' las' cent! Dass right! I'm good f'ler, an' I knows when an'body trea's me right!"

Between the times of the arrival and departure of the waiter, the man discoursed to the women on the tender regard he felt for all living things. He laid stress upon the purity of his motives in all dealings with men in the world, and spoke of the fervour of his friendship for those who were amiable. Tears welled slowly from his eyes. His voice quavered when he spoke to his companions.

Once when the waiter was about to depart with an empty tray, the man drew a coin from his pocket and held it forth. "Here," said he, quite magnificently, "here's quar'."

The waiter kept his hands on his tray. "I don't want yer money," he said.

The other put forth the coin with tearful insistence. "Here's quar'!" cried he, "take 't! Yer goo' f'ler an' I wan' yehs take 't!"

"Come, come, now," said the waiter, with the sullen air of a man who is forced into giving advice. "Put yer mon in yer pocket! Yer loaded an' yehs on'y makes a fool of yerself."

As the waiter passed out of the door the man turned pathetically to the women. "He don' know I'm goo' f'ler," cried he, dismally.

"Never you mind, Pete, dear," said the woman of brilliance and audacity, laying her hand with great affection upon his arm. "Never you mind, old boy! We'll stay by you, dear!"

"Dass ri'!" cried the man, his face lighting up at the soothing tones of the woman's voice. "Das ri'; I'm goo' f'ler an' w'en any one trea's me ri', I trea's zem ri'! Shee?"

"Sure!" cried the woman. "And we're not goin' back on you, old man."

The man turned appealing eyes to the woman. He felt that if he could be convicted of a contemptible action he would die. "Shay, Nell, I allus trea's yehs shquare, didn' I? I allus been go' f'ler wi' yehs, ain't I, Nell?"

"Sure you have, Pete," assented the woman. She delivered an oration to her companions. "Yessir, that's a fact. Pete's a square fellah, he is. He never goes back on a friend. He's the right kind an' we stay by him, don't we, girls?"

"Sure!" they exclaimed. Looking lovingly at him they raised their glasses and drank his health.

"Girlsh," said the man, beseechingly, "I allus trea's yehs ri', didn' I? I'm goo' f'ler, ain' I, girlsh?"

"Sure!" again they chorused.

"Well," said he finally, "le's have nozzer drink, zen."

"That's right," hailed a woman, "that's right. Yer no bloomin' jay! Yer spends yer money like a man. Dat's right."

The man pounded the table with his quivering fists. "Yessir," he cried, with deep earnestness, as if some one disputed him. "I'm goo' f'ler, an' w'en any one trea's me ri', I allus trea's—le's have nozzer drink." He began to beat the wood with his glass. "Shay!" howled he, growing suddenly impatient. As the waiter did not then come, the man swelled with wrath. "Shay!" howled he again. The waiter appeared at the door. "Bringsh drinksh," said the man.

The waiter disappeared with the orders.

"Zat f'ler fool!" cried the man. "He insul' me! I'm ge' man! Can' stan' be insul'! I'm goin' lick 'im when comes!"

"No, no!" cried the women, crowding about and trying to subdue him. "He's all right! He didn't mean anything! Let it go! He's a good fellah!"

"Di'n' he insul' me?" asked the man earnestly.

"No," said they. "Of course he didn't! He's all right!"

"Sure he didn' insul' me?" demanded the man, with deep anxiety in his voice.

"No, no! We know him! He's a good fellah. He didn't mean anything."

"Well, zen," said the man resolutely, "I'm go' 'pol'gize!"

When the waiter came, the man struggled to the middle of the floor. "Girlsh shed you insul' me! I shay—lie! I 'pol'gize!"

"All right," said the waiter.

The man sat down. He felt a sleepy but strong desire to straighten things out and have a perfect understanding with everybody. "Nell,

I allus trea's yeh shquare, di'n' I? Yeh likes me, don' yehs, Nell? I'm goo' f'ler?"

"Sure!" said the woman.

"Yeh knows I'm stuck on yehs, don' yehs, Nell?"

"Sure!" she repeated carelessly.

Overwhelmed by a spasm of drunken adoration, he drew two or three bills from his pocket and, with the trembling fingers of an offering priest, laid them on the table before the woman. "Yehs knows yehs kin have all I got, 'cause I'm stuck on yehs, Nell, I— I'm stuck on yehs, Nell—buy drinksh—we're havin' grea' time— w'en any one trea's me ri'—I—Nell—we're havin' heluva—time."

Presently he went to sleep with his swollen face fallen forward on his chest.

The women drank and laughed, not heeding the slumbering man in the corner. Finally he lurched forward and fell groaning to the floor.

The women screamed in disgust and drew back their skirts. "Come ahn!" cried one, starting up angrily, "let's get out of here."

The woman of brilliance and audacity stayed behind, taking up the bills and stuffing them into a deep, irregularly shaped pocket. A guttural snore from the recumbent man caused her to turn and look down at him. She laughed. "What a fool!" she said, and went.

The smoke from the lamps settled heavily down in the little compartment, obscuring the way out. The smell of oil, stifling in its intensity, pervaded the air. The wine from an overturned glass dripped softly down upon the blotches on the man's neck.

19

In a room a woman sat at a table eating like a fat monk in a picture.

A soiled, unshaven man pushed open the door and entered. "Well," said he, "Mag's dead."

"What?" said the woman, her mouth filled with bread.

"Mag's dead," repeated the man.

"Deh blazes she is!" said the woman. She continued her meal.

When she finished her coffee she began to weep. "I kin remember when her two feet was no bigger dan yer t'umb, and she weared worsted boots," moaned she.

"Well, what a' dat?" said the man.

"I kin remember when she weared worsted boots," she cried.

The neighbors began to gather in the hall, staring in at the weeping woman as if watching the contortions of a dying dog. A dozen women entered and lamented with her. Under their busy hands the room took on that appalling appearance of neatness and order with which death is greeted.

Suddenly the door opened and a woman in a black gown rushed in with outstretched arms. "Ah, poor Mary!" she cried, and tenderly embraced the moaning one. "Ah, what ter'ble affliction is dis!" continued she. Her vocabulary was derived from mission churches. "Me poor Mary, how I feel fer yehs! Ah, what ter'ble affliction is a disobed'ent chile." Her good, motherly face was wet with tears. She trembled in eagerness to express her sympathy.

The mourner sat with bowed head, rocking her body heavily to and fro, and crying out in a high, strained voice that sounded like a dirge on some forlorn pipe. "I kin remember when she weared worsted boots, an' her two feets was no bigger dan yer t'umb, an' she weared worsted boots, Miss Smith," she cried, raising her streaming eyes.

"Ah, me poor Mary!" sobbed the woman in black. With low, coddling cries, she sank on her knees by the mourner's chair, and put her arms about her. The other women began to groan in different keys.

"Yer poor misguided chil' is gone now, Mary, an' let us hope it's fer deh bes'. Yeh'll fergive her now, Mary, won't yehs, dear, all her disobed'ence? All her t'ankless behaviour to her mudder an' all her badness? She's gone where her ter'ble sins will be judged."

The woman in black raised her face and paused. The inevitable sunlight came streaming in at the window and shed a ghastly cheerfulness upon the faded hues of the room. Two or three of the spectators were sniffing, and one was weeping loudly.

The mourner arose and staggered into the other room. In a moment she emerged with a pair of faded baby shoes held in the hollow of her hand. "I kin remember when she used to wear dem!" cried she. The women burst anew into cries as if they had all been stabbed. The mourner turned to the soiled and unshaven man. "Jimmie, boy, go git yer sister! Go git yer sister an' we'll put deh boots on her feets!"

"Dey won't fit her now, yeh fool," said the man.

"Go git yer sister, Jimmie!" shrieked the woman, confronting him fiercely.

The man swore sullenly. He went over to a corner and slowly began to put on his coat. He took his hat and went out, with a dragging, reluctant step.

The woman in black came forward and again besought the mourner. "Yeh'll fergive her, Mary! Yeh'll fergive yer bad, bad chil'! Her life was a curse an' her days were black, an' yeh'll fergive yer bad girl? She's gone where her sins will be judged."

"She's gone where her sins will be judged!" cried the other women, like a choir at a funeral.

"Deh Lord gives and deh Lord takes away," said the woman in black, raising her eyes to the sunbeams.

"Deh Lord gives and deh Lord takes away," responded the others.

"Yeh'll fergive her, Mary?" pleaded the woman in black.

The mourner essayed to speak, but her voice gave way. She shook her great shoulders frantically, in an agony of grief. The tears seemed to scald her face. Finally her voice came and arose in a scream of pain. "Oh, yes, I'll fergive her! I'll fergive her!"

Melanctha

1909

GERTRUDE STEIN

Melanctha

EACH ONE AS SHE MAY

ROSE JOHNSON made it very hard to bring her baby to its birth.

Melanctha Herbert who was Rose Johnson's friend, did everything that any woman could. She tended Rose, and she was patient, submissive, soothing, and untiring, while the sullen, childish, cowardly, black Rosie grumbled and fussed and howled and made herself to be an abomination and like a simple beast.

The child though it was healthy after it was born, did not live long. Rose Johnson was careless and negligent and selfish, and when Melanctha had to leave for a few days, the baby died. Rose Johnson had liked the baby well enough and perhaps she just forgot it for awhile, anyway the child was dead and Rose and Sam her husband were very sorry but then these things came so often in the negro world in Bridgepoint, that they neither of them thought about it very long.

Rose Johnson and Melanctha Herbert had been friends now for some years. Rose had lately married Sam Johnson a decent honest kindly fellow, a deck hand on a coasting steamer.

Melanctha Herbert had not yet been really married.

Rose Johnson was a real black, tall, well built, sullen, stupid, childlike, good looking negress. She laughed when she was happy and grumbled and was sullen with everything that troubled.

Rose Johnson was a real black negress but she had been brought up quite like their own child by white folks.

Rose laughed when she was happy but she had not the wide, abandoned laughter that makes the warm broad glow of negro sunshine. Rose was never joyous with the earth-born, boundless joy of negroes. Hers was just ordinary, any sort of woman laughter.

Rose Johnson was careless and was lazy, but she had been brought up by white folks and she needed decent comfort. Her white training had only made for habits, not for nature. Rose had the simple, promiscuous unmorality of the black people.

Rose Johnson and Melanctha Herbert like many of the twos with women were a curious pair to be such friends.

Melanctha Herbert was a graceful, pale yellow, intelligent, attractive negress. She had not been raised like Rose by white folks but then she had been half made with real white blood.

She and Rose Johnson were both of the better sort of negroes, there, in Bridgepoint.

"No, I ain't no common nigger," said Rose Johnson, "for I was raised by white folks, and Melanctha she is so bright and learned so much in school, she ain't no common nigger either, though she ain't got no husband to be married to like I am to Sam Johnson."

Why did the subtle, intelligent, attractive, half white girl Melanctha Herbert love and do for and demean herself in service to this coarse, decent, sullen, ordinary, black childish Rose, and why was this unmoral, promiscuous, shiftless Rose married, and that's not so common either, to a good man of the negroes, while Melanctha with her white blood and attraction and her desire for a right position had not yet been really married.

Sometimes the thought of how all her world was made, filled the complex, desiring Melanctha with despair. She wondered, often, how she could go on living when she was so blue.

Melanctha told Rose one day how a woman whom she knew had killed herself because she was so blue. Melanctha said, sometimes, she thought this was the best thing for her herself to do.

Rose Johnson did not see it the least bit that way.

"I don't see Melanctha why you should talk like you would kill yourself just because you're blue. I'd never kill myself Melanctha just 'cause I was blue. I'd maybe kill somebody else Melanctha 'cause I was blue, but I'd never kill myself. If I ever killed myself Melanctha it'd be by accident, and if I ever killed myself by accident Melanctha, I'd be awful sorry."

Rose Johnson and Melanctha Herbert had first met, one night, at church. Rose Johnson did not care much for religion. She had not enough emotion to be really roused by a revival. Melanctha Herbert had not come yet to know how to use religion. She was still too complex with desire. However, the two of them in negro fashion went very often to the negro church, along with all their friends, and they slowly came to know each other very well.

Rose Johnson had been raised not as a servant but quite like their own child by white folks. Her mother who had died when Rose was still a baby, had been a trusted servant in the family. Rose was a cute, attractive, good looking little black girl and these people had no children of their own and so they kept Rose in their house.

As Rose grew older she drifted from her white folks back to the colored people, and she gradually no longer lived in the old house. Then it happened that these people went away to some other town to live, and somehow Rose stayed behind in Bridgepoint. Her white folks left a little money to take care of Rose, and this money she got every little while.

Rose now in the easy fashion of the poor lived with one woman in her house, and then for no reason went and lived with some other woman in her house. All this time, too, Rose kept company, and was engaged, first to this colored man and then to that, and always she made sure she was engaged, for Rose had strong the sense of proper conduct.

"No, I ain't no common nigger just to go around with any man, nor you Melanctha shouldn't neither," she said one day when she was telling the complex and less sure Melanctha what was the right way for her to do. "No Melanctha, I ain't no common nigger to do so, for I was raised by white folks. You know very well Melanctha that I'se always been engaged to them."

And so Rose lived on, always comfortable and rather decent and very lazy and very well content.

After she had lived some time this way, Rose thought it would be nice and very good in her position to get regularly really married. She had lately met Sam Johnson somewhere, and she liked him and she knew he was a good man, and then he had a place where he worked every day and got good wages. Sam Johnson liked Rose very well and he was quite ready to be married. One day they had a grand real wedding and were married. Then with Melanctha Herbert's help to do the sewing and the nicer work, they furnished comfortably a little red brick house. Sam then went back to his work as deck hand on a coasting steamer, and Rose stayed home in her house and sat and bragged to all her friends how nice it was to be married really to a husband.

Life went on very smoothly with them all the year. Rose was lazy but not dirty and Sam was careful but not fussy, and then there was Melanctha to come in every day and help to keep things neat.

When Rose's baby was coming to be born, Rose came to stay in the house where Melanctha Herbert lived just then, with a big good natured colored woman who did washing.

Rose went there to stay, so that she might have the doctor from the hospital near by to help her have the baby, and then, too, Melanctha could attend to her while she was sick.

Here the baby was born, and here it died, and then Rose went back to her house again with Sam.

Melanctha Herbert had not made her life all simple like Rose Johnson. Melanctha had not found it easy with herself to make her wants and what she had, agree.

Melanctha Herbert was always losing what she had in wanting all the things she saw. Melanctha was always being left when she was not leaving others.

Melanctha Herbert always loved too hard and much too often. She was always full with mystery and subtle movements and denials and vague distrusts and complicated disillusions. Then Melanctha would be sudden and impulsive and unbounded in some faith, and then she would suffer and be strong in her repression.

Melanctha Herbert was always seeking rest and quiet, and always she could only find new ways to be in trouble.

Melanctha wondered often how it was she did not kill herself when she was so blue. Often she thought this would be really the best way for her to do.

Melanctha Herbert had been raised to be religious, by her mother. Melanctha had not liked her mother very well. This mother, 'Mis' Herbert, as her neighbors called her, had been a sweet appearing and dignified and pleasant, pale yellow, colored woman. 'Mis' Herbert had always been a little wandering and mysterious and uncertain in her ways.

Melanctha was pale yellow and mysterious and a little pleasant like her mother, but the real power in Melanctha's nature came through her robust and unpleasant and very unendurable black father.

Melanctha's father only used to come to where Melanctha and her mother lived, once in a while.

It was many years now that Melanctha had not heard or seen or known of anything her father did.

Melanctha Herbert almost always hated her black father, but she loved very well the power in herself that came through him. And so her feeling was really closer to her black coarse father, than her feeling had ever been toward her pale yellow, sweet-appearing mother.

The things she had in her of her mother never made her feel respect.

Melanctha Herbert had not loved herself in childhood. All of her youth was bitter to remember.

Melanctha had not loved her father and her mother and they had found it very troublesome to have her.

Melanctha's mother and her father had been regularly married. Melanctha's father was a big black virile negro. He only came once in a while to where Melanctha and her mother lived, but always that pleasant, sweet-appearing, pale yellow woman, mysterious and uncertain and wandering in her ways, was close in sympathy and thinking to her big black virile husband.

James Herbert was a common, decent enough, colored workman, brutal and rough to his one daughter, but then she was a most disturbing child to manage.

The young Melanctha did not love her father and her mother, and she had a break neck courage, and a tongue that could be very nasty. Then, too, Melanctha went to school and was very quick in all the learning, and she knew very well how to use this knowledge to annoy her parents who knew nothing.

Melanctha Herbert had always had a break neck courage. Melanctha always loved to be with horses; she loved to do wild things, to ride the horses and to break and tame them.

Melanctha, when she was a little girl, had had a good chance to live with horses. Near where Melanctha and her mother lived was the stable of the Bishops, a rich family who always had fine horses.

John, the Bishops' coachman, liked Melanctha very well and he always let her do anything she wanted with the horses. John was a decent, vigorous mulatto with a prosperous house and wife and children. Melanctha Herbert was older than any of his children. She was now a well grown girl of twelve and just beginning as a woman.

James Herbert, Melanctha's father, knew this John, the Bishops' coachman very well.

One day James Herbert came to where his wife and daughter lived, and he was furious.

"Where's that Melanctha girl of yours," he said fiercely, "if she is to the Bishops' stables again, with that man John, I swear I kill her. Why don't you see to that girl better you, you're her mother."

James Herbert was a powerful, loose built, hard handed, black, angry negro. Herbert never was a joyous negro. Even when he drank with other men, and he did that very often, he was never really joyous. In the days when he had been most young and free and open, he had never had the wide abandoned laughter that gives the broad glow to negro sunshine.

His daughter, Melanctha Herbert, later always made a hard forced laughter. She was only strong and sweet and in her nature when she was really deep in trouble, when she was fighting so with all she really had, that she did not use her laughter. This was always true of poor Melanctha who was so certain that she hated trouble. Melanctha Herbert was always seeking peace and quiet, and she could always only find new ways to get excited.

James Herbert was often a very angry negro. He was fierce and serious, and he was very certain that he often had good reason to be angry with Melanctha, who knew so well how to be nasty, and to use her learning with a father who knew nothing.

James Herbert often drank with John, the Bishops' coachman. John in his good nature sometimes tried to soften Herbert's feeling toward Melanctha. Not that Melanctha ever complained to John of her home life or her father. It was never Melanctha's way, even in the midst of her worst trouble to complain to any one of what happened to her, but nevertheless somehow every one who knew Melanctha always knew how much she suffered. It was only while one really loved Melanctha that one understood how to forgive her, that she never once complained nor looked unhappy, and was always handsome and in spirits, and yet one always knew how much she suffered.

The father, James Herbert, never told his troubles either, and he was so fierce and serious that no one ever thought of asking.

'Mis' Herbert as her neighbors called her was never heard even to speak of her husband or her daughter. She was always pleasant, sweet-appearing, mysterious and uncertain, and a little wandering in her ways.

The Herberts were a silent family with their troubles, but somehow every one who knew them always knew everything that happened.

The morning of one day when in the evening Herbert and the coachman John were to meet to drink together, Melanctha had to come to the stable joyous and in the very best of humors. Her good friend John on this morning felt very firmly how good and sweet she was and how very much she suffered.

John was a very decent colored coachman. When he thought about

Melanctha it was as if she were the eldest of his children. Really he felt very strongly the power in her of a woman. John's wife always liked Melanctha and she always did all she could to make things pleasant. And Melanctha all her life loved and respected kind and good and considerate people. Melanctha always loved and wanted peace and gentleness and goodness and all her life for herself poor Melanctha could only find new ways to be in trouble.

This evening after John and Herbert had drunk awhile together, the good John began to tell the father what a fine girl he had for a daughter. Perhaps the good John had been drinking a good deal of liquor, perhaps there was a gleam of something softer than the feeling of a friendly elder in the way John then spoke of Melanctha. There had been a good deal of drinking and John certainly that very morning had felt strongly Melanctha's power as a woman. James Herbert was always a fierce, suspicious, serious negro, and drinking never made him feel more open. He looked very black and evil as he sat and listened while John grew more and more admiring as he talked half to himself, half to the father, of the virtues and the sweetness of Melanctha.

Suddenly between them there came a moment filled full with strong black curses, and then sharp razors flashed in the black hands, that held them flung backward in the negro fashion, and then for some minutes there was fierce slashing.

John was a decent, pleasant, good natured, light brown negro, but he knew how to use a razor to do bloody slashing.

When the two men were pulled apart by the other negroes who were in the room drinking, John had not been much wounded but James Herbert had gotten one good strong cut that went from his right shoulder down across the front of his whole body. Razor fighting does not wound very deeply, but it makes a cut that looks most nasty, for it is so very bloody.

Herbert was held by the other negroes until he was cleaned and plastered, and then he was put to bed to sleep off his drink and fighting.

The next day he came to where his wife and daughter lived and he was furious.

"Where's that Melanctha, of yours?" he said to his wife, when he saw her. "If she is to the Bishops' stables now with that yellow John, I swear I kill her. A nice way she is going for a decent daughter. Why don't you see to that girl better you, ain't you her mother!"

Melanctha Herbert had always been old in all her ways and she knew very early how to use her power as a woman, and yet Melanctha with all her inborn intense wisdom was really very ignorant of evil. Melanctha had not yet come to understand what they meant, the things she so often heard around her, and which were just beginning to stir strongly in her.

Now when her father began fiercely to assail her, she did not really know what it was that he was so furious to force from her. In every way that he could think of in his anger, he tried to make her say a thing she did not really know. She held out and never answered anything he asked her, for Melanctha had a breakneck courage and she just then badly hated her black father.

When the excitement was all over, Melanctha began to know her power, the power she had so often felt stirring within her and which she now knew she could use to make her stronger.

James Herbert did not win this fight with his daughter. After awhile he forgot it as he soon forgot John and the cut of his sharp razor.

Melanctha almost forgot to hate her father, in her strong interest in the power she now knew she had within her.

Melanctha did not care much now, any longer, to see John or his wife or even the fine horses. This life was too quiet and accustomed and no longer stirred her to any interest or excitement.

Melanctha now really was beginning as a woman. She was ready, and she began to search in the streets and in dark corners to discover men and to learn their natures and their various ways of working.

In these next years Melanctha learned many ways that lead to wisdom. She learned the ways, and dimly in the distance she saw wisdom. These years of learning led very straight to trouble for Melanctha, though in these years Melanctha never did or meant anything that was really wrong.

Girls who are brought up with care and watching can always find moments to escape into the world, where they may learn the ways that lead to wisdom. For a girl raised like Melanctha Herbert, such escape was always very simple. Often she was alone, sometimes she was with a fellow seeker, and she strayed and stood, sometimes by railroad yards, sometimes on the docks or around new buildings where many men were working. Then when the darkness covered everything all over, she would begin to learn to know this man or that. She would advance, they would respond, and then she would withdraw a little, dimly, and always she did not know what it was that really held her. Sometimes she would almost go over, and then the strength in her of not really knowing, would stop the average man in his endeavor. It was a strange experience of ignorance and power and desire. Melanctha did not know what it was that she so badly wanted. She was afraid, and yet she did not understand that here she really was a coward.

Boys had never meant much to Melanctha. They had always been too young to content her. Melanctha had a strong respect for any kind of successful power. It was this that always kept Melanctha nearer, in her feeling toward her virile and unendurable black father, than she ever was in her feeling for her pale yellow, sweet-appearing mother. The things she had in her of her mother, never made her feel respect.

In these young days, it was only men that for Melanctha held anything there was of knowledge and power. It was not from men however that Melanctha learned to really understand this power.

From the time that Melanctha was twelve until she was sixteen she wandered, always seeking but never more than very dimly seeing wisdom. All this time Melanctha went on with her school learning; she went to school rather longer than do most of the colored children.

Melanctha's wanderings after wisdom she always had to do in secret and by snatches, for her mother was then still living and 'Mis' Herbert always did some watching, and Melanctha with all her hard courage dreaded that there should be much telling to her father, who came now quite often to where Melanctha lived with her mother.

In these days Melanctha talked and stood and walked with many kinds of men, but she did not learn to know any of them very deeply. They all supposed her to have world knowledge and experience. They, believing that she knew all, told her nothing, and thinking that she was deciding with them, asked for nothing, and so though Melanctha wandered widely, she was really very safe with all the wandering.

It was a very wonderful experience this safety of Melanctha in these days of her attempted learning. Melanctha herself did not feel the wonder, she only knew that for her it all had no real value.

Melanctha all her life was very keen in her sense for real experience. She knew she was not getting what she so badly wanted, but with all her break neck courage Melanctha here was a coward, and so she could not learn to really understand.

Melanctha liked to wander, and to stand by the railroad yard, and watch the men and the engines and the switches and everything that was busy there, working. Railroad yards are a ceaseless fascination. They satisfy every kind of nature. For the lazy man whose blood flows very slowly, it is a steady soothing world of motion which supplies him with the sense of a strong moving power. He need not work and yet he has it very deeply; he has it even better than the man who works in it or owns it. Then for natures that like to feel emotion without the trouble of having any suffering, it is very nice to get the swelling in the throat, and the fullness, and the heart beats, and all the flutter of excitement that comes as one watches the people come and go, and hears the engine pound and give a long drawn whistle. For a child watching through a hole in the fence above the yard, it is a wonder world of mystery and movement. The child loves all the noise, and then it loves the silence of the wind that comes before the full rush of the pounding train, that bursts out from the tunnel where it lost itself and all its noise in darkness, and the child loves all the smoke, that sometimes comes in rings, and always puffs with fire and blue color.

For Melanctha the yard was full of the excitement of many men, and perhaps a free and whirling future.

Melanctha came here very often and watched the men and all the things that were so busy working. The men always had time for, "Hullo sis, do you want to sit on my engine," and, "Hullo, that's a pretty lookin' yaller girl, do you want to come and see him cookin."

All the colored porters liked Melanctha. They often told her exciting things that had happened; how in the West they went through big tunnels where there was no air to breathe, and then out and winding around edges of great canyons on thin high spindling trestles, and sometimes cars, and sometimes whole trains fell from the narrow bridges, and always up from the dark places death and all kinds of queer devils looked up and laughed in their faces. And then they would tell how sometimes when the train went pounding down steep slippery mountains, great rocks would racket and roll down around them, and sometimes would smash in the car and kill men; and as the porters told these stories their round, black, shining faces would grow solemn, and their color would go grey beneath the greasy black, and their eyes would roll white in the fear and wonder of the things they could scare themselves by telling.

There was one, big, serious, melancholy, light brown porter who often told Melanctha stories, for he liked the way she had of listening with intelligence and sympathetic feeling, when he told how the white men in the far South tried to kill him because he made one of them who was drunk and called him a damned nigger, and who refused to pay money for his chair to a nigger, get off the train between stations. And then this porter had to give up going to that part of the Southern country, for all the white men swore that if he ever came there again they would surely kill him.

Melanctha liked this serious, melancholy light brown negro very well, and all her life Melanctha wanted and respected gentleness and goodness, and this man always gave her good advice and serious kindness, and Melanctha felt such things very deeply, but she could never let them help her or affect her to change the ways that always made her keep herself in trouble.

Melanctha spent many of the last hours of the daylight with the porters and with other men who worked hard, but when darkness came it was always different. Then Melanctha would find herself with the, for her, gentlemanly classes. A clerk, or a young express agent would begin to know her, and they would stand, or perhaps, walk a little while together.

Melanctha always made herself escape but often it was with an effort. She did not know what it was that she so badly wanted, but with all her courage Melanctha here was a coward, and so she could not learn to understand.

Melanctha and some man would stand in the evening and would talk together. Sometimes Melanctha would be with another girl and then it was much easier to stay or to escape, for then they could make way for themselves together, and by throwing words and laughter to each other, could keep a man from getting too strong in his attention.

But when Melanctha was alone, and she was so, very often, she would sometimes come very near to making a long step on the road that leads to wisdom. Some man would learn a good deal about her in the talk, never altogether truly, for Melanctha all her life did not know how to tell a story wholly. She always, and yet not with intention, managed to leave out big pieces which make a story very different, for when it came to what had happened and what she had said and what it was that she had really done, Melanctha never could remember right. The man would sometimes come a little nearer, would detain her, would hold her arm or make his jokes a little clearer, and then Melanctha would always make herself escape. The man thinking that she really had world wisdom would not make his meaning clear, and believing that she was deciding with him he never went so fast that he could stop her when at last she made herself escape.

And so Melanctha wandered on the edge of wisdom. "Say, Sis, why don't you when you come here stay a little longer?" they would all ask her, and they would hold her for an answer, and she would laugh, and sometimes she did stay longer, but always just in time she made herself escape.

Melanctha Herbert wanted very much to know and yet she feared the knowledge. As she grew older she often stayed a good deal longer, and sometimes it was almost a balanced struggle, but she always made herself escape.

Next to the railroad yard it was the shipping docks that Melanctha loved best when she wandered. Often she was alone, sometimes she was with some better kind of black girl, and she would stand a long time and watch the men working at unloading, and see the steamers do their coaling, and she would listen with full feeling to the yowling of the free swinging negroes, as they ran, with their powerful loose jointed bodies and their childish savage yelling, pushing, carrying, pulling great loads from the ships to the warehouses.

The men would call out, "Say, Sis, look out or we'll come and catch yer," or "Hi, there, you yaller girl, come here and we'll take you sailin'." And then, too, Melanctha would learn to know some of the serious foreign sailors who told her all sorts of wonders, and a cook would sometimes take her and her friends over a ship and show where he made his messes and where the men slept, and where the shops were, and how everything was made by themselves, right there, on ship board.

Melanctha loved to see these dark and smelly places. She always loved to watch and talk and listen with men who worked hard. But it was never from these rougher people that Melanctha tried to learn the ways that lead to wisdom. In the daylight she always liked to talk with rough men and to listen to their lives and about their work and their various ways of doing, but when the darkness covered everything all over, Melanctha would meet, and stand, and talk with a clerk or a young shipping agent who had seen her watching, and so it was that she would try to learn to understand.

And then Melanctha was fond of watching men work on new

buildings. She loved to see them hoisting, digging, sawing and stone cutting. Here, too, in the daylight, she always learned to know the common workmen. "Heh, Sis, look out or that rock will fall on you and smash you all up into little pieces. Do you think you would make a nice jelly?" And then they would all laugh and feel that their jokes were very funny. And "Say, you pretty yaller girl, would it scare you bad to stand up here on top where I be? See if you've got grit and come up here where I can hold you. All you got to do is to sit still on that there rock that they're just hoistin', and then when you get here I'll hold you tight, don't you be scared Sis."

Sometimes Melanctha would do some of these things that had much danger, and always with such men, she showed her power and her break neck courage. Once she slipped and fell from a high place. A workman caught her and so she was not killed, but her left arm was badly broken.

All the men crowded around her. They admired her boldness in doing and in bearing pain when her arm was broken. They all went along with her with great respect to the doctor, and then they took her home in triumph and all of them were bragging about her not squealing.

James Herbert was home where his wife lived, that day. He was furious when he saw the workmen and Melanctha. He drove the men away with curses so that they were all very nearly fighting, and he would not let a doctor come in to attend Melanctha. "Why don't you see to that girl better, you, you're her mother."

James Herbert did not fight things out now any more with his daughter. He feared her tongue, and her school learning, and the way she had of saying things that were very nasty to a brutal black man who knew nothing. And Melanctha just then hated him very badly in her suffering.

And so this was the way Melanctha lived the four years of her beginning as a woman. And many things happened to Melanctha, but she knew very well that none of them had led her on to the right way, that certain way that was to lead her to world wisdom.

Melanctha Herbert was sixteen when she first met Jane Harden. Jane was a negress, but she was so white that hardly any one could guess it. Jane had had a good deal of education. She had been two years at a colored college. She had had to leave because of her bad conduct. She taught Melanctha many things. She taught her how to go the ways that lead to wisdom.

Jane Harden was at this time twenty-three years old and she had had much experience. She was very much attracted by Melanctha, and Melanctha was very proud that this Jane would let her know her.

Jane Harden was not afraid to understand. Melanctha, who had strong the sense for real experience, knew that here was a woman who had learned to understand.

Jane Harden had many bad habits. She drank a great deal, and she wandered widely. She was safe though now, when she wanted to be safe, in this wandering.

Melanctha Herbert soon always wandered with her. Melanctha tried the drinking and some of the other habits, but she did not find that she cared very much to do them. But every day she grew stronger in her desire to really understand.

It was now no longer, even in the daylight, the rougher men that these two learned to know in their wanderings, and for Melanctha the better classes were now a little higher. It was no longer express agents and clerks that she learned to know, but men in business, commercial travelers, and even men above these, and Jane and she would talk and walk and laugh and escape from them all very often. It was still the same, the knowing of them and the always just escaping, only now for Melanctha somehow it was different, for though it was always the same thing that happened it had a different flavor, for now Melanctha was with a woman who had wisdom, and dimly she began to see what it was that she should understand.

It was not from the men that Melanctha learned her wisdom. It was always Jane Harden herself who was making Melanctha begin to understand.

Jane was a roughened woman. She had power and she liked to use it, she had much white blood and that made her see clear, she liked drinking and that made her reckless. Her white blood was strong in her and she had grit and endurance and a vital courage. She was always game, however much she was in trouble. She liked Melanctha Herbert for the things that she had like her, and then Melanctha was young, and she had sweetness, and a way of listening with intelligence and sympathetic interest, to the stories that Jane Harden often told out of her experience.

Jane grew always fonder of Melanctha. Soon they began to wander, more to be together than to see men and learn their various ways of working. Then they began not to wander, and Melanctha would spend long hours with Jane in her room, sitting at her feet and listening to her stories, and feeling her strength and the power of her affection, and slowly she began to see clear before her one certain way that would be sure to lead to wisdom.

Before the end came, the end of the two years in which Melanctha spent all her time when she was not at school or in her home, with Jane Harden, before these two years were finished, Melanctha had come to see very clear, and she had come to be very certain, what it is that gives the world its wisdom.

Jane Harden always had a little money and she had a room in the lower part of the town. Jane had once taught in a colored school. She had had to leave that too on account of her bad conduct. It was her drinking that always made all the trouble for her, for that can never be really covered over.

Jane's drinking was always growing worse upon her. Melanctha had tried to do the drinking but it had no real attraction for her.

In the first year, between Jane Harden and Melanctha Herbert, Jane had been much the stronger. Jane loved Melanctha and she found her always intelligent and brave and sweet and docile, and Jane meant to, and before the year was over she had taught Melanctha what it is that gives many people in the world their wisdom.

Jane had many ways in which to do this teaching. She told Melanctha many things. She loved Melanctha hard and made Melanctha feel it very deeply. She would be with other people and with men and with Melanctha, and she would make Melanctha understand what everybody wanted, and what one did with power when one had it.

Melanctha sat at Jane's feet for many hours in these days and felt Jane's wisdom. She learned to love Jane and to have this feeling very deeply. She learned a little in these days to know joy, and she was taught too how very keenly she could suffer. It was very different this suffering from that Melanctha sometimes had from her mother and from her very unendurable black father. Then she was fighting and she could be strong and valiant in her suffering, but here with Jane Harden she was longing and she bent and pleaded with her suffering.

It was a very tumultuous, very mingled year, this time for Melanctha, but she certainly did begin to really understand.

In every way she got it from Jane Harden. There was nothing good or bad in doing, feeling, thinking or in talking, that Jane spared her. Sometimes the lesson came almost too strong for Melanctha, but somehow she always managed to endure it and so slowly, but always with increasing strength and feeling, Melanctha began to really understand.

Then slowly, between them, it began to be all different. Slowly now between them, it was Melanctha Herbert, who was stronger. Slowly now they began to drift apart from one another.

Melanctha Herbert never really lost her sense that it was Jane Harden who had taught her, but Jane did many things that Melanctha now no longer needed. And then, too, Melanctha never could remember right when it came to what she had done and what had happened. Melanctha now sometimes quarreled with Jane, and they no longer went about together, and sometimes Melanctha really forgot how much she owed to Jane Harden's teaching.

Melanctha began now to feel that she had always had world wisdom. She really knew of course, that it was Jane who had taught her, but all that began to be covered over by the trouble between them, that was now always getting stronger.

Jane Harden was a roughened woman. Once she had been very strong, but now she was weakened in all her kinds of strength by her drinking. Melanctha had tried the drinking but it had had no real attraction for her.

Jane's strong and roughened nature and her drinking made it always harder for her to forgive Melanctha, that now Melanctha did not really need her any longer. Now it was Melanctha who was stronger and it was Jane who was dependent on her.

Melanctha was now come to be about eighteen years old. She was a graceful, pale yellow, good looking, intelligent, attractive negress, a little mysterious sometimes in her ways, and always good and pleasant, and always ready to do things for people.

Melanctha from now on saw very little of Jane Harden. Jane did not like that very well and sometimes she abused Melanctha, but her drinking soon covered everything all over.

It was not in Melanctha's nature to really lose her sense for Jane Harden. Melanctha all her life was ready to help Jane out in any of her trouble, and later, when Jane really went to pieces, Melanctha always did all that she could to help her.

But Melanctha Herbert was ready now herself to do teaching. Melanctha could do anything now that she wanted. Melanctha knew now what everybody wanted.

Melanctha had learned how she might stay a little longer; she had learned that she must decide when she wanted really to stay longer, and she had learned how when she wanted to, she could escape.

And so Melanctha began once more to wander. It was all now for her very different. It was never rougher men now that she talked to, and she did not care much now to know white men of the, for her, very better classes. It was now something realler that Melanctha wanted, something that would move her very deeply, something that would fill her fully with the wisdom that was planted now within her, and that she wanted badly, should really wholly fill her.

Melanctha these days wandered very widely. She was always alone now when she wandered. Melanctha did not need help now to know, or to stay longer, or when she wanted, to escape.

Melanctha tried a great many men, in these days before she was really suited. It was almost a year that she wandered and then she met with a young mulatto. He was a doctor who had just begun to practice. He would most likely do well in the future, but it was not this that concerned Melanctha. She found him good and strong and gentle and very intellectual, and all her life Melanctha liked and wanted good and considerate people, and then too he did not at first believe in Melanctha. He held off and did not know what it was that Melanctha wanted. Melanctha came to want him very badly. They began to know each other better. Things began to be very strong between them. Melanctha wanted him so badly that now she never wandered. She just gave herself to this experience.

Melanctha Herbert was now, all alone, in Bridgepoint. She lived now with this colored woman and now with that one, and she sewed, and sometimes she taught a little in a colored school as substitute for some teacher. Melanctha had now no home nor any regular employment. Life was just commencing for Melanctha. She had youth and had learned wisdom, and she was graceful and pale yellow and very pleasant, and always ready to do things for people, and she was mysterious in her ways and that only made belief in her more fervent.

During the year before she met Jefferson Campbell, Melanctha had tried many kinds of men but they had none of them interested Melanctha very deeply. She met them, she was much with them, she left them, she would think perhaps this next time it would be more exciting, and always she found that for her it all had no real meaning. She could now do everything she wanted, she knew now everything that everybody wanted, and yet it all had no excitement for her. With these men, she knew she could learn nothing. She wanted some one that could teach her very deeply and now at last she was sure that she had found him, yes she really had it, before she had thought to look if in this man she would find it.

During this year 'Mis' Herbert as her neighbors called her, Melanctha's pale yellow mother was very sick, and in this year she died.

Melanctha's father during these last years did not come very often to the house where his wife lived and Melanctha. Melanctha was not sure that her father was now any longer here in Bridgepoint. It was Melanctha who was very good now to her mother. It was always Melanctha's way to be good to any one in trouble.

Melanctha took good care of her mother. She did everything that any woman could, she tended and soothed and helped her pale yellow mother, and she worked hard in every way to take care of her, and make her dying easy. But Melanctha did not in these days like her mother any better, and her mother never cared much for this daughter who was always a hard child to manage, and who had a tongue that always could be very nasty.

Melanctha did everything that any woman could, and at last her mother died, and Melanctha had her buried. Melanctha's father was not heard from, and Melanctha in all her life after, never saw or heard or knew of anything that her father did.

It was the young doctor, Jefferson Campbell, who helped Melanctha toward the end, to take care of her sick mother. Jefferson Campbell had often before seen Melanctha Herbert, but he had never liked her very well, and he had never believed that she was any good. He had heard something about how she wandered. He knew a little too of Jane Harden, and he was sure that this Melanctha Herbert, who was her friend and who wandered, would never come to any good.

Dr. Jefferson Campbell was a serious, earnest, good young joyous doctor. He liked to take care of everybody and he loved his own colored people. He always found life very easy did Jeff Campbell, and everybody liked to have him with them. He was so good and sympathetic, and he was so earnest and so joyous. He sang when he was happy, and he laughed, and his was the free abandoned laughter that gives the warm broad glow to negro sunshine.

Jeff Campbell had never yet in his life had real trouble. Jefferson's father was a good, kind, serious, religious man. He was a very steady, very intelligent, and very dignified, light brown, grey haired negro. He was a butler and he had worked for the Campbell family many years, and his father and his mother before him had been in the service of this family as free people.

Jefferson Campbell's father and his mother had of course been regularly married. Jefferson's mother was a sweet, little, pale brown, gentle woman who reverenced and obeyed her good husband, and who worshipped and admired and loved hard her good, earnest, cheery, hard working doctor boy who was her only child.

Jeff Campbell had been raised religious by his people but religion had never interested Jeff very much. Jefferson was very good. He loved his people and he never hurt them, and he always did everything they wanted and that he could to please them, but he really loved best science and experimenting and to learn things, and he early wanted to be a doctor, and he was always very interested in the life of the colored people.

The Campbell family had been very good to him and had helped him on with his ambition. Jefferson studied hard, he went to a colored college, and then he learnt to be a doctor.

It was now two or three years, that he had started in to practice. Everybody liked Jeff Campbell, he was so strong and kindly and cheerful and understanding, and he laughed so with pure joy, and he always liked to help all his own colored people.

Dr. Jeff knew all about Jane Harden. He had taken care of her in some of her bad trouble. He knew about Melanctha too, though until her mother was taken sick he had never met her. Then he was called in to help Melanctha to take care of her sick mother. Dr. Campbell did not like Melanctha's ways and he did not think that she would ever come to any good.

Dr. Campbell had taken care of Jane Harden in some of her bad trouble. Jane sometimes had abused Melanctha to him. What right had that Melanctha Herbert who owed everything to her, Jane Harden, what right had a girl like that to go away to other men and leave her, but Melanctha Herbert never had any sense of how to act to anybody. Melanctha had a good mind, Jane never denied her that, but she never used it to do anything decent with it. But what could you expect when Melanctha had such a brute of a black nigger father, and Melanctha was always abusing her father and yet she was just like him, and really she admired him so much and he never had any sense of what he owed to anybody, and Melanctha was just like him and she was proud of it too, and it made Jane so tired to hear Melanctha talk all the time as if she wasn't. Jane Harden hated people who had good minds and didn't use them, and Melanctha always had that weakness, and wanting to keep in with people, and never really saying that she wanted to be like her father, and it was so silly of Melanctha to abuse her father, when she was so much like him and she really liked it. No, Jane Harden had no use for Melanctha. Oh yes, Melanctha always came around to be good to her. Melanctha was always sure to do that. She never really went away and left one. She didn't use her mind enough to do things straight out like that. Melanctha Herbert had a good mind, Jane never denied that to her, but she never wanted to see or hear about Melanctha Herbert any more, and she wished Melanctha wouldn't come in any more to see her. She didn't hate her, but she didn't want to hear about her father and all that talk Melanctha always made, and that just meant nothing to her. Jane Harden was very tired of all that now. She didn't have any use now any more for Melanctha, and if Dr. Campbell saw her he better tell her Jane didn't want to see her, and she could take her talk to somebody else, who was ready to believe her. And then Jane Harden would drop away and forget Melanctha and all her life before, and then she would begin to drink and so she would cover everything all over.

Jeff Campbell heard all this very often, but it did not interest him very deeply. He felt no desire to know more of this Melanctha. He heard her, once, talking to another girl outside of the house, when he was paying a visit to Jane Harden. He did not see much in the talk that he heard her do. He did not see much in the things Jane Harden said when she abused Melanctha to him. He was more interested in Jane herself than in anything he heard about Melanctha. He knew Jane Harden had a good mind, and she had had power, and she could really have done things, and now this drinking covered everything all over. Jeff Campbell was always very sorry when he had to see it. Jane Harden was a roughened woman, and yet Jeff found a great many strong good things in her, that still made him like her.

Jeff Campbell did everything he could for Jane Harden. He did not care much to hear about Melanctha. He had no feeling, much, about her. He did not find that he took any interest in her. Jane Harden was so much a stronger woman, and Jane really had had a good mind, and she had used it to do things with it, before this drinking business had taken such a hold upon her.

Dr. Campbell was helping Melanctha Herbert to take care of her sick mother. He saw Melanctha now for long times and very often, and they sometimes talked a good deal together, but Melanctha never said anything to him about Jane Harden. She never talked to him about anything that was not just general matters, or about medicine, or to tell him funny stories. She asked him many questions and always listened very well to all he told her, and she always remembered everything she heard him say about doctoring, and she always remembered everything that she had learned from all the others.

Jeff Campbell never found that all this talk interested him very deeply. He did not find that he liked Melanctha when he saw her so much, any better. He never found that he thought much about Melanctha. He never found that he believed much in her having a good mind, like Jane Harden. He found he liked Jane Harden always better, and that he wished very much that she had never begun that bad drinking.

Melanctha Herbert's mother was now always getting sicker. Melanctha really did everything that any woman could. Melanctha's mother never liked her daughter any better. She never said much, did 'Mis' Herbert, but anybody could see that she did not think much of this daughter.

Dr. Campbell now often had to stay a long time to take care of 'Mis' Herbert. One day 'Mis' Herbert was much sicker and Dr. Campbell thought that this night, she would surely die. He came back late to the house, as he had said he would, to sit up and watch 'Mis' Herbert, and to help Melanctha, if she should need anybody to be with her. Melanctha Herbert and Jeff Campbell sat up all that night together. 'Mis' Herbert did not die. The next day she was a little better.

This house where Melanctha had always lived with her mother was a little red brick, two story house. They had not much furniture to fill it and some of the windows were broken and not mended. Melanctha did not have much money to use now on the house, but with a colored woman, who was their neighbor and good natured and who had always helped them, Melanctha managed to take care of her mother and to keep the house fairly clean and neat.

Melanctha's mother was in bed in a room upstairs, and the steps from below led right up into it. There were just two rooms on this upstairs floor. Melanctha and Dr. Campbell sat down on the steps, that night they watched together, so that they could hear and see Melanctha's mother and yet the light would be shaded, and they could sit and read, if they wanted to, and talk low some, and yet not disturb 'Mis' Herbert.

Dr. Campbell was always very fond of reading. Dr. Campbell had not brought a book with him that night. He had just forgotten it.

He had meant to put something in his pocket to read, so that he could amuse himself, while he was sitting there and watching. When he was through with taking care of 'Mis' Herbert, he came and sat down on the steps just above where Melanctha was sitting. He spoke about how he had forgotten to bring his book with him. Melanctha said there were some old papers in the house, perhaps Dr. Campbell could find something in them that would help pass the time for a while for him. All right, Dr. Campbell said, that would be better than just sitting there with nothing. Dr. Campbell began to read through the old papers that Melanctha gave him. When anything amused him in them, he read it out to Melanctha. Melanctha was now pretty silent, with him. Dr. Campbell began to feel a little, about how she responded to him. Dr. Campbell began to see a little that perhaps Melanctha had a good mind. Dr. Campbell was not sure yet that she had a good mind, but he began to think a little that perhaps she might have one.

Jefferson Campbell always liked to talk to everybody about the things he worked at and about his thinking about what he could do for the colored people. Melanctha Herbert never thought about these things the way that he did. Melanctha had never said much to Dr. Campbell about what she thought about them. Melanctha did not feel the same as he did about being good and regular in life, and not having excitements all the time, which was the way that Jefferson Campbell wanted that everybody should be, so that everybody would be wise and yet be happy. Melanctha always had strong the sense for real experience. Melanctha Herbert did not think much of this way of coming to real wisdom.

Dr. Campbell soon got through with his reading, in the old newspapers, and then somehow he began to talk along about the things he was always thinking. Dr. Campbell said he wanted to work so that he could understand what troubled people, and not to just have excitements, and he believed you ought to love your father and your mother and to be regular in all your life, and not to be always wanting new things and excitements, and to always know where you were, and what you wanted, and to always tell everything just as you meant it. That's the only kind of life he knew or believed in, Jeff Campbell repeated. "No I ain't got any use for all the time being in excitements and wanting to have all kinds of experience all the time. I got plenty of experience just living regular and quiet and with my family, and doing my work, and taking care of people, and trying

to understand it. I don't believe much in this running around business and I don't want to see the colored people do it. I am a colored
man and I ain't sorry, and I want to see the colored people like
what is good and what I want them to have, and that's to live regular
and work hard and understand things, and that's enough to keep any
decent man excited." Jeff Campbell spoke now with some anger. Not
to Melanctha, he did not think of her at all when he was talking.
It was the life he wanted that he spoke to, and the way he wanted
things to be with the colored people.

But Melanctha Herbert had listened to him say all this. She knew
he meant it, but it did not mean much to her, and she was sure some
day he would find out, that it was not all, of real wisdom. Melanctha
knew very well what it was to have real wisdom. "But how about
Jane Harden?" said Melanctha to Jeff Campbell, "seems to me Dr.
Campbell you find her to have something in her, and you go there
very often, and you talk to her much more than you do to the nice
girls that stay at home with their people, the kind you say you are
really wanting. It don't seem to me Dr. Campbell, that what you say
and what you do seem to have much to do with each other. And
about your being so good Dr. Campbell," went on Melanctha, "You
don't care about going to church much yourself, and yet you always
are saying you believe so much in things like that, for people. It
seems to me, Dr. Campbell you want to have a good time just like
all us others, and then you just keep on saying that it's right to be
good and you ought not to have excitements, and yet you really don't
want to do it Dr. Campbell, no more than me or Jane Harden. No,
Dr. Campbell, it certainly does seem to me you don't know very well
yourself, what you mean, when you are talking."

Jefferson had been talking right along, the way he always did
when he got started, and now Melanctha's answer only made him
talk a little harder. He laughed a little, too, but very low, so as not
to disturb 'Mis' Herbert who was sleeping very nicely, and he looked
brightly at Melanctha to enjoy her, and then he settled himself down
to answer.

"Yes," he began, "it certainly does sound a little like I didn't know
very well what I do mean, when you put it like that to me, Miss
Melanctha, but that's just because you don't understand enough
about what I meant, by what I was just saying to you. I don't say,
never, I don't want to know all kinds of people, Miss Melanctha,
and I don't say there ain't many kinds of people, and I don't say

ever, that I don't find some like Jane Harden very good to know and talk to, but it's the strong things I like in Jane Harden, not all her excitements. I don't admire the bad things she does, Miss Melanctha, but Jane Harden is a strong woman and I always respect that in her. No I know you don't believe what I say, Miss Melanctha, but I mean it, and it's all just because you don't understand it when I say it. And as for religion, that just ain't my way of being good, Miss Melanctha, but it's a good way for many people to be good and regular in their way of living, and if they believe it, it helps them to be good, and if they're honest in it, I like to see them have it. No, what I don't like, Miss Melanctha, is this what I see so much with the colored people, their always wanting new things just to get excited."

Jefferson Campbell here stopped himself in this talking. Melanctha Herbert did not make any answer. They both sat there very quiet.

Jeff Campbell then began again on the old papers. He sat there on the steps just above where Melanctha was sitting, and he went on with his reading, and his head went moving up and down, and sometimes he was reading, and sometimes he was thinking about all the things he wanted to be doing, and then he would rub the back of his dark hand over his mouth, and in between he would be frowning with his thinking, and sometimes he would be rubbing his head hard to help his thinking. And Melanctha just sat still and watched the lamp burning, and sometimes she turned it down a little, when the wind caught it and it would begin to get to smoking.

And so Jeff Campbell and Melanctha Herbert sat there on the steps, very quiet, a long time, and they didn't seem to think much, that they were together. They sat there so, for about an hour, and then it came to Jefferson very slowly and as a strong feeling that he was sitting there on the steps, alone, with Melanctha. He did not know if Melanctha Herbert was feeling very much about their being there alone together. Jefferson began to wonder about it a little. Slowly he felt that surely they must both have this feeling. It was so important that he knew that she must have it. They both sat there, very quiet, a long time.

At last Jefferson began to talk about how the lamp was smelling. Jefferson began to explain what it is that makes a lamp get to smelling. Melanctha let him talk. She did not answer, and then he stopped in his talking. Soon Melanctha began to sit up straighter and then she started in to question.

"About what you was just saying Dr. Campbell about living regular and all that, I certainly don't understand what you meant by what you was just saying. You ain't a bit like good people Dr. Campbell, like the good people you are always saying are just like you. I know good people Dr. Campbell, and you ain't a bit like men who are good and got religion. You are just as free and easy as any man can be Dr. Campbell, and you always like to be with Jane Harden, and she is a pretty bad one and you don't look down on her and you never tell her she is a bad one. I know you like her just like a friend Dr. Campbell, and so I certainly don't understand just what it is you mean by all that you was just saying to me. I know you mean honest Dr. Campbell, and I am always trying to believe you, but I can't say as I see just what you mean when you say you want to be good and real pious, because I am very certain Dr. Campbell that you ain't that kind of a man at all, and you ain't never ashamed to be with queer folks Dr. Campbell, and you seem to be thinking what you are doing is just like what you are always saying, and Dr. Campbell, I certainly don't just see what you mean by what you say."

Dr. Campbell almost laughed loud enough to wake 'Mis' Herbert. He did enjoy the way Melanctha said these things to him. He began to feel very strongly about it that perhaps Melanctha really had a good mind. He was very free now in his laughing, but not so as to make Melanctha angry. He was very friendly with her in his laughing, and then he made his face get serious, and he rubbed his head to help him in his thinking.

"I know Miss Melanctha" he began, "It ain't very easy for you to understand what I was meaning by what I was just saying to you, and perhaps some of the good people I like so wouldn't think very much, any more than you do, Miss Melanctha, about the ways I have to be good. But that's no matter Miss Melanctha. What I mean Miss Melanctha by what I was just saying to you is, that I don't, no, never, believe in doing things just to get excited. You see Miss Melanctha I mean the way so many of the colored people do it. Instead of just working hard and caring about their working and living regular with their families and saving up all their money, so they will have some to bring up their children better, instead of living regular and doing like that and getting all their new ways from just decent living, the colored people just keep running around and perhaps drinking and doing everything bad they can ever think of, and not just because they like all those bad things that they are always doing, but only just because they want to get excited. No Miss Melanctha, you see I am a colored man myself and I ain't sorry, and I want to see the colored people being good and careful and always honest and living always just as regular as can be, and I am sure Miss Melanctha, that that way everybody can have a good time, and be happy and keep right and be busy, and not always have to be doing bad things for new ways to get excited. Yes Miss Melanctha, I certainly do like everything to be good, and quiet, and I certainly do think that is the best way for all us colored people. No, Miss Melanctha too, I don't mean this except only just the way I say it. I ain't got any other meaning Miss Melanctha, and it's that what I mean when I am saying about being really good. It ain't Miss Melanctha to be pious and not liking every kind of people, and I don't say ever Miss Melanctha that when other kind of people come regular into your life you shouldn't want to know them always. What I mean Miss Melanctha by what I am always saying is, you shouldn't try to know everybody just to run around and get excited. It's that kind of way of doing that I hate so always Miss Melanctha, and that is so bad for all us colored people. I don't know as you understand now any better what I mean by what I was just saying to you. But you certainly do know now Miss Melanctha, that I always mean it what I say when I am talking."

"Yes I certainly do understand you when you talk so Dr. Campbell. I certainly do understand now what you mean by what you was always saying to me. I certainly do understand Dr. Campbell that you mean you don't believe it's right to love anybody." "Why sure no, yes I do Miss Melanctha, I certainly do believe strong in loving, and in being good to everybody, and trying to understand what they all need, to help them." "Oh I know all about that way of doing Dr. Campbell, but that certainly ain't the kind of love I mean when I am talking. I mean real, strong, hot love Dr. Campbell, that makes you do anything for somebody that loves you." "I don't know much about that kind of love yet Miss Melanctha. You see it's this way with me always Miss Melanctha. I am always so busy with my thinking about my work I am doing and so I don't have time for just fooling, and then too, you see Miss Melanctha, I really certainly don't ever like to get excited, and that kind of loving hard does seem always to mean just getting all the time excited. That certainly is what I always think from what I see of them that have it bad Miss Melanctha, and that certainly would never suit a man like me. You

see Miss Melanctha I am a very quiet kind of fellow, and I believe in
a quiet life for all the colored people. No Miss Melanctha I certainly
never have mixed myself up in that kind of trouble."

"Yes I certainly do see that very clear Dr. Campbell," said Melanctha, "I see that's certainly what it is always made me not know
right about you and that's certainly what it is that makes you really
mean what you was always saying. You certainly are just too scared
Dr. Campbell to really feel things way down in you. All you are
always wanting Dr. Campbell, is just to talk about being good, and
to play with people just to have a good time, and yet always to
certainly keep yourself out of trouble. It don't seem to me Dr. Campbell that I admire that way to do things very much. It certainly ain't
really to me being very good. It certainly ain't any more to me Dr.
Campbell, but that you certainly are awful scared about really feeling
things way down in you, and that's certainly the only way Dr.
Campbell I can see that you can mean, by what it is that you are
always saying to me."

"I don't know about that Miss Melanctha, I certainly don't think
I can't feel things very deep in me, though I do say I certainly do
like to have things nice and quiet, but I don't see harm in keeping
out of danger Miss Melanctha, when a man knows he certainly don't
want to get killed in it, and I don't know anything that's more awful
dangerous Miss Melanctha than being strong in love with somebody.
I don't mind sickness or real trouble Miss Melanctha, and I don't
want to be talking about what I can do in real trouble, but you know
something about that Miss Melanctha, but I certainly don't see much
in mixing up just to get excited, in that awful kind of danger. No
Miss Melanctha I certainly do only know just two kinds of ways of
loving. One kind of loving seems to me, is like one has a good quiet
feeling in a family when one does his work, and is always living good
and being regular, and then the other way of loving is just like having
it like any animal that's low in the streets together, and that don't
seem to me very good Miss Melanctha, though I don't say ever that
it's not all right when anybody likes it, and that's all the kinds of
love I know Miss Melanctha, and I certainly don't care very much
to get mixed up in that kind of a way just to be in trouble."

Jefferson stopped and Melanctha thought a little.

"That certainly does explain to me Dr. Campbell what I been
thinking about you this long time. I certainly did wonder how you
could be so live, and knowing everything, and everybody, and talking

so big always about everything, and everybody always liking you so much, and you always looking as if you was thinking, and yet you really was never knowing about anybody and certainly not being really very understanding. It certainly is all Dr. Campbell because you is so afraid you will be losing being good so easy, and it certainly do seem to me Dr. Campbell that it certainly don't amount to very much that kind of goodness."

"Perhaps you are right Miss Melanctha," Jefferson answered. "I don't say never, perhaps you ain't right Miss Melanctha. Perhaps I ought to know more about such ways Miss Melanctha. Perhaps it would help me some, taking care of the colored people, Miss Melanctha. I don't say, no, never, but perhaps I could learn a whole lot about women the right way, if I had a real good teacher."

'Mis' Herbert just then stirred a little in her sleep. Melanctha went up the steps to the bed to attend her. Dr. Campbell got up too and went to help her. 'Mis' Herbert woke up and was a little better. Now it was morning and Dr. Campbell gave his directions to Melanctha, and then left her.

Melanctha Herbert all her life long, loved and wanted good, kind and considerate people. Jefferson Campbell was all the things that Melanctha had ever wanted. Jefferson was a strong, well built, good looking, cheery, intelligent and good mulatto. And then at first he had not cared to know Melanctha, and when he did begin to know her he had not liked her very well, and he had not thought that she would ever come to any good. And then Jefferson Campbell was so very gentle. Jefferson never did some things like other men, things that now were beginning to be ugly, for Melanctha. And then too Jefferson Campbell did not seem to know very well what it was that Melanctha really wanted, and all this was making Melanctha feel his power with her always getting stronger.

Dr. Campbell came in every day to see 'Mis' Herbert. 'Mis' Herbert, after that night they watched together, did get a little better, but 'Mis' Herbert was really very sick, and soon it was pretty sure that she would have to die. Melanctha certainly did everything, all the time, that any woman could. Jefferson never thought much better of Melanctha while she did it. It was not her being good, he wanted to find in her. He knew very well Jane Harden was right, when she said Melanctha was always being good to everybody but that that did not make Melanctha any better for her. Then too, 'Mis' Herbert never liked Melanctha any better, even on the last day of her living, and so Jefferson really never thought much of Melanctha's always being good to her mother.

Jefferson and Melanctha now saw each other, very often. They now always liked to be with each other, and they always now had a good time when they talked to one another. They, mostly in their talking to each other, still just talked about outside things and what they were thinking. Except just in little moments, and not those very often, they never said anything about their feeling. Sometimes Melanctha would tease Jefferson a little just to show she had not forgotten, but mostly she listened to his talking, for Jefferson still always liked to talk along about the things he believed in. Melanctha was liking Jefferson Campbell better every day, and Jefferson was beginning to know that Melanctha certainly had a good mind, and he was beginning to feel a little her real sweetness. Not in her being good to 'Mis' Herbert, that never seemed to Jefferson to mean much in her, but there was a strong kind of sweetness in Melanctha's nature that Jefferson began now to feel when he was with her.

'Mis' Herbert was now always getting sicker. One night again Dr. Campbell felt very certain that before it was morning she would surely die. Dr. Campbell said he would come back to help Melanctha watch her, and to do anything he could to make 'Mis' Herbert's dying more easy for her. Dr. Campbell came back that evening, after he was through with his other patients, and then he made 'Mis' Herbert easy, and then he came and sat down on the steps just above where Melanctha was sitting with the lamp, and looking very tired. Dr. Campbell was pretty tired too, and they both sat there very quiet.

"You look awful tired to-night, Dr. Campbell," Melanctha said at last, with her voice low and very gentle, "Don't you want to go lie down and sleep a little? You're always being much too good to everybody, Dr. Campbell. I like to have you stay here watching to-night with me, but it don't seem right you ought to stay here when you got so much always to do for everybody. You are certainly very kind to come back, Dr. Campbell, but I can certainly get along to-night without you. I can get help next door sure if I need it. You just go 'long home to bed, Dr. Campbell. You certainly do look as if you need it."

Jefferson was silent for some time, and always he was looking very gently at Melanctha.

"I certainly never did think, Miss Melanctha, I would find you to be so sweet and thinking, with me." "Dr. Campbell" said Melanctha, still more gentle, "I certainly never did think that you would ever feel it good to like me. I certainly never did think you would want to see for yourself if I had sweet ways in me."

They both sat there very tired, very gentle, very quiet, a long time. At last Melanctha in a low, even tone began to talk to Jefferson Campbell.

"You are certainly a very good man, Dr. Campbell, I certainly do feel that more every day I see you. Dr. Campbell, I sure do want to be friends with a good man like you, now I know you. You certainly, Dr. Campbell, never do things like other men, that's always ugly for me. Tell me true, Dr. Campbell, how you feel about being always friends with me. I certainly do know, Dr. Campbell, you are a good man, and if you say you will be friends with me, you certainly never will go back on me, the way so many kinds of them do to every girl they ever get to like them. Tell me for true, Dr. Campbell, will you be friends with me?"

"Why, Miss Melanctha," said Campbell slowly, "why you see I just can't say that right out that way to you. Why sure you know Miss Melanctha, I will be very glad if it comes by and by that we are always friends together, but you see, Miss Melanctha, I certainly am a very slow-minded quiet kind of fellow though I do say quick things all the time to everybody, and when I certainly do want to mean it what I am saying to you, I can't say things like that right out to everybody till I know really more for certain all about you, and how I like you, and what I really mean to do better for you. You certainly do see what I mean, Miss Melanctha." "I certainly do admire you for talking honest to me, Jeff Campbell," said Melanctha. "Oh, I am always honest, Miss Melanctha. It's easy enough for me always to be honest, Miss Melanctha. All I got to do is always just to say right out what I am thinking. I certainly never have got any real reason for not saying it right out like that to anybody."

They sat together, very silent. "I certainly do wonder, Miss Melanctha," at last began Jeff Campbell, "I certainly do wonder, if we know very right, you and me, what each other is really thinking. I certainly do wonder, Miss Melanctha, if we know at all really what each other means by what we are always saying." "That certainly do mean, by what you say, that you think I am a bad one, Jeff Campbell," flashed out Melanctha. "Why no, Miss Melanctha, why sure I don't mean any thing like that at all, by what I am saying to you. You know well as I do, Miss Melanctha, I think better of you every day I see you, and I like to talk with you all the time now, Miss Melanctha, and I certainly do think we both like it very well when we are together, and it seems to me always more, you are very good and sweet always to everybody. It only is, I am really so slow-minded in my ways, Miss Melanctha, for all I talk so quick to everybody, and I don't like to say to you what I don't know for very sure, and I certainly don't know for sure I know just all what you mean by what you are always saying to me. And you see, Miss Melanctha, that's what makes me say what I was just saying to you when you asked me."

"I certainly do thank you again for being honest to me, Dr. Campbell," said Melanctha. "I guess I leave you now, Dr. Campbell. I think I go in the other room and rest a little. I leave you here, so perhaps if I ain't here you will maybe sleep and rest yourself a little. Good night now, Dr. Campbell, I call you if I need you later to help me, Dr. Campbell, I hope you rest well, Dr. Campbell."

Jeff Campbell, when Melanctha left him, sat there and he was very quiet and just wondered. He did not know very well just what Melanctha meant by what she was always saying to him. He did not know very well how much he really knew about Melanctha Herbert. He wondered if he should go on being so much all the time with her. He began to think about what he should do now with her. Jefferson Campbell was a man who liked everybody and many people liked very much to be with him. Women liked him, he was so strong, and good, and understanding, and innocent, and firm, and gentle. Sometimes they seemed to want very much he should be with them. When they got so, they always had made Campbell very tired. Sometimes he would play a little with them, but he never had had any strong feeling for them. Now with Melanctha Herbert everything seemed different. Jefferson was not sure that he knew here just what he wanted. He was not sure he knew just what it was that Melanctha wanted. He knew if it was only play, with Melanctha, that he did not want to do it. But he remembered always how she had told him he never knew how to feel things very deeply. He remembered how she told him he was afraid to let himself ever know real feeling, and then too, most of all to him, she had told him he was not very understanding. That always troubled Jefferson very keenly, he wanted very badly to be really understanding. If Jefferson only knew better just what Melanctha meant by what she said.

Jefferson always had thought he knew something about women. Now he found that really he knew nothing. He did not know the least bit about Melanctha. He did not know what it was right that he should do about it. He wondered if it was just a little play that they were doing. If it was a play he did not want to go on playing, but if it was really that he was not very understanding, and that with Melanctha Herbert he could learn to really understand, then he was very certain he did not want to be a coward. It was very hard for him to know what he wanted. He thought and thought, and always he did not seem to know any better what he wanted. At last he gave up this thinking. He felt sure it was only play with Melanctha. "No, I certainly won't go on fooling with her any more this way," he said at last out loud to himself, when he was through with this thinking. "I certainly will stop fooling, and begin to go on with my thinking about my work and what's the matter with people like 'Mis' Herbert," and Jefferson took out his book from his pocket, and drew near to the lamp, and began with some hard scientific reading.

Jefferson sat there for about an hour reading, and he had really forgotten all about his trouble with Melanctha's meaning. Then 'Mis' Herbert had some trouble with her breathing. She woke up and was gasping. Dr. Campbell went to her and gave her something that would help her. Melanctha came out from the other room and did things as he told her. They together made 'Mis' Herbert more comfortable and easy, and soon she was again in her deep sleep. Dr. Campbell went back to the steps where he had been sitting. Melanctha came and stood a little while beside him, and then she sat down and watched him reading. By and by they began with their talking. Jeff Campbell began to feel that perhaps it was all different. Perhaps it was not just play, with Melanctha. Anyway he liked it very well that she was with him. He began to tell her about the book he was just reading.

Melanctha was very intelligent always in her questions. Jefferson knew now very well that she had a good mind. They were having a very good time, talking there together. And then they began again to get quiet.

"It certainly was very good in you to come back and talk to me Miss Melanctha," Jefferson said at last to her, for now he was almost certain, it was no game she was playing. Melanctha really was a good woman, and she had a good mind, and she had a real, strong sweetness, and she could surely really teach him. "Oh I always like to talk to you Dr. Campbell" said Melanctha, "And then you was only just honest to me, and I always like it when a man is really honest to me." Then they were again very silent, sitting there together, with the lamp between them, that was always smoking. Melanctha began to lean a little more toward Dr. Campbell, where he was sitting, and then she took his hand between her two and pressed it hard, but she said nothing to him. She let it go then and leaned a little nearer to him. Jefferson moved a little but did not do anything in answer. At last, "Well," said Melanctha sharply to him. "I was just thinking" began Dr. Campbell slowly, "I was just wondering," he was beginning to get ready to go on with his talking. "Don't you ever stop with your thinking long enough ever to have any feeling Jeff Campbell," said Melanctha a little sadly. "I don't know," said Jeff Campbell slowly, "I don't know Miss Melanctha much about that. No, I don't stop thinking much Miss Melanctha and if I can't ever feel without stopping thinking, I certainly am very much afraid Miss Melanctha that I never will do much with that kind of feeling. Sure you ain't worried Miss Melanctha, about my really not feeling very much all the time. I certainly do think I feel some, Miss Melanctha, even though I always do it without ever knowing how to stop with my thinking." "I am certainly afraid I don't think much of your kind of feeling Dr. Campbell." "Why I think you certainly are wrong Miss Melanctha. I certainly do think I feel as much for you Miss Melanctha, as you ever feel about me, sure I do. I don't think you know me right when you talk like that to me. Tell me just straight out how much do you care about me, Miss Melanctha." "Care about you Jeff Campbell," said Melanctha slowly. "I certainly do care for you Jeff Campbell less than you are always thinking and much more than you are ever knowing."

Jeff Campbell paused on this, and he was silent with the power of Melanctha's meaning. They sat there together very silent, a long time. "Well Jeff Campbell," said Melanctha. "Oh," said Dr. Campbell and he moved himself a little, and then they were very silent a long time. "Haven't you got nothing to say to me Jeff Campbell?" said Melanctha. "Why yes, what was it we were just saying about to one another. You see Miss Melanctha I am a very quiet, slow minded kind of fellow, and I am never sure I know just exactly what you mean by all that you are always saying to me. But I do like you very much Miss Melanctha and I am very sure you got very good things in you all the time. You sure do believe what I am saying to you Miss Melanctha." "Yes I believe it when you say it to me, Jeff Campbell," said Melanctha, and then she was silent and there was much sadness in it. "I guess I go in and lie down again Dr. Campbell," said Melanctha. "Don't go leave me Miss Melanctha," said Jeff Campbell quickly. "Why not, what you want of me Jeff Campbell?" said Melanctha. "Why," said Jeff Campbell slowly, "I just want to go on talking with you. I certainly do like talking about all kinds of things with you. You certainly know that all right, Miss Melanctha." "I guess I go lie down again and leave you here with your thinking," said Melanctha gently. "I certainly am very tired to-night Dr. Campbell. Good night I hope you rest well Dr. Campbell." Melanctha stooped over him, where he was sitting, to say this good night, and then, very quick and sudden, she kissed him and then, very quick again, she went away and left him.

Dr. Campbell sat there very quiet, with only a little thinking and sometimes a beginning feeling, and he was alone until it began to be morning, and then he went, and Melanctha helped him, and he made 'Mis' Herbert more easy in her dying. 'Mis' Herbert lingered on till about ten o'clock the next morning, and then slowly and without much pain she died away. Jeff Campbell stayed till the last moment, with Melanctha, to make her mother's dying easy for her. When it was over he sent in the colored woman from next door to help Melanctha fix things, and then he went away to take care of his other patients. He came back very soon to Melanctha. He helped her to have a funeral for her mother. Melanctha then went to live with the good natured woman, who had been her neighbor. Melanctha still saw Jeff Campbell very often. Things began to be very strong between them.

Melanctha now never wandered, unless she was with Jeff Campbell. Sometimes she and he wandered a good deal together. Jeff Campbell had not got over his way of talking to her all the time about all the things he was always thinking. Melanctha never talked much, now, when they were together. Sometimes Jeff Campbell teased her about her not talking to him. "I certainly did think Melanctha you was a great talker from the way Jane Harden and everybody said things to me, and from the way I heard you talk so much when I first met you. Tell me true Melanctha, why don't you talk more now to me, perhaps it is I talk so much I don't give you any chance to say things to me, or perhaps it is you hear me talk so

much you don't think so much now of a whole lot of talking. Tell
me honest Melanctha, why don't you talk more to me." "You know
very well Jeff Campbell," said Melanctha. "You certainly do know
very well Jeff, you don't think really much, of my talking. You think
a whole lot more about everything than I do Jeff, and you don't
care much what I got to say about it. You know that's true what I
am saying Jeff, if you want to be real honest, the way you always
are when I like you so much." Jeff laughed and looked fondly at
her. "I don't say ever I know, you ain't right, when you say things
like that to me, Melanctha. You see you always like to be talking
just what you think everybody wants to be hearing from you, and
when you are like that, Melanctha, honest, I certainly don't care
very much to hear you, but sometimes you say something that is
what you are really thinking, and then I like a whole lot to hear you
talking." Melanctha smiled, with her strong sweetness, on him, and
she felt her power very deeply. "I certainly never do talk very much
when I like anybody really, Jeff. You see, Jeff, it ain't much use to
talk about what a woman is really feeling in her. You see all that,
Jeff, better, by and by, when you get to really feeling. You won't
be so ready then always with your talking. You see, Jeff, if it don't
come true what I am saying." "I don't ever say you ain't always
right, Melanctha," said Jeff Campbell. "Perhaps what I call my
thinking ain't really so very understanding. I don't say, no never
now any more, you ain't right, Melanctha, when you really say
things to me. Perhaps I see it all to be very different when I come
to really see what you mean by what you are always saying to me."
"You is very sweet and good to me always, Jeff Campbell," said
Melanctha. " 'Deed I certainly am not good to you, Melanctha.
Don't I bother you all the time with my talking, but I really do like
you a whole lot, Melanctha," "And I like you, Jeff Campbell, and
you certainly are mother, and father, and brother, and sister, and
child and everything, always to me. I can't say much about how good
you been to me, Jeff Campbell, I never knew any man who was
good and didn't do things ugly, before I met you to take care of me,
Jeff Campbell. Good-by, Jeff, come see me to-morrow, when you
get through with your working." "Sure Melanctha, you know that
already," said Jeff Campbell, and then he went away and left her.

These months had been an uncertain time for Jeff Campbell. He
never knew how much he really knew about Melanctha. He saw
her now for long times and very often. He was beginning always

more and more to like her. But he did not seem to himself to know
very much about her. He was beginning to feel he could almost
trust the goodness in her. But then, always, really, he was not very
sure about her. Melanctha always had ways that made him feel
uncertain with her, and yet he was so near, in his feeling for her.
He now never thought about all this in real words any more. He
was always letting it fight itself out in him. He was now never taking
any part in this fighting that was always going on inside him.

Jeff always loved now to be with Melanctha and yet he always
hated to go to her. Somehow he was always afraid when he was to
go to her, and yet he had made himself very certain that here he
would not be a coward. He never felt any of this being afraid,
when he was with her. Then they always were very true, and near
to one another. But always when he was going to her, Jeff would
like anything that could happen that would keep him a little longer
from her.

It was a very uncertain time, all these months, for Jeff Campbell.
He did not know very well what it was that he really wanted. He
was very certain that he did not know very well what it was that
Melanctha wanted. Jeff Campbell had always all his life loved to be
with people, and he had loved all his life always to be thinking,
but he was still only a great boy, was Jeff Campbell, and he had
never before had any of this funny kind of feeling. Now, this evening,
when he was free to go and see Melanctha, he talked to anybody he
could find who would detain him, and so it was very late when at
last he came to the house where Melanctha was waiting to receive
him.

Jeff came in to where Melanctha was waiting for him, and he
took off his hat and heavy coat, and then drew up a chair and sat
down by the fire. It was very cold that night, and Jeff sat there,
and rubbed his hands and tried to warm them. He had only said
"How do you do" to Melanctha, he had not yet begun to talk to
her. Melanctha sat there, by the fire, very quiet. The heat gave a
pretty pink glow to her pale yellow and attractive face. Melanctha
sat in a low chair, her hands, with their long, fluttering fingers,
always ready to show her strong feeling, were lying quiet in her
lap. Melanctha was very tired with her waiting for Jeff Campbell.
She sat there very quiet and just watching. Jeff was a robust, dark,
healthy, cheery negro. His hands were firm and kindly and unimpassioned. He touched women always with his big hands, like a

brother. He always had a warm broad glow, like southern sunshine. He never had anything mysterious in him. He was open, he was pleasant, he was cheery and always he wanted, as Melanctha once had wanted, always now he too wanted really to understand.

Jeff sat there this evening in his chair and was silent a long time, warming himself with the pleasant fire. He did not look at Melanctha who was watching. He sat there and just looked into the fire. At first his dark, open face was smiling, and he was rubbing the back of his black-brown hand over his mouth to help him in his smiling. Then he was thinking, and he frowned and rubbed his head hard, to help him in his thinking. Then he smiled again, but now his smiling was not very pleasant. His smile was now wavering on the edge of scorning. His smile changed more and more, and then he had a look as if he were deeply down, all disgusted. Now his face was darker, and he was bitter in his smiling, and he began, without looking from the fire, to talk to Melanctha, who was now very tense with her watching.

"Melanctha Herbert," began Jeff Campbell, "I certainly after all this time I know you, I certainly do know little, real about you. You see, Melanctha, it's like this way with me"; Jeff was frowning, with his thinking and looking very hard into the fire, "You see it's just this way, with me now, Melanctha. Sometimes you seem like one kind of a girl to me, and sometimes you are like a girl that is all different to me, and the two kinds of girls is certainly very different to each other, and I can't see any way they seem to have much to do, to be together in you. They certainly don't seem to be made much like as if they could have anything really to do with each other. Sometimes you are a girl to me I certainly never would be trusting, and you got a laugh then so hard, it just rattles, and you got ways so bad, I can't believe you mean them hardly, and yet all that I just been saying is certainly you one way I often see you, and it's what your mother and Jane Harden always found you, and it's what makes me hate so, to come near you. And then certainly sometimes, Melanctha, you certainly is all a different creature, and sometimes then there comes out in you what is certainly a thing, like a real beauty. I certainly, Melanctha, never can tell just how it is that it comes so lovely. Seems to me when it comes it's got a real sweetness, that is more wonderful than a pure flower, and a gentleness, that is more tender than the sunshine, and a kindness, that makes one feel like summer, and then a way to know, that makes everything all over, and all that, and it does certainly seem to be real for the little while it's lasting, for the little while that I can surely see it, and it gives me to feel like I certainly had got real religion. And then when I got rich with such a feeling, comes all that other girl, and then that seems more likely that that is really you what's honest, and then I certainly do get awful afraid to come to you, and I certainly never do feel I could be very trusting with you. And then I certainly don't know anything at all about you, and certainly don't know which is a real Melanctha Herbert, and I certainly don't feel no longer, I ever want to talk to you. Tell me honest, Melanctha, which is the way that is you really, when you are alone, and real, and all honest. Tell me, Melanctha, for I certainly do want to know it."

Melanctha did not make him any answer, and Jeff, without looking at her, after a little while, went on with his talking. "And then, Melanctha, sometimes you certainly do seem sort of cruel, and not to care about people being hurt or in trouble, something so hard about you it makes me sometimes real nervous, sometimes somehow like you always, like your being, with 'Mis' Herbert. You sure did do everything that any woman could, Melanctha, I certainly never did see anybody do things any better, and yet, I don't know how to say just what I mean, Melanctha, but there was something awful hard about your feeling, so different from the way I'm always used to see good people feeling, and so it was the way Jane Harden and 'Mis' Herbert talked when they felt strong to talk about you, and yet, Melanctha, somehow I feel so really near to you, and you certainly have got an awful wonderful, strong kind of sweetness. I certainly would like to know for sure, Melanctha, whether I got really anything to be afraid for. I certainly did think once, Melanctha, I knew something about all kinds of women. I certainly know now really, how I don't know anything sure at all about you, Melanctha, though I been with you so long, and so many times for whole hours with you, and I like so awful much to be with you, and I can always say anything I am thinking to you. I certainly do awful wish, Melanctha, I really was more understanding. I certainly do that same, Melanctha."

Jeff stopped now and looked harder than before into the fire. His face changed from his thinking back into that look that was so like as if he was all through and through him, disgusted with what he had been thinking. He sat there a long time, very quiet, and then slowly, somehow, it came strongly to him that Melanctha

Herbert, there beside him, was trembling and feeling it all to be very bitter. "Why, Melanctha," cried Jeff Campbell, and he got up and put his arm around her like a brother. "I stood it just so long as I could bear it, Jeff," sobbed Melanctha, and then she gave herself away, to her misery, "I was awful ready, Jeff, to let you say anything you liked that gave you any pleasure. You could say all about me what you wanted, Jeff, and I would try to stand it, so as you would be sure to be liking it, Jeff, but you was too cruel to me. When you do that kind of seeing how much you can make a woman suffer, you ought to give her a little rest, once sometimes, Jeff. They can't any of us stand it so for always, Jeff. I certainly did stand it just as long as I could, so you would like it, but I,—oh Jeff, you went on too long to-night Jeff. I couldn't stand it not a minute longer the way you was doing of it, Jeff. When you want to be seeing how the way a woman is really made of, Jeff, you shouldn't never be so cruel, never to be thinking how much she can stand, the strong way you always do it, Jeff." "Why, Melanctha," cried Jeff Campbell, in his horror, and then he was very tender to her, and like a good, strong, gentle brother in his soothing of her, "Why Melanctha dear, I certainly don't now see what it is you mean by what you was just saying to me. Why Melanctha, you poor little girl, you certainly never did believe I ever knew I was giving you real suffering. Why, Melanctha, how could you ever like me if you thought I ever could be so like a red Indian?" "I didn't just know, Jeff," and Melanctha nestled to him, "I certainly never did know just what it was you wanted to be doing with me, but I certainly wanted you should do anything you liked, you wanted, to make me more understanding for you. I tried awful hard to stand it, Jeff, so as you could do anything you wanted with me." "Good Lord and Jesus Christ, Melanctha!" cried Jeff Campbell. "I certainly never can know anything about you real, Melanctha, you poor little girl," and Jeff drew her closer to him, "But I certainly do admire and trust you a whole lot now, Melanctha. I certainly do, for I certainly never did think I was hurting you at all, Melanctha, by the things I always been saying to you. Melanctha, you poor little, sweet, trembling baby now, be good, Melanctha. I certainly can't ever tell you how awful sorry I am to hurt you so, Melanctha. I do anything I can to show you how I never did mean to hurt you, Melanctha." "I know, I know," murmured Melanctha, clinging to him. "I know you are a good man, Jeff. I always know that, no matter how much you can hurt me."

"I sure don't see how you can think so, Melanctha, if you certainly did think I was trying so hard just to hurt you." "Hush, you are only a great big boy, Jeff Campbell, and you don't know nothing yet about real hurting," said Melanctha, smiling up through her crying, at him. "You see, Jeff, I never knew anybody I could know real well and yet keep on always respecting, till I came to know you real well, Jeff." "I sure don't understand that very well Melanctha. I ain't a bit better than just lots of others of the colored people. You certainly have been unlucky with the kind you met before me, that's all, Melanctha. I certainly ain't very good, Melanctha." "Hush, Jeff, you don't know nothing at all about what you are," said Melanctha. "Perhaps you are right, Melanctha. I don't say ever any more, you ain't right, when you say things to me, Melanctha," and Jefferson sighed, and then he smiled, and then they were quiet a long time together, and then after some more kindness, it was late, and then Jeff left her.

Jeff Campbell, all these months, had never told his good mother anything about Melanctha Herbert. Somehow he always kept his seeing her so much now, to himself. Melanctha too had never had any of her other friends meet him. They always acted together, these two, as if their being so much together was a secret, but really there was no one who would have made it any harder for them. Jeff Campbell did not really know how it had happened that they were so secret. He did not know if it was what Melanctha wanted. Jeff had never spoken to her at all about it. It just seemed as if it were well understood between them that nobody should know that they were so much together. It was as if it were agreed between them, that they should be alone by themselves always, and so they would work out together what they meant by what they were always saying to each other.

Jefferson often spoke to Melanctha about his good mother. He never said anything about whether Melanctha would want to meet her. Jefferson never quite understood why all this had happened so, in secret. He never really knew what it was that Melanctha really wanted. In all these ways he just, by his nature, did, what he sort of felt Melanctha wanted. And so they continued to be alone and much together, and now it had come to be the spring time, and now they had all out-doors to wander.

They had many days now when they were very happy. Jeff every day found that he really liked Melanctha better. Now surely he was beginning to have real, deep feeling in him. And still he loved to talk himself out to Melanctha, and he loved to tell her how good it all was to him, and how he always loved to be with her, and to tell her always all about it. One day, now Jeff arranged, that Sunday they would go out and have a happy, long day in the bright fields, and they would be all day just alone together. The day before, Jeff was called in to see Jane Harden.

Jane Harden was very sick almost all day and Jeff Campbell did everything he could to make her better. After a while Jane became more easy and then she began to talk to Jeff about Melanctha. Jane did not know how much Jeff was now seeing of Melanctha. Jane these days never saw Melanctha. Jane began to talk of the time when she first knew Melanctha. Jane began to tell how in these days Melanctha had very little understanding. She was young then and she had a good mind. Jane Harden never would say Melanctha never had a good mind, but in those days Melanctha certainly had not been very understanding. Jane began to explain to Jeff Campbell how in every way, she Jane, had taught Melanctha. Jane then began to explain how eager Melanctha always had been for all that kind of learning. Jane Harden began to tell how they had wandered. Jane began to tell how Melanctha once had loved her, Jane Harden. Jane began to tell Jeff of all the bad ways Melanctha had used with her. Jane began to tell all she knew of the way Melanctha had gone on, after she had left her. Jane began to tell all about the different men, white ones and blacks, Melanctha never was particular about things like that, Jane Harden said in passing, not that Melanctha was a bad one, and she had a good mind, Jane Harden never would say that she hadn't, but Melanctha always liked to use all the under-standing ways that Jane had taught her, and so she wanted to know everything, always, that they knew how to teach her.

Jane was beginning to make Jeff Campbell see much clearer. Jane Harden did not know what it was that she was really doing with all this talking. Jane did not know what Jeff was feeling. Jane was always honest when she was talking, and now it just happened she had started talking about her old times with Melanctha Herbert. Jeff understood very well that it was all true what Jane was saying. Jeff Campbell was beginning now to see very clearly. He was be-ginning to feel very sick inside him. He knew now many things Melanctha had not yet taught him. He felt very sick and his heart was very heavy, and Melanctha certainly did seem very ugly to him. Jeff was at last beginning to know what it was to have deep feeling. He took care a little longer of Jane Harden, and then he went to his other patients, and then he went home to his room, and he sat down and at last he had stopped thinking. He was very sick and his heart was very heavy in him. He was very tired and all the world was very dreary to him, and he knew very well now at last, he was really feeling. He knew it now from the way it hurt him. He knew very well that now at last he was beginning to really have understanding. The next day he had arranged to spend, long and happy, all alone in the spring fields with Melanctha, wandering. He wrote her a note and said he could not go, he had a sick patient and would have to stay home with him. For three days after, he made no sign to Melanctha. He was very sick all these days, and his heart was very heavy in him, and he knew very well that now at last he had learned what it was to have deep feeling.

At last one day he got a letter from Melanctha. "I certainly don't rightly understand what you are doing now to me Jeff Campbell," wrote Melanctha Herbert. "I certainly don't rightly understand Jeff Campbell why you ain't all these days been near me, but I certainly do suppose it's just another one of the queer kind of ways you have to be good, and repenting of yourself all of a sudden. I certainly don't say to you Jeff Campbell I admire very much the way you take to be good Jeff Campbell. I am sorry Dr. Campbell, but I certainly am afraid I can't stand it no more from you the way you have been just acting. I certainly can't stand it any more the way you act when you have been as if you thought I was always good enough for anybody to have with them, and then you act as if I was a bad one and you always just despise me. I certainly am afraid Dr. Campbell I can't stand it any more like that. I certainly can't stand it any more the way you are always changing. I certainly am afraid Dr. Campbell you ain't man enough to deserve to have anybody care so much to be always with you. I certainly am awful afraid Dr. Campbell I don't ever any more want to really see you. Good-by Dr. Campbell I wish you always to be real happy."

Jeff Campbell sat in his room, very quiet, a long time, after he got through reading this letter. He sat very still and first he was very angry. As if he, too, did not know very badly what it was to suffer keenly. As if he had not been very strong to stay with Melanctha when he never knew what it was that she really wanted. He knew he was very right to be angry, he knew he really had not been a coward. He knew Melanctha had done many things it was very hard for him to forgive her. He knew very well he had done his best to be kind, and to trust her, and to be loyal to her, and now;— and then Jeff suddenly remembered how one night Melanctha had been so strong to suffer, and he felt come back to him the sweetness in her, and then Jeff knew that really, he always forgave her, and that really, it all was that he was so sorry he had hurt her, and he wanted to go straight away and be a comfort to her. Jeff knew very well, that what Jane Harden had told him about Melanctha and her bad ways, had been a true story, and yet he wanted very badly to be with Melanctha. Perhaps she could teach him to really understand it better. Perhaps she could teach him how it could be all true, and yet how he could be right to believe in her and to trust her.

Jeff sat down and began his answer to her. "Dear Melanctha," Jeff wrote to her. "I certainly don't think you got it all just right in the letter, I just been reading, that you just wrote me. I certainly don't think you are just fair or very understanding to all I have to suffer to keep straight on to really always to believe in you and trust you. I certainly don't think you always are fair to remember right how hard it is for a man, who thinks like I was always thinking, not to think you do things very bad very often. I certainly don't think, Melanctha, I ain't right when I was so angry when I got your letter to me. I know very well, Melanctha, that with you, I never have been a coward. I find it very hard, and I never said it any different, it is hard to me to be understanding, and to know really what it is you wanted, and what it is you are meaning by what you are always saying to me. I don't say ever, it ain't very hard for you to be standing that I ain't very quick to be following whichever way that you are always leading. You know very well, Melanctha, it hurts me very bad and way inside me when I have to hurt you, but I always got to be real honest with you. There ain't no other way for me to be, with you, and I know very well it hurts me too, a whole lot, when I can't follow so quick as you would have me. I don't like to be a coward to you, Melanctha, and I don't like to say what I ain't meaning to you. And if you don't want me to do things honest, Melanctha, why I can't ever talk to you, and you are right when you say, you never again want to see me, but if you got any real sense of what I always been feeling with you, and if you got any right sense, Melanctha, of how hard I been trying to think and to feel right for you, I will be very glad to come and see you, and to begin again with you. I don't say anything now, Melanctha, about how bad I been this week, since I saw you, Melanctha. It don't ever do any good to talk such things over. All I know is I do my best, Melanctha, to you, and I don't say, no, never, I can do any different than just to be honest and come as fast as I think it's right for me to be going in the ways you teach me to be really understanding. So don't talk any more foolishness, Melanctha, about my always changing. I don't change, never, and I got to do what I think is right and honest to me, and I never told you any different, and you always knew it very well that I always would do just so. If you like me to come and see you to-morrow, and go out with you, I will be very glad to, Melanctha. Let me know right away, what it is you want me to be doing for you, Melanctha.

Very truly yours,

JEFFERSON CAMPBELL

"Please come to me, Jeff." Melanctha wrote back for her answer. Jeff went very slowly to Melanctha, glad as he was, still to be going to her. Melanctha came, very quick, to meet him, when she saw him from where she had been watching for him. They went into the house together. They were very glad to be together. They were very good to one another.

"I certainly did think, Melanctha, this time almost really, you never did want me to come to you at all any more to see you," said Jeff Campbell to her, when they had begun again with their talking to each other. "You certainly did make me think, perhaps really this time, Melanctha, it was all over, my being with you ever, and I was very mad, and very sorry, too, Melanctha."

"Well you certainly was very bad to me, Jeff Campbell," said Melanctha, fondly.

"I certainly never do say any more you ain't always right, Melanctha," Jeff answered and he was very ready now with cheerful laughing, "I certainly never do say that any more, Melanctha, if I know it, but still, really, Melanctha, honest, I think perhaps I wasn't real bad to you any more than you just needed from me."

Jeff held Melanctha in his arms and kissed her. He sighed then and was very silent with her. "Well, Melanctha," he said at last, with some more laughing, "well, Melanctha, any way you can't say ever it ain't, if we are ever friends good and really, you can't say, no, never, but that we certainly have worked right hard to get both of us together for it, so we shall sure deserve it then, if we can ever really get it." "We certainly have worked real hard, Jeff, I can't say that ain't all right the way you say it," said Melanctha. "I certainly never can deny it, Jeff, when I feel so worn with all the trouble you been making for me, you bad boy, Jeff," and then Melanctha smiled and then she sighed, and then she was very silent with him.

At last Jeff was to go away. They stood there on the steps for a long time trying to say good-by to each other. At last Jeff made himself really say it. At last he made himself, that he went down the steps and went away.

On the next Sunday they arranged, they were to have the long happy day of wandering that they had lost last time by Jane Harden's talking. Not that Melanctha Herbert had heard yet of Jane Harden's talking.

Jeff saw Melanctha every day now. Jeff was a little uncertain all this time inside him, for he had never yet told to Melanctha what it was that had so nearly made him really want to leave her. Jeff knew that for him, it was not right he should not tell her. He knew they could only have real peace between them when he had been honest, and had really told her. On this long Sunday Jeff was certain that he would really tell her.

They were very happy all that day in their wandering. They had taken things along to eat together. They sat in the bright fields and they were happy, they wandered in the woods and they were happy. Jeff always loved in this way to wander. Jeff always loved to watch everything as it was growing, and he loved all the colors in the trees and on the ground, and the little, new, bright colored bugs he found in the moist ground and in the grass he loved to lie on and in which he was always so busy searching. Jeff loved everything that moved and that was still, and that had color, and beauty, and real being.

Jeff loved very much this day while they were wandering. He almost forgot that he had any trouble with him still inside him. Jeff loved to be there with Melanctha Herbert. She was always so sympathetic to him for the way she listened to everything he found and told her, the way she felt his joy in all this being, the way she never said she wanted anything different from the way they had it. It was certainly a busy and a happy day, this their first long day of really wandering.

Later they were tired, and Melanctha sat down on the ground, and Jeff threw himself his full length beside her. Jeff lay there, very quiet, and then he pressed her hand and kissed it and murmured to her, "You certainly are very good to me, Melanctha." Melanctha felt it very deep and did not answer. Jeff lay there a long time, looking up above him. He was counting all the little leaves he saw above him. He was following all the little clouds with his eyes as they sailed past him. He watched all the birds that flew high beyond him, and all the time Jeff knew he must tell to Melanctha what it was he knew now, that which Jane Harden, just a week ago, had told him. He knew very well that for him it was certain that he had to say it. It was hard, but for Jeff Campbell the only way to lose it was to say it, the only way to know Melanctha really, was to tell her all the struggle he had made to know her, to tell her so she could help him to understand his trouble better, to help him so that never again he could have any way to doubt her.

Jeff lay there a long time, very quiet, always looking up above him, and yet feeling very close now to Melanctha. At last he turned a little toward her, took her hands closer in his to make him feel it stronger, and then very slowly, for the words came very hard for him, slowly he began his talk to her.

"Melanctha," began Jeff, very slowly, "Melanctha, it ain't right I shouldn't tell you why I went away last week and almost never got the chance again to see you. Jane Harden was sick, and I went in to take care of her. She began to tell everything she ever knew about you. She didn't know how well now I know you. I didn't tell her not to go on talking. I listened while she told me everything about you. I certainly found it very hard with what she told me. I know she was talking truth in everything she said about you. I knew you had been free in your ways, Melanctha, I knew you liked to get excitement the way I always hate to see the colored people take it. I didn't know, till I heard Jane Harden say it, you had done things so bad, Melanctha. When Jane Harden told me, I got very sick, Melanctha. I couldn't bear hardly, to think, perhaps I was just another like them to you, Melanctha. I was wrong not to trust you perhaps, Melanctha, but it did make things very ugly to me. I try to be honest to you, Melanctha, the way you say you really want it from me."

Melanctha drew her hands from Jeff Campbell. She sat there, and there was deep scorn in her anger.

"If you wasn't all through just selfish and nothing else, Jeff Campbell, you would take care you wouldn't have to tell me things like this, Jeff Campbell."

Jeff was silent a little, and he waited before he gave his answer. It was not the power of Melanctha's words that held him, for, for them, he had his answer, it was the power of the mood that filled Melanctha, and for that he had no answer. At last he broke through this awe, with his slow fighting resolution, and he began to give his answer.

"I don't say ever, Melanctha," he began, "it wouldn't have been more right for me to stop Jane Harden in her talking and to come to you to have you tell me what you were when I never knew you. I don't say it, no never to you, that that would not have been the right way for me to do, Melanctha. But I certainly am without any kind of doubting, I certainly do know for sure, I had a good right to know about what you were and your ways and your trying to use your understanding, every kind of way you could to get your learning. I certainly did have a right to know things like that about you, Melanctha. I don't say it ever, Melanctha, and I say it very often, I don't say ever I shouldn't have stopped Jane Harden in her talking and come to you and asked you yourself to tell me all about it, but I guess I wanted to keep myself from how much it would hurt me more, to have you yourself say it to me. Perhaps it was I wanted to keep you from having it hurt you so much more, having you to have to tell it to me. I don't know, I don't say it was to help you from being hurt most, or to help me. Perhaps I was a coward to let Jane Harden tell me 'stead of coming straight to you, to have you tell me, but I certainly am sure, Melanctha, I certainly had a right to know such things about you. I don't say it ever, ever, Melanctha, I hadn't the just right to know those things about you." Melanctha laughed her harsh laugh. "You needn't have been under no kind of worry, Jeff Campbell, about whether you should have asked me. You could have asked, it wouldn't have hurt nothing. I certainly never would have told you nothing." "I am not so sure of that, Melanctha," said Jeff Campbell. "I certainly do think you would have told me. I certainly do think I could make you feel it right to tell me. I certainly do think all I did wrong was to let Jane Harden tell me. I certainly do know I never did wrong, to learn what she told me. I certainly know very well, Melanctha, if I had come here to you, you would have told it all to me, Melanctha."

He was silent, and this struggle lay there, strong, between them.

It was a struggle, sure to be going on always between them. It was a struggle that was as sure always to be going on between them, as their minds and hearts always were to have different ways of working.

At last Melanctha took his hand, leaned over him and kissed him. "I sure am very fond of you, Jeff Campbell," Melanctha whispered to him.

Now for a little time there was not any kind of trouble between Jeff Campbell and Melanctha Herbert. They were always together now for long times, and very often. They got much joy now, both of them, from being all the time together.

It was summer now, and they had warm sunshine to wander. It was summer now, and Jeff Campbell had more time to wander, for colored people never get sick so much in summer. It was summer now, and there was a lovely silence everywhere, and all the noises, too, that they heard around them were lovely ones, and added to the joy, in these warm days, they loved so much to be together.

They talked some to each other in these days, did Jeff Campbell and Melanctha Herbert, but always in these days their talking more and more was like it always is with real lovers. Jeff did not talk so much now about what he before always had been thinking. Sometimes Jeff would be, as if he was just waking from himself to be with Melanctha, and then he would find he had been really all the long time with her, and he had really never needed to be doing any thinking.

It was sometimes pure joy Jeff would be talking to Melanctha, in these warm days he loved so much to wander with her. Sometimes Jeff would lose all himself in a strong feeling. Very often now, and always with more joy in his feeling, he would find himself, he did not know how or what it was he had been thinking. And Melanctha always loved very well to make him feel it. She always now laughed a little at him, and went back a little in him to his before, always thinking, and she teased him with his always now being so good with her in his feeling, and then she would so well and freely, and with her pure, strong ways of reaching, she would give him all the love she knew now very well, how much he always wanted to be sure he really had it.

And Jeff took it straight now, and he loved it, and he felt, strong, the joy of all this being, and it swelled out full inside him, and he poured it all out back to her in freedom, in tender kindness, and in joy, and in gentle brother fondling. And Melanctha loved him for it always, her Jeff Campbell now, who never did things ugly, for her, like all the men she always knew before always had been doing to her. And they loved it always, more and more, together, with this new feeling they had now, in these long summer days so warm; they, always together now, just these two so dear, more and more to each other always, and the summer evenings when they wandered, and the noises in the full streets, and the music of the organs, and the dancing, and the warm smell of the people, and of dogs and of the horses, and all the joy of the strong, sweet pungent, dirty, moist, warm negro southern summer.

Every day now, Jeff seemed to be coming nearer, to be really loving. Every day now, Melanctha poured it all out to him, with more freedom. Every day now, they seemed to be having more and more, both together, of this strong, right feeling. More and more every day now they seemed to know more really, what it was each other one was always feeling. More and more now every day Jeff found in himself, he felt more trusting. More and more every day now, he did not think anything in words about what he was always doing. Every day now more and more Melanctha would let out to Jeff her real, strong feeling.

One day there had been much joy between them, more than they ever yet had had with their new feeling. All the day they had lost themselves in warm wandering. Now they were lying there and resting, with a green, bright, light-flecked world around them.

What was it that now really happened to them? What was it that Melanctha did, that made everything get all ugly for them? What was it that Melanctha felt then, that made Jeff remember all the feeling he had had in him when Jane Harden told him how Melanctha had learned to be so very understanding? Jeff did not know how it was that it had happened to him. It was all green, and warm, and very lovely to him, and now Melanctha somehow had made it all so ugly for him. What was it Melanctha was now doing with him? What was it he used to be thinking was the right way for him and all the colored people to be always trying to make it right, the way they should be always living? Why was Melanctha Herbert now all so ugly for him?

Melanctha Herbert somehow had made him feel deeply just then, what very more it was that she wanted from him. Jeff Campbell now felt in him what everybody always had needed to make them really understanding, to him. Jeff felt a strong disgust inside him; not for Melanctha herself, to him, not for himself really, in him, not for what it was that everybody wanted, in them; he only had disgust because he never could know really in him, what it was he wanted, to be really right in understanding, from him, he only had disgust because he never could know really what it was really right to him to be always doing, in the things he had before believed in, the things he before had believed in for himself and for all the colored people, the living regular, and the never wanting to be always having new things, just to keep on, always being in excitements. All the old thinking now came up very strong inside him. He sort of turned away then, and threw Melanctha from him.

Jeff never, even now, knew what it was that moved him. He never, even now, was ever sure, he really knew what Melanctha was, when she was real herself, and honest. He thought he knew, and then there came to him some moment, just like this one, when she really woke him up to be strong in him. Then he really knew he could know nothing. He knew then, he never could know what it was she really wanted with him. He knew then he never could know really what it was he felt inside him. It was all so mixed up inside him. All he knew was he wanted very badly Melanctha should be there beside him, and he wanted very badly, too, always to throw her from him. What was it really that Melanctha wanted with him? What was it really, he, Jeff Campbell, wanted she should give him? "I certainly did think now," Jeff Campbell groaned inside him, "I certainly did think now I really was knowing all right, what I wanted. I certainly did really think now I was knowing how to be trusting with Melanctha. I certainly did think it was like that now with me sure, after all I've been through all this time with her. And now I certainly do know I don't know anything that's very real about her. Oh the good Lord help and keep me!" and Jeff groaned hard inside him, and he buried his face deep in the green grass underneath him, and Melanctha Herbert was very silent there beside him.

Then Jeff turned to look and see her. She was lying very still there by him, and the bitter water on her face was biting. Jeff was so very sorry then, all over and inside him, the way he always was when Melanctha had been deep hurt by him. "I didn't mean to be so bad again to you, Melanctha, dear one," and he was very tender to her. "I certainly didn't never mean to go to be so bad to you, Melanctha, darling. I certainly don't know, Melanctha, darling, what it is makes me act so to you sometimes, when I certainly ain't meaning anything like I want to hurt you. I certainly don't mean to be so bad, Melanctha, only it comes so quick on me before I know what I am acting to you. I certainly am all sorry, hard, to be so bad to you, Melanctha, darling." "I suppose, Jeff," said Melanctha, very low and bitter, "I suppose you are always thinking, Jeff, somebody had ought to be ashamed with us two together, and you certainly do think you don't see any way to it, Jeff, for me to be feeling that way ever, so you certainly don't see any way to it, only to do it just so often for me. That certainly is the way always with you, Jeff Campbell, if I understand you right the way you are always acting to me. That certainly is right the way I am saying it to you now, Jeff Campbell. You certainly didn't anyway trust me now no more, did you, when you just acted so bad to me. I certainly am right the way I say it Jeff now to you. I certainly am right when I ask you for it now, to tell me what I ask you, about not trusting me more then again, Jeff, just like you never really knew me. You certainly never did trust me just then, Jeff, you hear me?" "Yes, Melanctha," Jeff answered slowly. Melanctha paused. "I guess I certainly never can forgive you this time, Jeff Campbell," she said firmly. Jeff paused too, and thought a little. "I certainly am afraid you never can no more now again, Melanctha," he said sadly.

They lay there very quiet now a long time, each one thinking very hard on their own trouble. At last Jeff began again to tell Melanctha what it was he was always thinking with her. "I certainly do know, Melanctha, you certainly now don't want any more to be hearing me just talking, but you see, Melanctha, really, it's just like this way always with me. You see, Melanctha, it's like this way now all the time with me. You remember, Melanctha, what I was once telling to you, when I didn't know you very long together, about how I certainly never did know more than just two kinds of ways of loving, one way the way it is good to be in families and the other kind of way, like animals are all the time just with each other, and how I didn't ever like that last kind of way much for any of the colored people. You see Melanctha, it's like this way with me. I got a new feeling now, you been teaching to me, just like I told you once, just like a new religion to me, and I see perhaps what really loving is like, like really having everything together, new things, little pieces all different, like I always before been thinking was bad to be having, all go together like, to make one good big feeling. You see,

Melanctha, it's certainly like that you make me been seeing, like I never know before any way there was of all kinds of loving to come together to make one way really truly lovely. I see that now, sometimes, the way you certainly been teaching me, Melanctha, really, and then I love you those times, Melanctha, like a real religion, and then it comes over me all sudden, I don't know anything real about you Melanctha, dear one, and then it comes over me sudden, perhaps I certainly am wrong now, thinking all this way so lovely, and not thinking now any more the old way I always before was always thinking, about what was the right way for me, to live regular and all the colored people, and then I think, perhaps, Melanctha you are really just a bad òne, and I think, perhaps I certainly am doing it so because I just am too anxious to be just having all the time excitements, like I don't ever like really to be doing when I know it, and then I always get so bad to you, Melanctha, and I can't help it with myself then, never, for I want to be always right really in the ways, I have to do them. I certainly do very badly want to be right, Melanctha, the only way I know is right Melanctha really, and I don't know any way, Melanctha, to find out really, whether my old way, the way I always used to be thinking, or the new way, you make so like a real religion to me sometimes, Melanctha, which way certainly is the real right way for me to be always thinking, and then I certainly am awful good and sorry, Melanctha, I always gave you so much trouble, hurting you with the bad ways I am acting. Can't you help me to any way, to make it all straight for me, Melanctha, so I know right and real what it is I should be acting. You see, Melanctha, I don't want always to be a coward with you, if I only could know certain what was the right way for me to be acting. I certainly am real sure, Melanctha, that would be the way I would be acting, if I only knew it sure for certain now, Melanctha. Can't you help me any way to find out real and true, Melanctha, dear one. I certainly do badly want to know always, the way I should be acting."

"No, Jeff, dear, I certainly can't help you much in that kind of trouble you are always having. All I can do now, Jeff, is to just keep certainly with my believing you are good always, Jeff, and though you certainly do hurt me bad, I always got strong faith in you, Jeff, more in you certainly, than you seem to be having in your acting to me, always so bad, Jeff."

"You certainly are very good to me, Melanctha, dear one," Jeff said, after a long, tender silence. "You certainly are very good to me, Melanctha, darling, and me so bad to you always, in my acting. Do you love me good, and right, Melanctha, always?" "Always and always, you be sure of that now you have me. Oh you Jeff, you always be so stupid." "I certainly never can say now you ain't right, when you say that to me so, Melanctha," Jeff answered. "Oh, Jeff dear, I love you always, you know that now, all right, for certain. If you don't know it right now, Jeff, really, I prove it to you now, for good and always." And they lay there a long time in their loving, and then Jeff began again with his happy free enjoying.

"I sure am a good boy to be learning all the time the right way you are teaching me, Melanctha, darling," began Jeff Campbell, laughing, "You can't say no, never, I ain't a good scholar for you to be teaching now, Melanctha, and I am always so ready to come to you every day, and never playing hooky ever from you. You can't say ever, Melanctha, now can you, I ain't a real good boy to be always studying to be learning to be real bright, just like my teacher. You can't say ever to me, I ain't a good boy to you now, Melanctha." "Not near so good, Jeff Campbell, as such a good, patient kind of teacher, like me, who never teaches any ways it ain't good her scholars should be knowing, ought to be really having, Jeff, you hear me? I certainly don't think I am right for you, to be forgiving always, when you are so bad, and I so patient, with all this hard teaching always." "But you do forgive me always, sure, Melanctha, always?" "Always and always, you be sure Jeff, and I certainly am afraid I never can stop with my forgiving, you always are going to be so bad to me, and I always going to have to be so good with my forgiving." "Oh! Oh!" cried Jeff Campbell, laughing, "I ain't going to be so bad for always, sure I ain't, Melanctha, my own darling. And sure you do forgive me really, and sure you love me true and really, sure, Melanctha?" "Sure, sure, Jeff, boy, sure now and always, sure now you believe me, sure you do, Jeff, always." "I sure hope I does, with all my heart, Melanctha, darling." "I sure do that same, Jeff, dear boy, now you really know what it is to be loving, and I prove it to you now so, Jeff, you never can be forgetting. You see now, Jeff, good and certain, what I always before been saying to you, Jeff, now." "Yes, Melanctha, darling," murmured Jeff, and he was very happy in it, and so the two of them now in the warm air of the sultry, southern, negro sunshine, lay there for a long time just resting.

And now for a real long time there was no open trouble any more between Jeff Campbell and Melanctha Herbert. Then it came that Jeff knew he could not say out any more, what it was he wanted, he could not say out any more, what it was, he wanted to know about, what Melanctha wanted.

Melanctha sometimes now, when she was tired with being all the time so much excited, when Jeff would talk a long time to her about what was right for them both to be always doing, would be, as if she gave way in her head, and lost herself in a bad feeling. Sometimes when they had been strong in their loving, and Jeff would have rise inside him some strange feeling, and Melanctha felt it in him as it would soon be coming, she would lose herself then in this bad feeling that made her head act as if she never knew what it was they were doing. And slowly now, Jeff soon always came to be feeling that his Melanctha would be hurt very much in her head in the ways he never liked to think of, if she would ever now again have to listen to his trouble, when he was telling about what it was he still was wanting to make things for himself really understanding.

Now Jeff began to have always a strong feeling that Melanctha could no longer stand it, with all her bad suffering, to let him fight out with himself what was right for him to be doing. Now he felt he must not, when she was there with him, keep on, with this kind of fighting that was always going on inside him. Jeff Campbell never knew yet, what he thought was the right way, for himself and for all the colored people to be living. Jeff was coming always each time closer to be really understanding, but now Melanctha was so bad in her suffering with him, that he knew she could not any longer have him with her while he was always showing that he never really yet was sure what it was, the right way, for them to be really loving.

Jeff saw now he had to go so fast, so that Melanctha never would have to wait any to get from him always all that she ever wanted. He never could be honest now, he never could be now, any more, trying to be really understanding, for always every moment now he felt it to be a strong thing in him, how very much it was Melanctha Herbert always suffered.

Jeff did not know very well these days, what it was, was really happening to him. All he knew every now and then, when they were getting strong to get excited, the way they used to when he gave his feeling out so that he could be always honest, that Melanctha somehow never seemed to hear him, she just looked at him and looked as if her head hurt with him, and then Jeff had to keep himself from being honest, and he had to go so fast, and to do everything Melanctha ever wanted from him.

Jeff did not like it very well these days, in his true feeling. He knew now very well Melanctha was not strong enough inside her to stand any more of his slow way of doing. And yet now he knew he was not honest in his feeling. Now he always had to show more to Melanctha than he was ever feeling. Now she made him go so fast, and he knew it was not real with his feeling, and yet he could not make her suffer so any more because he always was so slow with his feeling.

It was very hard for Jeff Campbell to make all this way of doing, right, inside him. If Jeff Campbell could not be straight out, and real honest, he never could be very strong inside him. Now Melanctha, with her making him feel, always, how good she was and how very much she suffered in him, made him always go so fast then, he could not be strong then, to feel things out straight then inside him. Always now when he was with her, he was being more, than he could already yet, be feeling for her. Always now, with her, he had something inside him always holding in him, always now, with her, he was far ahead of his own feeling.

Jeff Campbell never knew very well these days what it was that was going on inside him. All he knew was, he was uneasy now always to be with Melanctha. All he knew was, that he was always uneasy when he was with Melanctha, not the way he used to be from just not being very understanding, but now, because he never could be honest with her, because he was now always feeling her strong suffering, in her, because he knew now he was having a straight, good feeling with her, but she went so fast, and he was so slow to her; Jeff knew his right feeling never got a chance to show itself as strong, to her.

All this was always getting harder for Jeff Campbell. He was very proud to hold himself to be strong, was Jeff Campbell. He was very tender not to hurt Melanctha, when he knew she would be sure to feel it badly in her head a long time after, he hated that he could not now be honest with her, he wanted to stay away to work it out all alone, without her, he was afraid she would feel it to suffer, if he kept away now from her. He was uneasy always, with her, he was uneasy when he thought about her, he knew now he had a good, straight, strong feeling of right loving for her, and yet now he never could use it to be good and honest with her.

Jeff Campbell did not know, these days, anything he could do to make it better for her. He did not know anything he could do, to set himself really right in his acting and his thinking toward her. She pulled him so fast with her, and he did not dare to hurt her, and he could not come right, so fast, the way she always needed he should be doing it now, for her.

These days were not very joyful ones now any more, to Jeff Campbell, with Melanctha. He did not think it out to himself now, in words, about her. He did not know enough, what was his real trouble, with her.

Sometimes now and again with them, and with all this trouble for a little while well forgotten by him, Jeff, and Melanctha with him, would be very happy in a strong, sweet loving. Sometimes then, Jeff would find himself to be soaring very high in his true loving. Sometimes Jeff would find then, in his loving, his soul swelling out full inside him. Always Jeff felt now in himself, deep feeling.

Always now Jeff had to go so much faster than was real with his feeling. Yet always Jeff knew now he had a right, strong feeling. Always now when Jeff was wondering, it was Melanctha he was doubting, in the loving. Now he would often ask her, was she real now to him, in her loving. He would ask her often, feeling something queer about it all inside him, though yet he was never really strong in his doubting, and always Melanctha would answer to him, "Yes Jeff, sure, you know it, always," and always Jeff felt a doubt now, in her loving.

Always now Jeff felt in himself, deep loving. Always now he did not know really, if Melanctha was true in her loving.

All these days Jeff was uncertain in him, and he was uneasy about which way he should act so as not to be wrong and put them both into bad trouble. Always now he was, as if he must feel deep into Melanctha to see if it was real loving he would find she now had in her, and always he would stop himself, with her, for always he was afraid now that he might badly hurt her.

Always now he liked it better when he was detained when he had to go and see her. Always now he never liked to go to be with her, although he never wanted really, not to be always with her. Always now he never felt really at ease with her, even when they were good friends together. Always now he felt, with her, he could not be really honest to her. And Jeff never could be happy with her when he could not feel strong to tell all his feeling to her. Always now every day he found it harder to make the time pass, with her, and not let his feeling come so that he would quarrel with her.

And so one evening, late, he was to go to her. He waited a little long, before he went to her. He was afraid, in himself, to-night, he would surely hurt her. He never wanted to go when he might quarrel with her.

Melanctha sat there looking very angry, when he came in to her. Jeff took off his hat and coat and then sat down by the fire with her.

"If you come in much later to me just now, Jeff Campbell, I certainly never would have seen you no more never to speak to you, 'thout your apologising real humble to me." "Apologising Melanctha," and Jeff laughed and was scornful to her, "Apologising, Melanctha, I ain't proud that kind of way, Melanctha, I don't mind apologising to you, Melanctha, all I mind, Melanctha is to be doing of things wrong, to you." "That's easy, to say things that way, Jeff to me. But you never was very proud Jeff, to be courageous to me." "I don't know about that Melanctha. I got courage to say some things hard, when I mean them, to you." "Oh, yes, Jeff, I know all about that, Jeff, to me. But I mean real courage, to run around and not care nothing about what happens, and always to be game in any kind of trouble. That's what I mean by real courage, to me, Jeff, if you want to know it." "Oh, yes, Melanctha, I know all that kind of courage. I see plenty of it all the time with some kinds of colored men and with some girls like you Melanctha, and Jane Harden. I know all about how you are always making a fuss to be proud because you don't holler so much when you run in to where you ain't got any business to be, and so you get hurt, the way you ought to. And then, you kind of people are very brave then, sure, with all your kinds of suffering, but the way I see it, going around with all my patients, that kind of courage makes all kind of trouble, for them who ain't so noble with their courage, and then they got it, always to be bearing it, when the end comes, to be hurt the hardest. It's like running around and being game to spend all your money always, and then a man's wife and children are the ones do all the starving and they don't ever get a name for being brave, and they don't ever want to be doing all that suffering, and they got to stand it and say nothing. That's the way I see it a good deal now with all that kind of braveness in some of the colored people. They always make a lot of noise to show they are so brave not to holler, when they got so much suffering they always bring all on themselves just by doing things they got no business to be doing. I don't say, never Melanctha, they ain't got good courage not to holler, but I never did see much in looking for that kind of trouble just to show you ain't going to holler. No it's all right being brave every day, just living regular and not having new ways all the time just to get excitements, the way I hate to see it in all the colored people. No I don't see much, Melanctha, in being brave just to get it good, where you've got no business. I ain't ashamed Melanctha, right here to tell you, I ain't ashamed ever to say I ain't got no longing to be brave, just to go around and look for trouble." "Yes that's just like you always, Jeff, you never understand things right, the way you are always feeling in you. You ain't got no way to understand right, how it depends what way somebody goes to look for new things, the way it makes it right for them to get excited." "No Melanctha, I certainly never do say I understand much anybody's got a right to think they won't have real bad trouble, if they go and look hard where they are certain sure to find it. No Melanctha, it certainly does sound very pretty all this talking about danger and being game and never hollering, and all that way of talking, but when two men are just fighting, the strong man mostly gets on top with doing good hard pounding, and the man that's getting all that pounding, he mostly never likes it so far as I have been able yet to see it, and I don't see much difference what kind of noble way they are made of when they ain't got any kind of business to get together there to be fighting. That certainly is the only way I ever see it happen right, Melanctha, whenever I happen to be anywhere I can be looking." "That's because you never can see anything that ain't just so simple, Jeff, with everybody, the way you always think it. It do make all the difference the kind of way anybody is made to do things game Jeff Campbell." "Maybe Melanctha, I certainly never say no you ain't right, Melanctha. I just been telling it to you all straight, Melanctha, the way I always see it. Perhaps if you run around where you ain't got any business, and you stand up very straight and say, I am so brave, nothing can ever ever hurt me, maybe nothing will ever hurt you then Melanctha. I never have seen it do so. I never can say truly any differently to you Melanctha, but I always am ready to be learning from you, Melanctha. And perhaps when somebody cuts into you real hard, with a brick he is throwing, perhaps you never will do any hollering then, Melanctha. I certainly don't ever say no, Melanctha to you, I only say that ain't the way yet I ever see it happen when I had a chance to be there looking."

They sat there together, quiet by the fire, and they did not seem to feel very loving.

"I certainly do wonder," Melanctha said dreamily, at last breaking into their long unloving silence. "I certainly do wonder why always it happens to me I care for anybody who ain't no ways good enough for me ever to be thinking to respect him."

Jeff looked at Melanctha. Jeff got up then and walked a little up and down the room, and then he came back, and his face was set and dark and he was very quiet to her.

"Oh dear, Jeff, sure, why you look so solemn now to me. Sure Jeff I never am meaning anything real by what I just been saying. What was I just been saying Jeff to you. I only certainly was just thinking how everything always was just happening to me."

Jeff Campbell sat very still and dark, and made no answer.

"Seems to me, Jeff you might be good to me a little to-night when my head hurts so, and I am so tired with all the hard work I have been doing, thinking, and I always got so many things to be a trouble to me, living like I do with nobody ever who can help me. Seems to me you might be good to me Jeff to-night, and not get angry, every little thing I am ever saying to you."

"I certainly would not get angry ever with you, Melanctha, just because you say things to me. But now I certainly been thinking you really mean what you have been just then saying to me." "But you say all the time to me Jeff, you ain't no ways good enough in your loving to me, you certainly say to me all the time you ain't no ways good or understanding to me." "That certainly is what I say to you always, just the way I feel it to you Melanctha always, and I got it right in me to say it, and I have got a right in me to be very strong and feel it, and to be always sure to believe it, but it ain't right for you Melanctha to feel it. When you feel it so Melanctha, it does certainly make everything all wrong with our loving. It makes it so I certainly never can bear to have it."

They sat there then a long time by the fire, very silent, and not loving, and never looking to each other for it. Melanctha was moving and twitching herself and very nervous with it. Jeff was heavy and sullen and dark and very serious in it.

"Oh why can't you forget I said it to you Jeff now, and I certainly am so tired, and my head and all now with it."

Jeff stirred, "All right Melanctha, don't you go make yourself sick now in your head, feeling so bad with it," and Jeff made himself do it, and he was a patient doctor again now with Melanctha when he felt her really having her head hurt with it. "It's all right now Melanctha darling, sure it is now I tell you. You just lie down now a little, dear one, and I sit here by the fire and just read awhile and just watch with you so I will be here ready, if you need me to give you something to help you resting." And then Jeff was a good doctor to her, and very sweet and tender with her, and Melanctha loved him to be there to help her, and then Melanctha fell asleep a little, and Jeff waited there beside her until he saw she was really sleeping, and then he went back and sat down by the fire.

And Jeff tried to begin again with his thinking, and he could not make it come clear to himself, with all his thinking, and he felt everything all thick and heavy and bad, now inside him, everything that he could not understand right, with all the hard work he made, with his thinking. And then he moved himself a little, and took a book to forget his thinking, and then as always, he loved it when he was reading, and then very soon he was deep in his reading, and so he forgot now for a little while that he never could seem to be very understanding.

And so Jeff forgot himself for awhile in his reading, and Melanctha was sleeping. And then Melanctha woke up and she was screaming. "Oh, Jeff, I thought you gone away for always from me. Oh, Jeff, never now go away no more from me. Oh, Jeff, sure, sure, always be just so good to me."

There was a weight in Jeff Campbell from now on, always with him, that he could never lift out from him, to feel easy. He always was trying not to have it in him and he always was trying not to let Melanctha feel it, with him, but it was always there inside him. Now Jeff Campbell always was serious, and dark, and heavy, and sullen, and he would often sit a long time with Melanctha without moving.

"You certainly never have forgiven to me, what I said to you that night, Jeff, now have you?" Melanctha asked him after a long silence, late one evening with him. "It ain't ever with me a question like forgiving, Melanctha, I got in me. It's just only what you are feeling for me, makes any difference to me. I ain't ever seen anything since in you, makes me think you didn't mean it right, what you said about not thinking now any more I was good, to make it right for you to be really caring so very much to love me."

"I certainly never did see no man like you, Jeff. You always wanting to have it all clear out in words always, what everybody is always feeling. I certainly don't see a reason, why I should always be explaining to you what I mean by what I am just saying. And you ain't got no feeling ever for me, to ask me what I meant, by what I was saying when I was so tired, that night. I never know anything right I was saying." "But you don't ever tell me now, Melanctha, so I really hear you say it, you don't mean it the same way, the way you said it to me." "Oh Jeff, you so stupid always to me and always just bothering with your always asking to me. And I don't never any way remember ever anything I been saying to you, and I am always my head, so it hurts me it half kills me, and my heart jumps so, sometimes I think I die so when it hurts me, and I am so blue always, I think sometimes I take something to just kill me, and I got so much to bother thinking always and doing, and I got so much to worry, and all that, and then you come and ask me what I mean by what I was just saying to you. I certainly don't know, Jeff, when you ask me. Seems to me, Jeff, sometimes you might have some kind of a right feeling to be careful to me." "You ain't got no right Melanctha Herbert," flashed out Jeff through his dark, frowning anger, "you certainly ain't got no right always to be using your being hurt and being sick, and having pain, like a weapon, so as to make me do things it ain't never right for me to be doing for you. You certainly ain't got no right to be always holding your pain out to show me." "What do you mean by them words. Jeff Campbell." "I certainly do mean them just like I am saying them, Melanctha. You act always, like I been responsible all myself for all our loving one another. And if it's anything anyway that ever hurts you; you act like as if it was me made you just begin it all with me. I ain't no coward, you hear me, Melanctha? I never put my trouble back on anybody, thinking that they made me. I certainly am right ready always, Melanctha, you certainly had ought to know me, to stand all my own trouble for me, but I tell you straight now, the way I think it Melanctha, I ain't going to be as if I was the reason why you wanted to be loving, and to be suffering so now with me." "But ain't you certainly ought to be feeling it so, to be right, Jeff Campbell. Did I ever do anything but just let you do everything you wanted to me. Did I ever try to make you be loving to me. Did I ever do nothing except just sit there ready to endure your loving with me. But I certainly never, Jeff Campbell, did make any kind of way as if I wanted really to be having you for me."

Jeff stared at Melanctha. "So that's the way you say it when you are thinking right about it all, Melanctha. Well I certainly ain't got a word to say ever to you any more, Melanctha, if that's the way it's straight out to you now, Melantha." And Jeff almost laughed out to her, and he turned to take his hat and coat, and go away now forever from her.

Melanctha dropped her head on her arms, and she trembled all over and inside her. Jeff stopped a little and looked very sadly at her. Jeff could not so quickly make it right for himself, to leave her.

"Oh, I certainly shall go crazy now, I certainly know that," Melanctha moaned as she sat there, all fallen and miserable and weak together.

Jeff came and took her in his arms, and held her. Jeff was very good then to her, but they neither of them felt inside all right, as they once did, to be together.

From now on, Jeff had real torment in him.

Was it true what Melanctha had said that night to him? Was it true that he was the one had made all this trouble for them? Was it true, he was the only one, who always had had wrong ways in him? Waking or sleeping Jeff now always had this torment going on inside him.

Jeff did not know now any more, what to feel within him. He did not know how to begin thinking out this trouble that must always now be bad inside him. He just felt a confused struggle and resentment always in him, a knowing, no, Melanctha was not right in what she had said that night to him, and then a feeling, perhaps he always had been wrong in the way he never could be understanding. And then would come strong to him, a sense of the deep sweetness in Melanctha's loving and a hating the cold slow way he always had to feel things in him.

Always Jeff knew, sure, Melanctha was wrong in what she had said that night to him, but always Melanctha had had deep feeling with him, always he was poor and slow in the only way he knew how to have any feeling. Jeff knew Melanctha was wrong, and yet he always had a deep doubt in him. What could he know, who had such slow feeling in him? What could he ever know, who always had to find his way with just thinking. What could he know, who had to be taught such a long time to learn about what was really loving? Jeff now always had this torment in him.

Melanctha was now always making him feel her way, strong whenever she was with him. Did she go on to do it just to show him, did she do it so now because she was no longer loving, did she do it so because that was her way to make him be really loving. Jeff never did know how it was that it all hapened so to him.

Melanctha acted now the way she had said it always had been with them. Now it was always Jeff who had to do the asking. Now it was always Jeff who had to ask when would be the next time he should come to see her. Now always she was good and patient to him, and now always she was kind and loving with him, and always Jeff felt it was, that she was good to give him anything he ever asked or wanted, but never now any more for her own sake to make her happy in him. Now she did these things, as if it was just to please her Jeff Campbell who needed she should now have kindness for him. Always now he was the beggar, with them. Always now Melanctha gave it, not of her need, but from her bounty to him. Always now Jeff found it getting harder for him.

Sometimes Jeff wanted to tear things away from before him, always now he wanted to fight things and be angry with them, and always now Melanctha was so patient to him.

Now, deep inside him, there was always a doubt with Jeff, of Melanctha's loving. It was not a doubt yet to make him really doubting, for with that, Jeff never could be really loving, but always now he knew that something, and that not in him, something was wrong with their loving. Jeff Campbell could not know any right way to think out what was inside Melanctha with her loving, he could not use any way now to reach inside her to find if she was true in her loving, but now something had gone wrong between them, and now he never felt sure in him, the way once she had made him, that now at last he really had got to be understanding.

Melanctha was too many for him. He was helpless to find out the way she really felt now for him. Often Jeff would ask her, did she really love him. Always she said, "Yes Jeff, sure, you know that," and now instead of a full sweet strong love with it, Jeff only felt a patient, kind endurance in it.

Jeff did not know. If he was right in such a feeling, he certainly never any more did want to have Melanctha Herbert with him. Jeff Campbell hated badly to think Melanctha ever would give him love, just for his sake, and not because she needed it herself, to be with him. Such a way of loving would be very hard for Jeff to be enduring.

"Jeff what makes you act so funny to me. Jeff you certainly now are jealous to me. Sure Jeff, now I don't see ever why you be so foolish to look so to me." "Don't you ever think I can be jealous of anybody ever Melanctha, you hear me. It's just, you certainly don't ever understand me. It's just this way with me always now Melanctha. You love me, and I don't care anything what you do or what you ever been to anybody. You don't love me, then I don't care any more about what you ever do or what you ever be to anybody. But I never want you to be being good Melanctha to me, when it ain't your loving makes you need it. I certainly don't ever want to be having any of your kind of kindness to me. If you don't love me, I can stand it. All I never want to have is your being good to me from kindness. If you don't love me, then you and I certainly do quit right here Melanctha, all strong feeling, to be always living to each other. It certainly never is anybody I ever am thinking about when I am thinking with you Melanctha darling. That's the true way I am telling you Melanctha, always. It's only your loving me ever gives me anything to bother me Melanctha, so all you got to do, if you don't really love me, is just certainly to say so to me. I won't bother you more then than I can help to keep from it Melanctha. You certainly need never to be in any worry, never, about me Melanctha. You just tell me straight out Melanctha, real, the way you feel it. I certainly can stand it all right, I tell you true Melanctha. And I never will care to know why or nothing Melanctha. Loving is just living Melanctha to me, and if you don't really feel it now Melanctha to me, there ain't ever nothing between us then Melanctha, is there? That's straight and honest just the way I always feel it to you now Melanctha. Oh Melanctha, darling, do you love me? Oh Melanctha, please, please, tell me honest, tell me, do you really love me?"

"Oh you so stupid Jeff boy, of course I always love you. Always and always Jeff and I always just so good to you. Oh you so stupid Jeff and don't know when you got it good with me. Oh dear, Jeff I certainly am so tired Jeff to-night, don't you go be a bother to me. Yes I love you Jeff, how often you want me to tell you. Oh you so stupid Jeff, but yes I love you. Now I won't say it no more now to-night Jeff, you hear me. You just be good Jeff now to me or else I certainly get awful angry with you. Yes I love you, sure, Jeff, though you don't any way deserve it from me. Yes, yes I love you. Yes Jeff I say it till I certainly am very sleepy. Yes I love you now Jeff, and you certainly must stop asking me to tell you. Oh you great silly boy Jeff Campbell, sure I love you, oh you silly stupid, my own boy

Jeff Campbell. Yes I love you and I certainly never won't say it one more time to-night Jeff, now you hear me."

Yes Jeff Campbell heard her, and he tried hard to believe her. He did not really doubt her but somehow it was wrong now, the way Melanctha said it. Jeff always now felt baffled with Melanctha. Something, he knew, was not right now in her. Something in her always now was making stronger the torment that was tearing every minute at the joy he once always had had with her.

Always now Jeff wondered did Melanctha love him. Always now he was wondering, was Melanctha right when she said, it was he had made all their beginning. Was Melanctha right when she said, it was he had the real responsibility for all the trouble they had and still were having now between them. If she was right, what a brute he always had been in his acting. If she was right, how good she had been to endure the pain he had made so bad so often for her. But no, surely she had made herself to bear it, for her own sake, not for his to make him happy. Surely he was not so twisted in all his long thinking. Surely he could remember right what it was had happened every day in their long loving. Surely he was not so poor a coward as Melanctha always seemed to be thinking. Surely, surely, and then the torment would get worse every minute in him.

One night Jeff Campbell was lying in his bed with his thinking, and night after night now he could not do any sleeping for his thinking. To-night suddenly he sat up in his bed, and it all came clear to him, and he pounded his pillow with his fist, and he almost shouted out alone there to him, "I ain't a brute the way Melanctha has been saying. It's all wrong the way I been worried thinking. We did begin fair, each not for the other but for ourselves, what we were wanting. Melanctha Herbert did it just like I did it, because she liked it bad enough to want to stand it. It's all wrong in me to think it any way except the way we really did it. I certainly don't know now whether she is now real and true in her loving. I ain't got any way ever to find out if she is real and true now always to me. All I know is I didn't ever make her to begin to be with me. Melanctha has got to stand for her own trouble, just like I got to stand for my own trouble. Each man has got to do it for himself when he is in real trouble. Melanctha, she certainly don't remember right when she says I made her begin and then I made her trouble. No by God, I ain't no coward nor a brute either ever to her. I been the way I felt it honest, and that certainly is all about it now between us, and everybody always has just got to stand for their own trouble. I certainly am right this time the way I see it." And Jeff lay down now, at last in comfort, and he slept, and he was free from his long doubting torment.

"You know Melanctha," Jeff Campbell began, the next time he was alone to talk a long time to Melanctha. "You know Melanctha, sometimes I think a whole lot about what you like to say so much about being game and never doing any hollering. Seems to me Melanctha, I certainly don't understand right what you mean by not hollering. Seems to me it certainly ain't only what comes right away when one is hit, that counts to be brave to be bearing, but all that comes later from your getting sick from the shock of being hurt once in a fight, and all that, and all the being taken care of for years after, and the suffering of your family, and all that, you certainly must stand and not holler, to be certainly really brave the way I understand it." "What you mean Jeff by your talking." "I mean, seems to me really not to holler, is to be strong not to show you ever have been hurt. Seems to me, to get your head hurt from your trouble and to show it, ain't certainly no braver than to say, oh, oh, how bad you hurt me, please don't hurt me mister. It just certainly seems to me, like many people think themselves so game just to stand what we all of us always just got to be standing, and everybody stands it, and we don't certainly none of us like it, and yet we don't ever most of us think we are so much being game, just because we got to stand it."

"I know what you mean now by what you are saying to me now Jeff Campbell. You make a fuss now to me, because I certainly just have stopped standing everything you like to be always doing so cruel to me. But that's just the way always with you Jeff Campbell, if you want to know it. You ain't got no kind of right feeling for all I always been forgiving to you." "I said it once for fun, Melanctha, but now I certainly do mean it, you think you got a right to go where you got no business, and you say, I am so brave nothing can hurt me, and then something, like always, it happens to hurt you, and you show your hurt always so everybody can see it, and you say, I am so brave nothing did hurt me except he certainly didn't have any right to, and see how bad I suffer, but you never hear me make a holler, though certainly anybody got any feeling, to see me suffer, would certainly never touch me except to take good care of me. Sometimes I certainly don't rightly see Melanctha, how much more game that is than just the ordinary kind of holler." "No, Jeff Campbell, and made the way you is you certainly ain't likely ever to be much more understanding." "No, Melanctha, nor you neither. You think always, you are the only one who ever can do any way to really suffer." "Well, and ain't I certainly always been the only person knows how to bear it. No, Jeff Campbell, I certainly be glad to love anybody really worthy, but I made so, I never seem to be able in this world to find him." "No, and your kind of way of thinking, you certainly Melanctha never going to any way be able ever to be finding of him. Can't you understand Melanctha, ever, how no man certainly ever really can hold your love for long times together. You certainly Melanctha, you ain't got down deep loyal feeling, true inside you, and when you ain't just that moment quick with feeling, then you certainly ain't ever got anything more there to keep you. You see Melanctha, it certainly is this way with you, it is, that you ain't ever got any way to remember right what you been doing, or anybody else that has been feeling with you. You certainly Melanctha, never can remember right, when it comes what you have done and what you think happens to you." "It certainly is all easy for you Jeff Campbell to be talking. You remember right, because you don't remember nothing till you get home with your thinking everything all over, but I certainly don't think much ever of that kind of way of remembering right, Jeff Campbell. I certainly do call it remembering right Jeff Campbell, to remember right just when it happens to you, so you have a right kind of feeling not to act the way you always been doing to me, and then you go home Jeff Campbell, and you begin with your thinking, and then it certainly is very easy for you to be good and forgiving with it. No, that ain't to me, the way of remembering Jeff Campbell, not as I can see it not to make people always suffer, waiting for you certainly to get to do it. Seems to me like Jeff Campbell, I never could feel so like a man was low and to be scorning of him, like that day in the summer, when you threw me off just because you got one of those fits of your remembering. No Jeff Campbell, it's real feeling every moment when it's needed, that certainly does seem to me like real remembering. And that way, certainly, you don't never know nothing like what should be right Jeff Campbell. No Jeff, it's me that always certainly has had to bear it with you. It's always me that certainly has had to suffer, while you go home to remember. No you certainly ain't got no sense yet Jeff, what you need to make you really feeling. No, it certainly is me Jeff Campbell, that always has got to be remembering for us both, always. That's what's the true way with us Jeff Campbell, if you want to know what it is I am always thinking." "You is certainly real modest Melanctha, when you do this kind of talking, you sure is Melanctha," said Jeff Campbell laughing. "I think sometimes Melanctha I am certainly awful conceited, when I think sometimes I am all out doors, and I think I certainly am so bright, and better than most everybody I ever got anything now to do with, but when I hear you talk this way Melanctha, I certainly do think I am a real modest kind of fellow." "Modest!" said Melanctha, angry, "Modest, that certainly is a queer thing for you Jeff to be calling yourself even when you are laughing." "Well it certainly does depend a whole lot what you are thinking with," said Jeff Campbell. "I never did use to think I was so much on being real modest Melanctha, but now I know really I am, when I hear you talking. I see all the time there are many people living just as good as I am, though they are a little different to me. Now with you Melanctha if I understand you right what you are talking, you don't think that way of no other one that you are ever knowing." "I certainly could be real modest too, Jeff Campbell," said Melanctha, "If I could meet somebody once I could keep right on respecting when I got so I was really knowing with them. But I certainly never met anybody like that yet, Jeff Campbell, if you want to know it." "No Melanctha, and with the way you got of thinking, it certainly don't look like as if you ever will Melanctha, with your never remembering anything only what you just then are feeling in you, and you not understanding what any one else is ever feeling, if they don't holler just the way you are doing. No Melanctha, I certainly don't see any ways you are likely ever to meet one, so good as you are always thinking you be." "No, Jeff Campbell, it certainly ain't that way with me at all the way you say it. It's because I am always knowing what it is I am wanting, when I get it. I certainly don't never have to wait till I have it, and then throw away what I got in me, and then come back and say, that's a mistake I just been making, it ain't that never at all like I understood it, I want to have, bad, what I didn't think it was I wanted. It's that way of knowing right what I am wanting, makes me feel nobody can come right with me, when I am feeling things, Jeff Campbell. I certainly do say Jeff Campbell, I certainly don't think much of the way you always do it, always never knowing what it is you are ever really wanting and everybody always got to suffer. No Jeff, I don't certainly think there is much doubting which is better and the stronger with us two, Jeff Campbell."

"As you will, Melanctha Herbert," cried Jeff Campbell, and he rose up, and he thundered out a black oath, and he was fierce to leave her now forever, and then with the same movement, he took her in his arms and held her.

"What a silly goose boy you are, Jeff Campbell," Melanctha whispered to him fondly.

"Oh yes," said Jeff, very dreary. "I never could keep really mad with anybody, not when I was a little boy and playing. I used most to cry sometimes, I couldn't get real mad and keep on a long time with it, the way everybody always did it. It's certainly no use to me Melanctha, I certainly can't ever keep mad with you Melanctha, my dear one. But don't you ever be thinking it's because I think you right in what you been just saying to me. I don't Melanctha really think it that way, honest, though I certainly can't get mad the way I ought to. No Melanctha, little girl, really truly, you ain't right the way you think it. I certainly do know that Melanctha, honest. You certainly don't do me right Melanctha, the way you say you are thinking. Good-bye Melanctha, though you certainly is my own little girl for always." And then they were very good a little to each other, and then Jeff went away for that evening, from her.

Melanctha had begun now once more to wander. Melanctha did not yet always wander, but a little now she needed to begin to look for others. Now Melanctha Herbert began again to be with some of the better kind of black girls, and with them she sometimes wandered. Melanctha had not yet come again to need to be alone, when she wandered.

Jeff Campbell did not know that Melanctha had begun again to wander. All Jeff knew, was that now he could not be so often with her.

Jeff never knew how it had come to happen to him, but now he never thought to go to see Melanctha Herbert, until he had before, asked her if she could be going to have time then to have him with her. Then Melanctha would think a little, and then she would say to him, "Let me see Jeff, to-morrow, you was just saying to me. I certainly am awful busy you know Jeff just now. It certainly does seem to me this week Jeff, I can't anyways fix it. Sure I want to see you soon Jeff. I certainly Jeff got to do a little more now, I been giving so much time, when I had no business, just to be with you when you asked me. Now I guess Jeff, I certainly can't see you no more this week Jeff, the way I got to do things." "All right Melanctha," Jeff would answer and he would be very angry. "I want to come only just certainly as you want me now Melanctha." "Now Jeff you know I certainly can't be neglecting always to be with everybody just to see you. You come see me next week Tuesday Jeff, you hear me. I don't think Jeff I certainly be so busy, Tuesday." Jeff Campbell would then go away and leave her, and he would be hurt and very angry, for it was hard for a man with a great pride in himself, like Jeff Campbell, to feel himself no better than a beggar. And yet he always came as she said he should, on the day she had fixed for him, and always Jeff Campbell was not sure yet that he really understood what it was Melanctha wanted. Always Melanctha said to him, yes she loved him, sure he knew that. Always Melanctha said to him, she certainly did love him just the same as always, only sure he knew now she certainly did seem to be right busy with all she certainly now had to be doing.

Jeff never knew what Melanctha had to do now, that made her always be so busy, but Jeff Campbell never cared to ask Melanctha such a question. Besides Jeff knew Melanctha Herbert would never, in such a matter give him any kind of a real answer. Jeff did not know whether it was that Melanctha did not know how to give a simple answer. And then how could he, Jeff, know what was important to her. Jeff Campbell always felt strongly in him, he had no right to interfere with Melanctha in any practical kind of a matter. There they had always, never asked each other any kind of question. There they had felt always in each other, not any right to take care of one another. And Jeff Campbell now felt less than he had ever, any right to claim to know what Melanctha thought it right that she should do in any of her ways of living. All Jeff felt a right in himself to question, was her loving.

Jeff learned every day now, more and more, how much it was that he could really suffer. Sometimes it hurt so in him, when he was alone, it would force some slow tears from him. But every day, now that Jeff Campbell, knew more how it could hurt him, he lost his feeling of deep awe that he once always had had for Melanctha's feeling. Suffering was not so much after all, thought Jeff Campbell, if even he could feel it so it hurt him. It hurt him bad, just the way he knew he once had hurt Melanctha, and yet he too could have it and not make any kind of a loud holler with it.

In tender hearted natures, those that mostly never feel strong passion, suffering often comes to make them harder. When these do not know in themselves what it is to suffer, suffering is then very awful to them and they badly want to help everyone who ever has to suffer, and they have a deep reverence for anybody who knows really how to always suffer. But when it comes to them to really suffer, they soon begin to lose their fear and tenderness and wonder. Why it isn't so very much to suffer, when even I can bear to do it. It isn't very pleasant to be having all the time, to stand it, but they are not so much wiser after all, all the others just because they know too how to bear it.

Passionate natures who have always made themselves, to suffer, that is all the kind of people who have emotions that come to them as sharp as a sensation, they always get more tender-hearted when they suffer, and it always does them good to suffer. Tender-hearted, unpassionate, and comfortable natures always get much harder when they suffer, for so they lose the fear and reverence and wonder they once had for everybody who ever has to suffer, for now they know themselves what it is to suffer and it is not so awful any longer to them when they know too, just as well as all the others, how to have it.

And so it came in these days to Jeff Campbell. Jeff knew now always, way inside him, what it is to really suffer, and now every day with it, he knew how to understand Melanctha better. Jeff Campbell still loved Melanctha Herbert and he still had a real trust in her and he still had a little hope that some day they would once more get together, but slowly, every day, this hope in him would keep growing always weaker. They still were a good deal of time together, but now they never any more were really trusting with each other. In the days when they used to be together, Jeff had felt he did not know much what was inside Melanctha, but he knew very well, how very deep always was his trust in her; now he knew Melanctha Herbert better, but now he never felt a deep trust in her. Now Jeff never could be really honest with her. He never doubted yet, that she was steady only to him, but somehow he could not believe much really in Melanctha's loving.

Melanctha Herbert was a little angry now when Jeff asked her, "I never give nobody before Jeff, ever more than one chance with me, and I certainly been giving you most a hundred Jeff, you hear me." "And why shouldn't you Melanctha, give me a million, if you really love me!" Jeff flashed out very angry. "I certainly don't know as you deserve that anyways from me, Jeff Campbell." "It ain't deserving, I am ever talking about to you Melanctha. It's loving, and if you are really loving to me you won't certainly never any ways call them chances." "Deed Jeff, you certainly are getting awful wise Jeff now, ain't you, to me." "No I ain't Melanctha, and I ain't jealous either to you. I just am doubting from the way you are always acting to me." "Oh yes Jeff, that's what they all say, the same way, when they certainly got jealousy all through them. You ain't got no cause to be jealous with me Jeff, and I am awful tired of all this talking now, you hear me."

Jeff Campbell never asked Melanctha any more if she loved him. Now things were always getting worse between them. Now Jeff was always very silent with Melanctha. Now Jeff never wanted to be honest to her, and now Jeff never had much to say to her.

Now when they were together, it was Melanctha always did most of the talking. Now she often had other girls there with her. Melanctha was always kind to Jeff Campbell but she never seemed to need to be alone now with him. She always treated Jeff, like her best friend, and she always spoke so to him and yet she never seemed now to very often want to see him.

Every day it was getting harder for Jeff Campbell. It was as if now, when he had learned to really love Melanctha, she did not need any more to have him. Jeff began to know this very well inside him.

Jeff Campbell did not know yet that Melanctha had begun again to wander. Jeff was not very quick to suspect Melanctha. All Jeff knew was, that he did not trust her to be now really loving to him.

Jeff was no longer now in any doubt inside him. He knew very well now he really loved Melanctha. He knew now very well she was not any more a real religion to him. Jeff Campbell knew very well too now inside him, he did not really want Melanctha, now if he could no longer trust her, though he loved her hard and really knew now what it was to suffer.

Every day Melanctha Herbert was less and less near to him. She always was very pleasant in her talk and to be with him, but somehow now it never was any comfort to him.

Melanctha Herbert now always had a lot of friends around her. Jeff Campbell never wanted to be with them. Now Melanctha began to find it, she said it often to him, always harder to arrange to be alone now with him. Sometimes she would be late for him. Then Jeff always would try to be patient in his waiting, for Jeff Campbell knew very well how to remember, and he knew it was only right that he should now endure this from her.

Then Melanctha began to manage often not to see him, and once she went away when she had promised to be there to meet him.

Then Jeff Campbell was really filled up with his anger. Now he knew he could never really want her. Now he knew he never any more could really trust her.

Jeff Campbell never knew why Melanctha had not come to meet him. Jeff had heard a little talking now, about how Melanctha Herbert had commenced once more to wander. Jeff Campbell still sometimes saw Jane Harden, who always needed a doctor to be often there to help her. Jane Harden always knew very well what happened to Melanctha. Jeff Campbell never would talk to Jane Harden anything about Melanctha. Jeff was always loyal to Melanctha. Jeff never let Jane Harden say much to him about Melanctha, though he never let her know that now he loved her. But somehow Jeff did know now about Melanctha, and he knew about some men that Melanctha met with Rose Johnson very often.

Jeff Campbell would not let himself really doubt Melanctha, but Jeff began to know now very well, he did not want her. Melanctha Herbert did not love him ever, Jeff knew it now, the way he once had thought that she could feel it. Once she had been greater for him than he had thought he could ever know how to feel it. Now Jeff had come to where he could understand Melanctha Herbert. Jeff was not bitter to her because she could not really love him, he was bitter only that he had let himself have a real illusion in him. He was a little bitter too, that he had lost now, what he had always felt real in the world, that had made it for him always full of beauty, and now he had not got this new religion really, and he had lost what he before had to know what was good and had real beauty.

Jeff Campbell was so angry now in him, because he had begged Melanctha always to be honest to him. Jeff could stand it in her not to love him, he could not stand it in her not to be honest to him.

Jeff Campbell went home from where Melanctha had not met him, and he was sore and full of anger in him.

Jeff Campbell could not be sure what to do, to make it right inside him. Surely he must be strong now and cast this loving from him, and yet, was he sure he now had real wisdom in him. Was he sure that Melanctha Herbert never had had a real deep loving for him.

Was he sure Melanctha Herbert never had deserved a reverence from him. Always now Jeff had this torment in him, but always now he felt more that Melanctha never had real greatness for him.

Jeff waited to see if Melanctha would send any word to him. Melanctha Herbert never sent a line to him.

At last Jeff wrote his letter to Melanctha. "Dear Melanctha, I certainly do know you ain't been any way sick this last week when you never met me right the way you promised, and never sent me any word to say why you acted a way you certainly never could think was the right way you should do it to me. Jane Harden said she saw you that day and you went out walking with some people you like now to be with. Don't be misunderstanding me now any more Melanctha. I love you now because that's my slow way to learn what you been teaching, but I know now you certainly never had what seems to me real kind of feeling. I don't love you Melanctha any more now like a real religion, because now I know you are just made like all us others. I know now no man can ever really hold you because no man can ever be real to trust in you, because you mean right Melanctha, but you never can remember, and so you certainly never have got any way to be honest. So please you understand me right now Melanctha, it never is I don't know how to love you. I do know now how to love you, Melanctha, really. You sure do know that, Melanctha, in me. You certainly always can trust me. And so now Melanctha, I can say to you certainly real honest with you, I am better than you are in my right kind of feeling. And so Melanctha, I don't never any more want to be a trouble to you. You certainly make me see things Melanctha, I never any other way could be knowing. You been very good and patient to me, when I was certainly below you in my right feeling. I certainly never have been near so good and patient to you ever any way Melanctha, I certainly know that Melanctha. But Melanctha, with me, it certainly is, always to be good together, two people certainly must be thinking each one as good as the other, to be really loving right Melanctha. And it certainly must never be any kind of feeling, of one only taking, and one only just giving, Melanctha, to me. I know you certainly don't really ever understand me now Melanctha, but that's no matter. I certainly do know what I am feeling now with you real Melanctha. And so good-by now for good Melanctha. I say I can never ever really trust you real Melanctha, that's only just certainly from your way of not being ever equal in your feeling to anybody real, Melanctha, and your way never to know right how to remember. Many ways I really trust you deep Melanctha, and I certainly do feel deep all the good sweetness you certainly got real in you Melanctha. It's only just in your loving me Melanctha. You never can be equal to me and that way I certainly never can bear any more to have it. And so now Melanctha, I always be your friend, if you need me, and now we never see each other any more to talk to."

And then Jeff Campbell thought and thought, and he could never make any way for him now, to see it different, and so at last he sent this letter to Melanctha.

And now surely it was all over in Jeff Campbell. Surely now he never any more could know Melanctha. And yet, perhaps Melanctha really loved him. And then she would know how much it hurt him never any more, any way, to see her, and perhaps she would write a line to tell him. But that was a foolish way for Jeff ever to be thinking. Of course Melanctha never would write a word to him. It was all over now for always, everything between them, and Jeff felt it a real relief to him.

For many days now Jeff Campbell only felt it as a relief in him. Jeff was all locked up and quiet now inside him. It was all settling down heavy in him, and these days when it was sinking so deep in him, it was only the rest and quiet of not fighting that he could really feel inside him. Jeff Campbell could not think now, or feel anything else in him. He had no beauty nor any goodness to see around him. It was a dull, pleasant kind of quiet he now had inside him. Jeff almost began to love this dull quiet in him, for it was more nearly being free for him than anything he had known in him since Melanctha Herbert first had moved him. He did not find it a real rest yet for him, he had not really conquered what had been working so long in him, he had not learned to see beauty and real goodness yet in what had happened to him, but it was rest even if he was sodden now all through him. Jeff Campbell liked it very well, not to have fighting always going on inside him.

And so Jeff went on every day, and he was quiet, and he began again to watch himself in his working; and he did not see any beauty now around him, and it was dull and heavy always now inside him, and yet he was content to have gone so far in keeping steady to what he knew was the right way for him to come back to, to be regular, and see beauty in every kind of quiet way of living, the way he had always wanted it for himself and for all the colored people. He knew he had lost the sense he once had of joy all through him, but he could work, and perhaps he would bring some real belief back into him about the beauty that he could not now any more see around him.

And so Jeff Campbell went on with his working, and he stayed home every evening, and he began again with his reading, and he did not do much talking, and he did not seem to himself to have any kind of feeling.

And one day Jeff thought perhaps he really was forgetting, one day he thought he could soon come back and be happy in his old way of regular and quiet living.

Jeff Campbell had never talked to any one of what had been going on inside him. Jeff Campbell liked to talk and he was honest, but it never came out from him, anything he was ever really feeling, it only came out from him, what it was that he was always thinking. Jeff Campbell always was very proud to hide what he was really feeling. Always he blushed hot to think things he had been feeling. Only to Melanctha Herbert, had it ever come to him, to tell what it was that he was feeling.

And so Jeff Campbell went on with this dull and sodden, heavy, quiet always in him, and he never seemed to be able to have any feeling. Only sometimes he shivered hot with shame when he remembered some things he once had been feeling. And then one day it all woke up, and was sharp in him.

Dr. Campbell was just then staying long times with a sick man who might soon be dying. One day the sick man was resting. Dr. Campbell went to the window to look out a little, while he was waiting. It was very early now in the southern springtime. The trees were just beginning to get the little zigzag crinkles in them, which the young buds always give them. The air was soft and moist and pleasant to them. The earth was wet and rich and smelling for them. The birds were making sharp fresh noises all around them. The wind was very gentle and yet urgent to them. And the buds and the long earthworms, and the negroes, and all the kinds of children, were coming out every minute farther into the new spring, watery, southern sunshine.

Jeff Campbell too began to feel a little his old joy inside him. The sodden quiet began to break up in him. He leaned far out of the window to mix it all up with him. His heart went sharp and then it almost stopped inside him. Was it Melanctha Herbert he had just seen passing by him? Was it Melanctha, or was it just some other girl, who made him feel so bad inside him? Well, it was no matter, Melanctha was there in the world around him, he did certainly always know that in him. Melanctha Herbert was always in the same town with him, and he could never any more feel her near him. What a fool he was to throw her from him. Did he know she did not really love him. Suppose Melanctha was now suffering through him. Suppose she really would be glad to see him. And did anything else he did, really mean anything now to him? What a fool he was to cast her from him. And yet did Melanctha Herbert want him, was she honest to him, had Melanctha ever loved him, and did Melanctha now suffer by him? Oh! Oh! Oh! and the bitter water once more rose up in him.

All that long day, with the warm moist young spring stirring in him, Jeff Campbell worked, and thought, and beat his breast, and wandered, and spoke aloud, and was silent, and was certain, and then in doubt and then keen to surely feel, and then all sodden in him; and he walked, and he sometimes ran fast to lose himself in his rushing, and he bit his nails to pain and bleeding, and he tore his hair so that he could be sure he was really feeling, and he never could know what it was right, he now should be doing. And then late that night he wrote it all out to Melanctha Herbert, and he made himself quickly send it without giving himself any time to change it.

"It has come to me strong to-day Melanctha, perhaps I am wrong the way I now am thinking. Perhaps you do want me badly to be with you. Perhaps I have hurt you once again the way I used to. I certainly Melanctha, if I ever think that really, I certainly do want bad not to be wrong now ever any more to you. If you do feel the way to-day it came to me strong may-be you are feeling, then say so Melanctha to me, and I come again to see you. If not, don't say anything any more ever to me. I don't want ever to be bad to you Melanctha, really. I never want ever to be a bother to you. I never can stand it to think I am wrong; really, thinking you don't want me to come to you. Tell me Melanctha, tell me honest to me, shall I come now any more to see you." "Yes" came the answer from Melanctha, "I be home Jeff to-night to see you."

Jeff Campbell went that evening late to see Melanctha Herbert. As Jeff came nearer to her, he doubted that he wanted really to be with her, he felt that he did not know what it was he now wanted from her. Jeff Campbell knew very well now, way inside him, that they could never talk their trouble out between them. What was it Jeff wanted now to tell Melanctha Herbert? What was it that Jeff Campbell now could tell her? Surely he never now could learn to trust her. Surely Jeff knew very well all that Melanctha always had inside her. And yet it was awful, never any more to see her.

Jeff Campbell went into Melanctha, and he kissed her, and he held her, and then he went away from her and he stood still and looked at her. "Well Jeff!" "Yes Melanctha!" "Jeff what was it made you act so to me?" "You know very well Melanctha, it's always I am thinking you don't love me, and you are acting to me good out of kindness, and then Melanctha you certainly never did say anything to me why you never came to meet me, as you certainly did promise to me you would that day I never saw you!" "Jeff don't you really know for certain, I always love you?" "No Melanctha, deed I don't know it in me. Deed and certain sure Melanctha, if I only know that in me, I certainly never would give you any bother." "Jeff, I certainly do love you more seems to me always, you certainly had ought to feel that in you." "Sure Melanctha?" "Sure Jeff boy, you know that." "But then Melanctha why did you act so to me?" "Oh Jeff you certainly been such a bother to me. I just had to go away that day Jeff, and I certainly didn't mean not to tell you, and then that letter you wrote came to me and something happened to me. I don't know right what it was Jeff, I just kind of fainted, and what could I do Jeff, you said you certainly never any more wanted to come and see me!" "And no matter Melanctha, even if you knew, it was just killing me to act so to you, you never would have said nothing to me?" "No of course, how could I Jeff when you wrote that way to me. I know how you was feeling Jeff to me, but I certainly couldn't say nothing to you." "Well Melanctha, I certainly know I am right proud too in me, but I certainly never could act so to you Melanctha, if I ever knew any way at all you ever really loved me. No Melanctha darling, you and me certainly don't feel much the same way ever. Any way Melanctha, I certainly do love you true Melanctha." "And I love you too Jeff, even though you don't never certainly seem to believe me." "No I certainly don't any way believe you Melanctha, even when you say it to me. I don't know Melanctha how, but sure I certainly do trust you, only I don't believe now ever in your really being loving to me. I certainly do know you trust me always Melanctha, only somehow it ain't ever all right to me. I certainly don't know any way otherwise Melanctha, how I can say it to you." "Well I certainly can't help you no ways any more Jeff Campbell, though you certainly say it right when you say I trust you Jeff now always. You certainly is the best man Jeff Campbell, I ever can know, to me. I never been anyways thinking it can be ever different to me." "Well you trust me then Melanctha, and I certainly love you Melanctha, and seems like to me Melanctha, you and me had ought to be a little better than we certainly ever are doing now to be together. You certainly do think that way, too, Melanctha to me. But may be you do really love me. Tell me, please, real honest now Melanctha darling, tell me so I really always know it in me, do you really truly love me?" "Oh you stupid, stupid boy, Jeff Campbell. Love you, what do you think makes me always to forgive you. If I certainly didn't always love you Jeff, I certainly never would let you be always being all the time such a bother to me the way you certainly Jeff always are to me. Now don't you dass ever any more say words like that ever to me. You hear me now Jeff, or I do something real bad sometime, so I really hurt you. Now Jeff you just be good to me. You know Jeff how bad I need it, now you should always be good to me!"

Jeff Campbell could not make an answer to Melanctha. What was it he should now say to her? What words could help him to make their feeling any better? Jeff Campbell knew that he had learned to love deeply, that, he always knew very well now in him, Melanctha had learned to be strong to be always trusting, that he knew too now inside him, but Melanctha did not really love him, that he felt always too strong for him. The factor always was there in him, and it always thrust itself firm, between them. And so this talk did not make things really better for them.

Jeff Campbell was never any more a torment to Melanctha, he was only silent to her. Jeff often saw Melanctha and he was very friendly with her and he never any more was a bother to her. Jeff never any more now had much chance to be loving with her. Melanctha never was alone now when he saw her.

Melanctha Herbert had just been getting thick in her trouble with Jeff Campbell, when she went to that church where she first met Rose, who later was married regularly to Sam Johnson. Rose was a good-looking, better kind of black girl, and had been brought up quite like their own child by white folks. Rose was living now with colored people. Rose was staying just then with a colored woman, who had known 'Mis' Herbert and her black husband and this girl Melanctha.

Rose soon got to like Melanctha Herbert and Melanctha now always wanted to be with Rose, whenever she could do it. Melanctha Herbert always was doing everything for Rose that she could think of that Rose ever wanted. Rose always liked to be with nice people who would do things for her. Rose had strong common sense and she was lazy. Rose liked Melanctha Herbert, she had such kind of fine ways in her. Then, too, Rose had it in her to be sorry for the subtle, sweet-natured, docile, intelligent Melanctha Herbert who always was so blue sometimes, and always had had so much trouble. Then, too, Rose could scold Melanctha, for Melanctha Herbert never could know how to keep herself from trouble, and Rose was always strong to keep straight, with her simple selfish wisdom.

But why did the subtle, intelligent, attractive, half white girl Melanctha Herbert, with her sweetness and her power and her wisdom, demean herself to do for and to flatter and to be scolded, by this lazy, stupid, ordinary, selfish black girl. This was a queer thing in Melanctha Herbert.

And so now in these new spring days, it was with Rose that Melanctha began again to wander. Rose always knew very well in herself what was the right way to do when you wandered. Rose knew very well, she was not just any common kind of black girl, for she had been raised by white folks, and Rose always saw to it that she was engaged to him when she had any one man with whom she ever always wandered. Rose always had strong in her the sense for proper conduct. Rose always was telling the complex and less sure Melanctha, what was the right way she should do when she wandered.

Rose never knew much about Jeff Campbell with Melanctha Herbert. Rose had not known about Melanctha Herbert when she had been almost all her time with Dr. Campbell.

Jeff Campbell did not like Rose when he saw her with Melanctha. Jeff would never, when he could help it, meet her. Rose did not think much about Dr. Campbell. Melanctha never talked much about him to her. He was not important now to be with her.

Rose did not like Melanctha's old friend Jane Harden when she saw her. Jane despised Rose for an ordinary, stupid, sullen black girl. Jane could not see what Melanctha could find in that black girl, to endure her. It made Jane sick to see her. But then Melanctha had a good mind, but she certainly never did care much to really use it. Jane Harden now really never cared any more to see Melanctha, though Melanctha still always tried to be good to her. And Rose, she hated that stuck up, mean speaking, nasty, drunk thing, Jane Harden. Rose did not see how Melanctha could bear to ever see her, but Melanctha always was so good to everybody, she never would know how to act to people the way they deserved that she should do it.

Rose did not know much about Melanctha, and Jeff Campbell and Jane Harden. All Rose knew about Melanctha was her old life with her mother and her father. Rose was always glad to be good to poor Melanctha, who had had such an awful time with her mother and her father, and now she was alone and had nobody who could help her. "He was a awful black man to you Melanctha, I like to get my hands on him so he certainly could feel it. I just would Melanctha, now you hear me."

Perhaps it was this simple faith and simple anger and simple moral way of doing in Rose, that Melanctha now found such a comfort to her. Rose was selfish and was stupid and was lazy, but she was decent and knew always what was the right way she should do, and what she wanted, and she certainly did admire how bright was her friend Melanctha Herbert, and she certainly did feel how very much it was she always suffered and she scolded her to keep her from more trouble, and she never was angry when she found some of the different ways Melanctha Herbert sometimes had to do it.

And so always Rose and Melanctha were more and more together, and Jeff Campbell could now hardly ever any more be alone with Melanctha.

Once Jeff had to go away to another town to see a sick man. "When I come back Monday Melanctha, I come Monday evening to see you. You be home alone once Melanctha to see me." "Sure Jeff, I be glad to see you!"

When Jeff Campbell came to his house on Monday there was a note there from Melanctha. Could Jeff come day after to-morrow, Wednesday? Melanctha was so sorry she had to go out that evening. She was awful sorry and she hoped Jeff would not be angry.

Jeff was angry and he swore a little, and then he laughed, and then he sighed. "Poor Melanctha, she don't know any way to be real honest, but no matter, I sure do love her and I be good if only she will let me."

Jeff Campbell went Wednesday night to see Melanctha. Jeff Campbell took her in his arms and kissed her. "I certainly am awful sorry not to see you Jeff Monday, the way I promised, but I just couldn't Jeff, no way I could fix it." Jeff looked at her and then he laughed a little at her. "You want me to believe that really now Melanctha. All right I believe it if you want me to Melanctha. I certainly be good to you to-night the way you like it. I believe you certainly did want to see me Melanctha, and there was no way you could fix it." "Oh Jeff dear," said Melanctha, "I sure was wrong to act so to you. It's awful hard for me ever to say it to you, I have been wrong in my acting to you, but I certainly was bad this time Jeff to you. It do certainly come hard to me to say it Jeff, but I certainly was wrong to go away from you the way I did it. Only you always certainly been so bad Jeff, and such a bother to me, and making everything always so hard for me, and I certainly got some way to do it to make it come back sometimes to you. You bad boy Jeff, now you hear me and this certainly is the first time Jeff I ever yet said it to anybody, I ever been wrong, Jeff, you hear me!" "All right Melanctha, I sure do forgive you, cause it's certainly the first time I ever heard you say you ever did anything wrong the way you shouldn't," and Jeff Campbell laughed and kissed her, and Melanctha laughed and loved him, and they really were happy now for a little time together.

And now they were very happy in each other and then they were silent and then they became a little sadder and then they were very quiet once more with each other.

"Yes I certainly do love you Jeff!" Melanctha said and she was very dreamy. "Sure, Melanctha." "Yes Jeff sure, but not the way you are now ever thinking. I love you more and more seems to me Jeff always, and I certainly do trust you more and more always to me when I know you. I do love you Jeff, sure yes, but not the kind of way of loving you are ever thinking it now Jeff with me. I ain't got certainly no hot passion any more now in me. You certainly have killed all that kind of feeling now Jeff in me. You certainly do know that Jeff, now the way I am always, when I am loving with you. You certainly do know that Jeff, and that's the way you certainly do like it now in me. You certainly don't mind now Jeff, to hear me say this to you."

Jeff Campbell was hurt so that it almost killed him. Yes he certainly did know now what it was to have real hot love in him, and yet Melanctha certainly was right, he did not deserve she should ever give it to him. "All right Melanctha I ain't ever kicking. I always will give you certainly always everything you want that I got in me. I take anything you want now to give me. I don't say never Melanctha it don't hurt me, but I certainly don't say ever Melanctha it ought ever to be any different to me." And the bitter tears rose up in Jeff Campbell, and they came and choked his voice to be silent, and he held himself hard to keep from breaking.

"Good-night Melanctha," and Jeff was very humble to her. "Good-night Jeff, I certainly never did mean any way to hurt you. I do love you, sure Jeff every day more and more, all the time I know you." "I know Melanctha, I know, it's never nothing to me. You can't help it, anybody ever the way they are feeling. It's all right now Melanctha, you believe me, good-night now Melanctha, I got now to leave you, good-by Melanctha, sure don't look so worried to me, sure Melanctha I come again soon to see you." And then Jeff stumbled down the steps, and he went away fast to leave her.

And now the pain came hard and harder in Jeff Campbell, and he groaned, and it hurt him so, he could not bear it. And the tears came, and his heart beat, and he was hot and worn and bitter in him.

Now Jeff knew very well what it was to love Melanctha. Now Jeff Campbell knew he was really understanding. Now Jeff knew what it was to be good to Melanctha. Now Jeff was good to her always.

Slowly Jeff felt it a comfort in him to have it hurt so, and to be good to Melanctha always. Now there was no way Melanctha ever had had to bear things from him, worse than he now had it in him. Now Jeff was strong inside him. Now with all the pain there was peace in him. Now he knew he was understanding, now he knew he had a hot love in him, and he was good always to Melanctha Herbert who was the one had made him have it. Now he knew he could be good, and not cry out for help to her to teach him how to bear it. Every day Jeff felt himself more a strong man, the way he once had thought was his real self, the way he knew it. Now Jeff Campbell had real wisdom in him, and it did not make him bitter when it hurt him, for Jeff knew now all through him that he was really strong to bear it.

And so now Jeff Campbell could see Melanctha often, and he was patient, and always very friendly to her, and every day Jeff Campbell understood Melanctha Herbert better. And always Jeff saw Melanctha could not love him the way he needed she should do it. Melanctha Herbert had no way she ever really could remember.

And now Jeff knew there was a man Melanctha met very often, and perhaps she wanted to try to have this man to be good, for her. Jeff Campbell never saw the man Melanctha Herbert perhaps now wanted. Jeff Campbell only knew very well that there was one. Then there was Rose that Melanctha now always had with her when she wandered.

Jeff Campbell was very quiet to Melanctha. He said to her, now he thought he did not want to come any more especially to see her. When they met, he always would be glad to see her, but now he never would go anywhere any more to meet her. Sure he knew she always would have a deep love in him for her. Sure she knew that. "Yes Jeff, I always trust you Jeff, I certainly do know that all right." Jeff Campbell said, all right he never could say anything to reproach her. She knew always that he really had learned all through him how to love her. "Yes, Jeff, I certainly do know that." She knew now she could always trust him. Jeff always would be loyal to her though now she never was any more to him like a religion, but he never could forget the real sweetness in her. That Jeff must remember always, though now he never can trust her to be really loving to any man for always, she never did have any way she ever could remember. If she ever needed anybody to be good to her, Jeff Campbell always would do anything he could to help her. He never can forget the things she taught him so he could be really understanding, but he never any more wants to see her. He be like a brother to her always, when she needs it, and he always will be a good friend to her. Jeff Campbell certainly was sorry never any more to see her, but it was good that they now knew each other really. "Good-by Jeff you always been very good always to me." "Good-by Melanctha you know you always can trust yourself to me." "Yes, I know, I know Jeff, really." "I certainly got to go now Melanctha, from you. I go this time, Melanctha really," and Jeff Campbell went away and this time he never looked back to her. This time Jeff Campbell just broke away and left her.

Jeff Campbell loved to think now he was strong again to be quiet, and to live regular, and to do everything the way he wanted it to be right for himself and all the colored people. Jeff went away for a little while to another town to work there, and he worked hard, and he was very sad inside him, and sometimes the tears would rise up in him, and then he would work hard, and then he would begin once more to see some beauty in the world around him. Jeff had behaved right and he had learned to have a real love in him. That was very good to have inside him.

Jeff Campbell never could forget the sweetness in Melanctha Herbert, and he was always very friendly to her, but they never any more came close to one another. More and more Jeff Campbell and Melanctha fell away from all knowing of each other, but Jeff never could forget Melanctha. Jeff never could forget the real sweetness she had in her, but Jeff never any more had the sense of a real religion for her. Jeff always had strong in him the meaning of all the new kind of beauty Melanctha Herbert once had shown him, and always more and more it helped him with his working for himself and for all the colored people.

Melanctha Herbert, now that she was all through with Jeff Campbell, was free to be with Rose and the new men she met now.

Rose was always now with Melanctha Herbert. Rose never found any way to get excited. Rose always was telling Melanctha Herbert the right way she should do, so that she would not always be in trouble. But Melanctha Herbert could not help it, always she would find new ways to get excited.

Melanctha was all ready now to find new ways to be in trouble. And yet Melanctha Herbert never wanted not to do right. Always Melanctha Herbert wanted peace and quiet, and always she could only find new ways to get excited.

"Melanctha," Rose would say to her, "Melanctha, I certainly have got to tell you, you ain't right to act so with that kind of feller. You better just had stick to black men now, Melanctha, you hear me what I tell you, just the way you always see me do it. They're real bad men, now I tell you Melanctha true, and you better had hear to me. I been raised by real nice kind of white folks, Melanctha, and I certainly knows awful well, soon as ever I can see 'em acting, what is a white man will act decent to you and the kind it ain't never no good to a colored girl to ever go with. Now you know real Melanctha how I always mean right good to you, and you ain't got no way like me Melanctha, what was raised by white folks, to know right what is the way you should be acting with men. I don't never want to see you have bad trouble come hard to you now Melanctha, and so you just hear to me now Melanctha, what I tell you, for I

knows it. I don't say never certainly to you Melanctha, you never
had ought to have nothing to do ever with no white men, though it
ain't never to me Melanctha, the best kind of a way a colored girl
can have to be acting, no I never do say to you Melanctha, you
hadn't never ought to be with white men, though it ain't never
the way I feel it ever real right for a decent colored girl to be always
doing, but not never Melanctha, now you hear me, no not never no
kind of white men like you been with always now Melanctha when
I see you. You just hear to me Melanctha, you certainly had ought
to hear to me Melanctha, I say it just like I knows it awful well,
Melanctha, and I knows you don't know no better, Melanctha, how
to act so, the ways I seen it with them kind of white fellers, them as
never can know what to do right by a decent girl they have ever got
to be with them. Now you hear to me Melanctha, what I tell you."

And so it was Melanctha Herbert found new ways to be in
trouble. But it was not very bad this trouble, for these white men
Rose never wanted she should be with, never meant very much to
Melanctha. It was only that she liked it to be with them, and they
knew all about fine horses, and it was just good to Melanctha, now a
little, to feel real reckless with them. But mostly it was Rose and
other better kind of colored girls and colored men with whom Melanctha Herbert now always wandered.

It was summer now and the colored people came out into the
sunshine, full blown with the flowers. And they shone in the streets
and in the fields with their warm joy, and they glistened in their
black heat, and they flung themselves free in their wide abandonment of shouting laughter.

It was very pleasant in some ways, the life Melanctha Herbert
now led with Rose and all the others. It was not always that Rose
had to scold her.

There was not anybody of all these colored people, excepting only
Rose, who ever meant much to Melanctha Herbert. But they all
liked Melanctha, and the men all liked to see her do things, she was
so game always to do anything anybody ever could do, and then she
was good and sweet to do anything anybody ever wanted from her.

These were pleasant days then, in the hot southern negro sunshine, with many simple jokes and always wide abandonment of
laughter. "Just look at that Melanctha there a running. Don't she
just go like a bird when she is flying. Hey Melanctha there, I come
and catch you, hey Melanctha, I put salt on your tail to catch you."

and then the man would try to catch her, and he would fall full on
the earth and roll in an agony of wide-mouthed shouting laughter.
And this was the kind of way Rose always liked to have Melanctha
do it, to be engaged to him, and to have a good warm nigger time
with colored men, not to go about with that kind of white man, never
could know how to act right, to any decent kind of girl they could
ever get to be with them.

Rose, always more and more, liked Melanctha Herbert better.
Rose often had to scold Melanctha Herbert, but that only made her
like Melanctha better. And then Melanctha always listened to her,
and always acted every way she could to please her. And then Rose
was so sorry for Melanctha, when she was so blue sometimes, and
wanted somebody should come and kill her.

And Melanctha Herbert clung to Rose in the hope that Rose
could save her. Melanctha felt the power of Rose's selfish, decent
kind of nature. It was so solid, simple, certain to her. Melanctha
clung to Rose, she loved to have her scold her, she always wanted
to be with her. She always felt a solid safety in her. Rose always
was, in her way, very good to let Melanctha be loving to her. Melanctha never had any way she could really be a trouble to her.
Melanctha never had any way that she could ever get real power,
to come close inside to her. Melanctha was always very humble to
her. Melanctha was always ready to do anything Rose wanted from
her. Melanctha needed badly to have Rose always willing to let
Melanctha cling to her. Rose was a simple, sullen, selfish, black
girl, but she had a solid power in her. Rose had strong the sense of
decent conduct, she had strong the sense for decent comfort. Rose
always knew very well what it was she wanted, and she knew very
well what was the right way to do to get everything she wanted, and
she never had any kind of trouble to perplex her. And so the subtle
intelligent attractive half white girl Melanctha Herbert loved and
did for, and demeaned herself in service to this coarse, decent, sullen,
ordinary, black, childish Rose and now this unmoral promiscuous
shiftless Rose was to be married to a good man of the negroes, while
Melanctha Herbert with her white blood and attraction and her
desire for a right position was perhaps never to be really regularly
married. Sometimes the thought of how all her world was made
filled the complex, desiring Melanctha with despair. She wondered
often how she could go on living when she was so blue. Sometimes

Melanctha thought she would just kill herself, for sometimes she thought this would be really the best thing for her to do.

Rose was now to be married to a decent good man of the negroes. His name was Sam Johnson, and he worked as a deck-hand on a coasting steamer, and he was very steady, and he got good wages.

Rose first met Sam Johnson at church, the same place where she had met Melanctha Herbert. Rose liked Sam when she saw him, she knew he was a good man and worked hard and got good wages, and Rose thought it would be very nice and very good now in her position to get really, regularly married.

Sam Johnson liked Rose very well and he always was ready to do anything she wanted. Sam was a tall, square shouldered, decent, a serious, straightforward, simple, kindly, colored workman. They got on very well together, Sam and Rose, when they were married. Rose was lazy, but not dirty, and Sam was careful but not fussy. Sam was a kindly, simple, earnest, steady workman, and Rose had good common decent sense in her, of how to live regular, and not to have excitements, and to be saving so you could be always sure to have money, so as to have everything you wanted.

It was not very long that Rose knew Sam Johnson, before they were regularly married. Sometimes Sam went into the country with all the other young church people, and then he would be a great deal with Rose and with her Melanctha Herbert. Sam did not care much about Melanctha Herbert. He liked Rose's ways of doing, always better. Melanctha's mystery had no charm for Sam ever. Sam wanted a nice little house to come to when he was tired from his working, and a little baby all his own he could be good to. Sam Johnson was ready to marry as soon as ever Rose wanted he should do it. And so Sam Johnson and Rose one day had a grand real wedding and were married. Then they furnished completely, a little red brick house and then Sam went back to his work as deck-hand on a coasting steamer.

Rose had often talked to Sam about how good Melanctha was and how much she always suffered. Sam Johnson never really cared about Melanctha Herbert, but he always did almost everything Rose ever wanted, and he was a gentle, kindly creature, and so he was very good to Rose's friend Melanctha. Melanctha Herbert knew very well Sam did not like her, and so she was very quiet, and always let Rose do the talking for her. She only was very good to always help Rose, and to do anything she ever wanted from her,

and to be very good and listen and be quiet whenever Sam had anything to say to her. Melanctha liked Sam Johnson, and all her life
Melanctha loved and wanted good and kind and considerate people,
and always Melanctha loved and wanted people to be gentle to her,
and always she wanted to be regular, and to have peace and quiet in
her, and always Melanctha could only find new ways to be in
trouble. And Melanctha needed badly to have Rose, to believe her,
and to let her cling to her. Rose was the only steady thing Melanctha had to cling to and so Melanctha demeaned herself to be like a
servant, to wait on, and always to be scolded, by this ordinary,
sullen, black, stupid, childish woman.

Rose was always telling Sam he must be good to poor Melanctha.
"You know Sam," Rose said very often to him. "You certainly had
ought to be very good to poor Melanctha, she always do have so
much trouble with her. You know Sam how I told you she had such
a bad time always with that father, and he was awful mean to her
always that awful black man, and he never took no kind of care
ever to her, and he never helped her when her mother died so hard,
that poor Melanctha. Melanctha's ma you know Sam, always was
just real religious. One day Melanctha was real little, and she heard
her ma say to her pa, it was awful sad to her, Melanctha had not
been the one the Lord had took from them stead of the little brother
who was dead in the house there from fever. That hurt Melanctha
awful when she heard her ma say it. She never could feel it right,
and I don't no ways blame Melanctha, Sam, for not feeling better
to her ma always after, though Melanctha, just like always she is,
always was real good to her ma after, when she was so sick, and
died so hard, and nobody never to help Melanctha do it, and she
just all alone to do everything without no help come to her no way,
and that ugly awful black man she have for a father never all the
time come near her. But that's always the way Melanctha is just
doing Sam, the way I been telling to you. She always is being just
so good to everybody and nobody ever there to thank her for it.
I never did see nobody ever Sam, have such bad luck, seems to me
always with them, like that poor Melanctha always has it, and
she always so good with it, and never no murmur in her, and never
no complaining from her, and just never saying nothing with it.
You be real good to her Sam, now you hear me, now you and me
is married right together. He certainly was an awful black man to
her Sam, that father she had, acting always just like a brute to her

and she so game and never to tell anybody how it hurt her. And she so sweet and good always to do anything anybody ever can be wanting. I don't see Sam how some men can be to act so awful. I told you Sam, how once Melanctha broke her arm bad and she was so sick and it hurt her awful and he never would let no doctor come near to her and he do some things so awful to her, she don't never want to tell nobody how bad he hurt her. That's just the way Sam with Melanctha always, you never can know how bad it is, it hurts her. You hear me Sam, you always be real good to her now you and me is married right to each other."

And so Rose and Sam Johnson were regularly married, and Rose sat at home and bragged to all her friends how nice it was to be married really to a husband.

Rose did not have Melanctha to live with her, now Rose was married. Melanctha was with Rose almost as much as ever but it was a little different now their being together.

Rose Johnson never asked Melanctha to live with her in the house, now Rose was married. Rose liked to have Melanctha come all the time to help her, Rose liked Melanctha to be almost always with her, but Rose was shrewd in her simple selfish nature, she did not ever think to ask Melanctha to live with her.

Rose was hard headed, she was decent, and she always knew what it was she needed. Rose needed Melanctha to be with her, she liked to have her help her, the quick, good Melanctha to do for the slow, lazy, selfish, black girl, but Rose could have Melanctha to do for her and she did not need her to live with her.

Sam never asked Rose why she did not have her. Sam always took what Rose wanted should be done for Melanctha, as the right way he should act toward her.

It could never come to Melanctha to ask Rose to let her. It never could come to Melanctha to think that Rose would ask her. It would never ever come to Melanctha to want it, if Rose should ask her, but Melanctha would have done it for the safety she always felt when she was near her. Melanctha Herbert wanted badly to be safe now, but this living with her, that, Rose would never give her. Rose had strong the sense for decent comfort, Rose had strong the sense for proper conduct, Rose had strong the sense to get straight always what she wanted, and she always knew what was the best thing she needed, and always Rose got what she wanted.

And so Rose had Melanctha Herbert always there to help her,

and she sat and was lazy and she bragged and she complained a little and she told Melanctha how she ought to do, to get good what she wanted like she Rose always did it, and always Melanctha was doing everything Rose ever needed. "Don't you bother so, doing that Melanctha, I do it or Sam when he comes home to help me. Sure you don't mind lifting it Melanctha? You is very good Melanctha to do it, and when you go out Melanctha, you stop and get some rice to bring me to-morrow when you come in. Sure you won't forget Melanctha. I never see anybody like you Melanctha to always do things so nice for me." And then Melanctha would do some more for Rose, and then very late Melanctha would go home to the colored woman where she lived now.

And so though Melanctha still was so much with Rose Johnson, she had times when she could not stay there. Melanctha now could not really cling there. Rose had Sam, and Melanctha more and more lost the hold she had had there.

Melanctha Herbert began to feel she must begin again to look and see if she could find what it was she had always wanted. Now Rose Johnson could no longer help her.

And so Melanctha Herbert began once more to wander and with men Rose never thought it was right she should be with.

One day Melanctha had been very busy with the different kinds of ways she wandered. It was a pleasant late afternoon at the end of a long summer. Melanctha was walking along, and she was free and excited. Melanctha had just parted from a white man and she had a bunch of flowers he had left with her. A young buck, a mulatto, passed by and snatched them from her. "It certainly is real sweet in you sister, to be giving me them pretty flowers," he said to her.

"I don't see no way it can make them sweeter to have with you," said Melanctha. "What one man gives, another man had certainly just as much good right to be taking." "Keep your old flowers then, I certainly don't never want to have them." Melanctha Herbert laughed at him and took them. "No, I didn't nohow think you really did want to have them. Thank you kindly mister, for them. I certainly always do admire to see a man always so kind of real polite to people." The man laughed, "You ain't nobody's fool I can say for you, but you certainly are a damned pretty kind of girl, now I look at you. Want men to be polite to you? All right, I can love you, that's real polite now, want to see me try it." "I certainly ain't got no time this evening just only left to thank you. I certainly got to be real busy now, but I certainly always will admire to see you." The man tried to catch and stop her, Melanctha Herbert laughed and dodged so that he could not touch her. Melanctha went quickly down a side street near her and so the man for that time lost her.

For some days Melanctha did not see any more of her mulatto. One day Melanctha was with a white man and they saw him. The white man stopped to speak to him. Afterwards Melanctha left the white man and she then soon met him. Melanctha stopped to talk to him. Melanctha Herbert soon began to like him.

Jem Richards, the new man Melanctha had begun to know now, was a dashing kind of fellow, who had to do with fine horses and with racing. Sometimes Jem Richards would be betting and would be good and lucky, and be making lots of money. Sometimes Jem would be betting badly, and then he would not be having any money.

Jem Richards was a straight man. Jem Richards always knew that by and by he would win again and pay it, and so Jem mostly did win again, and then he always paid it.

Jem Richards was a man other men always trusted. Men gave him money when he lost all his, for they all knew Jem Richards would win again, and when he did win they knew, and they were right, that he would pay it.

Melanctha Herbert all her life had always loved to be with horses. Melanctha liked it that Jem knew all about fine horses. He was a reckless man was Jem Richards. He knew how to win out, and always all her life, Melanctha Herbert loved successful power.

Melanctha Herbert always liked Jem Richards better. Things soon began to be very strong between them.

Jem was more game even than Melanctha. Jem always had known what it was to have real wisdom. Jem had always all his life been understanding.

Jem Richards made Melanctha Herbert come fast with him. He never gave her any time with waiting. Soon Melanctha always had Jem with her. Melanctha did not want anything better. Now in Jem Richards, Melanctha found everything she had ever needed to content her.

Melanctha was now less and less with Rose Johnson. Rose did not think much of the way Melanctha now was going. Jem Richards was all right, only Melanctha never had no sense of the right kind of way she should be doing. Rose often was telling Sam now, she did not like the fast way Melanctha was going. Rose told it to Sam, and to all the girls and men, when she saw them. But Rose was nothing just then to Melanctha. Melanctha Herbert now only needed Jem Richards to be with her.

And things were always getting stronger between Jem Richards and Melanctha Herbert. Jem Richards began to talk now as if he wanted to get married to her. Jem was deep in his love now for her. And as for Melanctha, Jem was all the world now to her. And so Jem gave her a ring, like white folks, to show he was engaged to her, and would by and by be married to her. And Melanctha was filled full with joy to have Jem so good to her.

Melanctha always loved to go with Jem to the races. Jem had been lucky lately with his betting, and he had a swell turn-out to drive in, and Melanctha looked very handsome there beside him.

Melanctha was very proud to have Jem Richards want her. Melanctha loved it the way Jem knew how to do it. Melanctha loved Jem and loved that he should want her. She loved it too, that he wanted to be married to her. Jem Richards was a straight decent man, whom other men always looked up to and trusted. Melanctha needed badly a man to content her.

Melanctha's joy made her foolish. Melanctha told everybody about how Jem Richards, that swell man who owned all those fine horses and was so game, nothing ever scared him, was engaged to be married to her, and that was the ring he gave her.

Melanctha let out her joy very often to Rose Johnson. Melanctha had begun again now to go there.

Melanctha's love for Jem made her foolish. Melanctha had to have some one always now to talk to and so she went often to Rose Johnson.

Melanctha put all herself into Jem Richards. She was mad and foolish in the joy she had there.

Rose never liked the way Melanctha did it. "No Sam I don't say never Melanctha ain't engaged to Jem Richards the way she always says it, and Jem he is all right for that kind of a man he is, though he do think himself so smart and like he owns the earth and everything he can get with it, and he sure gave Melanctha a ring like he really meant he should be married right soon with it, only Sam, I don't ever like it the way Melanctha is going. When she is engaged to him Sam, she ain't not right to take on so excited. That ain't no decent kind of a way a girl ever should be acting. There ain't no kind of a man going stand that, not like I knows men Sam, and I sure does know them. I knows them white and I knows them colored, for I was raised by white folks, and they don't none of them like a girl to act so. That's all right to be so when you is just only loving, but it ain't no ways right to be acting so when you is engaged to him, and when he says, all right he get really regularly married to you. You see Sam I am right like I am always and I knows it. Jem Richards, he ain't going to the last to get real married, not if I knows it right, the way Melanctha now is acting to him. Rings or anything ain't nothing to them, and they don't never do no good for them, when a girl acts foolish like Melanctha always now is acting. I certainly will be right sorry Sam, if Melanctha has real bad trouble come now to her, but I certainly don't no ways like it Sam the kind of way Melanctha is acting to him. I don't never say nothing to her Sam. I just listens to what she is saying always, and I thinks it out like I am telling to you Sam but I don't never say nothing no more now to Melanctha. Melanctha didn't say nothing to me about that Jem Richards till she was all like finished with him, and I never did like it Sam, much, the way she was acting, not coming here never when she first ran with those men and met him. And I didn't never say nothing to her, Sam, about it, and it ain't nothing ever to me, only I don't never no more want to say nothing to her, so I just listens to what she got to tell like she wants it. No Sam, I don't never want to say nothing to her. Melanctha just got to go her own way, not as I want to see her have bad trouble ever come hard to her, only it ain't in me never Sam, after Melanctha did so, ever to say nothing more to her how she should be acting. You just see Sam like I tell you, what way Jem Richards will act to her, you see Sam I just am right like I always am when I knows it."

Melanctha Herbert never thought she could ever again be in trouble. Melanctha's joy had made her foolish.

And now Jem Richards had some bad trouble with his betting. Melanctha sometimes felt now when she was with him that there was something wrong inside him. Melanctha knew he had had trouble with his betting but Melanctha never felt that that could make any difference to them.

Melanctha once had told Jem, sure he knew she always would love to be with him, if he was in jail or only just a beggar. Now Melanctha said to him, "Sure you know Jem that it don't never make any kind of difference you're having any kind of trouble, you just try me Jem and be game, don't look so worried to me. Jem sure I know you love me like I love you always, and it's all I ever could be wanting Jem to me, just your wanting me always to be with you. I get married Jem to you soon ever as you can want me, if you once say it Jem to me. It ain't nothing to me ever, anything like having any money Jem, why you look so worried to me."

Melanctha Herbert's love had surely made her mad and foolish. She thrust it always deep into Jem Richards and now that he had trouble with his betting, Jem had no way that he ever wanted to be made to feel it. Jem Richards never could want to marry any girl while he had trouble. That was no way a man like him should do it. Melanctha's love had made her mad and foolish, she should be silent now and let him do it. Jem Richards was not a kind of man to want a woman to be strong to him, when he was in trouble with his betting. That was not the kind of a time when a man like him needed to have it.

Melanctha needed so badly to have it, this love which she had always wanted, she did not know what she should do to save it. Melanctha saw now, Jem Richards always had something wrong inside him. Melanctha soon dared not ask him. Jem was busy now, he had to sell things and see men to raise money. Jem could not meet Melanctha now so often.

It was lucky for Melanctha Herbert that Rose Johnson was coming now to have her baby. It had always been understood between them, Rose should come and stay then in the house where Melanctha lived with an old colored woman, so that Rose could have the Doctor from the hospital near by to help her, and Melanctha there to take care of her the way Melanctha always used to do it.

Melanctha was very good now to Rose Johnson. Melanctha did everything that any woman could, she tended Rose, and she was patient, submissive, soothing and untiring, while the sullen, childish, cowardly, black Rosie grumbled, and fussed, and howled, and made herself to be an abomination and like a simple beast.

All this time Melanctha was always being every now and then with Jem Richards. Melanctha was beginning to be stronger with Jem Richards. Melanctha was never so strong and sweet and in her nature as when she was deep in trouble, when she was fighting so with all she had, she could not do any foolish thing with her nature.

Always now Melanctha Herbert came back again to be nearer to

Rose Johnson. Always now Melanctha would tell all about her troubles to Rose Johnson. Rose had begun now a little again to advise her.

Melanctha always told Rose now about the talks she had with Jem Richards, talks where they neither of them liked very well what the other one was saying. Melanctha did not know what it was Jem Richards wanted. All Melanctha knew was, he did not like it when she wanted to be good friends and get really married, and then when Melanctha would say, "all right, I never wear your ring no more Jem, we ain't not any more to meet ever like we ever going to get really regular married," then Jem did not like it either. What was it Jem Richards really wanted?

Melanctha stopped wearing Jem's ring on her finger. Poor Melanctha, she wore it on a string she tied around her neck so that she could always feel it, but Melanctha was strong now with Jem Richards, and he never saw it. And sometimes Jem seemed to be awful sorry for it, and sometimes he seemed kind of glad of it. Melanctha never could make out really what it was Jem Richards wanted.

There was no other woman yet to Jem, that Melanctha knew, and so she always trusted that Jem would come back to her, deep in his love, the way once he had had it and had made all the world like she once had never believed anybody could really make it. But Jem Richards was more game than Melanctha Herbert. He knew how to fight to win out, better. Melanctha really had already lost it, in not keeping quiet and waiting for Jem to do it.

Jem Richards was not yet having better luck in his betting. He never before had had such a long time without some good coming to him in his betting. Sometimes Jem talked as if he wanted to go off on a trip somewhere and try some other place for luck with his betting. Jem Richards never talked as if he wanted to take Melanctha with him.

And so Melanctha sometimes was really trusting, and sometimes she was all sick inside her with her doubting. What was it Jem really wanted to do with her? He did not have any other woman, in that Melanctha could be really trusting, and when she said no to him, no she never would come near him, now he did not want to have her, then Jem would change and swear, yes sure he did want her, now and always right here near him, but he never now any more said he wanted to be married soon to her. But then Jem Richards never would marry a girl, he said that very often, when he was in this kind of trouble, and now he did not see any way he could get out of his trouble. But Melanctha ought to wear his ring, sure she knew he never had loved any kind of woman like he loved her. Melanctha would wear the ring a little while, and then they would have some more trouble, and then she would say to him, no she certainly never would any more wear anything he gave her, and then she would wear it on the string so nobody could see it but she could always feel it on her.

Poor Melanctha, surely her love had made her mad and foolish.

And now Melanctha needed always more and more to be with Rose Johnson, and Rose had commenced again to advise her, but Rose could not help her. There was no way now that anybody could advise her. The time when Melanctha could have changed it with Jem Richards was now all past for her. Rose knew it, and Melanctha too, she knew it, and it almost killed her to let herself believe it.

The only comfort Melanctha ever had now was waiting on Rose till she was so tired she could hardly stand it. Always Melanctha did everything Rose ever wanted. Sam Johnson began now to be very gentle and a little tender to Melanctha. She was so good to Rose and Sam was so glad to have her there to help Rose and to do things and to be a comfort to her.

Rose had a hard time to bring her baby to its birth and Melanctha did everything that any woman could.

The baby though it was healthy after it was born did not live long. Rose Johnson was careless and negligent and selfish and when Melanctha had to leave for a few days the baby died. Rose Johnson had liked her baby well enough and perhaps she just forgot it for a while, anyway the child was dead and Rose and Sam were very sorry, but then these things came so often in the negro world in Bridgepoint that they neither of them thought about it very long. When Rose had become strong again she went back to her house with Sam. And Sam Johnson was always now very gentle and kind and good to Melanctha who had been so good to Rose in her bad trouble.

Melanctha Herbert's troubles with Jem Richards were never getting any better. Jem always now had less and less time to be with her. When Jem was with Melanctha now he was good enough to her. Jem Richards was worried with his betting. Never since Jem had first begun to make a living had he ever had so much trouble

for such a long time together with his betting. Jem Richards was
good enough now to Melanctha but he had not much strength to
give her. Melanctha could never any more now make him quarrel
with her. Melanctha never now could complain of his treatment of
her, for surely, he said it always by his actions to her, surely she
must know how a man was when he had trouble on his mind with
trying to make things go a little better.

Sometimes Jem and Melanctha had long talks when they neither
of them liked very well what the other one was saying, but mostly
now Melanctha could not make Jem Richards quarrel with her, and
more and more, Melanctha could not find any way to make it right
to blame him for the trouble she now always had inside her. Jem
was good to her, and she knew, for he told her, that he had trouble
all the time now with his betting. Melanctha knew very well that for
her it was all wrong inside Jem Richards, but Melanctha had now
no way that she could really reach him.

Things between Melanctha and Jem Richards were now never
getting any better. Melanctha now more and more needed to be
with Rose Johnson. Rose still liked to have Melanctha come to her
house and do things for her, and Rose liked to grumble to her and
to scold her and to tell Melanctha what was the way Melanctha
always should be doing so she could make things come out better
and not always be so much in trouble. Sam Johnson in these days
was always very good and gentle to Melanctha. Sam was now beginning to be very sorry for her.

Jem Richards never made things any better for Melanctha. Often
Jem would talk so as to make Melanctha almost certain that he
never any more wanted to have her. Then Melanctha would get
very blue, and she would say to Rose, sure she would kill herself,
for that certainly now was the best way she could do.

Rose Johnson never saw it the least bit that way. "I don't see
Melanctha why you should talk like you would kill yourself just
because you're blue. I'd never kill myself Melanctha cause I was
blue. I'd maybe kill somebody else but I'd never kill myself. If I
ever killed myself, Melanctha it'd be by accident and if I ever killed
myself by accident, Melanctha, I'd be awful sorry. And that certainly is the way you should feel it Melanctha, now you hear me,
not just talking foolish like you always do. It certainly is only your
way just always being foolish makes you all that trouble to come
to you always now, Melanctha, and I certainly right well knows

that. You certainly never can learn no way Melanctha ever with all I certainly been telling to you, ever since I know you good, that it ain't never no way like you do always is the right way you be acting ever and talking, the way I certainly always have seen you do so Melanctha always. I certainly am right Melanctha about them ways you have to do it, and I knows it; but you certainly never can noways learn to act right Melanctha, I certainly do know that, I certainly do my best Melanctha, to help you with it only you certainly never do act right Melanctha, not to nobody ever, I can see it. You never act right by me Melanctha no more than by everybody. I never say nothing to you Melanctha when you do so, for I certainly never do like it when I just got to say it to you, but you just certainly done with that Jem Richards you always say wanted real bad to be married to you, just like I always said to Sam you certainly was going to do it. And I certainly am real kind of sorry like for you Melanctha, but you certainly had ought to have come to see me to talk to you, when you first was engaged to him so I could show you, and now you got all this trouble come to you Melanctha like I certainly know you always catch it. It certainly ain't never Melanctha I ain't real sorry to see trouble come so hard to you, but I certainly can see Melanctha it all is always just the way you always be having it in you not never to do right. And now you always talk like you just kill yourself because you are so blue, that certainly never is Melanctha, no kind of a way for any decent kind of a girl to do."

Rose had begun to be strong now to scold Melanctha and she was impatient very often with her, but Rose could now never any more be a help to her. Melanctha Herbert never could know now what it was right she should do. Melanctha always wanted to have Jem Richards with her and now he never seemed to want her, and what could Melanctha do. Surely she was right now when she said she would just kill herself, for that was the only way now she could do.

Sam Johnson always, more and more, was good and gentle to Melanctha. Poor Melanctha, she was so good and sweet to do anything anybody ever wanted, and Melanctha always liked it if she could have peace and quiet, and always she could only find new ways to be in trouble. Sam often said this now to Rose about Melanctha.

"I certainly don't never want Sam to say bad things about Melanctha, for she certainly always do have most awful kind of trouble come hard to her, but I never can say I like it real right Sam the way Melanctha always has to do it. It's now just the same with her like it is always she has got to do it, now the way she is with that Jem Richards. He certainly now don't never want to have her but Melanctha she ain't got no right kind of spirit. No Sam I don't never like the way any more Melanctha is acting to him, and then Sam, she ain't never real right honest, the way she always should do it. She certainly just don't kind of never Sam tell right what way she is doing with it. I don't never like to say nothing Sam no more to her about the way she always has to be acting. She always say, yes all right Rose, I do the way you say it, and then Sam she don't never noways do it. She certainly is right sweet and good, Sam, is Melanctha, nobody ever can hear me say she ain't always ready to do things for everybody any way she ever can see to do it, only Sam some ways she never does act real right ever, and some ways, Sam, she ain't ever real honest with it. And Sam sometimes I hear awful kind of things she been doing, some girls know about her how she does it, and sometimes they tell me what kind of ways she has to do it, and Sam it certainly do seem to me like more and more I certainly am awful afraid Melanctha never will come to any good. And then Sam, sometimes, you hear it, she always talk like she kill herself all the time she is so blue, and Sam that certainly never is no kind of way any decent girl ever had ought to do. You see Sam, how I am right like I always is when I knows it. You just be careful, Sam, now you hear me, you be careful Sam sure, I tell you, Melanctha more and more I see her I certainly do feel Melanctha no way is really honest. You be careful, Sam now, like I tell you, for I knows it, now you hear to me, Sam, what I tell you, for I certainly always is right, Sam, when I knows it."

At first Sam tried a little to defend Melanctha, and Sam always was good and gentle to her, and Sam liked the ways Melanctha had to be quiet to him, and to always listen as if she was learning, when she was there and heard him talking, and then Sam liked the sweet way she always did everything so nicely for him; but Sam never liked to fight with anybody ever, and surely Rose knew best about Melanctha and anyway Sam never did really care much about Melanctha. Her mystery never had had any interest for him. Sam liked it that she was sweet to him and that she always did everything Rose ever wanted that she should be doing, but Melanctha never could be important to him. All Sam ever wanted was to have a little house and to live regular and to work hard and to come home to his dinner, when he was tired with his working and by and by he wanted to have some children all his own to be good to, and so Sam was real sorry for Melanctha, she was so good and so sweet always to them, and Jem Richards was a bad man to behave so to her, but that was always the way a girl got it when she liked that kind of a fast fellow. Anyhow Melanctha was Rose's friend, and Sam never cared to have anything to do with the kind of trouble always came to women, when they wanted to have men, who never could know how to behave good and steady to their women.

And so Sam never said much to Rose about Melanctha. Sam was always very gentle to her, but now he began less and less to see her. Soon Melanctha never came any more to the house to see Rose and Sam never asked Rose anything about her.

Melanctha Herbert was beginning now to come less and less to the house to be with Rose Johnson. This was because Rose seemed always less and less now to want her, and Rose would not let Melanctha now do things for her. Melanctha was always humble to her and Melanctha always wanted in every way she could to do things for her. Rose said no, she guessed she do that herself like she likes to have it better. Melanctha is real good to stay so long to help her, but Rose guessed perhaps Melanctha better go home now, Rose don't need nobody to help her now, she is feeling real strong, not like just after she had all that trouble with the baby, and then Sam, when he comes home for his dinner he likes it when Rose is all alone there just to give him his dinner. Sam always is so tired now, like he always is in the summer, so many people always on the steamer, and they make so much work so Sam is real tired now, and he likes just to eat his dinner and never have people in the house to be a trouble to him.

Each day Rose treated Melanctha more and more as if she never wanted Melanctha any more to come there to the house to see her. Melanctha dared not ask Rose why she acted in this way to her. Melanctha badly needed to have Rose always there to save her. Melanctha wanted badly to cling to her and Rose had always been so solid for her. Melanctha did not dare to ask Rose if she now no longer wanted her to come and see her.

Melanctha now never any more had Sam to be gentle to her. Rose always sent Melanctha away from her before it was time for Sam to come home to her. One day Melanctha had stayed a little longer, for Rose that day had been good to let Melanctha begin to do things for her. Melanctha then left her and Melanctha met Sam Johnson who stopped a minute to speak kindly to her.

The next day Rose Johnson would not let Melanctha come in to her. Rose stood on the steps, and there she told Melanctha what she thought now of her.

"I guess Melanctha it certainly ain't no ways right for you to come here no more just to see me. I certainly don't Melanctha no ways like to be a trouble to you. I certainly think Melanctha I get along better now when I don't have nobody like you are, always here to help me, and Sam he do so good now with his working, he pay a little girl something to come every day to help me. I certainly do think Melanctha I don't never want you no more to come here just to see me." "Why Rose, what I ever done to you, I certainly don't think you is right Rose to be so bad now to me." "I certainly don't no ways Melanctha Herbert think you got any right ever to be complaining the way I been acting to you. I certainly never do think Melanctha Herbert, you hear to me, nobody ever been more patient to you than I always been to like you, only Melanctha, I hear more things now so awful bad about you, everybody always is telling to me what kind of a way you always have been doing so much, and me always so good to you, and you never no ways, knowing how to be honest to me. No Melanctha it ain't ever in me, not to want you to have good luck come to you, and I like it real well Melanctha when you some time learn how to act the way it is decent and right for a girl to be doing, but I don't no ways ever like it the kind of things everybody tell me now about you. No Melanctha, I can't never any more trust you. I certainly am real sorry to have never any more to see you, but there ain't no other way, I ever can be acting to you. That's all I ever got any more to say to you now Melanctha." "But Rose, deed; I certainly don't know, no more than the dead, nothing I ever done to make you act so to me. Anybody say anything bad about me Rose, to you, they just a pack of liars to you, they certainly is Rose, I tell you true. I certainly never done nothing I ever been ashamed to tell you. Why you act so bad to me Rose. Sam he certainly don't think ever like you do, and Rose I always do everything I can, you ever want me to do for you." "It ain't never no use standing there talking, Melanctha Herbert. I just can tell it to you, and Sam, he don't know nothing about women ever the way they can be acting. I certainly am very sorry Melanctha, to have to act so now to you, but I certainly can't do no other way with you, when you do things always so bad, and everybody is talking so about you. It ain't no use to you to stand there and say it different to me Melanctha. I certainly am always right Melanctha Herbert, the way I certainly always have been when I knows it, to you. No Melanctha, it just is, you never can have no kind of a way to act right, the way a decent girl has to do, and I done my best always to be telling it to you Melanctha Herbert, but it don't never do no good to tell nobody how to act right; they certainly never can learn when they ain't got no sense right to know it, and you never have no sense right Melanctha to be honest, and I ain't never wishing no harm to you ever Melanctha Herbert, only I don't never want any more to see you come here. I just say to you now, like I always been saying to you, you don't know never the right way, any kind of decent girl has to be acting, and so Melanctha Herbert, me and Sam, we don't never any more want you to be setting your foot in my house here Melanctha Herbert, I just tell you. And so you just go along now, Melanctha Herbert, you hear me, and I don't never wish no harm to come to you."

Rose Johnson went into her house and closed the door behind her. Melanctha stood like one dazed, she did not know how to bear this blow that almost killed her. Slowly then Melanctha went away without even turning to look behind her.

Melanctha Herbert was all sore and bruised inside her. Melanctha had needed Rose always to believe her, Melanctha needed Rose always to let her cling to her, Melanctha wanted badly to have somebody who could make her always feel a little safe inside her, and now Rose had sent her from her. Melanctha wanted Rose more than she had ever wanted all the others. Rose always was so simple, solid, decent, for her. And now Rose had cast her from her. Melanctha was lost, and all the world went whirling in a mad weary dance around her.

Melanctha Herbert never had any strength alone ever to feel safe inside her. And now Rose Johnson had cast her from her, and Melanctha could never any more be near her. Melanctha Herbert knew now, way inside her, that she was lost, and nothing any more could ever help her.

Melanctha went that night to meet Jem Richards who had promised to be at the old place to meet her. Jem Richards was absent in his manner to her. By and by he began to talk to her, about the trip he was going to take soon, to see if he could get some luck back in his betting. Melanctha trembled, was Jem too now going to leave her. Jem Richards talked some more then to her, about the bad luck he always had now, and how he needed to go away to see if he could make it come out any better.

Then Jem stopped, and then he looked straight at Melanctha.

"Tell me Melanctha right and true, you don't care really nothing more about me now Melanctha," he said to her.

"Why you ask me that, Jem Richards," said Melanctha.

"Why I ask you that Melanctha, God Almighty, because I just don't give a damn now for you any more Melanctha. That's the reason I was asking."

Melanctha never could have for this an answer. Jem Richards waited and then he went away and left her.

Melanctha Herbert never again saw Jem Richards. Melanctha never again saw Rose Johnson, and it was hard to Melanctha never any more to see her. Rose Johnson had worked in to be the deepest of all Melanctha's emotions.

"No, I don't never see Melanctha Herbert no more now," Rose would say to anybody who asked her about Melanctha. "No, Melanctha she never comes here no more now, after we had all that trouble with her acting so bad with them kind of men she liked so much to be with. She don't never come to no good Melanctha Herbert don't, and me and Sam don't want no more to see her. She didn't do right ever the way I told her. Melanctha just wouldn't, and I always said it to her, if she don't be more kind of careful, the way she always had to be acting, I never did want no more she should come here in my house no more to see me. I ain't no ways ever against any girl having any kind of a way, to have a good time like she wants it, but not that kind of a way Melanctha always had to do it. I expect some day Melanctha kill herself, when she act so bad like she do always, and then she get so awful blue. Melanctha always says that's the only way she ever can think it a easy way for her to do. No, I always am real sorry for Melanctha, she never was no just common kind of nigger, but she don't never know not with all the time I always was telling it to her, no she never no way could learn, what was the right way she should do. I certainly don't never want no kind of harm to come bad to Melanctha, but I certainly do think she will most kill herself some time, the way she always say it would be easy way for her to do. I never see nobody ever could be so awful blue."

But Melanctha Herbert never really killed herself because she was so blue, though often she thought this would be really the best way for her to do. Melanctha never killed herself, she only got a bad fever and went into the hospital where they took good care of her and cured her.

When Melanctha was well again, she took a place and began to work and to live regular. Then Melanctha got very sick again, she began to cough and sweat and be so weak she could not stand to do her work.

Melanctha went back to the hospital, and there the Doctor told her she had the consumption, and before long she would surely die. They sent her where she would be taken care of, a home for poor consumptives, and there Melanctha stayed until she died.

False Dawn

[THE 'FORTIES]

1924

EDITH WHARTON

False Dawn

[THE 'FORTIES]

I

HAY, verbena and mignonette scented the languid July day. Large strawberries, crimsoning through sprigs of mint, floated in a bowl of pale yellow cup on the verandah table: an old Georgian bowl, with complex reflections on polygonal flanks, engraved with the Raycie arms between lions' heads. Now and again the gentlemen, warned by a menacing hum, slapped their cheeks, their brows or their bald crowns; but they did so as furtively as possible, for Mr. Halston Raycie, on whose verandah they sat, would not admit that there were mosquitoes at High Point.

The strawberries came from Mr. Raycie's kitchen garden; the Georgian bowl came from his great-grandfather (father of the Signer); the verandah was that of his country-house, which stood on a height above the Sound, at a convenient driving distance from his town house in Canal Street.

"Another glass, Commodore," said Mr. Raycie, shaking out a cambric handkerchief the size of a table-cloth, and applying a corner of it to his steaming brow.

Mr. Jameson Ledgely smiled and took another glass. He was known as "the Commodore" among his intimates because of having been in the Navy in his youth, and having taken part, as a midshipman under Admiral Porter, in the war of 1812. This jolly sunburnt bachelor, whose face resembled that of one of the bronze idols he might have brought back with him, had kept his naval air, though long retired from the service; and his white duck trousers, his gold-braided cap and shining teeth, still made him look as if he might be in command of a frigate. Instead of that, he had just sailed over a party of friends from his own place on the Long Island shore; and his trim white sloop was now lying in the bay below the point.

The Halston Raycie house overlooked a lawn sloping to the Sound. The lawn was Mr. Raycie's pride: it was mown with a scythe once a fortnight, and rolled in the spring by an old white horse specially shod for the purpose. Below the verandah the turf was broken by three round beds of rose-geranium, heliotrope and Bengal roses, which Mrs. Raycie tended in gauntlet gloves, under a small hinged sunshade that folded back on its carved ivory handle. The house, remodelled and enlarged by Mr. Raycie on his marriage, had played a part in the Revolutionary war as the settler's cottage where Benedict Arnold had had his headquarters. A contemporary print of it hung in Mr. Raycie's study; but no one could have detected the humble outline of the old house in the majestic stone-coloured dwelling built of tongued-and-grooved boards, with an angle tower, tall narrow windows, and a verandah on chamfered posts, that figured so confidently as a "Tuscan Villa" in Downing's "Landscape Gardening in America." There was the same difference between the rude lithograph of the earlier house and the fine steel engraving of its successor (with a "specimen" weeping beech on the lawn) as between the buildings themselves. Mr. Raycie had reason to think well of his architect.

He thought well of most things related to himself by ties of blood or interest. No one had ever been quite sure that he made Mrs. Raycie happy, but he was known to have the highest opinion of her. So it was with his daughters, Sarah Anne and Mary Adeline, fresher replicas of the lymphatic Mrs. Raycie; no one would have sworn that they were quite at ease with their genial parent, yet every one knew how loud he was in their praises. But the most remarkable object within the range of Mr. Raycie's self-approval was his son Lewis. And yet, as Jameson Ledgely, who was given to speaking his mind, had once observed, you wouldn't have supposed young Lewis was exactly the kind of craft Halston would have turned out if he'd had the designing of his son and heir.

Mr. Raycie was a monumental man. His extent in height, width and thickness was so nearly the same that whichever way he was turned one had an almost equally broad view of him; and every inch of that mighty circumference was so exquisitely cared for that to a farmer's eye he might have suggested a great agricultural estate of which not an acre is untilled. Even his baldness, which was in proportion to the rest, looked as if it received a special daily polish; and on a hot day his whole person was like some wonderful example of the costliest irrigation. There was so much of him, and he had so many planes, that it was fascinating to watch each runnel of moisture follow its own particular watershed. Even on his large fresh-looking hands the drops divided, trickling in different ways from the ridges of the fingers; and as for his forehead and temples, and the raised cushion of cheek beneath each of his lower lids, every one of these slopes had its own particular stream, its hollow pools and sudden cataracts; and the sight was never unpleasant, because his whole vast bubbling surface was of such a clean and hearty pink, and the exuding moisture so perceptibly flavoured with expensive eau de Cologne and the best French soap.

Mrs. Raycie, though built on a less heroic scale, had a pale amplitude which, when she put on her best watered silk (the kind that stood alone), and framed her countenance in the innumerable blonde lace ruffles and clustered purple grapes of her newest Paris cap, almost balanced her husband's bulk. Yet from this full-rigged pair, as the Commodore would have put it, had issued the lean little runt of a Lewis, a shrimp of a baby, a shaver of a boy, and now a youth as scant as an ordinary man's midday shadow.

All these things, Lewis himself mused, dangling his legs from the verandah rail, were undoubtedly passing through the minds of the four gentlemen grouped about his father's bowl of cup.

Mr. Robert Huzzard, the banker, a tall broad man, who looked big in any company but Mr. Raycie's, leaned back, lifted his glass, and bowed to Lewis.

"Here's to the Grand Tour!"

"Don't perch on that rail like a sparrow, my boy," Mr. Raycie said reprovingly; and Lewis dropped to his feet, and returned Mr. Huzzard's bow.

"I wasn't thinking," he stammered. It was his too frequent excuse.

Mr. Ambrose Huzzard, the banker's younger brother, Mr. Ledgely and Mr. Donaldson Kent, all raised their glasses and cheerily echoed: "The Grand Tour!"

Lewis bowed again, and put his lips to the glass he had forgotten. In reality, he had eyes only for Mr. Donaldson Kent, his father's cousin, a silent man with a lean hawk-like profile, who looked like a retired Revolutionary hero, and lived in daily fear of the most trifling risk or responsibility.

To this prudent and circumspect citizen had come, some years earlier, the unexpected and altogether inexcusable demand that he should look after the daughter of his only brother, Julius Kent. Julius had died in Italy—well, that was his own business, if he chose to live there. But to let his wife die before him, and to leave a minor daughter, and a will entrusting her to the guardianship of his esteemed elder brother, Donaldson Kent Esquire, of Kent's Point, Long Island, and Great Jones Street, New York—well, as Mr. Kent himself said, and as his wife said for him, there had never been anything, anything whatever, in Mr. Kent's attitude or behaviour, to justify the ungrateful Julius (whose debts he had more than once paid) in laying on him this final burden.

The girl came. She was fourteen, she was considered plain, she was small and black and skinny. Her name was Beatrice, which was bad enough, and made worse by the fact that it had been shortened by ignorant foreigners to Treeshy. But she was eager, serviceable and good-tempered, and as Mr. and Mrs. Kent's friends pointed out, her plainness made everything easy. There were two Kent boys growing up, Bill and Donald; and if this penniless cousin had been compounded of cream and roses—well, she would have taken more watching, and might have rewarded the kindness of her uncle and aunt by some act of wicked ingratitude. But this risk being obviated by her appearance, they could be good-natured to her without afterthought, and to be good-natured was natural to them. So, as the years passed, she gradually became the guardian of her guardians; since it was equally natural to Mr. and Mrs. Kent to throw themselves in helpless reliance on every one whom they did not nervously fear or mistrust.

"Yes, he's off on Monday," Mr. Raycie said, nodding sharply at Lewis, who had set down his glass after one sip. "Empty it, you shirk!" the nod commanded; and Lewis, throwing back his head, gulped down the draught, though it almost stuck in his lean throat. He had already had to take two glasses, and even this scant conviviality was too much for him, and likely to result in a mood of excited volubility, followed by a morose evening and a head the next morning. And he wanted to keep his mind clear that day, and to think steadily and lucidly of Treeshy Kent.

Of course he couldn't marry her—yet. He was twenty-one that very day, and still entirely dependent on his father. And he wasn't altogether sorry to be going first on this Grand Tour. It was what he had always dreamed of, pined for, from the moment when his infant eyes had first been drawn to the prints of European cities in the long upper passage that smelt of matting. And all that Treeshy had told him about Italy had confirmed and intensified the longing.

Oh, to have been going there with her—with her as his guide, his Beatrice! (For she had given him a little Dante of her father's, with a steel-engraved frontispiece of Beatrice; and his sister Mary Adeline, who had been taught Italian by one of the romantic Milanese exiles, had helped her brother out with the grammar.)

The thought of going to Italy with Treeshy was only a dream; but later, as man and wife, they would return there, and by that time, perhaps, it was Lewis who would be her guide, and reveal to her the historic marvels of her birthplace, of which after all she knew so little, except in minor domestic ways that were quaint but unimportant.

The prospect swelled her suitor's bosom, and reconciled him to the idea of their separation. After all, he secretly felt himself to be still a boy, and it was as a man that he would return: he meant to tell her that when they met the next day. When he came back his character would be formed, his knowledge of life (which he already thought considerable) would be complete; and then no one could keep them apart. He smiled in advance to think how little his father's shouting and booming would impress a man on his return from the Grand Tour. . . .

The gentlemen were telling anecdotes about their own early experiences in Europe. None of them—not even Mr. Raycie—had travelled as extensively as it was intended that Lewis should; but the two Huzzards had been twice to England on banking matters, and Commodore Ledgely, a bold man, to France and Belgium as well—not to speak of his early experiences in the Far East. All three had kept a vivid and amused recollection, slightly tinged with disapprobation, of what they had seen— "Oh, those French wenches," the Commodore chuckled through his white teeth—but poor Mr. Kent, who had gone abroad on his honeymoon, had been caught in Paris by the revolution of 1830, had had the fever in Florence, and had nearly been arrested as a spy in Vienna; and the only satisfactory episode in this disastrous, and never repeated, adventure, had been the fact of his having been mistaken for the Duke of Wellington (as he was trying to slip out of a Viennese hotel in his courier's blue surtout) by a crowd who had been—"Well, very gratifying in their enthusiasm," Mr. Kent admitted.

"How my poor brother Julius could have lived in Europe! Well, look at the consequences—" he used to say, as if poor Treeshy's plainness gave an awful point to his moral.

"There's one thing in Paris, my boy, that you must be warned against: those gambling-hells in the Pally Royle," Mr. Kent insisted. "I never set foot in the places myself; but a glance at the outside was enough."

"I knew a feller that was fleeced of a fortune there," Mr. Henry Huzzard confirmed; while the Commodore, at his tenth glass, chuckled with moist eyes: "The trollops, oh, the trollops—"

"As for Vienna—" said Mr. Kent.

"Even in London," said Mr. Ambrose Huzzard, "a young man must be on his look-out against gamblers. Every form of swindling is practised, and the touts are always on the look-out for greenhorns; a term," he added apologetically, "which they apply to any traveller new to the country."

"In Paris," said Mr. Kent, "I was once within an ace of being challenged to fight a duel." He fetched a sigh of horror and relief, and glanced reassuredly down the Sound in the direction of his own peaceful roof-tree.

"Oh, a duel," laughed the Commodore. "A man can fight duels here. I fought a dozen when I was a young feller in New Erleens." The Commodore's mother had been a southern lady, and after his father's death had spent some years with her parents in Louisiana, so that her son's varied experiences had begun early. "'Bout women," he smiled confidentially, holding out his empty glass to Mr. Raycie.

"The ladies—!" exclaimed Mr. Kent in a voice of warning.

The gentlemen rose to their feet, the Commodore quite as promptly and steadily as the others. The drawing-room window opened, and from it emerged Mrs. Raycie, in a ruffled sarsenet dress and Point de Paris cap, followed by her two daughters in starched organdy with pink spencers. Mr. Raycie looked with proud approval at his womenkind.

"Gentlemen," said Mrs. Raycie, in a perfectly even voice, "supper is on the table, and if you will do Mr. Raycie and myself the favour—"

"The favour, ma'am," said Mr. Ambrose Huzzard, "is on your side, in so amiably inviting us."

Mrs. Raycie curtsied, the gentlemen bowed, and Mr. Raycie said: "Your arm to Mrs. Raycie, Huzzard. This little farewell party is a family affair, and the other gentlemen must content themselves with my two daughters. Sarah Anne, Mary Adeline—"

The Commodore and Mr. John Huzzard advanced ceremoniously toward the two girls, and Mr. Kent, being a cousin, closed the procession between Mr. Raycie and Lewis.

Oh, that supper-table! The vision of it used sometimes to rise before Lewis Raycie's eyes in outlandish foreign places; for though not a large or fastidious eater when he was at home, he was afterward, in lands of chestnut-flour and garlic and queer bearded sea-things, to suffer many pangs of hunger at the thought of that opulent board. In the centre stood the Raycie *épergne* of pierced silver, holding aloft a bunch of June roses surrounded by dangling baskets of sugared almonds and striped peppermints; and grouped about this decorative "motif" were Lowestoft platters heavy with piles of raspberries, strawberries and the first Delaware peaches. An outer flanking of heaped-up cookies, crullers, strawberry short-cake, piping hot corn-bread and deep golden butter in moist blocks still bedewed from the muslin swathings of the dairy, led the eye to the Virginia ham in front of Mr. Raycie, and the twin dishes of scrambled eggs on toast and broiled blue-fish over which his wife presided. Lewis could never afterward fit into this intricate pattern the "side-dishes" of devilled turkey legs and creamed chicken hash, the sliced cucumbers and tomatoes, the heavy silver jugs of butter-coloured cream, the floating-island, "slips" and lemon jellies that were somehow interwoven with the solider elements of the design; but they were all there, either together or successively, and so were the towering piles of waffles reeling on their foundations, and the slender silver jugs of maple syrup perpetually escorting them about the table as black Dinah replenished the supply.

They ate—oh, how they all ate!—though the ladies were supposed only to nibble; but the good things on Lewis's plate remained untouched until, ever and again, an admonishing glance from Mr. Raycie, or an entreating one from Mary Adeline, made him insert a languid fork into the heap.

And all the while Mr. Raycie continued to hold forth.

"A young man, in my opinion, before setting up for himself, must see the world; form his taste; fortify his judgment. He must study the most famous monuments, examine the organization of foreign societies, and the habits and customs of those older civilizations whose yoke it has been our glory to cast off. Though he may see in them much to deplore and to reprove—" ("Some of the gals, though," Commodore Ledgely was heard to interject)—"much that will make him give thanks for the privilege of having been born and brought up under our own Free Institutions, yet I believe he will also"—Mr. Raycie conceded it with magnanimity—"be able to learn much."

"The Sundays, though," Mr. Kent hazarded warningly; and Mrs. Raycie breathed across to her son: "Ah, that's what *I* say!"

Mr. Raycie did not like interruption; and he met it by growing visibly larger. His huge bulk hung a moment, like an avalanche, above the silence which followed Mr. Kent's interjection and Mrs. Raycie's murmur; then he crashed down on both.

"The Sundays—the Sundays? Well, what of the Sundays? What is there to frighten a good Episcopalian in what we call the Continental Sunday? I presume that we're all Churchmen here, eh? No puling Methodists or atheistical Unitarians at my table tonight, that I'm aware of? Nor will I offend the ladies of my household by assuming that they have secretly lent an ear to the Baptist ranter in the chapel at the foot of our lane. No? I thought not! Well, then, I say, what's all this flutter about the Papists? Far be it from me to approve of their heathenish doctrines—but, damn it, they go to church, don't they? And they have a real service, as we do, don't they? And real clergy, and not a lot of nondescripts dressed like laymen, and damned badly at that, who chat familiarly with the Almighty in their own vulgar lingo? No, sir"—he swung about on the shrinking Mr. Kent—"it's not the Church I'm afraid of in foreign countries, it's the sewers, sir!"

Mrs. Raycie had grown very pale: Lewis knew that she too was deeply perturbed about the sewers. "And the night air," she scarce-audibly sighed.

But Mr. Raycie had taken up his main theme again. "In my opinion, if a young man travels at all, he must travel as extensively as his—er—means permit; must see as much of the world as he can. Those are my son's sailing orders, Commodore; and here's to his carrying them out to the best of his powers!"

Black Dinah, removing the Virginia ham, or rather such of its bony structure as alone remained on the dish, had managed to make room for a bowl of punch from which Mr. Raycie poured deep ladlefuls of perfumed fire into the glasses ranged before him on a silver tray. The gentlemen rose, the ladies smiled and wept, and Lewis's health and the success of the Grand Tour were toasted with an eloquence which caused Mrs. Raycie, with a hasty nod to her daughters, and a covering rustle of starched flounces, to shepherd them softly from the room.

"After all," Lewis heard her murmur to them on the threshold, "your father's using such language shows that he's in the best of humor with dear Lewis."

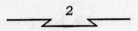

2

In spite of his enforced potations, Lewis Raycie was up the next morning before sunrise.

Unlatching his shutters without noise, he looked forth over the wet lawn merged in a blur of shrubberies, and the waters of the Sound dimly seen beneath a sky full of stars. His head ached but his heart glowed; what was before him was thrilling enough to clear a heavier brain than his.

He dressed quickly and completely (save for his shoes), and then, stripping the flowered quilt from his high mahogany bed, rolled it in a tight bundle under his arm. Thus enigmatically equipped he was feeling his way, shoes in hand, through the darkness of the upper story to the slippery oak stairs, when he was startled by a candle-gleam in the pitch-blackness of the hall below. He held his breath, and leaning over the stair-rail saw with amazement his sister Mary Adeline come forth, cloaked and bonneted, but also in stocking-feet, from the passage leading to the pantry. She too carried a double burden: her shoes and the candle in one hand, in the other a large covered basket that weighed down her bare arm.

Brother and sister stopped and stared at each other in the blue dusk: the upward slant of the candle-light distorted Mary Adeline's mild features, twisting them into a frightened grin as Lewis stole down to join her.

"Oh—" she whispered. "What in the world are you doing here? I was just getting together a few things for that poor young Mrs. Poe down the lane, who's so ill—before mother goes to the store-room. You won't tell, will you?"

Lewis signalled his complicity, and cautiously slid open the bolt of the front door. They durst not say more till they were out of ear-shot. On the doorstep they sat down to put on their shoes; then they hastened on without a word through the ghostly shrubberies till they reached the gate into the lane.

"But you, Lewis?" the sister suddenly questioned, with an astonished stare at the rolled-up quilt under her brother's arm.

"Oh, I—. Look here, Addy—" he broke off and began to grope in his pocket—"I haven't much about me . . . the old gentleman keeps me as close as ever . . . but here's a dollar, if you think that poor Mrs. Poe could use it . . . I'd be too happy . . . consider it a privilege . . ."

"Oh, Lewis, Lewis, how noble, how generous of you! Of course I can buy a few extra things with it . . . they never see meat unless I can bring them a bit, you know . . . and I fear she's dying of a decline . . . and she and her mother are so fiery-proud . . ." She wept with gratitude, and Lewis drew a breath of relief. He had diverted her attention from the bed-quilt.

"Ah, there's the breeze," he murmured, sniffing the suddenly chilled air.

"Yes; I must be off; I must be back before the sun is up," said Mary Adeline anxiously, "and it would never do if mother knew—"

"She doesn't know of your visits to Mrs. Poe?"

A look of childish guile sharpened Mary Adeline's undeveloped face. "She *does*, of course; but yet she doesn't . . . we've arranged it so. You see, Mr. Poe's an Atheist; and so father—"

"I see," Lewis nodded. "Well, we part here; I'm off for a swim," he said glibly. But abruptly he turned back and caught his sister's arm. "Sister, tell Mrs. Poe, please, that I heard her husband give a reading from his poems in New York two nights ago—"

("Oh, Lewis—*you?* But father says he's a blasphemer!")

"—And that he's a great poet—a Great Poet. Tell her that from me, will you, please, Mary Adeline?"

"Oh, brother, I couldn't . . . we never speak of him," the startled girl faltered, hurrying away.

In the cove where the Commodore's sloop had ridden a few hours earlier a biggish rowing-boat took the waking ripples. Young Raycie paddled out to her, fastened his skiff to the moorings, and hastily clambered into the boat.

From various recesses of his pockets he produced rope, string, a carpet-layer's needle, and other unexpected and incongruous tackle; then, lashing one of the oars across the top of the other, and jamming the latter upright between the forward thwart and the bow, he rigged the flowered bed-quilt on this mast, knotted a rope to the free end of the quilt, and sat down in the stern, one hand on the rudder, the other on his improvised sheet.

Venus, brooding silverly above a line of pale green sky, made a pool of glory in the sea as the dawn-breeze plumped the lover's sail. . . .

On the shelving pebbles of another cove, two or three miles down the Sound, Lewis Raycie lowered his queer sail and beached his boat. A clump of willows on the shingle-edge mysteriously stirred and parted, and Treeshy Kent was in his arms.

The sun was just pushing above a belt of low clouds in the east, spattering them with liquid gold, and Venus blanched as the light spread upward. But under the willows it was still dusk, a watery green dusk in which the secret murmurs of the night were caught.

"Treeshy—Treeshy!" the young man cried, kneeling beside her—and then, a moment later: "My angel, are you sure that no one guesses—?"

The girl gave a faint laugh which screwed up her funny nose. She leaned her head on his shoulder, her round forehead and rough braids pressed against his cheek, her hands in his, breathing quickly and joyfully.

"I thought I should never get here," Lewis grumbled, "with that ridiculous bed-quilt—and it'll be broad day soon! To think that I was of age yesterday, and must come to you in a boat rigged like a child's toy on a duck-pond! If you knew how it humiliates me—"

"What does it matter, dear, since you're of age now, and your own master?"

"But am I, though? He says so—but it's only on his own terms; only while I do what he wants! You'll see . . . I've a credit of ten thousand dollars . . . ten . . . thou . . . sand . . . d'you hear? . . . placed to my name in a London bank; and not a penny here to bless myself with meanwhile . . . Why, Treeshy darling, why, what's the matter?"

She flung her arms about his neck, and through their innocent kisses he could taste her tears. "What *is* it, Treeshy?" he implored her.

"I . . . oh, I'd forgotten it was to be our last day together till you spoke of London—cruel, cruel!" she reproached him; and through the green twilight of the willows her eyes blazed on him like two stormy stars. No other eyes he knew could express such elemental rage as Treeshy's.

"You little spitfire, you!" he laughed back somewhat chokingly. "Yes, it's our last day—but not for long; at our age two years are not so very long, after all, are they? And when I come back to you I'll come as my own master, independent, free—come to claim you in face of everything and everybody! Think of that, darling, and be brave for my sake . . . brave and patient . . . as I mean to be!" he declared heroically.

"Oh, but you—you'll see other girls; heaps and heaps of them; in those wicked old countries where they're so lovely. My uncle Kent says the European countries are all wicked, even my own poor Italy . . ."

"But you, Treeshy; you'll be seeing cousins Bill and Donald meanwhile—seeing them all day long and every day. And you know you've a weakness for that great hulk of a Bill. Ah, if only I stood six-foot-one in my stockings I'd go with an easier heart, you fickle child!" he tried to banter her.

"Fickle? Fickle? Me—oh, Lewis!"

He felt the premonitory sweep of sobs, and his untried courage failed him. It was delicious, in theory, to hold weeping beauty to one's breast, but terribly alarming, he found, in practice. There came a responsive twitching in his throat.

"No, no; firm as adamant, true as steel; that's what we both mean to be, isn't it, cara?"

"Caro, yes," she sighed, appeased.

"And you'll write to me regularly, Treeshy—long long letters? I may count on that, mayn't I, wherever I am? And they must all be numbered, every one of them, so that I shall know at once if I've missed one; remember!"

"And, Lewis, you'll wear them here?" (She touched his breast.) "Oh, not all," she added, laughing, "for they'd make such a big bundle that you'd soon have a hump in front like Pulcinella—but always at least the last one, just the last one. Promise!"

"Always, I promise—as long as they're kind," he said, still struggling to take a spirited line.

"Oh, Lewis, they will be, as long as yours are—and long long afterward . . ."

Venus failed and vanished in the sun's uprising.

3

The crucial moment, Lewis had always known, would be not that of his farewell to Treeshy, but of his final interview with his father.

On that everything hung: his immediate future as well as his more distant prospects. As he stole home in the early sunlight, over the dew-drenched grass, he glanced up apprehensively at Mr. Raycie's windows, and thanked his stars that they were still tightly shuttered.

There was no doubt, as Mrs. Raycie said, that her husband's "using language" before ladies showed him to be in high good humor, relaxed and slippered, as it were—a state his family so seldom saw him in that Lewis had sometimes impertinently wondered to what awful descent from the clouds he and his two sisters owed their timorous being.

It was all very well to tell himself, as he often did, that the bulk of the money was his mother's, and that he could turn her round his little finger. What difference did that make? Mr. Raycie, the day after his marriage, had quietly taken over the management of his wife's property, and deducted, from the very moderate allowance he accorded her, all her little personal expenses, even to the postage-stamps she used, and the dollar she put in the plate every Sunday. He called the allowance her "pin-money," since, as he often re-minded her, he paid all the household bills himself, so that Mrs. Raycie's quarterly pittance could be entirely devoted, if she chose, to frills and feathers.

"And will be, if you respect my wishes, my dear," he always added. "I like to see a handsome figure well set-off, and not to have our friends imagine, when they come to dine, that Mrs. Raycie is sick above-stairs, and I've replaced her by a poor relation in *alla-pacca*." In compliance with which Mrs. Raycie, at once flattered and terrified, spent her last penny in adorning herself and her daughters, and had to stint their bedroom fires, and the servants' meals, in order to find a penny for any private necessity.

Mr. Raycie had long since convinced his wife that this method of dealing with her, if not lavish, was suitable, and in fact "hand-some"; when she spoke of the subject to her relations it was with tears of gratitude for her husband's kindness in assuming the man-agement of her property. As he managed it exceedingly well, her hard-headed brothers (glad to have the responsibility off their hands, and convinced that, if left to herself, she would have muddled her money away in ill-advised charities) were disposed to share her approval of Mr. Raycie; though her old mother sometimes said helplessly: "When I think that Lucy Ann can't as much as have a drop of gruel brought up to her without his weighing the oatmeal . . ." But even that was only whispered, lest Mr. Raycie's mysterious faculty of hearing what was said behind his back should bring sudden reprisals on the venerable lady to whom he always alluded, with a tremor in his genial voice, as "my dear mother-in-law—unless indeed she will allow me to call her, more briefly but more truly, my dear mother."

To Lewis, hitherto, Mr. Raycie had meted the same measure as to the females of the household. He had dressed him well, educated him expensively, lauded him to the skies—and counted every penny of his allowance. Yet there was a difference; and Lewis was as well aware of it as any one.

The dream, the ambition, the passion of Mr. Raycie's life, was (as his son knew) to found a Family; and he had only Lewis to found it with. He believed in primogeniture, in heirlooms, in entailed estates, in all the ritual of the English "landed" tradition. No one was louder than he in praise of the democratic institutions under which he lived; but he never thought of them as affecting that more private but more important institution, the Family; and to the Family all his care and all his thoughts were given. The result, as Lewis dimly guessed, was, that upon his own shrinking and inadequate head was centred all the passion contained in the vast expanse of Mr. Raycie's breast. Lewis was his very own, and Lewis represented what was most dear to him; and for both these reasons Mr. Raycie set an inordinate value on the boy (a quite different thing, Lewis thought, from loving him).

Mr. Raycie was particularly proud of his son's taste for letters. Himself not a wholly unread man, he admired intensely what he called the "cultivated gentleman"—and that was what Lewis was evidently going to be. Could he have combined with this tendency a manlier frame, and an interest in the few forms of sport then popular among gentlemen, Mr. Raycie's satisfaction would have been complete; but whose is, in this disappointing world? Meanwhile he flattered himself that, Lewis being still young and malleable, and his health certainly mending, two years of travel and adventure might send him back a very different figure, physically as well as mentally. Mr. Raycie had himself travelled in his youth, and was persuaded that the experience was formative; he secretly hoped for the return of a bronzed and broadened Lewis, seasoned by independence and adventure, and having discreetly sown his wild oats in foreign pastures, where they would not contaminate the home crop.

All this Lewis guessed; and he guessed as well that these two wander-years were intended by Mr. Raycie to lead up to a marriage and an establishment after Mr. Raycie's own heart, but in which Lewis's was not to have even a consulting voice.

"He's going to give me all the advantages—for his own purpose," the young man summed it up as he went down to join the family at the breakfast table.

Mr. Raycie was never more resplendent than at that moment of the day and season. His spotless white duck trousers, strapped under kid boots, his thin kerseymere coat, and drab *piqué* waistcoat crossed below a snowy stock, made him look as fresh as the morning and as appetizing as the peaches and cream banked before him.

Opposite sat Mrs. Raycie, immaculate also, but paler than usual, as became a mother about to part from her only son; and between the two was Sarah Anne, unusually pink, and apparently occupied in trying to screen her sister's empty seat. Lewis greeted them, and seated himself at his mother's right.

Mr. Raycie drew out his *guillochée* repeating watch, and detaching it from its heavy gold chain laid it on the table beside him.

"Mary Adeline is late again. It is a somewhat unusual thing for a sister to be late at the last meal she is to take—for two years— with her only brother."

"Oh, Mr. Raycie!" Mrs. Raycie faltered.

"I say, the idea is peculiar. Perhaps," said Mr. Raycie sarcastically, "I am going to be blessed with a *peculiar* daughter."

"I'm afraid Mary Adeline is beginning a sick headache, sir. She tried to get up, but really could not," said Sarah Anne in a rush.

Mr. Raycie's only reply was to arch ironic eyebrows, and Lewis hastily intervened: "I'm sorry, sir; but it may be my fault—"

Mrs. Raycie paled, Sarah Anne, purpled, and Mr. Raycie echoed with punctilious incredulity: "Your—fault?"

"In being the occasion, sir, of last night's too-sumptuous festivity—"

"Ha—ha—ha!" Mr. Raycie laughed, his thunders instantly dispelled.

He pushed back his chair and nodded to his son with a smile; and the two, leaving the ladies to wash up the teacups (as was still the habit in genteel families) betook themselves to Mr. Raycie's study.

What Mr. Raycie studied in this apartment—except the accounts, and ways of making himself unpleasant to his family—Lewis had never been able to discover. It was a small bare formidable room; and the young man, who never crossed the threshold but with a sinking of his heart, felt it sink lower than ever. "*Now!*" he thought.

Mr. Raycie took the only easy-chair, and began.

"My dear fellow, our time is short, but long enough for what I have to say. In a few hours you will be setting out on your great journey: an important event in the life of any young man. Your talents and character—combined with your means of improving the opportunity—make me hope that in your case it will be decisive. I expect you to come home from this trip a man—"

So far, it was all to order, so to speak; Lewis could have recited it beforehand. He bent his head in acquiescence.

"A man," Mr. Raycie repeated, "prepared to play a part, a considerable part, in the social life of the community. I expect you to be a figure in New York; and I shall give you the means to be so." He cleared his throat. "But means are not enough—though you must never forget that they are essential. Education, polish, experience of the world; these are what so many of our men of standing lack. What do they know of Art or Letters? We have had little time here to produce either as yet—you spoke?" Mr. Raycie broke off with a crushing courtesy.

"I—oh, no," his son stammered.

"Ah; I thought you might be about to allude to certain blasphemous penny-a-liners whose poetic ravings are said to have given them a kind of pothouse notoriety."

Lewis reddened at the allusion but was silent, and his father went on:

"Where is our Byron—our Scott—our Shakespeare? And in painting it is the same. Where are our Old Masters? We are not without contemporary talent; but for works of genius we must still look to the past; we must in most cases, content ourselves with copies . . . Ah, here, I know, my dear boy, I touch a responsive chord! Your love of the arts has not passed unperceived; and I mean, I desire, to do all I can to encourage it. Your future position in the world—your duties and obligations as a gentleman and a man of fortune—will not permit you to become, yourself, an eminent painter or a famous sculptor; but I shall raise no objection to your dabbling in these arts as an amateur—at least while you are travelling abroad. It will form your taste, strengthen your judgment, and give you, I hope, the discernment necessary to select for me a few masterpieces which shall *not* be copies. Copies," Mr. Raycie pursued with a deepening emphasis, "are for the less discriminating, or for those less blessed with this world's goods. Yes, my dear Lewis, I wish to create a gallery: a gallery of Heirlooms. Your mother participates in this ambition—she desires to see on our walls a few original specimens of the Italian genius. Raphael, I fear, we can hardly aspire to; but a Domenichino, an Albano, a Carlo Dolci, a Guercino, a Carlo Maratta—one or two of Salvator Rosa's noble landscapes . . . you see my idea? There shall be a Raycie Gallery; and it shall be your mission to get together its nucleus." Mr. Raycie paused, and mopped his flowing forehead. "I believe I could have given my son no task more to his liking."

"Oh, no, sir, none indeed!" Lewis cried, flushing and paling. He had in fact never suspected this part of his father's plan, and his heart swelled with the honour of so unforeseen a mission. Nothing, in truth, could have made him prouder or happier. For a moment he forgot love, forgot Treeshy, forgot everything but the rapture of moving among the masterpieces of which he had so long dreamed, moving not as a mere hungry spectator but as one whose privilege it should at least be to single out and carry away some of the lesser treasures. He could hardly take in what had happened, and the shock of the announcement left him, as usual, inarticulate.

He heard his father booming on, developing the plan, explaining with his usual pompous precision that one of the partners of the London bank in which Lewis's funds were deposited was himself a noted collector, and had agreed to provide the young traveller with letters of introduction to other connoisseurs, both in France and Italy, so that Lewis's acquisitions might be made under the most enlightened guidance.

"It is," Mr. Raycie concluded, "in order to put you on a footing of equality with the best collectors that I have placed such a large sum at your disposal. I reckon that for ten thousand dollars you can travel for two years in the very best style; and I mean to place another five thousand to your credit"—he paused, and let the syllables drop slowly into his son's brain: "five thousand dollars for the purchase of works of art, which eventually—remember—will be yours; and will be handed on, I trust, to your sons' sons as long as the name of Raycie survives"—a length of time, Mr. Raycie's tone seemed to imply, hardly to be measured in periods less extensive than those of the Egyptian dynasties.

Lewis heard him with a whirling brain. *Five thousand dollars!* The sum seemed so enormous, even in dollars, and so incalculably larger when translated into any continental currency, that he wondered why his father, in advance, had given up all hope of a Raphael. . . "If I travel economically," he said to himself, "and deny myself unnecessary luxuries, I may yet be able to surprise him by bringing one back. And my mother—how magnanimous, how splendid! Now I see why she has consented to all the little economies that sometimes seemed so paltry and so humiliating. . ."

The young man's eyes filled with tears, but he was still silent, though he longed as never before to express his gratitude and admiration to his father. He had entered the study expecting a parting sermon on the subject of thrift, coupled with the prospective announcement of a "suitable establishment" (he could even guess the particular Huzzard girl his father had in view); and instead he had been told to spend his princely allowance in a princely manner, and to return home with a gallery of masterpieces. "At least," he murmured to himself, "it shall contain a Correggio."

"Well, sir?" Mr. Raycie boomed.

"Oh, sir—" his son cried, and flung himself on the vast slope of the parental waistcoat.

Amid all these accumulated joys there murmured deep down in him the thought that nothing had been said or done to interfere with his secret plans about Treeshy. It seemed almost as if his father had tacitly accepted the idea of their unmentioned engagement; and Lewis felt half guilty at not confessing to it then and there. But the gods are formidable even when they unbend; never more so, perhaps, than at such moments . . .

PART II

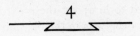

4

Lewis Raycie stood on a projecting rock and surveyed the sublime spectacle of Mont Blanc.

It was a brilliant August day, and the air, at that height, was already so sharp that he had had to put on his fur-lined pelisse. Behind him, at a respectful distance, was the travelling servant who, at a signal, had brought it up to him; below, in the bend of the mountain road, stood the light and elegant carriage which had carried him thus far on his travels.

Scarcely more than a year had passed since he had waved a farewell to New York from the deck of the packet-ship headed down the bay; yet, to the young man confidently facing Mont Blanc, nothing seemed left in him of that fluid and insubstantial being, the former Lewis Raycie, save a lurking and abeyant fear of Mr. Raycie senior. Even that, however, was so attenuated by distance and time, so far sunk below the horizon, and anchored on the far side of the globe, that it stirred in its sleep only when a handsomely folded and wafered letter in his parent's writing was handed out across the desk of some continental counting-house. Mr. Raycie senior did not write often, and when he did it was in a bland and stilted strain. He felt at a disadvantage on paper, and his natural sarcasm was swamped in the rolling periods which it cost him hours of labour to bring forth; so that the dreaded quality lurked for his son only in the curve of certain letters, and in a positively awful way of writing out, at full length, the word *Esquire*.

It was not that Lewis had broken with all the memories of his past of a year ago. Many still lingered in him, or rather had been transferred to the new man he had become—as for instance his tenderness for Treeshy Kent, which, somewhat to his surprise, had obstinately resisted all the assaults of English keepsake beauties and almond-eyed houris of the East. It startled him, at times, to find Treeshy's short dusky face, with its round forehead, the widely spaced eyes and the high cheek-bones, starting out at him suddenly in the street of some legendary town, or in a landscape of languid beauty, just as he had now and again been arrested in an exotic garden by the very

scent of the verbena under the verandah at home. His travels had
confirmed rather than weakened the family view of Treeshy's plainness; she could not be made to fit into any of the patterns of female
beauty so far submitted to him; yet there she was, ensconced in his
new heart and mind as deeply as in the old, though her kisses seemed
less vivid, and the peculiar rough notes of her voice hardly reached
him. Sometimes, half irritably, he said to himself that with an effort
he could disperse her once for all; yet she lived on in him, unseen yet
ineffaceable, like the image on a daguerreotype plate, no less there
because so often invisible.

To the new Lewis, however, the whole business was less important
than he had once thought it. His suddenly acquired maturity made
Treeshy seem a petted child rather than the guide, the Beatrice, he
had once considered her; and he promised himself, with an elderly
smile, that as soon as he got to Italy he would write her the long
letter for which he was now considerably in her debt.

His travels had first carried him to England. There he spent some
weeks in collecting letters and recommendations for his tour, in
purchasing his travelling-carriage and its numerous appurtenances,
and in driving in it from cathedral town to storied castle, omitting
nothing, from Abbotsford to Kenilworth, which deserved the attention of a cultivated mind. From England he crossed to Calais, moving
slowly southward to the Mediterranean; and there, taking ship for
the Piræus, he plunged into pure romance, and the tourist became a
Giaour.

It was the East which had made him into a new Lewis Raycie; the
East, so squalid and splendid, so pestilent and so poetic, so full of
knavery and romance and fleas and nightingales, and so different,
alike in its glories and its dirt, from what his studious youth had
dreamed. After Smyrna and the bazaars, after Damascus and Pal-
myra, the Acropolis, Mytilene and Sunium, what could be left in his
mind of Canal Street and the lawn above the Sound? Even the
mosquitoes, which seemed at first the only connecting link, were
different, because he fought with them in scenes so different; and a
young gentleman who had journeyed across the desert in Arabian
dress, slept under goats'-hair tents, been attacked by robbers in the
Peloponnesus and despoiled by his own escort at Baalbek, and by
customs' officials everywhere, could not but look with a smile on the
terrors that walk New York and the Hudson river. Encased in
security and monotony, that other Lewis Raycie, when his little figure

bobbed up to the surface, seemed like a new-born babe preserved in alcohol. Even Mr. Raycie senior's thunders were now no more than the far-off murmur of summer lightning on a perfect evening. Had Mr. Raycie ever really frightened Lewis? Why, now he was not even frightened by Mont Blanc!

He was still gazing with a sense of easy equality at its awful pinnacles when another travelling-carriage paused near his own, and a young man, eagerly jumping from it, and also followed by a servant with a cloak, began to mount the slope. Lewis at once recognized the carriage, and the light springing figure of the young man, his blue coat and swelling stock, and the scar slightly distorting his handsome and eloquent mouth. It was the Englishman who had arrived at the Montanvert inn the night before with a valet, a guide, and such a cargo of books, maps and sketching-materials as threatened to overshadow even Lewis's outfit.

Lewis, at first, had not been greatly drawn to the newcomer, who, seated aloof in the dining-room, seemed not to see his fellow-traveller. The truth was that Lewis was dying for a little conversation. His astonishing experiences were so tightly packed in him (with no outlet save the meagre trickle of his nightly diary) that he felt they would soon melt into the vague blur of other people's travels unless he could give them fresh reality by talking them over. And the stranger with the deep-blue eyes that matched his coat, the scarred cheek and eloquent lip, seemed to Lewis a worthy listener. The Englishman appeared to think otherwise. He preserved an air of moody abstraction, which Lewis's vanity imagined him to have put on as the gods becloud themselves for their secret errands; and the curtness of his goodnight was (Lewis flattered himself) surpassed only by the young New Yorker's.

But today all was different. The stranger advanced affably, raised his hat from his tossed statue-like hair, and enquired with a smile: "Are you by any chance interested in the forms of cirrus clouds?"

His voice was as sweet as his smile, and the two were reinforced by a glance so winning that it made the odd question seem not only pertinent but natural. Lewis, though surprised, was not disconcerted. He merely coloured with the unwonted sense of his ignorance, and replied ingenuously: "I believe, sir, I am interested in everything."

"A noble answer!" cried the other, and held out his hand.

"But I must add," Lewis continued with courageous honesty, "that

I have never as yet had occasion to occupy myself particularly with the forms of cirrus clouds.'

His companion looked at him merrily. "That," said he, "is no reason why you shouldn't begin to do so now!" To which Lewis as merrily agreed. "For in order to be interested in things," the other continued more gravely, "it is only necessary to see them; and I believe I am not wrong in saying that you are one of the privileged beings to whom the seeing eye has been given."

Lewis blushed his agreement, and his interlocutor continued: "You are one of those who have been on the road to Damascus."

"On the road? I've been to the place itself!" the wanderer exclaimed, bursting with the particulars of his travels; and then blushed more deeply at the perception that the other's use of the name had of course been figurative.

The young Englishman's face lit up. "You've been to Damascus—literally been there yourself? But that may be almost as interesting, in its quite different way, as the formation of clouds or lichens. For the present," he continued with a gesture toward the mountain, "I must devote myself to the extremely inadequate rendering of some of these delicate *aiguilles*; a bit of drudgery not likely to interest you in the face of so sublime a scene. But perhaps this evening—if, as I think, we are staying in the same inn—you will give me a few minutes of your society, and tell me something of your travels. My father," he added with his engaging smile, "has had packed with my paintbrushes a few bottles of a wholly trustworthy Madeira; and if you will favour me with your company at dinner. . ."

He signed to his servant to undo the sketching materials, spread his cloak on the rock, and was already lost in his task as Lewis descended to the carriage.

The Madeira proved as trustworthy as his host had promised. Perhaps it was its exceptional quality which threw such a golden lustre over the dinner; unless it were rather the conversation of the blue-eyed Englishman which made Lewis Raycie, always a small drinker, feel that in his company every drop was nectar.

When Lewis joined his host it had been with the secret hope of at last being able to talk; but when the evening was over (and they kept it up to the small hours) he perceived that he had chiefly listened. Yet there had been no sense of suppression, of thwarted volubility; he had been given all the openings he wanted. Only, whenever he produced a little fact it was instantly overflowed by the other's imagination till it burned like a dull pebble tossed into a rushing stream. For whatever Lewis said was seen by his companion from a new angle, and suggested a new train of thought; each commonplace item of experience became a many-faceted crystal flashing with unexpected fires. The young Englishman's mind moved in a world of associations and references far more richly peopled than Lewis's; but his eager communicativeness, his directness of speech and manner, instantly opened its gates to the simpler youth. It was certainly not the Madeira which sped the hours and flooded them with magic; but the magic gave the Madeira—excellent, and reputed of its kind, as Lewis afterward learned—a taste no other vintage was to have for him.

"Oh, but we must meet again in Italy—there are many things there that I could perhaps help you to see," the young Englishman declared as they swore eternal friendship on the stairs of the sleeping inn.

5

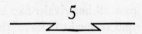

It was in a tiny Venetian church, no more than a chapel, that Lewis Raycie's eyes had been unsealed—in a dull-looking little church not even mentioned in the guide-books. But for his chance encounter with the young Englishman in the shadow of Mont Blanc, Lewis would never have heard of the place; but then what else that was worth knowing would he ever have heard of, he wondered?

He had stood a long time looking at the frescoes, put off at first—he could admit it now—by a certain stiffness in the attitudes of the people, by the childish elaboration of their dress (so different from the noble draperies which Sir Joshua's Discourses on Art had taught him to admire in the great painters), and by the innocent inexpressive look in their young faces—for even the gray-beards seemed young. And then suddenly his gaze had lit on one of these faces in particular: that of a girl with round cheeks, high cheek-bones and widely set eyes under an intricate head-dress of pearl-woven braids. Why, it was Treeshy—Treeshy Kent to the life! And so far from being thought "plain," the young lady was no other than the peerless princess about whom the tale revolved. And what a fairy-land she lived in —full of lithe youths and round-faced pouting maidens, rosy old men and burnished blackamoors, pretty birds and cats and nibbling rabbits—and all involved and enclosed in golden balustrades, in colonnades of pink and blue, laurel-garlands festooned from ivory balconies, and domes and minarets against summer seas! Lewis's imagination lost itself in the scene; he forgot to regret the noble draperies, the exalted sentiments, the fuliginous backgrounds, of the artists he had come to Italy to admire—forgot Sassoferrato, Guido Reni, Carlo Dolce, Lo Spagnoletto, the Carracci, and even the Transfiguration of Raphael, though he knew it to be the greatest picture in the world.

After that he had seen almost everything else that Italian art had to offer; had been to Florence, Naples, Rome; to Bologna to study the Eclectic School, to Parma to examine the Correggios and the Giulio Romanos. But that first vision had laid a magic seed between his lips; the seed that makes you hear what the birds say and the grasses whisper. Even if his English friend had not continued at his side, pointing out, explaining, inspiring, Lewis Raycie flattered himself that the round face of the little Saint Ursula would have led him safely and confidently past all her rivals. She had become his touchstone, his star: how insipid seemed to him all the sheep-faced Virgins draped in red and blue paint after he had looked into her wondering girlish eyes and traced the elaborate pattern of her brocades! He could remember now, quite distinctly, the day when he had given up even Beatrice Cenci . . . and as for that fat naked Magdalen of Carlo Dolce's, lolling over the book she was not reading, and ogling the spectator in the good old way . . . faugh! Saint Ursula did not need to rescue him from *her*. . .

His eyes had been opened to a new world of art. And this world it was his mission to reveal to others—he, the insignificant and ignorant Lewis Raycie, as "but for the grace of God," and that chance encounter on Mont Blanc, he might have gone on being to the end! He shuddered to think of the army of Neapolitan beggar-boys, bituminous monks, whirling prophets, languishing Madonnas and pink-rumped *amorini* who might have been travelling home with him in the hold of the fast new steampacket.

His excitement had something of the apostle's ecstasy. He was not only, in a few hours, to embrace Treeshy, and be reunited to his honoured parents; he was also to go forth and preach the new gospel to them that sat in the darkness of Salvator Rosa and Lo Spagnoletto. . .

The first thing that struck Lewis was the smallness of the house on the Sound, and the largeness of Mr. Raycie.

He had expected to receive the opposite impression. In his recollection the varnished Tuscan villa had retained something of its impressiveness, even when compared to its supposed originals. Perhaps the very contrast between their draughty distances and naked floors, and the expensive carpets and bright fires of High Point, magnified his memory of the latter—there were moments when the thought of its groaning board certainly added to the effect. But the image of Mr. Raycie had meanwhile dwindled. Everything about him, as his son looked back, seemed narrow, juvenile, almost childish. His bluster about Edgar Poe, for instance—true poet still to Lewis, though he had since heard richer notes; his fussy tyranny of his womenkind; his unconscious but total ignorance of most of the things, books, people, ideas, that now filled his son's mind; above all, the arrogance and incompetence of his artistic judgments. Beyond a narrow range of reading—mostly, Lewis suspected, culled in drowsy after-dinner snatches from Knight's "Half-hours with the Best Authors"—Mr. Raycie made no pretence to book-learning; left *that*, as he handsomely said, "to the professors." But on matters of art he was dogmatic and explicit, prepared to justify his opinions by the citing of eminent authorities and of market-prices, and quite clear, as his farewell talk with his son had shown, as to which Old Masters should be privileged to figure in the Raycie collection.

The young man felt no impatience of these judgments. America was a long way from Europe, and it was many years since Mr. Raycie had travelled. He could hardly be blamed for not knowing that the things he admired were no longer admirable, still less for not knowing why. The pictures before which Lewis had knelt in spirit had been virtually undiscovered, even by art-students and critics, in his father's youth. How was an American gentleman, filled with his own self-importance, and paying his courier the highest salary to show him the accredited "Masterpieces"—how was he to guess that whenever he stood rapt before a Sassoferrato or a Carlo Dolce one of those unknown treasures lurked near by under dust and cobwebs?

No; Lewis felt only tolerance and understanding. Such a view was not one to magnify the paternal image; but when the young man entered the study where Mr. Raycie sat immobilized by gout, the swathed leg stretched along his sofa seemed only another reason for indulgence . . .

Perhaps, Lewis thought afterward, it was his father's prone position, the way his great bulk billowed over the sofa, and the lame leg reached out like a mountain-ridge, that made him suddenly seem to fill the room; or else the sound of his voice booming irritably across the threshold, and scattering Mrs. Raycie and the girls with a fierce: "And now, ladies, if the hugging and kissing are over, I should be glad of a moment with my son." But it was odd that, after mother and daughters had withdrawn with all their hoops and flounces, the study seemed to grow even smaller, and Lewis himself to feel more like a David without the pebble.

"Well, my boy," his father cried, crimson and puffing, "here you are at home again, with many adventures to relate, no doubt; and a few masterpieces to show me, as I gather from the drafts on my exchequer."

"Oh, as to the masterpieces, sir, certainly," Lewis simpered, wondering why his voice sounded so fluty, and his smile was produced with such a conscious muscular effort.

"Good—good," Mr. Raycie approved, waving a violet hand which seemed to be ripening for a bandage. "Reedy carried out my orders, I presume? Saw to it that the paintings were deposited with the bulk of your luggage in Canal Street?"

"Oh, yes, sir; Mr. Reedy was on the dock with precise instructions. You know he always carries out your orders," Lewis ventured with a faint irony.

Mr. Raycie stared. "Mr. Reedy," he said, "does what I tell him, if that's what you mean; otherwise he would hardly have been in my employ for over thirty years."

Lewis was silent, and his father examined him critically. "You appear to have filled out; your health is satisfactory? Well . . . well . . . Mr. Robert Huzzard and his daughters are dining here this evening, by the way, and will no doubt be expecting to see the latest French novelties in stocks and waistcoats. Malvina has become a very elegant figure, your sisters tell me." Mr. Raycie chuckled, and Lewis thought: "I *knew* it was the oldest Huzzard girl!" while a slight chill ran down his spine.

"As to the pictures," Mr. Raycie pursued with growing animation, "I am laid low, as you see, by this cursèd affliction, and till the doctors get me up again, here must I lie and try to imagine how your treasures will look in the new gallery. And meanwhile, my dear boy, I need hardly say that no one is to be admitted to see them till they

have been inspected by me and suitably hung. Reedy shall begin
unpacking at once; and when we move to town next month Mrs.
Raycie, God willing, shall give the handsomest evening party New
York has yet seen, to show my son's collection, and perhaps . . . eh,
well? . . . to celebrate another interesting event in his history."

Lewis met this with a faint but respectful gurgle, and before his
blurred eyes rose the wistful face of Treeshy Kent.

"Ah, well, I shall see her tomorrow," he thought, taking heart
again as soon as he was out of his father's presence.

6

Mr. Raycie stood silent for a long time after making the round of
the room in the Canal Street house where the unpacked pictures had
been set out.

He had driven to town alone with Lewis, sternly rebuffing his
daughters' timid hints, and Mrs. Raycie's mute but visible yearning
to accompany him. Though the gout was over he was still weak and
irritable, and Mrs. Raycie, fluttered at the thought of "crossing him,"
had swept the girls away at his first frown.

Lewis's hopes rose as he followed his parent's limping progress.
The pictures, though standing on chairs and tables, and set clumsily
askew to catch the light, bloomed out of the half-dusk of the empty
house with a new and persuasive beauty. Ah, how right he had been
—how inevitable that his father should own it!

Mr. Raycie halted in the middle of the room. He was still silent,
and his face, so quick to frown and glare, wore the calm, almost
expressionless look known to Lewis as the mask of inward perplexity.
"Oh, of course it will take a little time," the son thought, tingling
with the eagerness of youth.

At last, Mr. Raycie woke the echoes by clearing his throat; but
the voice which issued from it was as inexpressive as his face. "It is
singular," he said, "how little the best copies of the Old Masters
resemble the originals. For these *are* Originals?" he questioned, suddenly swinging about on Lewis.

"Oh, absolutely, sir! Besides—" The young man was about to add:
"No one would ever have taken the trouble to copy them"—but
hastily checked himself.

"Besides——?"

"I meant, I had the most competent advice obtainable."

"So I assume; since it was the express condition on which I authorized your purchases."

Lewis felt himself shrinking and his father expanding; but he sent a glance along the wall, and beauty shed her reviving beam on him.

Mr. Raycie's brows projected ominously; but his face remained smooth and dubious. Once more he cast a slow glance about him.

"Let us," he said pleasantly, "begin with the Raphael." And it was evident that he did not know which way to turn.

"Oh, sir, a Raphael nowadays—I warned you it would be far beyond my budget."

Mr. Raycie's face fell slightly. "I had hoped nevertheless . . . for an inferior specimen. . . ." Then, with an effort: "The Sassoferrato, then."

Lewis felt more at his ease; he even ventured a respectful smile. "Sassoferrato is *all* inferior, isn't he? The fact is, he no longer stands . . . quite as he used to. . . ."

Mr. Raycie stood motionless: his eyes were vacuously fixed on the nearest picture.

"Sassoferrato . . . no longer . . . ?"

"Well, sir, *no;* not for a collection of this quality."

Lewis saw that he had at last struck the right note. Something large and uncomfortable appeared to struggle in Mr. Raycie's throat; then he gave a cough which might almost have been said to cast out Sassoferrato.

There was another pause before he pointed with his stick to a small picture representing a snub-nosed young woman with a high forehead and jewelled coif, against a background of delicately interwoven columbines. "Is *that*," he questioned, "your Carlo Dolce? The style is much the same, I see; but it seems to me lacking in his peculiar sentiment."

"Oh, but it's not a Carlo Dolce: it's a Piero della Francesca, sir!" burst in triumph from the trembling Lewis.

His father sternly faced him. "It's a *copy*, you mean? I thought so!"

"No, no; not a copy; it's by a great painter . . . a much greater . . ."

Mr. Raycie had reddened sharply at his mistake. To conceal his natural annoyance he assumed a still more silken manner. "In that case," he said, "I think I should like to see the inferior painters first. Where *is* the Carlo Dolce?"

"There *is* no Carlo Dolce," said Lewis, white to the lips.

The young man's next distinct recollection was of standing, he knew not how long afterward, before the armchair in which his father had sunk down, almost as white and shaken as himself.

"This," stammered Mr. Raycie, "this is going to bring back my gout. . . . " But when Lewis entreated: "Oh, sir, do let us drive back quietly to the country, and give me a chance later to explain . . . to put my case" . . . the old gentleman had struck through the pleading with a furious wave of his stick.

"Explain later? Put your case later? It's just what I insist upon your doing here and now!" And Mr. Raycie added hoarsely, and as if in actual physical anguish: "I understand that young John Huzzard returned from Rome last week with a Raphael."

After that, Lewis heard himself—as if with the icy detachment of a spectator—marshalling his arguments, pleading the cause he hoped his pictures would have pleaded for him, dethroning the old Powers and Principalities, and setting up these new names in their place. It was first of all the names that stuck in Mr. Raycie's throat: after spending a life-time in committing to memory the correct pronunciation of words like Lo Spagnoletto and Giulio Romano, it was bad enough, his wrathful eyes seemed to say, to have to begin a new set of verbal gymnastics before you could be sure of saying to a friend with careless accuracy: "And *this* is my Giotto da Bondone."

But that was only the first shock, soon forgotten in the rush of greater tribulation. For one might conceivably learn how to pronounce Giotto da Bondone, and even enjoy doing so, provided the friend in question recognized the name and bowed to its authority. But to have your effort received by a blank stare, and the playful request: "You'll have to say that over again, please"—to know that, in going the round of the gallery (the Raycie Gallery!) the same stare and the same request were likely to be repeated before each picture; the bitterness of this was so great that Mr. Raycie, without exaggeration, might have likened his case to that of Agag.

"God! God! God! Carpatcher, you say this other fellow's called? Kept him back till the last because it's the gem of the collection, did you? Carpatcher—well, he'd have done better to stick to his trade. Something to do with those new European steam-cars, I suppose, eh?" Mr. Raycie was so incensed that his irony was less subtle than usual. "And Angelico you say did that kind of Noah's Ark soldier in pink armour on gold-leaf? Well, *there* I've caught you tripping, my boy. Not Angelico, Angelic*a*; Angelica Kauffman was a lady. And the damned swindler who foisted that barbarous daub on you as a picture of hers deserves to be drawn and quartered—and shall be, sir, by God, if the law can reach him! He shall disgorge every penny he's rooked you out of, or my name's not Halston Raycie! A bargain . . . you say the thing was a *bargain*? Why, the price of a clean postage stamp would be too dear for it! God—my son; do you realize you had a *trust* to carry out?"

"Yes, sir, yes; and it's just because—"

"You might have written; you might at least have placed your views before me . . ."

How could Lewis say: "If I had, I knew you'd have refused to let me buy the pictures?" He could only stammer: "I *did* allude to the revolution in taste . . . new names coming up . . . you may remember . . . "

"Revolution! New names! Who says so? I had a letter last week from the London dealers to whom I especially recommended you, telling me that an undoubted Guido Reni was coming into the market this summer."

"Oh, the dealers—*they* don't know!"

"The dealers . . . don't? . . . Who does . . . except yourself?" Mr. Raycie pronounced in a white sneer.

Lewis, as white, still held his ground. "I wrote you, sir, about my friends; in Italy, and afterward in England."

"Well, God damn it, I never heard of one of *their* names before, either; no more'n of these painters of yours here. I supplied you with the names of all the advisers you needed, and all the painters, too; I all but made the collection for you myself, before you started. . . . I was explicit enough, in all conscience, wasn't I?"

Lewis smiled faintly. "That's what I hoped the pictures would be . . . "

"What? Be what? What'd you mean?"

"Be explicit . . . Speak for themselves . . . make you see that their painters are already superseding some of the better-known . . ."

Mr. Raycie gave an awful laugh. "They are, are they?" In whose estimation? Your friends', I suppose. What's the name, again, of that fellow you met in Italy, who picked 'em out for you?"

"Ruskin—John Ruskin," said Lewis.

Mr. Raycie's laugh, prolonged, gathered up into itself a fresh shower of expletives. "Ruskin—Ruskin—just plain John Ruskin, eh? And who *is* this great John Ruskin, who sets God A'mighty right in his judgments? Who'd you say John Ruskin's father was, now?"

"A respected wine-merchant in London, sir."

Mr. Raycie ceased to laugh: he looked at his son with an expression of unutterable disgust.

"Retail?"

"I . . . believe so . . ."

"Faugh!" said Mr. Raycie.

"It wasn't only Ruskin, father. . . . I told you of those other friends in London, whom I met on the way home. They inspected the pictures, and all of them agreed that . . . that the collection would some day be very valuable."

"*Some day*—did they give you a date . . . the month and the year? Ah, those other friends; yes. You said there was a Mr. Brown and a Mr. Hunt and a Mr. Rossiter, was it? Well, I never heard of any of those names, either—except perhaps in a trades' directory."

"It's not Rossiter, father: Dante Rossetti."

"Excuse me: Rossetti. And what does Mr. Dante Rossetti's father do? Sell macaroni, I presume?"

Lewis was silent, and Mr. Raycie went on, speaking now with a deadly steadiness: "The friends I sent you to were judges of art, sir; men who know what a picture's worth; not one of 'em but could pick out a genuine Raphael. Couldn't you find 'em when you got to England? Or hadn't they the time to spare for you? You'd better not," Mr. Raycie added, "tell me *that*, for I know how they'd have received your father's son."

"Oh, most kindly . . . they did indeed, sir . . ."

"Ay; but that didn't suit you. You didn't *want* to be advised. You wanted to show off before a lot of ignoramuses like yourself. You wanted—how'd I know what you wanted? It's as if I'd never given you an instruction or laid a charge on you! And the money—God! Where'd it go to? Buying *this*? Nonsense—." Mr. Raycie raised himself heavily on his stick and fixed his angry eyes on his son. "Own up, Lewis; tell me they got it out of you at cards. Professional gamblers the lot, I make no doubt; your Ruskin and your Brown and your Rossiter. Make a business to pick up young American greenhorns on their travels, I daresay. . . No? Not that, you say? Then—women? . . . God A'mighty, Lewis," gasped Mr. Raycie, tottering toward his son with outstretched stick, "I'm no bluenosed Puritan, sir, and I'd a damn sight rather you told me you'd spent it on a woman, every penny of it, than let yourself be fleeced like a simpleton, buying these things that look more like cuts out o' Foxe's Book of Martyrs than Originals of the Old Masters for a Gentleman's

Gallery. . . Youth's youth. . . Gad, sir, I've been young myself . . . a fellow's got to go through his apprenticeship. . . Own up now: women?"

"Oh, not women——"

"Not even!" Mr. Raycie groaned. "All in pictures, then? Well, say no more to me now. . . I'll get home, I'll get home. . ." He cast a last apoplectic glance about the room. "The Raycie Gallery! That pack of bones and mummers' finery! . . . Why, let alone the rest, there's not a full-bodied female among 'em. . . Do you know what those Madonnas of yours are like, my son? Why, there ain't one of 'em that don't remind me of a bad likeness of poor Treeshy Kent. . . I should say you'd hired half the sign-painters of Europe to do her portrait for you—if I could imagine your wanting it. . . No, sir! I don't need your arm," Mr. Raycie snarled, heaving his great bulk painfully across the hall. He withered Lewis with a last look from the doorstep. "And to buy *that* you overdrew your account?—No, I'll drive home alone."

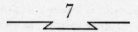

7

Mr. Raycie did not die till nearly a year later; but New York agreed it was the affair of the pictures that had killed him.

The day after his first and only sight of them he sent for his lawyer, and it became known that he had made a new will. Then he took to his bed with a return of the gout, and grew so rapidly worse that it was thought "only proper" to postpone the party Mrs. Raycie was to have given that autumn to inaugurate the gallery. This enabled the family to pass over in silence the question of the works of art themselves; but outside of the Raycie house, where they were never mentioned, they formed, that winter, a frequent and fruitful topic of discussion.

Only two persons besides Mr. Raycie were known to have seen them. One was Mr. Donaldson Kent, who owed the privilege to the fact of having once been to Italy; the other, Mr. Reedy, the agent, who had unpacked the pictures. Mr. Reedy, beset by Raycie cousins and old family friends, had replied with genuine humility: "Why, the truth is, I never was taught to see any difference between one picture and another, except as regards the size of them; and these struck me as smallish . . . on the small side, I would say. . ."

Mr. Kent was known to have unbosomed himself to Mr. Raycie with considerable frankness—he went so far, it was rumored, as to declare that he had never seen any pictures in Italy like those brought back by Lewis, and begged to doubt if they really came from there. But in public he maintained that noncommittal attitude which passed for prudence, but proceeded only from timidity; no one ever got anything from him but the guarded statement: "The subjects are wholly inoffensive."

It was believed that Mr. Raycie dared not consult the Huzzards. Young John Huzzard had just brought home a Raphael; it would have been hard not to avoid comparisons which would have been too galling. Neither to them, nor to any one else, did Mr. Raycie ever again allude to the Raycie Gallery. But when his will was opened it was found that he had bequeathed the pictures to his son. The rest of his property was left absolutely to his two daughters. The bulk of the estate was Mrs. Raycie's; but it was known that Mrs. Raycie had had her instructions, and among them, perhaps, was the order to fade away in her turn after six months of widowhood. When she had been laid beside her husband in Trinity churchyard her will (made in the same week as Mr. Raycie's, and obviously at his dictation) was found to allow five thousand dollars a year to Lewis during his life-time; the residue of the fortune, which Mr. Raycie's thrift and good management had made into one of the largest in New York, was divided between the daughters. Of these, the one promptly married a Kent and the other a Huzzard; and the latter, Sarah Anne (who had never been Lewis's favourite), was wont to say in later years: "Oh, no, I never grudged my poor brother those funny old pictures. You see, we have a Raphael."

The house stood on the corner of Third Avenue and Tenth Street. It had lately come to Lewis Raycie as his share in the property of a distant cousin, who had made an "old New York will" under which all his kin benefited in proportion to their consanguinity. The neighbourhood was unfashionable, and the house in bad repair; but Mr. and Mrs. Lewis Raycie, who, since their marriage, had been living in retirement at Tarrytown, immediately moved into it.

Their arrival excited small attention. Within a year of his father's death, Lewis had married Treeshy Kent. The alliance had not been encouraged by Mr. and Mrs. Kent, who went so far as to say that their niece might have done better; but as that one of their sons who was still unmarried had always shown a lively sympathy for Treeshy, they yielded to the prudent thought, that, after all, it was better than having her entangle Bill.

The Lewis Raycies had been four years married, and during that time had dropped out of the memory of New York as completely as if their exile had covered half a century. Neither of them had ever cut a great figure there. Treeshy had been nothing but the Kents' Cinderella, and Lewis's ephemeral importance, as heir to the Raycie millions, had been effaced by the painful episode which resulted in his being deprived of them.

So secluded was their way of living, and so much had it come to be a habit, that when Lewis announced that he had inherited Uncle Ebenezers' house his wife hardly looked up from the baby-blanket she was embroidering.

"Uncle Ebenezer's house in New York?"

He drew a deep breath. "Now I shall be able to show the pictures."

"Oh, Lewis—" She dropped the blanket. "Are we going to live there?"

"Certainly. But the house is so large that I shall turn the two corner rooms on the ground floor into a gallery. They are very suitably lighted. It was there that Cousin Ebenezer was laid out."

"Oh, Lewis——"

If anything could have made Lewis Raycie believe in his own strength of will it was his wife's attitude. Merely to hear that unquestioning murmur of submission was to feel something of his father's tyrannous strength arise in him; but with the wish to use it more humanely.

"You'll like that, Treeshy? It's been dull for you here, I know."

She flushed up. "Dull? With you, darling? Besides, I like the country. But I shall like Tenth Street too. Only—you said there were repairs?"

He nodded sternly. "I shall borrow money to make them. If necessary—" he lowered his voice—"I shall mortgage the pictures."

He saw her eyes fill. "Oh, but it won't be! There are so many ways still in which I can economize."

He laid his hand on hers and turned his profile toward her, because he knew it was so much stronger than his full face. He did not feel sure that she quite grasped his intention about the pictures; was not even certain that he wished her to. He went in to New York every week now, occupying himself mysteriously and importantly with plans, specifications and other business transactions with long names; while Treeshy, through the hot summer months, sat in Tarry-town and waited for the baby.

A little girl was born at the end of the summer and christened Louisa; and when she was a few weeks old the Lewis Raycies left the country for New York.

"*Now!*" thought Lewis, as they bumped over the cobblestones of Tenth Street in the direction of Cousin Ebenezer's house.

The carriage stopped, he handed out his wife, the nurse followed with the baby, and they all stood and looked up at the house-front.

"Oh, Lewis—" Treeshy gasped; and even little Louisa set up a sympathetic wail.

Over the door—over Cousin Ebenezer's respectable, conservative and intensely private front-door—hung a large signboard bearing, in gold letters on a black ground, the inscription:

GALLERY OF CHRISTIAN ART
OPEN ON WEEK-DAYS FROM 2 TO 4
ADMISSION 25 CENTS.   CHILDREN 10 CENTS

Lewis saw his wife turn pale, and pressed her arm in his. "Believe me, it's the only way to make the pictures known. And they *must* be made known," he said with a thrill of his old ardour.

"Yes, dear, of course. But . . . to every one? Publicly?"

"If we showed them only to our friends, of what use would it be? Their opinion is already formed."

She sighed her acknowledgment. "But the . . . the entrance fee . . ."

"If we can afford it later, the gallery will be free. But mean-while——"

"Oh, Lewis, I quite understand!" And clinging to him, the still-protesting baby in her wake, she passed with a dauntless step under the awful signboard.

"At last I shall see the pictures properly lighted!" she exclaimed, and turned in the hall to fling her arms about her husband.

"It's all they need . . . to be appreciated," he answered, aglow with her encouragement.

Since his withdrawal from the world it had been a part of Lewis's system never to read the daily papers. His wife eagerly conformed to his example, and they lived in a little air-tight circle of aloofness, as if the cottage at Tarrytown had been situated in another and happier planet.

Lewis, nevertheless, the day after the opening of the Gallery of Christian Art, deemed it his duty to derogate from this attitude, and sallied forth secretly to buy the principal journals. When he re-entered his house he went straight up to the nursery where he knew that, at that hour, Treeshy would be giving the little girl her bath. But it was later than he supposed. The rite was over, the baby lay asleep in its modest cot, and the mother sat crouched by the fire, her face hidden in her hands. Lewis instantly guessed that she too had seen the papers.

"Treeshy—you mustn't . . . consider this of any consequence. . . ," he stammered.

She lifted a tear-stained face. "Oh, my darling! I thought you never read the papers."

"Not usually. But I thought it my duty——"

"Yes; I see. But, as you say, what earthly consequence——?"

"None whatever; we must just be patient and persist."

She hesitated, and then, her arms about him, her head on his breast: "Only, dearest, I've been counting up again, ever so carefully; and even if we give up fires everywhere but in the nursery, I'm afraid the wages of the door-keeper and the guardian . . . especially if the gallery's open to the public every day . . ."

"I've thought of that already, too; and I myself shall hereafter act as door-keeper and guardian."

He kept his eyes on hers as he spoke. "This is the test," he thought. Her face paled under its brown glow, and the eyes dilated in her effort to check her tears. Then she said gaily: "That will be . . . very interesting, won't it, Lewis? Hearing what the people say. . . Because, as they begin to know the pictures better, and to understand them, they can't fail to say very interesting things . . . can they?" She turned and caught up the sleeping Louisa. "Can they . . . oh, you darling—darling?"

Lewis turned away too. Not another woman in New York would have been capable of that. He could hear all the town echoing with this new scandal of his showing the pictures himself—and she, so much more sensitive to ridicule, so much less carried away by apostolic ardour, how much louder must that mocking echo ring in her ears! But his pang was only momentary. The one thought that possessed him for any length of time was that of vindicating himself by making the pictures known; he could no longer fix his attention on lesser matters. The derision of illiterate journalists was not a thing to wince at; once let the pictures be seen by educated and intelligent people, and they would speak for themselves—especially if he were at hand to interpret them.

8

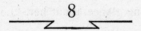

For a week or two a great many people came to the gallery; but, even with Lewis as interpreter, the pictures failed to make themselves heard. During the first days, indeed, owing to the unprecedented idea of holding a paying exhibition in a private house, and to the mockery of the newspapers, the Gallery of Christian Art was thronged with noisy curiosity-seekers; once the astonished metropolitan police had to be invited in to calm their comments and control their movements. But the name of "Christian Art" soon chilled this class of sightseer, and before long they were replaced by a dumb and respectable throng, who roamed vacantly through the rooms and out again, grumbling that it wasn't worth the money. Then these too diminished; and once the tide had turned, the ebb was rapid. Every day from two to four Lewis still sat shivering among his treasures, or patiently measured the length of the deserted gallery: as long as there was a chance of any one coming he would not admit that he was beaten. For the next visitor might always be the one who understood.

One snowy February day he had thus paced the rooms in unbroken solitude for above an hour when carriage-wheels stopped at the door. He hastened to open it, and in a great noise of silks his sister Sarah Anne Huzzard entered.

Lewis felt for a moment as he used to under his father's glance. Marriage and millions had given the moon-faced Sarah something of the Raycie awfulness; but her brother looked into her empty eyes, and his own kept their level.

"Well, Lewis," said Mrs. Huzzard with a simpering sternness, and caught her breath.

"Well, Sarah Anne—I'm happy that you've come to take a look at my pictures."

"I've come to see you and your wife." She gave another nervous gasp, shook out her flounces, and added in a rush: "And to ask you how much longer this . . . this spectacle is to continue. . . ."

"The exhibition?" Lewis smiled. She signed a flushed assent.

"Well, there has been a considerable falling-off lately in the number of visitors——"

"Thank heaven!" she interjected.

"But as long as I feel that any one wishes to come . . . I shall be here . . . to open the door, as you see."

She sent a shuddering glance about her. "Lewis—I wonder if you realize . . . ?"

"Oh, fully."

"Then *why* do you go on? Isn't it enough—aren't you satisfied?"

"With the effect they have produced?"

"With the effect *you* have produced—on your family and on the whole of New York. With the slur on poor Papa's memory."

"Papa left me the pictures, Sarah Anne."

"Yes. But not to make yourself a mountebank about them."

Lewis considered this impartially. "Are you sure? Perhaps, on the contrary, he did it for that very reason."

"Oh, don't heap more insults on our father's memory! Things are bad enough without that. How your wife can allow it I can't see. Do you ever consider the humiliation to *her*?"

Lewis gave another dry smile. "She's used to being humiliated. The Kents accustomed her to that."

Sarah Anne reddened. "I don't know why I should stay to be spoken to in this way. But I came with my husband's approval."

"Do you need that to come and see your brother?"

"I need it to—to make the offer I am about to make; and which he authorizes."

Lewis looked at her in surprise, and she purpled up to the lace ruffles inside her satin bonnet.

"Have you come to make an offer for my collection?" he asked her, humorously.

"You seem to take pleasure in insinuating preposterous things. But anything is better than this public slight on our name." Again she ran a shuddering glance over the pictures. "John and I," she announced, "are prepared to double the allowance mother left you on condition that this . . . this ends . . . for good. That that horrible sign is taken down tonight."

Lewis seemed mildly to weigh the proposal. "Thank you very much, Sarah Anne," he said at length. "I'm touched . . . touched and . . . and surprised . . . that you and John should have made this offer. But perhaps, before I decline it, you will accept *mine*: simply to show you my pictures. When once you've looked at them I think you'll understand——"

Mrs. Huzzard drew back hastily, her air of majesty collapsing. "Look at the pictures? Oh, thank you . . . but I can see them very well from here. And besides, I don't pretend to be a judge . . ."

"Then come up and see Treeshy and the baby," said Lewis quietly.

She stared at him, embarrassed. "Oh, thank you," she stammered again; and as she prepared to follow him: "Then it's *no*, really no, Lewis? Do consider, my dear! You say yourself that hardly any one comes. What harm can there be in closing the place?"

"What—when tomorrow the man may come who understands?"

Mrs. Huzzard tossed her plumes despairingly and followed him in silence.

"What—Mary Adeline?" she exclaimed, pausing abruptly on the threshold of the nursery. Treeshy, as usual, sat holding her baby by the fire; and from a low seat opposite her rose a lady as richly furred and feathered as Mrs. Huzzard, but with far less as-surance to carry off her furbelows. Mrs. Kent ran to Lewis and laid her plump cheek against his, while Treeshy greeted Sarah Anne.

"I had no idea you were here, Mary Adeline," Mrs. Huzzard murmured. It was clear that she had not imparted her philanthropic project to her sister, and was disturbed at the idea that Lewis might be about to do so. "I just dropped in for a minute," she continued, "to see that darling little pet of an angel child—" and she enveloped the astonished baby in her ample rustlings and flutterings.

"I'm very glad to see you here, Sarah Anne," Mary Adeline answered with simplicity.

"Ah, it's not for want of wishing that I haven't come before! Treeshy knows that, I hope. But the cares of a household like mine . . ."

"Yes; and it's been so difficult to get about in the bad weather," Treeshy suggested sympathetically.

Mrs. Huzzard lifted the Raycie eyebrows. "Has it really? With two pairs of horses one hardly notices the weather. . . Oh, the pretty, pretty, *pretty* baby! . . . Mary Adeline," Sarah Anne continued, turning severely to her sister, "I shall be happy to offer you a seat in my carriage if you're thinking of leaving."

But Mary Adeline was a married woman too. She raised her mild head and her glance crossed her sister's quietly. "My own carriage is at the door, thank you kindly, Sarah Anne," she said; and the baffled Sarah Anne withdrew on Lewis's arm. But a moment later the old habit of subordination reasserted itself. Mary Adeline's gentle countenance grew as timorous as a child's, and she gathered up her cloak in haste.

"Perhaps I was too quick. . . I'm sure she meant it kindly," she exclaimed, overtaking Lewis as he turned to come up the stairs; and with a smile he stood watching his two sisters drive off together in the Huzzard coach.

He returned to the nursery, where Treeshy was still crooning over her daughter.

"Well, my dear," he said, "what do you suppose Sarah Anne came for?" And, in reply to her wondering gaze: "To buy me off from showing the pictures!"

His wife's indignation took just the form he could have wished. She simply went on with her rich cooing laugh and hugged the baby tighter. But Lewis felt the perverse desire to lay a still greater strain upon her loyalty.

"Offered to double my allowance, she and John, if only I'll take down the sign!"

"No one shall touch the sign!" Treeshy flamed.

"Not till I do," said her husband grimly.

She turned about and scanned him with anxious eyes. "Lewis . . . *you?*"

"Oh, my dear . . . they're right. . . It can't go on forever . . ." He went up to her, and put his arm about her and the child. "You've been braver than an army of heroes; but it won't do. The expenses have been a good deal heavier than I was led to expect. And I . . . I can't raise a mortgage on the pictures. Nobody will touch them."

She met this quickly. "No; I know. That was what Mary Adeline came about."

The blood rushed angrily to Lewis's temples. "Mary Adeline— how the devil did *she* hear of it?"

"Through Mr. Reedy, I suppose. But you must not be angry. She was kindness itself: she doesn't want you to close the gallery, Lewis . . . that is, not as long as you really continue to believe in it. . . She and Donald Kent will lend us enough to go on with for a year longer. That is what she came to say."

For the first time since the struggle had begun, Lewis Raycie's throat was choked with tears. His faithful Mary Adeline! He had a sudden vision of her, stealing out of the house at High Point before daylight to carry a basket of scraps to the poor Mrs. Edgar Poe who was dying of a decline down the lane. . . He laughed aloud in his joy.

"Dear old Mary Adeline! How magnificent of her! Enough to give me a whole year more . . ." He pressed his wet cheek against his wife's in a long silence. "Well, dear," he said at length, "it's for you to say—do we accept?"

He held her off, questioningly, at arm's length, and her wan little smile met his own and mingled with it.

"Of course we accept!"

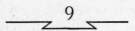

9

Of the Raycie family, which prevailed so powerfully in the New York of the 'forties, only one of the names survived in my boyhood, half a century later. Like so many of the descendants of the proud little Colonial society, the Raycies had totally vanished, forgotten by everyone but a few old ladies, one or two genealogists and the sexton of Trinity Church, who kept the record of their graves.

The Raycie blood was of course still to be traced in various allied families: Kents, Huzzards, Cosbys and many others, proud to claim cousinship with a "Signer," but already indifferent or incurious as to the fate of his progeny. These old New Yorkers, who lived so well and spent their money so liberally, vanished like a pinch of dust when they disappeared from their pews and their dinner-tables.

If I happen to have been familiar with the name since my youth, it is chiefly because its one survivor was a distant cousin of my mother's, whom she sometimes took me to see on days when she thought I was likely to be good because I had been promised a treat for the morrow.

Old Miss Alethea Raycie lived in a house I had always heard spoken of as "Cousin Ebenezer's." It had evidently, in its day, been an admired specimen of domestic architecture; but was now regarded as the hideous though venerable relic of a bygone age. Miss Raycie, being crippled by rheumatism, sat above stairs in a large cold room, meagerly furnished with beadwork tables, rosewood étagères and portraits of pale sad-looking people in odd clothes. She herself was large and saturnine, with a battlemented black lace

cap, and so deaf that she seemed a survival of forgotten days, a
Rosetta Stone to which the clue was lost. Even to my mother, nursed
in that vanished tradition, and knowing instinctively to whom Miss
Raycie alluded when she spoke of Mary Adeline, Sarah Anne or
Uncle Doctor, intercourse with her was difficult and languishing,
and my juvenile interruptions were oftener encouraged than re-
proved.

In the course of one of these visits my eye, listlessly roaming,
singled out among the pallid portraits a three-crayon drawing of a
little girl with a large forehead and dark eyes, dressed in a plaid
frock and embroidered pantalettes, and sitting on a grass-bank. I
pulled my mother's sleeve to ask who she was, and my mother answered: "Ah, that was poor little Louisa Raycie, who died of a
decline. How old was little Louisa when she died, Cousin Alethea?"

To batter this simple question into Cousin Alethea's brain was the
affair of ten laborious minutes; and when the job was done, and Miss
Raycie, with an air of mysterious displeasure, had dropped a deep
"Eleven," my mother was too exhausted to continue. So she turned
to me to add, with one of the private smiles we kept for each other:
"It was the poor child who would have inherited the Raycie Gallery."
But to a little boy of my age this item of information lacked interest,
nor did I understand my mother's surreptitious amusement.

This far-off scene suddenly came back to me last year, when, on
one of my infrequent visits to New York, I went to dine with my
old friend, the banker, John Selwyn, and came to an astonished stand
before the mantelpiece in his new library.

"Hallo!" I said, looking up at the picture above the chimney.

My host squared his shoulders, thrust his hands into his pockets,
and affected the air of modesty which people think it proper to
assume when their possessions are admired. "The Macrino d'Alba?
Y—yes . . . it was the only thing I managed to capture out of the
Raycie collection."

"The only thing? Well——"

"Ah, but you should have seen the Mantegna; *and* the Giotto;
and the Piero della Francesca—hang it, one of the most beautiful
Piero della Francescas in the world. . . A girl in profile, with her hair
in a pearl net, against a background of columbines; *that* went back
to Europe—the National Gallery, I believe. And the Carpaccio, the
most exquisite little St. George . . . that went to California . . .
Lord!" He sat down with the sigh of a hungry man turned away

from a groaning board. "Well, it nearly broke me buying *this*!" he murmured, as if at least that fact were some consolation.

I was turning over my early memories in quest of a clue to what he spoke of as the Raycie collection, in a tone which implied that he was alluding to objects familiar to all art-lovers.

Suddenly: "They weren't poor little Louisa's pictures, by any chance?" I asked, remembering my mother's cryptic smile.

Selwyn looked at me perplexedly. "Who the deuce is poor little Louisa?" And, without waiting for my answer, he went on: "They were that fool Netta Cosby's until a year ago—and she never even knew it."

We looked at each other interrogatively, my friend perplexed at my ignorance, and I now absorbed in trying to run down the genealogy of Netta Cosby. I did so finally. "Netta Cosby—you don't mean Netta Kent, the one who married Jim Cosby?"

"That's it. They were cousins of the Raycies', and she inherited the pictures."

I continued to ponder. "I wanted awfully to marry her, the year I left Harvard," I said presently, more to myself than to my hearer.

"Well, if you had you'd have annexed a prize fool; *and* one of the most beautiful collections of Italian Primitives in the world."

"In the world?"

"Well—you wait till you see them; if you haven't already. And I seem to make out that you haven't—that you can't have. How long have you been in Japan? Four years? I thought so. Well, it was only last winter that Netta found out."

"Found out what?"

"What there was in old Alethea Raycie's attic. You must remember the old Miss Raycie who lived in that hideous house in Tenth Street when we were children. She was a cousin of your mother's, wasn't she? Well, the old fool lived there for nearly half a century, with five millions' worth of pictures shut up in the attic over her head. It seems they'd been there ever since the death of a poor young Raycie who collected them in Italy years and years ago. I don't know much about the story; I never was strong on genealogy, and the Raycies have always been rather dim to me. They were everybody's cousins, of course; but as far as one can make out that seems to have been their principal if not their only function. Oh— and I suppose the Raycie Building was called after them; only *they* didn't build it!

"But there was this one young fellow—I wish I could find out more about him. All that Netta seems to know (or to care, for that matter) is that when he was very young—barely out of college— he was sent to Italy by his father to buy Old Masters—in the 'forties, it must have been—and came back with this extraordinary, this unbelievable collection . . . a boy of that age! . . . and was disinherited by the old gentleman for bringing home such rubbish. The young fellow and his wife died ever so many years ago, both of them. It seems he was so laughed at for buying such pictures that they went away and lived like hermits in the depths of the country. There were some funny spectral portraits of them that old Alethea had up in her bedroom. Netta showed me one of them that last time I went to see her: a pathetic drawing of the only child, an anæmic little girl with a big forehead. Jove, but that must have been your little Louisa!"

I nodded. "In a plaid frock and embroidered pantalettes?"

"Yes, something of the sort. Well, when Louisa and her parents died, I suppose the pictures went to old Miss Raycie. At any rate, at some time or other—and it must have been longer ago than you or I can remember—the old lady inherited them with the Tenth Street house; and when *she* died, three or four years ago, her relations found she'd never even been upstairs to look at them."

"Well——?"

"Well, she died intestate, and Netta Kent—Netta Cosby—turned out to be the next of kin. There wasn't much to be got out of the estate (or so they thought) and, as the Cosbys are always hard up, the house in Tenth Street had to be sold, and the pictures were very nearly sent off to the auction room with all the rest of the stuff. But nobody supposed they would bring anything, and the auctioneer said that if you tried to sell pictures with carpets and bedding and kitchen furniture it always depreciated the whole thing; and so, as the Cosbys had some bare walls to cover, they sent for the lot—there were about thirty—and decided to have them cleaned and hang them up. 'After all,' Netta said, 'as well as I can make out through the cobwebs, some of them look like rather jolly copies of early Italian things.' But as she was short of cash she decided to clean them at home instead of sending them to an expert; and one day, while she was operating on this very one before you, with her sleeves rolled up, the man called who always *does* call on such occasions; the man who knows. In the given case, it was a quiet fellow connected with the Louvre, who'd brought her a letter from Paris, and whom she'd invited to one of her stupid dinners. He was announced, and she thought it would be a joke to let him see what she was doing; she has pretty arms, you may remember. So he was asked into the dining-room, where he found her with a pail of hot water and soap-suds, and *this* laid out on the table; and the first thing he did was to grab her pretty arm so tight that it was black and blue, while he shouted out: 'God in heaven! Not *hot* water!'"

My friend leaned back with a sigh of mingled resentment and satisfaction, and we sat silently looking up at the lovely "Adoration" above the mantelpiece.

"That's how I got it a little cheaper—most of the old varnish was gone for good. But luckily for her it was the first picture she had attacked; and as for the others—you must see them, that's all I can say. . . . Wait; I've got the catalogue somewhere about . . ."

He began to rummage for it, and I asked, remembering how nearly I had married Netta Kent: "Do you mean to say she didn't keep a single one of them?"

"Oh, yes—in the shape of pearls and Rolls-Royces. And you've seen their new house in Fifth Avenue?" He ended with a grin of irony: "The best of the joke is that Jim was just thinking of divorcing her when the pictures were discovered."

"Poor little Louisa!" I sighed.

The Great Gatsby

1 9 2 5

F. SCOTT FITZGERALD

The Great Gatsby

I

IN MY younger and more vulnerable years my father gave me some advice that I've been turning over in my mind ever since. "Whenever you feel like criticising any one," he told me, "just remember that all the people in this world haven't had the advantages that you've had."

He didn't say any more, but we've always been unusually communicative in a reserved way, and I understood that he meant a great deal more than that. In consequence, I'm inclined to reserve all judgments, a habit that has opened up many curious natures to me and also made me the victim of not a few veteran bores. The abnormal mind is quick to detect and attach itself to this quality when it appears in a normal person, and so it came about that in college I was unjustly accused of being a politician, because I was privy to the secret griefs of wild, unknown men. Most of the confidences were unsought—frequently I have feigned sleep, preoccupation, or a hostile levity when I realized by some unmistakable sign that an intimate revelation was quivering on the horizon; for the intimate revelations of young men, or at least the terms in which they express them, are usually plagiaristic and marred by obvious suppressions. Reserving judgments is a matter of infinite hope. I am still a little afraid of missing something if I forget that, as my father snobbishly suggested, and I snobbishly repeat, a sense of the fundamental decencies is parcelled out unequally at birth.

And, after boasting this way of my tolerance, I come to the admission that it has a limit. Conduct may be founded on the hard rock or the wet marshes, but after a certain point I don't care what it's founded on. When I came back from the East last autumn I felt that I wanted the world to be in uniform and at a sort of moral attention forever; I wanted no more riotous excursions with privileged glimpses into the human heart. Only Gatsby, the man who gives his name to this book, was exempt from my reaction—Gatsby, who represented everything for which I have an unaffected scorn.

If personality is an unbroken series of successful gestures, then there was something gorgeous about him, some heightened sensitivity to the promises of life, as if he were related to one of those intricate machines that register earthquakes ten thousand miles away. This responsiveness had nothing to do with that flabby impressionability which is dignified under the name of the "creative temperament"— it was an extraordinary gift for hope, a romantic readiness such as I have never found in any other person and which it is not likely I shall ever find again. No—Gatsby turned out all right at the end; it is what preyed on Gatsby, what foul dust floated in the wake of his dreams that temporarily closed out my interest in the abortive sorrows and short-winded elations of men.

My family have been prominent, well-to-do people in this Middle Western city for three generations. The Carraways are something of a clan, and we have a tradition that we're descended from the Dukes of Buccleuch, but the actual founder of my line was my grandfather's brother, who came here in fifty-one, sent a substitute to the Civil War, and started the wholesale hardware business that my father carries on to-day.

I never saw this great-uncle, but I'm supposed to look like him— with special reference to the rather hard-boiled painting that hangs in father's office. I graduated from New Haven in 1915, just a quarter of a century after my father, and a little later I participated in that delayed Teutonic migration known as the Great War. I enjoyed the counter-raid so thoroughly that I came back restless. Instead of being the warm centre of the world, the Middle West now seemed like the ragged edge of the universe—so I decided to go East and learn the bond business. Everybody I knew was in the bond business, so I supposed it could support one more single man. All my aunts and uncles talked it over as if they were choosing a prep school for me, and finally said, "Why—ye-es," with very grave, hesitant faces. Father agreed to finance me for a year, and after various delays I came East, permanently, I thought, in the spring of twenty-two.

The practical thing was to find rooms in the city, but it was a warm season, and I had just left a country of wide lawns and friendly trees, so when a young man at the office suggested that we take a house together in a commuting town, it sounded like a great idea. He found the house, a weatherbeaten cardboard bungalow at eighty a month, but at the last minute the firm ordered him to Washington, and I went out to the country alone. I had a dog—at least I had him for a few days until he ran away—and an old Dodge and a Finnish woman, who made my bed and cooked breakfast and muttered Finnish wisdom to herself over the electric stove.

It was lonely for a day or so until one morning some man, more recently arrived than I, stopped me on the road.

"How do you get to West Egg village?" he asked helplessly.

I told him. And as I walked on I was lonely no longer. I was a guide, a pathfinder, an original settler. He had casually conferred on me the freedom of the neighborhood.

And so with the sunshine and the great bursts of leaves growing on the trees, just as things grow in fast movies, I had that familiar conviction that life was beginning over again with the summer.

There was so much to read, for one thing, and so much fine health to be pulled down out of the young breath-giving air. I bought a dozen volumes on banking and credit and investment securities, and they stood on my shelf in red and gold like new money from the mint, promising to unfold the shining secrets that only Midas and Morgan and Mæcenas knew. And I had the high intention of reading many other books besides. I was rather literary in college— one year I wrote a series of very solemn and obvious editorials for the *Yale News*—and now I was going to bring back all such things into my life and become again that most limited of all specialists, the "well-rounded man." This isn't just an epigram—life is much more successfully looked at from a single window, after all.

It was a matter of chance that I should have rented a house in one of the strangest communities in North America. It was on that slender riotous island which extends itself due east of New York —and where there are, among other natural curiosities, two unusual formations of land. Twenty miles from the city a pair of enormous eggs, identical in contour and separated only by a courtesy bay, jut out into the most domesticated body of salt water in the Western hemisphere, the great wet barnyard of Long Island Sound. They are not perfect ovals—like the egg in the Columbus story, they are both crushed flat at the contact end—but their physical resemblance must be a source of perpetual wonder to the gulls that fly overhead. To the wingless a more interesting phenomenon is their dissimilarity in every particular except shape and size.

I lived at West Egg, the—well, the less fashionable of the two, though this is a most superficial tag to express the bizarre and not a little sinister contrast between them. My house was at the very tip of the egg, only fifty yards from the Sound, and squeezed between two huge places that rented for twelve or fifteen thousand a season. The one on my right was a colossal affair by any standard—it was a factual imitation of some Hôtel de Ville in Normandy, with a tower on one side, spanking new under a thin beard of raw ivy, and a marble swimming pool, and more than forty acres of lawn and garden. It was Gatsby's mansion. Or, rather, as I didn't know Mr. Gatsby, it was a mansion, inhabited by a gentleman of that name. My own house was an eyesore, but it was a small eyesore, and it had been overlooked, so I had a view of the water, a partial view of my neighbor's lawn, and the consoling proximity of millionaires—all for eighty dollars a month.

Across the courtesy bay the white palaces of fashionable East Egg glittered along the water, and the history of the summer really begins on the evening I drove over there to have dinner with the Tom Buchanans. Daisy was my second cousin once removed, and I'd known Tom in college. And just after the war I spent two days with them in Chicago.

Her husband, among various physical accomplishments, had been one of the most powerful ends that ever played football at New Haven—a national figure in a way, one of those men who reach such an acute limited excellence at twenty-one that everything afterward savors of anticlimax. His family were enormously wealthy—even in college his freedom with money was a matter for reproach—but now he'd left Chicago and come East in a fashion that rather took your breath away; for instance, he'd brought down a string of polo ponies from Lake Forest. It was hard to realize that a man in my own generation was wealthy enough to do that.

Why they came East I don't know. They had spent a year in France for no particular reason, and then drifted here and there unrestfully wherever people played polo and were rich together. This was a permanent move, said Daisy over the telephone, but I didn't believe it—I had no sight into Daisy's heart, but I felt that Tom would drift on forever seeking, a little wistfully, for the dramatic turbulence of some irrecoverable football game.

And so it happened that on a warm windy evening I drove over to East Egg to see two old friends whom I scarcely knew at all. Their house was even more elaborate than I expected, a cheerful red-and-white Georgian Colonial mansion, overlooking the bay. The lawn started at the beach and ran toward the front door for a quarter of a mile, jumping over sun-dials and brick walks and burning gardens—finally when it reached the house drifting up the side in bright vines as though from the momentum of its run. The front was broken by a line of French windows, glowing now with reflected gold and wide open to the warm windy afternoon, and Tom Buchanan in riding clothes was standing with his legs apart on the front porch.

He had changed since his New Haven years. Now he was a sturdy straw-haired man of thirty with a rather hard mouth and a supercilious manner. Two shining arrogant eyes had established dominance over his face and gave him the appearance of always leaning aggressively forward. Not even the effeminate swank of his riding clothes could hide the enormous power of that body—he seemed to fill those glistening boots until he strained the top lacing, and you could see a great pack of muscle shifting when his shoulder moved under his thin coat. It was a body capable of enormous leverage— a cruel body.

His speaking voice, a gruff husky tenor, added to the impression of fractiousness he conveyed. There was a touch of paternal contempt in it, even toward people he liked—and there were men at New Haven who had hated his guts.

"Now, don't think my opinion on these matters is final," he seemed to say, "just because I'm stronger and more of a man than you are." We were in the same senior society, and while we were never intimate I always had the impression that he approved of me and wanted me to like him with some harsh, defiant wistfulness of his own.

We talked for a few minutes on the sunny porch.

"I've got a nice place here," he said, his eyes flashing about restlessly.

Turning me around by one arm, he moved a broad flat hand along the front vista, including in its sweep a sunken Italian garden, a half acre of deep, pungent roses, and a snub-nosed motor-boat that bumped the tide offshore.

"It belonged to Demaine, the oil man." He turned me around again, politely and abruptly. "We'll go inside."

We walked through a high hallway into a bright rosy-colored space, fragilely bound into the house by French windows at either end. The windows were ajar and gleaming white against the fresh grass outside that seemed to grow a little way into the house. A breeze blew through the room, blew curtains in at one end and out the other like pale flags, twisting them up toward the frosted wedding-cake of the ceiling, and then rippled over the wine-colored rug, making a shadow on it as wind does on the sea.

The only completely stationary object in the room was an enormous couch on which two young women were buoyed up as though upon an anchored balloon. They were both in white, and their dresses were rippling and fluttering as if they had just been blown back in after a short flight around the house. I must have stood for a few moments listening to the whip and snap of the curtains and the groan of a picture on the wall. Then there was a boom as Tom Buchanan shut the rear windows and the caught wind died out about the room, and the curtains and the rugs and the two young women ballooned slowly to the floor.

The younger of the two was a stranger to me. She was extended full length at her end of the divan, completely motionless, and with her chin raised a little, as if she were balancing something on it which was quite likely to fall. If she saw me out of the corner of her eyes she gave no hint of it—indeed, I was almost surprised into murmuring an apology for having disturbed her by coming in.

The other girl, Daisy, made an attempt to rise—she leaned slightly forward with a conscientious expression—then she laughed, an absurd, charming little laugh, and I laughed too and came forward into the room.

"I'm p-paralyzed with happiness."

She laughed again, as if she said something very witty, and held my hand for a moment, looking up into my face, promising that there was no one in the world she so much wanted to see. That was a a way she had. She hinted in a murmur that the surname of the balancing girl was Baker. (I've heard it said that Daisy's murmur was only to make people lean toward her; an irrelevant criticism that made it no less charming.)

At any rate, Miss Baker's lips fluttered, she nodded at me almost imperceptibly, and then quickly tipped her head back again—the object she was balancing had obviously tottered a little and given her something of a fright. Again a sort of apology arose to my lips. Almost any exhibition of complete self-sufficiency draws a stunned tribute from me.

I looked back at my cousin, who began to ask me questions in her low, thrilling voice. It was the kind of voice that the ear follows up and down, as if each speech is an arrangement of notes that will never be played again. Her face was sad and lovely with bright things in it, bright eyes and a bright passionate mouth, but there was an excitement in her voice that men who had cared for her found difficult to forget: a singing compulsion, a whispered "Listen," a promise that she had done gay, exciting things just a while since and that there were gay, exciting things hovering in the next hour.

I told her how I had stopped off in Chicago for a day on my way East, and how a dozen people had sent their love through me.

"Do they miss me?" she cried ecstatically.

"The whole town is desolate. All the cars have the left rear wheel painted black as a mourning wreath, and there's a persistent wail all night along the north shore."

"How gorgeous! Let's go back, Tom. To-morrow!" Then she added irrelevantly: "You ought to see the baby."

"I'd like to."

"She's asleep. She's three years old. Haven't you ever seen her?"

"Never."

"Well, you ought to see her. She's——"

Tom Buchanan, who had been hovering restlessly about the room, stopped and rested his hand on my shoulder.

"What you doing, Nick?"

"I'm a bond man."

"Who with?"

I told him.

"Never heard of them," he remarked decisively.

This annoyed me.

"You will," I answered shortly. "You will if you stay in the East."

"Oh, I'll stay in the East, don't you worry," he said, glancing at Daisy and then back at me, as if he were alert for something more. "I'd be a God damned fool to live anywhere else."

At this point Miss Baker said: "Absolutely!" with such suddenness that I started—it was the first word she had uttered since I came into the room. Evidently it surprised her as much as it did me, for she yawned and with a series of rapid, deft movements stood up into the room.

"I'm stiff," she complained, "I've been lying on that sofa for as long as I can remember."

"Don't look at me," Daisy retorted, "I've been trying to get you to New York all afternoon."

"No, thanks," said Miss Baker to the four cocktails just in from the pantry, "I'm absolutely in training."

Her host looked at her incredulously.

"You are!" He took down his drink as if it were a drop in the bottom of a glass. "How you ever get anything done is beyond me."

I looked at Miss Baker, wondering what it was she "got done." I enjoyed looking at her. She was a slender, small-breasted girl, with an erect carriage, which she accentuated by throwing her body backward at the shoulders like a young cadet. Her gray sun-strained eyes looked back at me with polite reciprocal curiosity out of a wan, charming, discontented face. It occurred to me now that I had seen her, or a picture of her, somewhere before.

"You live in West Egg," she remarked contemptuously. "I know somebody there."

"I don't know a single——"

"You must now Gatsby."

"Gatsby?" demanded Daisy. "What Gatsby?"

Before I could reply that he was my neighbor dinner was announced; wedging his tense arm imperatively under mine, Tom Buchanan compelled me from the room as though he were moving a checker to another square.

Slenderly, languidly, their hands set lightly on their hips, the two young women preceded us out onto a rosy-colored porch, open toward the sunset, where four candles flickered on the table in the diminished wind.

"Why *candles*?" objected Daisy, frowning. She snapped them out with her fingers. "In two weeks it'll be the longest day in the year." She looked at us all radiantly. "Do you always watch for the longest day of the year and then miss it? I always watch for the longest day in the year and then miss it."

"We ought to plan something," yawned Miss Baker, sitting down at the table as if she were getting into bed.

"All right," said Daisy. "What'll we plan?" She turned to me helplessly: "What do people plan?"

Before I could answer her eyes fastened with an awed expression on her little finger.

"Look!" she complained; "I hurt it."

We all looked—the knuckle was black and blue.

"You did it, Tom," she said accusingly. "I know you didn't mean to, but you *did* do it. That's what I get for marrying a brute of a man, a great, big, hulking physical specimen of a——"

"I hate that word hulking," objected Tom crossly, "even in kidding."

"Hulking," insisted Daisy.

Sometimes she and Miss Baker talked at once, unobtrusively and with a bantering inconsequence that was never quite chatter, that was as cool as their white dresses and their impersonal eyes in the absence of all desire. They were here, and they accepted Tom and me, making only a polite pleasant effort to entertain or to be entertained. They knew that presently dinner would be over and a little later the evening, too, would be over and casually put away. It was sharply different from the West, where an evening was hurried from phase to phase toward its close, in a continually disappointed anticipation or else in sheer nervous dread of the moment itself.

"You make me feel uncivilized, Daisy," I confessed on my second glass of corky but rather impressive claret. "Can't you talk about crops or something?"

I meant nothing in particular by this remark, but it was taken up in an unexpected way.

"Civilization's going to pieces," broke out Tom violently. "I've gotten to be a terrible pessimist about things. Have you read 'The Rise of the Colored Empires' by this man Goddard?"

"Why, no," I answered, rather surprised by his tone.

"Well, it's a fine book, and everybody ought to read it. The idea is if we don't look out the white race will be—will be utterly submerged. It's all scientific stuff; it's been proved."

"Tom's getting very profound," said Daisy, with an expression of unthoughtful sadness. "He reads deep books with long words in them. What was that word we——"

"Well, these books are all scientific," insisted Tom, glancing at her impatiently. "This fellow has worked out the whole thing. It's up to us, who are the dominant race, to watch out or these other races will have control of things."

"We've got to beat them down," whispered Daisy, winking ferociously toward the fervent sun.

"You ought to live in California——" began Miss Baker, but Tom interrupted her by shifting heavily in his chair.

"This idea is that we're Nordics. I am, and you are, and you are, and—" After an infinitesimal hesitation he included Daisy with a slight nod, and she winked at me again. "—And we've produced all the things that go to make civilization—oh, science and art, and all that. Do you see?"

There was something pathetic in his concentration, as if his complacency, more acute than of old, was not enough to him any more. When, almost immediately, the telephone rang inside and the butler left the porch Daisy seized upon the momentary interruption and leaned toward me.

"I'll tell you a family secret," she whispered enthusiastically. "It's about the butler's nose. Do you want to hear about the butler's nose?"

"That's why I came over to-night."

"Well, he wasn't always a butler; he used to be the silver polisher for some people in New York that had a silver service for two hundred people. He had to polish it from morning till night, until finally it began to affect his nose——"

"Things went from bad to worse," suggested Miss Baker.

"Yes. Things went from bad to worse, until finally he had to give up his position."

For a moment the last sunshine fell with romantic affection upon her glowing face; her voice compelled me forward breathlessly as I listened—then the glow faded, each light deserting her with lingering regret, like children leaving a pleasant street at dusk.

The butler came back and murmured something close to Tom's ear, whereupon Tom frowned, pushed back his chair, and without a word went inside. As if his absence quickened something within her, Daisy leaned forward again, her voice glowing and singing.

"I love to see you at my table, Nick. You remind me of a—of a rose, an absolute rose. Doesn't he?" She turned to Miss Baker for confirmation: "An absolute rose?"

This was untrue. I am not even faintly like a rose. She was only extemporizing, but a stirring warmth flowed from her, as if her heart was trying to come out to you concealed in one of those breathless, thrilling words. Then suddenly she threw her napkin on the table and excused herself and went into the house.

Miss Baker and I exchanged a short glance consciously devoid of meaning. I was about to speak when she sat up alertly and said "Sh!" in a warning voice. A subdued impassioned murmur was audible in the room beyond, and Miss Baker leaned forward unashamed, trying to hear. The murmur trembled on the verge of coherence, sank down, mounted excitedly, and then ceased altogether.

"This Mr. Gatsby you spoke of is my neighbor—" I began.

"Don't talk. I want to hear what happens."

"Is something happening?" I inquired innocently.

"You mean to say you don't know?" said Miss Baker, honestly surprised. "I thought everybody knew."

"I don't."

"Why—" she said hesitantly, "Tom's got some woman in New York."

"Got some woman?" I repeated blankly.

Miss Baker nodded.

"She might have the decency not to telephone him at dinner time. Don't you think?"

Almost before I had grasped her meaning there was the flutter of a dress and the crunch of leather boots, and Tom and Daisy were back at the table.

"It couldn't be helped!" cried Daisy with tense gayety.

She sat down, glanced searchingly at Miss Baker and then at me, and continued: "I looked outdoors for a minute, and it's very romantic outdoors. There's a bird on the lawn that I think must be a nightingale come over on the Cunard or White Star Line. He's singing away—" Her voice sang: "It's romantic, isn't it, Tom?"

"Very romantic," he said, and then miserably to me: "If it's light enough after dinner, I want to take you down to the stables."

The telephone rang inside, startlingly, and as Daisy shook her head decisively at Tom the subject of the stables, in fact all subjects, vanished into air. Among the broken fragments of the last five minutes at table I remember the candles being lit again, pointlessly, and I was conscious of wanting to look squarely at every one, and yet to avoid all eyes. I couldn't guess what Daisy and Tom were thinking, but I doubt if even Miss Baker, who seemed to have mastered a certain hardy scepticism, was able utterly to put this fifth guest's shrill metallic urgency out of mind. To a certain temperament the situation might have seemed intriguing—my own instinct was to telephone immediately for the police.

The horses, needless to say, were not mentioned again. Tom and Miss Baker, with several feet of twilight between them, strolled back into the library, as if to a vigil beside a perfectly tangible body, while, trying to look pleasantly interested and a little deaf, I followed Daisy around a chain of connecting verandas to the porch in front. In its deep gloom we sat down side by side on a wicker settee.

Daisy took her face in her hands as if feeling its lovely shape, and her eyes moved gradually out into the velvet dusk. I saw that turbulent emotions possessed her, so I asked what I thought would be some sedative questions about her little girl.

"We don't know each other very well, Nick," she said suddenly. "Even if we are cousins. You didn't come to my wedding."

"I wasn't back from the war."

"That's true." She hesitated. "Well, I've had a very bad time, Nick, and I'm pretty cynical about everything."

Evidently she had reason to be. I waited but she didn't say any more, and after a moment I returned rather feebly to the subject of her daughter.

"I suppose she talks, and—eats, and everything."

"Oh, yes." She looked at me absently. "Listen, Nick; let me tell you what I said when she was born. Would you like to hear?"

"Very much."

"It'll show you how I've gotten to feel about—things. Well, she was less than an hour old and Tom was God knows where. I woke up out of the ether with an utterly abandoned feeling, and asked the nurse right away if it was a boy or a girl. She told me it was a girl, and so I turned my head away and wept. 'All right,' I said, 'I'm glad it's a girl. And I hope she'll be a fool—that's the best thing a girl can be in this world, a beautiful little fool.'

"You see I think everything's terrible anyhow," she went on in a convinced way. "Everybody thinks so—the most advanced people. And I *know*. I've been everywhere and seen everything and done everything." Her eyes flashed around her in a defiant way, rather like Tom's, and she laughed with thrilling scorn. "Sophisticated— God, I'm sophisticated!"

The instant her voice broke off, ceasing to compel my attention, my belief, I felt the basic insincerity of what she had said. It made me uneasy, as though the whole evening had been a trick of some sort to exact a contributary emotion from me. I waited, and sure enough, in a moment she looked at me with an absolute smirk on her lovely face, as if she had asserted her membership in a rather distinguished secret society to which she and Tom belonged.

Inside, the crimson room bloomed with light. Tom and Miss Baker sat at either end of the long couch and she read aloud to him from

The Saturday Evening Post—the words, murmurous and uninfected, running together in a soothing tune. The lamp-light, bright on his boots and dull on the autumn-leaf yellow of her hair, glinted along the paper as she turned a page with a flutter of slender muscles in her arms.

When we came in she held us silent for a moment with a lifted hand.

"To be continued," she said, tossing the magazine on the table, "in our very next issue."

Her body asserted itself with a restless movement of her knee, and she stood up.

"Ten o'clock," she remarked, apparently finding the time on the ceiling. "Time for this good girl to go to bed."

"Jordan's going to play in the tournament to-morrow," explained Daisy, "over at Westchester."

"Oh—you're *Jor*dan Baker."

I knew now why her face was familiar—its pleasing contemptuous expression had looked out at me from many rotogravure pictures of the sporting life at Asheville and Hot Springs and Palm Beach. I had heard some story of her too, a critical, unpleasant story, but what it was I had forgotten long ago.

"Good night," she said softly. "Wake me at eight, won't you?"

"If you'll get up."

"I will. Good night Mr. Carraway. See you anon."

"Of course you will," confirmed Daisy. "In fact, I think I'll arrange a marriage. Come over often, Nick, and I'll sort of—oh—fling you together. You know—lock you up accidentally in linen closets and push you out to sea in a boat, and all that sort of thing——"

"Good night," called Miss Baker from the stairs. "I haven't heard a word."

"She's a nice girl," said Tom after a moment. "They oughtn't to let her run around the country this way."

"Who oughtn't to?" inquired Daisy coldly.

"Her family."

"Her family is one aunt about a thousand years old. Besides, Nick's going to look after her, aren't you, Nick? She's going to spend lots of week-ends out here this summer. I think the home influence will be very good for her."

Daisy and Tom looked at each other for a moment in silence.

"Is she from New York?" I asked quickly.

"From Louisville. Our white girlhood was passed together there. Our beautiful white——"

"Did you give Nick a little heart-to-heart talk on the veranda?" demanded Tom suddenly.

"Did I?" She looked at me. "I can't seem to remember, but I think we talked about the Nordic race. Yes, I'm sure we did. It sort of crept up on us and first thing you know——"

"Don't believe everything you hear, Nick," he advised me.

I said lightly that I had heard nothing at all, and a few minutes later I got up to go home. They came to the door with me and stood side by side in a cheerful square of light. As I started my motor Daisy peremptorily called: "Wait!

"I forgot to ask you something, and it's important. We heard you were engaged to a girl out West."

"That's right," corroborated Tom kindly. "We heard that you were engaged."

"It's a libel. I'm too poor."

"But we heard it," insisted Daisy, surprising me by opening up again in a flower-like way. "We heard it from three people, so it must be true."

Of course I knew what they were referring to, but I wasn't even vaguely engaged. The fact that gossip had published the banns was one of the reasons I had come East. You can't stop going with an old friend on account of rumors, and on the other hand I had no intention of being rumored into marriage.

Their interest rather touched me and made them less remotely rich—nevertheless, I was confused and a little disgusted as I drove away. It seemed to me that the thing for Daisy to do was to rush out of the house, child in arms—but apparently there were no such intentions in her head. As for Tom, the fact that he "had some woman in New York" was really less surprising than that he had been depressed by a book. Something was making him nibble at the edge of stale ideas as if his sturdy physical egotism no longer nourished his peremptory heart.

Already it was deep summer on roadhouse roofs and in front of wayside garages, where new red gas-pumps sat out in pools of light, and when I reached my estate at West Egg I ran the car under its shed and sat for a while on an abandoned grass roller in the yard. The wind had blown off, leaving a loud, bright night, with wings beating in the trees and a persistent organ sound as the full bellows of the earth blew the frogs full of life. The silhouette of a moving cat wavered across the moonlight, and turning my head to watch it, I saw that I was not alone—fifty feet away a figure had emerged from the shadow of my neighbor's mansion and was standing with his hands in his pockets regarding the silver pepper of the stars. Something in his leisurely movements and the secure position of his feet upon the lawn suggested that it was Mr. Gatsby himself, come out to determine what share was his of our local heavens.

I decided to call to him. Miss Baker had mentioned him at dinner, and that would do for an introduction. But I didn't call to him, for he gave a sudden intimation that he was content to be alone—he stretched out his arms toward the dark water in a curious way, and, far as I was from him, I could have sworn he was trembling. Involuntarily I glanced seaward—and distinguished nothing except a single green light, minute and far away, that might have been the end of a dock. When I looked once more for Gatsby he had vanished, and I was alone again in the unquiet darkness.

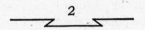

2

About half way between West Egg and New York the motor road hastily joins the railroad and runs beside it for a quarter of a mile, so as to shrink away from a certain desolate area of land. This is a valley of ashes—a fantastic farm where ashes grow like wheat into ridges and hills and grotesque gardens; where ashes take the forms of houses and chimneys and rising smoke and, finally, with a transcendent effort, of ash-gray men who move dimly and already crumbling through the powdery air. Occasionally a line of gray cars crawls along an invisible track, gives out a ghastly creak, and comes to rest, and immediately the ash-gray men swarm up with leaden spades and stir up an impenetrable cloud, which screens their obscure operations from your sight.

But above the gray land and the spasms of bleak dust which drift endlessly over it, you perceive, after a moment, the eyes of Doctor T. J. Eckleburg. The eyes of Doctor T. J. Eckleburg are blue and gigantic—their retinas are one yard high. They look out of no face, but, instead, from a pair of enormous yellow spectacles which pass over a non-existent nose. Evidently some wild wag of an oculist set them there to fatten his practice in the borough of Queens, and then sank down himself into eternal blindness, or forgot them and moved away. But his eyes, dimmed a little by many paintless days, under sun and rain, brood on over the solemn dumping ground.

The valley of ashes is bounded on one side by a small foul river, and, when the drawbridge is up to let barges through, the passengers on waiting trains can stare at the dismal scene for as long as half an hour. There is always a halt there of at least a minute, and it was because of this that I first met Tom Buchanan's mistress.

The fact that he had one was insisted upon wherever he was known. His acquaintances resented the fact that he turned up in popular cafés with her and, leaving her at a table, sauntered about, chatting with whomsoever he knew. Though I was curious to see her, I had no desire to meet her—but I did. I went up to New York with Tom on the train one afternoon, and when we stopped by the ashheaps he jumped to his feet and, taking hold of my elbow, literally forced me from the car.

"We're getting off," he insisted. "I want you to meet my girl."

I think he'd tanked up a good deal at luncheon, and his determination to have my company bordered on violence. The supercilious assumption was that on Sunday afternoon I had nothing better to do.

I followed him over a low whitewashed railroad fence, and we walked back a hundred yards along the road under Doctor Eckleburg's persistent stare. The only building in sight was a small block of yellow brick sitting on the edge of the waste land, a sort of compact Main Street ministering to it, and contiguous to absolutely nothing. One of the three shops it contained was for rent and another was an all-night restaurant, approached by a trail of ashes; the third was a garage—*Repairs*. George B. Wilson. *Cars bought and sold*.—and I followed Tom inside.

The interior was unprosperous and bare; the only car visible was the dust-covered wreck of a Ford which crouched in a dim corner. It had occurred to me that this shadow of a garage must be a blind, and that sumptuous and romantic apartments were concealed overhead, when the proprietor himself appeared in the door of an office, wiping his hands on a piece of waste. He was a blond, spiritless man, anæmic, and faintly handsome. When he saw us a damp gleam of hope sprang into his light blue eyes.

"Hello, Wilson, old man," said Tom, slapping him jovially on the shoulder. "How's business?"

"I can't complain," answered Wilson unconvincingly. "When are you going to sell me that car?"

"Next week; I've got my man working on it now."

"Works pretty slow, don't he?"

"No, he doesn't," said Tom coldly. "And if you feel that way about it, maybe I'd better sell it somewhere else after all."

"I don't mean that," explained Wilson quickly. "I just meant——"

His voice faded off and Tom glanced impatiently around the garage. Then I heard footsteps on a stairs, and in a moment the thickish figure of a woman blocked out the light from the office door. She was in the middle thirties, and faintly stout, but she carried her flesh sensuously as some women can. Her face, above a spotted dress of dark blue crêpe-de-chine, contained no facet or gleam of beauty, but there was an immediately perceptible vitality about her as if the nerves of her body were continually smouldering. She smiled slowly and, walking through her husband as if he were a ghost, shook hands with Tom, looking him flush in the eye. Then she wet her lips, and without turning around spoke to her husband in a soft, coarse voice:

"Get some chairs, why don't you, so somebody can sit down."

"Oh, sure," agreed Wilson hurriedly, and went toward the little office mingling immediately with the cement color of the walls. A white ashen dust veiled his dark suit and his pale hair as it veiled everything in the vicinity—except his wife, who moved close to Tom.

"I want to see you," said Tom intently. "Get on the next train."

"All right."

"I'll meet you by the news-stand on the lower level."

She nodded and moved away from him just as George Wilson emerged with two chairs from his office door.

We waited for her down the road and out of sight. It was a few days before the Fourth of July, and a gray, scrawny Italian child was setting torpedoes in a row along the railroad track.

"Terrible place, isn't it," said Tom, exchanging a frown with Doctor Eckleburg.

"Awful."

"It does her good to get away."

"Doesn't her husband object?"

"Wilson? He thinks she goes to see her sister in New York. He's so dumb he doesn't know he's alive."

So Tom Buchanan and his girl and I went up together to New York—or not quite together, for Mrs. Wilson sat discreetly in another car. Tom deferred that much to the sensibilities of those East Eggers who might be on the train.

She had changed her dress to a brown figured muslin, which stretched tight over her rather wide hips as Tom helped her to the platform in New York. At the news-stand she bought a copy of *Town Tattle* and a moving-picture magazine, and in the station drug-store some cold cream and a small flask of perfume. Up-stairs, in the solemn echoing drive she let four taxicabs drive away before she selected a new one, lavender-colored with gray upholstery, and in this we slid out from the mass of the station into the glowing sun-shine. But immediately she turned sharply from the window and, leaning forward, tapped on the front glass.

"I want to get one of those dogs," she said earnestly. "I want to get one for the apartment. They're nice to have—a dog."

We backed up to a gray old man who bore an absurd resemblance to John D. Rockefeller. In a basket swung from his neck cowered a dozen very recent puppies of an indeterminate breed.

"What kind are they?" asked Mrs. Wilson eagerly, as he came to the taxi-window.

"All kinds. What kind do you want, lady?"

"I'd like to get one of those police dogs; I don't suppose you got that kind?"

The man peered doubtfully into the basket, plunged in his hand and drew one up, wriggling, by the back of the neck.

"That's no police dog," said Tom.

"No, it's not exactly a po*lice* dog," said the man with disappoint-ment in his voice. "It's more of an Airedale." He passed his hand over the brown washrag of a back. "Look at that coat. Some coat. That's a dog that'll never bother you with catching cold."

"I think it's cute," said Mrs. Wilson enthusiastically. "How much is it?"

"That dog?" He looked at it admiringly. "That dog will cost you ten dollars."

The Airedale—undoubtedly there was an Airedale concerned in it somewhere, though its feet were startlingly white—changed hands and settled down into Mrs. Wilson's lap, where she fondled the weatherproof coat with rapture.

"Is it a boy or a girl?" she asked delicately.

"That dog? That dog's a boy."

"It's a bitch," said Tom decisively. "Here's your money. Go and buy ten more dogs with it."

We drove over to Fifth Avenue, warm and soft, almost pastoral, on the summer Sunday afternoon. I wouldn't have been surprised to see a great flock of white sheep turn the corner.

"Hold on," I said, "I have to leave you here."

"No, you don't," interposed Tom quickly. "Myrtle'll be hurt if you don't come up to the apartment. Won't you, Myrtle?"

"Come on," she urged. "I'll telephone my sister Catherine. She's said to be very beautiful by people who ought to know."

"Well, I'd like to, but——"

We went on, cutting back again over the Park toward the West Hundreds. At 158th Street the cab stopped at one slice in a long white cake of apartment-houses. Throwing a regal homecoming glance around the neighborhood, Mrs. Wilson gathered up her dog and her other purchases, and went haughtily in.

"I'm going to have the McKees come up," she announced as we rose in the elevator. "And, of course, I got to call up my sister, too."

The apartment was on the top floor—a small living-room, a small dining-room, a small bedroom, and a bath. The living-room was crowded to the doors with a set of tapestried furniture entirely too large for it, so that to move about was to stumble continually over scenes of ladies swinging in the gardens of Versailles. The only picture was an over-enlarged photograph, apparently a hen sitting on a blurred rock. Looked at from a distance, however, the hen resolved itself into a bonnet, and the countenance of a stout old lady beamed down into the room. Several old copies of *Town Tattle* lay on the table together with a copy of *Simon Called Peter*, and some of the small scandal magazines of Broadway. Mrs. Wilson was first concerned with the dog. A reluctant elevator-boy went for a box full of straw and some milk, to which he added on his own initiative a tin of large, hard dog-biscuits—one of which decomposed apathetically in the saucer of milk all afternoon. Meanwhile Tom brought out a bottle of whiskey from a locked bureau door.

I have been drunk just twice in my life, and the second time was that afternoon; so everything that happened has a dim, hazy cast over it, although until after eight o'clock the apartment was full of cheerful sun. Sitting on Tom's lap Mrs. Wilson called up several people on the telephone; then there were no cigarettes, and I went out to buy some at the drugstore on the corner. When I came back they had both disappeared, so I sat down discreetly in the living-room and read a chapter of *Simon Called Peter*—either it was terrible stuff or the whiskey distorted things, because it didn't make any sense to me.

Just as Tom and Myrtle (after the first drink Mrs. Wilson and I called each other by our first names) reappeared, company commenced to arrive at the apartment-door.

The sister, Catherine, was a slender, worldly girl of about thirty, with a solid, sticky bob of red hair, and a complexion powdered milky white. Her eyebrows had been plucked and then drawn on again at a more rakish angle but the efforts of nature toward the restoration of the old alignment gave a blurred air to her face. When she moved about there was an incessant clicking as innumerable pottery bracelets jingled up and down upon her arms. She came in with such a proprietary haste, and looked around so possessively at the furniture that I wondered if she lived here. But when I asked her she laughed immoderately, repeated my question aloud, and told me she lived with a girl friend at a hotel.

Mr. McKee was a pale, feminine man from the flat below. He had just shaved, for there was a white spot of lather on his cheekbone, and he was most respectful in his greeting to every one in the room. He informed me that he was in the "artistic game," and I gathered later that he was a photographer and had made the dim enlargement of Mrs. Wilson's mother which hovered like an ectoplasm on the wall. His wife was shrill, languid, handsome, and horrible. She told me with pride that her husband had photographed her a hundred and twenty-seven times since they had been married.

Mrs. Wilson had changed her costume some time before, and was now attired in an elaborate afternoon dress of cream-colored chiffon, which gave out a continual rustle as she swept about the room. With the influence of the dress her personality had also undergone a change. The intense vitality that had been so remarkable in the garage was converted into impressive hauteur. Her laughter, her gestures, her assertions became more violently affected moment by moment, and as she expanded the room grew smaller around her, until she seemed to be revolving on a noisy, creaking pivot through the smoky air.

"My dear," she told her sister in a high, mincing shout, "most of these fellas will cheat you every time. All they think of is money. I had a woman up here last week to look at my feet, and when she gave me the bill you'd of thought she had my appendicitis out."

"What was the name of the woman?" asked Mrs. McKee.

"Mrs. Eberhardt. She goes around looking at people's feet in their own homes."

"I like your dress," remarked Mrs. McKee, "I think it's adorable."

Mrs. Wilson rejected the compliment by raising her eyebrow in disdain.

"It's just a crazy old thing," she said. "I just slip it on sometimes when I don't care what I look like."

"But it looks wonderful on you, if you know what I mean," pursued Mrs. McKee. "If Chester could only get you in that pose I think he could make something of it."

We all looked in silence at Mrs. Wilson, who removed a strand of hair from over her eyes and looked back at us with a brilliant smile. Mr. McKee regarded her intently with his head on one side, and then moved his hand back and forth slowly in front of his face.

"I should change the light," he said after a moment. "I'd like to bring out the modelling of the features. And I'd try to get hold of all the back hair."

"I wouldn't think of changing the light," cried Mrs. McKee. "I think it's——"

Her husband said "Sh!" and we all looked at the subject again, whereupon Tom Buchanan yawned audibly and got to his feet.

"You McKees have something to drink," he said. "Get some more ice and mineral water, Myrtle, before everybody goes to sleep."

"I told that boy about the ice." Myrtle raised her eyebrows in despair at the shiftlessness of the lower orders. "These people! You have to keep after them all the time."

She looked at me and laughed pointlessly. Then she flounced over to the dog, kissed it with ecstasy, and swept into the kitchen, implying that a dozen chefs awaited her orders there.

"I've done some nice things out on Long Island," asserted Mr. McKee.

Tom looked at him blankly.

"Two of them we have framed down-stairs."

"Two what?" demanded Tom.

"Two studies. One of them I call *Montauk Point—The Gulls*, and the other I call *Montauk Point—The Sea*."

The sister Catherine sat down beside me on the couch.

"Do you live down on Long Island, too?" she inquired.

"I live at West Egg."

"Really? I was down there at a party about a month ago. At a man named Gatsby's. Do you know him?"

"I live next door to him."

"Well, they say he's a nephew or a cousin of Kaiser Wilhelm's. That's where all his money comes from."

"Really?"

She nodded.

"I'm scared of him. I'd hate to have him get anything on me."

This absorbing information about my neighbor was interrupted by Mrs. McKee's pointing suddenly at Catherine:

"Chester, I think you could do something with *her*," she broke out, but Mr. McKee only nodded in a bored way, and turned his attention to Tom.

"I'd like to do more work on Long Island, if I could get the entry. All I ask is that they should give me a start."

"Ask Myrtle," said Tom, breaking into a short shout of laughter as Mrs. Wilson entered with a tray. "She'll give you a letter of introduction, won't you, Myrtle?"

"Do what?" she asked, startled.

"You'll give McKee a letter of introduction to your husband, so he can do some studies of him." His lips moved silently for a moment as he invented. "*George B. Wilson at the Gasoline Pump*, or something like that."

Catherine leaned close to me and whispered in my ear:

"Neither of them can stand the person they're married to."

"Can't they?"

"Can't *stand* them." She looked at Myrtle and then at Tom. "What I say is, why go on living with them if they can't stand them? If I was them I'd get a divorce and get married to each other right away."

"Doesn't she like Wilson either?"

The answer to this was unexpected. It came from Myrtle, who had overheard the question, and it was violent and obscene.

"You see," cried Catherine triumphantly. She lowered her voice again. "It's really his wife that's keeping them apart. She's a Catholic, and they don't believe in divorce."

Daisy was not a Catholic, and I was a little shocked at the elaborateness of the lie.

"When they do get married," continued Catherine, "they're going West to live for a while until it blows over."

"It'd be more discreet to go to Europe."

"Oh, do you like Europe?" she exclaimed surprisingly. "I just got back from Monte Carlo."

"Really."

"Just last year. I went over there with another girl."

"Stay long?"

"No, we just went to Monte Carlo and back. We went by way of Marseilles. We had over twelve hundred dollars when we started, but we got gypped out of it all in two days in the private rooms. We had an awful time getting back, I can tell you. God, how I hated that town!"

The late afternoon sky bloomed in the window for a moment like the blue honey of the Mediterranean—then the shrill voice of Mrs. McKee called me back into the room.

"I almost made a mistake, too," she declared vigorously. "I almost married a little kike who'd been after me for years. I knew he was below me. Everybody kept saying to me: 'Lucille, that man's 'way below you!' But if I hadn't met Chester, he'd of got me sure."

"Yes, but listen," said Myrtle Wilson, nodding her head up and down, "at least you didn't marry him."

"I know I didn't."

"Well, I married him," said Myrtle, ambiguously. "And that's the difference between your case and mine."

"Why did you, Myrtle?" demanded Catherine. "Nobody forced you to."

Myrtle considered.

"I married him because I thought he was a gentleman," she said finally. "I thought he knew something about breeding, but he wasn't fit to lick my shoe."

"You were crazy about him for a while," said Catherine.

"Crazy about him!" cried Myrtle incredulously. "Who said I was crazy about him? I never was any more crazy about him than I was about that man there."

She pointed suddenly at me, and every one looked at me accusingly. I tried to show by my expression that I expected no affection.

"The only *crazy* I was was when I married him. I knew right away I made a mistake. He borrowed somebody's best suit to get married in, and never even told me about it, and the man came after it one day when he was out: 'Oh, is that your suit?' I said. 'This is the first I ever heard about it.' But I gave it to him and then I lay down and cried to beat the band all afternoon."

"She really ought to get away from him," resumed Catherine to me. "They've been living over that garage for eleven years. And Tom's the first sweetie she ever had."

The bottle of whiskey—a second one—was now in constant demand by all present, excepting Catherine, who "felt just as good on nothing at all." Tom rang for the janitor and sent him for some celebrated sandwiches, which were a complete supper in themselves. I wanted to get out and walk eastward toward the park through the soft twilight, but each time I tried to go I became entangled in some wild, strident argument which pulled me back, as if with ropes, into my chair. Yet high over the city our line of yellow windows must have contributed their share of human secrecy to the casual watcher in the darkening streets, and I saw him too, looking up and wondering. I was within and without, simultaneously enchanted and repelled by the inexhaustible variety of life.

Myrtle pulled her chair close to mine, and suddenly her warm breath poured over me the story of her first meeting with Tom.

"It was on the two little seats facing each other that are always the last ones left on the train. I was going up to New York to see my sister and spend the night. He had on a dress suit and patent leather shoes, and I couldn't keep my eyes off him, but every time he looked at me I had to pretend to be looking at the advertisement over his head. When we came into the station he was next to me, and his white shirt-front pressed against my arm, and so I told him I'd have to call a policeman, but he knew I lied. I was so excited that when I got into a taxi with him I didn't hardly know I wasn't getting into a subway train. All I kept thinking about, over and over, was 'You can't live forever; you can't live forever.'"

She turned to Mrs. McKee and the room rang full of her artificial laughter.

"My dear," she cried, "I'm going to give you this dress as soon as I'm through with it. I've got to get another one tomorrow. I'm going to make a list of all the things I've got to get. A massage and a wave, and a collar for the dog, and one of those cute little ash-trays where you touch a spring, and a wreath with a black silk bow for mother's grave that'll last all summer. I got to write down a list so I won't forget all the things I got to do."

It was nine o'clock—almost immediately afterward I looked at my watch and found it was ten. Mr. McKee was asleep on a chair with his fists clenched in his lap, like a photograph of a man of action. Taking out my handkerchief I wiped from his cheek the spot of dried lather that had worried me all the afternoon.

The little dog was sitting on the table looking with blind eyes through the smoke, and from time to time groaning faintly. People disappeared, reappeared, made plans to go somewhere, and then lost each other, searched for each other, found each other a few feet away. Some time toward midnight Tom Buchanan and Mrs. Wilson stood face to face discussing in impassioned voices, whether Mrs. Wilson had any right to mention Daisy's name.

"Daisy! Daisy! Daisy!" shouted Mrs. Wilson. "I'll say it whenever I want to! Daisy! Dai——"

Making a short deft movement, Tom Buchanan broke her nose with his open hand.

Then there were bloody towels upon the bathroom floor, and women's voices scolding, and high over the confusion a long broken wail of pain. Mr. McKee awoke from his doze and started in a daze toward the door. When he had gone halfway he turned around and stared at the scene—his wife and Catherine scolding and consoling as they stumbled here and there among the crowded furniture with articles of aid, and the despairing figure on the coach, bleeding fluently, and trying to spread a copy of *Town Tattle* over the tapestry scenes of Versailles. Then Mr. McKee turned and continued on out the door. Taking my hat from the chandelier, I followed.

"Come to lunch some day," he suggested, as we groaned down in the elevator.

"Where?"

"Anywhere."

"Keep your hands off the lever," snapped the elevator boy.

"I beg your pardon," said Mr. McKee with dignity, "I didn't know I was touching it."

"All right," I agreed, "I'll be glad to."

. . . I was standing beside his bed and he was sitting up between the sheets, clad in his underwear, with a great portfolio in his hands.

"Beauty and the Beast . . . Loneliness . . . Old Grocery Horse . . . Brook'n Bridge. . . ."

Then I was lying half asleep in the cold lower level of the Pennsylvania Station, staring at the morning Tribune, and waiting for the four o'clock train.

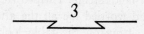

3

There was music from my neighbor's house through the summer nights. In his blue gardens men and girls came and went like moths among the whisperings and the champagne and the stars. At high tide in the afternoon I watched his guests diving from the tower of his raft, or taking the sun on the hot sand of his beach while his two motor-boats slit the waters of the Sound, drawing aquaplanes over cataracts of foam. On week-ends his Rolls-Royce became an omnibus, bearing parties to and from the city between nine in the morning and long past midnight, while his station wagon scampered like a brisk yellow bug to meet all trains. And on Mondays eight servants, including an extra gardener, toiled all day with mops and scrubbing-brushes and hammers and garden-shears, repairing the ravages of the night before.

Every Friday five crates of oranges and lemons arrived from a fruiterer in New York—every Monday these same oranges and lemons left his back door in a pyramid of pulpless halves. There was a machine in the kitchen which could extract the juice of two hundred oranges in half an hour if a little button was pressed two hundred times by a butler's thumb.

At least once a fortnight a corps of caterers came down with several hundred feet of canvas and enough colored lights to make a Christmas tree of Gatsby's enormous garden. On buffet tables, garnished with glistening hors-d'œuvre, spiced baked hams crowded against salads of harlequin designs and pastry pigs and turkeys bewitched to a dark gold. In the main hall a bar with a real brass rail was set up, and stocked with gins and liquors and with cordials so long forgotten that most of his female guests were too young to know one from another.

By seven o'clock the orchestra has arrived, no thin five-piece affair, but a whole pitful of oboes and trombones and saxophones and viols and cornets and piccolos, and low and high drums. The last swimmers have come in from the beach now and are dressing up-stairs; the cars from New York are parked five deep in the drive, and already the halls and salons and verandas are gaudy with primary colors, and hair bobbed in strange new ways, and shawls beyond the dreams of Castile. The bar is in full swing, and floating rounds of cocktails permeate the garden outside, until the air is alive with chatter and laughter, and casual innuendo and introductions forgotten on the spot, and enthusiastic meetings between women who never knew each other's names.

The lights grow brighter as the earth lurches away from the sun, and now the orchestra is playing yellow cocktail music, and the opera of voices pitches a key higher. Laughter is easier minute by minute, spilled with prodigality, tipped out at a cheerful word. The groups change more swiftly, swell with new arrivals, dissolve and form in the same breath; already there are wanderers, confident girls who weave here and there among the stouter and more stable, become for a sharp, joyous moment the center of a group, and then, excited with triumph, glide on through the sea-change of faces and voices and color under the constantly changing light.

Suddenly one of these gypsies, in trembling opal, seizes a cocktail out of the air, dumps it down for courage and, moving her hands like Frisco, dances out alone on the canvas platform. A momentary hush; the orchestra leader varies his rhythm obligingly for her, and there is a burst of chatter as the erroneous news goes around that she is Gilda Gray's understudy from the *Follies*. The party has begun.

I believe that on the first night I went to Gatsby's house I was one of the few guests who had actually been invited. People were not invited—they went there. They got into automobiles which bore them out to Long Island, and somehow they ended up at Gatsby's door. Once there they were introduced by somebody who knew Gatsby, and after that they conducted themselves according to the rules of behavior associated with an amusement park. Sometimes they came and went without having met Gatsby at all, came for the party with a simplicity of heart that was its own ticket of admission.

I had been actually invited. A chauffeur in a uniform of robin's-egg blue crossed my lawn early that Saturday morning with a surprisingly formal note from his employer: the honor would be entirely Gatsby's, it said, if I would attend his "little party" that night. He had seen me several times, and had intended to call on me long before, but a peculiar combination of circumstances had prevented it— signed Jay Gatsby, in a majestic hand.

Dressed up in white flannels I went over to his lawn a little after seven, and wandered around rather ill at ease among swirls and eddies of people I didn't know—though here and there was a face I had noticed on the commuting train. I was immediately struck by the number of young Englishmen dotted about; all well dressed, all looking a little hungry, and all talking in low, earnest voices to solid and prosperous Americans. I was sure that they were selling something: bonds or insurance or automobiles. They were at least agonizingly aware of the easy money in the vicinity and convinced that it was theirs for a few words in the right key.

As soon as I arrived I made an attempt to find my host, but the two or three people of whom I asked his whereabouts stared at me in such an amazed way, and denied so vehemently any knowledge of his movements, that I slunk off in the direction of the cocktail table—the only place in the garden where a single man could linger without looking purposeless and alone.

I was on my way to get roaring drunk from sheer embarrassment when Jordan Baker came out of the house and stood at the head of the marble steps, leaning a little backward and looking with contemptuous interest down into the garden.

Welcome or not, I found it necessary to attach myself to some one before I should begin to address cordial remarks to the passers-by.

"Hello!" I roared, advancing toward her. My voice seemed unnaturally loud across the garden.

"I thought you might be here," she responded absently as I came up. "I remembered you lived next door to——"

She held my hand impersonally, as a promise that she'd take care of me in a minute, and gave ear to two girls in twin yellow dresses, who stopped at the foot of the steps.

"Hello!" they cried together. "Sorry you didn't win."

That was for the golf tournament. She had lost in the finals the week before.

"You don't know who we are," said one of the girls in yellow, "but we met you here about a month ago."

"You've dyed your hair since then," remarked Jordan, and I started, but the girls had moved casually on and her remark was addressed to the premature moon, produced like the supper, no doubt, out of a caterer's basket. With Jordan's slender golden arm resting in mine, we descended the steps and sauntered about the garden. A tray of cocktails floated at us through the twilight, and we sat down at a table with the two girls in yellow and three men, each one introduced to us as Mr. Mumble.

"Do you come to these parties often?" inquired Jordan of the girl beside her.

"The last one was the one I met you at," answered the girl, in an alert confident voice. She turned to her companion: "Wasn't it for you, Lucille?"

It was for Lucille, too.

"I like to come," Lucille said. "I never care what I do, so I always have a good time. When I was here last I tore my gown on a chair, and he asked me my name and address—inside of a week I got a package from Groirier's with a new evening gown in it."

"Did you keep it?" asked Jordan.

"Sure I did. I was going to wear it tonight, but it was too big in the bust and had to be altered. It was gas blue with lavender beads. Two hundred and sixty-five dollars."

"There's something funny about a fellow that'll do a thing like that," said the other girl eagerly. "He doesn't want any trouble with *any*body."

"Who doesn't?" I inquired.

"Gatsby. Somebody told me——"

The two girls and Jordan leaned together confidentially.

"Somebody told me they thought he killed a man once."

A thrill passed over all of us. The three Mr. Mumbles bent forward and listened eagerly.

"I don't think it's so much *that*," argued Lucille sceptically; "it's more that he was a German spy during the war."

One of the men nodded in confirmation.

"I heard that from a man who knew all about him, grew up with him in Germany," he assured us positively.

"Oh, no," said the first girl, "it couldn't be that, because he was in the American army during the war." As our credulity switched back to her she leaned forward with enthusiasm. "You look at him sometimes when he thinks nobody's looking at him. I'll bet he killed a man."

She narrowed her eyes and shivered. Lucille shivered. We all turned and looked around for Gatsby. It was testimony to the romantic speculation he inspired that there were whispers about him from those who had found little that it was necessary to whisper about in this world.

The first supper—there would be another one after midnight—was now being served, and Jordan invited me to join her own party, who were spread around a table on the other side of the garden. There were three married couples and Jordan's escort, a persistent undergraduate given to violent innuendo, and obviously under the impression that sooner or later Jordan was going to yield him up her person to a greater or lesser degree. Instead of rambling, this party had preserved a dignified homogeneity, and assumed to itself the function of representing the staid nobility of the country-side—East Egg condescending to West Egg, and carefully on guard against its spectroscopic gayety.

"Let's get out," whispered Jordan, after a somehow wasteful and inappropriate half-hour; "this is much too polite for me."

We got up, and she explained that we were going to find the host: I had never met him, she said, and it was making me uneasy. The undergraduate nodded in a cynical, melancholy way.

The bar, where we glanced first, was crowded, but Gatsby was not there. She couldn't find him from the top of the steps, and he wasn't on the veranda. On a chance we tried an important-looking door, and walked into a high Gothic library, panelled with carved English oak, and probably transported complete from some ruin overseas.

A stout, middle-aged man, with enormous owl-eyed spectacles, was sitting somewhat drunk on the edge of a great table, staring with unsteady concentration at the shelves of books. As we entered he wheeled excitedly around and examined Jordan from head to foot.

"What do you think?" he demanded impetuously.

"About what?"

He waved his hand toward the book-shelves.

"About that. As a matter of fact you needn't bother to ascertain. I ascertained. They're real."

"The books?"

He noddded.

"Absolutely real—have pages and everything. I thought they'd be a nice durable cardboard. Matter of fact, they're absolutely real. Pages and—Here! Lemme show you."

Taking our scepticism for granted, he rushed to the bookcases and returned with Volume One of the "Stoddard Lectures."

"See!" he cried triumphantly. "It's a bona-fide piece of printed matter. It fooled me. This fella's a regular Belasco. It's a triumph. What thoroughness! What realism! Knew when to stop, too—didn't cut the pages. But what do you want? What do you expect?"

He snatched the book from me and replaced it hastily on its shelf, muttering that if one brick was removed the whole library was liable to collapse.

"Who brought you?" he demanded. "Or did you just come? I was brought. Most people were brought."

Jordan looked at him alertly, cheerfully, without answering.

"I was brought by a woman named Roosevelt," he continued. "Mrs. Claude Roosevelt. Do you know her? I met her somewhere last night. I've been drunk for about a week now, and I thought it might sober me up to sit in a library."

"Has it?"

"A little bit, I think. I can't tell yet. I've only been here an hour. Did I tell you about the books? They're real. They're——"

"You told us."

We shook hands with him gravely and went back outdoors.

There was dancing now on the canvas in the garden; old men pushing young girls backward in eternal graceless circles, superior couples holding each other tortuously, fashionably, and keeping in the corners—and a great number of single girls dancing individualistically or relieving the orchestra for a moment of the burden of the banjo or the traps. By midnight the hilarity had increased. A celebrated tenor had sung in Italian, and a notorious contralto had sung in jazz, and between the numbers people were doing "stunts" all over the garden, while happy, vacuous bursts of laughter rose toward the summer sky. A pair of stage twins, who turned out to be the girls in yellow, did a baby act in costume, and champagne was served in glasses bigger than finger-bowls. The moon had risen higher, and floating in the Sound was a triangle of silver scales, trembling a little to the stiff, tinny drip of the banjoes on the lawn.

I was still with Jordan Baker. We were sitting at a table with a man of about my age and a rowdy little girl, who gave way upon the slightest provocation to uncontrollable laughter. I was enjoying myself now. I had taken two finger-bowls of champagne, and the scene had changed before my eyes into something significant, elemental, and profound.

At a lull in the entertainment the man looked at me and smiled. "Your face is familiar," he said, politely. "Weren't you in the First Division during the war?"

"Why, yes. I was in the Twenty-eighth Infantry."

"I was in the Sixteenth until June nineteen-eighteen. I knew I'd seen you somewhere before."

We talked for a moment about some wet, gray little villages in France. Evidently he lived in this vicinity, for he told me that he had just bought a hydroplane, and was going to try it out in the morning.

"Want to go with me, old sport? Just near the shore along the Sound."

"What time?"

"Any time that suits you best."

It was on the tip of my tongue to ask his name when Jordan looked around and smiled.

"Having a gay time now?" she inquired.

"Much better." I turned again to my new acquaintance. "This is an unusual party for me. I haven't even seen the host. I live over there—" I waved my hand at the invisible hedge in the distance, "and this man Gatsby sent over his chauffeur with an invitation."

For a moment he looked at me as if he failed to understand.

"I'm Gatsby," he said suddenly.

"What!" I exclaimed. "Oh, I beg your pardon."

"I thought you knew, old sport. I'm afraid I'm not a very good host."

He smiled understandingly—much more than understandingly. It was one of those rare smiles with a quality of eternal reassurance in it, that you may come across four or five times in life. It faced—or seemed to face—the whole eternal world for an instant, and then concentrated on *you* with an irresistible prejudice in your favor. It understood you just as far as you wanted to be understood, believed in you as you would like to believe in yourself, and assured you that it had precisely the impression of you that, at your best, you hoped to convey. Precisely at that point it vanished—and I was looking at an elegant young roughneck, a year or two over thirty, whose elaborate formality of speech just missed being absurd. Some time before he introduced himself I'd got a strong impression that he was picking his words with care.

Almost at the moment when Mr. Gatsby identified himself, a butler hurried toward him with the information that Chicago was calling him on the wire. He excused himself with a small bow that included each of us in turn.

"If you want anything just ask for it, old sport," he urged me. "Excuse me. I will rejoin you later."

When he was gone I turned immediately to Jordan—constrained to assure her of my surprise. I had expected that Mr. Gatsby would be a florid and corpulent person in his middle years.

"Who is he?" I demanded. "Do you know?"

"He's just a man named Gatsby."

"Where is he from, I mean? And what does he do?"

"Now *you're* started on the subject," she answered with a wan smile. "Well, he told me once he was an Oxford man."

A dim background started to take shape behind him, but at her next remark it faded away.

"However, I don't believe it."

"Why not?"

"I don't know," she insisted, "I just don't think he went there."

Something in her tone reminded me of the other girl's "I think he killed a man," and had the effect of stimulating my curiosity. I would have accepted without question the information that Gatsby sprang from the swamps of Louisiana or from the lower East Side of New York. That was comprehensible. But young men didn't—at least in my provincial inexperience I believed they didn't—drift coolly out of nowhere and buy a palace on Long Island Sound.

"Anyhow, he gives large parties," said Jordan, changing the subject with an urban distaste for the concrete. "And I like large parties. They're so intimate. At small parties there isn't any privacy."

There was the boom of a bass drum, and the voice of the orchestra leader rang out suddenly above the echolalia of the garden.

"Ladies and gentlemen," he cried. "At the request of Mr. Gatsby we are going to play for you Mr. Vladimir Tostoff's latest work, which attracted so much attention at Carnegie Hall last May. If you read the papers, you know there was a big sensation." He smiled with jovial condescension, and added: "Some sensation!" Whereupon everybody laughed.

"The piece is known," he concluded lustily, "as Vladimir Tostoff's *Jazz History of the World.*"

The nature of Mr. Tostoff's composition eluded me, because just as it began my eyes fell on Gatsby, standing alone on the marble steps and looking from one group to another with approving eyes. His tanned skin was drawn attractively tight on his face and his short hair looked as though it were trimmed every day. I could see nothing sinister about him. I wondered if the fact that he was not drinking helped to set him off from his guests, for it seemed to me that he grew more correct as the fraternal hilarity increased. When the *Jazz History of the World* was over, girls were putting their heads on men's shoulders in a puppyish, convivial way, girls were swooning backward playfully into men's arms, even into groups, knowing that some one would arrest their falls—but no one swooned backward on Gatsby, and no French bob touched Gatsby's shoulder, and no singing quartets were formed for Gatsby's head for one link.

"I beg your pardon."

Gatsby's butler was suddenly standing beside us.

"Miss Baker?" he inquired. "I beg your pardon, but Mr. Gatsby would like to speak to you alone."

"With me?" she exclaimed in surprise.

"Yes, madame."

She got up slowly, raising her eyebrows at me in astonisthment, and followed the butler toward the house. I noticed that she wore her evening-dress, all her dresses, like sports clothes—there was a jauntiness about her movements as if she had first learned to walk upon golf courses on clean, crisp mornings.

I was alone and it was almost two. For some time confused and intriguing sounds had issued from a long, many-windowed room which overhung the terrace. Eluding Jordan's undergraduate, who was now engaged in an obstetrical conversation with two chorus girls, and who implored me to join him, I went inside.

The large room was full of people. One of the girls in yellow was playing the piano, and beside her stood a tall, red-haired young lady from a famous chorus, engaged in song. She had drunk a quantity of champagne, and during the course of her song she had decided, ineptly, that everything was very, very sad—she was not only singing, she was weeping too. Whenever there was a pause in the song she filled it with gasping, broken sobs, and then took up the lyric again in a quavering soprano. The tears coursed down her cheeks—not freely, however, for when they came into contact with her heavily beaded eyelashes they assumed an inky color, and pursued the rest of their way in slow black rivulets. A humorous suggestion was made that she sing the notes on her face, whereupon she threw up her hands, sank into a chair, and went off into a deep vinous sleep.

"She had a fight with a man who says he's her husband," explained a girl at my elbow.

I looked around. Most of the remaining women were now having fights with men said to be their husbands. Even Jordan's party, the quartet from East Egg, were rent asunder by dissension. One of the men was talking with curious intensity to a young actress, and his wife, after attempting to laugh at the situation in a dignified and indifferent way, broke down entirely and resorted to flank attacks— at intervals she appeared suddenly at his side like an angry diamond, and hissed: "You promised!" into his ear.

The reluctance to go home was not confined to wayward men. The hall was at present occupied by two deplorably sober men and their highly indignant wives. The wives were sympathizing with each other in slightly raised voices.

"Whenever he sees I'm having a good time he wants to go home."

"Never heard anything so selfish in my life."

"We're always the first ones to leave."

"So are we."

"Well, we're almost the last tonight," said one of the men sheepishly. "The orchestra left half an hour ago."

In spite of the wives' agreement that such malevolence was beyond credibility, the dispute ended in a short struggle, and both wives were lifted, kicking, into the night.

As I waited for my hat in the hall the door of the library opened and Jordan Baker and Gatsby came out together. He was saying some last word to her, but the eagerness in his manner tightened abruptly into formality as several people approached him to say good-by.

Jordan's party were calling impatiently to her from the porch, but she lingered for a moment to shake hands.

"I've just heard the most amazing thing," she whispered. "How long were we in there?"

"Why, about an hour."

"It was . . . simply amazing," she repeated abstractedly. "But I swore I wouldn't tell it and here I am tantalizing you." She yawned gracefully in my face. "Please come and see me. . . . Phone book. . . . Under the name of Mrs. Sigourney Howard. . . . My aunt. . . ." She was hurrying off as she talked—her brown hand waved a jaunty salute as she melted into her party at the door.

Rather ashamed that on my first appearance I had stayed so late, I joined the last of Gatsby's guests, who were clustered around him. I wanted to explain that I'd hunted for him early in the evening and to apologize for not having known him in the garden.

"Don't mention it," he enjoined me eagerly. "Don't give it another thought, old sport." The familiar expression held no more familiarity than the hand which reassuringly brushed my shoulder. "And don't forget we're going up in the hydroplane tomorrow morning, at nine o'clock."

Then the butler, behind his shoulder:

"Philadelphia wants you on the 'phone sir."

"All right, in a minute. Tell them I'll be right there. . . . Good night."

"Good night."

"Good night." He smiled—and suddenly there seemed to be a pleasant significance in having been among the last to go, as if he had desired it all the time. "Good night, old sport. . . . Good night."

But as I walked down the steps I saw that the evening was not quite over. Fifty feet from the door a dozen headlights illuminated a bizarre and tumultuous scene. In the ditch beside the road, right side up, but violently shorn of one wheel, rested a new coupé which had left Gatsby's drive not two minutes before. The sharp jut of a wall accounted for the detachment of the wheel, which was now getting considerable attention from half a dozen curious chauffeurs. However, as they had left their cars blocking the road, a harsh, discordant din from those in the rear had been audible for some time, and added to the already violent confusion of the scene.

A man in a long duster had dismounted from the wreck and now stood in the middle of the road, looking from the car to the tire and from the tire to the observers in a pleasant, puzzled way.

"See!" he explained. "It went in the ditch."

The fact was infinitely astonishing to him, and I recognized first the unusual quality of wonder, and then the man—it was the late patron of Gatsby's library.

"How'd it happen?"

He shrugged his shoulders.

"I know nothing whatever about mechanics," he said decisively.

"But how did it happen? Did you run into the wall?"

"Don't ask me," said Owl Eyes, washing his hands of the whole matter. "I know very little about driving—next to nothing. It happened, and that's all I know."

"Well, if you're a poor driver you oughtn't to try driving at night."

"But I wasn't even trying," he explained indignantly, "I wasn't even trying."

An awed hush fell upon the bystanders.

"Do you want to commit suicide?"

"You're lucky it was just a wheel! A bad driver and not even *trying*!"

"You don't understand," explained the criminal. "I wasn't driving. There's another man in the car."

The shock that followed this declaration found voice in a sustained "Ah-h-h!" as the door of the coupé swung slowly open. The crowd—it was now a crowd—stepped back involuntarily, and when the door had opened wide there was a ghostly pause. Then, very gradually, part by part, a pale, dangling individual stepped out of the wreck, pawing tentatively at the ground with a large uncertain dancing shoe.

Blinded by the glare of the headlights and confused by the incessant groaning of the horns, the apparition stood swaying for a moment before he perceived the man in the duster.

"Wha's matter?" he inquired calmly. "Did we run outa gas?"

"Look!"

Half a dozen fingers pointed at the amputated wheel—he stared at it for a moment, and then looked upward as though he suspected that it had dropped from the sky.

"It came off," some one explained.

He nodded.

"At first I din' notice we'd stopped."

A pause. Then, taking a long breath and straightening his shoulders, he remarked in a determined voice:

"Wonder'ff tell me where there's a gas'line station?"

At least a dozen men, some of them a little better off than he was, explained to him that wheel and car were no longer joined by any physical bond.

"Back out," he suggested after a moment. "Put her in reverse."

"But the *wheel's* off!"

He hesitated.

"No harm in trying," he said.

The caterwauling horns had reached a crescendo and I turned away and cut across the lawn toward home. I glanced back once. A wafer of a moon was shining over Gatsby's house, making the night fine as before, and surviving the laughter and the sound of his still glowing garden. A sudden emptiness seemed to flow now from the windows and the great doors, endowing with complete isolation

the figure of the host, who stood on the porch, his hand up in a
formal gesture of farewell.

Reading over what I have written so far, I see I have given the
impression that the events of three nights several weeks apart were
all that absorbed me. On the contrary, they were merely casual
events in a crowded summer, and, until much later, they absorbed
me infinitely less than my personal affairs.

Most of the time I worked. In the early morning the sun threw
my shadow westward as I hurried down the white chasms of lower
New York to the Probity Trust. I knew the other clerks and young
bond-salesmen by their first names, and lunched with them in dark,
crowded restaurants on little pig sausages and mashed potatoes and
coffee. I even had a short affair with a girl who lived in Jersey City
and worked in the accounting department, but her brother began
throwing mean looks in my direction, so when she went on her
vacation in July I let it blow quietly away.

I took dinner usually at the Yale Club—for some reason it was
the gloomiest event of my day—and then I went upstairs to the
library and studied investments and securities for a conscientious
hour. There were generally a few rioters around, but they never
came into the library, so it was a good place to work. After that, if
the night was mellow, I strolled down Madison Avenue past the old
Murray Hill Hotel, and over 33d Street to the Pennsylvania Station.

I began to like New York, the racy, adventurous feel of it at
night, and the satisfaction that the constant flicker of men and
women and machines gives to the restless eye. I liked to walk up
Fifth Avenue and pick out romantic women from the crowd and
imagine that in a few minutes I was going to enter into their lives,
and no one would ever know or disapprove. Sometimes, in my mind,
I followed them to their apartments on the corners of hidden streets,
and they turned and smiled back at me before they faded through a
door into warm darkness. At the enchanted metropolitan twilight I
felt a haunting loneliness sometimes, and felt it in others—poor
young clerks who loitered in front of windows waiting until it was
time for a solitary restaurant dinner—young clerks in the dusk,
wasting the most poignant moments of night and life.

Again at eight o'clock, when the dark lanes of the Forties were
lined five deep with throbbing taxicabs, bound for the theater district, I felt a sinking in my heart. Forms leaned together in the taxis

as they waited, and voices sang, and there was laughter from unheard jokes, and lighted cigarettes made unintelligible circles inside. Imagining that I, too, was hurrying toward gayety and sharing their intimate excitement, I wished them well.

For a while I lost sight of Jordan Baker, and then in midsummer I found her again. At first I was flattered to go places with her, because she was a golf champion, and everyone knew her name. Then it was something more. I wasn't actually in love, but I felt a sort of tender curiosity. The bored haughty face that she turned to the world concealed something—most affectations conceal something eventually, even though they don't in the beginning—and one day I found what it was. When we were on a house-party together up in Warwick, she left a borrowed car out in the rain with the top down, and then lied about it—and suddenly I remembered the story about her that had eluded me that night at Daisy's. At her first big golf tournament there was a row that nearly reached the newspapers —a suggestion that she had moved her ball from a bad lie in the semi-final round. The thing approached the proportions of a scandal—then died away. A caddy retracted his statement, and the only other witness admitted that he might have been mistaken. The incident and the name had remained together in my mind.

Jordan Baker instinctively avoided clever, shrewd men, and now I saw that this was because she felt safer on a plane where any divergence from a code would be thought impossible. She was incurably dishonest. She wasn't able to endure being at a disadvantage and, given this unwillingness, I suppose she had begun dealing in subterfuges when she was very young in order to keep that cool, insolent smile turned to the world and yet satisfy the demands of her hard, jaunty body.

It made no difference to me. Dishonesty in a woman is a thing you never blame deeply—I was casually sorry, and then I forgot. It was on that same house-party that we had a curious conversation about driving a car. It started because she passed so close to some workmen that our fender flicked a button on one man's coat.

"You're a rotten driver," I protested. "Either you ought to be more careful, or you oughtn't to drive at all."

"I am careful."

"No, you're not."

"Well, other people are," she said lightly.

"What's that got to do with it?"

"They'll keep out of my way," she insisted. "It takes two to make an accident."

"Suppose you met somebody just as careless as yourself."

"I hope I never will," she answered. "I hate careless people. That's why I like you."

Her gray, sun-strained eyes stared straight ahead, but she had deliberately shifted our relations, and for a moment I thought I loved her. But I am slow-thinking and full of interior rules that act as brakes on my desires, and I knew that first I had to get myself definitely out of that tangle back home. I'd been writing letters once a week and signing them: "Love, Nick," and all I could think of was how, when that certain girl played tennis, a faint mustache of perspiration appeared on her upper lip. Nevertheless there was a vague understanding that had to be tactfully broken off before I was free.

Every one suspects himself of at least one of the cardinal virtues, and this is mine: I am one of the few honest people that I have ever known.

4

On Sunday morning while church bells rang in the villages alongshore, the world and its mistress returned to Gatsby's house and twinkled hilariously on his lawn.

"He's a bootlegger," said the young ladies, moving somewhere between his cocktails and his flowers. "One time he killed a man who had found out that he was nephew to Von Hindenburg and second cousin to the devil. Reach me a rose, honey, and pour me a last drop into that there crystal glass."

Once I wrote down on the empty spaces of a timetable the names of those who came to Gatsby's house that summer. It is an old timetable now, disintegrating at its folds, and headed "This schedule in effect July 5th, 1922." But I can still read the gray names, and they will give you a better impression than my generalities of those who accepted Gatsby's hospitality and paid him the subtle tribute of knowing nothing whatever about him.

From East Egg, then, came the Chester Beckers and the Leeches, and a man named Bunsen, whom I knew at Yale, and Doctor Webster Civet, who was drowned last summer up in Maine. And the Hornbeams and the Willie Voltaires, and a whole clan named Blackbuck, who always gathered in a corner and flipped up their noses like goats at whosoever came near. And the Ismays and the Chrysties (or rather Hubert Auerbach and Mr. Chrystie's wife), and Edgar Beaver, whose hair, they say, turned cotton-white one winter afternoon for no good reason at all.

Clarence Endive was from East Egg, as I remember. He came only once, in white knickerbockers, and had a fight with a bum named Etty in the garden. From farther out on the Island came the Cheadles and the O. R. P. Schraeders, and the Stonewall Jackson Abrams of Georgia, and the Fishguards and the Ripley Snells. Snell was there three days before he went to the penitentiary, so drunk out on the gravel drive that Mrs. Ulysses Swett's automobile ran over his right hand. The Dancies came, too, and S. B. Whitebait, who was well over sixty, and Maurice A. Flink, and the Hammerheads, and Beluga the tobacco importer, and Beluga's girls.

From West Egg came the Poles and the Mulreadys and Cecil Roebuck and Cecil Schoen and Gulick the State senator and Newton Orchid, who controlled Films Par Excellence, and Eckhaust and Clyde Cohen and Don S. Schwartze (the son) and Arthur McCarty, all connected with the movies in one way or another. And the Catlips and the Bembergs and G. Earl Muldoon, brother to that Muldoon who afterward strangled his wife. Da Fontano the promoter came there, and Ed Legros and James B. ("Rot-Gut") Ferret and the De Jongs and Ernest Lilly—they came to gamble, and when Ferret wandered into the garden it meant he was cleaned out and Associated Traction would have to fluctuate profitably next day.

A man named Klipspringer was there so often and so long that he became known as "the boarder"—I doubt if he had any other home. Of theatrical people there were Gus Waize and Horace O'Donavan and Lester Myer and George Duckweed and Francis Bull. Also from New York were the Chromes and the Backhyssons and the Dennickerns and Russell Betty and the Corrigans and the Kellehers and the Dewers and the Scullys and S. W. Belcher and the Smirkes and the young Quinns, divorced now, and Henry L. Palmetto, who killed himself by jumping in front of a subway train in Times Square.

Benny McClenahan arrived always with four girls. They were never quite the same ones in physical person, but they were so identical one with another that it inevitably seemed they had been there before. I have forgotten their names—Jaqueline, I think, or else Consuela, or Gloria or Judy or June, and their last names were either the melodious names of flowers and months or the sterner ones of the great American capitalists whose cousins, if pressed, they would confess themselves to be.

In addition to all these I can remember that Faustina O'Brien came there at least once and the Baedeker girls and young Brewer, who had his nose shot off in the war, and Mr. Albrucksburger and Miss Haag, his fiancée, and Ardita Fitz-Peters and Mr. P. Jewett, once head of the American Legion, and Miss Claudia Hip, with a man reputed to be her chauffeur, and a prince of something, whom we called Duke, and whose name, if I ever knew it, I have forgotten.

All these people came to Gatsby's house in the summer.

At nine o'clock, one morning late in July, Gatsby's gorgeous car lurched up the rocky drive to my door and gave out a burst of melody from its three-noted horn. It was the first time he had called on me, though I had gone to two of his parties, mounted in his hydroplane, and, at his urgent invitation, made frequent use of his beach.

"Good morning, old sport. You're having lunch with me today and I thought we'd ride up together."

He was balancing himself on the dashboard of his car with that resourcefulness of movement that is so peculiarly American—that comes, I suppose, with the absence of lifting work in youth and, even more, with the formless grace of our nervous, sporadic games. This quality was continually breaking through his punctilious manner in the shape of restlessness. He was never quite still; there was always a tapping foot somewhere or the impatient opening and closing of a hand.

He saw me looking with admiration at his car.

"It's pretty, isn't it, old sport?" He jumped off to give me a better view. "Haven't you ever seen it before?"

I'd seen it. Everybody had seen it. It was a rich cream color, bright with nickel, swollen here and there in its monstrous length with triumphant hat-boxes and supper-boxes and tool-boxes, and terraced with a labyrinth of wind-shields that mirrored a dozen suns. Sitting down behind many layers of glass in a sort of green leather conservatory, we started to town.

I had talked with him perhaps half a dozen times in the past month and found, to my disappointment, that he had little to say. So my first impression, that he was a person of some undefined consequence, had gradually faded and he had become simply the proprietor of an elaborate road-house next door.

And then came that disconcerting ride. We hadn't reached West Egg Village before Gatsby began leaving his elegant sentences unfinished and slapping himself indecisively on the knees of his caramel-colored suit.

"Look here, old sport," he broke out surprisingly, "what's your opinion of me, anyhow?"

A little overwhelmed, I began the generalized evasions which that question deserves.

"Well, I'm going to tell you something about my life," he interrupted. "I don't want you to get a wrong idea of me from all these stories you hear."

So he was aware of the bizarre accusations that flavored conversation in his halls.

"I'll tell you God's truth." His right hand suddenly ordered divine retribution to stand by. "I am the son of some wealthy people in the Middle West—all dead now. I was brought up in America but educated at Oxford, because all my ancestors have been educated there for many years. It is a family tradition."

He looked at me sideways—and I knew why Jordan Baker had believed he was lying. He hurried the phrase "educated at Oxford," or swallowed it, or choked on it, as though it had bothered him before. And with this doubt, his whole statement fell to pieces, and I wondered if there wasn't something a little sinister about him, after all.

"What part of the Middle West?" I inquired casually.

"San Francisco."

"I see."

"My family all died and I came into a good deal of money."

His voice was solemn, as if the memory of that sudden extinction of a clan still haunted him. For a moment I suspected that he was pulling my leg, but a glance at him convinced me otherwise.

"After that I lived like a young rajah in all the capitals of Europe—Paris, Venice, Rome—collecting jewels, chiefly rubies, hunting big game, painting a little, things for myself only, and trying to forget something very sad that had happened to me long ago."

With an effort I managed to restrain my incredulous laughter.

The very phrases were worn so threadbare that they evoked no image except that of turbaned "character" leaking sawdust at every pore as he pursued a tiger through the Bois de Boulogne.

"Then came the war, old sport. It was a great relief, and I tried very hard to die, but I seemed to bear an enchanted life. I accepted a commission as first lieutenant when it began. In the Argonne Forest I took the remains of my machine-gun battalion so far forward that there was a half mile gap on either side of us where the infantry couldn't advance. We stayed there two days and two nights, a hundred and thirty men with sixteen Lewis guns, and when the infantry came up at last they found the insignia of three German divisions among the piles of dead. I was promoted to be a major, and every Allied government gave me a decoration—even Montenegro, little Montenegro down on the Adriatic Sea!"

Little Montenegro! He lifted up the words and nodded at them—with his smile. The smile comprehended Montenegro's troubled history and sympathized with the brave struggles of the Montenegrin people. It appreciated fully the chain of national circumstances which had elicited this tribute from Montenegro's warm little heart. My incredulity was submerged in fascination now; it was like skimming hastily through a dozen magazines.

He reached in his pocket, and a piece of metal, slung on a ribbon, fell into my palm.

"That's the one from Montenegro."

To my astonishment, the thing had an authentic look. "Orderi de Danilo," ran the circular legend, "Montenegro, Nicolas Rex."

"Turn it."

"Major Jay Gatsby," I read, "For Valour Extraordinary."

"Here's another thing I always carry. A souvenir of Oxford days. It was taken in Trinity Quad—the man on my left is now the Earl of Doncaster."

It was a photograph of half a dozen young men in blazers loafing in an archway through which were visible a host of spires. There was Gatsby, looking a little, not much, younger—with a cricket bat in his hand.

Then it was all true. I saw the skins of tigers flaming in his palace on the Grand Canal; I saw him opening a chest of rubies to ease, with their crimson-lighted depths, the gnawings of his broken heart.

"I'm going to make a big request of you today," he said, pocketing his souvenirs with satisfaction, "so I thought you ought to know something about me. I didn't want you to think I was just some nobody. You see, I usually find myself among strangers because I drift here and there trying to forget the sad thing that happened to me." He hesitated. "You'll hear about it this afternoon."

"At lunch?"

"No, this afternoon. I happened to find out that you're taking Miss Baker to tea."

"Do you mean you're in love with Miss Baker?"

"No, old sport, I'm not. But Miss Baker has kindly consented to speak to you about this matter."

I hadn't the faintest idea what "this matter" was, but I was more annoyed than interested. I hadn't asked Jordan to tea in order to discuss Mr. Jay Gatsby. I was sure the request would be something utterly fantastic, and for a moment I was sorry I'd ever set foot upon his overpopulated lawn.

He wouldn't say another word. His correctness grew on him as we neared the city. We passed Port Roosevelt, where there was a glimpse of red-belted ocean-going ships, and sped along a cobbled slum lined with the dark, undeserted saloons of the faded-gilt nineteen-hundreds. Then the valley of ashes opened out on both sides of us, and I had a glimpse of Mrs. Wilson straining at the garage pump with panting vitality as we went by.

With fenders spread like wings we scattered light through half Astoria—only half, for as we twisted among the pillars of the elevated I heard the familiar "jug-jug-*spat*!" of a motorcycle, and a frantic policeman rode alongside.

"All right, old sport," called Gatsby. We slowed down. Taking a white card from his wallet, he waved it before the man's eyes.

"Right you are," agreed the policeman, tipping his cap. "Know you next time, Mr. Gatsby. Excuse *me*!"

"What was that?" I inquired. "The picture of Oxford?"

"I was able to do the commissioner a favor once, and he sends me a Christmas card every year."

Over the great bridge, with the sunlight through the girders making a constant flicker upon the moving cars, with the city rising up across the river in white heaps and sugar lumps all built with a wish out of non-olfactory money. The city seen from the Queensboro Bridge is always the city seen for the first time, in its first wild promise of all the mystery and the beauty in the world.

A dead man passed us in a hearse heaped with blooms, followed by two carriages with drawn blinds, and by more cheerful carriages for friends. The friends looked out at us with the tragic eyes and short upper lips of southeastern Europe, and I was glad that the sight of Gatsby's splendid car was included in their somber holiday. As we crossed Blackwell's Island a limousine passed us, driven by a white chauffeur, in which sat three modish negroes, two bucks and a girl. I laughed aloud as the yolks of their eyeballs rolled toward us in haughty rivalry.

"Anything can happen now that we've slid over this bridge," I thought; "anything at all. . . ."

Even Gatsby could happen, without any particular wonder.

Roaring noon. In a well-fanned Forty-second Street cellar I met Gatsby for lunch. Blinking away the brightness of the street outside, my eyes picked him out obscurely in the anteroom, talking to another man.

"Mr. Carraway, this is my friend Mr. Wolfsheim."

A small, flat-nosed Jew raised his large head and regarded me with two fine growths of hair which luxuriated in either nostril. After a moment I discovered his tiny eyes in the half-darkness.

"—So I took one look at him," said Mr. Wolfsheim, shaking my hand earnestly, "and what do you think I did?"

"What?" I inquired politely.

But evidently he was not addressing me, for he dropped my hand and covered Gatsby with his expressive nose.

"I handed the money to Katspaugh and I said: 'All right, Katspaugh, don't pay him a penny till he shuts his mouth.' He shut it then and there."

Gatsby took an arm of each of us and moved forward into the restaurant, whereupon Mr. Wolfsheim swallowed a new sentence he was starting and lapsed into a somnambulatory abstraction.

"Highballs?" asked the head waiter.

"This is a nice restaurant here," said Mr. Wolfsheim, looking at the Presbyterian nymphs on the ceiling. "But I like across the street better!"

"Yes, highballs," agreed Gatsby, and then to Mr. Wolfsheim: "It's too hot over there."

"Hot and small—yes," said Mr. Wolfsheim, "but full of memories."

"What place is that?" I asked.

"The old Metropole."

"The old Metropole," brooded Mr. Wolfsheim gloomily. "Filled with faces dead and gone. Filled with friends gone now forever. I can't forget so long as I live the night they shot Rosy Rosenthal there. It was six of us at the table, and Rosy had eat and drunk a lot all evening. When it was almost morning the waiter came up to him with a funny look and says somebody wants to speak to him outside. 'All right,' says Rosy, and begins to get up, and I pulled him down in his chair.

" 'Let the bastards come in here if they want you, Rosy, but don't you, so help me, move outside this room.'

"It was four o'clock in the morning then, and if we'd of raised the blinds we'd of seen daylight."

"Did he go?" I asked innocently.

"Sure he went." Mr. Wolfsheim's nose flashed at me indignantly. "He turned around in the door and says: 'Don't let that waiter take away my coffee!' Then he went out on the sidewalk, and they shot him three times in his full belly and drove away."

"Four of them were electrocuted," I said, remembering.

"Five, with Becker." His nostrils turned to me in an interested way. "I understand you're looking for a business gonnegtion."

The juxaposition of these two remarks was startling. Gatsby answered for me:

"Oh, no," he exclaimed, "this isn't the man."

"No?" Mr. Wolfsheim seemed disappointed.

"This is just a friend. I told you we'd talk about that some other time."

"I beg your pardon," said Mr. Wolfsheim, "I had a wrong man."

A succulent hash arrived, and Mr. Wolfsheim, forgetting the more sentimental atmosphere of the old Metropole, began to eat with ferocious delicacy. His eyes, meanwhile, roved very slowly all around the room—he completed the arc by turning to inspect the people directly behind. I think that, except for my presence, he would have taken one short glance beneath our own table.

"Look here, old sport," said Gatsby leaning toward me, "I'm afraid I made you a little angry this morning in the car."

There was the smile again, but this time I held out against it.

"I don't like mysteries," I answered, "and I don't understand why you won't come out frankly and tell me what you want. Why has it all got to come through Miss Baker?"

"Oh, it's nothing underhand," he assured me. "Miss Baker's a great sportswoman, you know, and she'd never do anything that wasn't all right."

Suddenly he looked at his watch, jumped up, and hurried from the room, leaving me with Mr. Wolfsheim at the table.

"He has to telephone." said Mr. Wolfsheim, following him with his eyes. "Fine fellow, isn't he? Handsome to look at and a perfect gentleman."

"Yes."

"He's an Oggsford man."

"Oh!"

"He went to Oggsford College in England. You know Oggsford College?"

"I've heard of it."

"It's one of the most famous colleges in the world."

"Have you known Gatsby for a long time?" I inquired.

"Several years," he answered in a gratified way. "I made the pleasure of his acquaintance just after the war. But I knew I had discovered a man of fine breeding after I talked with him an hour. I said to myself: 'There's the kind of man you'd like to take home and introduce to your mother and sister.'" He paused. "I see you're looking at my cuff buttons."

I hadn't been looking at them, but I did now. They were composed of oddly familiar pieces of ivory.

"Finest specimens of human molars," he informed me.

"Well!" I inspected them. "That's a very interesting idea."

"Yeah." He flipped his sleeves up under his coat. "Yeah, Gatsby's very careful about women. He would never so much as look at a friend's wife."

When the subject of this instinctive trust returned to the table and sat down Mr. Wolfsheim drank his coffee with a jerk and got to his feet.

"I have enjoyed my lunch," he said, "and I'm going to run off from you two young men before I outstay my welcome."

"Don't hurry, Meyer," said Gatsby, without enthusiasm. Mr. Wolfsheim raised his hand in a sort of benediction.

"You're very polite, but I belong to another generation," he announced solemnly. "You sit here and discuss your sports and your young ladies and your—" He supplied an imaginary noun with another wave of his hand. "As for me, I am fifty years old, and I won't impose myself on you any longer."

As he shook hands and turned away his tragic nose was trembling. I wondered if I had said anything to offend him.

"He becomes very sentimental sometimes," explained Gatsby. "This is one of his sentimental days. He's quite a character around New York—a denizen of Broadway."

"Who is he, anyhow, an actor?"

"No."

"A dentist?"

"Meyer Wolfsheim? No, he's a gambler." Gatsby hesitated, then added coolly: "He's the man who fixed the World's Series back in 1919."

"Fixed the World's Series?" I repeated.

The idea staggered me. I remembered, of course, that the World's Series had been fixed in 1919, but if I had thought of it at all I would have thought of it as a thing that merely *happened*, the end of some inevitable chain. It never occurred to me that one man could start to play with the faith of fifty million people—with the single-mindedness of a burglar blowing a safe.

"How did he happen to do that?" I asked after a minute.

"He just saw the opportunity."

"Why isn't he in jail?"

"They can't get him, old sport. He's a smart man."

I insisted on paying the check. As the waiter brought my change I caught sight of Tom Buchanan across the crowded room.

"Come along with me for a minute," I said; "I've got to say hello to some one."

When he saw us Tom jumped up and took half a dozen steps in our direction.

"Where've you been?" he demanded eagerly. "Daisy's furious because you haven't called up."

"This is Mr. Gatsby, Mr. Buchanan."

They shook hands briefly, and a strained, unfamiliar look of embarrassment came over Gatsby's face.

"How've you been, anyhow?" demanded Tom of me. "How'd you happen to come up this far to eat?"

"I've been having lunch with Mr. Gatsby."

I turned toward Mr. Gatsby, but he was no longer there.

One October day in nineteen-seventeen——

(said Jordan Baker that afternoon, sitting up very straight on a straight chair in the tea-garden at the Plaza Hotel)

—I was walking along from one place to another, half on the sidewalks and half on the lawns. I was happier on the lawns because I had on shoes from England with rubber nobs on the soles that bit into the soft ground. I had on a new plaid skirt also that blew a little in the wind, and whenever this happened the red, white, and blue banners in front of all the houses stretched out stiff and said *tut-tut-tut-tut*, in a disapproving way.

The largest of the banners and the largest of the lawns belonged to Daisy Fay's house. She was just eighteen, two years older than me, and by far the most popular of all the young girls in Louisville. She dressed in white, and had a little white roadster, and all day long the telephone rang in her house and excited young officers from Camp Taylor demanded the privilege of monopolizing her that night. "Anyways, for an hour!"

When I came opposite her house that morning her white roadster was beside the curb, and she was sitting in it with a lieutenant I had never seen before. They were so engrossed in each other that she didn't see me until I was five feet away.

"Hello, Jordan," she called unexpectedly. "Please come here."

I was flattered that she wanted to speak to me, because of all the older girls I admired her most. She asked me if I was going to the Red Cross and make bandages. I was. Well, then, would I tell them that she couldn't come that day? The officer looked at Daisy while she was speaking, in a way that every young girl wants to be looked at some time, and because it seemed romantic to me I have remembered the incident ever since. His name was Jay Gatsby, and I didn't lay eyes on him again for over four years—even after I'd met him on Long Island I didn't realize it was the same man.

That was nineteen-seventeen. By the next year I had a few beaux myself, and I began to play in tournaments, so I didn't see Daisy very often. She went with a slightly older crowd—when she went with anyone at all. Wild rumors were circulating about her—how her mother had found her packing her bag one winter night to go to New York and say good-by to a soldier who was going overseas. She was effectually prevented, but she wasn't on speaking terms with her family for several weeks. After that she didn't play around with the soldiers any more, but only with a few flat-footed, shortsighted young men in town, who couldn't get into the army at all.

By the next autumn she was gay again, gay as ever. She had a début after the Armistice, and in February she was presumably engaged to a man from New Orleans. In June she married Tom Buchanan of Chicago, with more pomp and circumstance than Louisville ever knew before. He came down with a hundred people in four private cars, and hired a whole floor of the Muhlbach Hotel, and the day before the wedding he gave her a string of pearls valued at three hundred and fifty thousand dollars.

I was a bridesmaid. I came into her room half an hour before the bridal dinner, and found her lying on her bed as lovely as the June night in her flowered dress—and as drunk as a monkey. She had a bottle of Sauterne in one hand and a letter in the other.

" 'Gratulate me," she muttered. "Never had a drink before, but oh how I do enjoy it."

"What's the matter, Daisy?"

I was scared, I can tell you; I'd never seen a girl like that before.

"Here, deares'." She groped around in a waste-basket she had with her on the bed and pulled out the string of pearls. "Take 'em down-stairs and give 'em back to whoever they belong to. Tell 'em all Daisy's change' her mine. Say: 'Daisy's change' her mine!' "

She began to cry—she cried and cried. I rushed out and found her mother's maid, and we locked the door and got her into a cold bath. She wouldn't let go of the letter. She took it into the tub with her and squeezed it up into a wet ball, and only let me leave it in the soap-dish when she saw that it was coming to pieces like snow.

But she didn't say another word. We gave her spirits of ammonia and put ice on her forehead and hooked her back into her dress, and half an hour later, when we walked out of the room, the pearls were around her neck and the incident was over. Next day at five o'clock she married Tom Buchanan without so much as a shiver, and started off on a three months' trip to the South Seas.

I saw them in Santa Barbara when they came back, and I thought I'd never seen a girl so mad about her husband. If he left the room for a minute she'd look around uneasily, and say: "Where's Tom gone?" and wear the most abstracted expression until she saw him coming in the door. She used to sit on the sand with his head in her lap by the hour, rubbing her fingers over his eyes and looking at him with unfathomable delight. It was touching to see them together—it made you laugh in a hushed, fascinated way. That was in August. A week after I left Santa Barbara Tom ran into a wagon on the Ventura road one night, and ripped a front wheel off his car. The girl who was with him got into the papers, too, because her arm was broken—she was one of the chambermaids in the Santa Barbara Hotel.

The next April Daisy had her little girl, and they went to France for a year. I saw them one spring in Cannes, and later in Deauville, and then they came back to Chicago to settle down. Daisy was popular in Chicago, as you know. They moved with a fast crowd, all of them young and rich and wild, but she came out with an absolutely perfect reputation. Perhaps because she doesn't drink. It's a great advantage not to drink among hard-drinking people. You can hold your tongue, and, moreover, you can time any little irregularity of your own so that everybody else is so blind that they don't see or care. Perhaps Daisy never went in for amour at all—and yet there's something in that voice of hers. . . .

Well, about six weeks ago, she heard the name Gatsby for the first time in years. It was when I asked you—do you remember?—if you knew Gatsby in West Egg. After you had gone home she came into my room and woke me up, and said: "What Gatsby?" and when I described him—I was half asleep—she said in the strangest voice that it must be the man she used to know. It wasn't until then that I connected this Gatsby with the officer in her white car.

When Jordan Baker had finished telling all this we had left the Plaza for half an hour and were driving in a victoria through Central Park. The sun had gone down behind the tall apartments of the movie stars in the West Fifties, and the clear voices of children, already gathered like crickets on the grass, rose through the hot twilight:

> *"I'm the Sheik of Araby.*
> *Your love belongs to me.*
> *At night when you're asleep*
> *Into your tent I'll creep——"*

"It was a strange coincidence," I said.

"But it wasn't a coincidence at all."

"Why not?"

"Gatsby bought that house so that Daisy would be just across the bay."

Then it had not been merely the stars to which he had aspired on that June night. He came alive to me, delivered suddenly from the womb of his purposeless splendor.

"He wants to know," continued Jordan, "if you'll invite Daisy to your house some afternoon and then let him come over."

The modesty of the demand shook me. He had waited five years and bought a mansion where he dispensed starlight to casual moths—so that he could "come over" some afternoon to a stranger's garden.

"Did I have to know all this before he could ask such a little thing?"

"He's afraid, he's waited so long. He thought you might be offended. You see, he's regular tough underneath it all."

Something worried me.

"Why didn't he ask you to arrange a meeting?"

"He wants her to see his house," she explained. "And your house is right next door."

"Oh!"

"I think he half expected her to wander into one of his parties, some night," went on Jordan, "but she never did. Then he began asking people casually if they knew her, and I was the first one he found. It was that night he sent for me at his dance, and you should have heard the elaborate way he worked up to it. Of course, I immediately suggested a luncheon in New York—and I thought he'd go mad:

"'I don't want to do anything out of the way!' he kept saying. 'I want to see her right next door.'

"When I said you were a particular friend of Tom's, he started to abandon the whole idea. He doesn't know very much about Tom, though he says he's read a Chicago paper for years just on the chance of catching a glimpse of Daisy's name."

It was dark now, and as we dipped under a little bridge I put my arm around Jordan's golden shoulder and drew her toward me and asked her to dinner. Suddenly I wasn't thinking of Daisy and Gatsby any more, but of this clean, hard, limited person, who dealt in universal scepticism, and who leaned back jauntily just within the circle of my arm. A phrase began to beat in my ears with a sort of heady excitement: "There are only the pursued, the pursuing, the busy and the tired."

"And Daisy ought to have something in her life," murmured Jordan to me.

"Does she want to see Gatsby?"

"She's not to know about it. Gatsby doesn't want her to know. You're just supposed to invite her to tea."

We passed a barrier of dark trees, and then the façade of Fifty-ninth Street, a block of delicate pale light, beamed down into the park. Unlike Gatsby and Tom Buchanan, I had no girl whose disembodied face floated along the dark cornices and blinding signs, and so I drew up the girl beside me, tightening my arms. Her wan, scornful mouth smiled, and so I drew her up again closer, this time to my face.

5

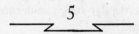

When I came home to West Egg that night I was afraid for a moment that my house was on fire. Two o'clock and the whole corner of the peninsula was blazing with light, which fell unreal on the shrubbery and made thin elongating glints upon the roadside wires. Turning a corner, I saw that it was Gatsby's house, lit from tower to cellar.

At first I thought it was another party, a wild rout that had resolved itself into "hide-and-go-seek" or "sardines-in-the-box" with all the house thrown open to the game. But there wasn't a sound. Only wind in the trees, which blew the wires and made the lights go off and on again as if the house had winked into the darkness. As my taxi groaned away I saw Gatsby walking toward me across his lawn.

"Your place looks like the World's Fair," I said.

"Does it?" He turned his eyes toward it absently. "I have been glancing into some of the rooms. Let's go to Coney Island, old sport. In my car."

"It's too late."

"Well, suppose we take a plunge in the swimming-pool? I haven't made use of it all summer."

"I've got to go to bed."

"All right."

He waited, looking at me with suppressed eagerness.

"I talked with Miss Baker," I said after a moment. "I'm going to call up Daisy tomorrow and invite her over here to tea."

"Oh, that's all right," he said carelessly. "I don't want to put you to any trouble."

"What day would suit you?"

"What day would suit *you*?" he corrected me quickly. "I don't want to put you to any trouble, you see."

"How about the day after tomorrow?"

He considered for a moment. Then, with reluctance:

"I want to get the grass cut," he said.

We both looked down at the grass—there was a sharp line where my ragged lawn ended and the darker, well-kept expanse of his began. I suspected that he meant my grass.

"There's another little thing," he said uncertainly, and hesitated.

"Would you rather put it off for a few days?" I asked.

"Oh, it isn't about that. At least—" He fumbled with a series of beginnings. "Why, I thought—why, look here, old sport, you don't make much money, do you?"

"Not very much."

This seemed to reassure him and he continued more confidently.

"I thought you didn't if you'll pardon my—you see, I carry on a little business on the side, a sort of side line, you understand. And I thought that if you don't make very much— You're selling bonds, aren't you, old sport?"

"Trying to."

"Well, this would interest you. It wouldn't take up much of your time and you might pick up a nice bit of money. It happens to be a rather confidential sort of thing."

I realize now that under different circumstances that conversation might have been one of the crises of my life. But, because the offer was obviously and tactlessly for a service to be rendered, I had no choice except to cut him off there.

"I've got my hands full," I said. "I'm much obliged but I couldn't take on any more work."

"You wouldn't have to do any business with Wolfsheim." Evidently he thought that I was shying away from the "gonnegtion" mentioned at lunch, but I assured him he was wrong. He waited a moment longer, hoping I'd begin a conversation, but I was too absorbed to be responsive, so he went unwillingly home.

The evening had made me light-headed and happy; I think I walked into a deep sleep as I entered my front door. So I don't know whether or not Gatsby went to Coney Island, or for how many hours he "glanced into rooms" while his house blazed gaudily on. I called up Daisy from the office next morning, and invited her to come to tea.

"Don't bring Tom," I warned her.

"What?"

"Don't bring Tom."

"Who is 'Tom'?" she asked innocently.

The day agreed upon was pouring rain. At eleven o'clock a man in a raincoat, dragging a lawn-mower, tapped at my front door and said that Mr. Gatsby had sent him over to cut my grass. This reminded me that I had forgotten to tell my Finn to come back, so I drove into West Egg Village to search for her among soggy white-washed alleys and to buy some cups and lemons and flowers.

The flowers were unnecessary, for at two o'clock a greenhouse arrived from Gatsby's, with innumerable receptacles to contain it. An hour later the front door opened nervously, and Gatsby, in a white flannel suit, silver shirt, and gold-colored tie, hurried in. He was pale, and there were dark signs of sleeplessness beneath his eyes.

"Is everything all right?" he asked immediately.

"The grass looks fine, if that's what you mean."

"What grass?" he inqured blankly. "Oh, the grass in the yard." He looked out the window at it, but, judging from his expression, I don't believe he saw a thing.

"Looks very good," he remarked vaguely. "One of the papers said they thought the rain would stop about four. I think it was *The Journal*. Have you got everything you need in the shape of—of tea?"

I took him into the pantry, where he looked a little reproachfully at the Finn. Together we scrutinized the twelve lemon cakes from the delicatessen shop.

"Will they do?" I asked.

"Of course, of course! They're fine!" and he added hollowly, ". . . old sport."

The rain cooled about half-past three to a damp mist, through which occasional thin drops swam like dew. Gatsby looked with vacant eyes through a copy of Clay's *Economics*, starting at the Finnish tread that shook the kitchen floor, and peering toward the bleared windows from time to time as if a series of invisible but alarming happenings were taking place outside. Finally he got up and informed me, in an uncertain voice, that he was going home.

"Why's that?"

"Nobody's coming to tea. It's too late!" He looked at his watch as if there was some pressing demand on his time elsewhere. "I can't wait all day."

"Don't be silly; it's just two minutes to four."

He sat down miserably, as if I had pushed him, and simultaneously there was the sound of a motor turning into my lane. We both jumped up, and, a little harrowed myself, I went out into the yard.

Under the dripping bare lilac-trees a large open car was coming up the drive. It stopped. Daisy's face, tipped sideways beneath a three-cornered lavender hat, looked out at me with a bright ecstatic smile.

"Is this absolutely where you live, my dearest one?"

The exhilarating ripple of her voice was a wild tonic in the rain. I had to follow the sound of it for a moment, up and down, with my ear alone, before any words came through. A damp streak of hair lay like a dash of blue paint across her cheek, and her hand was wet with glistening drops as I took it to help her from the car.

"Are you in love with me," she said low in my ear, "or why did I have to come alone?"

"That's the secret of Castle Rackrent. Tell your chauffeur to go far away and spend an hour."

"Come back in an hour, Ferdie." Then in a grave murmur: "His name is Ferdie."

"Does the gasoline affect his nose?"

"I don't think so," she said innocently. "Why?"

We went in. To my overwhelming surprise the living-room was deserted.

"Well, that's funny," I exclaimed.

"What's funny?"

She turned her head as there was a light dignified knocking at the front door. I went out and opened it. Gatsby, pale as death, with his hands plunged like weights in his coat pockets, was standing in a puddle of water glaring tragically into my eyes.

With his hands still in his coat pockets he stalked by me into the hall, turned sharply as if he were on a wire, and disappeared into the living-room. It wasn't a bit funny. Aware of the loud beating of my own heart I pulled the door to against the increasing rain.

For half a minute there wasn't a sound. Then from the living-room I heard a sort of choking murmur and part of a laugh, followed by Daisy's voice on a clear artificial note:

"I certainly am awfully glad to see you again."

A pause; it endured horribly. I had nothing to do in the hall, so I went into the room.

Gatsby, his hands still in his pockets, was reclining against the mantelpiece in a strained counterfeit of perfect ease, even of boredom. His head leaned back so far that it rested against the face of a defunct mantelpiece clock, and from this position his distraught eyes stared down at Daisy, who was sitting, frightened but graceful, on the edge of a stiff chair.

"We've met before," muttered Gatsby. His eyes glanced momentarily at me, and his lips parted with an abortive attempt at a laugh. Luckily the clock took this moment to tilt dangerously at the pressure of his head, whereupon he turned and caught it with trembling fingers and set it back in place. Then he sat down, rigidly, his elbow on the arm of the sofa and his chin in his hand.

"I'm sorry about the clock," he said.

My own face had now assumed a deep tropical burn. I couldn't muster up a single commonplace out of the thousand in my head.

"It's an old clock," I told them idiotically.

I think we all believed for a moment that it had smashed in pieces on the floor.

"We haven't met for many years," said Daisy, her voice as matter-of-fact as it could ever be.

"Five years next November."

The automatic quality of Gatsby's answer set us all back at least another minute. I had them both on their feet with the desperate suggestion that they help me make tea in the kitchen when the demoniac Finn brought it in on a tray.

Amid the welcome confusion of cups and cakes a certain physical decency established itself. Gatsby got himself into a shadow and, while Daisy and I talked, looked conscientiously from one to the other of us with tense, unhappy eyes. However, as calmness wasn't an end in itself, I made an excuse at the first possible moment, and got to my feet.

"Where are you going?" demanded Gatsby in immediate alarm.

"I'll be back."

"I've got to speak to you about something before you go."

He followed me wildly into the kitchen, closed the door, and whispered: "Oh, God!" in a miserable way.

"What's the matter?"

"This is a terrible mistake," he said, shaking his head from side to side, "a terrible, terrible mistake."

"You're just embarrassed, that's all," and luckily I added: "Daisy's embarrassed too."

"She's embarrassed?" he repeated incredulously.

"Just as much as you are."

"Don't talk so loud."

"You're acting like a little boy," I broke out impatiently. "Not only that, but you're rude. Daisy's sitting in there all alone."

He raised his hand to stop my words, looked at me with unforgettable reproach, and, opening the door cautiously, went back into the other room.

I walked out the back way—just as Gatsby had when he had made his nervous circuit of the house half an hour before—and ran for a huge black knotted tree, whose massed leaves made a fabric against the rain. Once more it was pouring, and my irregular lawn, well-shaved by Gatsby's gardener, abounded in small muddy swamps and prehistoric marshes. There was nothing to look at from under the tree except Gatsby's enormous house, so I stared at it, like Kant at his church steeple, for half an hour. A brewer had built it early in the "period" craze a decade before, and there was a story that he'd agreed to pay five years' taxes on all the neighboring cottages if the owners would have their roofs thatched with straw. Perhaps their refusal took the heart out of his plan to Found a Family— he went into an immediate decline. His children sold his house with the black wreath still on the door. Americans, while willing, even eager, to be serfs, have always been obstinate about being peasantry.

After half an hour, the sun shone again, and the grocer's automobile rounded Gatsby's drive with the raw material for his servants' dinner—I felt sure he wouldn't eat a spoonful. A maid began opening the upper windows of his house, appeared momentarily in each, and, leaning from the large central bay, spat meditatively into the garden. It was time I went back. While the rain continued it had seemed like the murmur of their voices, rising and swelling a little now and then with gusts of emotion. But in the new silence I felt that silence had fallen within the house too.

I went in—after making every possible noise in the kitchen, short of pushing over the stove—but I don't believe they heard a sound. They were sitting at either end of the couch, looking at each other as if some question had been asked, or was in the air, and every vestige of embarrassment was gone. Daisy's face was smeared with tears, and when I came in she jumped up and began wiping at it with her handkerchief before a mirror. But there was a change in Gatsby that was simply confounding. He literally glowed; without a word or a gesture of exultation a new well-being radiated from him and filled the little room.

"Oh, hello old sport," he said, as if he hadn't seen me for years. I thought for a moment he was going to shake hands.

"It's stopped raining."

"Has it?" When he realized what I was talking about, that there were twinkle-bells of sunshine in the room, he smiled like a weather man, like an ecstatic patron of recurrent light, and repeated the news to Daisy. "What do you think of that? It's stopped raining."

"I'm glad, Jay." Her throat, full of aching, grieving beauty, told only of her unexpected joy.

"I want you and Daisy to come over to my house," he said, "I'd like to show her around."

"You're sure you want me to come?"

"Absolutely, old sport."

Daisy went up-stairs to wash her face—too late I thought with humiliation of my towels—while Gatsby and I waited on the lawn.

"My house looks well, doesn't it?" he demanded. "See how the whole front of it catches the light."

I agreed that it was splendid.

"Yes." His eyes went over it, every arched door and square tower. "It took me just three years to earn the money that bought it."

"I thought you inherited your money."

"I did, old sport," he said automatically, "but I lost most of it in the big panic—the panic of the war."

I think he hardly knew what he was saying, for when I asked him what business he was in he answered: "That's my affair," before he realized that it wasn't an appropriate reply.

"Oh, I've been in several things," he corrected himself. "I was in the drug business and then I was in the oil business. But I'm not in either one now." He looked at me with more attention. "Do you mean you've been thinking over what I proposed the other night?"

Before I could answer, Daisy came out of the house and two rows of brass buttons on her dress gleamed in the sunlight.

"That huge place *there?*" she cried pointing.

"Do you like it?"

"I love it, but I don't see how you live there all alone."

"I keep it always full of interesting people, night and day. People who do interesting things. Celebrated people."

Instead of taking the short cut along the Sound we went down to the road and entered by the big postern. With enchanting murmurs Daisy admired this aspect or that of the feudal silhouette against the sky, admired the gardens, the sparkling odor of jonquils and the frothy odor of hawthorn and plum blossoms and the pale gold odor of kiss-me-at-the-gate. It was strange to reach the marble steps and find no stir of bright dresses in and out of the door, and hear no sound but bird voices in the trees.

And inside, as we wandered through Marie Antoinette music-rooms and Restoration Salons, I felt that there were guests concealed behind every couch and table, under orders to be breathlessly silent until we had passed through. As Gatsby closed the door of "the Merton College Library" I could have sworn I heard the owl-eyed man break into ghostly laughter.

We went upstairs, through period bedrooms swathed in rose and lavender silk and vivid with new flowers, through dressing-rooms and poolrooms, and bathrooms, with sunken baths—intruding into one chamber where a dishevelled man in pajamas was doing liver exercises on the floor. It was Mr. Klipspringer, the "boarder." I had seen him wandering hungrily about the beach that morning. Finally we came to Gatsby's own apartment, a bedroom and a bath, and an Adam study, where we sat down and drank a glass of some Chartreuse he took from a cupboard in the wall.

He hadn't once ceased looking at Daisy, and I think he revalued everything in his house according to the measure of response it drew from her well-loved eyes. Sometimes, too, he stared around at his possessions in a dazed way, as though in her actual and astounding presence none of it was any longer real. Once he nearly toppled down a flight of stairs.

His bedroom was the simplest room of all—except where the dresser was garnished with a toilet set of pure dull gold. Daisy took the brush with delight, and smoothed her hair, whereupon Gatsby sat down and shaded his eyes and began to laugh.

"It's the funniest thing, old sport," he said hilariously. "I can't— When I try to——"

He had passed visibly through two states and was entering upon a third. After his embarrassment and his unreasoning joy he was consumed with wonder at her presence. He had been full of the idea so long, dreamed it right through to the end, waited with his teeth set, so to speak, at an inconceivable pitch of intensity. Now, in the reaction, he was running down like an overwound clock.

Recovering himself in a minute he opened for us two hulking patent cabinets which held his massed suits and dressing-gowns and ties, and his shirts, piled like bricks in stacks a dozen high.

"I've got a man in England who buys me clothes. He sends over a selection of things at the beginning of each season, spring and fall."

He took out a pile of shirts and began throwing them, one by one, before us, shirts of sheer linen and thick silk and fine flannel, which lost their folds as they fell and covered the table in many-colored disarray. While we admired he brought more and the soft rich heap mounted higher—shirts with stripes and scrolls and plaids in coral and apple-green and lavender and faint orange, with monograms of Indian blue. Suddenly, with a strained sound, Daisy bent her head into the shirts and began to cry stormily.

"They're such beautiful shirts," she sobbed, her voice muffled in the thick folds. "It makes me sad because I've never seen such— such beautiful shirts before."

After the house, we were to see the grounds and the swimming-pool, and the hydroplane and the mid-summer flowers—but outside Gatsby's window it began to rain again, so we stood in a row looking at the corrugated surface of the Sound.

"If it wasn't for the mist we could see your home across the bay," said Gatsby. "You always have a green light that burns all night at the end of your dock."

Daisy put her arm through his abruptly, but he seemed absorbed in what he had just said. Possibly it had occurred to him that the colossal significance of that light had now vanished forever. Compared to the great distance that had separated him from Daisy it had seemed very near to her, almost touching her. It had seemed as close as a star to the moon. Now it was again a green light on a dock. His count of enchanted objects had diminished by one.

I began to walk about the room, examining various indefinite objects in the half darkness. A large photograph of an elderly man in yachting costume attracted me, hung on the wall over his desk.

"Who's this?"

"That? That's Mr. Dan Cody, old sport."

The name sounded faintly familiar.

"He's dead now. He used to be my best friend years ago."

There was a small picture of Gatsby, also in yachting costume, on the bureau—Gatsby with his head thrown back defiantly—taken apparently when he was about eighteen.

"I adore it," exclaimed Daisy. "The pompadour! You never told me you had a pompadour—or a yacht."

"Look at this," said Gatsby quickly. "Here's a lot of clippings—about you."

They stood side by side examining it. I was going to ask to see the rubies when the phone rang, and Gatsby took up the receiver.

"Yes.... Well, I can't talk now.... I can't talk now, old sport.... I said a *small* town. . . . He must know what a small town is. . . . Well, he's no use to us if Detroit is his idea of a small town. . . ."

He rang off.

"Come here *quick*!" cried Daisy at the window.

The rain was still falling, but the darkness had parted in the west, and there was a pink and golden billow of foamy clouds above the sea.

"Look at that," she whispered, and then after a moment: "I'd like to just get one of those pink clouds and put you in it and push you around."

I tried to go then, but they wouldn't hear of it; perhaps my presence made them feel more satisfactorily alone.

"I know what we'll do," said Gatsby, "we'll have Klipspringer play the piano."

He went out of the room calling "Ewing!" and returned in a few minutes accompanied by an embarrassed, slightly worn young man, with shell-rimmed glasses and scanty blond hair. He was now decently clothed in a "sport shirt," open at the neck, sneakers, and duck trousers of a nebulous hue.

"Did we interrupt your exercises?" inquired Daisy politely.

"I was asleep," cried Mr. Klipspringer, in a spasm of embarrassment. "That is, I'd *been* asleep. Then I got up . . ."

"Klipspringer plays the piano," said Gatsby, cutting him off. "Don't you, Ewing, old sport?"

"I don't play well. I don't—I hardly play at all. I'm all out of prac——"

"We'll go downstairs," interrupted Gatsby. He flipped a switch. The gray windows disappeared as the house glowed full of light.

In the music-room Gatsby turned on a solitary lamp beside the piano. He lit Daisy's cigarette from a trembling match, and sat down with her on a couch far across the room, where there was no light save what the gleaming floor bounced in from the hall.

When Klipspringer had played *The Love Nest* he turned around on the bench and searched unhappily for Gatsby in the gloom.

"I'm all out of practice, you see. I told you I couldn't play. I'm all out of prac——"

"Don't talk so much, old sport," commanded Gatsby. "Play!"

> *"In the morning,*
> *In the evening,*
> *Ain't we got fun——"*

Outside the wind was loud and there was a faint flow of thunder along the Sound. All the lights were going on in West Egg now; the electric trains, men-carrying, were plunging home through the rain from New York. It was the hour of a profound human change, and excitement was generating on the air.

> *"One thing's sure and nothing's surer*
> *The rich get richer and the poor get—children.*
> *In the meantime,*
> *In between time——"*

As I went over to say good-by I saw that the expression of bewilderment had come back into Gatsby's face, as though a faint doubt had occurred to him as to the quality of his present happiness. Almost five years! There must have been moments even that afternoon when Daisy tumbled short of his dreams—not through her own fault, but because of the colossal vitality of his illusion. It had gone beyond her, beyond everything. He had thrown himself into it with a creative passion, adding to it all the time, decking it out with every bright feather that drifted his way. No amount of fire or freshness can challenge what a man can store up in his ghostly heart.

As I watched him he adjusted himself a little, visibly. His hand took hold of hers, and as she said something low in his ear he turned toward her with a rush of emotion. I think that voice held him most, with its fluctuating, feverish warmth, because it couldn't be overdreamed—that voice was a deathless song.

They had forgotten me, but Daisy glanced up and held out her hand; Gatsby didn't know me now at all. I looked once more at them and they looked back at me, remotely, possessed by intense life. Then I went out of the room and down the marble steps into the rain, leaving them there together.

6

About this time an ambitious young reporter from New York arrived one morning at Gatsby's door and asked him if he had anything to say.

"Anything to say about what?" inquired Gatsby politely.

"Why—any statement to give out."

It transpired after a confused five minutes that the man had heard Gatsby's name around his office in a connection which he either wouldn't reveal or didn't fully understand. This was his day off and with laudable initiative he had hurried out "to see."

It was a random shot, and yet the reporter's instinct was right. Gatsby's notoriety, spread about by the hundreds who had accepted his hospitality and so become authorities upon his past, had increased all summer until he fell just short of being news. Contemporary legends such as the "underground pipe-line to Canada" attached themselves to him, and there was one persistent story that he didn't live in a house at all, but in a boat that looked like a house and was moved secretly up and down the Long Island shore. Just why these inventions were a source of satisfaction to James Gatz of North Dakota isn't easy to say.

James Gatz—that was really, or at least legally, his name. He had changed it at the age of seventeen and at the specific moment that witnessed the beginning of his career—when he saw Dan Cody's yacht drop anchor over the most insidious flat on Lake Superior. It was James Gatz who had been loafing along the beach that afternoon in a torn green jersey and a pair of canvas pants, but it was already Jay Gatsby who borrowed a rowboat, pulled out to the *Tuolomee*, and informed Cody that a wind might catch him and break him up in half an hour.

I suppose he'd had the name ready for a long time, even then. His parents were shiftless and unsuccessful farm people—his imagination had never really accepted them as his parents at all. The truth was that Jay Gatsby of West Egg, Long Island, sprang from his Platonic conception of himself. He was a son of God—a phrase which, if it means anything, means just that—and he must be about His Father's business, the service of vast, vulgar, and meretricious beauty. So he invented just the sort of Jay Gatsby that a seventeen-year-old boy would be likely to invent, and to this conception he was faithful to the end.

For over a year he had been beating his way along the south shore of Lake Superior as a clam-digger and a salmon-fisher or in any other capacity that brought him food and bed. His brown, hardening body lived naturally through the half-fierce, half-lazy work of the bracing days. He knew women early, and since they spoiled him he became contemptuous of them, of young virgins because they were ignorant, of the others because they were hysterical about things which in his overwhelming self-absorption he took for granted.

But his heart was in a constant, turbulent riot. The most grotesque and fantastic conceits haunted him in his bed at night. A universe of ineffable gaudiness spun itself out in his brain while the clock ticked on the wash-stand and the moon soaked with wet light his tangled clothes upon the floor. Each night he added to the pattern of his fancies until drowsiness closed down upon some vivid scene with an oblivious embrace. For a while these reveries provided an outlet for his imagination; they were a satisfactory hint of the unreality of reality, a promise that the rock of the world was founded securely on a fairy's wing.

An instinct toward his future glory had led him, some months before, to the small Lutheran College of St. Olaf's in southern Minnesota. He stayed there two weeks, dismayed at its ferocious indifference to the drums of his destiny, to destiny itself, and despising the janitor's work with which he was to pay his way through. Then he drifted back to Lake Superior, and he was still searching for something to do on the day that Dan Cody's yacht dropped anchor in the shallows alongshore.

Cody was fifty years old then, a product of the Nevada silver fields, of the Yukon, of every rush for metal since seventy-five. The transactions in Montana copper that made him many times a millionaire found him physically robust but on the verge of soft-mindedness, and, suspecting this, an infinite number of women tried to separate him from his money. The none too savory ramifications by which Ella Kaye, the newspaper woman, played Madame de Maintenon to his weakness and sent him to sea in a yacht, were common property of the turgid journalism of 1902. He had been coasting along all too hospitable shores for five years when he turned up as James Gatz's destiny in Little Girl Bay.

To young Gatz, resting on his oars and looking up at the railed deck, that yacht represented all the beauty and glamour in the world. I suppose he smiled at Cody—he had probably discovered that people liked him when he smiled. At any rate Cody asked him a few questions (one of them elicited the brand new name) and found that he was quick and extravagantly ambitious. A few days later he took him to Duluth and bought him a blue coat, six pair of white duck trousers, and a yachting cap. And when the *Tuolomee* left for the West Indies and the Barbary Coast Gatsby left too.

He was employed in a vague personal capacity—while he remained with Cody he was in turn steward, mate, skipper, secretary, and even jailor, for Dan Cody sober knew what lavish doings Dan Cody drunk might soon be about, and he provided for such contingencies by reposing more and more trust in Gatsby. The arrangement lasted five years, during which the boat went three times around the Continent. It might have lasted indefinitely except for the fact that Ella Kaye came on board one night in Boston and a week later Dan Cody inhospitably died.

I remember the portrait of him up in Gatsby's bedroom, a gray, florid man with a hard, empty face—the pioneer debauchee, who during one phase of American life brought back to the Eastern seaboard the savage violence of the frontier brothel and saloon. It was indirectly due to Cody that Gatsby drank so little. Sometimes in the course of gay parties women used to rub champagne into his hair; for himself he formed the habit of letting liquor alone.

And it was from Cody that he inherited money—a legacy of twenty-five thousand dollars. He didn't get it. He never understood the legal device that was used against him, but what remained of the millions went intact to Ella Kaye. He was left with his singularly appropriate education; the vague contour of Jay Gatsby had filled out to the substantiality of a man.

He told me all this very much later, but I've put it down here with the idea of exploding those first wild rumors about his antecedents, which weren't even faintly true. Moreover he told it to me at a time of confusion, when I had reached the point of believing everything and nothing about him. So I take advantage of this short halt, while Gatsby, so to speak, caught his breath, to clear this set of misconceptions away.

It was a halt, too, in my association with his affairs. For several weeks I didn't see him or hear his voice on the phone—mostly I was in New York, trotting around with Jordan and trying to ingratiate myself with her senile aunt—but finally I went over to his house one Sunday afternoon. I hadn't been there two minutes when somebody brought Tom Buchanan in for a drink. I was startled, naturally, but the really surprising thing was that it hadn't happened before.

They were a party of three on horseback—Tom and a man named Sloane and a pretty woman in a brown riding-habit, who had been there previously.

"I'm delighted to see you," said Gatsby, standing on his porch. "I'm delighted that you dropped in."

As though they cared!

"Sit right down. Have a cigarette or a cigar." He walked around the room quickly, ringing bells. "I'll have something to drink for you in just a minute."

He was profoundly affected by the fact that Tom was there. But he would be uneasy anyhow until he had given them something, realizing in a vague way that that was all they came for. Mr. Sloane wanted nothing. A lemonade? No, thanks. A little champagne? Nothing at all, thanks. . . . I'm sorry——

"Did you have a nice ride?"

"Very good roads around here."

"I suppose the automobiles——"

"Yeah."

Moved by an irresistible impulse, Gatsby turned to Tom, who had accepted the introduction as a stranger.

"I believe we've met somewhere before, Mr. Buchanan."

"Oh, yes," said Tom, gruffly polite, but obviously not remembering. "So we did. I remember very well."

"About two weeks ago."

"That's right. You were with Nick here."

"I know your wife," continued Gatsby, almost aggressively.

"That so?"

Tom turned to me.

"You live near here, Nick?"

"Next door."

"That so?"

Mr. Sloane didn't enter into the conversation, but lounged back haughtily in his chair; the woman said nothing either—until unexpectedly, after two highballs, she became cordial.

"We'll all come over to your next party, Mr. Gatsby," she suggested. "What do you say?"

"Certainly; I'd be delighted to have you."

"Be ver' nice," said Mr. Sloane, without gratitude. "Well—think ought to be starting home."

"Please don't hurry," Gatsby urged them. He had control of himself now, and he wanted to see more of Tom. "Why don't you— why don't you stay for supper? I wouldn't be surprised if some other people dropped in from New York."

"You come to supper with *me*," said the lady enthusiastically. "Both of you."

This included me. Mr. Sloane got to his feet.

"Come along," he said—but to her only.

"I mean it," she insisted. "I'd love to have you. Lots of room."

Gatsby looked at me questioningly. He wanted to go, and he didn't see that Mr. Sloane had determined he shouldn't.

"I'm afraid I won't be able to," I said.

"Well, you come," she urged, concentrating on Gatsby.

Mr. Sloane murmured something close to her ear.

"We won't be late if we start now," she insisted aloud.

"I haven't got a horse," said Gatsby. "I used to ride in the army, but I've never bought a horse. I'll have to follow you in my car. Excuse me for just a minute."

The rest of us walked out on the porch, where Sloane and the lady began an impassioned conversation aside.

"My God, I believe the man's coming," said Tom. "Doesn't he know she doesn't want him?"

"She says she does want him."

"She has a big dinner party and he won't know a soul there." He frowned. "I wonder where in the devil he met Daisy. By God, I may be old-fashioned in my ideas, but women run around too much these days to suit me. They meet all kinds of crazy fish."

Suddenly Mr. Sloane and the lady walked down the steps and mounted their horses.

"Come on," said Mr. Sloane to Tom, "we're late. We've got to go." And then to me: "Tell him we couldn't wait, will you?"

Tom and I shook hands, the rest of us exchanged a cool nod, and they trotted quickly down the drive, disappearing under the August foliage just as Gatsby, with hat and light overcoat in hand, came out the front door.

Tom was evidently perturbed at Daisy's running around alone, for on the following Saturday night he came with her to Gatsby's party. Perhaps his presence gave the evening its peculiar quality of oppressiveness—it stands out in my memory from Gatsby's other parties that summer. There were the same people, or at least the same sort of people, the same profusion of champagne, the same many-colored, many-keyed commotion, but I felt an unpleasantness in the air, a pervading harshness that hadn't been there before. Or perhaps I had merely grown used to it, grown to accept West Egg as a world complete in itself, with its own standards and its own great figures, second to nothing because it had no consciousness of being so, and now I was looking at it again, through Daisy's eyes. It is invariably saddening to look through new eyes at things upon which you have expended your own powers of adjustment.

They arrived at twilight, and, as we strolled out among the sparkling hundreds, Daisy's voice was playing murmurous tricks in her throat.

"These things excite me *so*," she whispered. "If you want to kiss me any time during the evening, Nick, just let me know and I'll be glad to arrange it for you. Just mention my name. Or present a green card. I'm giving out green——"

"Look around," suggested Gatsby.

"I'm looking around. I'm having a marvellous——"

"You must see the faces of many people you've heard about."

Tom's arrogant eyes roamed the crowd.

"We don't go around very much," he said; "in fact, I was just thinking I don't know a soul here."

"Perhaps you know that lady," Gatsby indicated a gorgeous, scarcely human orchid of a woman who sat in state under a white-plum tree. Tom and Daisy stared, with that particularly unreal feeling that accompanies the recognition of a hitherto ghostly celebrity of the movies."

"She's lovely," said Daisy.

"The man bending over her is her director."

He took them ceremoniously from group to group:

"Mrs. Buchanan . . . and Mr. Buchanan——" After an instant's hesitation he added: "the polo player."

"Oh, no," objected Tom quickly, "not me."

But evidently the sound of it pleased Gatsby, for Tom remained "the polo player" for the rest of the evening.

"I've never met so many celebrities," Daisy exclaimed. "I liked that man—what was his name?—with the sort of blue nose."

Gatsby identified him, adding that he was a small producer.

"Well, I liked him anyhow."

"I'd a little rather not be the polo player," said Tom pleasantly, "I'd rather look at all these famous people in—in oblivion."

Daisy and Gatsby danced. I remember being surprised by his graceful, conservative fox-trot—I had never seen him dance before. Then they sauntered over to my house and sat on the steps for half an hour, while at her request I remained watchfully in the garden. "In case there's a fire or a flood," she explained, "or any act of God."

Tom appeared from his oblivion as we were sitting down to supper together. "Do you mind if I eat with some people over here?" he said. "A fellow's getting off some funny stuff."

"Go ahead," answered Daisy genially, "and if you want to take down any addresses here's my little gold pencil." . . . She looked around after a moment and told me the girl was "common but pretty," and I knew that except for the half-hour she'd been alone with Gatsby she wasn't having a good time.

We were at a particularly tipsy table. That was my fault—Gatsby had been called to the phone, and I'd enjoyed these same people only two weeks before. But what had amused me then turned septic on the air now.

"How do you feel, Miss Baedeker?"

The girl addressed was trying, unsuccessfully, to slump against my shoulder. At this inquiry she sat up and opened her eyes.

"Wha'?"

A massive and lethargic woman, who had been urging Daisy to play golf with her at the local club to-morrow, spoke in Miss Baedeker's defence:

"Oh, she's all right now. When she's had five or six cocktails she always starts screaming like that. I tell her she ought to leave it alone."

"I do leave it alone," affirmed the accused hollowly.

"We heard you yelling, so I said to Doc Civet here: 'There's somebody that needs your help, Doc.'"

"She's much obliged, I'm sure," said another friend, without gratitude, "but you got her dress all wet when you stuck her head in the pool."

"Anything I hate is to get my head stuck in a pool," mumbled Miss Baedecker. "They almost drowned me once over in New Jersey."

"Then you ought to leave it alone," countered Doctor Civet.

"Speak for yourself!" cried Miss Baedecker violently. "Your hand shakes. I wouldn't let you operate on me!"

It was like that. Almost the last thing I remember was standing with Daisy and watching the moving-picture director and his Star. They were still under the white-plum tree and their faces were touching except for a pale, thin ray of moonlight between. It occurred to me that he had been very slowly bending toward her all evening to attain this proximity, and even while I watched I saw him stoop one ultimate degree and kiss at her cheek.

"I like her," said Daisy, "I think she's lovely."

But the rest offended her—and inarguably, because it wasn't a gesture but an emotion. She was appalled by West Egg, this unprecedented "place" that Broadway had begotten upon a Long Island fishing village—appalled by its raw vigor that chafed under the old euphemisms and by the too obtrusive fate that herded its inhabitants along a short-cut from nothing to nothing. She saw something awful in the very simplicity she failed to understand.

I sat on the front steps with them while they waited for their car. It was dark here in front; only the bright door sent ten square feet of light volleying out into the soft black morning. Sometimes a shadow moved against a dressing-room blind above, gave way to another shadow, an indefinite procession of shadows, that rouged and powdered in an invisible glass.

"Who is this Gatsby anyhow?" demanded Tom suddenly. "Some big bootlegger?"

"Where'd you hear that?" I inquired.

"I didn't hear it. I imagined it. A lot of these newly rich people are just big bootleggers, you know."

"Not Gatsby," I said shortly.

He was silent for a moment. The pebbles of the drive crunched under his feet.

"Well, he certainly must have strained himself to get this menagerie together."

A breeze stirred the gray haze of Daisy's fur collar.

"At least they are more interesting than the people we know," she said with an effort.

"You didn't look so interested."

"Well, I was."

Tom laughed and turned to me.

"Did you notice Daisy's face when that girl asked her to put her under a cold shower?"

Daisy began to sing with the music in a husky, rhythmic whisper, bringing out a meaning in each word that it had never had before and would never have again. When the melody rose, her voice broke up sweetly, following it, in a way contralto voices have, and each change tipped out a little of her warm human magic upon the air.

"Lots of people come who haven't been invited," she said suddenly. "That girl hadn't been invited. They simply force their way in and he's too polite to object."

"I'd like to know who he is and what he does," insisted Tom. "And I think I'll make a point of finding out."

"I can tell you right now," she answered. "He owned some drug-stores, a lot of drug-stores. He built them up himself."

The dilatory limousine came rolling up the drive.

"Good night, Nick," said Daisy.

Her glance left me and sought the lighted top of the steps, where *Three O'clock in the Morning*, a neat, sad little waltz of that year, was drifting out the open door. After all, in the very casualness of Gatsby's party there were romantic possibilities totally absent from her world. What was it up there in the song that seemed to be calling her back inside? What would happen now in the dim, incalculable hours? Perhaps some unbelievable guest would arrive, a person infinitely rare and to be marvelled at, some authentically radiant young girl who with one fresh glance at Gatsby, one moment of magical encounter, would blot out those five years of unwavering devotion.

I stayed late that night, Gatsby asked me to wait until he was free, and I lingered in the garden until the inevitable swimming party had run up, chilled and exalted, from the black beach, until the lights were extinguished in the guest-rooms overhead. When he came down the steps at last the tanned skin was drawn unusually tight on his face, and his eyes were bright and tired.

"She didn't like it," he said immediately.

"Of course she did."

"She didn't like it," he insisted. "She didn't have a good time."

He was silent, and I guessed at his unutterable depression.

"I feel far away from her," he said. "It's hard to make her understand."

"You mean about the dance?"

"The dance?" He dismissed all the dances he had given with a snap of his fingers. "Old sport, the dance is unimportant."

He wanted nothing less of Daisy than that she should go to Tom and say: "I never loved you." After she had obliterated four years with that sentence they could decide upon the more practical measures to be taken. One of them was that, after she was free, they were to go back to Louisville and be married from her house—just as if it were five years ago.

"And she doesn't understand," he said. "She used to be able to understand. We'd sit for hours——"

He broke off and began to walk up and down a desolate path of fruit rinds and discarded favors and crushed flowers.

"I wouldn't ask too much of her," I ventured. "You can't repeat the past."

"Can't repeat the past?" he cried incredulously. "Why of course you can!"

He looked around him wildly, as if the past were lurking here in the shadow of his house, just out of reach of his hand.

"I'm going to fix everything just the way it was before," he said, nodding determinedly. "She'll see."

He talked a lot about the past, and I gathered that he wanted to recover something, some idea of himself perhaps, that had gone into loving Daisy. His life had been confused and disordered since then, but if he could once return to a certain starting place and go over it all slowly, he could find out what that thing was. . . .

. . . One autumn night, five years before, they had been walking down the street when the leaves were falling, and they came to a place where there were no trees and the sidewalk was white with moonlight. They stopped here and turned toward each other. Now it was a cool night with that mysterious excitement in it which comes at the two changes of the year. The quiet lights in the houses were humming out into the darkness and there was a stir and bustle among the stars. Out of the corner of his eye Gatsby saw that the blocks of the sidewalks really formed a ladder and mounted to a secret place above the trees—he could climb to it, if he climbed alone, and once there he could suck on the pap of life, gulp down the incomparable milk of wonder.

His heart beat faster and faster as Daisy's white face came up to his own. He knew that when he kissed this girl, and forever wed his unutterable visions to her perishable breath, his mind would never romp again like the mind of God. So he waited, listening for a moment longer to the tuning-fork that had been struck upon a star. Then he kissed her. At his lips' touch she blossomed for him like a flower and the incarnation was complete.

Through all he said, even through his appalling sentimentality, I was reminded of something—an elusive rhythm, a fragment of lost words, that I had heard somewhere a long time ago. For a moment a phrase tried to take shape in my mouth and my lips parted like a dumb man's, as though there was more struggling upon them than a wisp of startled air. But they made no sound, and what I had almost remembered was uncommunicable forever.

7

It was when curiosity about Gatsby was at its highest that the lights in his house failed to go on one Saturday night—and, as obscurely as it had begun, his career as Trimalchio was over. Only gradually did I become aware that the automobiles which turned expectantly into his drive stayed for just a minute and then drove sulkily away. Wondering if he were sick I went over to find out—an unfamiliar butler with a villainous face squinted at me suspiciously from the door.

"Is Mr. Gatsby sick?"

"Nope." After a pause he added "sir" in a dilatory, grudging way.

"I hadn't seen him around, and I was rather worried. Tell him Mr. Carraway came over."

"Who?" he demanded rudely.

"Carraway."

"Carraway. All right, I'll tell him."

Abruptly he slammed the door.

My Finn informed me that Gatsby had dismissed every servant in his house a week ago and replaced them with half a dozen others, who never went into West Egg Village to be bribed by the tradesmen, but ordered moderate supplies over the telephone. The grocery boy reported that the kitchen looked like a pigsty, and the general opinion in the village was that the new people weren't servants at all.

Next day Gatsby called me on the phone.

"Going away?" I inquired.

"No, old sport."

"I hear you fired all your servants."

"I wanted somebody who wouldn't gossip. Daisy comes over quite often—in the afternoons."

So the whole caravansary had fallen in like a card house at the disapproval in her eyes.

"They're some people Wolfsheim wanted to do something for. They're all brothers and sisters. They used to run a small hotel."

"I see."

He was calling up at Daisy's request—would I come to lunch at her house to-morrow? Miss Baker would be there. Half an hour later Daisy herself telephoned and seemed relieved to find that I was coming. Something was up. And yet I couldn't believe that they would choose this occasion for a scene—especially for the rather harrowing scene that Gatsby had outlined in the garden.

The next day was broiling, almost the last, certainly the warmest, of the summer. As my train emerged from the tunnel into sunlight, only the hot whistles of the National Biscuit Company broke the simmering hush at noon. The straw seats of the car hovered on the edge of combustion; the woman next to me perspired delicately for a while into her white shirtwaist, and then, as her newspaper dampened under her fingers, lapsed despairingly into deep heat with a desolate cry. Her pocket-book slapped to the floor.

"Oh, my!" she gasped.

I picked it up with a weary bend and handed it back to her, holding it at arm's length and by the extreme tip of the corners to indicate that I had no designs upon it—but every one near by, including the woman, suspected me just the same.

"Hot!" said the conductor to familiar faces. "Some weather! . . . Hot! . . . Hot! . . . Hot! . . . Is it hot enough for you? Is it hot? Is it . . . ?"

My commutation ticket came back to me with a dark stain from his hand. That any one should care in this heat whose flushed lips he kissed, whose head made damp the pajama pocket over his heart!

. . . Through the hall of the Buchanans' house blew a faint wind, carrying the sound of the telephone bell out to Gatsby and me as we waited at the door.

"The master's body!" roared the butler into the mouthpiece. "I'm sorry, madame, but we can't furnish it—it's far too hot to touch this noon!"

What he really said was: "Yes . . . Yes . . . I'll see."

He set down the receiver and came toward us, glistening slightly, to take our stiff straw hats.

"Madame expects you in the salon!" he cried, needlessly indicating the direction. In this heat every extra gesture was an affront to the common store of life.

The room, shadowed well with awnings, was dark and cool. Daisy and Jordan lay upon an enormous couch, like silver idols weighing down their own white dresses against the singing breeze of the fans.

"We can't move," they said together.

Jordan's fingers, powdered white over their tan, rested for a moment in mine.

"And Mr. Thomas Buchanan, the athlete?" I inquired.

Simultaneously I heard his voice, gruff, muffled, husky, at the hall telephone.

Gatsby stood in the centre of the crimson carpet and gazed around with fascinated eyes. Daisy watched him and laughed, her sweet, exciting laugh; a tiny gust of powder rose from her bosom into the air.

"The rumor is," whispered Jordan, "that that's Tom's girl on the telephone."

We were silent. The voice in the hall rose high with annoyance: "Very well, then, I won't sell you the car at all. . . . I'm under no obligations to you at all . . . and as for your bothering me about it at lunch time, I won't stand that at all!"

"Holding down the receiver," said Daisy cynically.

"No, he's not," I assured her. "It's a bona-fide deal. I happen to know about it."

Tom flung open the door, blocked out its space for a moment with his thick body, and hurried into the room.

"Mr. Gatsby!" He put out his broad, flat hand with well-concealed dislike. "I'm glad to see you, sir. . . . Nick. . . ."

"Make us a cold drink," cried Daisy.

As he left the room again she got up and went over to Gatsby and pulled his face down, kissing him on the mouth.

"You know I love you," she murmured.

"You forget there's a lady present," said Jordan.

Daisy looked around doubtfully.

"You kiss Nick too."

"What a low, vulgar girl!"

"I don't care!" cried Daisy, and began to clog on the brick fireplace. Then she remembered the heat and sat down guiltily on the couch just as a freshly laundered nurse leading a little girl came into the room.

"Bles-sed pre-cious," she crooned, holding out her arms. "Come to your own mother that loves you."

The child, relinquished by the nurse, rushed across the room and rooted shyly into her mother's dress.

"The bles-sed pre-cious! Did mother get powder on your old yellowy hair? Stand up now, and say—How-de-do."

Gatsby and I in turn leaned down and took the small reluctant hand. Afterward he kept looking at the child with surprise. I don't think he had ever really believed in its existence before.

"I got dressed before luncheon," said the child, turning eagerly to Daisy.

"That's because your mother wanted to show you off." Her face bent into the single wrinkle of the small white neck. "You dream, you. You absolute little dream."

"Yes," admitted the child calmly. "Aunt Jordan's got on a white dress too."

"How do you like mother's friends?" Daisy turned her around so that she faced Gatsby. "Do you think they're pretty?"

"Where's Daddy?"

"She doesn't look like her father," explained Daisy. "She looks like me. She's got my hair and shape of the face."

Daisy sat back upon the couch. The nurse took a step forward and held out her hand.

"Come, Pammy."

"Good-by, sweetheart!"

With a reluctant backward glance the well-disciplined child held to her nurse's hand and was pulled out the door, just as Tom came back, preceding four gin rickeys that clicked full of ice.

Gatsby took up his drink.

"They certainly look cool," he said, with visible tension.

We drank in long, greedy swallows.

"I read somewhere that the sun's getting hotter every year," said Tom genially. "It seems that pretty soon the earth's going to fall into the sun—or wait a minute—it's just the opposite—the sun's getting colder every year."

"Come outside," he suggested to Gatsby, "I'd like you to have a look at the place."

I went with them out to the veranda. On the green Sound, stagnant in the heat, one small sail crawled slowly toward the fresher sea. Gatsby's eyes followed it momentarily; he raised his hand and pointed across the bay.

"I'm right across from you."

"So you are."

Our eyes lifted over the rose-beds and the hot lawn and the weedy refuse of the dog-days alongshore. Slowly the white wings of the boat moved against the blue cool limit of the sky. Ahead lay the scalloped ocean and the abounding blessed isles.

"There's sport for you," said Tom, nodding. "I'd like to be out there with him for about an hour."

We had luncheon in the dining-room, darkened too against the heat, and drank down nervous gayety with the cold ale.

"What'll we do with ourselves this afternoon?" cried Daisy, "and the day after that, and the next thirty years?"

"Don't be morbid," Jordan said. "Life starts all over again when it gets crisp in the fall."

"But it's so hot," insisted Daisy, on the verge of tears, "and everything's so confused. Let's all go to town!"

Her voice struggled on through the heat, beating against it, molding its senselessness into forms.

"I've heard of making a garage out of a stable," Tom was saying to Gatsby, "but I'm the first man who ever made a stable out of a garage."

"Who wants to go to town?" demanded Daisy insistently. Gatsby's eyes floated toward her. "Ah," she cried, "you look so cool."

Their eyes met, and they stared together at each other, alone in space. With an effort she glanced down at the table.

"You always look so cool," she repeated.

She had told him that she loved him, and Tom Buchanan saw. He was astounded. His mouth opened a little, and he looked at Gatsby, and then back at Daisy as if he had just recognized her as some one he knew a long time ago.

"You resemble the advertisement of the man," she went on innocently. "You know the advertisement of the man——"

"All right," broke in Tom quickly, "I'm perfectly willing to go to town. Come on—we're all going to town."

He got up, his eyes still flashing between Gatsby and his wife. No one moved.

"Come on!" His temper cracked a little. "What's the matter, anyhow? If we're going to town, let's start."

His hand, trembling with his effort at self-control, bore to his lips the last of his glass of ale. Daisy's voice got us to our feet and out on to the blazing gravel drive.

"Are we just going to go?" she objected. "Like this? Aren't we going to let any one smoke a cigarette first?"

"Everybody smoked all through lunch."

"Oh, let's have fun," she begged him. "It's too hot to fuss."

He didn't answer.

"Have it your own way," she said. "Come on, Jordan."

They went upstairs to get ready while we three men stood there shuffling the hot pebbles with our feet. A silver curve of the moon hovered already in the western sky. Gatsby started to speak, changed his mind, but not before Tom wheeled and faced him expectantly.

"Have you got your stables here?" asked Gatsby with an effort.

"About a quarter of a mile down the road."

"Oh."

A pause.

"I don't see the idea of going to town," broke out Tom savagely. "Women get these notions in their heads——"

"Shall we take anything to drink?" called Daisy from an upper window.

"I'll get some whiskey," answered Tom. He went inside.

Gatsby turned to me rigidly:

"I can't say anything in his house, old sport."

"She's got an indiscreet voice," I remarked. "It's full of—" I hesitated.

"Her voice is full of money," he said suddenly.

That was it. I'd never understood before. It was full of money—that was the inexhaustible charm that rose and fell in it, the jingle of it, the cymbals' song of it. . . . High in a white palace the king's daughter, the golden girl. . . .

Tom came out of the house wrapping a quart bottle in a towel, followed by Daisy and Jordan wearing small tight hats of metallic cloth and carrying light capes over their arms.

"Shall we all go in my car?" suggested Gatsby. He felt the hot, green leather of the seat. "I ought to have left it in the shade."

"Is it standard shift?" demanded Tom.

"Yes."

"Well, you take my coupé and let me drive your car to town."

The suggestion was distasteful to Gatsby.

"I don't think there's much gas," he objected.

"Plenty of gas," said Tom boisterously. He looked at the gauge. "And if it runs out I can stop at a drug-store. You can buy anything at a drug-store nowadays."

A pause followed this apparently pointless remark. Daisy looked at Tom frowning, and an indefinable expression, at once definitely unfamiliar and vaguely recognizable, as if I had only heard it described in words, passed over Gatsby's face.

"Come on, Daisy," said Tom, pressing her with his hand toward Gatsby's car. "I'll take you in this circus wagon."

He opened the door, but she moved out from the circle of his arm.

"You take Nick and Jordan. We'll follow you in the coupé."

She walked close to Gatsby, touching his coat with her hand. Jordan and Tom and I got into the front seat of Gatsby's car, Tom pushed the unfamiliar gears tentatively, and we shot off into the oppressive heat, leaving them out of sight behind.

"Did you see that?" demanded Tom.

"See what?"

He looked at me keenly, realizing that Jordan and I must have known all along.

"You think I'm pretty dumb, don't you?" he suggested. "Perhaps I am, but I have a—almost a second sight, sometimes, that tells me what to do. Maybe you don't believe that, but science——"

He paused. The immediate contingency overtook him, pulled him back from the edge of the theoretical abyss.

"I've made a small investigation of this fellow," he continued. "I could have gone deeper if I'd known——"

"Do you mean you've been to a medium?" inquired Jordan humorously.

"What?" Confused, he stared at us as we laughed. "A medium?"

"About Gatsby."

"About Gatsby! No, I haven't. I said I'd been making a small investigation of his past."

"And you found he was an Oxford man," said Jordan helpfully.

"An Oxford man!" He was incredulous. "Like hell he is! He wears a pink suit."

"Nevertheless he's an Oxford man."

"Oxford, New Mexico," snorted Tom contemptuously, "or something like that."

"Listen, Tom. If you're such a snob, why did you invite him to lunch?" demanded Jordan crossly.

"Daisy invited him; she knew him before we were married—God knows where!"

We were all irritable now with the fading ale, and aware of it we drove for a while in silence. Then as Doctor T. J. Eckleburg's faded eyes came into sight down the road, I remembered Gatsby's caution about gasoline.

"We've got enough to get us to town," said Tom.

"But there's a garage right here," objected Jordan. "I don't want to get stalled in this baking heat."

Tom threw on both brakes impatiently, and we slid to an abrupt dusty spot under Wilson's sign. After a moment the proprietor emerged from the interior of his establishment and gazed hollow-eyed at the car.

"Let's have some gas!" cried Tom roughly. "What do you think we stopped for—to admire the view?"

"I'm sick," said Wilson without moving. "Been sick all day."

"What's the matter?"

"I'm all run down."

"Well, shall I help myself?" Tom demanded. "You sounded well enough on the phone."

With an effort Wilson left the shade and support of the doorway and, breathing hard, unscrewed the cap of the tank. In the sunlight his face was green.

"I didn't mean to interrupt your lunch," he said. "But I need money pretty bad, and I was wondering what you were going to do with your old car."

"How do you like this one?" inquired Tom. "I bought it last week."

"It's a nice yellow one," said Wilson, as he strained at the handle.

"Like to buy it?"

"Big chance," Wilson smiled faintly. "No, but I could make some money on the other."

"What do you want money for, all of a sudden?"

"I've been here too long. I want to get away. My wife and I want to go West."

"Your wife does," exclaimed Tom, startled.

"She's been talking about it for ten years." He rested for a moment against the pump, shading his eyes. "And now she's going whether she wants to or not. I'm going to get her away."

The coupé flashed by us with a flurry of dust and the flash of a waving hand.

"What do I owe you?" demanded Tom harshly.

"I just got wised up to something funny the last two days," remarked Wilson. "That's why I want to get away. That's why I been bothering you about the car."

"What do I owe you?"

"Dollar twenty."

The relentless beating heat was beginning to confuse me and I had a bad moment there before I realized that so far his suspicions hadn't alighted on Tom. He had discovered that Myrtle had some sort of life apart from him in another world, and the shock had made him physically sick. I stared at him and then at Tom, who had made a parallel discovery less than an hour before—and it occurred to me that there was no difference between men, in intelligence or race, so profound as the difference between the sick and the well. Wilson was so sick that he looked guilty, unforgivably guilty—as if he had just got some poor girl with child.

"I'll let you have that car," said Tom. "I'll send it over to-morrow afternoon."

That locality was always vaguely disquieting, even in the broad glare of afternoon, and now I turned my head as though I had been warned of something behind. Over the ashheaps the giant eyes of Doctor T. J. Eckleburg kept their vigil, but I perceived, after a moment, that the other eyes were regarding us less than twenty feet away.

In one of the windows over the garage the curtains had been moved aside a little, and Myrtle Wilson was peering down at the car. So engrossed was she that she had no consciousness of being observed, and one emotion after another crept into her face like objects into a slowly developing picture. Her expression was curiously familiar—it was an expression I had often seen on women's faces, but on Myrtle Wilson's face it seemed purposeless and inexplicable until I realized that her eyes, wide with jealous terror, were fixed not on Tom, but on Jordan Baker, whom she took to be his wife.

There is no confusion like the confusion of a simple mind, and as we drove away Tom was feeling the hot whips of panic. His wife and his mistress, until an hour ago secure and inviolate, were slipping precipitately from his control. Instinct made him step on the accelerator with the double purpose of overtaking Daisy and leaving Wilson behind, and we sped along toward Astoria at fifty miles an hour, until, among the spidery girders of the elevated, we came in sight of the easy-going blue coupé.

"Those big movies around Fiftieth Street are cool," suggested Jordan. "I love New York on summer afternoons when every one's away. There's something very sensuous about it—overripe, as if all sorts of funny fruits were going to fall into your hands."

The word "sensuous" had the effect of further disquieting Tom, but before he could invent a protest the coupé came to a stop, and Daisy signaled us to draw up alongside.

"Where are we going?" she cried.

"How about the movies?"

"It's so hot," she complained. "You go. We'll ride around and meet you after." With an effort her wit rose faintly, "We'll meet you on some corner. I'll be the man smoking two cigarettes."

"We can't argue about it here," Tom said impatiently, as a truck gave out a cursing whistle behind us. "You follow me to the south side of Central Park, in front of the Plaza."

Several times he turned his head and looked back for their car, and if the traffic delayed them he slowed up until they came into sight. I think he was afraid they would dart down a side street and out of his life forever.

But they didn't. And we all took the less explicable step of engaging the parlor of a suite in the Plaza Hotel.

The prolonged and tumultuous argument that ended by herding us into that room eludes me, though I have a sharp physical memory that, in the course of it, my underwear kept climbing like a damp snake around my legs and intermittent beads of sweat raced cool across my back. The notion originated with Daisy's suggestion that we hire five bathrooms and take cold baths, and then assumed more tangible form as "a place to have a mint julep." Each of us said over and over that it was a "crazy idea"—we all talked at once to a baffled clerk and thought, or pretended to think, that we were being very funny . . .

The room was large and stifling, and, though it was already four o'clock, opening the windows admitted only a gust of hot shrubbery from the Park. Daisy went to the mirror and stood with her back to us, fixing her hair.

"It's a swell suite," whispered Jordan respectfully, and every one laughed.

"Open another window," commanded Daisy, without turning around.

"There aren't any more."

"Well, we'd better telephone for an axe——"

"The thing to do is to forget about the heat," said Tom impatiently. "You make it ten times worse by crabbing about it."

He unrolled the bottle of whiskey from the towel and put it on the table.

"Why not let her alone, old sport?" remarked Gatsby. "You're the one that wanted to come to town."

There was a moment of silence. The telephone book slipped from its nail and splashed to the floor, whereupon Jordan whispered, "Excuse me"—but this time no one laughed.

"I'll pick it up," I offered.

"I've got it." Gatsby examined the parted string, muttered "Hum!" in an interested way, and tossed the book on a chair.

"That's a great expression of yours, isn't it?" said Tom sharply.

"What is?"

"All this 'old sport' business. Where'd you pick that up?"

"Now see here, Tom," said Daisy, turning around from the mirror, "if you're going to make personal remarks I won't stay here a minute. Call up and order some ice for the mint julep."

As Tom took up the receiver the compressed heat exploded into sound and we were listening to the portentous chords of Mendelssohn's Wedding March from the ballroom below.

"Imagine marrying anybody in this heat!" cried Jordan dismally.

"Still—I was married in the middle of June," Daisy remembered, "Louisville in June! Somebody fainted. Who was it fainted, Tom?"

"Biloxi," he answered shortly.

"A man named Biloxi. 'Blocks' Biloxi, and he made boxes—that's a fact—and he was from Biloxi, Tennessee."

"They carried him into my house," appended Jordan, "because we lived just two doors from the church. And he stayed three weeks, until Daddy told him he had to get out. The day after he left Daddy died." After a moment she added. "There wasn't any connection."

"I used to know a Bill Biloxi from Memphis," I remarked.

"That was his cousin. I knew his whole family history before he left. He gave me an aluminum putter that I use today."

The music had died down as the ceremony began and now a long cheer floated in at the window, followed by intermittent cries of "Yea—ea—ea!" and finally by a burst of jazz as the dancing began.

"We're getting old," said Daisy. "If we were young we'd rise and dance."

"Remember Biloxi," Jordan warned her. "Where'd you know him, Tom?"

"Biloxi?" He concentrated with an effort. "I didn't know him. He was a friend of Daisy's."

"He was not," she denied. "I'd never seen him before. He came down in the private car."

"Well, he said he knew you. He said he was raised in Louisville. Asa Bird brought him around at the last minute and asked if we had room for him."

Jordan smiled.

"He was probably bumming his way home. He told me he was president of your class at Yale."

Tom and I looked at each other blankly.

"Biloxi?"

"First place, we didn't have any president——"

Gatsby's foot beat a short, restless tattoo and Tom eyed him suddenly.

"By the way, Mr. Gatsby, I understand you're an Oxford man."

"Not exactly."

"Oh, yes, I understand you went to Oxford."

"Yes—I went there."

A pause. Then Tom's voice incredulous and insulting:

"You must have gone there about the time Biloxi went to New Haven."

Another pause. A waiter knocked and came in with crushed mint and ice, but the silence was unbroken by his "thank you" and the soft closing of the door. This tremendous detail was to be cleared up at last.

"I told you I went there," said Gatsby.

"I heard you, but I'd like to know when."

"It was in nineteen-nineteen. I only stayed five months. That's why I can't really call myself an Oxford man."

Tom glanced around to see if we mirrored his unbelief. But we were all looking at Gatsby.

"It was an opportunity they gave to some of the officers after the Armistice," he continued. "We could go to any of the universities in England or France."

I wanted to get up and slap him on the back. I had one of those renewals of complete faith in him that I'd experienced before.

Daisy rose, smiling faintly, and went to the table.

"Open the whiskey, Tom," she ordered, "and I'll make you a mint julep. Then you won't seem so stupid to yourself. . . . Look at the mint!"

"Wait a minute," snapped Tom, "I want to ask Mr. Gatsby one more question."

"Go on," Gatsby said politely.

"What kind of a row are you trying to cause in my house anyhow?"

They were out in the open at last and Gatsby was content.

"He isn't causing a row," Daisy looked desperately from one to the other. "You're causing a row. Please have a little self-control."

"Self-control!" repeated Tom incredulously. "I suppose the latest thing is to sit back and let Mr. Nobody from Nowhere make love to your wife. Well, if that's the idea you can count me out. . . . Nowadays people begin by sneering at family life and family institutions, and next they'll throw everything overboard and have intermarriage between black and white."

Flushed with his impassioned gibberish, he saw himself standing alone on the last barrier of civilization.

"We're all white here," murmured Jordan.

"I know I'm not very popular. I don't give big parties. I suppose you've got to make your house into a pigsty in order to have any friends—in the modern world."

Angry as I was, as we all were, I was tempted to laugh whenever he opened his mouth. The transition from libertine to prig was so complete.

"I've got somthing to tell *you*, old sport—" began Gatsby. But Daisy guessed at his intention.

"Please don't!" she interrupted helplessly. "Please let's all go home. Why don't we all go home?"

"That's a good idea." I got up. "Come on, Tom. Nobody wants a drink."

"I want to know what Mr. Gatsby has to tell me."

"Your wife doesn't love you," said Gatsby. "She's never loved you. She loves me."

"You must be crazy!" exclaimed Tom automatically.

Gatsby sprang to his feet, vivid with excitement.

"She never loved you, do you hear?" he cried. "She only married you because I was poor and she was tired of waiting for me. It was a terrible mistake, but in her heart she never loved any one except me!"

At this point Jordan and I tried to go, but Tom and Gatsby insisted with competitive firmness that we remain—as though neither of them had anything to conceal and it would be a privilege to partake vicariously of their emotions.

"Sit down, Daisy," Tom's voice groped unsuccessfully for the paternal note. "What's been going on? I want to hear all about it."

"I told you what's been going on," said Gatsby. "Going on for five years—and you didn't know."

Tom turned to Daisy sharply.

"You've been seeing this fellow for five years?"

"Not seeing," said Gatsby. "No, we couldn't meet. But both of us loved each other all that time, old sport, and you didn't know. I used to laugh sometimes"—but there was no laughter in his eyes—"to think that you didn't know."

"Oh—that's all." Tom tapped his thick fingers together like a clergyman and leaned back in his chair.

"You're crazy!" he exploded. "I can't speak about what happened five years ago because I didn't know Daisy then—and I'll be damned if I see how you got within a mile of her unless you brought the groceries to the back door. But all the rest of that's a God damned lie. Daisy loved me when she married me and she loves me now."

"No," said Gatsby, shaking his head.

"She does, though. The trouble is that sometimes she gets foolish ideas in her head and doesn't know what she's doing." He nodded sagely. "And what's more I love Daisy too. Once in a while I go off on a spree and make a fool of myself, but I always come back, and in my heart I love her all the time."

"You're revolting," said Daisy. She turned to me, and her voice, dropping an octave lower, filled the room with thrilling scorn: "Do you know why we left Chicago? I'm surprised that they didn't treat you to the story of that little spree."

Gatsby walked over and stood beside her.

"Daisy, that's all over now," he said earnestly. "It doesn't matter any more. Just tell him the truth—that you never loved him—and it's all wiped out forever."

She looked at him blindly. "Why—how could I love him—possibly?"

"You never loved him."

She hesitated. Her eyes fell on Jordan and me with a sort of appeal, as though she realized at last what she was doing—and as though she had never, all along, intended doing anything at all. But it was done now. It was too late.

"I never loved him," she said, with perceptible reluctance.

"Not at Kapiolani?" demanded Tom suddenly.

"No."

From the ballroom beneath, muffled and suffocating chords were drifting up on hot waves of air.

"Not that day I carried you down from the Punch Bowl to keep your shoes dry?" There was a husky tenderness in his tone. . . . "Daisy?"

"Please don't." Her voice was cold, but the rancor was gone from it. She looked at Gatsby. "There, Jay," she said—but her hand as she tried to light a cigarette was trembling. Suddenly she threw the cigarette and the burning match on the carpet.

"Oh, you want too much!" she cried to Gatsby. "I love you now —isn't that enough? I can't help what's past." She began to sob helplessly. "I did love him once—but I loved you too."

Gatsby's eyes opened and closed.

"You loved me too?" he repeated.

"Even that's a lie," said Tom savagely. "She didn't know you were alive. Why—there're things between Daisy and me that you'll never know, things that neither of us can ever forget."

The words seemed to bite physically into Gatsby.

"I want to speak to Daisy alone," he insisted. "She's all excited now——"

"Even alone I can't say I never loved Tom,," she admitted in a pitiful voice. "It wouldn't be true."

"Of course it wouldn't," agreed Tom.

She turned to her husband.

"As if it mattered to you," she said.

"Of course it matters. I'm going to take better care of you from now on."

"You don't understand," said Gatsby, with a touch of panic. "You're not going to take care of her any more."

"I'm not?" Tom opened his eyes wide and laughed. He could afford to control himself now. "Why's that?"

"Daisy's leaving you."

"Nonsense."

"I am, though," she said with a visible effort.

"She's not leaving me!" Tom's words suddenly leaned down over Gatsby. "Certainly not for a common swindler who'd have to steal the ring he put on her finger."

"I won't stand this!" cried Daisy. "Oh, please let's get out."

"Who are you, anyhow?" broke out Tom. "You're one of that bunch that hangs around with Meyer Wolfsheim—that much I happen to know. I've made a little investigation into your affairs—and I'll carry it further to-morrow."

"You can suit yourself about that, old sport," said Gatsby steadily.

"I found out what your 'drug-stores' were." He turned to us and spoke rapidly. "He and this Wolfsheim bought up a lot of side-street drug-stores here and in Chicago and sold grain alcohol over the counter. That's one of his little stunts. I picked him for a bootlegger the first time I saw him, and I wasn't far wrong."

"What about it?" said Gatsby politely. "I guess your friend Walter Chase wasn't too proud to come in on it."

"And you left him in the lurch, didn't you? You let him go to jail for a month over in New Jersey. God! You ought to hear Walter on the subject of *you*."

"He came to us dead broke. He was very glad to pick up some money, old sport."

"Don't you call me 'old sport'!" cried Tom. Gatsby said nothing. "Walter could have you up on the betting laws too, but Wolfsheim scared him into shutting his mouth."

That unfamiliar yet recognizable look was back again in Gatsby's face.

"That drug-store business was just small change," continued Tom slowly, "but you've got something on now that Walter's afraid to tell me about."

I glanced at Daisy, who was staring terrified between Gatsby and her husband, and at Jordan, who had begun to balance an invisible but absorbing object on the tip of her chin. Then I turned back to Gatsby—and was startled at his expression. He looked—and this is said in all contempt for the babbled slander of his garden—as if he had "killed a man." For a moment the set of his face could be described in just that fantastic way.

It passed, and he began to talk excitedly to Daisy, denying everything, defending his name against accusations that had not been made. But with every word she was drawing further and further into herself, so he gave that up, and only the dead dream fought on as the afternoon slipped away, trying to touch what was no longer tangible, struggling unhappily, undespairingly, toward that lost voice across the room.

The voice begged again to go.

"*Please*, Tom! I can't stand this any more."

Her frightened eyes told that whatever intentions, whatever courage she had had, were definitely gone.

"You two start on home, Daisy," said Tom. "In Mr. Gatsby's car."

She looked at Tom, alarmed now, but he insisted with magnanimous scorn.

"Go on. He won't annoy you. I think he realizes that his presumptuous little flirtation is over."

They were gone, without a word, snapped out, made accidental, isolated, like ghosts, even from our pity.

After a moment Tom got up and began wrapping the unopened bottle of whiskey in the towel.

"Want any of this stuff? Jordan? ... Nick?"

I didn't answer.

"Nick?" He asked again.

"What?"

"Want any?"

"No ... I just remembered that today's my birthday."

I was thirty. Before me stretched the portentous, menacing road of a new decade.

It was seven o'clock when we got into the coupé with him and started for Long Island. Tom talked incessantly, exulting and laughing, but his voice was as remote from Jordan and me as the foreign clamor on the sidewalk or the tumult of the elevated overhead. Human sympathy has its limits, and we were content to let all their tragic arguments fade with the city lights behind. Thirty—the promise of a decade of loneliness, a thinning list of single men to know, a thinning brief-case of enthusiasm, thinning hair. But there was Jordan beside me, who, unlike Daisy, was too wise, ever to carry well-forgotten dreams from age to age. As we passed over the dark bridge her wan face fell lazily against my coat's shoulder and the formidable stroke of thirty died away with the reassuring pressure of her hand.

So we drove on toward death through the cooling twilight.

The young Greek, Michaelis, who ran the coffee joint beside the ashheaps was the principal witness at the inquest. He had slept through the heat until after five, when he strolled over to the garage, and found George Wilson sick in his office—really sick, pale as his own pale hair and shaking all over. Michaelis advised him to go to bed, but Wilson refused, saying that he'd miss a lot of business if he did. While his neighbor was trying to persuade him a violent racket broke out overhead.

"I've got my wife locked in up there," explained Wilson calmly. "She's going to stay there till the day after to-morrow, and then we're going to move away."

Michaelis was astonished; they had been neighbors for four years, and Wilson had never seemed faintly capable of such a statement. Generally he was one of these worn-out men: when he wasn't working, he sat on a chair in the doorway and stared at the people and the cars that passed along the road. When any one spoke to him he invariably laughed in an agreeable, colorless way. He was his wife's man and not his own.

So naturally Michaelis tried to find out what had happened, but Wilson wouldn't say a word—instead he began to throw curious, suspicious glances at his visitor and ask him what he'd been doing at certain times on certain days. Just as the latter was getting uneasy, some workmen came past the door bound for his restaurant, and Michaelis took the opportunity to get away, intending to come back later. But he didn't. He supposed he forgot to, that's all. When he came outside again, a little after seven, he was reminded of the conversation because he heard Mrs. Wilson's voice, loud and scolding, down-stairs in the garage.

"Beat me!" he heard her cry. "Throw me down and beat me, you dirty little coward!"

A moment later she rushed out into the dusk, waving her hands and shouting—before he could move from his door the business was over.

The "death car" as the newspapers called it, didn't stop; it came out of the gathering darkness, wavered tragically for a moment, and then disappeared around the next bend. Mavromichaelis wasn't even sure of its color—he told the first policeman that it was light green. The other car, the one going toward New York, came to rest a hundred yards beyond, and its driver hurried back to where Myrtle Wilson, her life violently extinguished, knelt in the road and mingled her thick dark blood with the dust.

Michaelis and this man reached her first, but when they had torn open her shirtwaist, still damp with perspiration, they saw that her left breast was swinging loose like a flap, and there was no need to listen for the heart beneath. The mouth was wide open and ripped a little at the corners, as though she had choked a little in giving up the tremendous vitality she had stored so long.

We saw the three or four automobiles and the crowd when we were still some distance away.

"Wreck!" said Tom. "That's good. Wilson'll have a little business at last."

He slowed down, but still without any intention of stopping, until, as we came nearer, the hushed, intent faces of the people at the garage door made him automatically put on the brakes.

"We'll take a look," he said doubtfully, "just a look."

I became aware now of a hollow, wailing sound which issued incessantly from the garage, a sound which as we got out of the coupé and walked toward the door resolved itself into the words "Oh, my God!" uttered over and over in a gasping moan.

"There's some bad trouble here," said Tom excitedly.

He reached up on tiptoes and peered over a circle of heads into the garage, which was lit only by a yellow light in a swinging metal basket overhead. Then he made a harsh sound in his throat, and with a violent thrusting movement of his powerful arms pushed his way through.

The circle closed up again with a running murmur of expostulation; it was a minute before I could see anything at all. Then new arrivals deranged the line, and Jordan and I were pushed suddenly inside.

Myrtle Wilson's body, wrapped in a blanket, and then in another blanket, as though she suffered from a chill in the hot night, lay on a work-table by the wall, and Tom, with his back to us, was bending over it, motionless. Next to him stood a motorcycle policeman taking down names with much sweat and correction in a little book. At first I couldn't find the source of the high, groaning words that echoed clamorously through the bare garage—then I saw Wilson standing on the raised threshold of his office, swaying back and forth and holding to the doorposts with both hands. Some man was talking to him in a low voice and attempting, from time to time, to lay a hand on his shoulder, but Wilson neither heard nor saw. His eyes would drop slowly from the swinging light to the laden table by the wall, and then jerk back to the light again, and he gave out incessantly his high, horrible call:

"Oh, my Ga-od! Oh, my Ga-od! Oh, Ga-od! Oh, my Ga-od!"

Presently Tom lifted his head with a jerk and, after staring around the garage with glazed eyes, addressed a mumbled incoherent remark to the policeman.

"M-a-y—" the policeman was saying, "—o——"

"No, r—" corrected the man, "M-a-v-r-o——"

"Listen to me!" muttered Tom fiercely.

"r" said the policeman, "o——"

"g——"

"g—" He looked up as Tom's broad hand fell sharply on his shoulder. "What you want, fella?"

"What happened?—that's what I want to know."

"Auto hit her. Ins'antly killed."

"Instantly killed," repeated Tom, staring.

"She ran out ina road. Son-of-a-bitch didn't even stopus car."

"There was two cars," said Michaelis, "one comin', one goin', see?"

"Going where?" asked the policeman keenly.

"One goin' each way. Well, she"—his hand rose toward the blankets but stopped half way and fell to his side—"she ran out there an' the one comin' from N'York knock right into her, goin' thirty or forty miles an hour."

"What's the name of this place here?" demanded the officer.

"Hasn't got any name."

A pale well-dressed negro stepped near.

"It was a yellow car," he said, "big yellow car. New."

"See the accident?" asked the policeman.

"No, but the car passed me down the road, going faster'n forty. Going fifty, sixty."

"Come here and let's have your name. Look out now. I want to get his name."

Some words of this conversation must have reached Wilson, swaying in the office door, for suddenly a new theme found voice among his gasping cries:

"You don't have to tell me what kind of car it was! I know what kind of car it was!"

Watching Tom, I saw the wad of muscle back of his shoulder tighten under his coat. He walked quickly over to Wilson and, standing in front of him, seized him firmly by the upper arms.

"You've got to pull yourself together," he said with soothing gruffness.

Wilson's eyes fell upon Tom; he started up on his tiptoes and then would have collapsed to his knees had not Tom held him upright.

"Listen," said Tom, shaking him a little. "I just got here a minute ago, from New York. I was bringing you that coupé we've been talking about. That yellow car I was driving this afternoon wasn't mine—do you hear? I haven't seen it all afternoon."

Only the negro and I were near enough to hear what he said, but the policeman caught something in the tone and looked over with truculent eyes.

"What's all that?" he demanded.

"I'm a friend of his." Tom turned his head but kept his hands firm on Wilson's body. "He says he knows the car that did it. . . . It was a yellow car."

Some dim impulse moved the policeman to look suspiciously at Tom.

"And what color's your car?"

"It's a blue car, a coupé."

"We've come straight from New York," I said.

Some one who had been driving a little behind us confirmed this, and the policeman turned away.

"Now, if you'll let me have that name again correct——"

Picking up Wilson like a doll, Tom carried him into the office, set him down in a chair, and came back.

"If somebody'll come here and sit with him," he snapped authoritatively. He watched while the two men standing closest glanced at each other and went unwillingly into the room. Then Tom shut the door on them and came down the single step, his eyes avoiding the table. As he passed close to me he whispered: "Let's get out."

Self-consciously, with his authoritative arms breaking the way, we pushed through the still gathering crowd, passing a hurried doctor, case in hand, who had been sent for in wild hope half an hour ago.

Tom drove slowly until we were beyond the bend—then his foot came down hard, and the coupé raced along through the night. In a little while I heard a low husky sob, and saw that the tears were overflowing down his face.

"The God damned coward!" he whimpered. "He didn't even stop his car."

The Buchanans' house floated suddenly toward us through the dark rustling trees. Tom stopped beside the porch and looked up at the second floor, where two windows bloomed with light among the vines.

"Daisy's home," he said. As we got out of the car he glanced at me and frowned slightly.

"I ought to have dropped you in West Egg, Nick. There's nothing we can do to-night."

A change had come over him, and he spoke gravely, and with decision. As we walked across the moonlight gravel to the porch he disposed of the situation in a few brisk phrases.

"I'll telephone for a taxi to take you home, and while you're waiting you and Jordan better go in the kitchen and have them get you some supper—if you want any." He opened the door. "Come in."

"No, thanks. But I'd be glad if you'd order me the taxi. I'll wait outside."

Jordan put her hand on my arm.

"Won't you come in, Nick?"

"No, thanks."

I was feeling a little sick and I wanted to be alone. But Jordan lingered for a moment more.

"It's only half-past nine," she said.

I'd be damned if I'd go in; I'd had enough of all of them for one day, and suddenly that included Jordan too. She must have seen something of this in my expression, for she turned abruptly away and ran up the porch steps into the house. I sat down for a few minutes with my head in my hands, until I heard the phone taken up inside and the butler's voice calling a taxi. Then I walked slowly down the drive away from the house, intending to wait by the gate.

I hadn't gone twenty yards when I heard my name and Gatsby stepped from between two bushes into the path. I must have felt pretty weird by that time, because I could think of nothing except the luminosity of his pink suit under the moon.

"What are you doing?" I inquired.

"Just standing here, old sport."

Somehow, that seemed a despicable occupation. For all I knew he was going to rob the house in a moment; I wouldn't have been surprised to see sinister faces, the faces of "Wolfsheim's people," behind him in the dark shrubbery.

"Did you see any trouble on the road?" he asked after a minute.

"Yes."

He hesitated.

"Was she killed?"

"Yes."

"I thought so; I told Daisy I thought so. It's better that the shock should all come at once. She stood it pretty well."

He spoke as if Daisy's reaction was the only thing that mattered.

"I got to West Egg by a side road," he went on, "and left the car in my garage. I don't think anybody saw us, but of course I can't be sure."

I disliked him so much by this time that I didn't find it necessary to tell him he was wrong.

"Who was the woman?" he inquired.

"Her name was Wilson. Her husband owns the garage. How the devil did it happen?"

"Well, I tried to swing the wheel—" He broke off, and suddenly I guessed at the truth.

"Was Daisy driving?"

"Yes," he said after a moment, "but of course I'll say I was. You see, when we left New York she was very nervous and she thought it would steady her to drive—and this woman rushed out at us just as we were passing a car coming the other way. It all happened in a minute, but it seemed to me that she wanted to speak to us, thought we were somebody she knew. Well, first Daisy turned away from the woman toward the other car, and then she lost her nerve and turned back. The second my hand reached the wheel I felt the shock —it must have killed her instantly."

"It ripped her open——"

"Don't tell me, old sport." He winced. "Anyhow—Daisy stepped on it. I tried to make her stop, but she couldn't, so I pulled on the emergency brake. Then she fell over into my lap and I drove on.

"She'll be all right tomorrow," he said presently. "I'm just going to wait here and see if he tries to bother her about that unpleasantness this afternoon. She's locked herself into her room, and if he tries any brutality she's going to turn the light out and on again."

"He won't touch her," I said. "He's not thinking about her."

"I don't trust him, old sport."

"How long are you going to wait?"

"All night, if necessary. Anyhow, till they all go to bed."

A new point of view occurred to me. Suppose Tom found out that Daisy had been driving. He might think he saw a connection in it— he might think anything. I looked at the house; there were two or three bright windows downstairs and the pink glow from Daisy's room on the second floor.

"You wait here," I said. "I'll see if there's any sign of a commotion."

I walked back along the border of the lawn, traversed the gravel softly, and tiptoed up the veranda steps. The drawing-room curtains were open, and I saw that the room was empty. Crossing the porch where we had dined that June night three months before, I came to a small rectangle of light which I guessed was the pantry window. The blind was drawn, but I found a rift at the sill.

Daisy and Tom were sitting opposite each other at the kitchen table, with a plate of cold fried chicken between them, and two bottles of ale. He was talking intently across the table at her, and in his earnestness his hand had fallen upon and covered her own. Once in a while she looked up at him and nodded in agreement.

They weren't happy, and neither of them had touched the chicken or the ale—and yet they weren't unhappy either. There was an unmistakable air of natural intimacy about the picture, and anybody would have said that they were conspiring together.

As I tiptoed from the porch I heard my taxi feeling its way along the dark road toward the house. Gatsby was waiting where I had left him in the drive.

"Is it all quiet up there?" he asked anxiously.

"Yes, it's all quiet." I hesitated. "You'd better come home and get some sleep."

He shook his head.

"I want to wait here till Daisy goes to bed. Good night, old sport."

He put his hands in his coat pockets and turned back eagerly to his scrutiny of the house, as though my presence marred the sacredness of the vigil. So I walked away and left him standing there in the moonlight—watching over nothing.

8

I couldn't sleep all night; a fog-horn was groaning incessantly on the Sound, and I tossed half-sick between grotesque reality and savage, frightening dreams. Toward dawn I heard a taxi go up Gatsby's drive, and immediately I jumped out of bed and began to dress—I felt that I had something to tell him, something to warn him about, and morning would be too late.

Crossing his lawn, I saw that his front door was still open and he was leaning against a table in the hall, heavy with dejection or sleep.

"Nothing happened," he said wanly. "I waited, and about four o'clock she came to the window and stood there for a minute and then turned out the light."

His house had never seemed so enormous to me as it did that night when we hunted through the great rooms for cigarettes. We pushed aside curtains that were like pavilions, and felt over innumerable feet of dark wall for electric light switches—once I tumbled with a sort of splash upon the keys of a ghostly piano. There was an inexplicable amount of dust everywhere, and the rooms were musty, as though they hadn't been aired for many days. I found the humidor on an unfamiliar table, with two stale, dry cigarettes inside. Throwing open the French windows of the drawing-room, we sat smoking out into the darkness.

"You ought to go away," I said. "It's pretty certain they'll trace your car."

"Go away *now*, old sport?"

"Go to Atlantic City for a week, or up to Montreal."

He wouldn't consider it. He couldn't possibly leave Daisy until he knew what she was going to do. He was clutching at some last hope and I couldn't bear to shake him free.

It was this night that he told me the strange story of his youth with Dan Cody—told it to me because "Jay Gatsby" had broken up like glass against Tom's hard malice, and the long secret extravaganza was played out. I think that he would have acknowledged anything now, without reserve, but he wanted to talk about Daisy.

She was the first "nice" girl he had ever known. In various unrevealed capacities he had come in contact with such people, but always with indiscernible barbed wire between. He found her excitingly desirable. He went to her house, at first with other officers from Camp Taylor, then alone. It amazed him—he had never been in such a beautiful house before. But what gave it an air of breathless intensity was that Daisy lived there—it was as casual a thing to her as his tent out at camp was to him. There was a ripe mystery about it, a hint of bedrooms upstairs more beautiful and cool than other bedrooms, of gay and radiant activities taking place through its corridors, and of romances that were not musty and laid away already in lavender, but fresh and breathing and redolent of this year's shining motor-cars and of dances whose flowers were scarcely withered. It excited him, too, that many men had already loved Daisy—it increased her value in his eyes. He felt their presence all about the house, pervading the air with the shades and echoes of still vibrant emotions.

But he knew that he was in Daisy's house by a colossal accident. However glorious might be his future as Jay Gatsby, he was at present a penniless young man without a past, and at any moment the invisible cloak of his uniform might slip from his shoulders. So he made the most of his time. He took what he could get, ravenously and unscrupulously—eventually he took Daisy one still October night, took her because he had no real right to touch her hand.

He might have despised himself, for he had certainly taken her under false pretenses. I don't mean that he had traded on his phantom millions, but he had deliberately given Daisy a sense of security; he let her believe that he was a person from much the same strata as herself—that he was fully able to take care of her. As a matter of fact, he had no such facilities—he had no comfortable family standing behind him, and he was liable at the whim of an impersonal government to be blown anywhere about the world.

But he didn't despise himself and it didn't turn out as he had imagined. He had intended, probably, to take what he could and go

—but now he found that he had committed himself to the following of a grail. He knew that Daisy was extraordinary, but he didn't realize just how extraordinary a "nice" girl could be. She vanished into her rich house, into her rich, full life, leaving Gatsby—nothing. He felt married to her, that was all.

When they met again, two days later, it was Gatsby who was breathless, who was, somehow, betrayed. Her porch was bright with the bought luxury of star-shine; the wicker of the settee squeaked fashionably as she turned toward him and he kissed her curious and lovely mouth. She had caught a cold, and it made her voice huskier and more charming than ever, and Gatsby was overwhelmingly aware of the youth and mystery that wealth imprisons and preserves, of the freshness of many clothes, and of Daisy, gleaming like silver, safe and proud above the hot struggles of the poor.

"I can't describe to you how surprised I was to find out I loved her, old sport. I even hoped for a while that she'd throw me over, but she didn't, because she was in love with me too. She thought I knew a lot because I knew different things from her . . . Well, there I was, 'way off my ambitions, getting deeper in love every minute, and all of a sudden I didn't care. What was the use of doing great things if I could have a better time telling her what I was going to do?"

On the last afternoon before he went abroad, he sat with Daisy in his arms for a long, silent time. It was a cold fall day, with fire in the room and her cheeks flushed. Now and then she moved and he changed his arm a little, and once he kissed her dark shining hair. The afternoon had made them tranquil for a while, as if to give them a deep memory for the long parting the next day promised. They had never been closer in their month of love, nor communicated more profoundly one with another, than when she brushed silent lips against his coat's shoulder or when he touched the end of her fingers, gently, as though she were asleep.

He did extraordinarily well in the war. He was a captain before he went to the front, and following the Argonne battles he got his majority and the command of the divisional machine-guns. After the Armistice he tried frantically to get home, but some complication or misunderstanding sent him to Oxford instead. He was worried now—there was a quality of nervous despair in Daisy's letters. She didn't see why he couldn't come. She was feeling the pressure of the world outside, and she wanted to see him and feel his presence beside her and be reassured that she was doing the right thing after all.

For Daisy was young and her artificial world was redolent of orchids and pleasant, cheerful snobbery and orchestras which set the rhythm of the year, summing up the sadness and suggestiveness of life in new tunes. All night the saxophones wailed the hopeless comment of the *Beale Street Blues* while a hundred pairs of golden and silver slippers shuffled the shining dust. At the gray tea hour there were always rooms that throbbed incessantly with this low, sweet fever, while fresh faces drifted here and there like rose petals blown by the sad horns around the floor.

Through this twilight universe Daisy began to move again with the season; suddenly she was again keeping half a dozen dates a day with half a dozen men, and drowsing asleep at dawn with the beads and chiffon of an evening dress tangled among dying orchids on the floor beside her bed. And all the time something within her was crying for a decision. She wanted her life shaped now, immediately—and the decision must be made by some force—of love, of money, of unquestionable practicality—that was close at hand.

That force took shape in the middle of spring with the arrival of Tom Buchanan. There was a wholesome bulkiness about his person and his position, and Daisy was flattered. Doubtless there was a certain struggle and a certain relief. The letter reached Gatsby while he was still at Oxford.

It was dawn now on Long Island and we went about opening the rest of the windows downstairs, filling the house with gray-turning, gold-turning light. The shadow of a tree fell abruptly across the dew and ghostly birds began to sing among the blue leaves. There was a slow, pleasant movement in the air, scarcely a wind, promising a cool, lovely day.

"I don't think she ever loved him," Gatsby turned around from a window and looked at me challengingly. "You must remember, old sport, she was very excited this afternoon. He told her those things in a way that frightened her—that made it look as if I was some kind of cheap sharper. And the result was she hardly knew what she was saying."

He sat down gloomily.

"Of course she might have loved him just for a minute, when

they were first married—and loved me more even then, do you see?"

Suddenly he came out with a curious remark.

"In any case," he said, "it was just personal."

What could you make of that, except to suspect some intensity in his conception of the affair that couldn't be measured?

He came back from France when Tom and Daisy were still on their wedding trip, and made a miserable but irresistible journey to Louisville on the last of his army pay. He stayed there a week, walking the streets where their footsteps had clicked together through the November night and revisiting the out-of-the-way places to which they had driven in her white car. Just as Daisy's house had always seemed to him more mysterious and gay than other houses, so his idea of the city itself, even though she was gone from it, was pervaded with a melancholy beauty.

He left, feeling that if he had searched harder, he might have found her—that he was leaving her behind. The day-coach—he was penniless now—was hot. He went out to the open vestibule and sat down on a folding-chair, and the station slid away and the backs of unfamiliar buildings moved by. Then out into the spring fields, where a yellow trolley raced them for a minute with people in it who might once have seen the pale magic of her face along the casual street.

The track curved and now it was going away from the sun, which, as it sank lower, seemed to spread itself in benediction over the vanishing city where she had drawn her breath. He stretched out his hand desperately as if to snatch only a wisp of air, to save a fragment of the spot that she had made lovely for him. But it was all going by too fast now for his blurred eyes and he knew that he had lost that part of it, the freshest and the best, forever.

It was nine o'clock when we finished breakfast and went out on the porch. The night had made a sharp difference in the weather and there was an autumn flavor in the air. The gardener, the last one of Gatsby's former servants, came to the foot of the steps.

"I'm going to drain the pool today, Mr. Gatsby. Leaves'll start falling pretty soon, and then there's always trouble with the pipes."

"Don't do it to-day," Gatsby answered. He turned to me apologetically. "You know, old sport, I've never used that pool all summer?"

I looked at my watch and stood up.

"Twelve minutes to my train."

I didn't want to go to the city. I wasn't worth a decent stroke of work, but it was more than that—I didn't want to leave Gatsby. I missed that train, and then another, before I could get myself away.

"I'll call you up," I said finally.

"Do, old sport."

"I'll call you about noon."

We walked slowly down the steps.

"I suppose Daisy'll call too." He looked at me anxiously, as if he hoped I'd corroborate this.

"I suppose so."

"Well, good-by."

We shook hands and I started away. Just before I reached the hedge I remembered something and turned around.

"They're a rotten crowd," I shouted across the lawn. "You're worth the whole damn bunch put together."

I've always been glad I said that. It was the only compliment I ever gave him, because I disapproved of him from beginning to end. First he nodded politely, and then his face broke into that radiant and understanding smile, as if we'd been in ecstatic cahoots on that fact all the time. His gorgeous pink rag of a suit made a bright spot of color against the white steps, and I thought of the night when I first came to his ancestral home, three months before. The lawn and drive had been crowded with the faces of those who guessed at his corruption—and he had stood on those steps, concealing his incorruptible dream, as he waved them good-by.

I thanked him for his hospitality. We were always thanking him for that—I and the others.

"Good-by," I called. "I enjoyed breakfast, Gatsby."

Up in the city, I tried for a while to list the quotations on an interminable amount of stock, then I fell asleeep in my swivel-chair. Just before noon the phone woke me, and I started up with sweat breaking out on my forehead. It was Jordan Baker; she often called me up at this hour because the uncertainty of her own movements between hotels and clubs and private houses made her hard to find in any other way. Usually her voice came over the wire as something fresh and cool, as if a divot from a green golf-links had come sailing in at the office window, but this morning it seemed harsh and dry.

"I've left Daisy's house," she said. "I'm at Hempstead, and I'm going down to Southampton this afternoon."

Probably it had been tactful to leave Daisy's house, but the act annoyed me, and her next remark made me rigid.

"You weren't so nice to me last night."

"How could it have mattered then?"

Silence for a moment. Then:

"However—I want to see you."

"I want to see you, too."

"Suppose I don't go to Southampton, and come into town this afternoon?"

"No—I don't think this afternoon."

"Very well."

"It's impossible this afternoon. Various——"

We talked like that for a while, and then abruptly we weren't talking any longer. I don't know which of us hung up with a sharp click, but I know I didn't care. I couldn't have talked to her across a tea-table that day if I never talked to her again in this world.

I called Gatsby's house a few minutes later, but the line was busy. I tried four times; finally an exasperated central told me the wire was being kept open for long distance from Detroit. Taking out my time-table, I drew a small circle around the three-fifty train. Then I leaned back in my chair and tried to think. It was just noon.

When I passed the ashheaps on the train that morning I had crossed deliberately to the other side of the car. I supposed there'd be a curious crowd around there all day with little boys searching for dark spots in the dust, and some garrulous man telling over and over what had happened, until it became less and less real even to him and he could tell it no longer, and Myrtle Wilson's tragic achievement was forgotten. Now I want to go back a little and tell what happened at the garage after we left there the night before.

They had difficulty in locating the sister, Catherine. She must have broken her rule against drinking that night, for when she arrived she was stupid with liquor and unable to understand that the ambulance had already gone to Flushing. When they convinced her of this, she immediately fainted, as if that was the intolerable part of the affair. Some one, kind or curious, took her in his car and drove her in the wake of her sister's body.

Until long after midnight a changing crowd lapped up against the front of the garage, while George Wilson rocked himself back and forth on the couch inside. For a while the door of the office was open, and every one who came into the garage glanced irresistibly through it. Finally some one said it was a shame, and closed the door. Michaelis and several other men were with him; first, four or five men, later two or three men. Still later Michaelis had to ask the last stranger to wait there fifteen minutes longer, while he went back to his own place and made a pot of coffee. After that, he stayed there alone with Wilson until dawn.

About three o'clock the quality of Wilson's incoherent muttering changed—he grew quieter and began to talk about the yellow car. He announced that he had a way of finding out whom the yellow car belonged to, and then he blurted out that a couple of months ago his wife had come from the city with her face bruised and her nose swollen.

But when he heard himself say this, he flinched and began to cry "Oh, my God!" again in his groaning voice. Michaelis made a clumsy attempt to distract him.

"How long have you been married, George? Come on there, try and sit still a minute and answer my question. How long have you been married?"

"Twelve years."

"Ever had any children? Come on, George, sit still—I asked you a question. Did you ever have any children?"

The hard brown beetles kept thudding against the dull light, and whenever Michaelis heard a car go tearing along the road outside it sounded to him like the car that hadn't stopped a few hours before. He didn't like to go into the garage, because the work bench was stained where the body had been lying, so he moved uncomfortably around the office—he knew every object in it before morning—and from time to time sat down beside Wilson trying to keep him more quiet.

"Have you got a church you go to sometimes, George? Maybe even if you haven't been there for a long time? Maybe I could call up the church and get a priest to come over and he could talk to you, see?"

"Don't belong to any."

"You ought to have a church, George, for times like this. You must have gone to church once. Didn't you get married in a church? Listen, George, listen to me. Didn't you get married in a church?"

"That was a long time ago."

The effort of answering broke the rhythm of his rocking—for a moment he was silent. Then the same half-knowing, half-bewildered look came back into his faded eyes.

"Look in the drawer there," he said, pointing at the desk.

"Which drawer?"

"That drawer—that one."

Michaelis opened the drawer nearest his hand. There was nothing in it but a small, expensive dog-leash, made of leather and braided silver. It was apparently new.

"This?" he inquired, holding it up.

Wilson stared and nodded.

"I found it yesterday afternoon. She tried to tell me about it, but I knew it was something funny."

"You mean your wife bought it?"

"She had it wrapped in tissue paper on her bureau."

Michaelis didn't see anything odd in that, and he gave Wilson a dozen reasons why his wife might have bought the dog-leash. But conceivably Wilson had heard some of these same explanations before, from Myrtle, because he began saying "Oh, my God!" again in a whisper—his comforter left several explanations in the air.

"Then he killed her," said Wilson. His mouth dropped open suddenly.

"Who did?"

"I have a way of finding out."

"You're morbid, George," said his friend. "This has been a strain to you and you don't know what you're saying. You'd better try and sit quiet till morning."

"He murdered her."

"It was an accident, George."

Wilson shook his head. His eyes narrowed and his mouth widened slightly with the ghost of a superior "Hm!"

"I know," he said definitely, "I'm one of these trusting fellas and I don't think any harm to *no*body, but when I get to know a thing I know it. It was the man in that car. She ran out to speak to him and he wouldn't stop."

Michaelis had seen this too, but it hadn't occurred to him that there was any special significance in it. He believed that Mrs. Wilson had been running away from her husband, rather than trying to stop any particular car.

"How could she of been like that?"

"She's a deep one," said Wilson, as if that answered the question. "Ah-h-h——"

He began to rock again, and Michaelis stood twisting the leash in his hand.

"Maybe you got some friend that I could telephone for, George?"

This was a forlorn hope—he was almost sure that Wilson had no friend: there was not enough of him for his wife. He was glad a little later when he noticed a change in the room, a blue quickening by the window, and realized that dawn wasn't far off. About five o'clock it was blue enough outside to snap off the light.

Wilson's glazed eyes turned out to the ashheaps, where small gray clouds took on fantastic shapes and scurried here and there in the faint dawn wind.

"I spoke to her," he muttered, after a long silence. "I told her she might fool me but she couldn't fool God. I took her to the window"—with an effort he got up and walked to the rear window and leaned with his face pressed against it—"and I said 'God knows what you've been doing, everything you've been doing. You may fool me, but you can't fool God!'"

Standing behind him, Michaelis saw with a shock that he was looking at the eyes of Doctor T. J. Eckleburg, which had just emerged, pale and enormous, from the dissolving night.

"God sees everything," repeated Wilson.

"That's an advertisement," Michaelis assured him. Something made him turn away from the window and look back into the room. But Wilson stood there a long time, his face close to the window pane, nodding into the twilight.

By six o'clock Michaelis was worn out, and grateful for the sound of a car stopping outside. It was one of the watchers of the night before who had promised to come back, so he cooked breakfast for three, which he and the other man ate together. Wilson was quieter now, and Michaelis went home to sleep; when he awoke four hours later and hurried back to the garage, Wilson was gone.

His movements—he was on foot all the time—were afterward traced to Port Roosevelt and then to Gad's Hill, where he bought a sandwich that he didn't eat, and a cup of coffee. He must have been tired and walking slowly, for he didn't reach Gad's Hill until noon. Thus far there was no difficulty in accounting for his time—there were boys who had seen a man "acting sort of crazy," and motorists at whom he stared oddly from the side of the road. Then for three hours he disappeared from view. The police, on the strength of what he said to Michaelis, that he "had a way of finding out," supposed that he spent that time going from garage to garage thereabout, inquiring for a yellow car. On the other hand, no garage man who had seen him ever came forward, and perhaps he had an easier, surer way of finding out what he wanted to know. By half-past two he was in West Egg, where he asked some one the way to Gatsby's house. So by that time he knew Gatsby's name.

At two o'clock Gatsby put on his bathing-suit and left word with the butler that if any one phoned word was to be brought to him at the pool. He stopped at the garage for a pneumatic mattress that had amused his guests during the summer, and the chauffeur helped him pump it up. Then he gave instructions that the open car wasn't to be taken out under any circumstances—and this was strange, because the front right fender needed repair.

Gatsby shouldered the mattress and started for the pool. Once he stopped and shifted it a little, and the chauffeur asked him if he needed help, but he shook his head and in a moment disappeared among the yellowing trees.

No telephone message arrived, but the butler went without his sleep and waited for it until four o'clock—until long after there was any one to give it to if it came. I have an idea that Gatsby himself didn't believe it would come, and perhaps he no longer cared. If that was true he must have felt that he had lost the old warm world, paid a high price for living too long with a single dream. He must have looked up at an unfamiliar sky through frightening leaves and shivered as he found what a grotesque thing a rose is and how raw the sunlight was upon the scarcely created grass. A new world, material without being real, where poor ghosts, breathing dreams like air, drifted fortuitously about . . . like that ashen, fantastic figure gliding toward him through the amorphous trees.

The chauffeur—he was one of Wolfsheim's protégés—heard the shots—afterward he could only say that he hadn't thought anything much about them. I drove from the station directly to Gatsby's house and my rushing anxiously up the front steps was the first thing that alarmed any one. But they knew then, I firmly believe. With scarcely a word said, four of us, the chauffeur, butler, gardener, and I, hurried down to the pool.

There was a faint, barely perceptible movement of the water as the fresh flow from one end urged its way toward the drain at the other. With little ripples that were hardly the shadows of waves, the laden mattress moved irregularly down the pool. A small gust of wind that scarcely corrugated the surface was enough to disturb its accidental course with its accidental burden. The touch of a cluster of leaves revolved it slowly, tracing, like the leg of transit, a thin red circle in the water.

It was after we started with Gatsby toward the house that the gardener saw Wilson's body a little way off in the grass, and the holocaust was complete.

9

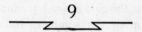

After two years I remember the rest of that day, and that night and the next day, only as an endless drill of police and photographers and newspaper men in and out of Gatsby's front door. A rope stretched across the main gate and a policeman by it kept out the curious, but little boys soon discovered that they could enter through my yard, and there were always a few of them clustered open-mouthed about the pool. Some one with a positive manner, perhaps a detective, used the expression "madman" as he bent over Wilson's body that afternoon, and the adventitious authority of his voice set the key for the newspaper reports next morning.

Most of those reports were a nightmare—grotesque, circumstantial, eager, and untrue. When Michaelis's testimony at the inquest brought to light Wilson's suspicions of his wife I thought the whole tale would shortly be served up in racy pasquinade—but Catherine, who might have said anything, didn't say a word. She showed a surprising amount of character about it too—looked at the coroner with determined eyes under that corrected brow of hers, and swore that her sister had never seen Gatsby, that her sister was completely happy with her husband, that her sister had been into no mischief whatever. She convinced herself of it, and cried into her handkerchief, as if the very suggestion was more than she could endure. So Wilson was reduced to a man "deranged by grief" in order that the case might remain in its simplest form. And it rested there.

But all this part of it seemed remote and unessential. I found myself on Gatsby's side, and alone. From the moment I telephoned news of the catastrophe to West Egg village, every surmise about him, and every practical question, was referred to me. At first I was surprised and confused; then, as he lay in his house and didn't move or breathe or speak, hour upon hour, it grew upon me that I was responsible, because no one else was interested—interested, I mean, with that intense personal interest to which every one has some vague right at the end.

I called up Daisy half an hour after we found him, called her instinctively and without hesitation. But she and Tom had gone away early that afternoon, and taken baggage with them.

"Left no address?"

"No."

"Say when they'd be back?"

"No."

"Any idea where they are? How I could reach them?"

"I don't know. Can't say."

I wanted to get somebody for him. I wanted to go into the room where he lay and reassure him: "I'll get somebody for you, Gatsby. Don't worry. Just trust me and I'll get somebody for you——"

Meyer Wolfsheim's name wasn't in the phone book. The butler gave me his office address on Broadway, and I called Information, but by the time I had the number it was long after five, and no one answered the phone.

"Will you ring again?"

"I've rung them three times."

"It's very important."

"Sorry. I'm afraid no one's there."

I went back to the drawing-room and thought for an instant that they were chance visitors, all these official people who suddenly filled it. But, though they drew back the sheet and looked at Gatsby with shocked eyes, his protest continued in my brain:

"Look here, old sport, you've got to get somebody for me. You've got to try hard. I can't go through this alone."

Some one started to ask me questions, but I broke away and going upstairs looked hastily through the unlocked parts of his desk—he'd never told me definitely that his parents were dead. But there was nothing—only the picture of Dan Cody, a token of forgotten violence, staring down from the wall.

Next morning I sent the butler to New York with a letter to Wolfsheim, which asked for information and urged him to come out on the next train. That request seemed superfluous when I wrote it. I was sure he'd start when he saw the newspapers, just as I was sure there'd be a wire from Daisy before noon—but neither a wire nor

Mr. Wolfsheim arrived; no one arrived except more police and photographers and newspaper men. When the butler brought back Wolfsheim's answer I began to have a feeling of defiance, of scornful solidarity between Gatsby and me against them all.

Dear Mr. Carraway. This has been one of the most terrible shocks of my life to me. I hardly can believe it that it is true at all. Such a mad act as that man did should make us all think. I cannot come down now as I am tied up in some very important business and cannot get mixed up in this thing now. If there is anything I can do a little later let me know in a letter by Edgar. I hardly know where I am when I hear about a thing like this and am completely knocked down and out.

Yours truly

Meyer Wolfsheim

and then hasty addenda beneath:

Let me know about the funeral etc do not know his family at all.

When the phone rang that afternoon and Long Distance said Chicago was calling I thought this would be Daisy at last. But the connection came through as a man's voice, very thin and far away.

"This is Slagle speaking . . ."

"Yes?" The name was unfamiliar.

"Hell of a note, isn't it? Get my wire?"

"There haven't been any wires."

"Young Parke's in trouble," he said rapidly. "They picked him up when he handed the bonds over the counter. They got a circular from New York giving 'em the numbers just five minutes before. What d'you know about that, hey? You never can tell in these hick towns——"

"Hello!" I interrupted breathlessly. "Look here—this isn't Mr. Gatsby. Mr. Gatsby's dead."

There was a long silence on the other end of the wire, followed by an exclamation . . . then a quick squawk as the connection was broken.

I think it was on the third day that a telegram signed Henry C. Gatz arrived from a town in Minnesota. It said only that the sender was leaving immediately and to postpone the funeral until he came.

It was Gatsby's father, a solemn old man, very helpless and dismayed, bundled up in a long cheap ulster against the warm September day. His eyes leaked continuously with excitement, and when I took the bag and umbrella from his hands he began to pull so incessantly at his sparse gray beard that I had difficulty in getting off his coat. He was on the point of collapse, so I took him into the music room and made him sit down while I sent for something to eat. But he wouldn't eat, and the glass of milk spilled from his trembling hand.

"I saw it in the Chicago newspaper," he said. "It was all in the Chicago newspaper. I started right away."

"I didn't know how to reach you."

His eyes, seeing nothing, moved ceaselessly about the room.

"It was a madman," he said. "He must have been mad."

"Wouldn't you like some coffee?" I urged him.

"I don't want anything. I'm all right now, Mr——"

"Carraway."

"Well, I'm all right now. Where have they got Jimmy?"

I took him into the drawing-room, where his son lay, and left him there. Some little boys had come up on the steps and were looking into the hall; when I told them who had arrived, they went reluctantly away.

After a little while Mr. Gatz opened the door and came out, his mouth ajar, his face flushed slightly, his eyes leaking isolated and unpunctual tears. He had reached an age where death no longer has the quality of ghastly surprise, and when he looked around him now for the first time and saw the height and splendor of the hall and the great rooms opening out from it into other rooms, his grief began to be mixed with an awed pride. I helped him to a bedroom upstairs; while he took off his coat and vest I told him that all arrangements had been deferred until he came.

"I didn't know what you'd want, Mr. Gatsby——"

"Gatz is my name."

"—Mr. Gatz. I thought you might want to take the body West." He shook his head.

"Jimmy always liked it better down East. He rose up to his position in the East. Were you a friend of my boy's, Mr.——?"

"We were close friends."

"He had a big future before him, you know. He was only a young man, but he had a lot of brain power here."

He touched his head impressively, and I nodded.

"If he'd of lived, he'd of been a great man. A man like James J. Hill. He'd of helped build up the country."

"That's true," I said, uncomfortably.

He fumbled at the embroidered coverlet, trying to take it from the bed, and lay down stiffly—was instantly asleep.

That night an obviously frightened person called up, and demanded to know who I was before he would give his name.

"This is Mr. Carraway," I said.

"Oh!" He sounded relieved. "This is Klipspringer."

I was relieved too, for that seemed to promise another friend at Gatsby's grave. I didn't want it to be in the papers and draw a sight-seeing crowd, so I'd been calling up a few people myself. They were hard to find.

"The funeral's tomorrow," I said. "Three o'clock, here at the house. I wish you'd tell anybody who'd be interested."

"Oh, I will," he broke out hastily. "Of course I'm not likely to see anybody, but if I do."

His tone made me suspicious.

"Of course you'll be there yourself."

"Well, I'll certainly try. What I called up about is——"

"Wait a minute," I interrupted. "How about saying you'll come?"

"Well, the fact is—the truth of the matter is that I'm staying with some people up here in Greenwich, and they rather expect me to be with them tomorrow. In fact, there's a sort of picnic or something. Of course I'll do my very best to get away."

I ejaculated an unrestrained "Huh!" and he must have heard me, for he went on nervously:

"What I called up about was a pair of shoes I left there. I wonder if it'd be too much trouble to have the butler send them on. You see, they're tennis shoes, and I'm sort of helpless without them. My address is care of B. F.——"

I didn't hear the rest of the name, because I hung up the receiver.

After that I felt a certain shame for Gatsby—one gentleman to whom I telephoned implied that he had got what he deserved. However, that was my fault, for he was one of those who used to sneer most bitterly at Gatsby on the courage of Gatsby's liquor, and I should have known better than to call him.

The morning of the funeral I went up to New York to see Meyer Wolfsheim; I couldn't seem to reach him any other way. The door

that I pushed open, on the advice of an elevator boy, was marked
"The Swastika Holding Company," and at first there didn't seem
to be any one inside. But when I'd shouted "hello" several times in
vain, an argument broke out behind a partition, and presently a
lovely Jewess appeared at an interior door and scrutinized me with
black hostile eyes.

"Nobody's in," she said. "Mr. Wolfsheim's gone to Chicago."

The first part of this was obviously untrue, for some one had
begun to whistle "The Rosary," tunelessly, inside.

"Please say that Mr. Carraway wants to see him."

"I can't get him back from Chicago, can I?"

At this moment a voice, unmistakably Wolfsheim's, called "Stella!"
from the other side of the door.

"Leave your name on the desk," she said quickly. "I'll give it to
him when he gets back."

"But I know he's there."

She took a step toward me and began to slide her hands indignantly up and down her hips.

"You young men think you can force your way in here any time,"
she scolded. "We're getting sickantired of it. When I say he's in
Chicago, he's in Chicago."

I mentioned Gatsby.

"Oh-h!" She looked at me over again. "Will you just— What was
your name?"

She vanished. In a moment Meyer Wolfsheim stood solemnly in
the doorway, holding out both hands. He drew me into his office,
remarking in a reverent voice that it was a sad time for all of us,
and offered me a cigar.

"My memory goes back to when first I met him," he said. "A young
major just out of the army and covered over with medals he got
in the war. He was so hard up he had to keep on wearing his uniform
because he couldn't buy some regular clothes. First time I saw him
was when he come into Winebrenner's poolroom at Forty-third
Street and asked for a job. He hadn't eat anything for a couple of
days. 'Come on have some lunch with me,' I said. He ate more than
four dollars' worth of food in half an hour."

"Did you start him in business?" I inquired.

"Start him! I made him."

"Oh."

"I raised him up out of nothing, right out of the gutter. I saw right away he was a fine-appearing, gentlemanly young man, and when he told me he was an Oggsford I knew I could use him good. I got him to join up in the American Legion and he used to stand high there. Right off he did some work for a client of mine up to Albany. We were so thick like that in everything"—he held up two bulbous fingers—"always together."

I wondered if this partnership had included the World's Series transaction in 1919.

"Now he's dead," I said after a moment. "You were his closest friend, so I know you'll want to come to his funeral this afternoon."

"I'd like to come."

"Well, come then."

The hair in his nostrils quivered slightly, and as he shook his head his eyes filled with tears.

"I can't do it—I can't get mixed up in it," he said.

"There's nothing to get mixed up in. It's all over now."

"When a man gets killed I never like to get mixed up in it in any way. I keep out. When I was a young man it was different—if a friend of mine died, no matter how, I stuck with them to the end. You may think that's sentimental, but I mean it—to the bitter end."

I saw that for some reason of his own he was determined not to come, so I stood up.

"Are you a college man?" he inquired suddenly.

For a moment I thought he was going to suggest a "gonnegtion," but he only nodded and shook my hand.

"Let us learn to show our friendship for a man when he is alive and not after he is dead," he suggested. "After that, my own rule is to let everything alone."

When I left his office the sky had turned dark and I got back to West Egg in a drizzle. After changing my clothes I went next door and found Mr. Gatz walking up and down excitedly in the hall. His pride in his son and in his son's possessions was continually increasing and now he had something to show me.

"Jimmy sent me this picture." He took out his wallet with trembling fingers. "Look there."

It was a photograph of the house, cracked in the corners and dirty with many hands. He pointed out every detail to me eagerly. "Look there!" and then sought admiration from my eyes. He had shown it so often that I think it was more real to him now than the house itself.

"Jimmy sent it to me. I think it's a very pretty picture. It shows up well."

"Very well. Had you seen him lately?"

"He come out to see me two years ago and bought me the house I live in now. Of course we was broke up when he run off from home, but I see now there was a reason for it. He knew he had a big future in front of him. And ever since he made a success he was very generous with me."

He seemed reluctant to put away the picture, held it for another minute, lingeringly, before my eyes. Then he returned the wallet and pulled from his pocket a ragged old copy of a book called *Hopalong Cassidy*.

"Look here, this is a book he had when he was a boy. It just shows you."

He opened it at the back cover and turned it around for me to see. On the last fly-leaf was printed the word SCHEDULE, and the date September 12, 1906. And underneath:

Rise from bed	6.00	A.M.
Dumbbell exercise and wall-scaling	6.15–6.30	"
Study electricity, etc.	7.15–8.15	"
Work	8.30–4.30	P.M.
Baseball and sports	4.30–5.00	"
Practice elocution, poise and how to attain it	5.00–6.00	"
Study needed inventions	7.00–9.00	"

GENERAL RESOLVES

No wasting time at Shafters or [a name, indecipherable]

No more smokeing or chewing.

Bath every other day

Read one improving book or magazine per week

Save $5.00 [crossed out] $3.00 per week

Be better to parents

"I come across this book by accident," said the old man. "It just shows you, don't it?

"Jimmy was bound to get ahead. He always had some resolves like this or something. Do you notice what he's got about improving his mind? He was always great for that. He told me I et like a hog once, and I beat him for it."

He was reluctant to close the book, reading each item aloud and then looking eagerly at me. I think he rather expected me to copy down the list for my own use.

A little before three the Lutheran minister arrived from Flushing, and I began to look involuntarily out the windows for other cars. So did Gatsby's father. And as the time passed and the servants came in and stood waiting in the hall, his eyes began to blink anxiously, and he spoke of the rain in a worried, uncertain way. The minister glanced several times at his watch, so I took him aside and asked him to wait for half an hour. But it wasn't any use. Nobody came.

About five o'clock our procession of three cars reached the cemetery and stopped in a thick drizzle beside the gate—first a motor hearse, horribly black and wet, then Mr. Gatz and the minister and I in the limousine, and a little later four or five servants and the postman from West Egg, in Gatsby's station wagon, all wet to the skin. As we started through the gate into the cemetery I heard a car stop and then the sound of some one splashing after us over the soggy ground. I looked around. It was the man with owl-eyed glasses whom I had found marvelling over Gatsby's books in the library one night three months before.

I'd never seen him since then. I don't know how he knew about the funeral, or even his name. The rain poured down his thick glasses, and he took them off and wiped them to see the protecting canvas unrolled from Gatsby's grave.

I tried to think about Gatsby then for a moment, but he was already too far away, and I could only remember, without resentment, that Daisy hadn't sent a message or a flower. Dimly I heard some one murmur "Blessed are the dead that the rain falls on," and then the owl-eyed man said "Amen to that," in a brave voice.

We straggled down quickly through the rain to the cars. Owl-eyes spoke to me by the gate.

"I couldn't get to the house," he remarked.

"Neither could anybody else."

"Go on!" He started. "Why, my God! they used to go there by the hundreds."

He took off his glasses and wiped them again, outside and in.

"The poor son-of-a-bitch," he said.

One of my most vivid memories is of coming back West from prep school and later from college at Christmas time. Those who went farther than Chicago would gather in the old dim Union Station at six o'clock of a December evening, with a few Chicago friends, already caught up into their own holiday gayeties, to bid them a hasty good-by. I remember the fur coats of the girls returning from Miss This-or-That's and the chatter of frozen breath and the hands waving overhead as we caught sight of old acquaintances, and the matchings of invitations: "Are you going to the Ordways'? the Herseys'? the Schultzes'?" and the long green tickets clasped tight in our gloved hands. And last the murky yellow cars of the Chicago, Milwaukee & St. Paul railroad looking cheerful as Christmas itself on the tracks beside the gate.

When we pulled out into the winter night and the real snow, our snow, began to stretch out beside us and twinkle against the windows, and the dim lights of small Wisconsin stations moved by, a sharp wild brace came suddenly into the air. We drew in deep breaths of it as we walked back from dinner through the cold vestibules, unutterably aware of our identity with this country for one strange hour, before we melted indistinguishably into it again.

That's my Middle West—not the wheat or the prairies or the lost Swede towns, but the thrilling returning trains of my youth, and the street lamps and sleigh bells in the frosty dark and the shadows of holly wreaths thrown by lighted windows on the snow. I am part of that, a little solemn with the feel of those long winters, a little complacent from growing up in the Carraway house in a city where dwellings are still called through decades by a family's name. I see now that this has been a story of the West, after all—Tom and Gatsby, Daisy and Jordan and I, were all Westerners, and perhaps we possessed some deficiency in common which made us subtly unadaptable to Eastern life.

Even when the East excited me most, even when I was most keenly aware of its superiority to the bored, sprawling, swollen towns beyond the Ohio, with their interminable inquisitions which spared only the children and the very old—even then it had always for me a quality of distortion. West Egg, especially, still figures in my more fantastic dreams. I see it as a night scene by El Greco: a hundred houses, at once conventional and grotesque, crouching under a sullen, overhanging sky and a lustreless moon. In the foreground four solemn men in dress suits are walking along the sidewalk with a stretcher on which lies a drunken woman in a white evening dress. Her hand, which dangles over the side, sparkles cold with jewels.

Gravely the men turn in at a house—the wrong house. But no one knows the woman's name, and no one cares.

After Gatsby's death the East was haunted for me like that, distorted beyond my eyes' power of correction. So when the blue smoke of brittle leaves was in the air and the wind blew the wet laundry stiff on the line I decided to come back home.

There was one thing to be done before I left, an awkward, unpleasant thing that perhaps had better have been let alone. But I wanted to leave things in order and not just trust that obliging and indifferent sea to sweep my refuse away. I saw Jordan Baker and talked over and around what had happened to us together, and what had happened afterward to me, and she lay perfectly still, listening, in a big chair.

She was dressed to play golf, and I remember thinking she looked like a good illustration, her chin raised a little jauntily, her hair the color of an autumn leaf, her face the same brown tint as the fingerless glove on her knee. When I had finished she told me without comment that she was engaged to another man. I doubted that, though there were several she could have married at a nod of her head, but I pretended to be surprised. For just a minute I wondered if I wasn't making a mistake, then I thought it all over again quickly and got up to say good-by.

"Nevertheless you did throw me over," said Jordan suddenly. "You threw me over on the telephone. I don't give a damn about you now, but it was a new experience for me, and I felt a little dizzy for a while."

We shook hands.

"Oh, and do you remember"—she added—"a conversation we had once about driving a car?"

"Why—not exactly."

"You said a bad driver was only safe until she met another bad driver? Well, I met another bad driver, didn't I? I mean it was careless of me to make such a wrong guess. I thought you were rather an honest, straightforward person. I thought it was your secret pride."

"I'm thirty," I said. "I'm five years too old to lie to myself and call it honor."

She didn't answer. Angry, and half in love with her, and tremendously sorry, I turned away.

One afternoon late in October I saw Tom Buchanan. He was

walking ahead of me along Fifth Avenue in his alert, aggressive way, his hands out a little from his body as if to fight off interference, his head moving sharply here and there, adapting itself to his restless eyes. Just as I slowed up to avoid overtaking him he stopped and began frowning into the windows of a jewelry store. Suddenly he saw me and walked back, holding out his hand.

"What's the matter, Nick? Do you object to shaking hands with me?"

"Yes. You know what I think of you."

"You're crazy, Nick," he said quickly. "Crazy as hell. I don't know what's the matter with you."

"Tom," I inquired, "what did you say to Wilson that afternoon?"

He stared at me without a word, and I knew I had guessed right about those missing hours. I started to turn away, but he took a step after me and grabbed my arm.

"I told him the truth," he said. "He came to the door while we were getting ready to leave, and when I sent down word that we weren't in he tried to force his way upstairs. He was crazy enough to kill me if I hadn't told him who owned the car. His hand was on a revolver in his pocket every minute he was in the house—" He broke off defiantly. "What if I did tell him? That fellow had it coming to him. He threw dust into your eyes just like he did in Daisy's, but he was a tough one. He ran over Myrtle like you'd run over a dog and never even stopped his car."

There was nothing I could say, except the one unutterable fact that it wasn't true.

"And if you think I didn't have my share of suffering—look here, when I went to give up that flat and saw that damn box of dog biscuits sitting there on the sideboard, I sat down and cried like a baby. By God it was awful——"

I couldn't forgive him or like him, but I saw that what he had done was, to him, entirely justified. It was all very careless and confused. They were careless people, Tom and Daisy—they smashed up things and creatures and then retreated back into their money or their vast carelessness, or whatever it was that kept them together, and let other people clean up the mess they had made. . . .

I shook hands with him; it seemed silly not to, for I felt suddenly as though I were talking to a child. Then he went into the jewelry store to buy a pearl necklace—or perhaps only a pair of cuff buttons—rid of my provincial squeamishness forever.

Gatsby's house was still empty when I left—the grass on his lawn had grown as long as mine. One of the taxi drivers in the village never took a fare past the entrance gate without stopping for a minute and pointing inside; perhaps it was he who drove Daisy and Gatsby over to East Egg the night of the accident, and perhaps he had made a story about it all his own. I didn't want to hear it and I avoided him when I got off the train.

I spent my Saturday nights in New York, because those gleaming, dazzling parties of his were with me so vividly that I could still hear the music and the laughter, faint and incessant, from his garden, and the cars going up and down his drive. One night I did hear a material car there, and saw its lights stop at his front steps. But I didn't investigate. Probably it was some final guest who had been away at the ends of the earth and didn't know that the party was over.

On the last night, with my trunk packed and my car sold to the grocer, I went over and looked at that huge incoherent failure of a house once more. On the white steps an obscene word, scrawled by some boy with a piece of brick, stood out clearly in the moonlight, and I erased it, drawing my shoe raspingly along the stone. Then I wandered down to the beach and sprawled out on the sand.

Most of the big shore places were closed now and there were hardly any lights except the shadowy, moving glow of a ferryboat across the Sound. And as the moon rose higher the inessential houses began to melt away until gradually I became aware of the old island here that flowered once for Dutch sailors' eyes—a fresh, green breast of the new world. Its vanished trees, the trees that had made way for Gatsby's house, had once pandered in whispers to the last and greatest of all human dreams; for a transitory enchanted moment man must have held his breath in the presence of this continent, compelled into an æsthetic contemplation he neither understood nor desired, face to face for the last time in history with something commensurate to his capacity for wonder.

And as I sat there brooding on the old, unknown world, I thought of Gatsby's wonder when he first picked out the green light at the end of Daisy's dock. He had come a long way to this blue lawn, and his dream must have seemed so close that he could hardly fail to grasp it. He did not know that it was already behind him, somewhere back in that vast obscurity beyond the city, where the dark fields of the republic rolled on under the night.

Gatsby believed in the green light, the orgiastic future that year by year recedes before us. It eluded us then, but that's no matter—tomorrow we will run faster, stretch out our arms farther. . . . And one fine morning——

So we beat on, boats against the current, borne back ceaselessly into the past.

Pale Horse, Pale Rider

1936

KATHERINE ANNE PORTER

Pale Horse, Pale Rider

IN SLEEP she knew she was in her bed, but not the bed she had lain down in a few hours since, and the room was not the same but it was a room she had known somewhere. Her heart was a stone lying upon her breast outside of her; her pulses lagged and paused, and she knew that something strange was going to happen, even as the early morning winds were cool through the lattice, the streaks of light were dark blue and the whole house was snoring in its sleep.

Now I must get up and go while they are all quiet. Where are my things? Things have a will of their own in this place and hide where they like. Daylight will strike a sudden blow on the roof startling them all up to their feet; faces will beam asking, Where are you going, What are you doing, What are you thinking, How do you feel, Why do you say such things, What do you mean? No more sleep. Where are my boots and what horse shall I ride? Fiddler or Graylie or Miss Lucy with the long nose and the wicked eye? How I have loved this house in the morning before we are all awake and tangled together like badly cast fishing lines. Too many people have been born here, and have wept too much here, and have laughed too much, and have been too angry and outrageous with each other here. Too many have died in this bed already, there are far too many ancestral bones propped up on the mantelpieces, there have been too damned many antimacassars in this house, she said loudly, and oh, what accumulation of storied dust never allowed to settle in peace for one moment.

And the stranger? Where is that lank greenish stranger I remember hanging about the place, welcomed by my grandfather, my great-aunt, my five times removed cousin, my decrepit hound and my silver kitten? Why did they take to him, I wonder? And where are they now? Yet I saw him pass the window in the evening. What else besides them did I have in the world? Nothing. Nothing is mine, I have only nothing but it is enough, it is beautiful and it is all mine. Do I even walk about in my own skin or is it something I have borrowed to spare my modesty? Now what horse shall I borrow for this journey I do not mean to take, Graylie or Miss Lucy or Fiddler who can jump ditches in the dark and knows how to get the bit between his teeth? Early morning is best for me because trees are trees in one stroke, stones are stones set in shades known to be grass, there are no false shapes or surmises, the road is still asleep with the crust of dew unbroken. I'll take Graylie because he is not afraid of bridges.

Come now, Graylie, she said, taking his bridle, we must outrun Death and the Devil. You are no good for it, she told the other horses standing saddled before the stable gate, among them the horse of the stranger, gray also, with tarnished nose and ears. The stranger swung into his saddle beside her, leaned far towards her and regarded her without meaning, the blank still stare of mindless malice that makes no threats and can bide its time. She drew Graylie around sharply, urged him to run. He leaped the low rose hedge and the narrow ditch beyond, and the dust of the lane flew heavily under his beating hoofs. The stranger rode beside her, easily, lightly, his reins loose in his half-closed hand, straight and elegant in dark shabby garments that flapped upon his bones; his pale face smiled in an evil trance, he did not glance at her. Ah, I have seen this fellow before, I know this man if I could place him. He is no stranger to me.

She pulled Graylie up, rose in her stirrups and shouted, I'm not going with you this time—ride on! Without pausing or turning his head the stranger rode on. Graylie's ribs heaved under her, her own ribs rose and fell, Oh, why am I so tired, I must wake up. "But let me get a fine yawn first," she said, opening her eyes and stretching, "a slap of cold water in my face, for I've been talking in my sleep again, I heard myself but what was I saying?"

Slowly, unwillingly, Miranda drew herself up inch by inch out of the pit of sleep, waited in a daze for life to begin again. A single word struck in her mind, a gong of warning, reminding her for the day long what she forgot happily in sleep, and only in sleep. The war, said the gong, and she shook her head. Dangling her feet idly with their slippers hanging, she was reminded of the way all sorts of persons sat upon her desk at the newspaper office. Every day she found someone there, sitting upon her desk instead of the chair provided, dangling his legs, eyes roving, full of his important affairs, waiting to pounce about something or other. "*Why* won't they sit in the chair? Should I put a sign on it, saying, 'For God's sake, sit here'?"

Far from putting up a sign, she did not even frown at her visitors. Usually she did not notice them at all until their determination to be seen was greater than her determination not to see them. Saturday, she thought, lying comfortably in her tub of hot water, will be pay day, as always. Or I hope always. Her thoughts roved hazily in a continual effort to bring together and unite firmly the disturbing oppositions in her day-to-day existence, where survival, she could see clearly, had become a series of feats of sleight of hand. I owe—let me see, I wish I had pencil and paper—well, suppose I *did* pay five dollars now on a Liberty Bond, I couldn't possibly keep it up. Or maybe. Eighteen dollars a week. So much for rent, so much for food, and I mean to have a few things besides. About five dollars' worth. Will leave me twenty-seven cents. I suppose I can make it. I suppose I should be worried. I am worried. Very well, now I am worried and what next? Twenty-seven cents. That's not so bad. Pure profit, really. Imagine if they should suddenly raise me to twenty I should then have two dollars and twenty-seven cents left over. But they aren't going to raise me to twenty. They are in fact going to throw me out if I don't buy a Liberty Bond. I hardly believe that. I'll ask Bill. (Bill was the city editor.) I wonder if a threat like that isn't a kind of blackmail. I don't believe even a Lusk Committeeman can get away with that.

Yesterday there had been two pairs of legs dangling, on either side of her typewriter, both pairs stuffed thickly into funnels of dark expensive-looking material. She noticed at a distance that one of them was oldish and one was youngish, and they both of them had a stale air of borrowed importance which apparently they had got from the same source. They were both much too well nourished and the younger one wore a square little mustache. Being what they were, no matter what their business was it would be something unpleasant. Miranda had nodded at them, pulled out her chair and without removing her cap or gloves had reached into a pile of letters and sheets from the copy desk as if she had not a moment to spare. They did not move, or take off their hats. At last she had said "Good morning" to them, and asked if they were, perhaps, waiting for her?

The two men slid off the desk, leaving some of her papers rumpled, and the oldish man had inquired why she had not bought a Liberty

Bond. Miranda had looked at him then, and got a poor impression. He was a pursy-faced man, gross-mouthed, with little lightless eyes, and Miranda wondered why nearly all of those selected to do the war work at home were of his sort. He might be anything at all, she thought; advance agent for a road show, promoter of a wildcat oil company, a former saloon keeper announcing the opening of a new cabaret, an automobile salesman—any follower of any one of the crafty, haphazard callings. But he was now all Patriot, working for the government. "Look here," he asked her, "do you know there's a war, or don't you?"

Did he expect an answer to that? Be quiet, Miranda told herself, this was bound to happen. Sooner or later it happens. Keep your head. The man wagged his finger at her, "Do you?" he persisted, as if he were prompting an obstinate child.

"Oh, the war," Miranda had echoed on a rising note and she almost smiled at him. It was habitual, automatic, to give that solemn, mystically uplifted grin when you spoke the words or heard them spoken. "*C'est la guerre*," whether you could pronounce it or not, was even better, and always, always, you shrugged.

"Yeah," said the younger man in a nasty way, "the war." Miranda, startled by the tone, met his eye; his stare was really stony, really viciously cold, the kind of thing you might expect to meet behind a pistol on a deserted corner. This expression gave temporary meaning to a set of features otherwise nondescript, the face of those men who have no business of their own. "We're having a war, and some people are buying Liberty Bonds and others just don't seem to get around to it," he said. "That's what we mean."

Miranda frowned with nervousness, the sharp beginnings of fear. "Are you selling them?" she asked, taking the cover off her typewriter and putting it back again.

"No, we're not selling them," said the older man. "We're just asking you why you haven't bought one." The voice was persuasive and ominous.

Miranda began to explain that she had no money, and did not know where to find any, when the older man interrupted: "That's no excuse, no excuse at all, and you know it, with the Huns overrunning martyred Belgium."

"With our American boys fighting and dying in Belleau Wood," said the younger man, "anybody can raise fifty dollars to help beat the Boche."

Miranda said hastily, "I have eighteen dollars a week and not another cent in the world. I simply cannot buy anything."

"You can pay for it five dollars a week," said the older man (they had stood there cawing back and forth over her head), "like a lot of other people in this office, and a lot of other offices besides are doing."

Miranda, desperately silent, had thought, "Suppose I were not a coward, but said what I really thought? Suppose I said to hell with this filthy war? Suppose I asked that little thug, What's the matter with you, why aren't you rotting in Belleau Wood? I wish you were . . ."

She began to arrange her letters and notes, her fingers refusing to pick up things properly. The older man went on making his little set speech. It was hard, of course. Everybody was suffering, naturally. Everybody had to do his share. But as to that, a Liberty Bond was the safest investment you could make. It was just like having the money in the bank. Of course. The government was back of it and where better could you invest?

"I agree with you about that," said Miranda, "but I haven't any money to invest."

And of course, the man had gone on, it wasn't so much her fifty dollars that was going to make any difference. It was just a pledge of good faith on her part. A pledge of good faith that she was a loyal American doing her duty. And the thing was safe as a church. Why, if he had a million dollars he'd be glad to put every last cent of it in these Bonds. . . . "You can't lose by it," he said, almost benevolently, "and you can lose a lot if you don't. Think it over. You're the only one in this whole newspaper office that hasn't come in. And every firm in this city has come in one hundred per cent. Over at the *Daily Clarion* nobody had to be asked twice."

"They pay better over there," said Miranda. "But next week, if I can. Not now, next week."

"See that you do," said the younger man. "This ain't any laughing matter."

They lolled away, past the Society Editor's desk, past Bill the City Editor's desk, past the long copy desk where old man Gibbons sat all night shouting at intervals, "Jarge! Jarge!" and the copy boy would come flying. "Never say *people* when you mean *persons*," old man Gibbons had instructed Miranda, "and never say *practically*, say *virtually*, and don't for God's sake ever so long as I am at this

desk use the barbarism *inasmuch* under any circumstances whatso-
ever. Now you're educated, you may go." At the head of the stairs
her inquisitors had stopped in their fussy pride and vainglory,
lighting cigars and wedging their hats more firmly over their eyes.

Miranda turned over in the soothing water, and wished she might
fall asleep there, to wake up only when it was time to sleep again.
She had a burning slow headache, and noticed it now, remembering
she had waked up with it and it had in fact begun the evening before.
While she dressed she tried to trace the insidious career of her headache, and it seemed reasonable to suppose it had started with the
war. "It's been a headache, all right, but not quite like this." After
the Committeemen had left, yesterday, she had gone to the cloakroom and had found Mary Townsend, the Society Editor, quietly
hysterical about something. She was perched on the edge of the
shabby wicker couch with ridges down the center, knitting on something rose-colored. Now and then she would put down her knitting,
seize her head with both hands and rock, saying, "My *God*," in a
surprised, inquiring voice. Her column was called Ye Towne Gossyp,
so of course everybody called her Towney. Miranda and Towney had
a great deal in common, and liked each other. They had both been
real reporters once, and had been sent together to "cover" a scandalous elopement, in which no marriage had taken place, after all,
and the recaptured girl, her face swollen, had sat with her mother,
who was moaning steadily under a mound of blankets. They had
both wept painfully and implored the young reporters to suppress the
worst of the story. They had suppressed it, and the rival newspaper
printed it all the next day. Miranda and Towney had then taken
their punishment together, and had been degraded publicly to routine
female jobs, one to the theaters, the other to society. They had this
in common, that neither of them could see what else they could possibly have done, and they knew they were considered fools by the
rest of the staff—nice girls, but fools. At sight of Miranda, Towney
had broken out in a rage, "I can't do it, I'll never be able to raise
the money, I told them, I can't, I can't, but they wouldn't listen."

Miranda said, "I knew I wasn't the only person in this office who
couldn't raise five dollars. I told them I couldn't, too, and I can't."

"My *God*," said Towney, in the same voice, "they told me I'd lose
my job—"

"I'm going to ask Bill," Miranda said; "I don't believe Bill would do that."

"It's not up to Bill," said Towney. "He'd have to if they got after him. Do you suppose they could put us in jail?"

"I don't know," said Miranda. "If they do, we won't be lone-some." She sat down beside Towney and held her own head. "What kind of soldier are you knitting that for? It's a sprightly color, it ought to cheer him up."

"Like hell," said Towney, her needles going again. "I'm making this for myself. That's that."

"Well," said Miranda, "we won't be lonesome and we'll catch up on our sleep." She washed her face and put on fresh make-up. Taking clean gray gloves out of her pocket she went out to join a group of young women fresh from the country club dances, the morn-ing bridge, the charity bazaar, the Red Cross workrooms, who were wallowing in good works. They gave tea dances and raised money, and with the money they bought quantities of sweets, fruit, cigarettes, and magazines for the men in the cantonment hospitals. With this loot they were now setting out, a gay procession of high-powered cars and brightly tinted faces to cheer the brave boys who already, you might very well say, had fallen in defense of their country. It must be frightfully hard on them, the dears, to be floored like this when they're all crazy to get overseas and into the trenches as quickly as possible. Yes, and some of them are the cutest things you ever saw, I didn't know there were so many good-looking men in this country, good heavens, I said, where do they come from? Well, my dear, you may ask yourself that question, who knows where they did come from? You're quite right, the way I feel about it is this, we must do everything we can to make them contented, but I draw the line at talking to them. I told the chaperons at those dances for enlisted men, I'll dance with them, every dumbbell who asks me, but I will NOT talk to them, I said, even if there is a war. So I danced hundreds of miles without opening my mouth except to say, Please keep your knees to yourself. I'm glad we gave those dances up. Yes, and the men stopped coming, anyway. But listen, I've heard that a great many of the enlisted men come from very good fam-ilies; I'm not good at catching names, and those I did catch I'd never heard before, so I don't know . . . but it seems to me if they were from good families, you'd know it, wouldn't you? I mean, if a man is well bred he doesn't step on your feet, does he? At least not that.

I used to have a pair of sandals ruined at every one of those dances. Well, I think any kind of social life is in very poor taste just now, I think we should all put on our Red Cross head dresses and wear them for the duration of the war—

Miranda, carrying her basket and her flowers, moved in among the young women, who scattered out and rushed upon the ward uttering girlish laughter meant to be refreshingly gay, but there was a grim determined clang in it calculated to freeze the blood. Miserably embarrassed at the idiocy of her errand, she walked rapidly between the long rows of high beds, set foot to foot with a narrow aisle between. The men, a selected presentable lot, sheets drawn up to their chins, not seriously ill, were bored and restless, most of them willing to be amused at anything. They were for the most part picturesquely bandaged as to arm or head, and those who were not visibly wounded invariably replied "Rheumatism" if some tactless girl, who had been solemnly warned never to ask this question, still forgot and asked a man what his illness was. The good-natured, eager ones, laughing and calling out from their hard narrow beds, were soon surrounded. Miranda, with her wilting bouquet and her basket of sweets and cigarettes, looking about, caught the unfriendly bitter eye of a young fellow lying on his back, his right leg in a cast and pulley. She stopped at the foot of his bed and continued to look at him, and he looked back with an unchanged, hostile face. Not having any, thank you and be damned to the whole business, his eyes said plainly to her, and will you be so good as to take your trash off my bed? For Miranda had set it down, leaning over to place it where he might be able to reach it if he would. Having set it down, she was incapable of taking it up again, but hurried away, her face burning, down the long aisle and out into the cool October sunshine, where the dreary raw barracks swarmed and worked with an aimless life of scurrying, dun-colored insects; and going around to a window near where he lay, she looked in, spying upon her soldier. He was lying with his eyes closed, his eyebrows in a sad bitter frown. She could not place him at all, she could not imagine where he came from nor what sort of being he might have been "in life," she said to herself. His face was young and the features sharp and plain, the hands were not laborer's hands but not well-cared-for hands either. They were good useful properly shaped hands, lying there on the coverlet. It occurred to her that it would be her luck to find him, instead of a jolly hungry puppy glad of a bite to eat and a little chatter. It is like turning a corner absorbed in your painful thoughts and meeting your state of mind embodied, face to face, she said. "My own feelings about this whole thing, made flesh. Never again will I come here, this is no sort of thing to be doing. This is disgusting," she told herself plainly. "Of course I would pick him out," she thought, getting into the back seat of the car she came in, "serves me right, I know better."

Another girl came out looking very tired and climbed in beside her. After a short silence, the girl said in a puzzled way, "I don't know what good it does, really. Some of them wouldn't take anything at all. I don't like this, do you?"

"I hate it," said Miranda.

"I suppose it's all right, though," said the girl, cautiously.

"Perhaps," said Miranda, turning cautious also.

That was for yesterday. At this point Miranda decided there was no good in thinking of yesterday, except for the hour after midnight she had spent dancing with Adam. He was in her mind so much, she hardly knew when she was thinking about him directly. His image was simply always present in more or less degree, he was sometimes nearer the surface of her thoughts, the pleasantest, the only really pleasant thought she had. She examined her face in the mirror between the windows and decided that her uneasiness was not all imagination. For three days at least she had felt odd and her expression was unfamiliar. She would have to raise that fifty dollars somehow, she supposed, or who knows what can happen? She was hardened to stories of personal disaster, of outrageous accusations and extraordinarily bitter penalties that had grown monstrously out of incidents very little more important than her failure—her refusal—to buy a Bond. No, she did not find herself a pleasing sight, flushed and shiny, and even her hair felt as if it had decided to grow in the other direction. I must do something about this, I can't let Adam see me like this, she told herself, knowing that even now at that moment he was listening for the turn of her door knob, and he would be in the hallway, or on the porch when she came out, as if by sheerest coincidence. The noon sunlight cast cold slanting shadows in the room where, she said, I suppose I live, and this day is beginning badly, but they all do now, for one reason or another. In a drowse, she sprayed perfume on her hair, put on her moleskin cap and jacket, now in their second winter, but still good, still nice to wear, again being glad she had paid a frightening price for them.

She had enjoyed them all this time, and in no case would she have had the money now. Maybe she could manage for that Bond. She could not find the lock without leaning to search for it, then stood undecided a moment possessed by the notion that she had forgotten something she would miss seriously later on.

Adam was in the hallway, a step outside his own door; he swung about as if quite startled to see her, and said, "Hello. I don't have to go back to camp today after all—isn't that luck?"

Miranda smiled at him gaily because she was always delighted at the sight of him. He was wearing his new uniform, and he was all olive and tan and tawny, hay colored and sand colored from hair to boots. She half noticed again that he always began by smiling at her; that his smile faded gradually; that his eyes became fixed and thoughtful as if he were reading in a poor light.

They walked out together into the fine fall day, scuffling bright ragged leaves under their feet, turning their faces up to a generous sky really blue and spotless. At the first corner they waited for a funeral to pass, the mourners seated straight and firm as if proud in their sorrow.

"I imagine I'm late," said Miranda, "as usual. What time is it?"

"Nearly half past one," he said, slipping back his sleeve with an exaggerated thrust of his arm upward. The young soldiers were still self-conscious about their wrist watches. Such of them as Miranda knew were boys from southern and southwestern towns, far off the Atlantic seaboard, and they had always believed that only sissies wore wrist watches. "I'll slap you on the wrist watch," one vaudeville comedian would simper to another, and it was always a good joke, never stale.

"I think it's a most sensible way to carry a watch," said Miranda. "You needn't blush."

"I'm nearly used to it," said Adam, who was from Texas. "We've been told time and again how all the he-manly regular army men wear them. It's the horrors of war," he said; "are we downhearted? I'll say we are."

It was the kind of patter going the rounds. "You look it," said Miranda.

He was tall and heavily muscled in the shoulders, narrow in the waist and flanks, and he was infinitely buttoned, strapped, harnessed into a uniform as tough and unyielding in cut as a strait jacket, though the cloth was fine and supple. He had his uniforms made by the best tailor he could find, he confided to Miranda one day when she told him how squish he was looking in his new soldier suit. "Hard enough to make anything of the outfit, anyhow," he told her. "It's the least I can do for my beloved country, not to go around looking like a tramp." He was twenty-four years old and a Second Lieutenant in an Engineers Corps, on leave because his outfit expected to be sent over shortly. "Came in to make my will," he told Miranda, "and get a supply of toothbrushes and razor blades. By what gorgeous luck do you suppose," he asked her, "I happened to pick on your rooming house? How did I know you were there?"

Strolling, keeping step, his stout polished well-made boots setting themselves down firmly beside her thin-soled black suède, they put off as long as they could the end of their moment together, and kept up as well as they could their small talk that flew back and forth over little grooves worn in the thin upper surface of the brain, things you could say and hear clink reassuringly at once without disturbing the radiance which played and darted about the simple and lovely miracle of being two persons named Adam and Miranda, twenty-four years old each, alive and on the earth at the same moment: "Are you in the mood for dancing, Miranda?" and "I'm always in the mood for dancing, Adam!" but there were things in the way, the day that ended with dancing was a long way to go.

He really did look, Miranda thought, like a fine healthy apple this morning. One time or another in their talking, he had boasted that he had never had a pain in his life that he could remember. Instead of being horrified at this monster, she approved his monstrous uniqueness. As for herself, she had had too many pains to mention, so she did not mention them. After working for three years on a morning newspaper she had an illusion of maturity and experience; but it was fatigue merely, she decided, from keeping what she had been brought up to believe were unnatural hours, eating casually at dirty little restaurants, drinking bad coffee all night, and smoking too much. When she said something of her way of living to Adam, he studied her face a few seconds as if he had never seen it before, and said in a forthright way, "Why, it hasn't hurt you a bit, I think you're beautiful," and left her dangling there, wondering if he had thought she wished to be praised. She did wish to be praised, but not at that moment. Adam kept unwholesome hours too, or had in the ten days they had known each other, staying awake until one o'clock to take her out for supper; he smoked also continually, though if she did not stop him he was apt to explain to her exactly what smoking did to the lungs. "But," he said, "does it matter so much if you're going to war, anyway?"

"No," said Miranda, "and it matters even less if you're staying at home knitting socks. Give me a cigarette, will you?" They paused at another corner, under a half-foliaged maple, and hardly glanced at a funeral procession approaching. His eyes were pale tan with orange flecks in them, and his hair was the color of a haystack when you turn the weathered top back to the clear straw beneath. He fished out his cigarette case and snapped his silver lighter at her, snapped it several times in his own face, and they moved on, smoking.

"I can see you knitting socks," he said. "That would be just your speed. You know perfectly well you can't knit."

"I do worse," she said, soberly; "I write pieces advising other young women to knit and roll bandages and do without sugar and help win the war."

"Oh, well," said Adam, with the easy masculine morals in such questions, "that's merely your job, that doesn't count."

"I wonder," said Miranda. "How did you manage to get an extension of leave?"

"They just gave it," said Adam, "for no reason. The men are dying like flies out there, anyway. This funny new disease. Simply knocks you into a cocked hat."

"It seems to be a plague," said Miranda, "something out of the Middle Ages. Did you ever see so many funerals, ever?"

"Never did. Well, let's be strong minded and not have any of it. I've got four days more straight from the blue and not a blade of grass must grow under our feet. What about tonight?"

"Same thing," she told him, "but make it about half past one. I've got a special job beside my usual run of the mill."

"What a job you've got," said Adam, "nothing to do but run from one dizzy amusement to another and then write a piece about it."

"Yes, it's too dizzy for words," said Miranda. They stood while a funeral passed, and this time they watched it in silence. Miranda pulled her cap to an angle and winked in the sunlight, her head swimming slowly "like goldfish," she told Adam, "my head swims. I'm only half awake, I must have some coffee."

They lounged on their elbows over the counter of a drug store.

"No more cream for the stay-at-homes," she said, "and only one lump of sugar. I'll have two or none; that's the kind of martyr I'm being. I mean to live on boiled cabbage and wear shoddy from now on and get in good shape for the next round. No war is going to sneak up on me again."

"Oh, there won't be any more wars, don't you read the newspapers?" asked Adam. "We're going to mop 'em up this time, and they're going to stay mopped, and this is going to be all."

"So they told me," said Miranda, tasting her bitter lukewarm brew and making a rueful face. Their smiles approved of each other, they felt they had got the right tone, they were taking the war properly. Above all, thought Miranda, no tooth-gnashing, no hair-tearing, it's noisy and unbecoming and it doesn't get you anywhere.

"Swill," said Adam rudely, pushing back his cup. "Is that all you're having for breakfast?"

"It's more than I want," said Miranda.

"I had buckwheat cakes, with sausage and maple syrup, and two bananas, and two cups of coffee, at eight o'clock, and right now, again, I feel like a famished orphan left in the ashcan. I'm all set," said Adam, "for broiled steak and fried potatoes and—"

"Don't go on with it," said Miranda, "it sounds delirious to me. Do all that after I'm gone." She slipped from the high seat, leaned against it slightly, glanced at her face in her round mirror, rubbed rouge on her lips and decided that she was past praying for.

"There's something terribly wrong," she told Adam. "I feel too rotten. It can't just be the weather, and the war."

"The weather is perfect," said Adam, "and the war is simply too good to be true. But since when? You were all right yesterday."

"I don't know," she said slowly, her voice sounding small and thin. They stopped as always at the open door before the flight of littered steps leading up to the newspaper loft. Miranda listened for a moment to the rattle of typewriters above, the steady rumble of presses below. "I wish we were going to spend the whole afternoon on a park bench," she said, "or drive to the mountains."

"I do too," he said; "let's do that tomorrow."

"Yes, tomorrow, unless something else happens. I'd like to run away," she told him; "let's both."

"Me?" said Adam. "Where I'm going there's no running to speak of. You mostly crawl about on your stomach here and there among the debris. You know, barbed wire and such stuff. It's going to be the kind of thing that happens once in a lifetime." He reflected a moment, and went on, "I don't know a darned thing about it, really, but they make it sound awfully messy. I've heard so much about it I feel as if I had been there and back. It's going to be an anticlimax," he said, "like seeing the pictures of a place so often you can't see it at all when you actually get there. Seems to me I've been in the army all my life."

Six months, he meant. Eternity. He looked so clear and fresh, and he had never had a pain in his life. She had seen them when they had been there and back and they never looked like this again. "Already the returned hero," she said, "and don't I wish you were."

"When I learned the use of the bayonet in my first training camp," said Adam, "I gouged the vitals out of more sandbags and sacks of hay than I could keep track of. They kept bawling at us, 'Get him, get that Boche, stick him before he sticks you'—and we'd go for those sandbags like wildfire, and honestly, sometimes I felt a perfect fool for getting so worked up when I saw the sand trickling out. I used to wake up in the night sometimes feeling silly about it."

"I can imagine," said Miranda. "It's perfect nonsense." They lingered, unwilling to say good-by. After a little pause, Adam, as if keeping up the conversation, asked, "Do you know what the average life expectation of a sapping party is after it hits the job?"

"Something speedy, I suppose."

"Just nine minutes," said Adam; "I read that in your own newspaper not a week ago."

"Make it ten and I'll come along," said Miranda.

"Not another second," said Adam, "exactly nine minutes, take it or leave it."

"Stop bragging," said Miranda. "Who figured that out?"

"A noncombatant," said Adam, "a fellow with rickets."

This seemed very comic, they laughed and leaned towards each other and Miranda heard herself being a little shrill. She wiped the tears from her eyes. "My, it's a funny war," she said; "isn't it? I laugh every time I think about it."

Adam took her hand in both of his and pulled a little at the tips of her gloves and sniffed them. "What nice perfume you have," he said, "and such a lot of it, too. I like a lot of perfume on gloves and hair," he said, sniffing again.

"I've got probably too much," she said. "I can't smell or see or hear today. I must have a fearful cold."

"Don't catch cold," said Adam; "my leave is nearly up and it will be the last, the very last." She moved her fingers in her gloves as he pulled at the fingers and turned her hands as if they were something new and curious and of great value, and she turned shy and quiet. She liked him, she liked him, and there was more than this but it was no good even imagining, because he was not for her nor for any woman, being beyond experience already, committed without any knowledge or act of his own to death. She took back her hands. "Good-by," she said finally, "until tonight."

She ran upstairs and looked back from the top. He was still watching her, and raised his hand without smiling. Miranda hardly ever saw anyone look back after he had said good-by. She could not help turning sometimes for one glimpse more of the person she had been talking with, as if that would save too rude and too sudden a snapping of even the lightest bond. But people hurried away, their faces already changed, fixed, in their straining towards their next stopping place, already absorbed in planning their next act or encounter. Adam was waiting as if he expected her to turn, and under his brows fixed in a strained frown, his eyes were very black.

At her desk she sat without taking off jacket or cap, slitting envelopes and pretending to read the letters. Only Chuck Rouncivale, the sports reporter, and Ye Towne Gossyp were sitting on her desk today, and them she liked having there. She sat on theirs when she pleased. Towney and Chuck were talking and they went on with it.

"They say," said Towney, "that it is really caused by germs brought by a German ship to Boston, a camouflaged ship, naturally, it didn't come in under its own colors. Isn't that ridiculous?"

"Maybe it was a submarine," said Chuck, "sneaking in from the bottom of the sea in the dead of night. Now that sounds better."

"Yes, it does," said Towney; "they always slip up somewhere in these details . . . and they think the germs were sprayed over the city—it started in Boston, you know—and somebody reported seeing a strange, thick, greasy-looking cloud float up out of Boston Harbor and spread slowly all over that end of town. I think it was an old woman who saw it."

"Should have been," said Chuck.

"I read it in a New York newspaper," said Towney; "so it's bound to be true."

Chuck and Miranda laughed so loudly at this that Bill stood up

and glared at them. "Towney still reads the newspapers," explained
Chuck.

"Well, what's funny about that?" asked Bill, sitting down again
and frowning into the clutter before him.

"It was a noncombatant saw that cloud," said Miranda.

"Naturally," said Towney.

"Member of the Lusk Committee, maybe," said Miranda.

"The Angel of Mons," said Chuck, "or a dollar-a-year man."

Miranda wished to stop hearing, and talking, she wished to think
for just five minutes of her own about Adam, really to think about
him, but there was no time. She had seen him first ten days ago, and
since then they had been crossing streets together, darting between
trucks and limousines and pushcarts and farm wagons; he had waited
for her in doorways and in little restaurants that smelled of stale
frying fat; they had eaten and danced to the urgent whine and bray
of jazz orchestras, they had sat in dull theaters because Miranda was
there to write a piece about the play. Once they had gone to the
mountains and, leaving the car, had climbed a stony trail, and had
come out on a ledge upon a flat stone, where they sat and watched
the lights change on a valley landscape that was, no doubt, Miranda
said, quite apocryphal—"We need not believe it, but it is fine poetry,"
she told him; they had leaned their shoulders together there, and
had sat quite still, watching. On two Sundays they had gone to the
geological museum, and had pored in shared fascination over bits of
meteors, rock formations, fossilized tusks and trees, Indian arrows,
grottoes from the silver and gold lodes. "Think of those old miners
washing out their fortunes in little pans beside the streams," said
Adam, "and inside the earth there was this—" and he had told her
he liked better those things that took long to make; he loved air-
planes too, all sorts of machinery, things carved out of wood or stone.
He knew nothing much about them, but he recognized them when he
saw them. He had confessed that he simply could not get through a
book, any kind of book except textbooks on engineering; reading
bored him to crumbs; he regretted now he hadn't brought his roadster, but he hadn't thought he would need a car; he loved driving, he
wouldn't expect her to believe how many hundreds of miles he could
get over in a day . . . he had showed her snapshots of himself at the
wheel of his roadster; of himself sailing a boat, looking very free and
windblown, all angles, hauling on the ropes; he would have joined the
air force, but his mother had hysterics every time he mentioned it.

She didn't seem to realize that dog fighting in the air was a good deal safer than sapping parties on the ground at night. But he hadn't argued, because of course she did not realize about sapping parties. And here he was, stuck, on a plateau a mile high with no water for a boat and his car at home, otherwise they could really have had a good time. Miranda knew he was trying to tell her what kind of person he was when he had his machinery with him. She felt she knew pretty well what kind of person he was, and would have liked to tell him that if he thought he had left himself at home in a boat or an automobile, he was much mistaken. The telephones were ringing, Bill was shouting at somebody who kept saying, "Well, but listen, well, but listen—" but nobody was going to listen, of course, nobody. Old man Gibbons bellowed in despair, "Jarge, Jarge—"

"Just the same," Towney was saying in her most complacent patriotic voice, "Hut Service is a fine idea, and we should all volunteer even if they don't want us." Towney does well at this, thought Miranda, look at her; remembering the rose-colored sweater and the tight rebellious face in the cloakroom. Towney was now all open-faced glory and goodness, willing to sacrifice herself for her country. "After all," said Towney, "I *can* sing and dance well enough for the Little Theater, and I could write their letters for them, and at a pinch I might drive an ambulance. I have driven a Ford for years."

Miranda joined in: "Well, I can sing and dance too, but who's going to do the bed-making and the scrubbing up? Those huts are hard to keep, and it would be a dirty job and we'd be perfectly miserable; and as I've got a hard dirty job and am perfectly miserable, I'm going to stay at home."

"I think the women should keep out of it," said Chuck Rouncivale. "They just add skirts to the horrors of war." Chuck had bad lungs and fretted a good deal about missing the show. "I could have been there and back with a leg off by now; it would have served the old man right. Then he'd either have to buy his own hooch or sober up."

Miranda had seen Chuck on pay day giving the old man money for hooch. He was a good-humored ingratiating old scoundrel, too, that was the worst of him. He slapped his son on the back and beamed upon him with the bleared eye of paternal affection while he took his last nickel.

"It was Florence Nightingale ruined wars," Chuck went on. "What's the idea of petting soldiers and binding up their wounds and soothing their fevered brows? That's not war. Let 'em perish where they fall. That's what they're there for."

"You can talk," said Towney, with a slantwise glint at him.

"What's the idea?" asked Chuck, flushing and hunching his shoulders. "You know I've got this lung, or maybe half of it anyway by now."

"You're much too sensitive," said Towney. "I didn't mean a thing."

Bill had been raging about, chewing his half-smoked cigar, his hair standing up in a brush, his eyes soft and lambent but wild, like a stag's. He would never, thought Miranda, be more than fourteen years old if he lived for a century, which he would not, at the rate he was going. He behaved exactly like city editors in the moving pictures, even to the chewed cigar. Had he formed his style on the films, or had scenario writers seized once for all on the type Bill in its inarguable purity? Bill was shouting to Chuck: "*And* if he comes back here take him up the alley and saw his head off *by hand!*"

Chuck said, "He'll be back, don't worry." Bill said mildly, already off on another track, "Well, saw him off." Towney went to her own desk, but Chuck sat waiting amiably to be taken to the new vaudeville show. Miranda, with two tickets, always invited one of the reporters to go with her on Monday. Chuck was lavishly hardboiled and professional in his sports writing, but he had told Miranda that he didn't give a damn about sports, really; the job kept him out in the open, and paid him enough to buy the old man's hooch. He preferred shows and didn't see why women always had the job.

"Who does Bill want sawed today?" asked Miranda.

"That hoofer you panned in this morning's," said Chuck. "He was up here bright and early asking for the guy that writes up the show business. He said he was going to take the goof who wrote that piece up the alley and bop him in the nose. He said . . ."

"I hope he's gone," said Miranda; "I do hope he had to catch a train."

Chuck stood up and arranged his maroon-colored turtle-necked sweater, glanced down at the peasoup tweed plus fours and the hobnailed tan boots which he hoped would help to disguise the fact that he had a bad lung and didn't care for sports, and said, "He's long gone by now, don't worry. Let's get going; you're late as usual."

Miranda, facing about, almost stepped on the toes of a little drab man in a derby hat. He might have been a pretty fellow once, but now his mouth drooped where he had lost his side teeth, and his sad red-rimmed eyes had given up coquetry. A thin brown wave of hair was combed out with brilliantine and curled against the rim of the derby. He didn't move his feet, but stood planted with a kind of inert resistance, and asked Miranda: "Are you the so-called dramatic critic on this hick newspaper?"

"I'm afraid I am," said Miranda.

"Well," said the little man, "I'm just asking for one minute of your valuable time." His underlip shot out, he began with shaking hands to fish about in his waistcoat pocket. "I just hate to let you get away with it, that's all." He riffled through a collection of shabby newspaper clippings. "Just give these the once-over, will you? And then let me ask you if you think I'm gonna stand for being knocked by a tanktown critic," he said, in a toneless voice; "look here, here's Buffalo, Chicago, Saint Looey, Philadelphia, Frisco, besides New York. Here's the best publications in the business, *Variety*, the *Billboard*, they all broke down and admitted that Danny Dickerson knows his stuff. So you don't think so, hey? That's all I wanta ask you."

"No, I don't," said Miranda, as bluntly as she could, "and I can't stop to talk about it."

The little man leaned nearer, his voice shook as if he had been nervous for a long time. "Look here, what was there you didn't like about me? Tell me that."

Miranda said, "You shouldn't pay any attention at all. What does it matter what I think?"

"I don't care what you think, it ain't that," said the little man, "but these things get round and booking agencies back East don't know how it is out here. We get panned in the sticks and they think it's the same as getting panned in Chicago, see? They don't know the difference. They don't know that the more high class an act is the more the hick critics pan it. But I've been called the best in the business by the best in the business and I wanta know what you think is wrong with me."

Chuck said, "Come on, Miranda, curtain's going up." Miranda handed the little man his clippings, they were mostly ten years old, and tried to edge past him. He stepped before her again and said without much conviction, "If you was a man I'd knock your block off." Chuck got up at that and lounged over, taking his hands out of his pockets, and said, "Now you've done your song and dance you'd better get out. Get the hell out now before I throw you downstairs."

The little man pulled at the top of his tie, a small blue tie with red polka dots, slightly frayed at the knot. He pulled it straight and repeated as if he had rehearsed it, "Come out in the alley." The tears filled his thickened red lids. Chuck said, "Ah, shut up," and followed Miranda, who was running towards the stairs. He overtook her on the sidewalk. "I left him sniveling and shuffling his publicity trying to find the joker," said Chuck, "the poor old heel."

Miranda said, "There's too much of everything in this world just now. I'd like to sit down here on the curb, Chuck, and die, and never again see—I wish I could lose my memory and forget my own name . . . I wish—"

Chuck said, "Toughen up, Miranda. This is no time to cave in. Forget that fellow. For every hundred people in show business, there are ninety-nine like him. But you don't manage right, anyway. You bring it on yourself. All you have to do is play up the headliners, and you needn't even mention the also-rans. Try to keep in mind that Rypinsky has got show business cornered in this town; please Rypinsky and you'll please the advertising department, please them and you'll get a raise. Hand-in-glove, my poor dumb child, will you never learn?"

"I seem to keep learning all the wrong things," said Miranda, hopelessly.

"You do for a fact," Chuck told her cheerfully. "You are as good at it as I ever saw. Now do you feel better?"

"This is a rotten show you've invited me to," said Chuck. "Now what are you going to do about it? If I were writing it up, I'd—"

"Do write it up," said Miranda. "You write it up this time. I'm getting ready to leave, anyway, but don't tell anybody yet."

"You mean it? All my life," said Chuck, "I've yearned to be a so-called dramatic critic on a hick newspaper, and this is positively my first chance."

"Better take it," Miranda told him. "It may be your last." She thought, This is the beginning of the end of something. Something terrible is going to happen to me. I shan't need bread and butter where I'm going. I'll will it to Chuck, he has a venerable father to buy hooch for. I hope they let him have it. Oh, Adam, I hope I see you once more before I go under with whatever is the matter with me. "I wish the war were over," she said to Chuck, as if they had been talking about that. "I wish it were over and I wish it had never begun."

Chuck had got out his pad and pencil and was already writing his review. What she had said seemed safe enough but how would he take it? "I don't care how it started or when it ends," said Chuck, scribbling away, "I'm not going to be there."

All the rejected men talked like that, thought Miranda. War was the one thing they wanted, now they couldn't have it. Maybe they had wanted badly to go, some of them. All of them had a sidelong eye for the women they talked with about it, a guarded resentment which said, "Don't pin a white feather on me, you bloodthirsty female. I've offered my meat to the crows and they won't have it." The worst thing about war for the stay-at-homes is there isn't anyone to talk to any more. The Lusk Committee will get you if you don't watch out. Bread will win the war. Work will win, sugar will win, peach pits will win the war. Nonsense. *Not* nonsense, I tell you, there's some kind of valuable high explosive to be got out of peach pits. So all the happy housewives hurry during the canning season to lay their baskets of peach pits on the altar of their country. It keeps them busy and makes them feel useful, and all these women running wild with the men away are dangerous, if they aren't given something to keep their little minds out of mischief. So rows of young girls, the intact cradles of the future, with their pure serious faces framed becomingly in Red Cross wimples, roll cock-eyed bandages that will never reach a base hospital, and knit sweaters that will never warm a manly chest, their minds dwelling lovingly on all the blood and mud and the next dance at the Acanthus Club for the officers of the flying corps. Keeping still and quiet will win the war.

"I'm simply not going to be there," said Chuck, absorbed in his review. No, Adam will be there, thought Miranda. She slipped down in the chair and leaned her head against the dusty plush, closed her eyes and faced for one instant that was a lifetime the certain, the overwhelming and awful knowledge that there was nothing at all ahead for Adam and for her. Nothing. She opened her eyes and held her hands together palms up, gazing at them and trying to understand oblivion.

"Now look at this," said Chuck, for the lights had come on and the audience was rustling and talking again. "I've got it all done, even before the headliner comes on. It's old Stella Mayhew, and she's always good, she's been good for forty years, and she's going to sing 'O the blues ain't nothin' but the easy-going heart disease.' That's all you need to know about her. Now just glance over this. Would you be willing to sign it?"

Miranda took the pages and stared at them conscientiously, turning them over, she hoped, at the right moment, and gave them back. "Yes, Chuck, yes, I'd sign that. But I won't. We must tell Bill you wrote it, because it's your start, maybe."

"You don't half appreciate it," said Chuck. "You read it too fast. Here, listen to this—" and he began to mutter excitedly. While he was reading she watched his face. It was a pleasant face with some kind of spark of life in it, and a good severity in the modeling of the brow above the nose. For the first time since she had known him she wondered what Chuck was thinking about. He looked preoccupied and unhappy, he wasn't so frivolous as he sounded. The people were crowding into the aisle, bringing out their cigarette cases ready to strike a match the instant they reached the lobby; women with waved hair clutched at their wraps, men stretched their chins to ease them of their stiff collars, and Chuck said, "We might as well go now." Miranda, buttoning her jacket, stepped into the moving crowd, thinking, What did I ever know about them? There must be a great many of them here who think as I do, and we dare not say a word to each other of our desperation, we are speechless animals letting ourselves be destroyed, and why? Does anybody here believe the things we say to each other?

Stretched in unease on the ridge of the wicker couch in the cloakroom, Miranda waited for time to pass and leave Adam with her. Time seemed to proceed with more than usual eccentricity, leaving twilight gaps in her mind for thirty minutes which seemed like a second, and then hard flashes of light that shone clearly on her watch proving that three minutes is an intolerable stretch of waiting, as if she were hanging by her thumbs. At last it was reasonable to imagine Adam stepping out of the house in the early darkness into the blue mist that might soon be rain, he would be on the way, and there was nothing to think about him, after all. There was only the wish to see him and the fear, the present threat, of not seeing him again; for every step they took towards each other seemed perilous, drawing them apart instead of together, as a swimmer in spite of his most determined strokes is yet drawn slowly backward by the tide. "I don't want to love," she would think in spite of herself, "not Adam, there is no time and we are not ready for it and yet this is all we have—"

And there he was on the sidewalk, with his foot on the first step, and Miranda almost ran down to meet him. Adam, holding her hands, asked, "Do you feel well now? Are you hungry? Are you tired? Will you feel like dancing after the show?"

"Yes to everything," said Miranda, "yes, yes. . . ." Her head was like a feather, and she steadied herself on his arm. The mist was still mist that might be rain later, and though the air was sharp and clean in her mouth, it did not, she decided, make breathing any easier. "I hope the show is good, or at least funny," she told him, "but I promise nothing."

It was a long, dreary play, but Adam and Miranda sat very quietly together waiting patiently for it to be over. Adam carefully and seriously pulled off her glove and held her hand as if he were accustomed to holding her hand in theaters. Once they turned and their eyes met, but only once, and the two pairs of eyes were equally steady and noncommittal. A deep tremor set up in Miranda, and she set about resisting herself methodically as if she were closing windows and doors and fastening down curtains against a rising storm. Adam sat watching the monotonous play with a strange shining excitement, his face quite fixed and still.

When the curtain rose for the third act, the third act did not take place at once. There was instead disclosed a backdrop almost covered with an American flag improperly and disrespectfully exposed, nailed at each upper corner, gathered in the middle and nailed again, sagging dustily. Before it posed a local dollar-a-year man, now doing his bit as a Liberty Bond salesman. He was an ordinary man past middle life, with a neat little melon buttoned into his trousers and waistcoat, an opinionated tight mouth, a face and figure in which nothing could be read save the inept sensual record of fifty years. But for once in his life he was an important fellow in an impressive situation, and he reveled, rolling his words in an actorish tone.

"Looks like a penguin," said Adam. They moved, smiled at each other, Miranda reclaimed her hand, Adam folded his together and they prepared to wear their way again through the same old moldy speech with the same old dusty backdrop. Miranda tried not to listen, but she heard. These vile Huns—glorious Belleau Wood—our keyword is Sacrifice—Martyred Belgium—give till it hurts—our noble boys Over There—Big Berthas—the death of civilization—the Boche—

"My head aches," whispered Miranda. "Oh, why won't he hush?"

"He won't," whispered Adam. "I'll get you some aspirin."

"In Flanders Field the poppies grow, Between the crosses row on row"—"He's getting into the home stretch," whispered Adam—atrocities, innocent babes hoisted on Boche bayonets—your child and my child—if our children are spared these things, then let us say with all reverence that these dead have not died in vain—the war, the *war*, the WAR to end WAR, war for Democracy, for humanity, a safe world forever and ever—and to prove our faith in Democracy to each other, and to the world, let everybody get together and buy Liberty Bonds and do without sugar and wool socks—was that it? Miranda asked herself, Say that over, I didn't catch the last line. Did you mention Adam? If you didn't I'm not interested. What about Adam, you little pig? And what are we going to sing this time, "Tipperary" or "There's a Long, Long Trail"? Oh, please do let the show go on and get over with. I must write a piece about it before I can go dancing with Adam and we have no time. Coal, oil, iron, gold, international finance, why don't you tell us about them, you little liar?

The audience rose and sang, "There's a Long, Long Trail A-winding," their opened mouths black and faces pallid in the reflected footlights; some of the faces grimaced and wept and had shining streaks like snail's tracks on them. Adam and Miranda joined in at the tops of their voices, grinning shamefacedly at each other once or twice.

In the street, they lit their cigarettes and walked slowly as always. "Just another nasty old man who would like to see the young ones killed," said Miranda in a low voice; "the tomcats try to eat the little tomkittens, you know. They don't fool you really, do they, Adam?"

The young people were talking like that about the business by then. They felt they were seeing pretty clearly through that game. She went on, "I hate these potbellied baldheads, too fat, too old, too cowardly, to go to war themselves, they know they're safe; it's you they are sending instead—"

Adam turned eyes of genuine surprise upon her. "Oh, *that* one," he said. "Now what could the poor sap do if they did take him? It's not his fault," he explained, "he can't do anything but talk." His pride in his youth, his forbearance and tolerance and contempt for that unlucky being breathed out of his very pores as he strolled, straight and relaxed in his strength. "What *could* you expect of him, Miranda?"

She spoke his name often, and he spoke hers rarely. The little shock of pleasure the sound of her name in his mouth gave her stopped her answer. For a moment she hesitated, and began at another point of attack. "Adam," she said, "the worst of war is the fear and suspicion and the awful expression in all the eyes you meet . . . as if they had pulled down the shutters over their minds and their hearts and were peering out at you, ready to leap if you make one gesture or say one word they do not understand instantly. It frightens me; I live in fear too, and no one should have to live in fear. It's the skulking about, and the lying. It's what war does to the mind and the heart, Adam, and you can't separate these two—what it does to them is worse than what it can do to the body."

Adam said soberly, after a moment, "Oh, yes, but suppose one comes back whole? The mind and the heart sometimes get another chance, but if anything happens to the poor old human frame, why, it's just out of luck, that's all."

"Oh, yes," mimicked Miranda. "It's just out of luck, that's all."

"If I didn't go," said Adam, in a matter-of-fact voice, "I couldn't look myself in the face."

So that's all settled. With her fingers flattened on his arm, Miranda was silent, thinking about Adam. No, there was no resentment or revolt in him. Pure, she thought, all the way through, flawless, complete, as the sacrificial lamb must be. The sacrificial lamb strode along casually, accommodating his long pace to hers, keeping her on the inside of the walk in the good American style, helping her across street corners as if she were a cripple—"I hope we don't come to a mud puddle, he'll carry me over it"—giving off whiffs of tobacco smoke, a manly smell of scentless soap, freshly cleaned leather and freshly washed skin, breathing through his nose and carrying his chest easily. He threw back his head and smiled into the sky which still misted, promising rain. "Oh, boy," he said, "what a night. Can't you hurry that review of yours so we can get started?"

He waited for her before a cup of coffee in the restaurant next to the pressroom, nicknamed The Greasy Spoon. When she came down at last, freshly washed and combed and powdered, she saw Adam first, sitting near the dingy big window, face turned to the street, but looking down. It was an extraordinary face, smooth and fine and golden in the shabby light, but now set in a blind melancholy, a look of pained suspense and disillusion. For just one split second she got a glimpse of Adam when he would have been older, the face of the man he would not live to be. He saw her then, rose, and the bright glow was there.

Adam pulled their chairs together at their table; they drank hot tea and listened to the orchestra jazzing "Pack Up Your Troubles."

"In an old kit bag, and smoil, smoil, smoil," shouted half a dozen boys under the draft age, gathered around a table near the orchestra. They yelled incoherently, laughed in great hysterical bursts of something that appeared to be merriment, and passed around under the tablecloth flat bottles containing a clear liquid—for in this western city founded and built by roaring drunken miners, no one was allowed to take his alcohol openly—splashed it into their tumblers of ginger ale, and went on singing, "It's a Long Way to Tipperary." When the tune changed to "Madelon," Adam said, "Let's dance." It was a tawdry little place, crowded and hot and full of smoke, but there was nothing better. The music was gay; and life is completely crazy anyway, thought Miranda, so what does it matter? This is what we have, Adam and I, this is all we're going to get, this is the way it is with us. She wanted to say, "Adam, come out of your dream and listen to me. I have pains in my chest and my head and my heart and they're real. I am in pain all over, and you are in such danger as I can't bear to think about, and why can we not save each other?" When her hand tightened on his shoulder his arm tightened about her waist instantly, and stayed there, holding firmly. They said nothing but smiled continually at each other, odd changing smiles as though they had found a new language. Miranda, her face near Adam's shoulder, noticed a dark young pair sitting at a corner table, each with an arm around the waist of the other, their heads together, their eyes staring at the same thing, whatever it was, that hovered in space before them. Her right hand lay on the table, his hand over it, and her face was a blur with weeping. Now and then he raised her hand and kissed it, and set it down and held it, and her eyes would fill again. They were not shameless, they had merely forgotten where they were, or they had no other place to go, perhaps. They said not a word, and the small pantomime repeated itself, like a melancholy short film running monotonously over and over again. Miranda envied them. She envied that girl. At least she can weep if that helps, and he does not even have to ask, What is the matter? Tell me. They had cups of coffee before them, and after a long while —Miranda and Adam had danced and sat down again twice—when the coffee was quite cold, they drank it suddenly, then embraced as before, without a word and scarcely a glance at each other. Something was done and settled between them, at least; it was enviable, enviable, that they could sit quietly together and have the same expression on their faces while they looked into the hell they shared, no matter what kind of hell, it was theirs, they were together.

At the table nearest Adam and Miranda a young woman was leaning on her elbow, telling her young man a story. "And I don't like him because he's too fresh. He kept on asking me to take a drink and I kept telling him, I don't drink and he said, Now look here, I want a drink the worst way and I think it's mean of you not to drink with me, I can't sit up here and drink by myself, he said. I told him, You're not by yourself in the first place; I like that, I said, and if you want a drink go ahead and have it, I told him, why drag *me* in? So he called the waiter and ordered ginger ale and two glasses and I drank straight ginger ale like I always do but he poured a shot of hooch in his. He was awfully proud of that hooch, said he made it himself out of potatoes. Nice homemade likker, warm from the pipe, he told me, three drops of this and your ginger ale will taste like Mumm's Extry. But I said, No, and I mean no, can't you get that through your bean? He took another drink and said, Ah, come on, honey, don't be so stubborn, this'll make your shimmy shake. So I just got tired of the argument, and I said, I don't need to drink, to shake my shimmy, I can strut my stuff on tea, I said. Well, why don't you then, he wanted to know, and I just told him—"

She knew she had been asleep for a long time when all at once without even a warning footstep or creak of the door hinge, Adam was in the room turning on the light, and she knew it was he, though at first she was blinded and turned her head away. He came over at once and sat on the side of the bed and began to talk as if he were going on with something they had been talking about before. He crumpled a square of paper and tossed it in the fireplace.

"You didn't get my note," he said. "I left it under the door. I was called back suddenly to camp for a lot of inoculations. They kept me longer than I expected, I was late. I called the office and they told me you were not coming in today. I called Miss Hobbe here and she said you were in bed and couldn't come to the telephone. Did she give you my message?"

"No," said Miranda drowsily, "but I think I have been asleep all day. Oh, I do remember. There was a doctor here. Bill sent him. I was at the telephone once, for Bill told me he would send an ambulance and have me taken to the hospital. The doctor tapped my chest and left a prescription and said he would be back, but he hasn't come."

"Where is it, the prescription?" asked Adam.

"I don't know. He left it, though, I saw him."

Adam moved about searching the tables and the mantelpiece. "Here it is," he said. "I'll be back in a few minutes. I must look for an all-night drug store. It's after one o'clock. Good-by."

Good-by, good-by. Miranda watched the door where he had disappeared for quite a while, then closed her eyes, and thought, When I am not here I cannot remember anything about this room where I have lived for nearly a year, except that the curtains are too thin and there was never any way of shutting out the morning light. Miss Hobbe had promised heavier curtains, but they had never appeared. When Miranda in her dressing gown had been at the telephone that morning, Miss Hobbe had passed through, carrying a tray. She was a little red-haired nervously friendly creature, and her manner said all too plainly that the place was not paying and she was on the ragged edge.

"My dear *child*," she said sharply, with a glance at Miranda's attire, "what is the matter?"

Miranda, with the receiver to her ear, said, "Influenza, I think."

"*Horrors,*" said Miss Hobbe, in a whisper, and the tray wavered in her hands. "Go back to bed at once . . . go at *once!*"

"I must talk to Bill first," Miranda had told her, and Miss Hobbe had hurried on and had not returned. Bill had shouted directions at her, promising everything, doctor, nurse, ambulance, hospital, her check every week as usual, everything, but she was to get back to bed and stay there. She dropped into bed, thinking that Bill was the only person she had ever seen who actually tore his own hair when he was excited enough . . . I suppose I should ask to be sent home, she thought, it's a respectable old custom to inflict your death on the family if you can manage it. No, I'll stay here, this is my business, but not in this room, I hope . . . I wish I were in the cold mountains in the snow, that's what I should like best; and all about her rose the measured ranges of the Rockies wearing their perpetual snow, their majestic blue laurels of cloud, chilling her to the bone with their sharp breath. Oh, no, I must have warmth—and her memory turned and roved after another place she had known first and loved best, that now she could see only in drifting fragments of palm and cedar, dark shadows and a sky that warmed without dazzling, as this strange sky had dazzled without warming her; there was the long slow wavering of gray moss in the drowsy oak shade, the spacious hovering of buzzards overhead, the smell of crushed water herbs along a bank, and without warning a broad tranquil river into which flowed all the rivers she had known. The walls shelved away in one deliberate silent movement on either side, and a tall sailing ship was moored near by, with a gangplank weathered to blackness touching the foot of her bed. Back of the ship was jungle, and even as it appeared before her, she knew it was all she had ever read or had been told or felt or thought about jungles; a writhing terribly alive and secret place of death, creeping with tangles of spotted serpents, rainbow-colored birds with malign eyes, leopards with humanly wise faces and extravagantly crested lions; screaming long-armed monkeys tumbling among broad fleshy leaves that glowed with sulphur-colored light and exuded the ichor of death, and rotting trunks of unfamiliar trees sprawled in crawling slime. Without surprise, watching from her pillow, she saw herself run swiftly down this gangplank to the slanting deck, and standing there, she leaned on the rail and waved gaily to herself in bed, and the slender ship spread its wings and sailed away into the jungle. The air trembled with the shattering scream and the hoarse bellow of voices all crying together, rolling and colliding above her like ragged stormclouds, and the words became two words only rising and falling and clamoring about her head. Danger, danger, danger, the voices said, and War, war, war. There was her door half open, Adam standing with his hand on the knob, and Miss Hobbe with her face all out of shape with terror was crying shrilly, "I tell you, they must come for her *now*, or I'll put her on the sidewalk . . . I tell you, this is a plague, a plague, my God, and I've got a houseful of people to think about!"

Adam said, "I know that. They'll come for her tomorrow morning."

"Tomorrow morning, my God, they'd better come now!"

"They can't get an ambulance," said Adam, "and there aren't any beds. And we can't find a doctor or a nurse. They're all busy. That's all there is to it. You stay out of the room, and I'll look after her."

"Yes, you'll look after her, I can see that," said Miss Hobbe, in a particularly unpleasant tone.

"Yes, that's what I said," answered Adam, drily, "and you keep out."

He closed the door carefully. He was carrying an assortment of misshapen packages, and his face was astonishingly impassive.

"Did you hear that?" he asked, leaning over and speaking very quietly.

"Most of it," said Miranda, "it's a nice prospect, isn't it?"

"I've got your medicine," said Adam, "and you're to begin with it this minute. She can't put you out."

"So it's really as bad as that," said Miranda.

"It's as bad as anything can be," said Adam, "all the theaters and nearly all the shops and restaurants are closed, and the streets have been full of funerals all day and ambulances all night—"

"But not one for me," said Miranda, feeling hilarious and light-headed. She sat up and beat her pillow into shape and reached for her robe. "I'm glad you're here, I've been having a nightmare. Give me a cigarette, will you, and light one for yourself and open all the windows and sit near one of them. You're running a risk," she told him, "don't you know that? Why do you do it?"

"Never mind," said Adam, "take your medicine," and offered her two large cherry-colored pills. She swallowed them promptly and instantly vomited them up. "*Do* excuse me," she said, beginning to laugh. "I'm so sorry." Adam without a word and with a very concerned expression washed her face with a wet towel, gave her some cracked ice from one of the packages, and firmly offered her two more pills. "That's what they always did at home," she explained to him, "and it worked." Crushed with humiliation, she put her hands over her face and laughed again, painfully.

"There are two more kinds yet," said Adam, pulling her hands from her face and lifting her chin. "You've hardly begun. And I've got other things, like orange juice and ice cream—they told me to feed you ice cream—and coffee in a thermos bottle, and a thermometer. You have to work through the whole lot so you'd better take it easy."

"This time last night we were dancing," said Miranda, and drank something from a spoon. Her eyes followed him about the room, as he did things for her with an absent-minded face, like a man alone; now and again he would come back, and slipping his hand under her head, would hold a cup or a tumbler to her mouth, and she drank, and followed him with her eyes again, without a clear notion of what was happening.

"Adam," she said, "I've just thought of something. Maybe they forgot St. Luke's Hospital. Call the sisters there and ask them not to be so selfish with their silly old rooms. Tell them I only want a very small dark ugly one for three days, or less. Do try them, Adam."

He believed, apparently, that she was still more or less in her right mind, for she heard him at the telephone explaining in his deliberate voice. He was back again almost at once, saying, "This seems to be my day for getting mixed up with peevish old maids. The sister said that even if they had a room you couldn't have it without doctor's orders. But they didn't have one, anyway. She was pretty sour about it."

"Well," said Miranda in a thick voice, "I think that's abominably rude and mean, don't you?" She sat up with a wide gesture of both arms, and began to retch again, violently.

"Hold it, as you were," called Adam, fetching the basin. He held her head, washed her face and hands with ice water, put her head straight on the pillow, and went over and looked out of the window. "Well," he said at last, sitting beside her again, "they haven't got a room. They haven't got a bed. They haven't even got a baby crib, the way she talked. So I think that's straight enough, and we may as well dig in."

"Isn't the ambulance coming?"

"Tomorrow, maybe."

He took off his tunic and hung it on the back of a chair. Kneeling before the fireplace, he began carefully to set kindling sticks in the shape of an Indian tepee, with a little paper in the center for them to lean upon. He lighted this and placed other sticks upon them, and larger bits of woods. When they were going nicely he added still heavier wood, and coal a few lumps at a time, until there was a good blaze, and a fire that would not need rekindling. He rose and dusted his hands together, the fire illuminated him from the back and his hair shone.

"Adam," said Miranda, "I think you're very beautiful." He laughed out at this, and shook his head at her. "What a hell of a word," he said, "for me." "It was the first that occurred to me," she said, drawing up on her elbow to catch the warmth of the blaze. "That's a good job, that fire."

He sat on the bed again, dragging up a chair and putting his feet on the rungs. They smiled at each other for the first time since he had come in that night. "How do you feel now?" he asked.

"Better, much better," she told him. "Let's talk. Let's tell each other what we meant to do."

"You tell me first," said Adam. "I want to know about you."

"You'd get the notion I had a very sad life," she said, "and perhaps it was, but I'd be glad enough to have it now. If I could have it back, it would be easy to be happy about almost anything at all. That's not true, but that's the way I feel now." After a pause, she said, "There's nothing to tell, after all, if it ends now, for all this time I was getting ready for something that was going to happen later, when the time came. So now it's nothing much."

"But it must have been worth having until now, wasn't it?" he asked seriously as if it were something important to know.

"Not if this is all," she repeated obstinately.

"Weren't you ever—happy?" asked Adam, and he was plainly afraid of the word; he was shy of it as he was of the word *love*, he seemed never to have spoken it before, and was uncertain of its sound or meaning.

"I don't know," she said; "I just lived and never thought about it. I remember things I liked, though, and things I hoped for."

"I was going to be an electrical engineer," said Adam. He stopped short. "And I shall finish up when I get back," he added, after a moment.

"Don't you love being alive?" asked Miranda. "Don't you love weather and the colors at different times of the day, and all the sounds and noises like children screaming in the next lot, and automobile horns and little bands playing in the street and the smell of food cooking?"

"I love to swim, too," said Adam.

"So do I," said Miranda; "we never did swim together."

"Do you remember any prayers?" she asked him suddenly. "Did you ever learn anything at Sunday School?"

"Not much," confessed Adam without contrition. "Well, the Lord's Prayer."

"Yes, and there's Hail Mary," she said, "and the really useful one beginning, I confess to Almighty God and to blessed Mary ever virgin and to the holy Apostles Peter and Paul—"

"Catholic," he commented.

"Prayers just the same, you big Methodist. I'll bet you *are* a Methodist."

"No, Presbyterian."

"Well, what others do you remember?"

"Now I lay me down to sleep—" said Adam.

"Yes, that one, and Blessed Jesus meek and mild—you see that my religious education wasn't neglected either. I even know a prayer beginning O Apollo. Want to hear it?"

"No," said Adam, "you're making fun."

"I'm not," said Miranda, "I'm trying to keep from going to sleep. I'm afraid to go to sleep, I may not wake up. Don't let me go to sleep, Adam. Do you know Matthew, Mark, Luke and John? Bless the bed I lie upon?"

"If I should die before I wake, I pray the Lord my soul to take. Is that it?" asked Adam. "It doesn't sound right, somehow."

"Light me a cigarette, please, and move over and sit near the window. We keep forgetting about fresh air. You must have it." He lighted the cigarette and held it to her lips. She took it between her fingers and dropped it under the edge of her pillow. He found it and crushed it out in the saucer under the water tumbler. Her head swam in darkness for an instant, cleared, and she sat up in panic, throwing off the covers and breaking into a sweat. Adam leaped up with an alarmed face, and almost at once was holding a cup of hot coffee to her mouth.

"You must have some too," she told him, quiet again, and they sat huddled together on the edge of the bed, drinking coffee in silence.

Adam said, "You must lie down again. You're awake now."

"Let's sing," said Miranda. "I know an old spiritual, I can remember some of the words." She spoke in a natural voice. "I'm fine now." She began in a hoarse whisper, " 'Pale horse, pale rider, done taken my lover away . . .' Do you know that song?"

"Yes," said Adam, "I heard Negroes in Texas sing it, in an oil field."

"I heard them sing it in a cotton field," she said; "it's a good song." They sang that line together. "But I can't remember what comes next," said Adam.

" 'Pale horse, pale rider,' " said Miranda, "(We really need a good banjo) 'done taken my lover away—' " Her voice cleared and she said, "But we ought to get on with it. What's the next line?"

"There's a lot more to it than that," said Adam, "about forty verses, the rider done taken away mammy, pappy, brother, sister, the whole family besides the lover—"

"But not the singer, not yet," said Miranda. "Death always leaves one singer to mourn. 'Death,' " she sang, " 'oh, leave one singer to mourn—' "

" 'Pale horse, pale rider,' " chanted Adam, coming in on the beat, " 'done taken my lover away!' (I think we're good, I think we ought to get up an act—)"

"Go in Hut Service," said Miranda, "entertain the poor defenseless heroes Over There."

"We'll play banjos," said Adam; "I always wanted to play the banjo."

Miranda sighed, and lay back on the pillow and thought, I must give up, I can't hold out any longer. There was only that pain, only that room, and only Adam. There were no longer any multiple planes of living, no tough filaments of memory and hope pulling taut backwards and forwards holding her upright between them. There was only this one moment and it was a dream of time, and Adam's face, very near hers, eyes still and intent, was a shadow, and there was to be nothing more. . . .

"Adam," she said out of the heavy soft darkness that drew her down, down, "I love you, and I was hoping you would say that to me, too."

He lay down beside her with his arm under her shoulder, and pressed his smooth face against hers, his mouth moved towards her mouth and stopped. "Can you hear what I am saying? . . . What do you think I have been trying to tell you all this time?"

She turned towards him, the cloud cleared and she saw his face for an instant. He pulled the covers about her and held her, and said, "Go to sleep, darling, darling; if you will go to sleep now for one hour I will wake you up and bring you hot coffee and tomorrow we will find somebody to help. I love you, go to sleep—"

Almost with no warning at all, she floated into the darkness, holding his hand, in sleep that was not sleep but clear evening light in a small green wood, an angry dangerous wood full of inhuman concealed voices singing sharply like the whine of arrows and she saw Adam transfixed by a flight of these singing arrows that struck him in the heart and passed shrilly cutting their path through the leaves. Adam fell straight back before her eyes, and rose again unwounded and alive; another flight of arrows loosed from the invisible bow struck him again and he fell, and yet he was there before her untouched in a perpetual death and resurrection. She threw herself before him, angrily and selfishly she interposed between him and

the track of the arrow, crying, No, no, like a child cheated in a game,
It's my turn now, why must you always be the one to die? and the
arrows struck her cleanly through the heart and through his body and
he lay dead, and she still lived, and the wood whistled and sang and
shouted, every branch and leaf and blade of grass had its own terrible accusing voice. She ran then, and Adam caught her in the
middle of the room, running, and said, "Darling, I must have been
asleep too. What happened, you screamed terribly?"

After he had helped her to settle again, she sat with her knees
drawn up under her chin, resting her head on her folded arms and
began carefully searching for her words because it was important to
explain clearly. "It was a very odd sort of dream, I don't know why
it could have frightened me. There was something about an old-
fashioned valentine. There were two hearts carved on a tree, pierced
by the same arrow—you know, Adam—"

"Yes, I know, honey," he said in the gentlest sort of way, and sat
kissing her on the cheek and forehead with a kind of accustomedness,
as if he had been kissing her for years, "one of those lace paper
things."

"Yes, and yet they were alive, and were us, you understand—this
doesn't seem to be quite the way it was, but it was something like
that. It was in a wood—"

"Yes," said Adam. He got up and put on his tunic and gathered
up the thermos bottle. "I'm going back to that little stand and get us
some ice cream and hot coffee," he told her, "and I'll be back in five
minutes, and you keep quiet. Good-by for five minutes," he said,
holding her chin in the palm of his hand and trying to catch her eye,
"and you be very quiet."

"Good-by," she said. "I'm awake again." But she was not, and
the two alert young internes from the County hospital who had arrived, after frantic urgings from the noisy city editor of the Blue
Mountain *News*, to carry her away in a police ambulance, decided
that they had better go down and get the stretcher. Their voices
roused her, she sat up, got out of bed at once and stood glancing
about brightly. "Why, you're all right," said the darker and stouter
of the two young men, both extremely fit and competent-looking in
their white clothes, each with a flower in his buttonhole. "I'll just
carry you." He unfolded a white blanket and wrapped it around her.
She gathered up the folds and asked, "But where is Adam?" taking

hold of the doctor's arm. He laid a hand on her drenched forehead, shook his head, and gave her a shrewd look. "Adam?"

"Yes," Miranda told him, lowering her voice confidentially, "he was here and now he is gone."

"Oh, he'll be back," the interne told her easily, "he's just gone round the block to get cigarettes. Don't worry about Adam. He's the least of your troubles."

"Will he know where to find me?" she asked, still holding back.

"We'll leave him a note," said the interne. "Come now, it's time we got out of here."

He lifted and swung her up to his shoulder. "I feel very badly," she told him; "I don't know why."

"I'll bet you do," said he, stepping out carefully, the other doctor going before them, and feeling for the first step of the stairs. "Put your arms around my neck," he instructed her. "It won't do you any harm and it's a great help to me."

"What's your name?" Miranda asked as the other doctor opened the front door and they stepped out into the frosty sweet air.

"Hildesheim," he said, in the tone of one humoring a child.

"Well, Dr. Hildesheim, aren't we in a pretty mess?"

"We certainly are," said Dr. Hildesheim.

The second young interne, still quite fresh and dapper in his white coat, though his carnation was withering at the edges, was leaning over listening to her breathing through a stethoscope, whistling thinly, "There's a Long, Long Trail—" From time to time he tapped her ribs smartly with two fingers, whistling, Miranda observed him for a few moments until she fixed his bright busy hazel eye not four inches from hers. "I'm not unconscious," she explained, "I know what I want to say." Then to her horror she heard herself babbling nonsense, knowing it was nonsense though she could not hear what she was saying. The flicker of attention in the eye near her vanished, the second interne went on tapping and listening, hissing softly under his breath.

"I wish you'd stop whistling," she said clearly. The sound stopped. "It's a beastly tune," she added. Anything, anything at all to keep her small hold on the life of human beings, a clear line of communication, no matter what, between her and the receding world. "Please let me see Dr. Hildesheim," she said, "I have something important to say to him. I must say it now." The second interne vanished. He did not walk away, he fled into the air without a sound, and Dr. Hildesheim's face appeared in his stead.

"Dr. Hildesheim, I want to ask you about Adam."

"That young man? He's been here, and left you a note, and has gone again," said Dr. Hildesheim, "and he'll be back tomorrow and the day after." His tone was altogether too merry and flippant.

"I don't believe you," said Miranda, bitterly, closing her lips and eyes and hoping she might not weep.

"Miss Tanner," called the doctor, "have you got that note?"

Miss Tanner appeared beside her, handed her an unsealed envelope, took it back, unfolded the note and gave it to her.

"I can't see it," said Miranda, after a pained search of the page full of hasty scratches in black ink.

"Here, I'll read it," said Miss Tanner. "It says, 'They came and took you while I was away and now they will not let me see you. Maybe tomorrow they will, with my love, Adam,'" read Miss Tanner in a firm dry voice, pronouncing the words distinctly. "Now, do you see?" she asked soothingly.

Miranda, hearing the words one by one, forgot them one by one. "Oh, read it again, what does it say?" she called out over the silence that pressed upon her, reaching towards the dancing words that just escaped as she almost touched them. "That will do," said Dr. Hildesheim, calmly authoritarian. "Where is that bed?"

"There is no bed yet," said Miss Tanner, as if she said, We are short of oranges. Dr. Hildesheim said, "Well, we'll manage something," and Miss Tanner drew the narrow trestle with bright crossed metal supports and small rubbery wheels into a deep jut of the corridor, out of the way of the swift white figures darting about, whirling and skimming like water flies all in silence. The white walls rose sheer as cliffs, a dozen frosted moons followed each other in perfect self-possession down a white lane and dropped mutely one by one into a snowy abyss.

What is this whiteness and silence but the absence of pain? Miranda lay lifting the nap of her white blanket softly between eased fingers, watching a dance of tall deliberate shadows moving behind a wide screen of sheets spread upon a frame. It was there, near her, on her side of the wall where she could see it clearly and enjoy it, and it was so beautiful she had no curiosity as to its meaning. Two dark figures nodded, bent, curtsied to each other, retreated and bowed again, lifted long arms and spread great hands against the white shadow of the screen; then with a single round movement, the sheets were folded back, disclosing two speechless men in white, standing, and another speechless man in white, lying on the bare springs of a white iron bed. The man on the springs was swathed smoothly from head to foot in white, with folded bands across the face, and a large stiff bow like merry rabbit ears dangled at the crown of his head.

The two living men lifted a mattress standing hunched against the wall, spread it tenderly and exactly over the dead man. Wordless and white they vanished down the corridor, pushing the wheeled bed before them. It had been an entrancing and leisurely spectacle, but now it was over. A pallid white fog rose in their wake insinuatingly and floated before Miranda's eyes, a fog in which was concealed all terror and all weariness, all the wrung faces and twisted backs and broken feet of abused, outraged living things, all the shapes of their confused pain and their estranged hearts; the fog might part at any moment and loose the horde of human torments. She put up her hands and said, Not yet, not yet, but it was too late. The fog parted and two executioners, white clad, moved towards her pushing between them with marvelously deft and practiced hands the misshapen figure of an old man in filthy rags whose scanty beard waggled under his opened mouth as he bowed his back and braced his feet to resist and delay the fate they had prepared for him. In a high weeping voice he was trying to explain to them that the crime of which he was accused did not merit the punishment he was about to receive; and except for this whining cry there was silence as they advanced. The soiled cracked bowls of the old man's hands were held before him beseechingly as a beggar's as he said, "Before God I am not guilty," but they held his arms and drew him onward, passed, and were gone.

The road to death is a long march beset with all evils, and the heart fails little by little at each new terror, the bones rebel at each step, the mind sets up its own bitter resistance and to what end? The barriers sink one by one, and no covering of the eyes shuts out the landscape of disaster, nor the sight of crimes committed there. Across the field came Dr. Hildesheim, his face a skull beneath his German helmet, carrying a naked infant writhing on the point of his bayonet, and a huge stone pot marked Poison in Gothic letters. He stopped before the well that Miranda remembered in a pasture on her father's farm, a well once dry but now bubbling with

living water, and into its pure depths he threw the child and the
poison, and the violated water sank back soundlessly into the earth.
Miranda, screaming, ran with her arms above her head; her voice
echoed and came back to her like a wolf's howl, Hildesheim is a
Boche, a spy, a Hun, kill him, kill him before he kills you. . . . She
woke howling, she heard the foul words accusing Dr. Hildesheim
tumbling from her mouth; opened her eyes and knew she was in a
bed in a small white room, with Dr. Hildesheim sitting beside her,
two firm fingers on her pulse. His hair was brushed sleekly and his
buttonhole flower was fresh. Stars gleamed through the window, and
Dr. Hildesheim seemed to be gazing at them with no particular
expression, his stethoscope dangling around his neck. Miss Tanner
stood at the foot of the bed writing something on a chart.

"Hello," said Dr. Hildesheim, "at least you take it out in shouting.
You don't try to get out of bed and go running around." Miranda
held her eyes open with a terrible effort, saw his rather heavy, patient
face clearly even as her mind tottered and slithered again, broke
from its foundation and spun like a cast wheel in a ditch. "I didn't
mean it, I never believed it, Dr. Hildesheim, you musn't remember
it—" and was gone again, not being able to wait for an answer.

The wrong she had done followed her and haunted her dream:
this wrong took vague shapes of horror she could not recognize
or name, though her heart cringed at sight of them. Her mind, split
in two, acknowledged and denied what she saw in the one instant,
for across an abyss of complaining darkness her reasoning coherent
self watched the strange frenzy of the other coldly, reluctant to admit
the truth of its visions, its tenacious remorses and despairs.

"I know those are your hands," she told Miss Tanner, "I know it,
but to me they are white tarantulas, don't touch me."

"Shut your eyes," said Miss Tanner.

"Oh, no," said Miranda, "for then I see worse things," but her eyes
closed in spite of her will, and the midnight of her internal torment
closed about her.

Oblivion, thought Miranda, her mind feeling among her memories
of words she had been taught to describe the unseen, the un-
knowable, is a whirlpool of gray water turning upon itself for all
eternity . . . eternity is perhaps more than the distance to the farthest
star. She lay on a narrow ledge over a pit that she knew to be bot-
tomless, though she could not comprehend it; the ledge was her childhood dream of danger, and she strained back against a reassuring

wall of granite at her shoulders, staring into the pit, thinking, There it is, there it is at last, it is very simple; and soft carefully shaped words like oblivion and eternity are curtains hung before nothing at all. I shall not know when it happens, I shall not feel or remember, why can't I consent now, I am lost, there is no hope for me. Look, she told herself, there it is, that is death and there is nothing to fear. But she could not consent, still shrinking stiffly against the granite wall that was her childhood dream of safety, breathing slowly for fear of squandering breath, saying desperately, Look, don't be afraid, it is nothing, it is only eternity.

Granite walls, whirlpools, stars are things. None of them is death, nor the image of it. Death is death, said Miranda, and for the dead it has no attributes. Silenced she sank easily through deeps under deeps of darkness until she lay like a stone at the farthest bottom of life, knowing herself to be blind, deaf, speechless, no longer aware of the members of her own body, entirely withdrawn from all human concerns, yet alive with a peculiar lucidity and coherence; all notions of the mind, the reasonable inquiries of doubt, all ties of blood and the desires of the heart, dissolved and fell away from her, and there remained of her only a minute fiercely burning particle of being that knew itself alone, that relied upon nothing beyond itself for its strength; not susceptible to any appeal or inducement, being itself composed entirely of one single motive, the stubborn will to live. This fiery motionless particle set itself unaided to resist destruction, to survive and to be in its own madness of being, motiveless and planless beyond that one essential end. Trust me, the hard unwinking angry point of light said. Trust me. I stay.

At once it grew, flattened, thinned to a fine radiance, spread like a great fan and curved out into a rainbow through which Miranda, enchanted, altogether believing, looked upon a deep clear landscape of sea and sand, of soft meadow and sky, freshly washed and glistening with transparencies of blue. Why, of course, of course, said Miranda, without surprise but with serene rapture as if some promise made to her had been kept long after she had ceased to hope for it. She rose from her narrow ledge and ran lightly through the tall portals of the great bow that arched in its splendor over the burning blue of the sea and the cool green of the meadow on either hand.

The small waves rolled in and over unhurriedly, lapped upon the sand in silence and retreated; the grasses flurried before a breeze that made no sound. Moving towards her leisurely as clouds through the shimmering air came a great company of human beings, and Miranda saw in an amazement of joy that they were all the living she had known. Their faces were transfigured, each in its own beauty, beyond what she remembered of them, their eyes were clear and untroubled as good weather, and they cast no shadows. They were pure identities and she knew them every one without calling their names or remembering what relation she bore to them. They surrounded her smoothly on silent feet, then turned their entranced faces again towards the sea, and she moved among them easily as a wave among waves. The drifting circle widened, separated, and each figure was alone but not solitary; Miranda, alone too, questioning nothing, desiring nothing, in the quietude of her ecstasy, stayed where she was, eyes fixed on the overwhelming deep sky where it was always morning.

Lying at ease, arms under her head, in the prodigal warmth which flowed evenly from sea and sky and meadow, within touch but not touching the serenely smiling familiar beings about her, Miranda felt without warning a vague tremor of apprehension, some small flick of distrust in her joy; a thin frost touched the edges of this confident tranquillity; something, somebody, was missing, she had lost something, she had left something valuable in another country, oh, what could it be? There are no trees, no trees here, she said in fright, I have left something unfinished. A thought struggled at the back of her mind, came clearly as a voice in her ear. Where are the dead? We have forgotten the dead, oh, the dead, where are they? At once as if a curtain had fallen, the bright landscape faded, she was alone in a strange stony place of bitter cold, picking her way along a steep path of slippery snow, calling out, Oh, I must go back! But in what direction? Pain returned, a terrible compelling pain running through her veins like heavy fire, the stench of corruption filled her nostrils, the sweetish sickening smell of rotting flesh and pus; she opened her eyes and saw pale light through a coarse white cloth over her face, knew that the smell of death was in her own body, and struggled to lift her hand. The cloth was drawn away; she saw Miss Tanner filling a hypodermic needle in her methodical expert way, and heard Dr. Hildesheim saying, "I think that will do the trick. Try another." Miss Tanner plucked firmly at Miranda's arm near the shoulder, and the unbelievable current of agony ran burning through her veins again. She struggled to cry out, saying, Let me go, let me go; but heard only incoherent sounds of animal suffering. She saw doctor and nurse glance at each other with the glance of initiates at a mystery, nodding in silence, their eyes alive with knowledgeable pride. They looked briefly at their handiwork and hurried away.

Bells screamed all off key, wrangling together as they collided in mid air, horns and whistles mingled shrilly with cries of human distress; sulphur colored light exploded through the black window pane and flashed away in darkness. Miranda waking from a dreamless sleep asked without expecting an answer, "What is happening?" for there was a bustle of voices and footsteps in the corridor, and a sharpness in the air; the far clamor went on, a furious exasperated shrieking like a mob in revolt.

The light came on, and Miss Tanner said in a furry voice, "Hear that? They're celebrating. It's the Armistice. The war is over, my dear." Her hands trembled. She rattled a spoon in a cup, stopped to listen, held the cup out to Miranda. From the ward for old bedridden women down the hall floated a ragged chorus of cracked voices singing, "My country, 'tis of thee . . ."

Sweet land . . . oh, terrible land of this bitter world where the sound of rejoicing was a clamor of pain, where ragged tuneless old women, sitting up waiting for their evening bowl of cocoa, were singing, "Sweet land of Liberty—"

"Oh, say, can you see?" their hopeless voices were asking next, the hammer strokes of metal tongues drowning them out. "The war is over," said Miss Tanner, her underlip held firmly, her eyes blurred. Miranda said, "Please open the window, please, I smell death in here."

Now if real daylight such as I remember having seen in this world would only come again, but it is always twilight or just before morning, a promise of day that is never kept. What has become of the sun? That was the longest and loneliest night and yet it will not end and let the day come. Shall I ever see light again?

Sitting in a long chair, near a window, it was in itself a melancholy wonder to see the colorless sunlight slanting on the snow, under a sky drained of its blue. "Can this be my face?" Miranda asked her mirror. "Are these my own hands?" she asked Miss Tanner, holding them up to show the yellow tint like melted wax glimmering between the closed fingers. The body is a curious monster, no place to live in, how could anyone feel at home there? Is it possible I can ever accustom myself to this place? she asked herself. The human faces around her seemed dulled and tired, with no radiance of skin and eyes as Miranda remembered radiance; the once white walls of her room were now a soiled gray. Breathing slowly, falling asleep and waking again, feeling the splash of water on her flesh, taking food, talking in bare phrases with Dr. Hildesheim and Miss Tanner, Miranda looked about her with the covertly hostile eyes of an alien who does not like the country in which he finds himself, does not understand the language nor wish to learn it, does not mean to live there and yet is helpless, unable to leave it at his will.

"It is morning," Miss Tanner would say, with a sigh, for she had grown old and weary once for all in the past month, "morning again, my dear," showing Miranda the same monotonous landscape of dulled evergreens and leaden snow. She would rustle about in her starched skirts, her face bravely powdered, her spirit unbreakable as good steel, saying, "Look, my dear, what a heavenly morning, like a crystal," for she had an affection for the salvaged creature before her, the silent ungrateful human being whom she, Cornelia Tanner, a nurse who knew her business, had snatched back from death with her own hands. "Nursing is nine-tenths, just the same," Miss Tanner would tell the other nurses; "keep that in mind." Even the sunshine was Miss Tanner's own prescription for the further recovery of Miranda, this patient the doctors had given up for lost, and who yet sat here, visible proof of Miss Tanner's theory. She said, "Look at the sunshine, now," as she might be saying, "I ordered this for you, my dear, do sit up and take it."

"It's beautiful," Miranda would answer, even turning her head to look, thanking Miss Tanner for her goodness, most of all her goodness about the weather, "beautiful, I always loved it." And I might love it again if I saw it, she thought, but truth was, she could not see it. There was no light, there might never be light again, compared as it must always be with the light she had seen beside the blue sea that lay so tranquilly along the shore of her paradise. That was a child's dream of the heavenly meadow, the vision of repose that comes to a tired body in sleep, she thought, but I have seen it when I did not know it was a dream. Closing her eyes she would rest for a moment remembering that bliss which had repaid all the pain of the journey to reach it; opening them again she saw with a new anguish the dull world to which she was condemned, where the light seemed filmed over with cobwebs, all the bright surfaces corroded, the sharp planes melted and formless, all objects and beings meaningless, ah, dead and withered things that believed themselves alive!

At night, after the long effort of lying in her chair, in her extremity of grief for what she had so briefly won, she folded her painful body together and wept silently, shamelessly, in pity for herself and her lost rapture. There was no escape. Dr. Hildesheim, Miss Tanner, the nurses in the diet kitchen, the chemist, the surgeon, the precise machine of the hospital, the whole humane conviction and custom of society, conspired to pull her inseparable rack of bones and wasted flesh to its feet, to put in order her disordered mind, and to set her once more safely in the road that would lead her again to death.

Chuck Rouncivale and Mary Townsend came to see her, bringing her a bundle of letters they had guarded for her. They brought a basket of delicate small hothouse flowers, lilies of the valley with sweet peas and feathery fern, and above these blooms their faces were merry and haggard.

Mary said, "You *have* had a tussle, haven't you?" and Chuck said, "Well, you made it back, didn't you?" Then after an uneasy pause, they told her that everybody was waiting to see her again at her desk. "They've put me back on sports already, Miranda," said Chuck. For ten minutes Miranda smiled and told them how gay and what a pleasant surprise it was to find herself alive. For it will not do to betray the conspiracy and tamper with the courage of the living; there is nothing better than to be alive, everyone has agreed on that; it is past argument, and who attempts to deny it is justly outlawed. "I'll be back in no time at all," she said; "this is almost over."

Her letters lay in a heap in her lap and beside her chair. Now and then she turned one over to read the inscription, recognized this handwriting or that, examined the blotted stamps and the postmarks, and let them drop again. For two or three days they lay upon the table beside her, and she continued to shrink from them. "They will all be telling me again how good it is to be alive, they will say again they love me, they are glad I am living too, and what can I answer to that?" and her hardened, indifferent heart shuddered in despair at itself, because before it had been tender and capable of love.

Dr. Hildesheim said, "What, all these letters not opened yet?" and Miss Tanner said, "Read your letters, my dear, I'll open them for you." Standing beside the bed, she slit them cleanly with a paper knife. Miranda, cornered, picked and chose until she found a thin one in an unfamiliar handwriting. "Oh, no, now," said Miss Tanner, "take them as they come. Here, I'll hand them to you." She sat down, prepared to be helpful to the end.

What a victory, what triumph, what happiness to be alive, sang the letters in a chorus. The names were signed with flourishes like the circles in air of bugle notes, and they were the names of those she had loved best; some of those she had known well and pleasantly; and a few who meant nothing to her, then or now. The thin letter in the unfamiliar handwriting was from a strange man at the camp where Adam had been, telling her that Adam had died of influenza in the camp hospital. Adam had asked him, in case any-thing happened, to be sure to let her know.

If anything happened. To be sure to let her know. If anything happened. "Your friend, Adam Barclay," wrote the strange man. It had happened—she looked at the date—more than a month ago.

"I've been here a long time, haven't I?" she asked Miss Tanner, who was folding letters and putting them back in their proper envelopes.

"Oh, quite a while," said Miss Tanner, "but you'll be ready to go soon now. But you must be careful of yourself and not overdo, and you should come back now and then and let us look at you, because sometimes the aftereffects are very—"

Miranda, sitting up before the mirror, wrote carefully: "One lipstick, medium, one ounce flask Bois d'Hiver perfume, one pair of gray suède gauntlets without straps, two pairs gray sheer stockings without clocks—"

Towney, reading after her, said, "Everything without something so that it will be almost impossible to get?"

"Try it, though," said Miranda, "they're nicer without. One walking stick of silvery wood with a silver knob."

"That's going to be expensive," warned Towney. "Walking is hardly worth it."

"You're right," said Miranda, and wrote in the margin, "a nice one to match my other things. Ask Chuck to look for this, Mary. Good looking and not too heavy." Lazarus, come forth. Not unless you bring me my top hat and stick. Stay where you are then, you snob. Not at all. I'm coming forth. "A jar of cold cream," wrote Miranda, "a box of apricot powder—and, Mary, I don't need eye shadow, do I?" She glanced at her face in the mirror and away again. "Still, no one need pity this corpse if we look properly to the art of the thing."

Mary Townsend said, "You won't recognize yourself in a week."

"Do you suppose, Mary," asked Miranda, "I could have my old room back again?"

"That should be easy," said Mary. "We stored away all your things there with Miss Hobbe." Miranda wondered again at the time and trouble the living took to be helpful to the dead. But not quite dead now, she reassured herself, one foot in either world now; soon I shall cross back and be at home again. The light will seem real and I shall be glad when I hear that someone I know has escaped from death. I shall visit the escaped ones and help them dress and tell them how lucky they are, and how lucky I am still to have them. Mary will be back soon with my gloves and my walking stick, I must go now, I must begin saying good-by to Miss Tanner and Dr. Hildesheim. Adam, she said, now you need not die again, but still I wish you were here; I wish you had come back, what do you think I came back for, Adam, to be deceived like this?

At once he was there beside her, invisible but urgently present, a ghost but more alive than she was, the last intolerable cheat of her heart; for knowing it was false she still clung to the lie, the unpardonable lie of her bitter desire. She said, "I love you," and stood up trembling, trying by the mere act of her will to bring him to sight before her. If I could call you up from the grave I would, she said, if I could see your ghost I would say, I believe . . . "I believe," she said aloud. "Oh, let me see you once more." The room was silent, empty, the shade was gone from it, struck away by the sudden violence of her rising and speaking aloud. She came to herself as if out of sleep. Oh, no, that is not the way, I must never do that, she warned herself. Miss Tanner said, "Your taxicab is waiting, my dear," and there was Mary. Ready to go.

No more war, no more plague, only the dazed silence that follows the ceasing of the heavy guns; noiseless houses with the shades drawn, empty streets, the dead cold light of tomorrow. Now there would be time for everything.

The Pilgrim Hawk

1940

GLENWAY WESCOTT

The Pilgrim Hawk

THE Cullens were Irish; but it was in France that I met them and was able to form an impression of their love and their trouble. They were on their way to a property they had rented in Hungary; and one afternoon they came to Chancellet to see my great friend Alexandra Henry. That was in May of 1928 or 1929, before we all returned to America, and she met my brother and married him.

Needless to say, the twenties were very different from the thirties, and now the forties have begun. In the twenties it was not unusual to meet foreigners in some country as foreign to them as to you, your peregrination just crossing theirs; and you did your best to know them in an afternoon or so; and perhaps you called that little lightning knowledge, friendship. There was a kind of idealistic or optimistic curiosity in the air. And vagaries of character, and the various war and peace that goes on in the psyche, seemed of the greatest interest and even importance.

Chancellet must be a painful place in the forties, although one of the least changed in France, I suppose, because it is unimportant. As I remember, there was a school of what is now romantically called celestial navigation, with a modest flying field and a few hangars, two or three kilometers away, at Pelors; but if that is in use now the foreigners must have it. In our day, day in and day out, the old Duchesse de Challot and her poor relations and friends in tight coats on windbroken mounts used to hunt in the forest of Pelors. We could hear their hunting horns which sounded like a picnic of boy sopranos, lost. Meanwhile perhaps there have been anti-aircraft guns for the defense of Paris embedded all amid the earths of foxes: angry radio stammering in the well-kept branches. Now at least the foxes and the thrushes can come back. The old ex-cabinet-minister whose château and little park adjoined Alex's garden is dead.

Her house was just a section of the village street: two small dwellings and a large horse-stable combined and rebuilt and expensively furnished in the plain modern style. She or her architect made a mistake in the planning of the ground floor. The dining room and the chief guest-room were on the street, which is also the highway to Orléans and the tourist country of the Loire; so that the reckless French traffic practically brushed the walls, and heavy trucks alarmed one all night. Not only Alex's bedroom but the kitchen and pantry opened into the spacious and quiet garden. This delighted the new servants whom Alex had brought up from Morocco, a romantic pair named Jean and Eva. They promptly took a far corner of it under some plane trees for their own use; and all spring they passed every spare moment there, quarreling and occasionally weeping during the day, but like clockwork making peace and sealing it with kisses in the twilight or moonlight. . . . I mention this odd location of the servants' quarters because, that afternoon of the Cullens' visit, I went to speak to Jean and happened to look out the kitchen window and saw Cullen in the garden, futilely giving way to his awful jealousy, emancipated from love for a few minutes.

There had been no mention of their coming, or perhaps I had forgotten it. I heard the doorbell ring, then ring again. Jean and Eva must have been outdoors or napping. Alex had put through a telephone call to London upon some little annoying matter of business, and wished not to be disturbed. So I went to the door; and there was the long dark Daimler entirely occupying the cobbled space between the house and the highway, and there stood the Irishman about to ring a third time. "Oh, how d'ya do, is this Miss Henry's house, my name's Cullen," he said; and turned to help Mrs. Cullen out of the car, which was a delicate operation, for she bore a full-grown hooded falcon on her wrist. A dapper young chauffeur also helped. She was dressed with extreme elegance and she wore the highest heels I ever saw, on which, with one solicitous male at each elbow, she stumbled across the ancient cobblestones, the bird swaying a little and hunching its wings to steady itself.

I told them my name, and they repeated it after me and shook hands with a somewhat grand and vague affability. "I brought my hawk," Mrs. Cullen unnecessarily announced. "She's new. I thought Alex wouldn't mind. And I hope you too," she added and paused a moment, with bright eyes to flatter me just in case I felt entitled to authority of some sort in Alex's house, "I hope you won't mind." She had no way of knowing who or what I was: casual caller or one of Alex's kinsmen or perhaps a sweetheart.

Her eyes were a crystal blue, unmistakably Irish; and she was unmistakable in other ways too, in spite of her brisk London voice and fine French dress. Her make-up was better than you would have expected of a lady falconer; still you could see that her skin was naturally downy and her snub nose tended to be pink. There was also a crookedness, particularly in the alignment of her nostrils and her voluble little lips. How rare pulchritude is among the Irish, I said to myself; therefore what a trouble is made when it does appear: Emer and Deirdre, Mrs. O'Shea and Mrs. McBride. Then my glance fell upon Mrs. Cullen's snowy dimpled fingers, with a considerable diamond on one, a star sapphire on another. Between her sleeve and the rough gauntlet to which the falcon clung, her wrist showed like a bit of Easter lily; and her ankle was a match for it, perfectly straight in a mere glimmer of stocking. No doubt these fine points were enough to entitle her to a certain enchantment and disturbance of the opposite sex: her husband for one.

Meanwhile Jean had come running in a fine embarrassment, buttoning his white jacket; and I sent him to inform his mistress of the arrival of her guests and to guide their chauffeur to the garage, while I tried to usher them into the living room. But Mrs. Cullen went on explaining the hawk. "Her name's Lucy. Don't you think she's sweet? She's Scottish; I've only had her five or six weeks. A gamekeeper near Inverness trapped her, but she's all right, only one toe bent in the trap. D'you see, this toe?" She paused on the threshold and held up the gloved hand and wrist on which Lucy perched, and I saw: gripping the rugged and stained leather, one sharp talon that did not grip straight. The stain on the leather was dried blood.

"I call her Lucy because my old father used to make me read Scott to him in the winter whenever the weather got too beastly to hunt. I thought Alex would like to see her."

"We had to bring her anyway," her husband loudly chimed in. "The most awful things happen if we leave her in the hotel. She frightens the chambermaids, and they scream and weep. I have to give immense tips."

He was a large man, not really fat but with bulk and softness irregularly here and there, not so much in the middle as up and down his back, all around his head, in his hands. His British complexion suggested eating and drinking rather than hunting and shooting; certainly nothing about him suggested hawking. His hazel eyes were a little bloodshot, wavering golden now and then; and he had a way of opening and shutting his lips, like an unsympathetic pout, or a dispirited kiss, under the tufts of his mustache.

We were about to sit down in the living room when they both noticed it, and evidently felt obliged to comment. "What a splendid room, splendid," they said; "most unusual and modern and comfortable." It was not splendid, but it was very large: the entire former stable with the hayloft removed so that the roof constituted the ceiling, with old chestnut rafters gothically pointing up twenty-five or thirty feet; the woodwork darkly waxed and the walls painted white. It reminded me of a village church. At regular intervals all around hung certain modern pictures with only blunt rudimentary drawing and overflowing color, like stained glass. But on as fine a day as this, modern art was dimmed and dwarfed by the view of the garden and the park beyond it, Alex's architect having removed almost a third of the wall on that side and put in two great panes of plate glass.

Mrs. Cullen tripped over to this great window and courteously exclaimed once more: "Splendid garden. What luck to have a pond!" It was what the French call an English garden; no formal flower beds—a few blossoms amid the grass, paths along the water, and shrubs flourishing, in the muffled brilliance of late May. The characteristic Seine-et-Oise sky, foamy cloud and weak blue, lay at our feet also, daubed in a soft copy on the surface of the pond. In the background every tree was draped in a slightly different shade of the same ecstatic color.

But as Mrs. Cullen stood facing all this, I had an impression of indifference and mere courtesy; her look did not take in much. A little narrow frown, an efficient survey, only to discover if there was anything in it for her personally; and there was not. In a moment the light eyelashes began to flutter again, and the blue pupils loosened, merely sparkling. Her prolonged and expressive looks were all for her husband or her hawk.

Now, what seeing the garden chiefly reminded her of, was that the hawk could not see: its entire head except the beak encased in its plumed Dutch hood. "Poor Lucy, blind as a bat," she murmured; and very deftly, taking one drawstring in her teeth and the other between thumb and forefinger of her right hand, she unhooded it. It also frowned, and stared circularly at the room and blinked at the window. Then it opened out and rearranged the whitish and bluish feathers around its throat; combed its head between its tethered legs; smoothed its cheek against its powerful shoulder.

Mrs. Cullen paced up and down, evidently trying to decide which armchair would suit her and Lucy best. Then Alex came in from her long-distance business, with apologies for not welcoming them at once. They replied with another round of compliments upon the house and garden, and there was a new introduction of the falcon. "Lucy, for Lucy Ashton, Lucy of Lammermoor," Mrs. Cullen explained. "Don't you remember her song? *Easy live and quiet die, Vacant hand and heart and eye.*"

To my amusement Cullen hummed a few notes of the Mad Scene from "Lucia" in a manly Irish treble. His wife hushed him by murmuring his name, which was Larry; and went on informing Alex that they were at the Plaza-Honoré, busy shopping in Paris, eager to leave for Hungary via Strasbourg on the morrow. I was impatient for them to cease this small talk and be seated, because I wanted to sit down and admire the falcon comfortably, and to ask certain questions. At last Mrs. Cullen requested a straight chair, which I brought from the dining room.

I was much impressed by Alex's enthusiasm during this first part of the Cullens' visit. It reminded me that she must be lonely here in France with only myself and my cousin and a few other friends rather like us. She had spent a number of years in Scotland with her father, and in Morocco, and journeying around the Orient; and in London also the acquaintances of her girlhood had been outdoor people like these two, self-centered but without any introspection, strenuous but emotionally idle. It was a type of humanity that she no longer quite respected or trusted, but evidently still enjoyed.

Their enthusiasm about themselves and all that exactly appertained to them, always overflowing, coolly playing and bubbling over in mild agitation like a fountain, held your attention and mirrored itself in your mind; little by little you began to bubble with it. One of Alex's obvious characteristics was lack of curiosity; and I think that was chiefly fear of arousing or authorizing others' inquiry about herself. Perhaps selfishness reassured her and made her less shy. In any case, that afternoon she eagerly asked questions, including some that I had in mind; and Mrs. Cullen was charmed to answer; and Cullen was charmed to listen and give back his approximate echoes. Thus an odd kind of compatibility was established, in which I too gradually let myself be included, somewhat to my surprise.

For one thing, the bird charmed me so that nothing else mattered much. And it served as an embodiment or emblem for me of all the truly interesting subjects of conversation that these very sociable, traveling, sporting people leave out as a rule: illness, poverty, sex, religion, art. Whenever I began to be bored, a solemn glance of its maniacal eyes helped me to stop listening and to think concentratedly of myself instead, or for myself.

Furthermore the Cullens began to puzzle me, to charm me in that sense. Whether or not I finally arrive at a proper understanding of people, I often begin in the way of a vexed, intense superficiality. And indeed they were mere male and female of that species of well-to-do British which haunts the entire world with excess of energy and sedate manner. They were self-absorbed, coldly gregarious, mere passers of time. But nothing about them was authentically sedate or even peaceful. There Cullen plumply sat in Alex's softest armchair, his legs more widely spread or loosely crossed than you would expect of a conventional gentleman; licking his lips under his fringy mustache; evidently thinking of his dinner; interrupting his wife's conversation at regular intervals as if that were his life work. Yet he seemed to be constantly fighting against some strange feeling, and to be somehow outwitted by it. Whenever he spoke, his wife smiled or at least tilted her head toward him. This, I felt, was chiefly good breeding on her part; many of his remarks, and especially his tone of voice, seemed unpleasant. But between remarks, in her glances at him, there was affection as bright as tears. And during the loving fuss she made over the great bird on her arm, she kept shifting her eyes in his direction, imploring him to try to like it too. It might have been a baby, and he a lover; or was it the other way around?

Alex expressed surprise that they should willingly leave Ireland at this lovely time of year. Mrs. Cullen answered that, in season or out, there was nothing much to do in Ireland except hunt. "And our terrible sons pinch our hunters when they come home. We can't afford to keep enough for them. I can't bear a horse that others have been riding."

She also alluded mildly to the diminishment of the old quiet kind of fortune like theirs. The banshee in the draughty corridor or the weedy hedge crying not the deaths of relatives, but increase of taxes, decrease of rents and investments . . . Indeed they still appeared rich, in hand-woven silk with diamonds, in tweed as soft as silk, stopping at the Plaza-Honoré, en route to Budapest in a Daimler. But all that in fact is cheaper than an old country house full of guests, and the requisite stable and kennel and larder and cellar, and servants enough. Having closed Cullen Hall, Mrs. Cullen pointed out, they were in a position to accept invitations half the year; and the continent was cheap.

Evidently her telling us this vexed Cullen. He warmly informed us that one of his neighbors, a drunken idiot anyway, had sold everything that the entail permitted, and two of his cousins were obliged to rent; and so it went all over the British Isles. Their own circumstances were neither discreditable nor hopeless. There were still certain inheritances due them, on his side, not Mrs. Cullen's. His sons might be considered grown men, except by their mother; but they were still engaged in that great postponement, education, which is expensive. His brother and sister were happy to have them during their long vacations; but as a rule they preferred to loiter at Cullen Hall with two or three servants who were too old to dismiss anyway; and they hunted with the neighbors. It is easy for youngsters to get on with new people, even such as the latest in their county, a manufacturing peer named Bild, a Jew; not at all easy for him.

Mrs. Cullen said a word in defense of Lord Bild. Thank heaven it was he who had bought the estate adjoining Cullen Hall, on their youngsters' account especially. Although of common Germanic origin he was very strict about manners and sportsmanship and keeping fit; more so than they were. Neighborly influence is like education; the best teachers belong to the races and classes which have been learning themselves just lately.

Now Cullen had risen and was standing at his wife's elbow, shaking his finger at the falcon teasingly. I thought that the bird's great eyes showed only a slight natural bewilderment; whereas a slow sneer came over his face and he turned pale. It was the first revelation I had of the interesting fact that he hated Lucy. He would willingly have sacrificed a finger tip in order to have an excuse to retaliate, I thought; and I imagined him picking up a chair or a coffee table and going at her with smashing blows. What a difference there is between animals and humans! Lucy no doubt would be disgustingly fierce when her time came; but meanwhile sat pleasantly and idly, in abeyance. Whereas humanity is histrionic, and must prepare and practice every stroke of passion; so half our life is a vague and stormy make-believe.

Mrs. Cullen merely looked up at her husband and said in a velvety tone, "The trouble with Ireland, from my point of view, is that they don't like our having a falcon. Naturally Lord Bild disapproves; but I don't mind him. He's so unsure of himself; he's a Jew furthermore; you can scarcely expect him to live and let live. But our other neighbors and the family are almost as tiresome."

Cullen thrust the teasing hand in his pocket and returned to his armchair. Her eyes sparkled fast, perhaps with that form of contrition which pretends to be joking. Or perhaps it pleased her to break off the subject of their Irish circumstance and worldly situation and to resume the dear theme of hawk, which meant all the world to her.

The summer before, she told us, an old Hungarian had sold her a trained tiercel. "I took him with me last winter when we stayed with some pleasant Americans in Scotland. There's a bad ailment called croaks, and he caught that and died. They had installed their American heating, which I think makes an old house damp; don't you? Then their gamekeeper trapped Lucy and gave her to me. Wasn't that lucky? I've always wanted a real falcon, a haggard, to man and train myself."

In strict terminology of the sport, she explained, only a female is called a falcon; and a haggard is one that has already hunted on her own account, that is, at least a year old when caught.

Except for that one deformed bit of one foot, Lucy was a perfect example of her species, *Falco peregrinus*, pilgrim hawk. Her body was as long as her mistress's arm; the wing feathers in repose a little too long, slung across her back like a folded tent. Her back was an indefinable hue of iron; only a slight patina of the ruddiness of youth still shone on it. Her luxurious breast was white, with little tabs or tassels of chestnut. Out of tasseled pantaloons her legs came down straight to the perch with no apparent flesh on them, enameled a greenish yellow.

But her chief beauty was that of expression. It was like a little flame; it caught and compelled your attention like that, although it did not flicker and there was nothing bright about it nor any warmth in it. It is a look that men sometimes have; men of great energy, whose appetite or vocation has kept them absorbed every instant all their lives. They may be good men but they are often mistaken for evil men, and vice versa. In Lucy's case it appeared chiefly in her eyes, not black but funereally brown, and extravagantly large, set deep in her flattened head.

On each side of the upper beak there was a little tooth or tusk. Mrs. Cullen explained that the able bird in the prime of life uses this to snap the spinal cord of its quarry, which is the most merciful death in nature. It reminded me of the hooked gloves which our farmers wear to husk corn; and so in fact, I thought, it must work: the falcon in the sky like a large angelic hand, stripping the meat of pigeon or partridge out of its feathers, the soul out of its throat.

I think Mrs. Cullen was the most talkative woman I ever met; and it was hawk, hawk, all afternoon. A good many inhabitants of the British Isles are hell-bent all their lives upon killing some wild animal somehow, and naturally are keen about the domestic animals which assist them. Others, who know all about human nature, nevertheless prefer to converse about animals, perhaps because it is the better part of conversational valor. Mrs. Cullen's enthusiasm was nothing like that, and it probably would have annoyed or alarmed the majority of her compatriots. As it seemed to me after listening a while, she felt welling up in her mind some peculiar imagination, or some trouble impossible to ignore, which she tried to relieve by talking, with a kind of continuous double meaning. I think she would never have admitted the duplicity, and perhaps could not have expressed herself in plain terms. People as a rule do mean much more than they understand.

She informed us, for example, that in a state of nature hawks rarely die of disease; they starve to death. Their eyesight fails; some of their flight feathers break off or fall out; and their talons get dull or broken. They cease to be able to judge what quarry is worth flying at; or their flight slows up so that even the likely quarry gets away. Or, because they have lost weight, the victim is not stunned by their swooping down on it. Or when they have clutched it, they cannot hang on long enough to kill. Day after day they make fools of themselves. Then they have to depend upon very young birds or sick birds, or little animals on the ground, which are the hardest of all to see; and in any case there are not enough of these easy conquests to keep them in flesh. The hungrier they get, the more wearily and weakly they hunt. And the weaker they get, the more often they go hungry, in a miserable confusion of cause and effect. Finally what appears to be shame and morbid discouragement overcomes them. They simply sit on the rocks or in a tree somewhere waiting to die, as you might say philosophically, letting themselves die.

"I met a man on the staff of our great madhouse in Dublin last year," Mrs. Cullen added. "I was curious to see what it was like; so he took me with him one afternoon on a tour of inspection. Some of the mad people reminded me of hawks, exactly." The lethargically mad, sitting with their hands in their laps, imaginarily exhausted, unable to speak above a whisper, with burning but unfocusable eyes, unable to concentrate. . . .

Cullen cleared his throat boisterously, perhaps to protest against the curiosity of women or against this folly of reading meaning into the ways of mere birds.

Falconers believe that hunger must be worse for falcons than for other birds and animals, Mrs. Cullen said. It maddens them, with a soreness in every feather; an unrelievable itching in their awful feet; a bloody lump in their throats, with the light plumage wrapped loose around like a bandage. This painful greed, sick single-mindedness, makes it possible to tame them and to perfect the extraordinary technique of falconry, which is more than any other bird can learn. You hear it in their cry—*aik, aik*—as Mrs. Cullen then imitated it for us, ache, ache—a small flat scream with a bubbling or gargling undertone, as if their mouths were full of scalding water. "I suppose human beings never feel anything like it."

"But Madeleine, Madeleine, we're never hungry," her husband protested with a chuckle in which there was great satisfaction. "How can we tell?"

She begged him not to be silly. She had known people who had starved, Irish republicans hiding from the Black and Tans, Germans in 1922, and had inquired of them; and they had described it as rather a soft cool drowsy feeling.

I wondered about this. Although I had been a poor boy, on a Wisconsin farm and in a slum in Chicago and in Germany in 1922, I could not recollect any exact sensation of hunger, that is to say, hunger of the stomach. And I thought—as the relatively well-fed do think—of the other human hungers, mental and sentimental and so on. For example, my own undertaking in early manhood to be a literary artist. No one warned me that I really did not have talent enough. Therefore my hope of becoming a very good artist turned bitter, hot and nerve-racking; and it would get worse as I grew older. The unsuccessful artist also ends in an apathy, too proud and vexed to fly again, waiting upon withheld inspiration, bored to death. . . . Naturally I did not speak of this to Alex and the Cullens. It seemed rude and somehow abnormal even to be thinking of it, while they sat exchanging information about real life, really starving nations and greedy species of bird.

Whereupon our present bird mantled, that is, stood a moment on one leg, shook the other leg and wing downward, and spread that half of her plumage in a long fan, gazing at me, blinking or winking at me. But because my writing had gone badly all spring I could not bear to give her more than a passing thought with reference to that. I began to think of her as an image of amorous desire instead. That is the great relief of weariness of work in any case; the natural consolation for its not going well. Or perhaps the Cullens' feeling about each other suggested it to me. No doubt art is too exceptional to be worth talking about; but sex is not. At least in good countries such as France and the United States during prosperous periods like the twenties, it must be the keenest of all appetites for a majority of men most of their lives.

And highly sexed men, unless they give in and get married and stay married, more or less starve to death. I myself was still young then and I had been lucky in love. But little early quarrels and failures warn one; and in the confidences of friends and in gossip about other men, one discovers the vague beastly shape of what to expect. Life goes on and on after one's luck has run out. Youthfulness persists, alas, long after one has ceased to be young. Love-life goes on indefinitely, with less and less likelihood of being loved, less and less ability to love, and the stomach-ache of love still as sharp as ever. The old bachelor is like an old hawk.

Civilized human beings have learned how to avoid literal starvation and the fear of death and real enslavement; so at least it seemed in the twenties. They have this kind of thing instead: fear of old age, loss of charm, lack of love. Therefore I caught myself gazing at my young unmarried Alex anxiously, sentimentally, and at her. Irish guests with idle envy. But the Irish wife's uneasiness and the husband's captivated but uncomfortable look reminded me that I was making a false distinction. There is not as much sweet safety in marriage as one hopes. Hunger and its twin, disgust, are in it too; need and greed; and passage of time, the punishment. Of course true love and lust are not the same, neither are they inseparable, nor indistinguishable. Only they reflect and imitate and elucidate each other.

Looking back upon that afternoon's talk and thought, I am inclined to hold Mrs. Cullen responsible for this daydreaming of mine, personal worry and exhilaration, which made me inattentive to what she said now and then. In a woman as energetic and attractive as that, the hint of hidden emotion and the sense of double meaning naturally are exciting; and the excitement leads in one's own private direction. But as it were in a mirror, looking at myself, I could see something of her character and plight before the circumstances of the afternoon betrayed her. I think that was what she instinctively wanted.

Meanwhile she had gone on answering Alex's questions: something about the craftsmen who outfit falcons, generation after generation of avian haberdashers especially in India, and which bell resounds the clearest through the grass and bushes and breezes, and what hood is least likely to ulcerate the waxen lids and lips; and something about an ancient Persian text with a thrice-hyphenated title which is still the best handbook of falconry. I wanted to know all this, yet I failed to pay attention.

Then Lucy bated, that is, threw herself headlong off the fist. The leather jesses around her legs and the leash looped through Mrs. Cullen's fingers held her ignominiously, upside down. It was a painful sight, like an epileptic fit or an insane fit. There was no possibility of the thongs breaking; I half-expected her lean bright legs to snap instead. I expected her to scream, aik! But the only sound was the jingling of her bell and the convulsion of her plumage, air panting through her plumage. The tail feathers and the flight feathers, shooting out rigidly, threshed against herself and against her mistress from head to foot. Mrs. Cullen, not the least disconcerted, raised her left arm straight up over her head, and stood up and stood quite still, only turning her face away from the flapping and whipping. Her equanimity impressed me as much as her strength.

In a minute Lucy gave up little by little. It was extraordinary: you could see her self-control returning, recurring in one feather after another. Then she hung peacefully like a mere turkey or goose hooked up in a butchershop; only for an instant. The long wings began again, but in a different exertion: hugging the air, bracing against the air, until her talons got a grip on the gauntlet and she succeeded in pulling herself up again where she belonged. There she stared or glared at us, blinking the rush of blood back out of her embarrassed eyes and pulling her plumage together.

With a sigh and a half-smile Mrs. Cullen brought her burdened and shaken arm down, and seated herself again in the straight chair. Some such hopeless attempt to escape, crazy fit of freedom, comes over all domesticated falcons at fairly regular intervals, she explained, especially in their first year or two; all their lives if they have not been well manned. "They never get over being wild. It's like malaria or that other intermittent fever, the one you have to be so careful about in the Orient."

Lucy happened to be an unusually frank, active bird, so that you could often tell when her trouble was to be expected; by a soft repeated tinkle of her bells or a steady pull at one of her jesses. The leather might of course be loose or worn out. "And instead it pinches her, which makes her angry, and everything seems hopeless," Mrs. Cullen concluded. "She can't help it, can't bear it. It's like committing suicide."

"Give me liberty or give me death, ha, ha," cried Cullen, seeming to expect special applause from us because we were Americans, or perhaps because Alex's name was Henry like the American who first expressed that sentiment. His wife gave him that look of hers which was the opposite of applause; and he took it as usual. His hazel eyes stood out like jewels, the tip of his tongue brightened his lips.

Meanwhile she was slowly caressing Lucy's lower plumage and tired feet. She might have been a trained nurse and Lucy her patient, after a bout of illness or craziness. Or she might have been in love and Lucy her beloved, pleasure absent-mindedly ebbing . . . And every word she uttered added a little to the confused significance. "Sometimes I can prevent her independent fits. The way a governess gets to know a child, and can see its tantrums beginning and distract it somehow. . . . Being stroked like this often does the trick. At first I used a dried pigeon's wing as you're supposed to, but this suits Lucy as well."

Idly she went on with it: two dimpled fingers with long tinted nails and heavy rings just brushing the spent feathers. "Or if I notice it in time, I lift her over my head for a moment. She likes to perch as high as possible, so she can look down upon everything around her. I think it must frighten her to see things higher than she is.

We're like that sometimes ourselves, aren't we?" she added, smiling gently.

Time after time her transitions like this—from hawk to human, objective to subjective—startled me. To be sure, any woman greatly in love must know how a flattery in time saves trouble, how the illusion of superiority counteracts the illusion of inferiority, as well as any governess. But it had not occurred to me that her love for Cullen was great in that sense: cunning, instructive, curative.

Falcons, she informed us, do not breed in captivity. Various attempts have been made to induce them to, but with no success. Thus, the entire sport has to start again from scratch for each falconer, whenever he trains a new playmate. Little by little the perfectly wild creature surrenders, individually, in the awful difficulty of hunger. But surrender is all, domestication is all; they never feel at home. You can carry male and female side by side in the same cage year in and year out; nothing happens. They will cease to fight but they stay solitary. Scorn of each other for giving in, or self-scorn, seems to break their hearts. They never build a nest or lay an egg. Not one chick or eyas is ever reared in bondage. There is no real acceptance or inheritance of the state of surrender.

Mrs. Cullen mentioned, as a kind of exception, the make-hawks: old good-natured birds which some professionals use in the training of the young wild ones. But even their influence must be in the way of a rationalization of necessary evil, inculcation of vice, making the best of a bad bargain. For they too are born in the vacant rocks or uncomfortable trees; and they too keep sterile.

"Like schoolmasters," crowed Cullen. That appealed to my sense of humor. But Cullen's smile was a leer if I ever saw one, and evidently embarrassed his wife and Alex; so I kept from smiling.

Mrs. Cullen then quoted Buffon's famous sentence about falcons: *"L'individu seul est esclave; l'espèce est libre."* Buffon had been her father's second-best author, after Scott. Her French accent was incorrect but very pretty. Only the individual hawk is a slave; the species is free. . . .

Then Alex spoke up, in what was a loud voice for her: "Oh, dear, it is the opposite of human beings. We are slaves in the mass, aren't we? Only one man can hope to free himself; one at a time, then another, and another."

"Oh, I dare say," Mrs. Cullen assented. "Yes, perhaps." But she smiled patronizingly. I think she was congratulating herself upon knowing a freer and stronger type of humanity than our pampered, subtle, self-questioning American type; and perhaps she did: Irish republicans, wild Hungarians with hawks, Germans during their defeat.

"But it is true, isn't it?" Alex insisted. "The man who really loves freedom is the exception."

"Oh, quite. How right you are," our lady falconer dubiously murmured.

But her husband disagreed. "No, Alex! What a disgusting idea! Love of liberty is the deepest instinct we have—if you will excuse my saying so."

We silently considered this for a moment; the three of us, it seemed, regretfully. Alex wanted freedom more than anything; and if others as a rule did not, she might have a lonely life. In any case it would take a better man than Cullen to dispel her young misanthropy. I myself regretted never having been able to decide what to think: how much liberty is a true human motive, and how much is wasteful and foolish? And for the first time that afternoon Mrs. Cullen gazed at her husband sadly, that is, weakly. She agreed with him, I felt sure. But there are circumstances in which it may be obvious that at least one human being requires freedom; and you bitterly regret that it is so: because you need to keep that one captive.

"Why, hang it all," Cullen still sputtered, "why, independence is the only thing that is human about hawks. Don't you agree, Madeleine?"

She slightly turned her back to him and contemplated Alex and me rather unkindly. It was the careful absence of expression, absence of frown, that you see on a clever lecturer's face when the irrelevant questioning or heckling begins. There was also a sadness about it which, if I read it aright, I have often felt myself. She did not want us to take her hawk, her dear subject-matter, her hobby and symbol —whatever it meant to her—and turn it this way and that to mean what we liked. It was hers and we were spoiling it. Around her eyes and mouth there were lines of that caricatural weariness which is peculiar to those who talk too much.

Indeed our sociability as a whole had gone off; something a little sour and dark had developed in it. We had been sitting there too long. Alex, I fancied, was counting the minutes until they departed. But suddenly she grew hospitable. "You'll stay to dinner, Madeleine, won't you? Please, Larry, do. I can promise you a good dinner," she added with an indulgent smile.

I wondered whether she had mentioned this invitation to Jean and

Eva, and whether the short notice would exasperate or inspire them. Mrs. Cullen also thought of that. "Servants are devils, don't you know. Mine used to behave madly, when extra people turned up at Cullen Hall."

Poor Alex was accustomed to the madness of servants; but, as she explained, this new couple did not mind surprises. She had found them in Tangier, where the secretary of the pig-sticking club had engaged them to cook in camp for several tentfuls of unmarried members. With only primitive utensils, a few iron kettles and a spit over an outdoor fire, and unpredictable guests at all hours, it evidently was child's play for them, and a welcome opportunity to show off. One afternoon a French general and a party of eight had motored out from the town, and some thoughtless fellow had asked them to stay. Jean had taken a boar killed that morning, and by slicing it thin, rubbing it with certain herbs which grew there underfoot amid the tents, and marinating it in four bottles of brandy, rendered it quite edible by nightfall. Alex was inclined to think of her entire lifetime as an emergency of that sort. So she had hired the proud pair and secured passports for them and embarked them for France and Chancellet. And this, she told Mrs. Cullen, was what she had hired them for.

"If we do stay," Mrs. Cullen said, "my bird will have to be fed, toward six o'clock." Alex in any case intended to suggest to Jean a dish of pigeons baked with white currants. He would procure them from a neighbor who had an immense old dovecot; and one could be brought back alive for Lucy. The reminiscence of the brandied wild pig, the prospect of *pigeons aux groseilles*, charmed Cullen; you could see the gourmandise shining on his rosy lips.

Alex went to the kitchen, and by her comfortable air when she came back I judged that Jean was well disposed. Then she suggested our taking a walk until dinner-time, which also charmed Cullen, though his appetite did not need whetting. "By Jove," he said, "I do look forward to those squabs."

They were disappointed to learn that the park was not Alex's property. It belonged to the nation, along with the little château de Chancellet in the midst of it. Bidou, the illustrious aged ex-minister, was permitted to live there. But he kept the gates open in the daytime, and the entire village strolled in and out. Meeting all classes when he took his daily exercise perhaps made him think proudly how democratic a statesman he had been all his life. He gave everyone a *bon jour*. He especially liked meeting Alex because she was an American and he vaguely remembered having advocated the payment of the war debts.

"Oh, aren't politicians a bore?" Cullen exclaimed with an odd proud laugh. "Worse than poets."

"Larry, please," his wife said in haste, "please let's not talk about that." I wondered what that meant.

Alex unlocked the little gate on the far side of the pond, and we strolled along an *allée* of ancient beeches. She warned us that if Bidou should appear in the distance, she would have to turn back. He had a way of inviting her to dine, and Mme. Bidou had asked her not to accept on account of the failing of his health, the folly of his old manhood.

We all felt happier now that we were outdoors. It was beautiful in the park. The trees had been so lovingly tended ever since a pupil of Lenôtre's set them out, that each had developed its maximum character. The way they stood in informal groups, or in line, or alone at a little distance, seemed not only to conform to the art of parks but to express their feelings about each other: idiosyncrasies of affection or obedience, pride or pain. And unlike human characters in such an assembly, they promised or threatened nothing more; no episodes or developments.

Cullen walked up ahead with Alex. Now in the open air he not only laughed but shouted; so that I could hear him telling her a yarn about an old English politician who had attached himself to a young married woman. And one day he and the husband had gone out alone together on the moor for a bit of rough shooting; and he had shot the husband by accident, so to speak. Then he had married her. But he had worried about it all the rest of his life, which was not long; and he had impoverished her in his will. It was ancient gossip: I had heard it before; and at the time I did not see any oddity in Cullen's telling it, except that it seemed funny to him and not to me. When love is diabolic, I thought, a triangle is the simplest form it can take; and a convenient form, if it cannot be endured. The lovers to be pitied perhaps are those who have no one to hate— what they long to kill, and what the killing would be for, incorporated in one and the same person, the one they love—whose rough shooting therefore can take place only in imagination, and never ends.

Presently we came to a crossroads; and there we did see the short silhouette of old Bidou headed in our direction: his peculiar march or trudge, and the shrugging of his shoulders inside a great cape. All his life he had gone booted like a common soldier and blackly wrapped up, which had been a boon to caricaturists and a kind of electoral trade mark; which now made it easy to avoid him. Mrs. Cullen asked if they might go on ahead and have a look at the famous old fellow.

Alex and I turned back alone toward her house, by a short cut through a dense plantation of young trees, with vernal branches of old trees rounded overhead. It was like walking inside a great recumbent telescope, pointed at the château half a kilometer away. In the nineteenth century, under the personal supervision of Viollet-le-Duc and his friend the author of *Carmen*, Chancellet had been entirely and fussily restored. In the round bit of sunshine afar off, the lens of our telescope, it looked too good to be true, amid the patchy flower beds and the moat, where a few ducks were splashing and lovemaking.

I was in as foolish a good humor as Cullen; everything seemed mysterious and sentimental. The rounded frame of branches in which we strolled, looking ahead into pinkish sunlight; the tidy little architecture enframed, with its associations literary as well as historical; the dying, absent-minded, erotic statesman exercising daily in an immutable circle around it; our odd guests walking to meet him, woman with hawk and greedy man, whose eyes turned golden when he looked at her, whose spit ran at the mere mention of his dinner—all were gathered around me, I vainly fancied, to make one great vague thing very simple and clear to me. What more could I ask? But it is always foolish to expect simplicity. All one can do is to substitute little facts for great speculations, little performances for immense desire, and call this, simplification.

The return by ourselves gave me a chance to question Alex about the Cullens. They had come to Tangier two or three years before for the pig-sticking. Madeleine rode ideally, but the rule of the club forebade women to carry a spear. Cullen had shown a definite lack of enthusiasm and indeed a lack of talent; however, he had gone out every day and not done badly. When one of the vile brave beasts appeared in the distance—flickering along the shrub, suddenly fleeing out across open ground like the shadow of a flying bird—the Irish woman would gallop out with the very first riders; her husband following hard, looking as if he might fall any minute but not falling. At the last minute, when the spears began to point down along the shoulders of the horses, she would rein up short or turn aside. Suddenly she would not be there any longer, and Cullen still would be. Her ambition for him and his poor horsemanship—so it appeared to the others—betrayed him into prowess. Alex heard a club member say that once or twice at the kill his audacity and ferocity had been rather too much of a good thing; shocking. One morning his horse stepped into a hole and threw him right down beside the boar, a big wicked one already wounded; and he behaved with great sense and courage, and kept his horse away from its tushes, although he was not quite sober. His not being quite sober was the trouble in general.

One afternoon Mrs. Cullen had said as much to Alex. "Poor Larry, when we're in Ireland or in London with nothing to do, is inclined to overeat, and furthermore to drink far too much." Alex must have been impressed by this confession, for she quoted some of it word for word. "Most things are a beastly bore for him, you know; that's his real weakness. But you can't say anything to a grown man about drinking, after all, can you? It's such a horrid little unimportant thing. They're proud, and they resent having to think of it. I had an aunt who talked about it, and it made my uncle worse." As discreetly as she could therefore, she told Alex, she tried to keep him distracted; busy doing things, in good company which inspired him to do well; abroad, and outdoors as much as possible. He often complained that it was no way to live; but it had kept him fit and good-natured.

She was younger than he, Alex pointed out; and she had money of her own; and she was a clever, unconventional, and rather self-indulgent woman. Yet she devoted herself entirely to him, every instant, year in and year out. He on the other hand was not perfectly faithful, in spite of his devotion to her. When they were in Tangier a pretty young American named Baroness Levene came across from Malaga, and flirted with Cullen; and he obviously responded to it. One of the Tangier residents asked them all to dine, and while the men stayed in the dining room, Madeleine had been very rude to the little interloper. A day or two later she spoke of it apologetically. It was disgraceful of her, she assured Alex, to mind her husband's virile frivolity. She never doubted for an instant that he loved her, and no other woman. His response to the others was all make-believe or in fun. She alluded again to his deadly tedium; his need of some novelty to pass the time somehow, every day of his life, every hour; and his other weaknesses in direct consequence. A little philandering, like eating and drinking, gave him something to think about.

Whereas marriage was infinitely simple for her, she said; she never needed the attention of other men. She supposed this to be so settled and so apparent in her character that it bored men and they let her alone. Alex had observed a number of acceptable men not letting her alone in the least; rather smitten. Yet there seemed to be no affectation or insincerity in Mrs. Cullen's account of herself. Women who have been spoiled by the many, tormented by one, often have an air of innocence.

Alex had seen a great deal of them the following winter in London; and there they were engaged in a very odd sport indeed: underground activity of Irish rebellion. Cullen was perfectly and anciently Irish, and one of his brothers had been a friend of Casement's. Whereas Madeleine was not a Catholic; and she had Ulster blood and English blood; and as a child she had lived in Canada. Yet she was the rebel, or she ardently played the part of one; Larry followed. Alex heard him speak very angrily of the British, disgustedly of de Valera. But he loved joining in others' opinion, no matter what, and embellishing his repetition of it, as best he could—how could one tell what he thought? Perhaps it was hard for him to tell himself.

All that winter they were at home informally almost every evening to the oddest patriots. At first glance it looked like a literary salon. The ringleader was the poet McVoy: a young man of great conversation, with a half-rapacious, half-religious face. Alex also met a man who had done a little bombing, another with a bit of his cheek shot away, and certain bereaved and cruel women, and a bizarre priest. Their political opinion was all tinged with piety, even puritanism. They would have been ashamed to eat or drink or be merry in any way, with so much to be done for Eire. Cullen yielded to the general austerity. Furthermore, he told Alex, they could not afford to live well that winter, because of their contributions to the cause. Alex had never seen him in better form, lean and youthful and if not exactly cheerful, amiable. Rebellion evidently served as an excellent exercise and diet. There was also amorous anxiety: he thought McVoy in love with Madeleine. Alex indeed thought so too. But all Madeleine appeared to want of the poet was to keep on his political high horse, in his fascinating conspiratorial vein, for Larry's amusement. Rioting and sabotage and perhaps even assassination—as it were sticking of the Ulster pig, mort of the English stag—with poor Larry in the thick of it, because it would be good for him. . . . Suddenly all that ceased, Alex never heard why. They sublet their house and spent the summer in Vienna and Budapest. That was the summer Mrs. Cullen bought her first hawk, the tiercel that died of the croaks.

This little information Alex gave me as we sauntered slowly through the ex-minister's park. Now we were back near our gate, under the great beeches. Alex had been a little anxious lest the Cullens get lost. But there in the broken light, pallid shade, there they came at a brisk pace, engaged in a vivacious discussion of some sort, which they ceased as soon as they saw us. "He's a dear, your old politician," Mrs. Cullen said. "He spoke to us, and then what do you suppose he did? He did bird imitations for Lucy; I mean to say, he whistled at her."

Evidently Cullen preferred French politicians to Irish. "A good old boy! He did a nightingale and a lark and some bird I didn't know. He told us what it was, but it was French. Quite good."

"And Larry, wasn't he cheerful and civil? Perhaps he thought that if he kept whistling long enough, Lucy would answer. Wasn't it funny?"

I thought it touching as well as funny: that old man had been whistling to his compatriots like that for half a century, and as a rule a majority had answered; but, alas, nothing much had come of it, for France.

Now Mrs. Cullen was ready to feed Lucy. But her chauffeur and Jean who had gone to the neighbor's dovecot, had not returned. Foolish Eva felt sure they were in a ditch somewhere, or quarreling, or lost. So we sat down again; and I like a fool inquired what they thought of French and English and German politics. Cullen was out of breath but he sniffed wonderfully and cleared his throat, preliminary to an opinion. "Please, Larry, no politics," his wife requested, smiling at me to make it less impolite.

She was fondling Lucy, gazing at her eye to eye, slowly shaking her head at her; and the wicked beak moved in exact obedience to the tip of her nose as if it were magnetized. "Lucy's hungry," she said solemnly.

"Feel her breast." She took my hand and held it against the

tasseled plumage; and indeed there was a humming and stiffening in it, like a little voltage of electricity. Her eyes were moist and explosive; and the instant her mistress's eyes released them, down they went to the gauntlet, as if expecting a feathery form in agony to materialize out of the leather.

"Feel her feet," Mrs. Cullen added; and I did, while she explained that birds always have a higher temperature than animals. Fever heat; and yet they were slick and dry like a serpent. I could feel what they wanted to do, what they wanted to have, swelling in them and ticking the dull minutes meanwhile with little throbs. My pleasure in touching them was half embarrassment; and it set my mind running back to the thought I had left off an hour ago; that this hawk's hunger was like amorous appetite. I call it thought— and it is thought now, as I remember and try to tell it—but at the time it was only a vague flashing daydream. It all came together like one large composite phrase: old bachelor hungry bird, aging-hungry-man-bird, and how I hate desire, how I need pleasure, how I adore love, how difficult middle age must be!

Then, I lamented to myself, if your judgment is poor you fall in love with those who could not possibly love you. If romance of the past has done you any harm, you will not be able to hold on to love when you do attain it; your grasp of it will be out of alignment. Or pity or self-pity may have blunted your hand so that it makes no mark. Back you fly to your perch, ashamed as well as frustrated. Life is almost all perch. There is no nest; and no one is with you, on exactly the same rock or out on the same limb. The circumstances of passion are all too petty to be companionable. So there you sit, and you try to sit still, and doze and dream to save trouble. It is the kind of thing you have to keep quiet about for others' sake, politeness's sake: itching palm and ugly tongue and unsighted eye and empty flatulent physiology as a whole; and your cry of desire, ache, ache, ringing in your own ears. No one else hears it; and you get so tired of it yourself that you can't wait to grow old. . . .

Thus in an instant I foolishly imagined myself growing old; and meanwhile Mrs. Cullen had not ceased speaking with that single-minded vivacity of hers, but a little somber. "Since we caught Lucy," she said, "she's never had a mouthful to eat except out of my hand, and I've always worn the same glove. Think what it must mean to her!"

It was an impressive unpleasant object, that glove, stiffened and

discolored by a hundred little sanguinary banquets. It resembled
things you see in cases in anthropological museums; fetishes of awful
religion, sacrificial utensils, witch-doctors' kits. And the feet with
crescent toenails trod it so passionately that you wondered how the
wrist inside endured it.

"You know, she's not really attached to me personally," Mrs.
Cullen said. "If I gave you the glove she'd be yours instead of
mine. It's as simple as that, I think. It's what's called behaviorism,
isn't it? Would you like to try it? Try taking her a moment."

She turned around and held Lucy some five or six inches below the
chair-back, and after a moment's hesitation Lucy hopped up there.
Mrs. Cullen's hand was large and mine is not; so that I was able to
squeeze into the gauntlet. It surprised me to see that she wore
another large diamond on that hand, which under the pressure of
the leather had bruised her finger a little. . . Then I held my wrist
five or six inches above the chair-back; and Lucy, with her belief in
food-stained leather added to her belief in the highest possible perch,
hopped again.

"That's what they call an inferiority complex, don't they?" Cullen
proudly demanded, not to be outdone by his wife's use of that other
catchword. "Madeleine can't understand one thing about psychol-
ogy."

"Very well, Larry. I tell you she's hungry," his wife answered.
And by the tone of her voice you would have thought her the
hungry one.

I drew a deep breath, in which I got the hawk odor, slightly
bloody, slightly peppery. I had noticed it before, but without dis-
tinguishing it from Mrs. Cullen's French scent. The body, well balanced on its hot feet, weighed less than I had supposed. At the least
move her talons pricked the leather and pulled it a bit—as fashionable women's fingernails do on certain fabrics—though evidently
she held them as loose and harmless as she could. Only her grip as
a whole was hard, like a pair of tight, heated iron bracelets.

Alex offered her congratulations upon Lucy's evident peace of
mind with me; I would make a good falconer. That reminded me
of my father and his magic with animals which filled me with envy
and antipathy when I was a boy. He could force a crazy colt to its
knees, or castrate a young boar, or chloroform a desperate trapped
owl; and their wretched muscles relaxed and surrendered, their eyes
blinked in perfect gentleness in alignment with his eyes. His eyes,

or perhaps it was his hands, seemed able to promise them something. Half my life, I said to myself, has been discovering that my character is not the antithesis or the contradiction of his; here was a new kinship. Perhaps I could cope with horse or hog or doomed bird too, if I had to; perhaps even with a wild antipathetic son, disinclined to live—who knows? This was a gratifying thought but not altogether happy: vast vague potentiality of things I did not wish to do in any case.

I happen to be a trifle long-sighted; and now Lucy was so close that I could not quite see her in focus; and I have always had a fear of going blind. One good flutter, one simple thrust, and she could have slit an eyelid or ruptured an eyeball in an instant. She did not shuffle much on the borrowed gauntlet. But the vague dilated dark of her eye, the naked ring around it, the inner eyelids opening and closing as instantly as bubbles, seemed worse than restlessness. I was ashamed to tell her mistress that I was afraid. No doubt the chances of her actually hurting me were negligible. Mrs. Cullen's half-supercilious glance at us was reassuring. Still, I felt rather as if I had a great thought of death concentrated and embodied and perched on me. Whatever had possessed me, I wondered, to think of this Lucy—bloodthirsty brute with a face like a gouge, feet like two sets of dirty scalpels—as significant of love? Perhaps those two things, imaginary death and hopeless desire, always lie close together in one's mind, foolishly interchangeable.

Mrs. Cullen meanwhile, with vacated wrist, seemed the most restless woman in the world. She kept crossing and uncrossing her perfect stilted feet; leaning this way and that in the soft armchair; clasping and unclasping her jeweled fingers. It suggested one more explanation of her attachment to Lucy; falconry made her sit still. Perhaps too she was slightly jealous of my successful deputyship. "The real reason Lucy likes you so much," she murmured, "is that it's getting on toward mealtime. She fancies you may have a little steak or half a pigeon in your pocket. You look promising to her. What do you suppose has become of your cook? I do hope he and Ricketts haven't gone off to get drunk together."

She rose and tripped across to the great window. She tripped back and paused beside us and teased Lucy as Cullen had done, but in the opposite spirit. The star sapphire slid a little from one teasing finger to the next, which Lucy observed with interest. It looked like an unsocketed eye, I thought.

"Oh, Alex," Mrs. Cullen said, "you're so intelligent. I'm afraid you think me very sentimental. I'm not really. I do not want a falcon to be attached to me personally. When animals get that sort of feeling, it's too awful. Knowing the sound of your voice, liking the way you smell, wanting to be touched, all that. I hate it. It's such a parody of us, it's worse than we are. A bird like Lucy is so simple and straight. You make a promise and she expects you to keep it, that's all. She knows what she wants, and who gives it to her, and that's that."

Cullen grunted, and assured us that his wife didn't mean a word of this cynical stuff. But he did agree about one thing: "Birds are selfish as the devil. That's why I can't care for them. I'd rather have a dog, I tell you."

"Do you hear, Lucy? He'd rather have a dog." She said this in the way of wicked affectation, perhaps toying with the idea of being hated by him for it.

Then she turned briskly to me: "I'll take her back now, Mr. Tower, if you please. I think she'll bate in a minute."

Once more we exchanged the glove. Once more Lucy considered, on the rough leather, the stain of yesterdays' meals and the hope of today's and tomorrow's, and leaped up with alacrity. Her mistress carefully fondled her to prevent her bating, but she bated nevertheless.

After that, Mrs. Cullen heaved a greater sigh than before, not because it had been a harder struggle, but because her own light but significant remarks had hurt her at last, I fancied. And now she added that, simple though hawks all were, you could never really trust one. "Oh, I shall have to be so careful, never to fly Lucy at things she cannot catch and kill. The least failure makes her hopeless. My man in Hungary says that if she misses her quarry twice, I must call it a day and keep her hooded; otherwise it's risky. Because if she should miss a third time she might leave me; fly off and never return. They're all alike: the haggard you've hunted with for years; even the eyas you have taken from the nest and babied all its life. . . ."

"Damned ungrateful, I say," Cullen jeered.

"No, Larry. Lucy gives up her freedom and stays with me because it's a better life, more food and more fun. If it doesn't work, after all, what's the use? If my falconry isn't good enough. . . ."

Cullen giggled. I didn't. For it is the way religious faith goes, in the sense of God's failure; and it is the way true love ends: missing the third time. That much of life I already knew; I had missed twice. I glanced at Alex, wondering if the mysterious turn this small talk was taking troubled her too. But her face had its pretty well-bred passivity; I could not tell. The light in the Irish woman's eyes was fantastic, focused like glass on her great weak husband, then on me for just a moment with something like embarrassing affection. She and I understood each other.

She seemed to me a very passionate woman, but it was a kind of plural passion, all confused or crossed: work and play and sense of beauty, the maternal and the conjugal and the misanthropic, mixed. Perhaps that is a peculiarity of childless women. Female character has a great many secondary traits and minor talents; the wear and tear of motherhood may weaken them or stamp them out. It is anarchy if they all flourish.

"Tower," she said, "you would make a good falconer. Why don't you take it up, in the States? And you too, Alex. Everyone should have some hobby, some pet, I think. And all the other pets really are too awful.

"Ugh, how I despise dogs!" she then exclaimed in a dull disgusted tone of voice. "Do you know what dogs remind me of? It's not a nice thing to say but I do mean it. Prostitutes; all things to all men, and all that. And all shapes and sizes, from adapting themselves to everything and everybody for centuries, with no integrity. Men love them for that; it's flattering.

"Falcons have never changed. Forty centuries of falconry, think of it! And still wild; every feather as it was, and the same everywhere. I tell you, there's nothing like it in nature. Cats have more character than dogs, if they only weren't so damned amorous. Kittens to be drowned every few months, isn't it awful!"

My well-bred Alex in spite of herself made a little shocked face. It startled me too, because just then like a fool I had been thinking of Mrs. Cullen as a childless woman. What about those wild Irish sons of hers, shifting for themselves at Cullen Hall, riding and spoiling her favorite hunters, hunting with Lord Bild? I said a kind of prayer for them. That is, I hoped that they really were wild. Cullen had spoken of them as practically mature men; but perhaps he himself was not mature enough to judge of it. I hoped that they did not love their mother much. If they were at all backward or sensitive it was good of her, wise of her, to keep out of Ireland.

At this point wild Lucy flung up her wings and let her mute drop to the floor. Mrs. Cullen cheerfully apologized, and also proudly called our attention to its whiteness. It meant that Lucy was in excellent health. A healthy falcon's mute is the cleanest wastage in nature, and by no stretch of imagination could Alex or I have been offended by it. Cullen offendedly stirred his great body about in the great soft armchair; his face got redder; his light eyes protruded. But they protruded at us rather than it. Perhaps he feared, or perhaps hoped, that we would somehow express disapprobation or disgust. Alex rang for Eva, and of course that simple creature did not mind; it rather amused her. She fetched a towel and some wax, and knelt beautifully, and gave the parquet a very good restoration.

During which, Jean came rushing in, sweaty and pleased with himself. When he saw his dear beauty there on her knees he made a gleeful sound and gave her a tap as he passed, which made her blush. He and Ricketts in the Daimler had had a blowout on the back road. But dinner would not be much delayed; for while Ricketts had changed the tire, he had seated himself by the roadside and dressed the pigeons with his jackknife.

Mrs. Cullen asked him how large Lucy's pigeon was; and he sent Eva after it: a rumpled thing in a basket with warm damned eyes. She instructed them to wring its neck and chop it in half and bring it back, with its feathers and half the giblets. Meanwhile she asked me to move the straight chair into a dusky corner under the staircase. Though the least shy hawk in the world, Lucy would not feed properly outdoors or with a light in her eyes. Next Mrs. Cullen requested a number of towels to protect her dress, and Eva brought a worn-out tablecloth; and Alex helped tie this under her chin like a bib and spread it out over her lap. She sat with her pretty legs far apart, no longer a fashionable woman but rather like a gypsy or a priestess; or as if this were to be some surgical operation or painful travail.

Whereupon Jean returned with the portion of pigeon. He let two or three drops of blood and a bit of gizzard fall on the waxed floor; and again Eva cheerfully mopped up. Mrs. Cullen took the half-bird in the hand on which Lucy perched, pinching it between gloved forefinger and thumb, at Lucy's feet; turning it temptingly. At first Lucy stared at Alex and me so insolently that we drew a few steps away from the staircase. Jean and Eva also wanted to watch, but Alex reminded them that we too were hungry.

I had been hearing so much and thinking so romantically of hawk-hunger, that I expected a lunge and a grab, like a wolf or a cat; it was not so at all. It took two or three minutes for Lucy's appetite to develop, to accumulate. In a state of nature, no doubt it depends upon the fun of pursuit, voluptuous air in her wings, and the hovering and teasing; and there would not be any real spasm of Lucy's love of food until the instant she felt food in her beak. Now there had to be time for some equivalent of all that to take place in her narrow mind; time at least to regret it. The tedium of this conjugal kind of repast had to be overcome somehow, so she doubted and deliberated and imagined.

"Damn your pride, Lucy," Mrs. Cullen muttered; then murmured to us in her schoolgirl French, because Lucy did not understand French, "*l'appétit vient en mangeant.*" Upon which I reminded myself that on the whole, throughout life as a whole, the appetites which do not arise until we have resolved to eat, which we cannot comprehend until we have eaten, are the noblest—marital, aesthetic, religious. . . .

At last Lucy's curly breast did throb; a few feathers bristled up; her wings stood out a few inches; her greenish fists clenched on the glove; then her whole body began to point down beak first like a water-diviner's stick. She set her feet a little farther apart on her mistress's wrist. Then she stooped straight between them and thrust into the piece of pigeon. Mrs. Cullen held it tight. Lucy braced her legs and pulled and straightened back up with a morsel, which after a moment she shifted away into her throat and with a sinuous motion or a toss, swallowed.

Until the end, until there was no more pigeon, Mrs. Cullen had to encourage her to keep her mind on what she was doing. "The important thing," she said, "is to get her to take feathers enough. Her digestion depends a good deal on that."

When Lucy paused and raised her weird face between mouthfuls, it seemed spiritual rather than sensual; a bigoted face. There was no histrionic angry temper, no showing off. Thoroughly and slowly it went on to the end, with meditation upon every feather, every crumb of meat, every sip of blood—sacramental. Once or twice, because she did not like the way some wisp of plumage or tiny tendon felt—or because she liked it extremely—she shook her head hard; and a spot of blood appeared on Mrs. Cullen's bib, a feather drifted to the floor. Perhaps you could not have watched it if you were squeamish; neither Alex nor I were. But after the fourth or fifth beakful Lucy had a bad moment, modesty or imaginary repletion, and Mrs. Cullen asked us to move still farther away; and we were glad to go. We sat down beside Cullen in front of the big window.

It interested me to observe, or to guess at, his feeling about this. When his wife first called for Lucy's banquet he had pulled a long face. I think that may have been only fond anxiety, lest in her serving of it she appear to Alex and me coarse, or comical. He kept his eyes averted, but it was not disgust, surely, for it put him in mind of his own eating. He talked to us of that with enthusiasm and in great detail. In Paris the past week someone had sent them away out on the Avenue Jean Jaurès for a steak: year after year they always telephoned a certain small unsuccessful restaurant to prepare a supreme *cassoulet* which took two days; and so forth. Which brought him finally to the present, the great casserole of pigeons which Jean was preparing. At that point, I think, Alex regarded him almost with detestation.

The half-pigeon out of the way, Mrs. Cullen decided to put Lucy outdoors to weather, as it is called. We followed her into the garden where she selected the back of a rustic bench as a suitable perch. But there had been signs of more than usual nervousness during the feeding: it seemed best to leave her hooded. Because of the unaccustomed warmth of the afternoon, after Scotland, Mrs. Cullen said, she had a slight headache; and she retired with Alex to the bedroom for some aspirin and a moment's repose.

Then I offered Cullen a cocktail. He rose with enthusiasm and followed me to what I called the choir loft, that is, the balcony, where Alex's decorator had seen fit to install a bar, in the fashion of the twenties: all chromium and copper with a fine hierarchy of glasses and remarkable liquors in odd bottles. My Irishman had never seen the like of it. There was a magnum of prewar vodka; and I suggested a kind of modified Alexander with that in it instead of gin. Missing a syllable, he thought it charming of me, and so American, to serve a drink named after our hostess. I tried to set him right on that point but he was too charmed to care. The drink itself also suited him and for a while he concentrated on it, without a word.

The ladies did not return, so presently I mixed a second shakerful; and Alex's silver shaker was large. It was indiscreet, perhaps a little perverse, and in a way characteristic of me. As a rule I dislike being with people who have had too much to drink. It often brings on in me a kind of misanthropic fit; pity verging upon repugnance, and a mean sense of humor which they sometimes notice. But just because I am aware of the old-maidishness and even injustice of this, whenever the hospitality of the bottle is up to me I am inclined to overdo it.

Cullen in fact had been a little tight all afternoon, and I had not realized it. Now as he got tighter I saw that it was the same thing. They had arrived at Chancellet about two-thirty; so probably it had happened at luncheon, perhaps at breakfast. That explained his wife's anxious and resentful air, and her rude motherly snubs to keep him in order. He must have been in misery the last few hours, while we failed to offer him anything: thoughtlessness on my part, perhaps prudence or dislike on Alex's. She of course knew him well and must have noticed.

Perhaps the unnoticeable sort of heavy daytime drinker has the worst trouble; certainly they are more troublesome to others than they think. And others—sobersides like myself—are often more unjust to them than to their reeling, roaring, festive confreres. Half the time they themselves are only half aware of any incapacity or lack of charm. Or perhaps they know, and they think that you do not, and you do, and of course it is not manners to tell them so. They make an effort, often a heroic effort; and you feel that you have to respect and applaud that, whether or not it is fun for you.

But the worst injustice must be when you scarcely know them, and you judge them without reference to their habit, as in my case with Cullen that afternoon. He had simply seemed to me mediocre; old for his age, and weak for his size, dull, vain, and rather cross. No one had warned me that I was not seeing him at his best. It was his character, for all I knew, the nature of the creature; take it or leave it. That is to say, I had left it. So now I felt a slight embarrassment and grudging contrition.

Perhaps at other times, I reminded myself, his character was ideal; his mind vigorous; his great physique fresh and energetic. That would explain the love his wife bore him. Suppose you have learned to like or to love such a man when he was sober; and you happen to dislike him when he is not; and he doesn't know the difference or can't help it. The temptation to interfere, the fond hope of reformation, must be very great. Thus I began to think indulgently of Mrs. Cullen's selfish nervousness and sharp tongue. Although, if what I had seen that afternoon was the worst of it, certainly she exaggerated and overemphasized the plight she was in with him. An ordinary boring conceited uneasy childish man! Yet out of his petty instability she seemed to expect something odious or dangerous to develop any minute—as if she felt the ground underfoot move a bit, like a landslide starting, and caught glimpses of little creeping sickening things close to the surface, coming up! Love itself is an exaggeration, and very likely to lead to others.

After the first pouring of the second round, suddenly Cullen began a long complaint of the merry chase she led him year in and year out: her Mediterranean cruises, her falcons, her Irish republicans. No home to speak of, no creature comforts; nothing like the good time Alex and I had here in Chancellet, this pretty bar for example. Nothing but wild men, wild birds, and two silly maids to mop up after the birds instead of a good cook: hotel food all the year round, never a leg of boar soaked in brandy nor squab with currants.

At first, I think his outburst embarrassed him as well as me. For he explained that if I were an Englishman he would not be talking to me in this way; nor, for that matter, if he were an Englishman! But the Irish are like Americans in this respect. He had been in the States three or four years when he was a young fellow; therefore he felt the likeness. "The English never talk freely, as we're talking now. They're sly; they simply rule, and have their own way about everything. Britannia rules the waves and so on. You know, Tower, my wife's English. . . ."

These little distinctions of nationality were what reminded him of their winter in London with the Irish republicans. He not only disliked that type of Irish; their political principle seemed suspect to him. "They're not really republicans, that's just talk. They're anarchists. It was beastly for me. I'm a fool, I'd do anything in the world for my wife, and she does whatever strikes her fancy. She kept asking those patriots to the house. It cost me a pretty penny too, I can tell you. I had to pay for a lot of pamphlets, I had to support two widows, I had to hire halls for their meetings. Then, if you please, some of 'em said they needed some guns and bombs. Can you believe it? Only I don't think they got any bombs. Nothing happened. It would serve the English right if they did blow things up, you know. I suppose my wife's little friends just pocketed the money; or they bought a poor make of bomb that wouldn't do. Nothing happened."

He also complained that they were comic little characters, not gentlemen. And all their women appeared half-crazed with loving them, weeping in the corridor, losing their tempers with each other; some of them occult, some religious, and all of course talking Ireland, Ireland. Not a class of women that a man of a sensual nature would look twice at, not if he had any self-respect; nothing soft or sweet or tidy about them. "But I must say I enjoyed it for a while," he admitted, "seeing how that class of people get on and hearing their stories. I could always shut them up when I felt like it, or chuck them all altogether, you understand, because I had the money."

Of course I had begun to feel my misanthropy; but still his monologue amused me, especially the vulgar touches like this last. No doubt he was a quite good county aristocrat of that modest rank which as a rule is less mixed than any other. But not even aristocracy can be expected to give good examples of itself all the time. It seems rather to secrete commonness little by little, and to keep it in reserve, along with those odds and ends of mere human nature which aristocratic manners are intended to hide. And every generation or two it purges itself, in the form of some odd son or daughter, perfect little shopkeeper or predestined courtesan, upon whom manners wear thin.

Cullen silently ruminated two or three minutes; and when he began again it was in the middle of a new bit of subject matter. Probably it seemed to him that he had told me something which he had been saying to himself, something about his wife. "Make no mistake, Tower, I respect my wife." And he went on to assure me, or to warn me, that anyone who doubted it or slighted her in the least was quite likely to be knocked down by him; in fact he had done it once. She was like a swan in his opinion; pure as snow, with never a harmful thought all her life. "Only she's thoughtless," he added. "She never thinks of anything except what she happens to want. She's spoiled. When I met her she was the prettiest girl in Dublin. Lovely breasts for one thing. And ankles; you saw her ankles! Her family wasn't well off either. I took her without a penny; and I've spoiled her."

Aristocracy had nothing to do with it. It was my own fault; the vodka and cream had done it. Alcohol is the great leveler. Given a stiff drink, the true descendant of princes boasts of it as if it were not true, the multimillionaire feels poor, and Tristan talks to you about Isolde like a pimp, I said to myself. My malice was beginning to keep pace with my companion's folly.

"I spoiled her myself," he continued. "That's why she's so restless. Damn it, Tower, for years now she's kept me on the go like a gypsy. We've done everything." He held up one large moist freckled hand and counted on its unsteady fingers the things they had done: salmon fishing and photography and pig-sticking and now hawking. They had also been everywhere, and he counted places too, with a boastful as well as pathetic intonation: Norway and America and Java and Morocco and Africa—to say nothing of that winter when she had insisted on Irish rebellion, the most expensive thing on earth.

"I've let her have all my money," he said proudly. "She isn't as pretty as she was; but you know, I let her go t> London for all her dresses, or Paris; and she] : two maids. Before I married her I had a man to look after me; I gave him up. Now we need this chauffeur, Ricketts, because we're always on the go. I have to keep an eye on him too, because he has an eye for a pretty woman. Funny thing, one day when we were shooting in Scotland with those Americans, I thought Ricketts was insolent about Mrs. Cullen, and I'd have killed him. But she said I imagined it."

All alcoholism in a nutshell, I foolishly mused. And while he, poor man, counted his sports and his travels on his fingers, I meanly ticked off the drunkard's faults and pitfalls of drink as it were on my fingers—indiscretion and boastfulness and snobbism; and sentimentality so nervous that it may switch any minute to the exact opposite; and the sexual note and the sadistic note, undesirable desire, improbable murder. All of it of course a bit unreal and unrealizable in fact. . . .

What exaggeration I had drifted into! Cullen really was not in very bad shape; I have spent afternoons with a hundred drunker men. The point is that I exaggerated at the time, item by item as he talked along; and I think he sensed it and played up to it: a fatalist and a play-actor. The presence of my fastidious Alex and his overwrought wife downstairs—my wishing they would hurry up and join us, and my dreading it at the same time—made his loose talk more exciting than it would have been in ordinary circumstances. I had been too happy all afternoon, thinking meanwhile of unhappiness; which is a heady combination. Sometimes I am as sensitive as a woman to others' temper or temperament; and it is a kind of sensitivity which may turn, almost by chance, for them or against them. Perhaps at the end of our tête-à-tête I was not much soberer than my companion.

I began to wonder whether, after all, he was not going to tell me the little tale of anxiety or jealousy that winter in London which Alex had half told me in the park. And then he did.

"That winter in London one of our patriots," he began, "had the insolence to fall in love with my wife. A brute of a young fellow named McVoy who was a poet. It got very sticky then. I made up my mind to show them the door, the lot of them. But the more I worried about it, the easier it was for my wife to get around me and have her own way. I didn't want to be unjust to her; and if I'd made a scene before I knew what was up, you see, I might never have known. Terrible, the power a woman has over a man of my nature. You see that side of it, don't you?"

He told it tranquilly enough, though with some breathing between words. He reached out and grasped the cocktail shaker; and having helped himself, kept a tight hold on it. Once or twice he slipped off the tall stool and took steps up and down, carrying the shaker with him instead of his glass, to gesture with; coming back to drink and refill. I had not poured any of this second shakerful for myself; it was almost empty. The whites of his eyes grew more and more untidy, the hazel pupils a harder color; sense of humor and self-knowledge dying down in them. The strong though puffy fingers fixed on the large silver vessel, melting the frostiness off it in patches. I thought of wresting it away from him; emptying it slyly down the little chromium sink; perhaps pretending to be getting drunk myself, and jollying and bullying him along downstairs. . . . Naturally I did nothing; I looked and listened; I nodded. I wiped the copper top of the bar more than it needed, like a bartender. Probably even bartenders feel a little ignominious curiosity amid their professional boredom.

"One fine day there had to be an end of it, McVoy and all that. Especially one night. The police misunderstood something about him, and were waiting for him at his lodgings; so we had to put him up for the night. I couldn't sleep a wink. I kept hearing him sneaking around in the dark after my wife, I thought. All imagination; I've too much imagination anyway. My wife and I shared a bedroom; we always do; and he'd never have had the courage to come in there.

"Then I had a disgusting dream. I woke up standing beside my wife's bed. There was a moon, and I could see her, and she was sleeping. But I couldn't sleep. So about three o'clock I got up and took a knife from the butler's pantry. I thought I'd tackle McVoy with it. But my wife woke up and came and followed me, across the hall. When she saw the knife naturally it frightened her terribly. And the funny thing was, she frightened me too: there on the landing in her white nightgown. She made me give her the knife and go back to our bedroom. The wonder is we didn't wake McVoy. If we had, there'd have been an awful fuss, I expect. But he slept through it all. Or perhaps he was listening and hiding, scared, under his bed.

"After that I think my wife saw my point of view about it, and was sorry for me. She wept, and it wasn't like her to weep. In a way I was sorry for her too. Think of it, Tower! Think of a common little fellow like that coming to your house, whinnying like a horse around a respectable married woman. He'd have had only himself to blame if I had knifed him. After that Mrs. Cullen sent them all packing, believe me. All the rebels."

He picked up the shaker and shook it hopefully. Now there was only the clunk of small ice in diluted cream, to which I was deaf: a poor host at last, now that it was too late. My feeling about it all really was an absurd mixture. I felt a certain compassion; all the world loves a lover, and especially I do. I also longed to laugh aloud and to tease him. I also itched to tell him the miserable truth about himself, and rather vengefully than for the good it might do. There are a number of circumstances in which the truth does no good; and oh, this was one. I began to feel a mixture of sadness with my malice; a fellow feeling in spite of myself.

Drunkenness does superimpose a certain peculiarity and opaqueness of its own—monotonous complexion, odd aroma, pitch of voice, and nervous twitch—on the rest of a man's humanity; over the personality that you have known sober. But worse still is the transparency and the revelation, as it were sudden little windows uncurtained, or little holes cut, into common recesses of character. It is an anatomy lesson: behold the ducts and sinuses and bladders of the soul, common to every soul ever born! Drunken tricks are nothing but basic human traits. Ordinary frame of mind is never altogether unlike this babble of morbid Irishman. I felt the sickish embarrassment of being mere human clay myself. It seems to me that only art has the right to make one feel that. I am inclined to detest anyone who makes me feel it, as you might say, socially.

"God, Tower, it's tragic," my man sighed. "There's always something. Now I have to keep an eye on our damned Ricketts." He kept it on me for a while then, flashing it or rolling it; sometimes as simply as Othello, sometimes with the imagination and abstraction of a eunuch.

"You know, Tower, it's very interesting. My wife and I are the ideal married couple, so to speak. It's real love. She wouldn't look at another man. I'm as good a man as ever in spite of my age; it runs in the family; and I understand women. Oh, it's not all roses; it never was all roses. There were times when I thought I'd leave her, after some of the mistreatment she's given me. At least I could pretend to, and she might learn to treat me better. All it would need to summon her back would be a wink and a beckoning. She'd do it; she'd stoop her proud neck, I tell you; she'd come on her hands and knees. But I'd never humiliate her, Tower; I never have. To me she's still the proud ignorant girl as I married her; the prettiest in all Dublin.

"The worst mistreatment I've had to bear, you know, is this hawk. There are things only a common fellow could bear peaceably, and a hawk is one of 'em. Funny about hawks, you know, they can't learn to control themselves. They make their messes when they feel the need. Oh, well, you saw it with your own eyes; I sympathized with you. It happens in the hotel, the maids mop up after it, and I can't tell you how ashamed I am. I can't look the man at the desk in the face; he might make a joke of it. Madeleine has to tell him what we want; I won't go near him. . . . Funny about women, isn't it? They haven't the same natural shame about things that men have. Let's face it: that's why the church has to keep them in their place, they can't help it. I suppose if they had finer feelings, we men would get left out in the cold, wouldn't we? They'd have none of our kisses. So there you are.

"My wife's a fine trainer of hawks; her crooked old Hungarian admits it himself. But that is one way she can't subdue 'em; it's their nature. She can't teach me much either. She's got to get rid of that hawk, pretty quick; I won't stand for it. You see, I love her, Tower; that's the trouble. Suppose I want to put my arm around her, and she has that hawk on her arm. Can I? No, Larry, no, dear, you'll break a feather, a very important flight feather! Day after day now on the way to Hungary I'll have to sit there pushed over in the corner of the back seat out of Lucy's way; and I tell you, it makes me sick.

"She's been keeping it in our bedroom, because it doesn't like the bathroom. She's sorry for it. I lie awake all night hearing it stir on the perch, and I never forget it for a minute. When I'm beginning to fall asleep I think it's coming to attack me with its nasty beak. You can't imagine what it means to me. I dream of it. I dream sometimes it's an obscene thing; and that wakes me and I reach my arm over to my wife's bed; but she's asleep and takes no notice of me. I tell you, it's not healthy. I dream sometimes it's death. You know, I had an old uncle who saw ghosts, in a big house we had in Galway. I inherited that kind of feeling, you see, and Lucy brings it on. I'll tell you another dream. When I was a boy my old nurse taught me to weave osier baskets; and the other night I dreamed Lucy was a basket. Her feathers weren't right for it because they were sticky, but I wove her; and I gave her to my wife. But this is the end! No more Lucy!"

That was a lovely moment, to my way of thinking. My animosity toward this fool husband suddenly wafted away. It is a manner of self-revelation that I especially delight in: by means of loose imagery, and dreams, and careless connection of odd bits of memory as they come. Even as he spoke I hoped that I should be able to remember every word.

For alcohol is a god, as the Greeks decided when it was first introduced from the East, although a god of vengeance. The drinker becomes the drunkard. Everyone is to blame. The soberest man or woman in the world at some time or another has helped the sad process along in some poor dear drinker's case. For example, I think someone must have looked at Cullen in his youth when drunkenness became him, and so loved or admired him in it that he began to regard that as the secret of love and admiration. There are men who master the trick of drink, and practically never take a drop without being made admirable by it. I have known one or two; they were extraordinary men in other ways as well.

But even for the average man, even in the poorest booze-fight—between the vanity of the beginning and the sickness at last—there is a fine moment. It is the mark of its oriental origin and the proof of the Greek belief in it. The fumes seem suddenly mixed with more light and air than usual, and it is the right mixture. The silly self-consciousness clears up; the chip falls from the shoulder. Your friend is drinking, and you are not, or not much; so naturally there is an undercurrent of quarrel between you; now suddenly it ceases, peaceful. His tipsy mind is as it were sitting quiet, like an oracle on a tripod, under the influence not of alcohol simply, but of himself, his very nature, his fatality, his childhood. Whatever has been kept secret, damped in ashes, smothered and contemptible, begins to come out; and for the average man there is no harm in it. The murderous man may murder then, the madman talk nonsense; who cares? For most of us the ashes are bad, the secrecy mistaken, the contempt and self-contempt contemptible—and the raking of the ashes is good. For a moment, drunk as a lord, instead of coarseness and looseness you have the intuition of a child or an old woman. . . .

Of course it does not last long. Ordinarily when it has occurred, befuddlement and some bodily incompetence are in the offing. Too much delight in it may cause one to keep the worst company in the world all one's life. But certainly it is one of the main things in human nature, worth experiencing and worth watching. Cullen did not quite reach it that afternoon, on vodka and cream in Alex's silly de luxe bar. But I thought he was about to, when we were interrupted. As I really did not like him anyway I did not care much.

It was Alex who interrupted us, coming into the big room under the balcony and calling to me. She wanted me to visit Jean and Eva in the kitchen, and encourage them about the impromptu dinner and hurry them up. She had been hearing strange tones of voice out there; and she was afraid that if she went herself, Jean might make speeches and Eva might weep.

It was a large, unmistakably French kitchen: the stove in a deep niche of brick; dim walls and array of copper; the open doorway and windows full of little landscape with afternoon sunlight slanting across it. The Cullens' chauffeur was there with our two servants, and somehow it seemed to me dramatic as well as picturesque. Jean was the classic manservant, a type that you find more or less the same all around the Mediterranean: doubtless very good-looking and amorous as a boy; forty now and the worse for wear, with a bald spot and dark jowls and several teeth missing; a man broken to harness but still apt to show off his emotions, and still amorous. He had acquired Eva in Morocco; and she certainly had Moorish blood though she called herself Italian. She was half his age and lovely, although of an increasing billowy fatness; pale in the way

that seems sallow at times, silvery at other times. Ricketts was a
fine Cockney, bright-eyed and sharp-nosed. He sat at the table in the
middle of the room in a spoiled young male attitude, with a bottle
of wine half empty and half a plate of Eva's little Moorish cakes.

Dinner was flourishing; that I could tell by the smell of it. Along
with which I breathed the early summer wafting in: a tart exhala-
tion of the sod, a scent of some shrub that was like a dark candy.
In spite of the open door, the stove going full tilt for the squabs
and the strawberry tart made the room hot, which brought out the
men's untidy healthy body odor. Eva had one of those cheap North
African perfumes in a little cake like a rubber eraser, and had put
that on to excess, which, alas, I fancied, was for the young Englishman's benefit. And the mood of the room, the morality or psychol-
ogy of the three together, was as confusing as this fragrant air in it.
Eva stood and stared at Ricketts. Her great eyes were a little reddened; probably she had been weeping; at the moment she was
smiling vaguely. Ricketts poured the sour red wine down his throat
half a glass at a time; and between throatfuls looked up at her
with a becoming brightness. Jean pretended to be busy beside the
stove with his back to them. But he agitated the pots and pans,
and flashed glances over his shoulder, and replied to my questions
about the tart and the cheese with a little more obscurity and more
assurance than I liked.

Then I happened to look outdoors. It pleased me to be able to see,
in a little interval between two shrubs, the dreamy hawk hunched
up on the rustic bench. And then, to my amazement, I saw Cullen
on the left coming across the lawn. Very slowly, with a kind of
noticeable alcoholic endeavor not to be noticed; on tiptoe, and as
if the grass were a loud and slippery surface like a ballroom floor.
. . . Instantly I sensed that it was abnormal and scandalous. But I
could not run out to see what he was up to, without making a little
scandal myself. Jean and Eva and Ricketts would follow or at least
watch. So there I stood, acting absent-minded, murmuring about the
Camembert and the iced hock.

Cullen vanished for a moment behind one of those two shrubs
near Lucy's perch. When he reappeared he was crouching, and
hitching along on the balls of his feet, and steadying himself with
one hand, closer and closer to her. The grotesque furtive approach
indicated for one thing that he had no rational plan, no serious intention. For Lucy was hooded as well as leashed; she could not

see him. He kept stretching out one hand, very tense; but he could scarcely have reached her from that quadruped position. I began to think it funny. But from the bedroom window Alex and Mrs. Cullen could have seen him as well as I: that was a pity. . . .

Perhaps it occurred to him. He scrambled to his feet, and somewhat assumed an attitude of knowing what he was about, and leaned over the bench with his back to me. Perhaps he was undoing the knot or knots of the leash. Evidently he was not alarming Lucy much; she opened her wings a few inches, as if expecting to be picked up. But he drew back, and to my dismay, my disgust, thrust his hand in his pocket and brought out a large pocketknife and opened it. Murder at last, I thought. It was Lucy's turn; no more Lucy!

Before I even got started to run out and stop him, he simply pushed her hard off the back of the bench, recoiling away from her at the same time. It was obvious how afraid of her he was. With a large indignant flutter she landed on the grass. He had cut the leash; he had not cut her throat. Also he had unhooded her. On the grass for a moment she took a rapid confused look in every direction. Then with a great lift of her legs and two or three strokes of her wings, she climbed up on top of the air, and above the lawn, and across the pond. It was lovely. Her searching looks still, this way and that— to discover why she had been loosed, what quarry there was for her—made her appear to be shaking her head, saying no, no.

I lost sight of her when she passed behind a tree; again, when she rose beyond the scope of the kitchen window. Down she came then, with neck and wing and tail and legs all out—in the shape of a sixpointed star, big and dim, collapsing. She rested her weight on the air again for an instant, and alighted on a post in the far corner of the garden. It was one of two posts from which Eva hung Alex's lingerie to dry early in the morning. The gesture of alighting was lovely: her rigid hands clutching the top of the post like a living victim. It might have been a little angel seizing a tall man by the hair. Then there she sat, still wondering what in the world—what, in terms of a hawk's simple murderous instinct—this liberation meant.

Meanwhile, of course Cullen too had gazed up at her, gazed across the pond at her. Now like a ninny he waved good-bye, good-bye. Then he turned and ambled back through the bushes. Jean and Eva and Ricketts, in their matrimonial or adulterous absorption, had not seen a thing. I was thankful for that; I also felt a childish optimism because of it. I waited a bit, to give Cullen time to get settled in the living room. Then I dashed out of the kitchen, and knocked at Alex's bedroom door, and shouted through it to Mrs. Cullen. I simply said that Lucy was no longer on her perch. Then I hastened away to see what state of mind Cullen was in. There he sat in the living room, one leg over the arm of his easy chair, stoutly puffing; sorrowful and also smug, I thought, and somewhat sobered by his exploit; that at least was a blessing.

"The hawk has got loose. It's not on the bench. I've called Mrs. Cullen. She's coming to look for it. It must have untied the leash itself." I said this as emphatically as I could, to suggest to him the line he should take.

"But what about the hood?" he asked in an infuriating little tone. "I cut the leash myself, damn it all."

Whereupon I groaned or I cursed; I can't remember which. I didn't want him to confess; I should have spoken to him before I called his wife; now it was too late. She came rushing from the bedroom; and it was as if the news had instantly disheveled her from head to foot. She shuffled, her fine shoes half unlaced. Her perfect dress hung or clung around her one-sidedly. She was pulling on the blood-stained gauntlet; and as she crossed the room she impatiently ran her other hand up through her hair, which fell down on that side over her cheek. She did not close her mouth between her voluble exclamations. "Damn, damn. Oh, I am so unhappy. I must get her back, I can't bear to lose her."

At the sight of her, Cullen pulled himself up out of the easy chair and stood at a kind of attention: but badly, not a bit brave. She must have seen him; she took no notice. I had a sense of her knowing what had happened, who had done it. She looked like the type of old Irishwoman who has second sight: countrified, frumpy, and frightened. And in spite of her outcries and panicky movements, it seemed to me that she had an air of experience and familiarity; familiarity with fright.

"Oh, Mr. Tower, can you get me the other half of that pigeon?" she begged. "The pigeon I fed her. She hasn't, I hope she hasn't, gone far away."

Upon which her husband behind us chimed in as usual, worse than usual: "Madeleine, Madelene, surely they've cooked it. That's the dinner, you know, pigeons with white currants."

She took notice of that. She swung around and answered in a devilish voice, "Of course they have not cooked it." For one second I thought she might strike him; perhaps he did too. He wrinkled his nose and flung up his hands.

I started toward the kitchen and she followed, explaining, "I'll never catch her without a lure. Thank heaven it was a small pigeon, she'll still be hungry." She gave me a perhaps affectionate pat on the shoulder which amounted to a push.

Then she ran back to the window and there gave a wonderful small shriek. It should have been hawklike, I said to myself; what it really made me think of was a valkyrie, a very small valkyrie. For in spite of my admiration of Lucy and sympathy for the other two, I was enjoying all this.

I met Alex at the kitchen door, and she had the half-pigeon. Mrs. Cullen called to us, "What in God's name did I do with my bag? My extra leash is in it. She must have broken hers."

Alex ran for the bag, handing me the pigeon. I dropped it, and it smudged the parquet. Jean and Eva were there beside me, but they were too thrilled to do any mopping now. Then Mrs. Cullen lost one shoe and stumbled into an armchair; and her husband knelt and tried to put it back on, fumbling around her silky ankle with those freckled fingers which could so easily have snapped it in two like a twig—until she lost patience and kicked the other shoe off, over his shoulder, and rose to go in her stocking-feet.

"Stay here, all of you," she ordered. "Please, please, let me go alone." She paused a moment on the threshold staring across the pond at heedless Lucy. She held her gloved fingers up to her mouth as you do when you blow a kiss. Then she swung around toward us, demanding, with a kind of loud lump in her throat, "Where in God's name is her hood? How wicked! Who did it? One of you, how wicked!"

It was poor Eva who answered, with her primitive sensibility, primitive expectation of blame: "Oh, Madame, Madame, Jean and I never left the kitchen," and began to cry.

Alex told her to hush, which she did, more or less. As I watched our angry birdcatcher, I still kept one eye on these other watchers, so assorted and attractive, there inside the house in a row close to the plate-glass window in the last murky sunshine. I thought that Alex glanced oddly back at me; perhaps my eyewitnessing and slight complicity had given me an odd expression. Certainly she hated this disorder: obscure common blundering around her house, and general self-betrayal, with the servants goggle-eyed. On the other hand catching a great runaway bird was the sort of problem she loved. Her mild brown eyes lit up, and she breathed like a happy child. Ricketts came tip-toeing in and stood behind us as close to Eva as he dared. Whereupon Jean began whispering to her in Italian, *prestissimo*, until Alex hushed him too. Eva dabbed her eyes with the corner of the towel, another corner of which had pigeon's blood on it. As for Cullen, his face was quite mottled with his mixed emotions; heaven knows what they were.

As Mrs. Cullen left us, across the lawn, along the left side of the pond, I was struck by the change this emergency had made in her appearance and carriage. Perhaps it was chiefly her going in stocking-feet. When she first descended from the Daimler, how delicately she had stumbled on the cobblestones; then foolishly tripped back and forth on the waxed parquet, and weakly strolled in the park! That French or Italian footwear of hers with three-inch heels not only incapacitated her but flattered her, and disguised her. Now her breasts seemed lower on her torso, out of the way of her nervous arms. Her hips were wide and her back powerful, with that curve from the shoulder blades to the head which you see in the nudes of Ingres. She walked with her legs well apart, one padding footfall after another, as impossible to trip up as a cat.

Suddenly she must have remembered that she had brought an extra leash but no extra hood. She hurried back along the water and across to the rustic bench, where she picked up the one Cullen had removed and let fall; then set out again, by the right bank, more slow and catlike as she approached her quarry. What followed took only a few moments. We heard the falconer's cry: *hai, hai*, a desolate sound, which probably has not varied much in the three or four thousand years of falconry, for it is based on eternal acoustics, agreeable to the changeless ears of hawks. I loved to hear it. Lucy's head stirred swiftly around in response to it. I wanted her to cry back, *aik*, which she did not. They were too far away for us to see much. We saw the swing of Mrs. Cullen's arm as she tossed the piece of the pigeon over the hedge, toward the foot of the post; and after a breathless instant, we saw Lucy's descent upon it, down in one smooth rush, like a large, dusky, finished flower off its stem. Instantly the birdcatcher bent over, lurked along the hedge, and squattingly slipped around behind it. Then we had to wait, wait—

until she briskly stood up and started back toward us with Lucy hooded on her wrist, where she belonged. Before hooding her, I suppose, she let her have a few good beakfuls of the unscheduled pigeon so that even this mishap or misdemeanor should be a lesson to her, as it was to us all in a sense.

Inside the house, before the great window, we were smiling from ear to ear, and murmuring or exclaiming each in his or her way. Only Cullen was deathly still, not even puffing. I moved far enough away from him to see his face, and found there, added to the bibulous pink, a pale light of wild relief, reprieve, even rapture, as if that horrid bird on his wife's arm returning to haunt him again had been his heart's desire. It was too much of a good thing; he was sober perhaps, but tormentedly sentimental; I should not have trusted him an instant.

Mrs. Cullen came down the left side of the pond, the long way. The sun, muffled all afternoon, was setting brightly. Some of its beams turned back up from the water, broken into a sparkle, through which we could not see her well. There were vague irises and something else up to her ankles; and branches of lilac occasionally hung between us and her. Her face looked to me calm, careless. Her hair still absurdly fell down one cheek; now and then she blew it out of her eyes. Dress disarranged and petticoat showing and stocking-feet and all, she walked back proudly, taking her time; a springy walk that reminded me of Isadora Duncan.

The five of us happy onlookers trooped out on the lawn to meet her. "Isn't it wonderful?" she rejoiced. "You see, she's perfectly manned. She understands. Otherwise I could never have caught her. I'll be hunting with her in no time. Larry, go and find the other leash; which I left on the bench." And she decidedly emphasized the I. She too wished him not to admit what he had done.

He went meekly for the leash. The servants returned to the kitchen. Mrs. Cullen asked permission to retire and put herself to rights, declining Alex's offer of company and assistance. "No more weathering for you, my haggard Lucy," I heard her mutter as she left us.

I had not dared hope that Lucy—haggard that she was, with only two months of the least comfortable phase of captivity to look back upon, and none of the pleasure of the chase so far, and one toe still sore from the trap—would allow herself to be caught. That had made the little spectacle of her capture or surrender the more exciting for me. On the other hand I had not wanted her to escape. I had not pictured her setting out lonelily over Normandy toward Scotland, or whatever resort in the summer she might instinctively choose. Given my sentimental imagination, it was an odd lapse. And it made me aware of my really not wanting Larry Cullen to escape from Mrs. Cullen either, or vice versa. Perhaps I do not believe in liberty, or I regard it as only episodic in life; a circumstance that one must be able to bear and profit by when it occurs; a kind of necessary evil. When love itself is at stake, love of liberty as a rule is only fear of captivity.

Alex thought a drink would help at this juncture, and started to the balcony; but with one glance in Cullen's direction and another in mine, she returned and sat down. Cullen slumped in his armchair, gazing at apparently nothing, in that calm which is only the entire expenditure of energy; the coming down of a dull curtain upon the drama in head or heart. But probably it was only entr'acte. There was something turgid if not turbulent throughout his aging bulky frame; his jaws stirred a bit in his double chin; his bloodshot eyes kept lighting up.

Then we heard a persistent ringing of the bell in Alex's room, and Alex went anxiously to see what it meant, and came back and informed us that Mrs. Cullen had decided to return to town at once, before dinner. She had a brother in Paris, and she had telephoned him; something had gone wrong in Paris, and he needed her. I did not believe a word of this, and Alex's expression confirmed my disbelief. Evidently it did not surprise Cullen. He sighed hard, which perhaps referred to *pigeons aux groseilles*; but he said nothing even about that.

Alex left it to me to inform Jean and Eva of the superfluity of their dinner. I could scarcely tell how Eva took it, not well in any case: she gaped at me and fled to her bedroom. Jean on the other hand chose to be superior and calm. Something always went wrong, he observed, when the English upper classes came to see poor Mademoiselle, in their automobiles as big as busses driven by idiotic little boys. In his opinion also the boy Ricketts had something to do with the escape of Madame Cullen's eagle. At that moment the idiot was paying a visit to the *bistrot* or bar at the corner. I let Jean go after him. The announcement of the Cullens' change of plan might somewhat relieve his evident personal desire to put him out of the house.

Meanwhile with a certain simplicity our unhappy guests gathered up their belongings here and there: severed leash and mislaid lipstick and cigarette case with a diamond button. As we waited in the hallway for the Daimler to be brought around Mrs. Cullen quietly asked, "Dear Alex, you don't need a new chauffeur, do you?"

As it happened Alex did need one. "What luck! I wish you'd take Ricketts," Mrs. Cullen quietly continued. "I'll be giving him notice when we get to Budapest. And I know he hates Ireland, and he speaks quite decent French. He's very good, very fast, and a mechanic and all that." And she recommended him in other particulars as well, including semi-genteel birth.

Cullen beside me was shuffling and loudly hemming, and at last could not hold his peace. "But Madeleine, really, my dear woman, you're fantastic. We've never had anybody as good as Ricketts. What in the world!"

Slightly embarrassed, Alex said that indeed they might have difficulty in finding a chauffeur in Hungary in summer; it should not be decided in haste on her account. Perhaps she sensed what was coming; I did.

"Oh, I shall easily find another," Mrs. Cullen said, "or I can do without. You see, Ricketts doesn't like Lucy. He laughs at me up his sleeve. I doubtless am an old fool, but I cannot have people around me who think so." She said this in a great sad false way; and it was unmistakably intended for her husband.

Again I could not see his banal but significant face when I wished, to read the emotion in it; we stood shoulder to shoulder facing our dear women. There was still some of that fine pre-bolshevik distillation on his somewhat accelerated and audible breath; but its troublesome effects must have passed. We all kept silent for a moment.

Mrs. Cullen was quite willing to look either of us in the eye; but her sparkle was all extinguished. It would have seemed healthier, more rational, if her eyes had looked angry; they looked nothing at all, nullified. Lucy was hooded now; under her mistress's chin the frivolous topknot on the stitched leather nodded very slightly; and Mrs. Cullen's crooked Irish face as a whole was not much more expressive than that. Her serenity, her stoical wit, her obscurity, were a sort of mental or moral craftsmanship; ornamentation. Inside all that, I suspected, her spirit was as bland as Lucy's. The point of not allowing a hawk to see is to keep it from being fright-

ened; and I hoped that Mrs. Cullen's grand, mean manner served
that purpose as well. I was afraid it did not.

Along the cobblestones under the plane trees I heard the Daimler
come purring, not a moment too soon. By that time I also felt—
as it seemed, aching in my bones and running in my veins and
tempering my nerves—something like the mixture of hot and cold,
good and bad, which troubled the difficult hearts of this odd couple.

Unrequited passion; romance put asunder by circumstances or
mistakes; sexually pretending to be love—all that is a matter of little
consequence, a mere voluntary temporary uneasiness, compared
with the long course of true love, especially marriage. In marriage,
insult arises again and again and again; and pain has to be not only
endured, but consented to; and the amount of forgiveness that it
necessitates is incredible and exhausting. When love has given satisfaction, then you discover how large a part of the rest of life is only
payment for it, installment after installment . . . That was the one
definite lesson which these petty scenes of the Cullens illustrated.
Early in life I had learned it for myself well enough. It was on
Alex's account that I minded. To see the cost of love before one has
felt what it is worth, is a pity; one may never have the courage to
begin.

There stood the Daimler; and Cullen and I helped Mrs. Cullen
and Lucy up into it, while Ricketts, cap in hand, held the door. I
observed that in fact Ricketts was laughing, in a silent subaltern way;
but surely it was not at his mistress or her bird. Thin lips very red,
rough eyelashes very shadowy: the effect of a Moorish-Italian kiss
behind the kitchen door, I fancied. Or perhaps—for Cockneys are
a malicious breed—the mere discomfiture of Jean amused him. He
glanced over my shoulder, then up at a likely window, and so did
I; but I did not discover the Mediterranean couple peeping out anywhere.

Neither the Cullens nor Alex and I had the heart for much repetition of farewell. Cullen had tears in his eyes. We turned back to the
house and shut the door before Ricketts could get the long car out
onto the highway, amid cars coming toward him from Paris.

There had been just time for us to reach the living room and sit
down and light cigarettes, when we heard a fearful grinding of
brakes; then several cars honking as in panic; and a Frenchman
shouting the usual insults. A moment after, a car drove in under

our plane trees. I got up and looked out a small window on that side: it was the Daimler.

Alex and I hastened back through the hall to see what had happened. There we heard Mrs. Cullen's voice, very loud and exclamatory but incomprehensible; and she was pushing the doorbell, rattling the doorknob, and calling, "Alex, Alex!" As I opened the door she stepped back, turning away from us, gesticulating and exclaiming, "No, Ricketts, stay where you are. Larry, please! Now wait for me, Ricketts. Oh, dear, you fool, you fool!"

She stumbled on the cobblestones; Lucy was having a hard time. Then she returned to us and grasped Alex's arm and motioned us back inside the house. "Don't get out of the car, Larry, I'll attend to it," she cried, over her shoulder.

"Alex, dear, I'm sorry, I've forgotten something. Poor damned fool," she repeated. By the heart-broken tone of her voice I judged that the fool was not Ricketts.

That young man was not laughing now, nor smacking his lips upon any recollection of pleasure or rivalry. His lips were white; he was badly frightened. The Daimler stood at a very odd angle between two trees; he must have made a U-turn on the highway. A little further along on the verge of a ditch stood an old Renault, with which, I supposed, they had narrowly escaped a collision. Its French driver stood beside it, still vehemently expressing himself, shaking his fist. But, oddly, neither the Cullens nor Ricketts even glanced in that Frenchman's direction. Something else must have happened; just before, just after, or at the same time. Inside the Daimler, Cullen had his great hand pressed over his mouth as if he were gnawing it, and he too was pale: the worst pallor in the world, like cooked veal. During the little drama of recapturing Lucy he had ceased to be drunk, I thought. But now I was afraid that he was going to be sick.

Alex and I followed Mrs. Cullen inside the house. She too was in a worse emotion and looked worse than before. Not only a portion of her lovely hair but her hat as well this time, hung over one ear. There were beads of sweat on her brow and her upper lip. "Oh, Alex, do forgive us," she kept saying, "I'm so ashamed, so ashamed;" and hurried past us into the living room.

Shame, I must say, was one thing which all this did not suggest. Across that great expanse of waxed parquet toward the garden door she sped ahead of us—her pretty feet on her too high heels wide apart, lest she skid and fall headlong—saying to Alex over her shoulder, "Excuse me. Please, dear. Don't mind me. Let me go into the garden alone a minute."

On her wrist of course Lucy still perched, that is, rode, with some difficulty: her green-gold feet also wide apart, ducking or dipping to keep her balance, with characteristic indignation of her shoulders and that nervous puffing of breast-feathers which, as Mrs. Cullen had informed us, is a good sign in a hunting hawk. Hawks are not really tree-birds; and if in a state of nature Lucy had ever found herself on a perch as agitated as this female arm, blown by any such passionate wind as this, whatever this was—she would have left it instantly and sought out a rock. It was absurd. Even her little blind headgear with parrot feathers seemed to me absurd; it matched the French hat which her mistress was wearing at so Irish an angle, except that it was provided with secure drawstrings. In spite of my bewilderment and alarm, I began to laugh. It struck me as a completion of the cycle of the afternoon, an end of the sequence of meanings I had been reading into everything, especially Lucy. The all-embracing symbolic bird; primitive image with iron wings and rusty tassels and enameled feet; airy murderess like an angel; young predatory sanguinary de luxe hen—now she was funny; she had not seemed funny before. Perhaps all pets, all domesticated animals, no matter how ancient or beautiful or strange, show a comic aspect sooner or later; a part of the shame of our humanity that we gradually convey to them.

Just then I saw what Mrs. Cullen had in her right hand, half concealed against her breast and behind Lucy's wing: a large revolver. Alex must have seen it before I did. She was clinging to my elbow and whispering, "Stay back. Don't laugh, don't follow her."

I am not a judge of firearms, but this was a grim important object, glimmering, apparently brand-new and in working order. "Shall I try to take it away from her?" I asked Alex in a whisper.

"Heavens, no. She'll be all right. Don't worry her." Women, even some young girls, have this ability to guess at degrees of trouble; this equanimity of a trained nurse. And, with or without much affection, they sometimes suddenly know each other as if they were twins.

There was more to it than that. Looking back on that moment I have wondered just how her friend's passion appeared to Alex. How could she tell, as the disheveled creature fled ahead of us into the garden, that she was not going to kill herself? Then it occurred to me that in my friend's character and way of life in those days there was a certain passivity; at least abstention from other's lives. Whatever she did not understand about them might, she felt, be more awful than anything she could imagine. If others said that things were unbearable, she could well believe it. If the Irishwoman's life had reached that point, the point of suicide, I think she might not have cared to interfere or prevent it.

Outside on the terrace Mrs. Cullen stopped; and grasping the gun by the barrel, brought it back over her shoulder and hurled it high above the shrubs, far across the lawn, so that it splashed into the pond.

This important gesture was too much for Lucy. Off the dear wrist she went, hung in a paroxysm once more. But this time it was not bating, not mystical dread or symbolical love of liberty; it was just ordinary loss of balance. Symbol or no symbol, I said to myself, if I were busy getting rid of a suicidal or murderous weapon I should hate to have a heavy hysterical bird tied to me, yanking my wrist, flapping in my face. Mrs. Cullen, the good sportswoman, did not mind. Perhaps because of her own hysteria—the real meaning of this episode pulling at her heartstrings and beating upon her intellect—she merely did the thing to do, as usual. Up went her embattled left arm over her head; stock-still she stood, until terrible Lucy grew tired, and recovered her self-control, and resumed her domestication.

From our viewpoint, behind her, seeing her through the sunset-streaked window, against the background of the old park and the shrubs and the gray pond with ripples unclosing away from the place where the gun had gone down, Mrs. Cullen was beautiful. Throughout her somewhat bulky body—motherly torso and panting breasts and round neck—there was wonderful strength; and between her absurd high heels and her fist in the rough glove, there was exact perpendicularity: the yard-wind wings now settling back on top. And the fact that she looked a bit ridiculous, disheveled and second-rate and past her prime, made it all the finer, I thought, as she turned and came slowly back indoors.

There were tears in her eyes, but she chuckled, or pretended to, or tried to. "Darling Alex," she said hoarsely, "did you ever have guests who behaved so madly? Don't, please, don't ever ask me what this was all about."

Then in her way, in a series of little dull, prosaic, but shameless statements, she told us what it was about. "You see, dear, why we can't live in Ireland. It's such a bad example for my silly sons."

My presence did not make her shy. For a moment that flattered me; upon second thought it seemed to me to have the opposite implication. Quite early in the afternoon, I suppose, she had perceived that Alex was not in love with me; therefore, in her view of life, I did not count, I was a supernumerary. What harm could I do with her secrets? Women are fantastic.

Holding her left arm and Lucy well out of the way, she threw her right arm somewhat around Alex and kissed her. "Dear, dear friend," she murmured. "You're so clever, you'll marry well when the time comes. Thank you so much for your patience with us." Alex shrank a little as she always did from female affection, but the odd compliment seemed to please her.

"Larry's been threatening to leave me for weeks," Mrs. Cullen added. "Oh, I'm so afraid he will one day. I don't know what would become of him by himself, the fool, the old darling."

Poor Larry, I sighed; poor supernumerary me! Women are no respecters of men. I also felt a little indignation on Lucy's account. Trapped out of the real wind and rock, and perverted rather than domesticated, kept blind and childish, at the mercy of every human absurdity, vodka and automobiles, guns and kisses: poor Lucy! She no doubt personified for Mrs. Cullen the deep problems of life; certainly. Mrs. Cullen now devoted a large part of her life to her. Yet again and again, splendid *falco's* position in fact, her proprietress's handling of her, was in the way of a handkerchief or a muff or a hat. Absorbed in her narration of what had just occurred on the highway in the Daimler, Mrs. Cullen forgot about her and gestured a little with her left hand as well as her right. Lucy had to embrace the air desperately to stabilize herself; her plumage all thickened up and homely, sick-looking. It afforded me an instant's characteristic grim amusement to think how often the great issues which I had taken this bird to augur, come down in fact to undignified appearance, petty neurasthenic anecdote; bring one in fact at last to a poor domestication like Lucy's. It also reminded me of the absurd position of the artist in the midst of the disorders of those who honor and support him, but who can scarcely be expected to keep quiet around him for art's sake.

"I don't even know which of us Larry thought of shooting," Mrs. Cullen said. "Wife or chauffeur or haggard. I dare say I never shall know, unless some day he does it. The minute you closed your door, he began saying things at the top of his voice about Lucy and Ricketts. It upset Ricketts, and there was a car coming toward us, and for a moment I really thought we would crash. I told Ricketts to stop at the side of the road, and instead he turned back here, with two other cars speeding around the corner. That was what made the little Frenchman in the Renault angry. In the midst of which poor Larry began to threaten us with the revolver. It was in the side pocket of the car. I can't imagine when he put it there, or where he got it. You know, I think the Frenchman saw it. Lucky for us he didn't call the police."

She began to have an almost cheerful expression. If you have been lonelily excited a long while, expecting the worst to happen, with no validation for your fear in fact, no excuse that others would understand—perhaps the trouble in question must always come as a slight relief. At least you know then that you have not morbidly made it all up out of whole cloth.

"I'll tell you an odd thing about myself," she said, with her vaguest smile. "I happen to be a very good shot; and d'you know, all the while I was trying to take that beastly gun away from Larry—with Ricketts driving like a fool, and poor Lucy on my arm so awfully in the way—I kept calculating every instant just where the bullet would go if he pulled the trigger. The trajectory and all that. I suppose I'm a born sportswoman; how childish it is! At the last moment I simply can't take things quite seriously. I suppose that's what made me good at lions in Kenya years ago."

She frowned and sighed then, as if ashamed of her coldness or lightheartedness. "Now Ricketts of course is quite out of patience with Larry. I suppose I shall have to give him notice; what a pity! If Larry wasn't quiet after I got out of the car, I expect Ricketts knocked him out. He did once before. There's nothing I can do; Larry is as strong as an ox. But I'd have gone mad, I'd have killed Ricketts—if I had waited to see what happened. Ricketts is so damned English; the instant he clenches his fist he makes a smug face, like a governess. But I say it's time to go back now; I've been cowardly long enough; perhaps at this point I can be of some comfort to my man."

She intended to give Alex another kiss, but Alex avoided it. "Oh, Alex, I do," she lamented, "do love that great fool desperately. Whatever shall I do with him? Oh, well, we'll see. Do you think I must get rid of Lucy? It was astonishing, you know, how well Larry hawked, last summer in Hungary. I thought he'd enjoy it so."

Then she laughed, and all afternoon I think she had not laughed; rather a bad sound, two loud liquid feverish notes. "Ho, ho, perhaps this may have done him good. He has bated, don't you know."

So she took her second departure. "Good-bye, Mr. Tower. Good-bye, Alex, dear child. I shall miss you. Larry will be ashamed to see you after all this, I'm afraid. Don't come out to the car; it would embarrass them." She slipped across the hall and out the door, opening it only a little and immediately slamming it.

"Well!" exclaimed Alex, as we returned to the living room, and her delivery of that syllable made me laugh: ooo-ell; the soft bark of a very small dog.

After so much disorder we thought it would be indiscreet to seem impatient for our dinner. We wandered into the garden, sighing, tired. "I hope Jean and Eva did not see this last bit of melodrama," Alex said. "It's not the kind of idea I should like him to get into his head and develop. He's no Cullen; he's an imitative Italian, and he might not muff it."

"That great comfortable greedy easy old boy," I mumbled, meaning Cullen. "Did you dream he had murder in him? Vodka or no vodka."

"But it was suicide surely, not murder," said Alex. "Madeleine Cullen has no imagination."

"I wonder. It overlaps in any case. People do kill themselves just because they want to murder someone," I replied in my quibbling way. "Someone they love."

Alex made a little face, expressive of skepticism of everything and practically universal disapproval. "You know, he wasn't really very drunk."

"Two shakerfuls of prewar vodka," I reminded her.

"No matter. That's not much for those immense Irishmen. I've seen him drunk and it wasn't anything like this. Or perhaps he pretended to be drunk for your benefit; and to have an excuse for what was happening anyway, what was bound to happen. You're such a sober creature, my dear; you naturally overestimate other people's intoxication."

Her saying that made me suddenly unhappy. I thought of the wicked way I had watched him as he drank, the grandiose theories of drunkenness I had spun for myself meanwhile; and I blushed.

Half the time, I am afraid, my opinion of people is just guessing; cartooning. Again and again I give way to a kind of inexact and vengeful lyricism; I cannot tell what right I have to be avenged, and I am ashamed of it. Sometimes I entirely doubt my judgment in moral matters; and so long as I propose to be a story-teller, that is the whisper of the devil for me.

But my dear Alex then sensed, as a good young woman should, my doubt and weak self-criticism; and she smiled. "You must tell me what he said to you, before you forget it. I gathered from your expression that he'd been weeping on your shoulder."

Then Eva, with even less etiquette than usual, came out of the kitchen waving a napkin, huskily imploring us to hurry in to dinner, half-spoiled in any case, she thought. As if to point the moral of the changes of the day from a cook's angle, Jean sent in to us eight pigeons, a veritable sheaf of asparagus, and two good-sized tarts. It was perfect; and melodrama all afternoon evidently gave us appetite. Eva shed a sequence of tears as she served, mutely and prettily, with a wan smile whenever I looked at her, like a seventeenth-century Magdalen. Jean brought the tart himself and thanked us for our overeating, as if it had been a special effort to console him.

After he had served our coffee in the living room, I told Alex what I had seen from the kitchen window. I was surprised to learn that she too had seen it, from her bedroom window, while Mrs. Cullen lay stretched on the bed with her eyes shut. But she had missed the jackknife. Then I tried to remember and report to her Cullen's confession to me, man to man over our vodka, which entertained her, although I think it shocked her.

Then she went to write a note and send a telegram, and she did not return for three-quarters of an hour. I sat there by myself, not even trying to read. I was still excited; and I fell into a form of fatigued stupidity which, while it lasts, often seems to me an important intellectual effort. It was an effort to compress the excessive details of the afternoon into an abstraction or two, a formula of a moral; in order to store that away in my head for future use, and yet leave room for something new, for the next thing. Morally speaking, those Cullens had crowded me out of myself. I also hoped to distinguish a little more clearly between what the Cullens meant to me and certain fine points of my own meaning to myself which had fascinated me in the midst of their afternoon's performance. Of course it was not possible.

I have learned—but again and again I forget—that abstraction is a bad thing, innumerable and infinitesimal and tiresome; worse than any amount of petty fact. The emotion that comes blurring my retrospect is warmer and weaker than the excitement of whatever happened, good or bad. It is like a useless, fruitless vegetation, spreading and twining and fading and corrrupting; even the ego disappears under it. . . . Therefore I scarcely noticed how long my dear friend stayed away in her bedroom; and therefore I was glad when she came back. For me, putting a stop to so-called thought is one of the functions of friendship.

It was not writing or telegraphing which had kept her; it was Eva weeping and denouncing Jean, laughing and worshiping Jean. They had quarreled about Ricketts, and after that he had gone to the village to get drunk. He would kill her, he had said, and sooner or later he might well, Eva thought; certainly he would beat her the minute he returned. He was the most jealous man alive, in her opinion, and she worshiped him.

In any case she was much to blame. She had a way of obviously reveling in the sense of her own beauty whenever a new man appeared in the kitchen; a look of being at the mercy of circumstances, or perhaps at the man's mercy. Neighbor or workman or tradesman would appear; and casually Eva would come up, and stand close by, with a sleepy stare, letting her eyes drop sideways in their wide sockets amid African eyelashes, giving off her sweetness like a flower bed—while Jean watched her, admiring and suffering, until his storm broke.

Alex had asked what made her behave so; why she flirted with men like Ricketts if she loved Jean and wanted to be at peace with him. Seriously she had explained that, when she flirted, it gave him a chance to come between her and the rival, which made her feel his love, and to that of course she promptly yielded; and her yielding also gave him assurance that she loved him. "And if you please, terrible female that she is," said Alex, "she laughed as she explained it, deep in her fat throat.

"But she would not go on laughing. This time, she thinks, it has gone too far. He will beat her, and he may kill her, and *tutti quanti*. Therefore she began to cry again, and she wanted to tell me their story again, from the beginning. I pretended to lose my temper and sent her to bed.

"I shall have to dismiss them, you know, if they go on like this,"

Alex added. "The lower classes have a way of making one ashamed of one's sex."

She always had trouble with servants. The trouble really was that her kind interest in them, if aroused at all, soon went too far. Shrinking from them, but pinned down by them at last, she gave a great deal of the warmth that lay in her. But between their demands upon her, she fancied that she had no sympathy for them at all. She often said that she wished she could be served by machinery.

The door stood open; but amid the breath of the garden, it seemed to me that I could detect, at least I could strongly remember, Lucy's little body odor of blood and honey. The talk of Jean and Eva and Ricketts had carried my imagination again to the Cullen triangle: the virtuous passionate hard-hearted woman, the sad man, and the bird; and I had a new notion. It was that Mrs. Cullen now loved Cullen less than she intended; and lived with him, lived for him, perhaps only to fulfil a dear bootless contract with herself. In any case she loved Lucy, and I hoped she would refuse to give her up.

In the garden, over by the kitchen door, we heard a few notes of mellow laughter. Jean had returned and it had not gone according to Eva's expectation. Laughter, and a rustle and scuffle—the make-believe fighting that when all goes well, relaxes and relieves the true struggle of love—and footsteps diminishing toward the far corner of the garden hidden by the plane trees. The moon that night was not a fine carved shape. It hung under a little loose cloud; only a piece of pallor, a bit of anti-darkness. The air was as warm as Tangier but one could not lie outdoors, I thought, for the grass would be splashed with dew.

"You'll never marry, dear," I said, to tease Alex. "Your friend Mrs. Cullen thinks you will, but she has no imagination. You'll be afraid to, after this fantastic bad luck."

"What bad luck, if you please?" she inquired, smiling to show that my mockery was welcome.

"Fantastic bad object lessons."

"You're no novelist," she said, to tease me. "I envy the Cullens, didn't you know?" And I concluded from the look on her face that she herself did not quite know whether she meant it.